Last
Licks

Books by Cynthia Baxter

MURDER WITH A CHERRY ON TOP

HOT FUDGE MURDER

LAST LICKS

Published by Kensington Publishing Corporation

Last Licks

Cynthia Baxter

KENSINGTON BOOKS
www.kensingtonbooks.com

KENSINGTON BOOKS are published by

Kensington Publishing Corp.
119 West 40th Street
New York, NY 10018

All Kensington titles, imprints and distributed lines are available at special quantity discounts for bulk purchases for sales promotion, premiums, fund-raising, educational or institutional use.

Special book excerpts or customized printings can also be created to fit specific needs. For details, write or phone the office of the Kensington Special Sales Manager: Kensington Publishing Corp., 119 West 40th Street, New York, NY, 10018. Attn. Special Sales Department. Phone: 1-800-221-2647.

Kensington and the K logo Reg. U.S. Pat. & TM Off.

Library of Congress Card Catalogue Number: 2019950880

ISBN-13: 978-1-4967-1418-3
ISBN-10: 1-4967-1418-0
First Kensington Hardcover Edition: January 2020

ISBN-13: 978-1-4967-1420-6 (e-book)
ISBN-10: 1-4967-1420-2 (e-book)

10 9 8 7 6 5 4 3 2 1

Printed in the United States of America

Last Licks

Chapter 1

Next to cookies, ice cream stands as the
best-selling treat in America.

—*www.icecream.com/icecreaminfo*

"How does this sound? Green ice cream—pistachio would be perfect—that's mixed with chocolate chips, nuts, crushed chocolate cookies, and—here's the best part—tiny eyeballs made of sugar!"

"It sounds amazing," I told my eighteen-year-old niece Emma, whose big brown eyes were lit up with excitement. "And I bet you have a great name for it."

"I do!" she replied gleefully. "Monster Mash!"

"I love it," I told her. "I'm adding it to the list. Of course, we'd have to find someone who actually *makes* sugar eyeballs."

Halloween was less than three weeks away, and Emma and I were sitting at one of the round marble tables at my ice cream store, the Lickety Splits Ice Cream Shoppe, trying to come up with fun flavors that had a spooky theme. We had just finished our usual breakfast of Cappuccino Crunch ice cream, which I consider a perfectly respectable substitute for a more normal breakfast since it contains coffee, cream, and protein-rich nuts.

But so far, our enthusiasm had greatly outweighed our

productivity. In fact, Monster Mash was only the second flavor I'd written on the list. The other was Smashed Pumpkins, which was pumpkin ice cream with pecans and pralines—both smashed into little pieces, of course.

Yet while we were still at the brainstorming stage for creative new flavors, thanks to my artistic niece, my shop already looked like Halloween Central. I had given her free reign with decorating, and the results had astounded me. Just looking around was enough to put me in a Halloween mood.

Emma had begun by hanging fake spiderwebs all around the shop. She'd made them by draping strips of gauzy fabric from the shiny tin ceiling and along the exposed brick wall. She had even put them on the huge, cartoon-like paintings of ice cream treats that my best friend, Willow, had painted for the shop. One was a picture of a huge ice cream cone, one was a banana split, and the third was an ice cream sandwich. The webs were anything but eerie, especially because of the furry stuffed spiders she had added here and there. In fact, the huge smiles she'd embroidered on their faces made them look positively cute.

Intertwined in the spiderwebs were strings of tiny orange lights. They nicely complemented the string of orange jack-o'-lantern lights that Emma had hung across the front display window that overlooked Hudson Street, Wolfert's Roost's main thoroughfare. To me, those grinning pumpkins captured all the fun of what had always been one of my favorite holidays. A second string of jack-o'-lantern lights festooned the glass display case that contained the giant tubs of ice cream.

But the best part of Lickety Splits' Halloween décor were the life-size creatures my clever niece had made out of papier-mâché, paint, fabric, and glue. At the moment, Count Dracula was sitting at the table behind me, his mitten-like hand holding a plastic spoon. In front of him was a ceramic coffin the size of a dinner plate piled high with fake ice cream made from balls of fabric. Emma had done an incredible job of replicating one of Lickety Splits' signature dishes, the Bananafana Split. And customers were more than welcome to share the Count's table while they ate their own ice cream.

Emma had also constructed a life-size witch, complete with a tall, pointed hat and a long, crooked nose. She stood at the front door, greeting customers. Well, scowling at them, actually. But when you're dealing with Halloween clichés, mean-looking witches are so much more effective than friendly ones.

Outside the shop, on the pink-and-lime-green bench I'd placed underneath the display window, sat Frankenstein. His face and hands were made from nubby green burlap. He even had bolts in his neck. He was grinning at the ice cream cone he held, which was piled high with three humongous scoops. Definitely a monster-size portion by anyone's standards.

To make these creatures, Emma had enlisted Grams's help. Night after night, my niece and my grandmother had sat up at the dining room table long after I'd gone to bed, bent over their sewing like pioneer women. But instead of quilts or gingham prairie dresses, they were creating these wonderful, lovable monsters.

True, I'd had to say no to Emma's idea about dripping fake blood over Count Dracula's banana split. After all, I was in the business of selling ice cream, not freaking out potential customers. But I'd said yes to the fuzzy black-felt bats she had wanted to sew onto his shoulders. The way I saw it, you could never have too many vampire touches.

I was astounded that Emma had found the time to work on such an ambitious project. A few weeks earlier, she had begun taking two classes at the local community college. One was Life Drawing, meant to feed her outstanding artistic talents. The other was some computer thing I never did understand. All this was in addition to working part-time at my ice cream shop. Since I hadn't been eighteen myself for a decade and a half, I didn't know if all young women her age had that much energy or if she just happened to be exceptional.

"How about ice cream concoctions that are based on popular costumes?" Emma suggested. "Like . . ." Her eyes traveled around the shop, taking in the characters she had created. "Like pirates and clowns and maybe even ghosts.

"We could make clowns whose heads are a scoop of ice cream and faces are made from pieces of candy," she went on. "And ice cream cone hats! We can put frosting on the cones and then stick on colored sprinkles—"

"Or pearls," I interjected. "We could decorate the hats with pearls. The candy variety, not the jewelry kind."

"What on earth are pearls?" Emma demanded.

"They're tiny round balls made of sugar," I explained. "They're also called dragées. They come in all colors, but my personal favorite is the shiny silver variety."

"Like miniature disco balls?" Emma asked, blinking.

I laughed. "Exactly," I said, adding ice cream clowns to the list. "How about ghost ice cream cones? A scoop of vanilla ice cream in a cone that's been dipped in white chocolate."

"And witches!" Emma cried. "Ice cream cones make perfect witches' hats! We can cover them with something smooth and black—fondant would work great. And we can make little brims . . ."

"Wonderful," I said, scribbling away.

"But we still need more Halloween-inspired flavors," Emma said, frowning. And then her face lit up. "How about Creepy Crawlers? We could start with chocolate, since it's brown like dirt, and mix in gummy centipedes and spiders." Excitedly, she added, "We could put in powdered cocoa, too, so it *really* looks like dirt. And maybe there's something we could use for pebbles . . ."

I grimaced. "I'll have to think about that one. It sounds fun, but I'm not sure anyone would actually want to eat it."

"I bet it'd be a real hit with ten-year-old boys," my niece countered.

"True," I replied. "Probably with forty-year-old boys, too."

I was in the midst of making notes about the Creepy Crawler flavor when the door to my shop opened. I glanced up, surprised to see a young woman striding inside confidently. Even though I'd unlocked the door when I'd come in that morning, the CLOSED sign was still hanging on it.

Yet even as the woman glanced around and saw that Emma and I were the only ones in the shop and that neither of us was standing behind the counter selling ice cream, she looked perfectly at ease as she surveyed my store.

She appeared to be in her late twenties or early thirties and was dressed in fashionable-looking jeans, a baggy, oatmeal-colored sweater, and brown-suede ankle boots. Her thick, flyaway red hair was pulled back into a messy bun, with lots of loose ends falling around her face and neck.

"I'm sorry, but we're not open yet," I told her.

"So I see," she said, still looking around. Her tone crisp and businesslike, she asked, "How big is this space?"

"About nine hundred square feet," I told her. "That includes the work area in back."

"Are you the manager here?" she asked.

My stomach suddenly tightened. I wondered if she was an inspector of some kind. I instantly felt guilty, even though I was pretty confident that I had nothing to feel guilty about.

"Yes," I replied, growing increasingly wary. "I'm also the owner. My name is Kate McKay."

"And I'm Chelsea Atkins," she said.

I glanced over at Emma, who looked as if she was just as puzzled as I was. "Is there something I can help you with?" I asked.

"I hope so," she said. "I'm the assistant director on a

movie that's being filmed here in the Hudson Valley. Which means that my job is basically to make sure that everything runs as smoothly as possible."

Once again, I looked over at Emma. Her expression had changed completely. Her eyes had grown wide, and her cheeks were now the color of my Strawberry Rhubarb Pie ice cream.

"A film? You mean like a big Hollywood movie?" she half-whispered.

"That's right," Chelsea said, her tone still brusque. "It's being made by a production company called Palm Frond Productions. It's based in Los Angeles, which is also where I live."

"Who's in it?" my star-struck niece asked.

"No one you're likely to have heard of," Chelsea replied. "At least, not yet. But this movie, *The Best Ten Days of My Life*, is going to make its star famous. Savannah Crane is destined to be the next big thing. Some people are even saying that she's about to become the new Jennifer Jordan."

Thoughtfully, she added, "Ironically, Jennifer Jordan tried out for this role. She really, really wanted it, too." She shrugged. "But that's Hollywood."

"I love Jennifer Jordan!" Emma cried. She reached into the purple backpack lying on the floor beside her and pulled out a tattered magazine. "Look! She's on the cover of this week's issue of *People*! I even follow her on Twitter and Instagram!"

I glanced at the actress pictured on the cover of the magazine. Jennifer Jordan was beautiful, with long, straight, jet-black hair and huge eyes the color of dark chocolate. Her cheekbones were so sharp that they practically stuck out of the page. I vaguely remembered seeing her in a movie, but I couldn't remember which one.

"But I've got a problem," Chelsea went on, "and I wondered if you might be able to help."

"We can help!" Emma cried. She began fluffing her mane

of wildly curly dark hair, not quite as black as Jennifer Jordan's but much more distinctive because of the blue streaks running through it. You'd have thought she was auditioning for a role in this movie herself.

I was much more cautious. "What exactly is the problem?" I asked.

"Tomorrow morning, we were scheduled to shoot a key scene at a diner that's a few miles from here, over in Woodstock," Chelsea explained. "But the owner called me late last night and said there'd been a small fire in the kitchen. The fire department has closed the restaurant, and no one is allowed on the premises until it's finished its investigation. So we suddenly find ourselves with no place to film the scene."

I could see where this was going. "But this isn't a diner," I said, pointing out the obvious.

"No, but the diner part isn't important," Chelsea said. "What we need is an eatery of some kind. A place that has some charm. Some style. And it just so happens that the main character, the role of Suzi Hamilton that Savannah Crane is playing, is eating ice cream in this scene. That's why I went online to look for ice cream shops in the Hudson Valley and found yours."

"I see," I said.

So did Emma. She looked as if she was about to burst.

"You want to film a scene for a big Hollywood movie *here*?" she cried. "At Lickety Splits?"

"It would sure be a quick fix for a disaster we didn't see coming," Chelsea said. "Normally, the location scout on a project like this spends a long time finding the spots where each scene will be filmed. But we don't have much time. Basically, we're stuck. And, well, you can help." She looked at me expectantly.

"What would I have to do?" I asked uneasily.

"Basically nothing," Chelsea said. "That is, aside from

closing your shop for whatever length of time we need to finish filming. Probably just a few hours, starting first thing tomorrow morning. Another thing is that the crew would have to come in beforehand to set up. Ideally, we'd show up late tonight, ideally around nine o'clock."

"But what about all these wonderful Halloween decorations my niece put up?" I asked, still doubtful.

"I promise you that by the time we leave, this place will look exactly the way it does now," Chelsea assured me. "The first thing we'll do is take plenty of photos. Once we're finished, we'll put everything back."

Glancing around, she added, "And if there's any damage, which hardly ever happens, we'll fix it. I can guarantee that at the end of the shoot you won't even know we were here."

I thought for a few seconds, then thought of something else. "What exactly happens in the scene?" I had visions of chaotic shoot-outs, ceilings caving in, and bad guys being pushed through windows.

"The scene opens with Savannah Crane's character sitting at a table by herself, eating ice cream," Chelsea explained. "Her boyfriend comes in and sits down. They have an argument, and then he gets up and leaves. End of scene."

"That's it?" I asked.

"That's it," she said.

Do it! Emma was mouthing, practically jumping out of her chair.

"Would it be okay if I was here during the shoot?" I asked, trying to sound casual. "With a few members of my staff, of course," I added, nodding toward Emma. "I'd feel much more comfortable if we could stick around to keep an eye on things."

"As long as you understand that you have to stay out of the way," Chelsea replied. "And that you have to remain absolutely silent while we're filming."

I was about to say yes when she reached into her bag and pulled out some papers.

"Here's a contract that outlines the terms," she said as she handed it to me.

I read through it quickly and found that it pretty much spelled out everything she'd just said. There was a bit of legal mumbo jumbo, too, wording I couldn't come close to understanding.

I should have Jake take a look at it, I thought. He *is* a lawyer, after all. And I want to be perfectly certain that—

And then I caught sight of a number at the bottom. With a dollar sign next to it.

"What's this number?" I asked, blinking. "This dollar amount?"

"That's what we'll pay you for the shoot," Chelsea explained patiently. "It's our normal fee. I'm afraid it's non-negotiable, but it is pretty standard."

I literally had to stop myself from letting my jaw drop. I was that flabbergasted.

It was a very large number.

"I'm sure all this is fine," I finally managed to say, "but I'll have to run it by my lawyer."

Out of the corner of my eye, I could see Emma's face fall. She started making histrionic gestures that were so distracting that I turned away.

"But that shouldn't take long," I added. "He can probably look at it this morning."

Chelsea nodded. "I'm sure he'll be fine with it. As I said, this is our standard contract, and we're offering the usual amount. How about if somebody stops by to pick up the contract later today?"

"That's fine," I said, still reeling. "I'll let you know when it's signed."

"So we're set," Chelsea said.

"I guess so," I replied, feeling a bit dazed. Emma was pumping her fist in the air in victory.

"Great. Here's my contact info," Chelsea said, handing me

a business card. I, in turn, grabbed one of the flyers I keep on the display counter, jotted down my cell phone number, and gave it to her. In addition to the shop's phone number and address, the flyer lists Lickety Splits' hours and a few of our most popular flavors. Emma designed it, of course. After all, she's my marketing department and my art department as well as my best employee.

"I'm so glad this is working out," Chelsea said, reaching over and shaking my hand. "And don't hesitate to get in touch if you have any more questions."

"I do have one more," I said. "Will anyone actually be eating any ice cream during the shoot? I just want to know what to have on hand."

"We will need ice cream," she replied. "We could supply it ourselves, but given how fast all this is happening, it would be great if you could do it."

"I'd be happy to," I told her. "I also have dishes and spoons, of course."

"Perfect," Chelsea said. "Sometimes the props people make a big deal about what they want to use, but the prop master on this shoot is pretty mellow."

As soon as she left, Emma exploded.

"O-M-G, this is the most exciting thing that's ever happened in this town!" she shrieked. "A real Hollywood movie, being filmed here—right in your shop!"

"It *is* pretty cool," I admitted. I was already busy with my phone, texting Jake about the movie shoot and asking him to stop by to look at the contract as soon as it was convenient. "I just hope that—"

"A Hollywood director! Real cameras! Movie stars!" Emma cried, waving her arms in the air excitedly.

"The actress playing the lead role isn't exactly a star," I pointed out. "At least not yet. And—"

"Just think, Kate, you can hang framed photos of the actors and the director on the wall!" she continued. "Auto-graphed!"

"Emma, that's a nice idea, but—"

I was about to tell her about my lingering concerns. One was the possibility of things getting broken and never really fixed correctly, no matter how well intentioned the film crew was. Another was disappointing my regular customers when they showed up to buy ice cream and found that my shop was closed.

But before I had a chance, the door opened once again.

Emma snapped her head around. I got the feeling she was expecting a famous movie star to walk in. Instead, Grams was coming into the shop.

When I was five years old, my father died. Soon afterward, my mother, my two older sisters, and I moved to the Hudson Valley to live with my grandmother. Then, when I was ten, my mom died. Grams became our mother then.

In fact, Grams was the reason I was living back in my hometown. She had fallen on the stairs back in March, seven months earlier. It immediately became clear that now that she was getting older, she needed help running the house. So I came up with the obvious solution: I left my job working for a public relations firm in New York and moved back to Wolfert's Roost.

My grandmother wasn't alone. There was a man with her. A tall, attractive man who appeared to be about her age.

Which I found at least as interesting as a movie star walking into Lickety Splits.

As usual, Grams was dressed comfortably. But over the last several weeks, as she'd gotten more and more involved with volunteer activities at the local senior center, she'd started wearing spiffier outfits. Today, for example, along with her beige pants and the black blazer she wore over a cream-colored blouse, she had draped a mint-green silk scarf around her neck. She had recently gotten a haircut at Lotsa Locks, the hair salon a few doors down from Lickety Splits. As a result, her gray, blunt-cut pageboy was doing an exceptional job of falling into place.

But there was something else I noticed. Today, she looked prettier than usual. More animated. Her eyes were bright, and her face seemed to be glowing, an effect that had nothing to do with makeup. I had a hunch that the good-looking man she was with was the reason.

He, too, was nicely dressed, wearing crisply-ironed khaki pants, a black knit golf shirt, and shiny black loafers. His silver hair was almost the same color as Grams's, and his eyes were a distinctive shade of hazel.

I had to admit that they made a cute couple.

"Hi, Grams!" I greeted her. "This is a nice surprise. What brings you into town this morning?"

"I have someone I'd like you both to meet," she replied, smiling. "A new friend I made at the senior center. Emma, Kate, this is George Vernon. George, this is my great-granddaughter, Emma, who's an amazingly talented artist as well as a computer genius. And this is my favorite granddaughter—although I guess I shouldn't admit that. Anyway, this is Kate."

"Pleased to meet you," George said, giving me a firm handshake. "And I'm afraid I have to add that old cliché about having heard so much about you. All of it positive, of course. Your grandmother raves about you both constantly. Emma, I've heard all about your creativity. As for you, Kate, it's pretty clear that you really are her favorite granddaughter."

"Grams is definitely at the top of my list of favorite people, too," I assured him, laughing.

"Mine, too," Emma piped up.

"Both of these young women deserve every bit of praise they get," Grams insisted. "Kate here isn't only a former public relations star who's made a great success of her new ice cream empire. She's also the sweetest, most considerate, strongest, cleverest—"

"You can see I wasn't exaggerating," George interrupted, his tone teasing.

"But Grams has been quite secretive about you," I told him, casting my grandmother a sly look. "In fact, I'm afraid I don't know a thing about you."

He shrugged. "There's not much to tell. I'm just one more retired businessman. And a widower who's still getting used to being on my own. Frankly, I was getting a little tired of playing golf every day, so I decided to check out the local senior center. I met your grandmother the first time I walked in. And the next thing I knew, she'd signed me up for the Halloween Hollow committee." Looking over at her fondly, he added, "The woman wouldn't take no for an answer. Which makes her my kind of gal."

"I didn't exactly have to twist your arm!" Grams exclaimed. But the flush of her cheeks told me she didn't mind his ribbing in the least.

"At least not after you agreed that I could still sneak off to play golf a few times a week!" George shot back.

"What's the Halloween Hollow committee?" Emma asked.

Grams pulled out a black wrought-iron chair and sat down on its pink-vinyl seat. "You know that I've gotten the folks at the senior center involved in volunteering, mainly working with kids in the community."

Emma and I both nodded.

"You also know that in recent years, trick or treating has pretty much gone out of style," Grams went on.

I did know that—and it made me sad. When I was growing up, Halloween was one of my favorite holidays. And trick or treating was what it was all about. I still remembered all the fun my two sisters and I had had planning our costumes weeks in advance, as well as agonizing over which shopping bag or pillowcase to carry to maximize the number of treats we could stash away. Then came the thrill of the big day itself, going house to house collecting candy. Even the final step was exhilarating: sorting through the day's haul that night, gleefully exclaiming over each Snickers bar or peanut-butter cup as if there was no other way in the world to acquire them.

"So I came up with an idea," Grams continued, her voice reflecting her growing excitement. "We're going to build a haunted house in the high school gym so all the kids in Wolfert's Roost can celebrate there—safely. And one of the women at the senior center came up with the perfect name for it: Halloween Hollow."

"What a great idea!" I exclaimed.

Grams was beaming. "It's going to be sensational. A few of the regulars at the senior center used to work in construction, and they're already drawing up plans. The house will be wonderfully creepy, with creaking doors and cobwebs and strange noises . . . and all the seniors who volunteer will dress up as ghosts and monsters and ghouls."

"Don't forget to tell her about the foam pit the kids can jump into," George interjected.

"A foam pit?" Emma exclaimed. "That sounds awesome!"

"There'll be plenty of candy, too," Grams said. "And we thought that you might be willing to donate some ice cream, Kate."

"Of course!" I exclaimed. "We can set up a do-it-yourself ice cream sundae station where kids can decorate a scoop of ice cream with all kinds of goodies. Not only syrups and whipped cream, but also rainbow sprinkles and sugar pearls in a lot of different colors and pieces of Halloween candy."

"I'll help!" Emma cried. "Can I dress up like a witch? I love wearing costumes, and I hardly ever get a chance. I could make them for all of us—"

"Actually, I kind of like what you're wearing," George commented, nodding at the shirts Emma and I had on.

The knit polo shirts were bubble-gum pink, their breast pockets embroidered in white with the words LICKETY SPLITS ICE CREAM SHOPPE. While I'd ordered them online for my staff members and me to wear whenever we catered events off-site, we'd also started wearing them at the shop sometimes. And if we weren't wearing the shirts, we put on cute black-and-white-checked aprons with LICKETY SPLITS ICE CREAM SHOPPE written on them in pink.

"Those matching shirts make you look very professional," George noted. "Wearing them at Halloween Hollow would give your shop some good exposure, too, since a lot of the parents would see them."

"That's true," Emma said. "But I can wear this shirt anytime. Wearing a witch costume would be much more fun!"

"Then witch costumes it is," Grams said with a nod.

"What about you, George?" I asked. "What's your role in all this?" Jokingly, I added, "I suspect that my hard-driving grandmother is putting you to work big-time."

"You got that right," he replied. "As soon as I mentioned that I'm handy with woodworking, Caroline here put me in charge of overseeing construction. The haunted house, the foam pit . . . I'm overseeing all of it." With a wink, he said, "Good thing I hung on to my tools when I retired."

"Our goal is to make it fun for kids of all ages," Grams noted. "The little ones will come to the gym right after school lets out. Then, in the late afternoon, the middle school kids will get a turn. In the evening, it will be open to high school students."

Beaming, she added, "It's the perfect way to give the children something fun to do without running around the streets of Wolfert's Roost throwing eggs and smashing pumpkins."

"Frankly, when I was a kid, I had a great time throwing

eggs and smashing pumpkins," George said with a grin. "It was what Halloween was all about!"

Grams swatted his arm playfully. "I have no doubt that you got into your share of trouble when you were young."

Feigning surprise, he asked, "What makes you think that's changed?"

"It all sounds wonderful," I said sincerely. "And I'll be happy to help as much as I can."

"Me, too," Emma offered. "Hey, how about if I build some more of these papier-mâché monsters, like Count Dracula here and Frankenstein out in front? Mummies or ghosts or funny monsters with purple faces and orange hair . . .

"And I can make posters advertising Haunted Hollow!" she went on, as full of good ideas as usual. "Bright orange poster board with those scary-looking letters that look like blood dripping . . . We can put them up on the schools' bulletin boards. We can even put some up around town, including in the window of this shop."

"These are all great ideas!" Grams said enthusiastically. "Thank you both so much for agreeing to be part of this. We've put together a marvelous crew, but we can still use every pair of hands we can get."

"You're not the only one with big news, Grams," Emma suddenly said. "Kate has some of her own!"

I'd been so absorbed in Grams's plans that I'd completely forgotten about what had happened right before she and George had shown up.

But before I had a chance to tell them, Emma exploded with, "A Hollywood crew is filming a scene for a movie here at Lickety Splits! *Tomorrow*!"

"My goodness," Grams cried. "That *is* big news."

"Who's in it?" George asked. "Anyone famous?"

"Well, no," Emma replied, her enthusiasm deflating just a little. "But it's supposed to be the breakout film for an actress named Savannah Crane. I've never heard of her, but I plan to get her autograph. It sounds as if she's going to be the next big star!"

"So you'll get to meet her?" Grams asked. "They'll allow you to be here in the shop while they're filming?"

"You bet," Emma said. "Kate made sure of it."

"This all sounds like great fun," George commented. "But won't you lose business if your shop is closed during the filming?"

"They're paying me a small fortune to use Lickety Splits as a movie set," I told him. "And it's just for one day. Tonight, the crew is coming in after I close a little early, at nine instead of eleven. They'll stay as late as necessary to get everything set up for the shoot. Then, first thing in the morning, the actors and the director and the camera people and everyone else will show up and start filming."

"And we get to watch!" Emma cried. "As long as we're quiet and stay out of the way."

"Are they using your ice cream?" George asked. Gesturing at the display case, he added, "It sure looks as if you have enough of it!"

I nodded. "My ice cream, my dishes, even my spoons. They seem really grateful that I'm being so helpful. It seems that Savannah Crane will be eating a dish of my ice cream when the scene opens. Then her boyfriend walks in, and they have an argument." Grinning, I said, "Maybe I won't get my fifteen minutes of fame this time around, but my ice cream will. It might even get a close-up!"

"It sounds thrilling," Grams said sincerely. "So, it looks as if we all have something to be excited about. You and Emma have your glamorous connection to Hollywood, I have my Halloween project—"

"And I get to build a giant foam pit," George added. "Which sounds a heck of a lot more rewarding than playing golf."

"Speaking of which," Grams said, standing up, "you and I

should be heading over to the high school gym. We need to take a few more measurements, and I want to find out if there's a place we can store supplies . . . I've got about a hundred other things to do today, too."

As soon as they had left, I turned to Emma.

Smiling, I said, "My goodness, George is certainly a cutie."

"He sure is," she agreed. "Was it my imagination or was Grams practically glowing?"

"I was thinking the exact same thing!" I exclaimed.

"I'm so happy for her," Emma said, pulling out her phone. "She could really use—oh my goodness, look what time it is! I've got to get to my Life Drawing class!" Hastily, she added, "But I'll be back as soon as it's over. You know, in case the movie people need help with anything."

"Such a dedicated employee," I teased.

"Hey, it's not every day that Hollywood comes to Wolfert's Roost!" she countered. "And if anything else happens, I don't want to miss it!"

The truth was that I was as excited as my niece. In fact, I didn't know how I was going to get through the rest of the day.

Chapter 2

The top six ice-cream-consuming countries in the world (per capita, gallons per year) are (1) New Zealand, (2) the United States, (3) Australia, (4) Finland, (5) Sweden, and (6) China.

—https://www.frozendessertsupplies.com/p-943-which-countries-eat-the-most-ice-cream-ice-cream-consumption-by-countries.aspx

Just as I'd expected, it wasn't easy focusing on ice cream for the next few hours.

For example, a customer requested a Melty Chocolate Malt waffle cone, and I was so distracted that I accidentally scooped out Chocolate Almond Fudge. (Not that the customer minded. At least not when I gave him both cones for the price of one.)

Serving up ice cream suddenly seemed terribly mundane, even if the flavors that surrounded me were as fantastically creative and irresistibly delicious as Honey Lavender and Banana Walnut Bread Pudding and Toasted Coconut with Maui Macadamia.

Not all the flavors in my display case were that exotic. My philosophy at Lickety Splits was to offer three kinds of ice cream. The first category was the classics—like chocolate, vanilla, and strawberry, but each one made with such delectable ingredients that all my customers would walk away feeling that the chocolate cone or scoop of vanilla I'd just served them was the absolute best they had ever tasted.

The ice creams in the second category were slightly more adventurous. These were more along the lines of the flavors that innovative ice cream shops all over the country have begun offering. With my own special touches, of course. The best example was Peanut Butter on the Playground, which is peanut butter ice cream made with freshly ground peanuts, then infused with generous blobs of luscious grape jelly.

The third type involved thinking totally outside the ice cream freezer. I'm talking about flavors that incorporate such unusual ingredients as cheese—any variety, from blue cheese to goat cheese. Chunks of biscotti. Pie crust. Bacon. Sweet potatoes. Potato chips. In short, all the foods people love but have probably never thought of in an ice cream context before.

But today I couldn't get excited about any of them. Not with visions of bright lights and stunningly glamorous actors and stern directors barking out commands dancing in my head.

Ice cream aside, I kept looking at the interior of my shop through the eyes of someone else. Someone like a movie director. Or a camera person. Or even a star who was about to burst onto the Hollywood scene—and onto the cover of a magazine like *People*.

I had to admit that I was certain that everyone involved in the film shoot would be bowled over by Lickety Splits.

When I'd decided to live out a lifelong fantasy by opening my own ice cream shop a mere four months earlier, I knew exactly how I wanted it to look. And the space that happened to be available for rent just as I was gearing up was perfect. Not only was the location fabulous and the size just right; the shop on Hudson Street had that gorgeous exposed brick wall that gave it a wonderful feeling of warmth as well as a sense of history. Then there was the shiny tin ceiling and the black-and-white tiled floor, two more remnants of Wolfert's Roost's past.

I'd painted the other walls bright pink, hung Willow's whimsical paintings of oversized ice cream treats, and out-fitted the sitting area with six small marble tables and black wrought-iron chairs with pink-vinyl seats. What could be cuter?

I was tickled that Chelsea Atkins, the assistant director, had immediately seen its charm. And thrilled that Lickety Splits was going to be in a real live Hollywood movie.

As long as Jake approved the contract, of course.

I was in agony during the hours that passed before he showed up.

"I'm so sorry I couldn't get here sooner," he greeted me breathlessly as he scurried through the door. He was wearing his usual jeans and snug-fitting T-shirt. Even though he probably hadn't played much baseball since high school, when he was our team's star, he'd retained his lean, muscular physique. "This has been a crazy morning. For some reason, everybody in the universe suddenly seems to want organic dairy products."

"It's fine," I assured him. Jake runs an organic dairy nearby called Juniper Hill. Local interest in healthy eating had helped what was once a sleepy family business boom. "The movie people aren't coming until nine o'clock tonight. Once you look at the contract and tell me it's okay to sign, I'll text Chelsea—she's the one who came in this morning—and tell her we're all set."

Jake sat down at one of the tables, running his hands through his light brown hair as he read the contract. It didn't take him very long, given the fact that the legal document was pretty concise.

"It looks okay to me," he finally said. And then, in a very

un-Jake-like movement, he flashed his fingers and palms in that theatrical gesture that's known as jazz hands and cried, "It's showtime!"

"That's great!" I told him. "I'll let Chelsea know right away. Where do I sign?"

"I only have one question," he said earnestly.

My stomach tightened. "What's that?"

Widening his blue eyes wistfully, he asked, "Are you going to remember the little people once you're part of the Hollywood scene? Or will you forget all about the folks who knew you way back when?"

I laughed. But it was a loaded question, so much so that I immediately felt a low-grade tension between us.

The "way back when" Jake was referring to, after all, had been the years we were growing up together. Specifically, back in high school. He and I were the Romeo and Juliet of what was then called Modderplaatz High. That was long before the powers that be decided that our scenic riverside town deserved a better moniker than its colonial name, which is Dutch for "muddy place."

Unfortunately, our story ended tragically, just like Romeo and Juliet's. Not quite as tragically, of course, since we were both still up and running. But Jake had left me stranded on prom night, and I'd never completely forgiven him. Not only for what happened that June evening fifteen years before, but perhaps even more for the fact that he'd never even tried to get in touch with me since. Not to explain, not to say hello, not even to post a LIKE on a video of a kitten eating an ice cream cone that I once posted on Facebook.

Now that I was back in town, he and I had started hanging out together. Occasionally. And with major reservations on my part.

So I was happy that his reference to our shared past, however humorous it was meant to be, was cut short by Emma, who'd hurried back to Lickety Splits as soon as her morning class ended.

"Kate," she called from behind the counter, "I'm sorry to interrupt, but I think we need to open a new tub of Cashew Brittle with Sea Salt. There's a little bit left, but it's looking kind of . . . swampy."

"And I'd better get going," Jake said. "Hey, good luck with the movie thing! And let me know if the male lead gets sick and they need a last-minute replacement."

"Everybody wants to be a star," I replied, laughing. "But I promise that you'll be the first person I call. Assuming they give me that much power."

"Hey, they picked your ice cream shop to be in the movie, didn't they?" he asked. "Why not choose your local organic dairy guy and part-time semi-retired lawyer to get a star on his dressing-room door?"

Finally, the infuriatingly sluggish hands of the clock positioned themselves at the right angle that meant it was nine o'clock. Or, to be more accurate, my cell phone said "9:00" when I checked it for the eighteen thousandth time that day.

By that point, Emma had already gone over to the window at least twenty times to see if there were any signs of the film crew. But it wasn't until a few minutes after the hour that the door opened and Chelsea Atkins popped her head in.

Tonight, she was carrying a clipboard, which gave her an official look. Then I noticed the T-shirt she was wearing under a light jacket. It was bright red with the words PALM FROND PRODUCTIONS printed on it in white.

"Hey, Kate," she greeted me, sounding as if we were old friends. "Are you ready for us?"

We've been ready for almost twelve hours, I felt like telling her. Instead, I simply said, "Yup."

"Great." She turned away and addressed the cluster of people I now saw standing behind her. "Okay, let's do this."

Suddenly a dozen people swarmed in, most of them carrying things. A couple of big husky guys were dragging in cables and heavy-looking black cases that no doubt contained some sort of equipment. A third guy was lugging huge lights. Someone started snapping photos of my shop, just as Chelsea had promised, no doubt so they could put everything back the way it was once they were done. Someone else had whipped out an electronic measuring device and was checking out the room's dimensions. Through it all, Chelsea was shouting directions.

And then, amid all the unfamiliar faces around me, I saw one that I recognized. Ethan, Emma's boyfriend, had just come through the door.

As usual, his eyes were barely visible, since a curtain of straight black hair covered much of the upper half of his face. Thanks to his scrawny build and choice of hairstyle, he looks about fifteen. But he's actually eighteen, just like Emma. He was wearing grungy jeans, the kind I suspected weren't designed to be stylishly grungy but had gotten that way through his own blood, sweat, and tears. But he was also wearing the bubble-gum-pink Lickety Splits polo shirt I'd given him. He sometimes helps out with catered events, so it makes sense for him to have one at home, ready to go. And hopefully clean. As had become his habit of late, he was carrying a thick, well-worn paperback, no doubt one of the novels that's routinely on the "100 Most Important Books of Our Time" list. Dostoevsky was one of his favorites. Jack Kerouac, too.

Yet Ethan didn't belong here any more than Fyodor or Jack did. Trying to keep my irritation in check, I turned to Emma.

"How did Ethan know about this?" I demanded.

"I called him!" Emma replied. "And I told him to wear his

pink Lickety Splits shirt, since I figured that was the only way they'd let him in."

"Emma, you shouldn't have—"

I stopped mid-sentence since I'd suddenly caught sight of another familiar face. Willow, my best friend since my very first day of middle school and currently Wolfert's Roost's resident yoga instructor, was also slipping through the crowd. She, too, was wearing her pink Lickety Splits shirt, paired with turquoise yoga pants.

"How did Willow know about this?" Emma asked, her tone neutral. "And how come she thought to wear her Lickety Splits shirt?"

She had me there.

"Okay, so it's not so terrible that we each invited one friend," I said. "Just as long as everyone keeps out of the way."

"Thanks for telling me about this!" Willow gushed as she hurried over to Emma and me. Her eyes were bright, and strands of her pale blond hair, worn in a pixie cut, were sticking up at odd angles. "This is so exciting! I wouldn't have missed it for the world!"

"It's totally chill," Ethan said, nodding enthusiastically so that his bangs swung like a surrey with a fringe on top. "Probably the most clutch thing that's ever happened in this town!"

I took that to mean he was happy.

The four of us stood huddled together in the corner, content to stay out of the way and watch. Emma and Ethan kept whispering to each other excitedly, pointing out various crew members and analyzing the tasks they were performing. Willow just stood very still, her eyes wide with wonder.

It was all terribly glamorous. All that activity, all those people who were so good at what they did, matter-of-factly dealing with lights and cameras and other equipment and carrying out every single step required to turn my little shop into a movie set. It was even interesting watching them gently pack up Count Dracula and the witch, wrapping them in Bubble Wrap and hauling them to the back of the store.

Suddenly, I noticed Chelsea Atkins making a beeline in my direction.

"I need your help with something important," she said.

I stood up a little straighter. "Of course," I told her. "Anything."

"Can you pick out the dish and spoon that you think we should use in this scene?" she asked. "The ones Savannah Crane will use to eat ice cream?" Scrunching up her face, she added, "I'd feel kind of weird scrounging around in your cabinets. Besides, you're the ice cream expert."

"I'd be happy to," I replied, feeling very important. I smoothed the front of my pink Lickety Splits polo shirt, ran my fingers through my hair, and headed behind the counter.

Without hesitation, I picked out a classic, clear-glass tulip dish. Then I chose a stainless-steel spoon with an extra-long handle. Somehow, a metal spoon seemed just a little more elegant than the brightly colored plastic ones that most of my customers opted for. I handed both to Chelsea, then watched with pride as she set them on the table that was closest to the display counter. I couldn't help feeling that I'd just played an instrumental role in this production.

"Thanks!" Chelsea called, then moved on to some other task.

"You're a set designer!" Emma whispered when I joined her and the others in the corner we'd staked out. "That's something you can put on your résumé!"

Or at least tell my grandchildren about, I thought.

Being part of this production, even in such a small way, was exhilarating. So I was surprised that, before long, the thrill began to wear off. After a couple of hours, I found myself growing bored with watching electricians plug things in and camera people position cameras and lighting people stand on step stools. It was after eleven by then, and I was starting to yawn.

I glanced at the little group I'd come to think of as my Ice Cream Team. Willow was texting someone, while Emma and Ethan were slumped against the wall. They were both still watching, but their eyes were drooping, and their shoulders were sagging.

"I think it's time for us to go home," I announced.

I half-expected protests. Instead, all three 'Cream Team members nodded in agreement.

I went over to Chelsea, who was scribbling furiously on her clipboard. "If you don't need me here," I told her, "I'm going to call it a night. Let me give you the keys to the shop . . ."

"That's fine," she replied, barely glancing at me as I put the keys into her hand. "I've got your cell phone number right here, so I'll get in touch if anything comes up."

So much for my first taste of Hollywood. I'd been expecting some sort of drama. Instead, I was sorely disappointed.

Maybe there will be more excitement tomorrow, I told myself as the four of us shuffled out of the shop. But frankly, I wasn't feeling very optimistic.

Early the next morning, Emma and I walked to Lickety Splits, rather than driving. It was a lovely autumn day, perfect for taking a walk. The bright October sun gently warmed the crisp, cool air, and all around us the trees were tinged with vibrant reds, oranges, and yellows. Emma chattered away nonstop, still scarcely able to believe that a scene in a real Hollywood movie was about to be filmed at her aunt's ice cream shop.

As we turned the corner of Wolfert's Roost's main intersection, I wondered if I'd even be able to tell that a film shoot was about to take place at Lickety Splits. I pictured a small van parked outside, perhaps with a half dozen cables running from the vehicle to the shop, a camera or two, and some of the people I'd seen the night before standing around with clipboards or cameras or lights.

So I froze when I saw the chaos outside my store.

A moving-van-size truck that took up several parking spaces stood in front of Lickety Splits. The sidewalk in front of the shop was cordoned off, preventing anyone from walking by.

And there was a huge crowd. People were standing out on the sidewalk or going in and out of Lickety Splits, all of them looking busy. Not only the men and women who'd shown up the night before to set up, but at least ten or fifteen others. Some were hauling equipment around, some were fiddling with the thick black cables that snaked across the pavement, and some were talking animatedly on cell phones.

"Wow!" Emma said breathlessly. "This really is a big deal, Kate. Look at all these people! I wish Ethan could be here!"

"Yes, jobs do tend to get in the way a lot of the time," I commented. But I had just been thinking that it was too bad that Willow had to teach three classes in a row that morning at her yoga studio, Heart, Mind & Soul.

I quickly spotted Chelsea. She was standing near Lickety Splits' front door, clutching her clipboard. I wondered if she'd slept with it.

"Good morning, Chelsea," I greeted her. "It looks like you're already in full swing."

"Time is money," she replied with her usual brusqueness. "Especially in the movie business."

"Are you allowed to close off the sidewalk like this?" I asked nervously, wondering how my neighboring shopkeepers would feel about all this disruption.

"Don't worry, I got all the necessary permits," she assured

me. With a shrug, she added, "I've done it a million times before. We cordon off the area in order to—hey, Carlos? Could you please move that boom pole? It's kind of in the way. Thanks."

"Who are all these people?" I asked.

"That guy over there is Skip DiFalco, the director," she said. She pointed at a man in a backward baseball cap who was standing inside the shop, earnestly addressing three people. "And those people he's talking to right now are the gaffer—the chief lighting technician—and two of the cameramen. Those women in the corner are the hair stylist and the makeup artist. The woman behind them is the prop master."

"Wow, I had no idea they needed so many people to shoot a simple scene like this," I said breathlessly.

Emma, I noticed, didn't say a word. But the expression on her face was that of someone who had been hypnotized. Her brown eyes were the size of ice cream scoops. And they were as glazed as if they were made of the same type of metal.

"That woman over there is the script supervisor," Chelsea went on. "She takes notes constantly, keeping track of what's been filmed, checking for continuity, noting any changes the actors have made to their lines, things like that. Carlos over there is the boom operator, who positions the microphone during filming. And that tall man over there is the best boy, the head electrician. Let's see, who else is here . . . ?"

I remembered seeing some of those terms in the screen credits at the end of movies. I'd always wondered what they meant. Now I knew.

Suddenly the door of the white truck opened. A tall, slender woman stepped out, blinking in the bright sunlight of the crisp October morning. Her long blond curls looked as if they'd been arranged strand by strand to fall in perfect symmetry across her shoulders. Her features were delicate: pale blue eyes, a patrician nose, high cheekbones. She wasn't conventionally beautiful, but she was definitely one of those people who gave off an inner light that somehow let everyone around her know that she was special.

She was wearing a flowing dress made from a fabric that reminded me of cotton candy. It looked as if it would dissolve in your hand if you touched it. The dress was a color that looked great on her: the same shade of peach as my Peaches and Cream ice cream.

She drifted past us, flashing Chelsea a dazzling smile.

"Who's that?" I asked, even though I already knew.

"That's Savannah Crane," Chelsea said. "She's the star."

Emma uttered a little throaty sound. I had a feeling she was picturing her on an upcoming issue of *People*.

I followed Savannah Crane with my eyes as she floated into my shop. As she neared the display case, the hair stylist stopped her. She began fussing with the long, blond strands that as far as I could tell were already flawless. The makeup artist leaped into action as well, frowning pensively as she brushed blush over the actress's cheekbones.

The door of the truck opened once again. This time, a young man who also had an air of specialness around him stepped out. He, too, was lean. On the short side, too. I remembered reading that short men came across especially well in movies because of the way the camera caught their proportions.

He was startlingly handsome, his rugged features an interesting contrast to his leading lady's delicate look. His dark hair and dark eyes would be a pleasing complement to her fair coloring, too.

Before I had a chance to ask the obvious question with the obvious answer, Chelsea said, "And that's Damian Reese. He's got the other lead role."

"I'm impressed that all these people are managing to fit inside my store," I commented. "This isn't exactly a large space."

"We're used to working in all kinds of situations," Chelsea

told me. "Besides, some of these people will be moving out shortly. We're about to begin filming."

By this point, Savannah had taken a seat at one of the round tables. In front of her was the glass tulip dish I'd picked out the night before, along with the long-handled spoon. She sat facing the front of the store, with her back to the display case. Frankly, I didn't consider that the best way to shoot the scene. I thought she should have her back to the display window, since it would provide a much better view of my shop. But no one had asked me.

"We're ready for the ice cream," someone suddenly called.

Chelsea turned to me. "That's your cue, Kate. Could you please put a nice big scoop of something chocolate in front of Savannah? Just use the dish that's already in place."

"Chocolate?" I repeated, wanting be sure I got it right.

"That's right," Chelsea replied. "The dark brown will be a nice contrast to the color of her dress."

"I'm on it," I said.

My heart was pounding as I strode through the shop, picked up the dish, and took my place behind the counter. My hands were actually shaking as I scooped out a big ball of Chocolate Almond Fudge. It was a lovely shade of brown, and I figured the darker-colored fudge running through it would add visual interest. Nice texture, too. I pressed it into the dish, then rounded off the top so it would have a pleasing shape.

I sashayed over to Savannah's table and set it down in front of her.

"Here you go," I said.

She looked up and flashed me the same dazzling smile I'd seen before. "Thanks," she said, sounding a little breathless. "I don't usually eat ice cream at this hour."

"I think you'll find this is the best ice cream you've ever had," I couldn't help saying.

She laughed. "I just hope we do this scene in one or two

takes. If I keep eating ice cream all morning, I won't fit in my costume for the scene we're shooting tomorrow!"

I laughed too. *Friends*. Savannah Crane and I were now friends. I was friends with a movie star. Or at least a soon-to-be movie star.

I glanced over at Emma, who was standing in the corner closest to the front door. She was so green with envy that she looked like a scoop of Mint Chocolate Chip.

I wove through the crowd and joined her in the corner. It was an excellent spot, one that enabled us both to see perfectly.

"Quiet on the set!" Chelsea called out.

Emma and I looked at each other and grinned.

Just as Chelsea had explained, the scene opened with Savannah, playing the role of Suzi Hamilton, sitting at the table eating ice cream. I was pleased to see that the two shades of brown in my Chocolate Almond Fudge did indeed provide a nice contrast to the peach color of her dress. Vanilla would have looked too washed out. Strawberry, forget it. Mint Chocolate Chip and Pistachio Almond would have worked well, too, but again, no one had asked me.

And then the director called, "Action!" Just like I'd seen in the movies.

The actor Damian Reese strode in, his fingers clenched into fists and his expression angry. As he passed by Emma and me, I got a whiff of his cologne. He headed over to the table, sat down opposite Savannah, and stuck his hands in his pockets.

"What are you doing here?" Savannah asked, her eyes growing wide. Her voice was much more even, and considerably more controlled, than it had been when she and I had spoken.

"I just talked to Steve," Damian replied. "He told me you're leaving tomorrow."

Savannah had the next line.

"Honestly, Shane," she said, casually reaching for the spoon lying on the table, "I don't see what you're so upset about."

"Cut!" Skip DiFalco yelled. Everything immediately came to a halt.

With great patience, Skip said, "Savannah, you're supposed to be infuriating. This scene should be fraught with tension. But you're sounding just a bit too nice. Can you put a little more coldness into what you're saying? Can you be meaner?"

Savannah nodded. I got the feeling she was someone who didn't find it easy to be mean. Then again, she was an actress.

She closed her eyes, relaxed her shoulders, and took a deep breath. A few seconds later, she straightened up again and said, "Okay, I'm ready."

"Action!" the director called.

For the second time, Damian Reese strode over to the table and sat down opposite Savannah, then stuck his hands in his pockets.

"What are you doing here?" Savannah asked. She widened her eyes in the exact same way she had before.

"I just talked to Steve," Damian said. "He told me you're leaving tomorrow."

"Honestly, Shane," she said, once again reaching for the spoon, "I don't see what you're so upset about."

I guess she sounded mean enough, because this time Damian got to say his next line. As Savannah scooped up one spoonful of ice cream, then another, then one more, he stared at her angrily.

"You don't?" he yelled. "You seriously mean you don't understand how much you mean to me?"

"I'm tired of hearing you say that," she replied, eating more ice cream. I was starting to get alarmed. At the rate she was downing the stuff, I was afraid she'd run out before the scene was finished. I wished someone had told me how many lines of dialogue there were so I'd have known how much to dish out.

"You know you're the most important person in my life," Damian-as-Shane insisted. "That's been true since the first time we met. Have you forgotten Paris? Didn't all those evenings at that piano bar mean anything? You said yourself that those were the best ten days of your life!"

By that point, Savannah Crane had eaten almost the entire dish of Chocolate Almond Fudge. I glanced at the director, but he seemed so intent on his two actors' performances that he didn't seem to notice.

Finally, she scraped up what remained of the ice cream, sucked it off her spoon, and looked at Damian defiantly. She was silent for a few seconds, just staring at him.

I had to admit, it was a pretty dramatic moment. This Savannah Crane was a good actress. Even I could see that.

I glanced at Skip DiFalco. He was positively glowing with satisfaction.

"Shane," Savannah finally said, speaking with the same cold indifference with which she'd delivered her earlier lines, "I've told you all along that I have to—I have to—"

A sense of stillness gripped the entire room as she stopped mid-sentence. I could feel the tension in the air even before I glanced at the director and saw the shock on his face.

Was it really possible that Savannah had forgotten her next line and was about to flub what had clearly been exactly the performance that Skip DiFalco had hoped for?

But I quickly saw that something entirely different was going on. Savannah hadn't simply forgotten her lines.

Her entire demeanor had changed, her expression becoming stricken and her body hunching up in a peculiar way.

"Savannah?" Chelsea called from across the room. "Is everything okay?"

Savannah didn't reply. Instead, her eyebrows shot up, and her eyes widened as she clasped both hands to her heart.

A buzz rose up in the room.

"Savannah?" Chelsea cried again. "What's going on?"

"I—there's—" Savannah whispered hoarsely.

"Cut!" the director finally remembered to yell.

Savannah was shaking her head hard. Her eyes fluttered for a few seconds, then her shoulders slumped, and her entire body seemed to go limp.

As she slid off her chair and onto the floor, somebody let out a scream.

Chapter 3

George Washington had an absolute sweet tooth,
and his real love was for ice cream. He was
introduced to it around 1768 or 1770, and then
he became an addict. He started serving it at
Mount Vernon all the way back in 1784. And
when they did a catalog of his possessions,
he had a 306-piece ice cream serving set.

—*Amy Ettinger, author of* Sweet Spot: An Ice Cream Binge
Across America, *in an interview on NPR's* All Things
Considered

Total chaos immediately descended upon my shop.
"Somebody call nine-one-one!" someone shrieked.

"I'm doing that right now!" another voice yelled back.

"I already called!" a third person chimed in. "They're on
their way!"

Meanwhile, several people crowded around Savannah as
she lay sprawled on the floor. A man hunched over her, doing
CPR. A young woman with tears streaming down her cheeks
was clutching her hand, crying, "Savannah, can you hear
me? Savannah, talk to me!"

Damian Reese sat frozen in his chair, looking as if he were
in shock.

"Stay calm, everybody," the director, Skip DiFalco, called.
"And please clear the room. Hopefully the EMTs will be here

any minute, and they'll need to get in. Wayne, keep administering CPR. You look like you know what you're doing."

Most of the crew members dutifully moved out to the street, their expressions distraught and their voices hushed. The few people who remained included Skip DiFalco, Chelsea Atkins, and the man named Wayne, who continued doing CPR. I noticed that Damian Reese had shot out of there, practically pushing his way through the crowd.

Emma and I were among the last ones out. I was feeling completely dazed by what had just happened, and I sensed that my niece felt the exact same way.

"How could this be happening, Aunt Kate?" she asked in a high-pitched, little-girl voice once we were standing outside on the sidewalk. "Do you think Savannah Crane is just sick, or do you think something worse happened? What should we do? Should we call Grams?"

"None of us know what's going on yet," I told her, putting my arm around her and doing my best to sound reassuring. "I hope she's just fallen a bit ill and that it's nothing serious. I think we should stand by until we find out more about what's going on. And to answer your other question, I don't think there's any reason to call Grams. Not at this point."

It took only a few minutes for the ambulance to arrive. Two EMTs hurried into Lickety Splits as everyone stood around watching them. The air was so thick with tension that it seemed as if the people who were gathered there were barely breathing.

The last thing I wanted was for my niece to see something she wouldn't be able to get out of her head. So I pulled her away and said, "Let's take a walk around the block. It's so crowded that the best thing we can do is give the EMTs some space."

She nodded, then silently followed me as I led her down the street.

It wasn't until I saw the ambulance driving back down

Hudson Street, its sirens blaring, that I veered back to my shop. The same crowd was still standing on the sidewalk. But there was a new addition: a black-and-white police car had pulled up in front of Lickety Splits. As we got close, the driver's door opened, and Pete Bonano got out, pulling his navy-blue hat over his head of curly, dark brown hair.

Officer Pete Bonano, I had to remind myself. It was still difficult to comprehend the fact that my high school's good-natured star football player, with his chubby cheeks and his big grin, had grown up to become a police officer.

"Can I have everybody's attention, please?" he said authoritatively, addressing the crew members as well as a small group of passersby who lingered on the sidewalk, eager to see what all the commotion was about. "I'm going to ask any of you who were inside the store this morning for the film shoot to remain right where you are. I'd like to speak with each one of you briefly, primarily to take down your name and contact information. Everyone else, please clear the scene."

As a few members of the crowd shuffled away, I turned to my niece.

"Emma, I think you should go home," I said.

"But, Kate! You shouldn't be alone right now!" Emma protested. "Besides, the police officer just said that everyone who was there when this happened should stay."

"I insist," I told her firmly. "I'll tell Pete you were there and answer any of his questions for both of us.

"Besides," I added, as I noticed someone crossing the street and heading in our direction, "I'm not going to be alone."

Jake rushed over to the spot where we were standing, his expression grim.

"Is the rumor true?" he immediately asked. "Was the actress in this movie poisoned?"

Emma let out a cry. "Savannah Crane was *poisoned*?" she wailed.

"That's the rumor that's going around," Jake replied somberly. "I just got a call from a friend of mine who knew they were filming here this morning, and he said that's what he heard. So, of course, I came right over."

"I wish Ethan was here," Emma said, her voice thin. "Is he coming, too, Jake?"

"He's still at the dairy," Jake said. "I had to leave somebody there to keep things running. But you should call him. I'm sure he's anxious to hear how you're doing."

Just then, another vehicle pulled up in front of my store. This one was a van bearing the logo of our local cable TV news station.

Jake gently took my arm. "Let's go inside."

I turned to my niece. "Go home, Emma," I instructed her. "In fact, you can do me a big favor by telling Grams what happened. If Savannah Crane really was poisoned, I don't want her hearing about this from someone else. And please convince her that I'm totally fine!"

Emma scooted off with her phone in hand, no doubt calling Ethan.

But as Jake and I started to go inside Lickety Splits, I saw that Pete Bonano was blocking the way. He was standing in the doorway with his back to us, leaning forward awkwardly. I couldn't imagine what he was doing.

And then he turned around and I found out. He had fastened yellow tape printed with the words CRIME SCENE DO NOT CROSS across the doorway.

"Pete!" I cried. "What are you doing?"

Pete's full cheeks reddened. "Sorry, Katy," he said. "I had no choice."

"But—but—!" I protested.

A hundred *buts* were running through my mind, the predominant one something along the lines of "But Lickety Splits is mine! You can't close it off to me! It's autumn, one of Wolfert's Roost's prime tourist seasons! The Hudson Valley is crawling with leaf peepers, tourists who came to the area to look at the beautiful autumn leaves—and hopefully eat ice cream while doing so!"

Following that one were some more practical *buts*: "But how will I make a living if I can't run my shop? But what about all the ice cream I've got stashed in the freezer? But what about the milk and cream and all the other ingredients in the refrigerator?"

Before I had a chance to ask any of those questions, Pete said, "I know it's tough to be shut out of your own store." His tone was sympathetic. "But I just got word that Savannah Crane died on the way to the hospital. We'll have to wait for the toxicology report, of course, but at this point it looks like she was poisoned. And that makes Lickety Splits the scene of a homicide investigation."

I suddenly felt like a blob of melting ice cream lying on a hot sidewalk.

Jake must have guessed that my knees had suddenly turned into something resembling soft serve because he grabbed hold of me.

"It's okay, Kate," he said. "This whole mess won't last long. They'll take that tape down in a day or two, as soon as the forensics people are done."

I nodded, trying to believe him.

"What now?" I asked him. "Should I just go home?"

"It looks as if that may not be an option," Jake replied warily. "At least, not yet."

Confused, I glanced over at him and saw that his gaze was fixed on something up the street. I followed his eyes and saw a gray car heading in our direction. The driver was tall with dark blond hair cut short. Just like Jake, I knew who he was immediately.

So I wasn't at all surprised when the car pulled up right in front of us and the driver rolled down his window.

"Ms. McKay?" Detective Stoltz said. "Would you mind coming down to the police station so I could ask you a few questions?"

I was grateful to have Jake with me in the small, dreary, windowless room in the Wolfert's Roost police station, a place I'd unfortunately been before. I found myself wondering if the Palm Frond Productions people knew about it. It would have been perfect for one of those tense, hard-to-watch scenes in a movie in which someone is being given the third degree.

Fake wood paneling, a scuffed linoleum floor, an ugly metal table, and impressively uncomfortable metal chairs . . . the room truly captured the demoralizing feeling that invariably accompanied being questioned by the police. A feeling that was impossible to shake even if you knew you hadn't done anything wrong.

Finally, after what seemed like a very long time, Detective Stoltz strode in. As usual, his posture was as upright and wooden as a four-star general's. His suit, meanwhile, was as far from a military uniform as it could be. In fact, it looked as if he had grabbed it off the clearance rack in a store that had particularly bad lighting and hadn't cared in the least that it wasn't actually his size.

"Ms. McKay," he said dryly as he sat down. "Here we are again." As usual, he was the picture of politeness. But there was a hard look in his eyes. They were a pale, nondescript shade of gray, something I didn't remember noticing before. Somehow, that seemed to suit his personality perfectly.

Turning to Jake, he curtly asked, "And you're here as her attorney?"

"That's right, I am," he replied, returning Stoltz's steely stare.

While Jake had taken over his family's dairy several years earlier, prior to that he had been a criminal defense lawyer, working for a big law firm in New York City. Since I'd come back to Wolfert's Roost, his background had come in handy. Repeatedly.

Detective Stoltz took out a spiral pad of paper and opened it to a blank page. I was glad that he still used a paper and pen, like in the old days. Somehow, it seemed less intimidating than having him type every word I said into a computer.

"I'd like you to tell me your version of what happened," he began, his voice showing not even a trace of emotion.

I didn't like the phrase "your version." Somehow it seemed to imply that my version wasn't the most valid version. Or even truthful.

But I glanced at Jake, and he nodded.

"I suppose I should start with what happened yesterday," I began, trying to sound as matter-of-fact about all of this as I could. "A woman named Chelsea Atkins came into my shop at around ten in the morning, before it had even opened. She said she was the assistant director on a movie that was being made in the Hudson Valley and she needed a place to film a scene in a hurry. The spot they'd planned to use had become unavailable at the last minute, and the director and the actors and the rest of the crew were all ready to go. She offered me a ton of money. And I have to admit that it sounded like fun. So I said yes.

"Later that evening," I went on, "at a time we'd agreed upon, nine o'clock, a bunch of people who were involved in making the movie showed up and began setting up—"

"Let me stop you there," Detective Stoltz interrupted. "Who, exactly, came into your shop last night?"

I squirmed in my seat, just a little, then forced myself to stop as soon as I realized what I was doing. "I don't really know. There were probably about a dozen people there, and

I didn't know any of them. To me they looked like camera people, lighting people . . ."

I shrugged. "I'm afraid I can't be very helpful about specifics. I suggest that you talk to Chelsea Atkins, the assistant director I mentioned, since she'll know exactly who was there. She was in charge of the setup last night."

Detective Stoltz nodded. "Who was there that you did know?"

"My niece was there," I replied. "Emma Pritchard is my sister Julie's daughter. She lives in Washington, D.C., but she's staying with my grandmother and me here in Wolfert's Roost right now. She's taking classes at the community college and working part-time at Lickety Splits. You've met her."

"Anyone else?"

"Willow Baines," I said. "She runs the Heart, Mind, and Soul yoga studio in town. And then there's Ethan—" I realized I didn't know his last name.

"Love," Jake said. "He works for me at the dairy."

"Really?" I couldn't help asking. "Ethan's last name is *Love*?"

Jake just shrugged.

"And that's it?" Detective Stoltz asked.

"Yes," I said. "Just the four of us."

"How long were you there?" he asked.

"Until a few minutes past eleven," I replied. Speaking more to myself than to him, I added, "We'd all had enough by then. I thought the setup would be exciting, but it was actually kind of boring."

"And this morning?" Detective Stoltz asked.

"Emma and I were the only ones who went to the shop," I said. "Willow had classes to teach, and Ethan had to work at the dairy. The two of us showed up at around nine. There was already a whole crowd of people there." I gave him an overview of who and what I'd seen.

"And while you were there," Detective Stoltz said when I'd finished, "either last night or this morning, did you notice anything out of the ordinary? Anything at all? Anyone who looked as if they shouldn't have been there? Anyone who seemed angry? Or was acting strangely?"

I shook my head.

"Did you see anyone who seemed to have a particular interest in watching what was going on?" he asked.

I shook my head again. "Everything seemed to be going along just fine. Of course, it's hard to say, since I've never been at a film shoot before," I noted. "At least not for a big Hollywood movie. I went to plenty when I worked in public relations. The firm I worked for was involved with corporate films. But this Hollywood thing is new to me."

"But you have had some exposure to film sets," Detective Stoltz prompted. "Did anything strike you as unusual?"

I thought for a few seconds. "Only how thorough everyone was," I finally replied. "They were meticulous about setting up everything that would be needed for the next morning. The idea was to make it possible for the actors and the director and everyone else to just show up and immediately get right to work."

"And that included putting the dishes and silverware on the table?" Detective Stoltz asked.

I stiffened. "Yes, that's right."

"Where did the dish and spoon that Savannah Crane was using to eat the ice cream come from?" he asked.

The fake wood paneling began swirling around me like a set in a horror movie.

"They were both mine," I finally managed to reply. "I mean, the dish and the spoon belong to my shop."

"I'm a little confused," Jake interjected. "Why do the dish and spoon matter so much?"

Detective Stoltz glanced at him coolly. "One theory I'm

considering is that the person who murdered Savannah
Crane did so by putting poison into the dish, rather than into
the ice cream. That way, it would have been in place no matter what flavor was used. The spoon could also have been
dipped in poison, but that's not as likely because it's smaller
and flatter and would therefore hold less."

"That sounds right," I said thoughtfully. "Especially since
no one knew in advance which flavor of ice cream would be
used."

I repeated what Chelsea Atkins had said on the morning of
the shoot, which was, "Could you please put a nice big scoop
of something chocolate in front of Savannah?" I also told
him that she had then added, "Just use the dish that's already
in place."

"So the poison *has* to have been in the dish," I concluded.

"The dish you told me *you* picked out and put on the
table," Detective Stoltz said.

The faux-wood panels were doing the boogie-woogie once
again.

"Look, Detective, I didn't even know Savannah," I said
firmly. "I'd never *heard* of her until Chelsea Atkins told me
her name yesterday. I had absolutely no reason to wish her
any harm. But there were plenty of people in that room who
did know her. Which means Savannah Crane's killer must
have been a member of the crew."

My mind continued to race as I tried to reconstruct what
had happen. "They were the only ones who had access to the
dish and the spoon. There was nobody else there last night or
this morning, at least not besides the three people I told you
about and me. And I know for certain that none of us had
anything to do with what happened."

"I can assure you that we'll look at all the crew members
carefully," he said. With a meaningful look, he added, "But
when it comes to murder, sometimes what seems like the

most obvious explanation doesn't turn out to be the correct one."

Jake leaned forward. "Surely you don't consider my client a suspect in this actress's murder," he said. "As she just told you, she had never even heard of her before yesterday, much less met her and had something transpire that gave her a reason to want her dead."

Detective Stoltz was silent for what seemed like a very long time before he said, "But we don't actually know that, do we?"

I opened my mouth to protest, then immediately snapped it shut. I'd just gotten the answer to Jake's question about whether or not I was a suspect.

Clearly, I was.

I was still trying to digest that ugly fact when Detective Stoltz said, "You can be sure that we'll be looking into every possible option. In the meantime, Ms. McKay, there's something you can do for me. Once your store is open again, I'd like you to pay extra attention to everyone who comes in."

I blinked. "What do you mean?"

"Often, a murderer can't resist the urge to return to the scene of the crime," he said. "If someone shows up who doesn't normally come into your shop, or if someone appears to be acting a little strange, take note."

There was something chilling about the idea of Savannah Crane's murderer sailing into Lickety Splits, pretending to crave ice cream but, in reality, wanting to be there for an entirely different reason. An unimaginably sinister reason.

"I will," I assured him.

The detective asked me a few more questions, mostly about logistics. He wanted to know about all the ways of gaining entrance into Lickety Splits, other people who may have had keys, and spots in the downtown area where someone might stand in order to get a good view of the shop. He also asked if I'd noticed anyone watching my store or asking unusual questions, not only the day before but at any time. I did my best to give helpful answers.

Finally, he shifted in his seat, his body language telling me that our interview was over.

"Thank you for your time, Ms. McKay," he said. Glancing at his notes, he added, "I'll also be talking to your niece, Emma Pritchard, as well as your other two associates."

"When can I go back to business as usual?" I asked.

"I'm afraid I can't answer that," Detective Stoltz replied seriously. "Your ice cream shop is now a crime scene. No one can go inside until the investigation has been completed. Or even touch anything on the exterior, for that matter, since that's been taped off, too."

"But—but—"

The same *buts* that had run through my head before were making a comeback. Big-time.

I never did have a chance to voice any of them since the detective was already on his feet. It was clear that, as far as he was concerned, we were done.

Lickety Splits was also done. At least for now.

"I don't think you should be alone right now," Jake said as the two of us stood outside the Wolfert's Roost police station. "It's still a little early, but let's go get lunch."

"Sounds good," I said. Especially since I didn't know where else to go.

Jake drove back into town, using a circuitous route that kept us from driving past Lickety Splits. But as soon as I realized what he was doing, I asked him to take me there.

"I just want to see it," I explained.

Hearing Detective Stoltz say that I had to keep Lickety Splits closed indefinitely had been bad enough. The actual experience of parking outside it and seeing the yellow crime-scene tape crisscrossed along the front was an experience that was on another level entirely.

My beautiful shop looked so forlorn. So miserable. So hopeless.

Which was exactly the way I felt.

Jake put his arm around me protectively. "Come on, Katy," he said softly. "Let's get out of here. And I know just the place to go."

Toastie's was the obvious place to recover from the morning's events. The small eatery was right in town, but not close enough to Lickety Splits that I'd have a view of my poor, pathetic shop. It was also the embodiment of homeyness. Familiarity, too, since it was a place I'd been coming to for so long that I used to have to climb up onto the seats.

Toastie's was a genuine, old-fashioned diner, rather than merely being a more modern place that was simply designed to look like one. That was a nice way of saying it was kind of a dump. The Formica on the tables was the real thing, probably there since the 1970s. The same went for the cigarette burns and mysterious stains that dotted it.

It was pretty empty, so Jake and I slid into one of the booths in front, next to the line of windows overlooking Hudson Street. My pants snagged a bit on the strip of duct tape that held the seat together.

Toasties's proprietor, Big Moe, immediately lumbered over to our table with two white mugs of steaming coffee. I swear, the man must be psychic. Tucked under his arm were two laminated menus, multipage tomes that listed everything from basic egg sandwiches to heavenly waffles with Nutella to turkey dinners complete with stuffing, gravy, and cranberry sauce. I knew from past experience that the menus would add to the diner's feeling of authenticity by being sticky.

Jake drank his coffee black, no sugar. I, meanwhile, always loaded mine up with enough cream and sugar that it practically became a melted version of Cappuccino Crunch ice cream.

He took a sip, then with mock serious said, "This seems to be becoming a tradition."

"What does?" I asked, tearing open a packet of sugar.

"You and me coming to Toastie's after you've been implicated in a murder," he replied.

"Ha ha," I said sullenly.

"Too soon, I guess," Jake said, shrugging. "Come on, Kate. I wouldn't be teasing you if I thought you had anything to worry about."

"No? What about the fact that someone was murdered— and it happened in my shop?" I shot back. "That doesn't exactly do much for my reputation. You know that saying about how there's no such thing as bad publicity? I, for one, have never believed that. And this is from someone who used to work as a publicist!"

My eyes were burning as I muttered, "I can't believe I'm in the middle of a murder investigation again."

I waited for Jake to say something comforting. Something like, "Yeah, but it's pretty clear that Detective Stoltz doesn't really believe you had anything to do with it." Or at least, "I'm sure Stoltz will get this case cleared up fast."

Instead, he said, "It's not good, is it?"

"Well, I guess the upside is that Lickety Splits being closed for a while because it's now considered a crime scene will give me plenty of free time," I quipped. I was trying to sound lighthearted, but I wasn't doing that great a job.

Jake eyed me warily. "Yeah, it will. And what exactly are you planning on doing with that free time?"

I kept my eyes on my coffee mug. "What do you *think* I'm planning on doing?" I asked.

"Kate, I hope you're not thinking of conducting your own investigation," Jake said earnestly.

I just shrugged, then took a big gulp of coffee. "I haven't actually thought about it," I replied.

He leaned forward so he was only a few inches away from me, studying my face.

"Is there something wrong?" I asked, frowning.

"I'm just checking to see if your nose is growing," he said, trying not to smile.

Personally, I wasn't in the mood to smile. "I haven't decided anything, Jake. But if I did decide to be a little—shall we say, *proactive*—in absolving myself of guilt, since I'm clearly a suspect in Detective Stoltz's mind, I don't see the problem with that."

"*I* see a problem," Jake said. "In fact, I see a serious problem. First, there's a killer out there. Someone dangerous. Second, you don't know anything about the movie business or the people in it. Third, you have no training, aside from the fact that you've gotten involved in murder investigations a couple of times before. Both times with nearly disastrous consequences, I might add—"

"Point taken," I said.

I hoped I was making it clear that I didn't want to have this discussion. Not now, possibly not ever. What I wanted was to drink my coffee, stuff my face with some comfort food, and find something else to talk about.

Besides, I got the feeling I wasn't going to change Jake's mind anyway.

So it was a great relief that Big Moe chose that moment to reappear. Jake and I ordered. We were both familiar enough with the menu that we already knew exactly what we wanted. A burger for him, emotional support in the form of strawberry-banana waffles smothered in whipped cream for me.

When Big Moe went off to make all our dreams come true, I immediately told Jake, "I can't think about this anymore. Let's talk about something else. Anything new with you?"

Jake leaned back in his seat and casually draped his arm across the back. "Funny you should ask," he said, his tone a bit strained. "Actually, there is. And, well, it has something to do with you."

"With me?" I repeated, blinking.

"It *might* have something to do with you," he corrected himself. Grinning, he added, "That is, if I can talk you into it."

"Okay, now you've got my attention," I told him.

"So, here's the thing," Jake said. He pushed aside his mug, folded his arms across his chest, and leaned forward so his elbows were on the table. "I've been thinking about expanding Juniper Hill's scope. Up until now, the dairy has been focusing on wholesale, but the Hudson Valley is going through a major shift—"

"Cut to the punch line," I interrupted.

He took a deep breath. "I want to open a store."

I was still trying to absorb what he'd just said when he went on. "I found the perfect place. It's this old roadside stand, right on Route 9 a few miles south of Wolfert's Roost. It's bigger than the usual roadside stand, though. I think it was a mom-and-pop operation a million years ago that mainly catered to tourists. They may even have had a gas pump there at one point, if the big concrete slab in front is any indication.

"Anyway," he went on, "a few other businesses have been in that building over the decades, but it's been sitting there empty for at least two years. I think I can get it cheap."

"And turn it into what?" I asked.

"A modern-day version of a roadside stand, with enough old-fashioned touches that it feels like an original," he replied proudly. "It would sell all the things that tourists like to shop for. Locally grown fruit and vegetables, when they're in season. Flowers, too. I can picture huge, colorful bouquets out front that would catch the eye of people driving by. And food, especially things made by local people. Jams and jellies, baked goods, cheeses, whatever I can find. Basics, too, so people who live around here would have a reason to stop in. Milk and other dairy products from Juniper Hill, for one thing.

"But it would have other things, too," he went on, growing more and more excited the longer he talked. "Local crafts, souvenirs . . ."

"You could call it something cute like the Broken Bucket," I said, thinking out loud. "Or something memorable, like, I don't know, the Flying Frog or the Happy Cow."

"One idea I came up with is simply calling it Pratt's," Jake added. "Or there's always the Juniper Hill Farm Stand."

"Tell you what: I'll put Emma on it," I told him. "She's great at this kind of thing."

"So it sounds as if you think this is a good idea," Jake said lightly.

"I absolutely do," I said. "I think that between the steady stream of day-trippers and all the city people with weekend houses around here, not to mention all the new people who are relocating to this area, you can't go wrong."

Suddenly I remembered that Jake had said something about me being part of this.

"But where do I fit in?" I asked, even though I already had an idea.

"Ice cream, of course," he replied. "I was hoping you'd be willing to let me sell Lickety Splits ice cream at my shop. It *is* made with Juniper Hill products, after all."

"Do you mean packed ice cream, like pint containers, or cups and cones that are scooped out on-site?" I asked.

"Up to you," he said. "But selling gourmet ice cream like yours would be a real plus for my shop. Especially since you've already built yourself a nice reputation."

"Have I?" I asked, genuinely surprised by his comment.

He laughed. "You obviously haven't Googled 'Lickety Splits' lately, have you? Check out the reviews on Yelp and TripAdvisor. You're pretty much getting five stars everywhere. Although there is this one guy who blasted Prune 'n' Raisin," he noted, chuckling.

"Not my finest hour," I admitted. "But at least I'm willing to experiment."

"Lickety Splits has even been mentioned on some special web sites that are geared toward ice cream lovers," Jake added. "This one web site, IceCreamFanatics.com, actually named you the number-three gourmet ice cream purveyor in the country."

I was dying to know who'd captured the top two spots on that list.

"In fact," Jake went on, suddenly breaking eye contact and instead acting as if the answer to the secret of life was written on Big Moe's sticky, cigarette-stained table, "I thought you might even consider becoming my business partner."

That comment sent my eyebrows jumping up to the stratosphere. "But—I'm not looking to—we don't—if it's start-up money you need, I could certainly—"

"It's nothing like that," Jake insisted. When he finally looked at me, his eyes positively bored into mine. "I thought it would be fun."

I had nothing to say to that.

Jake wanted the two of us to become partners. A pair. A unit.

I wasn't quite sure what he meant by that. Was he saying he wanted to be *business* partners or *partner* partners?

Either way, the complications could be monumental.

"Just think about it," Jake said. "I know it's a major decision. You've already got so much going on, what with running the shop and catering and all the other things you're doing—"

Jake was right. I did have a lot going on. And not all of it was related to ice cream.

Still, I had a feeling that no matter how distracted I was about Savannah Crane's murder, it would be difficult not to think about his proposition.

Chapter 4

Jacob Fussell of Baltimore, Maryland, was the
first to manufacture ice cream on a large scale.
Fussell bought fresh dairy products from farmers
in York County, Pennsylvania, and sold them in
Baltimore. An unstable demand for his dairy
products often left him with a surplus of cream,
which he made into ice cream. He built his first
ice cream factory in Seven Valleys, Pennsylvania,
in 1851.

—*https://en.wikipedia.org/wiki/Ice_cream*

Now that Lickety Splits was a crime scene, I had nowhere
to go but home. Fortunately, that was exactly where I
wanted to be.

As I drove up to 59 Sugar Maple Way, I could practically
feel the dilapidated old house reaching its arms out to me and
pulling me into a soothing bear hug. I had spent most of my
childhood there, ever since I was five years old. That was
when my father passed away and my mother brought my
two sisters and me to Wolfert's Roost to live with Grams.
Julie, the oldest of us three, was twelve, and Nina was ten.

I would have loved any house I lived in with the four of
them. But this particular house happened to be the very
image of—well, comfort.

Back in the 1880s, when the three-story Victorian was built, it had undoubtedly been majestic. It has a turret jutting out of the center, an elegant white porch that runs along the entire front, and curved bay windows on both sides of the front door, one in the living room and one in the dining room. Due to a misunderstanding between my great-great-great-grandfather and the builder, the shingles had been painted yellow—rather than "mellow," as my ancestor had intended.

The house was still dignified, but the past century and a half had taken a bit of a toll. These days the porch sagged, the paint on the shingles and window frames was chipped, and the front yard looked so bedraggled that I was actually grateful when it snowed.

Yet the house still epitomized hominess, at least in my eyes. Grams kept three rocking chairs on the front porch, one wicker, one wood, and one painted with peeling blue paint. There was a colorful needlepoint pillow featuring a different flower on each one. My grandmother's handiwork, of course. A line of flowerpots stood along the banister, and Grams had hung one of her dried-flower wreaths on the front door. Late that summer, she had even painted huge pink and purple flowers on the wooden ramp we'd had built to make it easier for her to get in and out of the house.

The inside of the house was filled with her creations, too. The sunny living room was dominated by large, well-worn furniture: a dark red velvet couch with gold carved legs, over-stuffed upholstered chairs, and three heavy wooden curio cabinets displaying souvenirs of Grams's countless trips all around the world. And superimposed over them were more items she had made. Spread along the back of the couch was an orange, gold, and lime-green afghan, the startling colors a throwback to the seventies, when she'd crocheted it. She had needlepointed the pillows crowding the back and hooked the footstool in front of the green upholstered chair that was her favorite. Her meticulously made patchwork quilts hung on the walls, all made with wonderfully bright fabrics.

As I opened the front door, I was immediately greeted by the two individuals charged with keeping the place cute. Digger is our resident cheerleader, always happy and full of energy—so much so that just being in his presence can often be exhausting. Then again, the scruffy little guy is a terrier mix, so he can't help having the personality of someone who's hit the espresso pot a little too hard.

Our feline, Chloe, is a grand dame who may be aging but still considers it her job to keep Digger under control. He's been a big influence on her as well, since she's almost as sociable as he is. If there's a human in the room, she has to be there, too.

Grams was in the living room, no doubt waiting for me. She was dressed comfortably in sweat pants and an apple-green, long-sleeved knit shirt, along with a hand-knit, dark green vest. Draped across her lap was her latest craft project, a small gold and brown patchwork quilt with appliquéd pumpkins. She jumped up as soon as I came in.

"Katydid!" she cried, still holding her needle and thread as she came into the foyer. "Are you all right?"

"I'm fine," I assured her, crouching down to give Digger and Chloe the welcoming tummy scratching they had both come to expect. "I take it Emma told you what happened?"

She nodded. "You must be devastated. What a horrible thing to witness!"

"It was pretty bad," I agreed. "And there's been a new development: Lickety Splits is closed. It's now a crime scene."

"Oh, my goodness," Grams said breathlessly. "Do you know how long it will be before you can reopen?"

"Probably not too long," I replied. "At least that's what Jake said."

"You've talked to Jake?" she said.

"He came to the police station with me," I told her. "Detective Stoltz wanted to question me. But that was mainly because Savannah Crane was killed inside my shop." I didn't see any reason to worry her about me being a suspect.

"You poor thing," she said. "What a morning!" And she gave me exactly what I needed: a long, hard hug.

I was still feeling pretty shaken up, but not so much that I didn't know exactly what to do next. I went into my bedroom and fired up my laptop, determined to find out everything I could about Savannah Crane.

Maybe the young actress was about to become a star, but she wasn't there yet. So even though she was on the verge of fame and fortune, the irony was that, at this point, there simply wasn't that much about her online aside from several articles about her murder that didn't tell me anything I didn't already know.

But plenty of photos came up. A string of pictures of the blond actress with the not-quite-perfect yet infinitely intriguing face stared back at me. In some of them, she looked as glamorous as an old-time movie star. In others, she looked much more down-to-earth, like someone you could talk to. Someone you could even joke around with. About eating too much ice cream, for example, and not fitting into her costume. Those were the photos that made me feel as if someone was squeezing my heart in their fist.

There were also listings for her on Wikipedia and the TV and film web site IMBD.com.

I learned that Savannah had been born in Columbus, Ohio, then majored in theater at Ohio State before moving to New York. She continued studying acting at the New York Acting Workshop, meanwhile doing television commercials and picking up small parts with small theater companies. Then came some tiny roles in movies, none of which I'd ever heard of.

I found it sad that *The Best Ten Days of My Life* was listed as one of her credits, with a release date one year in the future. Now, of course, that wasn't going to happen.

As for her personal life, the Internet was willing to tell me plenty. Her father was a high school math teacher, her mother was a real estate agent, and she had a brother who was in the military and stationed abroad.

She also had a serious boyfriend.

Timothy Scott, born Timothy Randall Scott, was an actor as well. The web pages about Savannah just mentioned him in passing, so I moved on to Googling him.

Once again, a line of photos came up. Timothy Scott was nice-looking, but not over-the-top handsome. More like the boy next door. Light brown hair, light brown eyes, an engaging smile. Late twenties or early thirties, I surmised. Nice build, but not exactly a muscleman.

Below the photos I found the same thing I'd found when I'd Googled Savannah: Wikipedia and IMBD.com listings. Timothy was born and raised in the New York area, then studied theater at New York University and a few different acting schools in the city. Since then he had landed small parts in a variety of television shows, including playing Thug with Knife in an episode of the popular crime drama *Mean City Streets* and Jogger in the comedy series *Miami Minutes*. He had also done some commercials, including one for Verizon that I figured must have paid the rent for quite some time.

I wondered if I'd ever seen him on television. I scrolled back to the photos and began studying them, one by one.

I didn't recognize him. But I suddenly froze as I realized I did recognize something.

In one photograph, Timothy and Savannah were standing with their arms around each other, grinning at the camera, in front of a house. It was a cute bungalow, nothing too fancy, with stone steps in front and window boxes dripping with flowers. The front door was painted a startling shade of lime green.

A weekend place, I figured. Interesting that two aspiring actors could afford something like that.

But I was much more interested in the truck parked in the driveway. Printed on the side were the words NEW PALTZ PLUMBING.

New Paltz was right across the Hudson River from Wolfert's Roost. Which meant that Savannah Crane's weekend getaway was close by.

Excitedly, I clicked on photo after photo, looking for more clues. And then I spotted something else that was familiar. I came across a photo of Timothy—alone, this time—sitting at a café, sipping a cold drink through a straw. Behind him was a sign identifying the restaurant as the Coffee Break Café.

I knew the Coffee Break Café. It was located on Main Street in Cold Spring, a charming village that overlooked the Hudson River and was located just a few miles south of Wolfert's Roost.

I did some more Googling. I put in Timothy's name again, this time adding "Cold Spring." Nothing.

I tried again, this time using Savannah Crane's name.

Bingo. An address in Cold Spring came up.

The house belongs to *Savannah*? I thought. An aspiring actress like her had had the money to buy a house? In a desirable place like Cold Spring, no less?

There were some perfectly good explanations for that, of course. They ranged from family money to a large inheritance to working hard from an early age and investing well.

But while the question of how Savannah had managed to buy a house was intriguing, what mattered to me even more was the fact that I'd just found my first good lead.

*   *   *

Once I had the address of Savannah's house in Cold Spring, finding it was easy. Thank you, Google Maps. And because of all the information available on real estate web sites like Trulia and Redfin, I was able to learn that the one-story ranch had three bedrooms and two bathrooms, occupied 1,296 square feet on a 1.1-acre lot, and was worth almost $400,000.

Quite a price tag for a struggling actress.

As I drove down her street, I spotted the house from a block away. The lime-green door was hard to miss. It was a charming little place, with white shingles, black shutters that looked as if they'd been painted recently, and an expansive front lawn.

I was nervous as I strode up the walkway, my heart pounding and my mouth dry. My anxiety was alleviated only slightly by the sight of a cute, foot-high ceramic garden gnome with a tall red hat, perched on the corner of the stone steps.

I was poised outside the door, rehearsing my opening lines one more time, when the sound of someone yelling made me freeze. It was a man's voice, coming from inside the house.

While my instincts told me to run, my determination to do what I'd come here to do propelled me a few steps forward.

And then: "What the hell do you think you're doing! I'm gonna kill you, you animal!"

I froze.

Maybe this isn't such a good time, I thought, glancing longingly at my truck.

"I'm gonna kill you, you animal!" I heard once again. And then, in a softer voice, "I'm gonna kill you, you animal!"

Something sounded wrong.

And then, in a low, gruff voice, I heard, "What the hell do you think you're doing? I'm gonna kill you, you animal! I'm gonna kill you, you—no, wait."

And then, a loud groan. One of frustration, not fury.

"I can't do this!" the voice from inside the house wailed.

Peering through the front window, I saw a man standing in the living room, alone. In one hand he held a stack of paper that I immediately surmised was a script.

But while the lines I'd just heard him screaming may have been nothing more than words he was reading off a page, the desperation that was now in his voice sounded real.

I watched him sink onto the couch, drop the script, and bury his face in his hands.

I realized that I'd come at a very bad time.

I turned away to retreat to my truck, thinking that I'd come back another day. But in my rush to get away, I accidentally kicked the garden gnome. It tumbled down the stone steps, landing on the walkway with a loud crash. At least it wasn't completely destroyed. Only the top of its red hat had broken off, like an ice cream cone that someone had snapped in two.

A few seconds later I heard the front door open behind me. I turned, certain that the guilt I was feeling was written all over my face. Not only guilt over breaking the garden ornament, either. I also felt bad that I'd come here so soon after the tragedy that Timothy had just suffered.

And the man standing in front of me was undoubtedly Timothy. I recognized him from the Internet immediately. He was wearing jeans and a rumpled navy-blue T-shirt. His shoulders were slumped, giving him a defeated look. His thick, light brown hair was shaggy, not in a cool way but in a way that said he needed a haircut. His eyes were rimmed in red, and his expression was distraught.

"Can I help you?" he asked, running one hand through his hair distractedly.

"I'm afraid I broke your gnome," I said apologetically, pointing to the ceramic figure lying on the ground.

"No big deal," he said. "Just give it to me, will you? I don't want anyone to trip on it."

I retrieved the gnome and its broken-off hat and handed them to Timothy.

"Is there a reason you're here?" he asked, sounding confused. "Aside from coming onto my property to break my stuff?"

"You're Timothy Scott, right?" I said. "I wondered if I could talk to you."

"Who are you?" he asked. He was cradling the gnome in his arms as his eyes traveled past me, toward the street. I suspected that he was looking for a van from a television station. Or maybe some other indication that I was a reporter or an overzealous fan or someone else who was anything but welcome.

"My name is Kate McKay," I said. "I hope I'm not interrupting . . ."

"What do you want?" he demanded.

I took a deep breath. "I'm really sorry to bother you," I said. "But I'm the owner of Lickety Splits, the ice cream parlor in Wolfert's Roost where—"

"Now I understand." Still looking puzzled, he added, "Sort of. Why are you here?"

"A few reasons, actually," I said. "One is to extend my condolences. I didn't know Savannah—in fact, I just met her briefly the day of the shoot, but—"

"Thanks," he said brusquely, "but there's got to be another reason."

I took a deep breath, then said, "I'm here because I'm involved. This terrible thing happened in my shop. I was standing just feet away from Savannah when she ate *my* ice cream out of one of *my* dishes with *my* spoon . . ."

Through some quirk of fate, a van emblazoned with the initials of a national cable television news station chose that exact moment to pull up in front of the house.

Timothy's expression immediately hardened. "Come inside," he instructed, waving me in.

As soon as we were in the foyer, he slammed the front door shut.

"Those idiots have been bothering me nonstop," he said. "As if I don't have enough to deal with right now."

"It's the kind of story that makes headlines," I said gently. "Unfortunately."

"Yes, I guess it is," Timothy said. He put the damaged gnome on the windowsill, gently placing the chunk that had broken off its hat beside it. Then he collapsed onto the couch and stared off into space for what seemed a very long time. I wondered if he'd forgotten I was there.

But then he turned to me. "Do the cops consider you a suspect?" he asked. The tension in his face told me he wasn't sure whether or not he should, too.

"Yes and no," I replied. "They brought me in for questioning simply because it happened in my store. As I said, I'd never met Savannah until two days ago. I'd never even heard her name. There's absolutely no reason why I would have wanted anything bad to happen to her."

Timothy's eyes narrowed. "I still don't understand why you're here."

I decided to be honest. "I'm trying to clear my name. And to solve this mess so my shop's reputation isn't tarnished— the faster, the better."

"Isn't that why we have homicide detectives?" he asked, sounding a bit skeptical.

"Of course," I said. "It's just that it's hard *not* to get involved in something like this when you're one of the people those homicide detectives are looking at. The sooner the case is solved, the faster I can get back to my normal life." I couldn't resist adding, "At the moment, my shop is closed for business. It's now a crime scene."

"I get it," he said.

"In that case," I said, "I wonder if there's anything you

can tell me about Savannah's life. Anything out of the ordinary that might have been going on. There was obviously someone who was very angry with her. Or who wanted her out of the way for some reason. Do you have any idea who that might be?"

He thought for a few seconds. "Believe me, I've been thinking about very little else for the past two days. But there are no obvious answers. Everybody loved Savannah. She was the sweetest, kindest, gentlest person—"

His face crumpled. "You know, I spent the morning arranging a memorial service for her. It'll be here in the Hudson Valley. Even though she lived in the city, this weekend place of hers was where she really felt at home, so it seemed like the right thing to do."

I blinked. So not only had Savannah bought this house; she had done so in order to have a second home—rather than, say, for rental income. It was her weekend place. I was more puzzled than ever about how she had managed to pull that off.

"I can't describe how horrible all this is," Timothy went on, his eyes moist. "She was twenty-six years old, for heaven's sake! And—and I loved her."

He dissolved into tears, his anguish erupting in deep choking sounds that made my eyes fill with tears, too.

Seeing how distraught this man was made it pretty much impossible to believe that he could have had anything to do with her death.

I left soon afterward, not wanting to intrude on his grief. It wasn't until I was driving away that I was able to put our meeting into perspective.

Timothy had seemed sincerely devastated. Then again, I reminded myself, he was an actor. And pretending was what actors did best.

Then there was his claim that Savannah Crane hadn't had

a single enemy. I found that difficult to believe about anyone, no matter how sweet she was. Someone had wanted her dead, and it was undoubtedly someone she knew. And Timothy, of all people, should have known that there were many possibilities. Actors became jealous of other actors' success, current and former lovers became possessive, people from one's past dug up old conflicts and became vengeful.

Timothy's insistence that everyone in the world was as crazy about Savannah as he was made me wonder if he was protecting someone.

Or even himself.

There was one—and only one—advantage to Lickety Splits being closed. And that was that I now had more time to spend with Grams.

That evening was one of those rare occasions when the three of us were able to sit down and enjoy a meal together. Grams had set the dining room table with her "good" china. She had also used her favorite tablecloth and matching napkins, a blue and green block-print design with elephants she'd bought on a trip to India.

Emma, meanwhile, had insisted on doing all the cooking. She had declared that the meal she was preparing had a theme: comfort food. She spent hours in the kitchen whipping up herbed meatloaf, made-from-scratch macaroni and cheese, carrots dripping with honey, and fluffy biscuits the size of baseballs. If a person couldn't find comfort in a menu like that, the poor sad sack was beyond being consoled.

As usual, I was in charge of dessert. For tonight, I'd made something I was thinking of selling at the shop: an Italian dessert called *affogato*, which means "drowned." It's simple enough to make, since it's basically vanilla ice cream that's been drowned in hot espresso.

But one of the fun things about *affogato* is that you don't have to use vanilla ice cream. The sky's the limit there, as long as you choose a flavor that's compatible with the flavor of the coffee. And you can add other things, such as shaved chocolate or nuts or coconut. You can even top it off with amaretto or hazelnut-flavored liquor. I was still experimenting with different combinations. But one thing I was certain of was that I would use decaf espresso in case the person who was eating it liked the flavor of coffee but didn't want a caffeine jolt.

Yet while all the trappings of our family dinner were festive, the bottom line was that even colorful cloth napkins and drippy melted cheese couldn't keep us from ruminating about the matters at hand.

"Did Detective Stoltz say anything about how long Lickety Splits will be closed?" Emma asked as she slathered butter on the cloud-like biscuit she'd just broken in half.

"You know how he is," I said, stabbing a piece of meatloaf with my fork. "He says as little as possible. Getting information out of that man is impossible."

"What about Jake?" Emma asked. "He was a criminal lawyer. Does he have any idea how long it usually takes the police to collect the evidence they need in a situation like this?"

"He said it shouldn't take too long," I replied. "But every day that goes by is costing me money." Not to mention what it's doing to my shop's good name, I thought. *And* mine.

As Emma and I talked, I gradually became aware of a strange sound in the background. It wasn't until Emma and I stopped talking long enough to pass the butter from her side of the table to mine that I realized what it was.

"Are you humming?" I asked, turning to Grams.

"Was I?" she replied, looking surprised. And, I thought, a little guilty. "I'm sorry. There's a song playing in my head, but I didn't realize I was humming it."

Emma and I exchanged puzzled looks.

"What's going on, Grams?" Emma demanded. Even though Caroline Whitman, my grandmother, is actually Emma's great-grandmother, she calls her Grams, the same way my two sisters and I do. Their husbands call her Grams, too. Somehow, coming up with another name for Emma to call her by would be, well, just too complicated.

Grams glanced up from her plate. "Nothing is going on!"

"Come on, Grams," I said. "I've never heard you hum while you were eating dinner before. Emma's spread of comfort food is truly spectacular, but I don't know that it's something to hum about."

She sighed. "All right. Maybe I am in a particularly good mood."

"And why would that be?" Emma asked teasingly. "I don't suppose it has anything to do with Georgie-Porgie, does it?"

I braced myself for a denial. Instead, Grams's face softened into a smile. "As a matter of fact, it does. My relationship with George is—let's just say it's suddenly going beyond planning the Halloween event for the kids."

"Do you mean he asked you out on a date?" Emma asked, widening her big brown eyes.

"As a matter of fact, he did," Grams replied. "He invited me to have dinner with him at Greenleaf this Sunday evening."

"Greenleaf!" I cried. "This guy is serious!"

Greenleaf is easily the best restaurant in Wolfert's Roost, if not the entire Hudson Valley. A few months earlier, the *New York Times'* restaurant critic had trekked up to our little town to check it out. After tasting the farm-to-table cuisine, brought to thrilling new levels with the addition of ingredients that most people didn't even know how to pronounce, he had awarded it the maximum number of stars.

Since then, foodies from all over the metropolitan area had been descending upon Wolfert's Roost to enjoy Greenleaf's exceptional cuisine. While the restaurant's founder and executive chef no longer lived in town, he apparently oversaw its menu from afar. I hadn't gotten around to eating there myself yet, but from what I heard, it was as fabulous as ever.

"George and Caroline, sitting in a tree," Emma began chanting, "K-I-S-S—"

"Oh, stop," Grams insisted, waving her hand in the air dismissively. "For all I know, it's not even an actual date. I may simply be leaping to conclusions. Maybe he just means it as a friendly gesture."

"Ri-i-ight," Emma said dryly. "A man takes you out for an expensive dinner because he wants to be friends."

"It's not impossible, is it?" Grams countered.

"Not impossible," I replied. "But I agree with Emma. It's highly unlikely."

"The important question," Emma said, waving her fork in the air, "is what are you going to wear?"

For the rest of the meal, the three of us had fun speculating about hilarious outfits, everything from an evening gown to a chef's hat and apron to show how much she appreciated fine cuisine. It was a welcome distraction, much better than talking about Savannah Crane's murder and the toll it was taking on me, my business, and every other aspect of my life.

"Maybe you and George could double-date with Ethan and me some time," Emma teased as we all cleared the table. "He keeps talking about this club he heard about that specializes in grunge music from the nineties. That's ancient history to me, but maybe that's your thing, Grams."

"Of course it's her thing," I joked. "Haven't you noticed the Nirvana T-shirt hanging in her closet?"

"Don't get ahead of yourself, Emma," Grams warned. "We're not at the double-date stage yet, and we might never be. I still think George may just be interested in an occasional dinner companion."

But I noticed that her eyes definitely had that same twinkle I'd seen in them before.

Later that evening, as Grams was beating me at Rummy 500, Emma came rushing into the living room, her cloud of dark, blue-streaked curls flying behind her. Her laptop computer was tucked under her arm.

"Kate, you're not going to believe what happened!" she cried.

"Whatever it is, I hope it's better than what's happening with this hand," I replied, grimacing at the mismatched twos, threes, and fours I was holding.

"Kate, this is serious!" Emma insisted.

That got my attention.

"What happened?" I asked.

"I was just checking some of the web sites I like to follow that have news about celebrities. And I just read that Jennifer Jordan has disappeared!" Emma exclaimed. "She was last spotted on Wednesday afternoon, picking up dry cleaning in Greenwich Village, the section of New York City where she lives. No one has seen her since then!"

Jennifer Jordan, Jennifer Jordan . . . I couldn't place the name. I certainly didn't have any idea why we should care.

"Who on earth is Jennifer Jordan?" I finally asked.

Emma rolled her eyes. "Ka-a-a-ate!" she moaned, as if I was the most clueless person in the universe. "Jennifer Jordan is the actress who lost the part of Suzi Hamilton in *The Best Ten Days* to Savannah Crane! According to this web site, she really, really wanted that role. And just a few hours after Savannah was murdered, she mysteriously vanished!"

Chapter 5

Rocky Road ice cream became the first widely
available flavor other than vanilla, chocolate, and
strawberry in 1929. It was invented in Oakland,
California, by William Dreyer, who had an ice
cream company with his partner, Joseph Edy.
Dreyer used his wife's sewing scissors to cut up
walnuts and marshmallows, which he added to
chocolate ice cream. The walnuts were later
replaced with toasted almonds. Dreyer and Edy
named the flavor after the period that followed
the Wall Street Crash of 1929 "to give folks something to smile about in the midst of the Great
Depression."

—https://en.wikipedia.org/wiki/Rocky_road_(ice_cream)

"She vanished?" I repeated, confused. "Where did she go?"

"Kate, that's the whole point of vanishing!" Emma exclaimed, sounding exasperated. "It means that no one *knows*
where she went!"

"But there could be all kinds of explanations, couldn't
there?" Grams said.

My mind raced as I tried to come up with a few. "Like she
decided she wanted to get out of the public eye for a while,"
I said. "Like a favorite aunt got sick and she flew off somewhere to take care of her. Like—like—"

"Here's one," Emma said breathlessly. "How about she disappeared because she just murdered her rival, Savannah Crane?"

My mind was still clicking away. "But was Jennifer Jordan even anywhere *near* the Hudson Valley?" I asked, trying to figure out a way that Emma's theory could hold water.

"That's something I hope to find out," Emma said. "But there's another possibility."

"What's that?" I asked.

"That she hired one of the crew members who was at the shoot to kill Savannah!" she said excitedly. She plopped down in the dark green upholstered chair. "Think about it. It makes perfect sense. Or maybe both Jennifer and the person she hired wanted Savannah dead, so Jennifer didn't actually have to hire him or her, since they were working together as a team. And now that she's a murderer, she's disappeared . . ."

"It's not impossible," I said thoughtfully. "Maybe it's not the most likely scenario, but it could be what happened."

Detective Stoltz's declaration about the most obvious explanation in murder cases not always being the correct one had stuck in my mind. So did the other side of it: that the correct explanation could sometimes be one that wasn't obvious at all.

"I've been doing some research on Jennifer Jordan," Emma went on animatedly. She opened her laptop and placed it on the coffee table so Grams and I could see the screen. "Apparently she and Savannah have been rivals for ages. The two of them went to the same acting school in New York together. According to this web site, CelebScoops.com, they were both the same type. You know, young, pretty, innocent-looking. What used to be called debutantes back in the old days. Anyway, every time there was a role that they were both suited for, they ended up competing."

"Who usually won?" Grams asked, craning her neck to get a better look at the computer.

Emma pointed at the screen. "Over here it makes it sound as if Savannah was the favorite most of the time. Jennifer Jordan didn't get famous until she married a big-shot movie producer." Turning her laptop so I could see the screen, she added, "He's the yucky-looking guy in this picture, Harry Steinberg."

"He looks as if he's much older than she is," I commented, peering at the photo. And that was being polite. He was also short, chubby, bald, and kind of ugly.

But Emma had made it sound as if he was very influential. Wealthy, too.

"They got divorced after only a couple of years," she went on. "But while they were married, she landed some great roles in a bunch of his movies. She even got an Oscar nomination for her performance in *Young Eleanor*. But as soon as she got famous, she ditched him."

"Marrying someone powerful is one way to get ahead in Hollywood, I suppose," I mused. "But if she's so famous, why would she give a hoot about Savannah Crane's career?"

Emma did some more clicking. "This website, StarGazer. com, says that once Jennifer Jordan divorced Harry Steinberg, no one would touch her. She couldn't get any good parts. But then the role of Suzi Hamilton in *The Best Ten Days of My Life* came up. Jennifer was sure that would be her big comeback. And apparently the studio that's making it was one of the few places where Harry Steinberg didn't have any influence. At any rate, she desperately wanted that role—"

"And instead Savannah Crane got it," I said, finishing her sentence. "Once again, Jennifer Jordan's longtime rival got something she really, really wanted."

The relationship between the two actresses reminded me of the one I'd had with my nemesis since childhood, Ashley

Winthrop. Ashley had resurfaced right after I'd opened Lickety Splits four months earlier. It turned out that she ran the bakery right across the street from my ice cream shop, and as soon as it opened, she put up a big sign announcing that the Sweet Things Pastry Palace was now selling ice cream.

That hadn't ended well. But it had certainly given me a good lesson in the bitter feelings that rivalries can cause.

"So Jennifer Jordan had a strong motive for killing Savannah Crane," I said, thinking aloud.

"She sure did," Emma agreed. "And now she's vanished! Kate, I think we may have found our murderer!"

"Not so fast," I warned. "There are a few other suspects, too, some of them right in the area."

I was mainly thinking about Savannah's boyfriend, Timothy. But there were also all the other people who were part of the film crew, people who had been at Lickety Splits at the time Savannah was poisoned. The possibility that one of them was working with the victim's rival was worth considering, but that still left us with the problem of figuring out who that person was.

And how on earth he or she had managed to put poison into Savannah's ice cream dish.

I was still lost in thought as Emma asked, "So you're going to do it again, right?"

I puzzled over her question, wondering if she was talking about some ice cream flavor I'd once made or an unusual catered event I'd put together . . .

But before I had a chance to figure out what she was talking about, she added, "You're going to see if you can figure out who killed Savannah Crane, aren't you?"

I was about to protest, to insist she had it all wrong. Instead, I let out a deep sigh.

"I don't think I have any choice, do you?" I said. "In fact,

I already tracked down her boyfriend. I wanted to ask him if he had any ideas about who might have been behind this."

I glanced over at Grams, nervous about her reaction.

So I was greatly relieved when she said, "Just be careful, Kate. I understand that this terrible thing really hit you close to home. After all, it happened right in your shop, with *your* ice cream in *your* dish . . . But please promise me that you won't put yourself in any danger."

"I promise," I told her earnestly.

"You know that I'll do everything I can to help you, right?" Emma said. "Computer stuff, research stuff, even going undercover."

I couldn't resist leaning over and giving my niece a big hug. "You're the absolute best, Emma," I told her. "Thank you."

"You're welcome," she replied. Snapping her computer shut, she added, "But so far, I'm betting on Jennifer Jordan. She played a killer in *Dark Days in Denmark*, and I always thought she was just a little too convincing. She was much better in that movie than any of the others I'd seen her in."

I doubted that that argument would hold up in a murder trial. But the two actresses' long-term rivalry, along with the fact that Jennifer Jordan had really wanted the role of Suzi Hamilton, were definitely worth taking into account.

Not to mention the reports that Jennifer Jordan had inexplicably disappeared.

I wondered if Detective Stoltz read CelebScoops.com or StarGazer.com. But since I was pretty sure he didn't, I decided this was a piece of information I should keep in mind.

The following morning, a Saturday, I was lingering over breakfast when my cell phone buzzed. I'd been sipping my second cup of coffee as I read and reread that day's *Daily Roost*. "MURDER STILL UNSOLVED!" the front-page headline screamed. It was a harsh reminder that I had work to do. Even with Detective Stoltz on the case.

Then came the call from the very same individual I'd been thinking about only moments earlier.

"The crime-scene tape has been taken down from your shop, Ms. McKay," Detective Stoltz informed me as soon as he'd identified himself. "You can open for business again."

At first, I was so thrilled that I let out a whoop that caused Digger's ears to jump up to the ceiling. The scruffy terrier gave me a look that said, "Hey, I thought *I* was the one who was supposed to do the barking around here!"

But two seconds later, I was in panic mode. It was already nine AM. That meant I had exactly two hours to get ready to reopen.

I gulped down the remains of my coffee, then shrieked, "Emma!"

Half an hour later, the two of us were bustling around the shop, getting ready for what would hopefully end up being a day that could be described as business as usual.

That turned out to be more demanding than I'd anticipated. Not the ice cream part, which by that point I'd pretty much mastered. It was the fact that my shop no longer looked like Halloween Central.

Despite Chelsea Atkins's promise about restoring Lickety Splits to its original state, Halloween decorations and all, that hadn't happened. Not when immediately after the movie shoot—right in the middle of it, in fact—my beloved little store had become a crime scene.

The cobwebs, the pumpkin lights, the lovable life size monsters . . . none of it was on display. Fortunately, we found all of it stashed in back, in the kitchen area where I whip up my fresh, homemade ice cream and all the other related concoctions.

"The bat fell off Dracula's shoulder!" Emma wailed as she pulled off the Bubble Wrap he'd been cocooned in.

"We can prop him up at the table anyway," I assured her. "And next time you come, bring a needle and thread, and you can perform emergency surgery."

Thanks to being highly motivated, not to mention downing that second cup of coffee, my niece and I quickly restored Lickety Splits to its original state. By five minutes to eleven, the Count was seated at a table, the witch was at the door, and Frankenstein was sitting outside, drooling over his towering ice cream cone. The cobwebs, the spiders, the lights . . . everything was back in place.

"It looks great," I told Emma. "Now all we need is customers."

I held my breath as I turned around my CLOSED sign so that it read OPEN.

It's showtime! I thought. But this time, the phrase had an entirely different meaning.

I usually love opening my shop in the morning, but today I was filled more with apprehension than optimism. I was truly worried about business being slow. A couple of months earlier, back in August, a similar incident had all but closed down Wolfert's Roost. The tourists and day-trippers were scared away.

And here we were, dealing with another murder.

So I was relieved that it didn't take long for customers to start drifting in.

Even though it was a Saturday, the most popular day for tourism in the Hudson Valley, foot traffic did seem lighter than usual. But Halloween being less than two weeks away seemed to have put the local residents in a holiday mood.

The first customer of the day was a young mother who ordered a dozen of Emma's ice cream characters for her seven-year-old son's Halloween party. She decided on an assortment of pirates, clowns, and monsters. Quite a few of the customers who followed were also up for seasonal treats, including the makeshift version of Monster Mash that Emma quickly put together by topping green mint ice cream with chocolate chips, two kinds of nuts, and crushed chocolate cookies. All that was missing from the original concept were the tiny eyeballs, but the new flavor proved to be pretty popular even without them.

Not everyone was in a Halloween mood. The two earnest teenage girls who came in, lugging heavy backpacks, for example. I suspected that they were gearing up for an intense studying session. After spending nearly ten minutes agonizing over what to get, they ended up sharing a Bananafana Split. Their choice of flavors: Dark Chocolate Hazelnut, Classic Tahitian Vanilla, and Berry Blizzard—an updated, very Lickety Splits version of the classic chocolate, vanilla, and strawberry. Then three businessmen came in and loudly ordered cones stuffed with all the ice cream that would fit. From the giddy way they were high-fiving each other, I got the feeling they'd just closed a deal.

But the customer who really made my day was the young man who wandered in. He was about Emma and Ethan's age, with a wild mane of jet-black hair. At least it managed to stay out of his eyes.

"I was totally into the thing you did the other day," he remarked after he ordered a Hudson's Hottest Hot Fudge Sundae made with English Toffee Caramel and Black Raspberry with Dark Chocolate Chunks.

"Thanks," I said automatically. Then I added, "What exactly are you talking about?"

"The crime-scene tape," he replied with a grin. "It took the concept of Halloween decorations to an awesome new level. It was totally chill! But I can see why you couldn't leave it up. It was kind of blocking the door."

I was smiling as I opened the cabinet to take out a glass tulip dish for the man's sundae. I hoped most other people had made the same assumption he had, that the crime-scene tape was just another clever Halloween decoration.

As I was reaching for the dish, I suddenly stopped, my hand frozen in midair. I had just spotted a single strand of human hair curled up on the shelf. At first, I assumed it was mine, and I told myself that I needed to be more careful. But when I pulled it out and studied it, I noticed it had a reddish tinge.

Definitely not mine.

A shock wave passed through me. I knew someone with long red hair. Chelsea Atkins, the assistant director.

My mind was racing. Of course, she had spent hours in the shop, both the night before the shoot and early that morning. But she had specifically said that she wanted *me* to pick out the dish and spoon that would be used during the film shoot because she felt uncomfortable scrounging around in my cabinets.

Now it looked as if she had done precisely that.

There could be a hundred different reasons why Chelsea had been rummaging through my cabinets, I thought. But I still felt uneasy about the fact that she had clearly done exactly that. I decided that this was a fact worth filing away. As for the hair, I wrapped it up in paper and stuck it on a shelf.

A few more customers wandered in, and then suddenly there was a lull. Lickety Splits was empty. Emma had plans to meet with two classmates from her computer course to work on a group project, and I assured her that I could handle the shop by myself while she focused on her schoolwork. The fact that she had her own car now was what made juggling her complicated life possible. Her parents had been so thrilled that she was taking classes at the community college that they had bought her one. It was practically an antique, but it gave her the mobility she needed.

Which left me alone in my shop. As I stood behind the counter, I looked around, still trying to digest the fact that this lovely place had actually been the scene of a murder.

I stared at the seat Savannah Crane had been sitting in, wondering if I'd ever again be able to see it as just another chair. It was difficult not to keep replaying that horrible morning over and over again in my head.

But what was even worse was the idea that Detective Stoltz thought I might have had something to do with it. That continued to plague me like a low-level headache that simply wouldn't go away.

I was sinking deeper and deeper into negative thoughts, so I was relieved when the door opened and another customer came in. At least, I assumed the woman was a customer. She looked as if she was in her late twenties, small in both height and build, with wavy, shoulder-length, dark brown hair. Her large brown eyes and full lips gave her round face a doll-like appearance.

She didn't come right up to the counter. That was what most customers did, either to scan the giant tubs of ice cream in the display case or to study the menu posted on the wall behind me. Instead, she immediately slumped into a chair. Then she looked around, as if she was trying to drink in her surroundings.

A wave of panic came over me as I realized that she might be a reporter. I'd prepared myself for that possibility, deciding in advance that I would refuse to talk to anyone looking for an inside scoop or even a catchy sound bite.

But this woman didn't strike me as someone who'd come here to interview me. In fact, I immediately picked up on the heavy sense of sadness she exuded.

An awkward silence hung over the shop. Finally, I asked, "Is there something I can get you?"

She glanced up, looking surprised. It was as if she'd just noticed that she wasn't alone. But instead of responding, she stared at me blankly.

"You're welcome to sample any of our flavors before deciding," I went on cheerfully. Gesturing at the listings behind me, I said, "And in addition to cones and cups, we have Hudson's Hottest Hot Fudge Sundaes, Bananafana Splits . . . and for Halloween, we've come up with a bunch of fun seasonal creations."

"Actually, I didn't come here for ice cream," the young woman said somberly.

Now I was really confused. But before I had a chance to ask what she *had* come in for, she added, "I was Savannah Crane's best friend." Tears welled up in her eyes as she choked out the words, "I wanted to see this place for myself."

"I see," I replied. I could feel my own shoulders slumping. "You're welcome to spend as much time here as you like."

"Thanks," she said. Her eyes filled with tears.

I desperately wanted to do something more for her. But the only thing I could come up with was giving her ice cream.

So I dished out big scoops of Classic Tahitian Vanilla, Chocolate Almond Fudge, and Blueberry Pomegranate, filling the biggest dish I had. Then I covered the ice cream with rainbow sprinkles. I figured the bright colors might cheer her up. And she was clearly someone who needed cheering up.

"I don't know about you," I said as I brought the concoction over to her table, "but I find that ice cream goes a long way in making even the worst situations just a little bit better."

"Thanks," she said, casting me a woeful glance as I set it down in front of her. "I don't know if I can eat it, though. I haven't had much of an appetite since . . ."

"I understand completely," I told her. "But another good

thing about ice cream it's that it's easy to eat, even if you don't have the least interest in food."

She picked up the spoon, treating it like it was made of lead.

"Do you mind if I sit down?" I asked, nodding at the seat opposite her.

She shrugged. I took that as permission.

Maybe it was because I was sitting a few inches away from her, but she finally forced a minuscule bit of vanilla into her mouth. I was glad to see that her tense expression softened, just a little.

"Hey, this is really good," she commented. "I'm not usually a big fan of vanilla, but this is delicious."

"The vanilla is imported from Tahiti," I told her, glad we'd found something lighthearted to talk about. "I call the flavor Classic Tahitian Vanilla. My intention in creating it was to bring regular old vanilla ice cream to a brand-new level."

"You sure managed to accomplish that," she said, helping herself to more.

Neither of us spoke as she continued to eat, scooping up one tiny spoonful of ice cream after another. Finally, the silence started to make me uncomfortable.

"By the way, I'm Kate McKay," I said.

"Nice to meet you," she replied. "I'm Amanda Huffner."

"Are you an actress, too?" I asked. "Is that how you know Savannah?"

She shook her head. "No, but we did meet through her acting career. It was while she was in an off-off-Broadway play. It was called *Next Stop: Brooklyn*." She grimaced. "Savannah was great in it, but it was a pretty terrible play."

"How did you come to be involved with it?" I asked.

"I work for a props house," Amanda said. "It's called Monarch Cinema Props. It's in Queens." She sounded proud as she added, "It's the biggest props house on the East Coast.

We handle everything: furniture, lamps, rugs, fake flowers, dishes, toys, you name it. We've got anything anyone could possibly need for movies, television, theater, commercials, fashion shoots ... Everything is stored in a one hundred thousand square foot warehouse that's also our showroom."

"Wow, that sounds fun!" I said. I was already wondering if it would be possible to go see it. Especially with Emma. Given my niece's artistic bent, not to mention her love of anything related to the entertainment industry, I had a feeling she'd get a real kick out of touring a place like that.

"It is fun," she agreed. "I really love my job."

Suddenly another thought occurred to me. "Did Monarch handle the props for *Ten Days*?" I asked.

Amanda shook her head. "Unfortunately not. It would have been cool to work on a film that my best friend was starring in. Especially since that connection is how we met in the first place. A few years ago, I was part of the crew that was delivering props to the theater where *Next Stop: Brooklyn* was rehearsing. Savannah and I started chatting, and before we knew it, we'd exchanged phone numbers." With a little shrug, she added, "That was about two years ago, right after Savannah moved to New York from Ohio. She didn't know many people, and we started hanging out together a lot."

Her voice had become strained, as if talking about her close friendship with Savannah was difficult. Instead, she went back to eating ice cream.

But after just one more mouthful, she set down her spoon. The corners of her mouth drooping downward, she mumbled, "I knew he was a creep, but I had no idea he was this psycho."

I blinked. "Who are we talking about?"

"Ragnar, of course. Ragnar Bruin." She practically spit out the syllables.

Ragnar Bruin, Ragnar Bruin . . . it took me a few seconds to remember why that name sounded familiar.

"The director?" I finally asked, my eyebrows shooting up. "The guy who directed *The Hartford Trilogy* and *Too Much Time*?"

"That's right," she replied, her tone colder than the ice cream in her dish. "The great Ragnar Bruin. Academy-Award-winning director, artistic genius, and total nutjob."

I knew that film directors had a reputation for having strong personalities. Egos as big as the Hollywood sign, in fact. But Amanda's take on Ragnar Bruin was in another realm entirely.

And she was clearly convinced that he was responsible for her friend Savannah's murder.

"I think I'd heard that Ragnar Bruin was a bit of an egomaniac," I said, trying to sound casual. "But I've never heard anything about him being—well, as extreme as you make him sound."

Amanda snorted. "That's because he's so good at making money that no one wants to get on his bad side.

"That's how Hollywood works," she went on. "People can get away with pretty much anything as long as they're good at turning out movies that make everyone rich. That's certainly true for actors, and it's especially true for directors."

I thought about all the scandals in recent years concerning powerful people in Hollywood who had exhibited despicable behavior. But I'd always suspected that there were plenty more we never heard about.

"Ragnar is exceptionally lucky because his scandalous behavior never got into the news," Amanda went on. "Maybe it will finally come out." Bitterly, she muttered, "Now that it's too late."

"So he and Savannah were . . . friends?" I prompted, still not understanding.

She let out a contemptuous snort. "That's not the word I'd use, but they did know each other."

"What word would you use?" I asked, now even more cautious.

"How about 'stalker'?" Amanda replied. "Yeah, that'd work."

"Ragnar Bruin was stalking Savannah?" I repeated, even though that was exactly what she had just told me. The problem was that I was having trouble digesting this bizarre bit of news. "When did it start? How did they meet? What did he do, exactly?" I had lots more questions, but those were the ones that immediately came to mind.

"It started when he met Savannah at the Academy Awards last year," Amanda said.

"Savannah went to the Oscars?" Another question. But I was still trying to wrap my head around all this.

"She was working at the Oscars," she explained. She paused to eat another spoonful of ice cream. This time, she went for the Blueberry Pomegranate. "She was there as a seat filler."

"I think I've read about that," I said. "Aren't they people who sit in an empty seat whenever one of the celebrities or anyone else in the audience gets up to go to the bathroom or make a phone call or whatever?"

"Exactly," Amanda replied. "It's usually a really fun gig— hey, this ice cream flavor is amazing! It tastes so fresh and fruity! What is it?"

"Thanks," I said. "It's Blueberry Pomegranate."

"That's new to me," Amanda said, shaking her head. "Anyway, as you can imagine, Savannah was beyond excited. She got all dressed up for it—fortunately, she found a fabulous gown at a resale shop in Los Angeles—and she got her hair and makeup done at a salon near where she was staying."

"And where was that?" I interjected. "Did she have an apartment in L.A.?"

Amanda shook her head. "No. She would crash with friends whenever she had to go to L.A. Like for an audition or to meet with her agent or some other career-related business. But that girl was a New Yorker at heart. She lived in Brooklyn."

"But she was up here at the weekend house, too," I interjected.

"True," Amanda agreed. "But she spent most of her time in the city."

"So she met Ragnar Bruin at the Oscar ceremony?" I prompted, anxious to get back to what she'd been telling me.

"That's right," Amanda said. "Apparently she ended up sitting next to him when one of the nominees for Best Actress went to the bathroom. And during the ten or fifteen minutes they spent sitting together, Ragnar became obsessed with her.

"Of course, at the time Savannah thought it was the best thing that could possibly happen to her career," she went on. "I mean, she gets a once-in-a-lifetime opportunity to meet this fabulously important, ridiculously famous movie director, and within minutes he's clearly infatuated with her.

"She called me that night," Amanda said. "It was two AM on the West Coast, which means that in New York, where I was, it was five AM. But she was so excited that I wasn't the least bit angry about her waking me up. In fact, I was as thrilled as she was. She told me that Ragnar had wanted to know who her agent was, as if he had a project in mind for her. But then he asked her for her personal number so he could get in touch with her directly. Naturally she gave it to him. She was certain that she'd just made the most important contact of her career. And I suppose she had. It was just that from that night on, he barely left her alone."

Amanda stopped eating and put down her spoon. "At first, she was flattered," she said. "Who wouldn't be? There she was, one of hundreds if not thousands of aspiring actresses living in New York and L.A., with Ragnar Bruin calling her and sending her flowers and texting her night and day—"

"Were they dating?" I interrupted, realizing she hadn't said anything about the two of them ever actually going out anywhere.

She shifted in her seat. "Not dating, exactly. After all, there was the issue of Ragnar's wife."

Of course. I suddenly remembered his wedding being all over the news. He had married a famous actress who was almost twenty years younger than he was. The couple had flown a hundred of their "closest friends" to a small island in French Polynesia, someplace near Bora Bora. The festivities had lasted three days. Helicopters had hovered overhead the whole time as daredevil paparazzi snapped photos of the famous pair and all the other celebrities who had gathered together for the glamorous event.

"So even though, at first, all the attention Savannah was getting from Ragnar was flattering, it started to get . . . creepy," Amanda continued. "And she felt stuck. She wanted to tell him to tone it down, but she was afraid of messing up her career. After all, he's a pretty powerful guy." She glanced around the shop. Even though no one else was there but the two of us, Count Dracula, and the witch standing near the door, she lowered her voice. "And then he started acting weird."

"Weird how?" I asked, my voice equally quiet.

"He began sending her . . . photos," Amanda said softly. "Of himself. Um, naked. Or doing . . . strange things."

"I see."

"And sending her presents like sexy underwear," she added. "*Really* sexy underwear. With notes saying he couldn't wait to see her wearing it."

"How did Timothy feel about all this?" I asked, trying to sound casual.

Amanda jerked her head up. "How do you know about Timothy?"

"I've been doing a little research," I replied. "Because Savannah was murdered in my shop, I'm on the list of suspects even though I'd never even met her before Thursday. I figured that the more I knew about her and her life, the better position I'd be in."

I was being honest, but not quite coming right out and telling her that I was trying to find out who had killed her.

"Makes sense," she said with a nod.

"Timothy seems utterly devastated," I commented.

Amanda's eyes widened. "Are you kidding? Of *course* he's devastated! Those two were absolutely crazy about each other. In fact, just before . . . all this happened . . ."

She stopped, unable to go on for a few seconds. Then she took a deep breath. "Just before all this happened, Savannah told me that she and Timothy had decided to get married."

My eyebrows shot up. "So they were pretty solid."

"*Very* solid," Amanda agreed. "And I was so happy for Savannah. I mean, Timothy is the sweetest guy in the whole world. He's perfect for her, since she's the nicest person you can imagine, too . . ." Her voice trailed off. "She *was* the nicest person," she corrected herself, choking on her words.

"How did they meet?" I asked.

"Through acting," Amanda replied. "They were in a play together. This one was much better than the one I told you about. It was actually off-Broadway as opposed to off-off-Broadway."

"How long ago?" I couldn't resist asking.

"About a year and a half ago," Amanda replied, "not long after she moved to New York. Savannah's relationship with Timothy was one more great thing in her life." She let out a deep sigh. "Everything was going so well for her. She'd found the love of her life, her acting career was about to take off . . . not that she was someone who cared about the money or the fame or any of the glitzy stuff. For her, it was all about the work. She truly loved acting. It was what mattered to her most. And she figured that once she'd broken out in a big-name film like *Ten Days*, she'd have enough clout to do the roles she wanted to do. Shakespeare, Chekhov, all the great plays.

"She was finally in a position give up her day job, too," she added. "She hated working at that big corporate machine, doing boring, low-level stuff."

My ears pricked up. This was the first I'd heard about Savannah doing anything besides acting. "What did she do?"

"She was basically an administrative assistant," Amanda explained. "Pretty low-level stuff. But that was the kind of job she wanted: something that would pay the rent but wouldn't be too taxing. She also needed to be able to take off time for auditions and the occasional acting gig. It's not like she was looking to climb the corporate ladder or anything.

"But even though the job was supposed to be as undemanding as possible, it still seemed to be taking a toll on her. She'd only been there about a year, but lately she kept talking about how she couldn't wait to get out. Landing that role in *Ten Days* was her ticket out of there." She laughed, then said, "Although she still didn't quite believe it. In fact, she didn't even quit her job. She took a leave of absence, just to be safe."

"Where did she work?" I asked.

She paused to eat another spoonful of ice cream. "A company in New York called Alpha Industries," she finally replied.

"I never heard of it," I commented. "What does it do?"

"It's one of those big companies that's involved in lots of different things," Amanda said with a wave of her hand. "She wasn't interested in talking about her day job. That's how little it mattered to her."

She gobbled down the rest of her ice cream, then began gathering up her things.

Gesturing at her empty dish, she asked, "That was truly amazing, especially the pomegranate thing. How much do I owe you?"

"It's on the house," I said.

"Thanks," she said, rising to her feet. Her voice was choked as she added, "And thanks for letting me be here. It was important to me."

"I'm so sorry," I told her sincerely.

Even though I'd only met Savannah once, my heart felt crushed. I'd lost enough people who mattered to me to understand only too well what she was going through. And as Amanda walked away, her body language spoke volumes. Her shoulders were still slumped, her head was lowered, and she moved as if the very effort was almost too demanding.

Once she was gone, I lingered at the table, thinking. Amanda and I hadn't talked for very long, but I'd learned a lot about Savannah Crane.

Mainly about her relationship with Ragnar Bruin.

I wondered how far jealousy had taken the famous director.

And then something else occurred to me. Ragnar Bruin was married. Which meant that his wife was undoubtedly as distressed about his obsession with Savannah as she was.

But Amanda had given me a second important lead: Savannah's day job. That struck me as something that I should be able to learn more about. I resolved to go into the city the first chance I got to do exactly that.

But as I sat alone at the table, it wasn't the investigation or even the details of Savannah's life that hung over me like a dark cloud. It was the heartbreaking fact that she was gone.

In the end, Savannah Crane had turned into a tragic heroine, just like a character in one of the Shakespearean plays she longed to be in.

Chapter 6

Most of the vanilla used to make ice cream
comes from Madagascar and Indonesia.

—www.icecream.com/icecreaminfo

Over the next several hours, business continued to be un-usually light. I hoped it was just a fluke and that Wol-fert's Roost—and Lickety Splits in particular—weren't suffering from the horrific crime that had been exploding in the headlines for the past few days.

When the door of my shop opened after a lull, I glanced up anxiously, assuming it was another customer. Instead, I was surprised to see that Chelsea Atkins had come into my shop.

I hadn't expected to see her again. And her presence in-stantly made me uncomfortable, thanks to that stray hair I'd found in my cabinet.

She was dressed more formally than the other times I'd seen her, in sleek black pants, a fitted jacket made of olive-green suede, and a tailored white shirt that looked like silk underneath it. While in the past her red hair had been pulled back into a haphazard knot with plenty of flyaway strands, today it hung loose, brushed into a sort of halo around her face.

She ignored me, instead looking around my shop critically the way she had the first time she'd come into Lickety Splits.

It was hard to believe that that had only been three days earlier.

"Hi, Chelsea," I said. "I didn't realize you were still in town."

She grimaced. "Not my choice," she said sullenly, ambling over to the counter. "I'd much rather be back home in Los Angeles, at least until Skip DiFalco decides what's going to happen with *Ten Days* now that Savannah is gone. But your local police department suggested that it would be a good idea if I stuck around for a while."

She seemed different from the other times I'd seen her. And it wasn't only what she was wearing or the way she wore her hair. She seemed . . . distracted. She was acting as if she was in a daze.

Her eyes traveled around my shop again. "You've put everything back," she observed, vaguely gesturing at Count Dracula. "Sorry I didn't make good on my promise to have the crew do all that. It must have been a big job."

"My niece and I worked on it together," I told her. "It didn't take us that long."

"Good." She was silent for a long time before saying, "That scary detective spent a long time questioning me." I could tell by the look on her face that she'd found the experience extremely unpleasant.

Not that I blamed her. Going head-to-head with Detective Stoltz wasn't exactly my favorite thing, either.

"Everything about this terrible event is awful," I said. "He questioned me, too. And I'd never even heard of Savannah Crane until Wednesday, when you first mentioned her to me."

I expected her to make a comment about her own relationship to Savannah. But she said nothing.

"I'm sure Detective Stoltz considers you an important source of information," I commented. "After all, you knew the names of everyone who came into Lickety Splits before and during the shoot."

She nodded. "I gave him a list. They were all people I'd worked with before, and frankly, I'd vouch for the innocence of each and every one of them."

"And no one came onto the set who didn't belong there?" I asked. "Maybe someone who said they were friends with Savannah or one of the other actors, or someone who didn't identify themselves at all . . . ?"

Chelsea shook her head. "It's just like I told the police: The only people on the set who I didn't know were the people from your shop."

A heavy silence hung between us. I was still trying to figure out why she'd come back. A quick phone call to apologize for my store's unexpected involvement in this horrific episode would have worked just as well as a personal visit.

Detective Stoltz's claim that the murderer might come back to my shop loomed large in my mind.

"Is there anything in particular I can help you with?" I finally asked.

"Not really," Chelsea replied. "I guess I just wanted to see this place one more time.

"I didn't know Savannah Crane well at all," she continued. "I'd only met her a few times before we started shooting this film. And I remember running into her at a restaurant one night while she was having dinner with her boyfriend, Timothy. But what happened to her was so horrible. I guess I thought that coming back here might give me some sense of—I don't know, closure."

She seemed so sincere that my heart melted, at least a little. "Is it working?" I asked gently.

She shook her head. "Things are never that simple, are they? But there's something else: I'd also like to apologize in person for all the disruption this nightmare caused for you. I feel responsible, since I'm the one who got you involved in the first place."

I didn't know how to respond. Frankly, I was finding this whole interaction a bit awkward. I was back to wondering if Chelsea really was looking for closure—or if perhaps there was some other reason for her visit.

But before I had a chance to try to find out, the door opened again. A man and a woman in their sixties, wearing jeans and tie-dye, sauntered in. The woman had a long, gray braid hanging below her waist, and the man's curly white mane gave him a distinct Jerry Garcia look. The Hudson Valley was home to a lot of people who had come to the area in the 1960s, fell in love with it, and never left. I had a feeling that this couple fit into that category.

"I see you have customers," Chelsea said. "I won't take up any more of your time."

I was actually relieved when she left, given her strange demeanor. I was still unsure if grief was behind it—or something else.

I turned to the couple, who were oohing and aahing over the display case. The woman, I noticed, had a blue streak in her hair, just like Emma. I liked her immediately.

"What can I get you?" I asked, anxious to spread a little joy in the form of ice cream. There had been too much bad karma in my shop over the past several days, and I hoped that a few generous scoops and a little chocolate syrup would work their usual magic.

"How about stopping over at the high school gym before you go into Lickety Splits this morning?" Grams suggested over breakfast the next morning. "I'm interested in what you think about the progress we're making."

"I thought you'd never ask," I replied. "I've been wondering how Halloween Hollow was shaping up."

From the excited expression on Grams's face, I had a feeling it was shaping up just fine. And I could hardly wait to get a peek. It wasn't only the local kids I was thinking about, either, since Halloween had been such a highlight of my childhood.

I found myself remembering that every year, my two sisters and I would start planning our costumes during the summer, usually while camped out on the front porch on a hot, lazy day, armed with lemonade. I remember one time in particular, when I was seven. My sister Julie would have been fourteen and Nina twelve—so the fact that they actually chose to hang out with me, their little sister, made it a particularly special occasion.

I could still hear myself telling my sisters that that year I wanted to dress up as either a princess or a pirate.

"I have a better idea," Julie said. As the oldest of three sisters, Julie frequently had a "better idea." And because of her status, we usually ended up doing whatever she had come up with.

"This year, let's coordinate our costumes," Julie continued. "We can have a theme. The Three Musketeers or the Three Stooges—"

"How about the three fairy godmothers from *Sleeping Beauty*?" Nina suggested. "Flora, Fauna, and Merryweather?"

In the end, we'd gone as characters from *Peter Pan*. Julie, being Julie, got to be Peter, decked out in green tights and a green felt tunic that Grams made. Nina was Captain Hook. And I was Tinkerbell, which I absolutely loved because I got to wear both a green, ballerina-style skirt *and* wings. True, the wings kept falling off, especially since it was windy and drizzly that year. But I still loved parading around in that costume.

The three of us always went trick-or-treating together, since until I was close to starting middle school, I was considered too young to go alone or even with friends my own age. Julie, in particular, always acted as if she was doing me a favor. But I always suspected she loved having an excuse to go house-to-house begging for candy, something her teenage friends considered uncool. And sometimes we got something even better, like the time we were invited into a neighbor's house for hot apple cider and freshly made cinnamon donuts.

Once we got home, exhausted but exhilarated, the sorting and trading began. My sisters and I each got two big bowls out of the kitchen cabinets and began dividing up our loot. The first bowl was for the good stuff we planned to keep for ourselves or share with Grams or our friends at school. The second bowl was for the rejects we were willing to trade away.

Our taste was generally similar. Everything made with chocolate ended up in the "keepers" bowl: Milky Ways, peanut butter cups, anything with a Hershey label on it.

But the rejects were much more personal, which turned out to be a good thing. Julie loved anything green—lollipops, jelly beans, green apple Skittles. And Nina went crazy for anything sour, from Sour Patch Kids to lemon lollipops. As for me, I liked candy that was cherry-flavored. We traded our goodies so that each McKay sister was able to load up on her sugary favorites.

Given my love of Halloween, I couldn't wait to see what Grams and her helpers had come up with. And as soon as I stepped into the high school gym, lugging a big box of rainbow sprinkles and round silver pearls and assorted Halloween candies for the do-it-yourself ice cream station, I saw that I wasn't about to be the least bit disappointed.

An actual, full-size house was under construction, complete with every scary element anyone could think of. Directly behind it, I could see the beginnings of a gigantic foam pit. I could practically hear the children's gleeful howls as they jumped off the edge, plunging into what amounted to a huge bowl filled with clumps of dense foam that would cushion their fall.

"Wow!" I cried. "This is a huge production! I had no idea you were doing this Halloween thing on such a grand scale!"

"I told you it was going to be fabulous," Grams said proudly.

At the sound of our voices, the front door of the dilapidated house in the center of the gym opened. George Vernon emerged, dressed in jeans and sneakers and carrying a paintbrush.

"I see the boss is taking a break," he quipped. "I guess that means the rest of us can, too."

"Halloween is less than two weeks away," Grams returned, sounding a bit flirtatious. "No slacking off!"

"Who, me?" George replied, flirting right back. "I've been here since seven!"

"Only because I read you the riot act," Grams countered. "I hope I finally convinced you that making sure the children have a wonderful Halloween is more important than that golf game of yours!"

He shrugged. "What can I say? The other guys depend on me. But I've been making up for it. I just finished painting the ballroom, and now I'm working on the front room."

"A ballroom?" I repeated, startled. I had to admit that I was dazzled by the scope of this project. "I can't believe you're building an actual mansion here in the gym!"

"That's exactly what we're doing," George said. "Come on, we'll show you around."

As we neared the front door, Grams said, "This house is going to be fabulous both outside *and* inside. Emma's already working on making more of those life-size monsters out of papier-mâché and duct tape and paint and whatever else she uses. But that's just the beginning. One of our volunteers has a daughter who runs a party store, and she donated some great props."

"Like this fog machine," George said, pointing at a large cardboard carton that had yet to be opened. "The haunted house will be surrounded by fog. We'll have more fog inside, as well."

"What's in here?" I asked, peering inside another box, this one full of big white rectangles with curved tops.

"Tombstones," George replied. "We're going to set up a fake cemetery out front. They'll have funny sayings written on them like, 'Charlie Chicken. He forgot to look both ways.'"

"On one of them," Grams added with a grin, "there'll be a bony hand that suddenly comes up from behind and reaches over the top."

I shivered at the thought. "Great effect," I said. "I hope the kids can handle it."

"That one's not for the youngest children," Grams explained. "We're going to have different effects at different times of the day, depending on which age group is here."

"The high school kids will get all the really fun stuff," George said, rubbing his hands together. I could tell he was getting a kick out of all this.

"On the outside," he went on, "we'll have twisting trees with creepy faces painted on the branches. One of the front windows will be broken, and another will be boarded up. The shutters will be falling off . . . and there'll be signs that say 'Danger!' and 'Enter at Your Own Risk!'"

"And the house itself will have one of those Gothic towers, like the Haunted Mansion at Disneyland," Grams said. "And glowing jack-o'-lanterns with snarling mouths and jagged teeth. Of course, cobwebs will be hanging everywhere. We can make those by taking pieces of gauze and shredding it. And someone is making a fake wrought-iron fence—"

"And there'll be a skull hanging over the front door!" George said.

I laughed. "Goodness, you've thought of everything!"

"Wait until you hear about what we've got planned for the inside!" Grams exclaimed as we passed through the front door. The interior was still mostly under construction. "When the children first walk inside, there'll be a room with a black light. That will make their white clothes glow. Their teeth, too!"

"And a cabinet will suddenly fly open and a white ghost will fly out at them!" George said. "Or maybe a skeleton." Frowning, he added, "Actually, I still haven't figured out how to make that happen. But I'm working on it."

"This front room will also have a strobe light in it," Grams said. "And in this corner, one of the volunteers who's dressed as a witch will be stirring a bubbling cauldron. You can get that effect by putting dry ice in warm water. If we throw in some glow sticks, we can make it yellow or green or whatever color we like."

"This area over here will have hundreds of spiders hanging from the ceiling," George said, pointing in a different direction.

"There'll be eerie music playing, too," Grams added.

"And other scary sounds," George said. "Growling, low chanting, rattling chains, and of course the classic evil laughter."

"You really have thought of everything!" I exclaimed.

"I've got a few other ideas up my sleeve, too," he said. With a wink, he teased, "But I'm not going to tell you about all of them. I'd rather let you experience everything for yourself!"

I laughed. "I can hardly wait," I told them both sincerely. "I'm overwhelmed by what a great job you're both doing."

And I wasn't only referring to what they were doing in the gym. Even more, I was talking about what they were clearly doing for each other.

*　*　*

Given how quiet the shop had been the day before, I suggested that Emma take the day off. I was hoping she'd spend the time studying, but instead she started texting Ethan before I'd even finished my sentence. Not that I was worried. She had already gotten A's on the first two quizzes in her computer course. As for her ability to do well in her art class, all I had to do was look around my shop to see how talented and committed she was.

So I was alone in the shop early Sunday afternoon when Brody Lundgren came striding in.

And *striding* is definitely the right word. Not walking, not wandering, but striding. The man has the longest legs I've ever seen, so every step he takes is a stride.

In fact, Brody looks like he just got off a Viking ship. In addition to his impressive height, he's got an equally impressive head of curly blond hair, which is ridiculously thick and just long enough to make him look as if he's been so busy climbing every mountain and fording every stream that he hasn't had time to schedule a haircut. His eyes are a remarkable shade of green, and his big smile shows off teeth so white they practically sparkle.

Two months earlier, back in August, Brody had opened a shop directly across the street from Lickety Splits. The name of his shop, Hudson Valley Adventure Tours, was written on the brick-red T-shirt he was wearing, his well-developed pectoral muscles distorting the letters a little. He was in the business of selling adventure. The sign outside his shop said it all: KAYAKING, CANOEING, TUBING, HIKING, BIKING, ROCK CLIMBING, SPELUNKING.

"Hey, Brody," I said. I tried not to let on that merely being in his presence always caused my heart to beat a little too fast and my breaths to become a little too short.

"Hey, Kate," he replied. Flashing me that blinding smile, he added, "You're looking fine today."

"That's a surprise," I told him, "given what's gone on this week."

"Yes, I heard all about it," he said, his smile fading. "I saw the crime-scene tape, too. I'm glad you were finally able to open your store again."

I wondered if he'd heard that I was considered a suspect, since Savannah Crane's murder had occurred in my shop.

"But I'm here to talk about happier things," Brody went on. "I wondered if you'd be able to take some time off this week. I'd like to take you hiking."

A *date*? I thought, my mind instantly racing. Is Brody asking me on a date? Or is he simply concerned about the ill effects of a life of too much ice cream and too little exercise, aside from pumping up my right arm with endless scooping?

I was still trying to figure that out when he added, "The weather couldn't be better. Sunshine and cool temperatures all week. Perfect for enjoying the mountains! And the autumn leaves are at their best. Not quite at peak yet, which means there's still enough green to make the reds and oranges look even more amazing." He paused. "I was wondering if you could get away for a few hours on Thursday."

It did sound like fun. And good for my health.

I couldn't think of a single reason to say no. So I said, "Yes!"

"Great!" he said, awarding me with another dazzling smile. "I'll swing by at three."

"That should work," I told him.

Seconds after he had left, Willow breezed in.

"I just saw Brody," she said. Teasingly, she said, "It seems the man can't stay away. Or is it your Toasted Coconut Fudge that keeps him coming back?"

"Actually, this is the first time he's been in the shop for days," I said, averting my eyes so she wouldn't see how red my cheeks were.

"Then what's behind his sudden interest in ice cream?" she

asked, grinning. "Or should I say his sudden *passion* for ice cream?"

"He invited me to go on a hike," I mumbled, my voice barely audible.

Willow heard me anyway. "A date! The man asked you on a date! I told you! I've been telling you all along—"

"I'm not sure it's a date," I told her. I realized I sounded just like Grams on the issue of George and his invitation to dinner at Greenleaf. "I think he just wanted somebody to go on a hike with."

"Right," Willow replied dryly. "And you're the obvious person, since your idea of a hike is walking from the parking lot to the mall."

"That's not true!" I protested. But she was close to correct. Unlike her, I wasn't one of those people who made exercise a priority in my life. I wasn't much of an outdoors girl, either. I'd always preferred indoor pursuits—including eating ice cream—to activities that made me sweaty and out of breath. With a few exceptions.

"I think he's just being friendly," I insisted.

Suddenly, Willow grew serious. "Honestly, Kate, why are you being so coy about this? The man clearly likes you! Why won't you admit that?"

I let out a deep sigh. "Because I'm still so conflicted about my feelings for Jake," I admitted. "If I can't figure out how Jake fits into the picture, how can I complicate things even further by bringing in somebody else?"

"Good point," she said. She patted me on the arm. "You've got a good head on your shoulders, Kate. I'm sure you'll figure out what's best for you. In the meantime, if you need a good pair of hiking boots, I have a pair that might fit you."

Hiking boots? I thought, horrified.

I was really starting to wonder what I'd gotten myself into.

* * *

I wasn't the only one with a blossoming social life. Tonight was Grams's dinner date with George.

I decided to close Lickety Splits a bit early. Sunday evenings were always slow, and business had continued to be quieter than usual. So I was in the dining room having dinner with Emma as Grams came out of her bedroom, wearing the same stretchy black pants and cushy gray Skechers walking shoes she'd worn all day. She had put on a different top, however; instead of the faded pink QUILTING IS MY HAPPY PLACE T-shirt she'd worn while giving Digger a bath, she had on a plain turquoise T-shirt.

"I'm ready!" Grams announced.

Emma and I exchanged a look of horror.

"Is that what you're planning on wearing tonight?" I asked.

Grams frowned. "Why not? I love these pants. They're so comfortable."

"This is a *date*, Grams!" Emma exclaimed. "Not a trip to the post office."

"It's just dinner," Grams insisted.

"It's dinner at one of the finest restaurants in the Hudson Valley," I pointed out. "If not the entire New York metropolitan area."

"Besides," Emma said, "this is your big chance to get dressed up. How often does anyone get to do that anymore? Go back to your closet and see if you can find something more formal."

"How about that blue dress?" I suggested. "The one you wore to the art opening back in September?"

"And put on that silver necklace with the blue beads," Emma added. "That will go with it really well."

Grams opened her mouth to protest, then immediately snapped it shut. I guess she understood that Emma and I weren't about to take no for an answer.

She retreated to her bedroom, then reemerged five minutes

later. This time, she was wearing a cobalt blue silk cocktail dress that was simply styled and extremely flattering. Around her neck was the necklace Emma had insisted on. She had also put on a pair of low-heeled, black patent-leather shoes. They looked almost as comfortable as the slouchy loafers, but considerably more elegant.

"Much better!" Emma declared. "But I think you need a little eyeliner."

"I suggest a bolder lipstick," I added. "Do you have one in a darker color?"

"Honestly!" Grams cried. "The way you two are fussing over me you'd think no one had ever gone out to dinner with a friend before!"

"As if George Vernon is just a friend," I scoffed. "Besides, how long has it been since you've been on a date?"

"It's not a—!"

"Grams!" Emma cried.

Grams thought for a few seconds, then said, "So many years that I couldn't even give you an answer."

When it was five minutes before the time George was scheduled to arrive, Emma and I fluttered around her like two mother hens.

"Take a light jacket," Emma instructed. "It's not that chilly now, but it will be later on."

"Do you have everything you need?" I asked. "Is your cell phone charged? Do you have—let's see, a comb? Tissues for a runny nose? Extra cash, in case you run into some sort of problem?"

"I'm fine," Grams insisted. "George and I are only going about three blocks away!"

"Even so, I don't want you staying out too late," Emma warned. "And feel free to text either one of us with updates. Or to ask us any questions." She took a deep breath. "And there's one more thing."

"What's that?" Grams asked, checking her reflection in

the mirror in the front hall and adjusting one of her pearl earrings.

"I don't think you should kiss George good night," Emma said firmly.

Both Grams and I let out a cry of surprise.

"Why not?" Grams asked. "For goodness' sake, Emma, if I really like him—and I think I do—why shouldn't I kiss him good night?"

"It just sends the wrong message," she replied. "There's plenty of time for that later. You two are still getting to know each other, and there's no reason to move things along too quickly."

Grams cast me a wary glance. "And you, Kate? Any more advice you'd like to give me before I walk out the door?"

"Yes," I said. "Have fun tonight."

"Thank you!" she cried. "I think that's the best advice I've gotten from either of you."

As if on cue, Digger ran over to the front door and started barking at it, acting as if sheer noise was what was required to let our visitor in. A few seconds later, we heard a knock.

Grams was about to put her hand on the doorknob when Emma whispered, "Not so fast. He can wait. You don't want to look too eager."

Grams and I exchanged another look. I'm sure we were thinking the same thing: Where on earth did this Victorian lady come from?

When Emma finally nodded, Grams opened the door. George stood on the doorstep, dressed in a suit and tie. He was holding a big, lush bouquet of yellow roses.

I immediately grabbed Digger by the collar, wanting to spare Grams's gentleman caller the horror of paw prints on his lovely suit.

"Aren't I lucky!" George greeted us. "Not one but three lovely ladies!"

Grinning at Grams and presenting her with the flowers, he added, "Maybe I shouldn't play favorites, but there really is one of you that I'm happiest to see."

"Just don't keep her out too late," Emma told him.

"I promise," George replied seriously. "I will be on my very best behavior tonight."

Once they were gone, Emma sank onto the couch as if she was exhausted by the ordeal of getting Grams out the door.

"Isn't it nice that Grams has a boyfriend!" I said with a sigh, lowering myself onto the green upholstered chair.

"Now we've all got one," Emma said.

"No, we don't!" I corrected her. "I don't have a boyfriend!"

"You have Jake," Emma pointed out. "I can see the sparks flying whenever you two are together. So can everyone else."

"Jake isn't my boyfriend," I insisted. Squirming in my chair, I added, "In fact, there's a new wrinkle in my life I want your advice on."

She was looking at me expectantly as I jumped right in and announced, "Brody asked me out. I said yes."

When she didn't say anything, I babbled on.

"And I'm not sure that I should have. You just said yourself that Jake and I have kind of a—a thing going on. At least we're trying to decide if we still have the connection we had back in high school—"

"You definitely have that connection," she said. "The only question is what you both want to do about it."

"Okay, so we're still feeling our way," I said seriously. "Which makes the idea of me going out with someone else even more complicated. Doesn't it?"

I suddenly realized the absurdity of me, a thirty-three-year-old woman, asking an eighteen-year-old for advice on my love life. A clever, insightful, worldly eighteen-year-old, but technically still a teenager.

Surely this represented a new low.

But then she said something very wise.

"Kate," Emma told me seriously, "I think you owe it to yourself to explore every option. I know that you haven't yet decided how you feel about Jake. The stuff that happened fifteen years ago, your anger over the fact that he never tried to get in touch with you afterward, the shock of him being back in your life all of a sudden . . . You still need time to sort all that out.

"But in the meantime, here's Brody. Charming, handsome Brody, who's been totally into you since the first time he laid eyes on you. So what I suggest is that at this point, you reserve judgment. You don't have to decide anything at this point. Go out with Brody—and go out with Jake. Sooner or later, you'll know what to do."

She really *was* clever and insightful.

Not that she wasn't telling me anything I didn't already know. It's just that by saying it out loud, by presenting it in such a matter-of-fact way, she was giving me permission to do what I'd pretty much decided to do already.

"You're right," I told her.

"I know I'm right," she said.

"Now let's have some ice cream to celebrate Grams's date," I suggested. "I've got another idea about making the perfect *affogato*. How about adding espresso *and* chocolate syrup?"

After all, I figured, there was no reason why Grams should be the only one who was eating well tonight.

Chapter 7

California produces the most ice cream in
America—and has since 1990.

—*www.californiadairypressroom.com/Products/Ice_Cream*

"You were certainly out late last night," Emma said the
following morning as she and I sat with Grams over
breakfast.

"Was I?" Grams replied, slathering orange marmalade
over half an English muffin. "I hope I didn't miss curfew. The
last thing I want is to be grounded. Especially with the Halloween dance coming up so soon."

I was glad that Grams was finding Emma's Mother Hen
act as amusing as I was. Neither of us would have ever
guessed that the youngest member of our little household
would turn out to be so protective.

"I was just worried, that's all," Emma said archly. She
paused to sip the banana-strawberry smoothie she'd whipped
up in the blender. "I was starting to think that maybe
George's car had broken down or something."

"George's car worked just fine," Grams said, her cheeks
reddening.

Before Emma had a chance to reply, I pushed back my
chair.

"I'm afraid I have to run," I announced. "Emma, could you

please drop me at the train station? I imagine you'd planned to head over to Lickety Splits soon, anyway."

Today, my niece would be running the shop by herself. Tomorrow, too, since I was about to embark on a two-day trip into Manhattan.

I had told Emma and Grams that I was going to take care of a few things in the city, then have dinner and stay overnight with Becca Collins, a friend from my job in public relations. And that was all true.

What I didn't explain was that the "things" I intended to do in the city were all related to my investigation of Savannah Crane's murder.

Less than an hour later, I was on an Amtrak train into New York City. While the ride would take less than two hours, I knew the trip I was embarking on would be transporting me to an entirely different world.

Sure enough, as the train chugged closer and closer to the city, the view outside my window changed dramatically. The open fields, the charming villages that looked as if they'd popped off the pages of a calendar, the calming sight of the mountains and the wide Hudson River, the breathtaking swaths of brilliant orange, red, and gold leaves . . . Before long, the quaint towns were replaced by clusters of buildings crowded together, many of them covered with graffiti. Trees became increasingly scarce. The streets the train sailed past were congested, and the sidewalks I glimpsed were filled with people, nearly all of them appearing to be in a hurry.

Still, while pastoral serenity was no longer part of the view, I could already feel the city's energy charging through me. It was as if there was electricity in the air, and it had the power to convey its spark to whoever was breathing it in.

I was simply one of those rare individuals who loved and appreciated both the big city and country life.

By the time my train pulled into Penn Station, my heart

was pounding with excitement. I hadn't been back in New York since the summer, when I'd asked Willow to fill in at the shop so I could take Emma to the city for lunch and a Broadway matinee. Only now that I had arrived did I realize how exhilarating it felt to be here.

Glancing at the address I'd jotted down on a slip of paper brought me back to reality with a big jolt. I suddenly remembered the reason why I'd come.

I took the subway uptown, eagerly drinking in the city's noise and crowds and busyness as I came up the stairs, onto the street. Alpha Industries was on Sixth Avenue, not far from Radio City Music Hall and Rockefeller Center. Those were two of my favorite spots during the holiday season.

But today, I made a beeline for the office building in which Savannah Crane had worked.

Alpha Industries was located on the fifty-fourth floor. After checking in with the security guard sitting behind a big desk and being given a name tag with the word VISITOR printed on it in red, I floated up in an elevator that was so smooth it didn't even feel as if it was moving.

I sneaked peeks at the other people crammed inside. All of them were stylishly dressed. The men wore well-cut suits, while the women favored separates in inoffensive colors like black and gray. I caught sight of more than one set of pearls.

Given the feeling of formality, it was difficult to imagine Savannah fitting in here. Then again, she was an actress. Maybe her ability to turn herself into different people had played an important role here as well as on a stage or a movie set.

When we arrived at the fifty-fourth floor, the doors opened onto what looked like a movie version of a thriving company in Manhattan. The walls and carpets were pale gray, and the chairs in the waiting area were low and sleek and uncomfortable-looking. An entire wall of windows off to the right afforded a spectacular view of Midtown, the tall, serious-looking buildings interspersed with crisscrossing streets far below that were crowded with slow-moving cars and yellow taxis.

In the center was a high counter, with a woman's neatly coiffed head bobbing above it. On the wall behind her, ALPHA INDUSTRIES was spelled out in huge silver letters.

I was finding it more and more difficult to picture Savannah working here.

The receptionist, I saw, was as conservatively dressed as everyone else I'd encountered so far. Her meticulously tailored black jacket made her look like a banker.

She turned her attention to me immediately. "Can I help you?" she asked pleasantly.

"I'm here to see Savannah Crane," I told her.

The woman's expression immediately changed to one of controlled horror. "May I ask what this is about?" she asked.

"Catering," I replied. "I'm meeting with her to talk about the company's holiday party. We made this appointment months ago."

"Holiday party!" the receptionist exclaimed. "But it isn't even Halloween yet!"

I shot her the most disdainful look I could manage. "Most firms have their entire holiday event planned by the end of the summer," I told her haughtily. "Perhaps you're not aware of how much competition there is to grab one of the top caterers."

Savannah wasn't the only one with acting abilities, I thought, surprised by how authoritative I sounded.

And she bought it. "I guess that makes sense," she said, clearly humbled. "I've never had to plan anything like that, so I wouldn't know . . . But Savannah isn't here any longer. I'll have to find out who I should put you in touch with instead—"

"What do you mean, Savannah isn't here?" I said. Now I was using my annoyed voice. "We had an appointment. She specifically told me that this would be a good time to meet! I have a *very* busy schedule!"

The receptionist was clearly growing more and more agitated by my insistence, biting her lip and tapping her tapered, blood-red fingernails nervously on the desk. "I'm going to have to make a few calls," she said.

"Why don't you give me Savannah Crane's cell phone number, and I'll talk to her myself?" I suggested, really getting into my "impatient" act. "Maybe she misunderstood and thought we were meeting somewhere off-site."

"You don't understand," the receptionist said. "Savannah Crane is—gone. As in she's not working here anymore. She took a leave a while ago, but now—"

I let out a yelp, moving on to "irritated." "And she didn't even bother to let me know?" I cried. "I'd like to speak to her supervisor."

That was my ploy for getting my foot in the door. Or, to be more accurate, my ploy for getting my entire body past the reception area, into the place in which Savannah had worked and in the midst of the people who had known her.

"This is—complicated," the receptionist said. "I'm going to ask you to leave your business card, and I'll have someone get back to you."

"But I came all the way from the Hudson Valley!" I protested. "That's a train ride of over two hours. Each way!"

"I'm sorry, but it's the best I can do," she said, sounding truly apologetic.

As we were having this exchange, a woman sailed into the reception area from the offices in back. I instantly picked up on the fact that she was one of those people who was inherently attractive. She was pretty, but in a quirky way that made her much more interesting than your standard Homecoming Queen–style beauty. She had wavy, white-blond hair cut in one of those tousled, irregular styles that made it look as if she had just gotten out of bed. Her long, slender nose had a bit of a hook in it, and her lips were pouty, colored with a swipe of pale pink lipstick.

She also was tall and slender, and walked with a sort of swagger that seemed to come to her naturally. Her outfit was simple: a gray pencil skirt that showed off her slim silhouette, an oversized pale blue sweater cut so wide at the neck that it kept slipping off one shoulder, and low-heeled black pumps.

She was one of those women who just exuded confidence. I wondered if she could give me lessons.

"Hey, Deb," she said breezily, glancing at the receptionist as she headed toward the elevators. "Quiet morning?"

"Hi, Coo," the receptionist replied. "Yup. Pretty much."

"I'm going out for coffee," the woman named Coo called over her shoulder as she pressed the DOWN button. "Want anything?"

Was it my imagination, or did she actually cast me a meaningful look?

"No, thanks," the receptionist said. Then she mumbled, "There's plenty of coffee in the snack room."

Coo glanced back at her and smiled winningly. "I have a sudden craving for a Starbucks Hazelnut Mocha Coconut Milk Macchiato. I'm addicted. What can I do but give in to my bodily urges?"

Is that a real thing? I wondered. Maybe I should be researching new flavor combinations at Starbucks instead of ice cream shops . . .

But I forced myself to focus on the moment at hand. The woman who was apparently called Coo appeared to be about my age, which meant she was about Savannah's age, too. And she had clearly worked on the same floor, which meant there was a good chance she'd known her.

"Thanks for your time," I told the receptionist. I dropped

one of my business cards on the counter in front of her, then trotted after Coo.

"That was so weird," I said to her as soon as the elevator doors closed, leaving the two of us alone. "I mean, if a person has an appointment, you'd think that would mean something."

"I guess you haven't heard about what happened," Coo replied. "And apparently Deb wasn't about to tell you."

"Tell me what?" I asked, playing innocent.

"Savannah Crane passed away last week," Coo said somberly. "Under very suspicious circumstances."

I took a deep breath, my mind racing as I planned my strategy. I decided to take a chance.

"Look, I know all about what happened to Savannah," I told her. "She was murdered in my ice cream shop in the Hudson Valley. In fact, she was poisoned by ice cream that I'd personally put into the dish she was eating out of."

Coo looked at me appraisingly. "You don't look like a murderer," she said.

"I didn't even know her!" I insisted. "Which is why I'm trying to find out whatever I can about the people who *did* know her. I'm doing everything I can to clear my name.

"That's why I came here today," I went on as the elevator's doors opened onto the lobby. "I was hoping for a chance to speak to some of the people she worked with. I thought someone might be able to tell me something that would give me some insight into what was going on in her life."

"Maybe I can help," Coo said. Gesturing toward the Starbucks across the street, she added, "Come on. The coffee's on me."

"I haven't even introduced myself," I said after the two of us grabbed a corner table with our coffee and a couple of scones I'd been unable to resist. "I'm Kate McKay."

"I'm Coo Jameson," she replied. "It's short for Cooper."

She wrinkled her nose. "My real name is Cornelia Cooper Jameson. I think Mummy had a vicious streak, naming me after my grandmother. My family called me Cornelia when I was kid. But as soon as I went off to prep school, my friends decided I needed a better name."

I was already getting a sense of where this young woman's self-confidence had come from. I watched her dump a packet of sugar into her macchiato. Then a second packet. Then a third. And this was a coffee concoction that already had more sweet flavors crammed into it than I could fit into my ice cream display case. I couldn't imagine how she managed to keep those hips of hers slim enough to pull off that skin-tight pencil skirt she was wearing.

She had clearly caught me staring. "What, you're surprised that I'm a sugar addict?" she asked, looking amused.

"I'm just jealous that you can eat so much of my favorite substance and still stay thin," I replied.

She laughed. "I'm one of those lucky people with a crazy-high metabolism. But it'll probably catch up with me one of these days. I just hope I don't end up gaining fifty pounds overnight. My worst nightmare is that all the calories I've ingested over the years will pile up on me in one fell swoop."

I laughed. Coo was a woman I liked. More importantly, she was someone I trusted.

She paused to stir all that sugar into her coffee. Grinning slyly, she asked, "Do you really cater corporate events? Or is that something you made up to try to get information out of Deb the Devil?"

"I actually do cater events," I told her. "I kind of fell into it, but over time it's become one of my shop's specialties." I hesitated, then added, "But you're right. I wasn't really planning anything at Alpha."

"Where is your shop, exactly?" she asked.

"A town called Wolfert's Roost. Have you ever heard of it?"

"Oh, sure," she replied, waving her hand in the air. "It used to be called Modderplaatz, right? Mummy had friends with a place in the Hudson Valley. I spent lots of summers up there, swimming in their private lake."

Did people really have private lakes? I wondered. I supposed they did, at least in the circles Coo seemed to travel in.

I noticed that even though her coffee was full of sugar, she didn't touch either of the scones I'd bought to go with my cappuccino, either the raspberry or the chocolate chip. I had a sudden urge to force some of my magnificent ice cream on this woman the first chance I got.

Suddenly, Coo leaned forward. Lowering her voice, she asked, "So tell me more about why you're trying to figure out who killed Savannah."

"It's partly because I'm considered a suspect," I replied, "and partly because I'm worried about my shop's reputation. But I also feel a weird sense of responsibility since this terrible thing happened in *my* store, with *my* ice cream."

"All good reasons," she commented, sipping her coffee.

"I've talked to a few people about Savannah's acting career," I went on, "but I don't know a thing about the rest of her life. And this job might not have meant much to her, but she undoubtedly spent a good chunk of her days here." I paused to drink some of my own coffee. "I'm also trying to find out more about what she was really like."

"She was great," Coo said. "She was one of the nicest people I've ever met. Everyone at Alpha liked her. She made a point of being as nice to the mail room guys as she was to the executives. She was one of those people who just exuded warmth." She frowned. "Which is why it's so puzzling that someone wanted to—you know."

"I was hoping you'd know who some of her enemies were," I said.

"Enemies?" She blinked. "I can't imagine Savannah having any enemies. You never met such a sweet, genuine person in your life."

"But there was clearly *someone* who didn't feel that way," I pointed out. "I was hoping you might have some idea of who that person might be."

Coo's expression suddenly changed. It was as if a rain cloud had passed over her face.

"You know something," I said without thinking.

"No," she insisted. She sat in silence for a few seconds, staring at her coffee cup.

And then, raising her eyes to me, she said, "But I did know that something was wrong. Savannah had begun acting strange."

"Strange?" I repeated. "In what way?"

Shifting in her seat, Coo said, "I'm not sure. She just seemed . . . *troubled* somehow. Her usual spark was missing."

"Was that before or after she got the role in *The Best Ten Days of My Life*?" I asked, aware that my heart had begun beating a lot faster than usual.

"Before," she replied without hesitating.

"Do you think that whatever seemed to be bothering her might have been related to her boyfriend?" I asked.

"Timothy?" Coo thought for a moment. "I guess it's possible. Especially since the last few times I saw them together I did notice some tension."

My ears pricked up. Amanda certainly hadn't said anything about there being any tension between Savannah and Timothy. In fact, she had claimed the opposite, insisting that the two of them were ecstatically happy together. That they'd even gotten engaged recently.

"Are you talking about the usual disagreements couples have?" I asked. "Even people who are madly in love have arguments sometimes."

Coo shook her head. "It struck me as more than that. I remember this one time . . . I came down the elevator around noon to go grab lunch. I saw Timothy standing in the lobby, looking as if he was waiting for someone. As soon as Savannah came down the elevator, the two of them started fighting. I was standing too far away to hear what they were saying, but you could tell from their body language that something was very wrong."

Why would Amanda lie? I wondered, swirling the foam in my cappuccino with my wooden stirrer. Was it possible that she and Savannah weren't as close as she claimed? Or that Savannah had simply been a private person, at least where her difficulties with her fiancé were concerned?

But that was unlikely. After all, I knew perfectly well that when it came to matters of the heart, it was pretty difficult for women *not* to tell their friends about whatever was going on—especially if it was something that was troubling them.

"What about that director, Ragnar Bruin?" I asked.

I half expected her to look puzzled. Instead, she said, "I wasn't sure if you knew about that." She shook her head and added, "Savannah was totally shocked when this past summer he moved his New York office to a building that's right around the corner from Alpha."

That was a new piece of information. "Ragnar opened an office close by?" I exclaimed, surprised. "I imagine she was terrified!"

Coo's eyebrows shot up. "Why on earth would she have been terrified?"

"Wasn't Ragnar stalking Savannah?" I asked. I was doing my best to sound matter-of-fact even though my thoughts were racing.

"Hardly," she said. "If anything, it was the other way around. Well, not stalking exactly. I mean, Savannah wasn't the type to stalk.

"But she was certainly into him," she continued after

pausing to sip her coffee. "She was constantly texting him, sending him little presents, like boxes of chocolate or, this one time, a huge bunch of balloons." She shook her head slowly. "It was no wonder that Ragnar's wife, Delia, was so jealous."

I had been wondering about how Ragnar's wife fit into all this ever since Amanda had told me about their involvement. But I was still stuck on what Coo had said about Savannah being totally into him, rather than him being an unwelcome stalker as her supposed best friend had claimed.

Coo leaned forward, meanwhile glancing around as if to see if anyone was listening. "There was this one time that Delia came to the office, screaming her head off," she said, her voice low.

"What was she screaming about?" I asked.

Coo grimaced. "What do you think? She was yelling at Savannah about keeping her hands off her husband."

I nodded. But then another thought occurred to me. "Are you sure their relationship was sexual? Is it possible that Savannah was simply cultivating Ragnar because he was an important Hollywood director and she was trying to get ahead?"

"I'm afraid I can't answer that," Coo said. "I always got the feeling that Timothy and Savannah were really committed to each other. I knew for sure that she was always texting Ragnar, and there was definitely a flirtation thing going on. But whether they were actually, you know, doing anything about it . . . that was something Savannah never talked to me about."

At that moment, Coo took out her phone and checked the time. "Sorry I haven't been more helpful. And now I should get back."

"You've been *very* helpful," I assured her. And I meant it.

"One thing's for sure: you've motivated me to do something I was assigned but which I've been dreading," Coo said as she crumpled up her napkin and stuffed it into her empty cup. "I'm going to clean out Savannah's office. Since she was just on leave, everything had been left pretty much the way it was. But now that she's gone . . ."

I was startled. "You mean no one has done that yet?"

She shook her head. "Our office manager was supposed to do it. At least that's what I heard, that she'd been instructed to clear everything out and just throw it away. Files for work, personal items, her coffee mug, and the dumb little stuffed animals she kept lined up on a shelf . . . Handling the cleanup that way struck me as a little cold, but apparently that was the word from the top."

"But that hasn't happened?" I asked.

"Not yet," Coo replied. Grimacing, she added, "Our office manager is one of the laziest people you ever met. It's practically impossible to get her to answer the phone, much less deal with somebody else's stuff. So, do you know what I'm going to do? I'm going to grab some empty boxes out of the storeroom as soon as I get a chance and pack up all of Savannah's things."

Once again, she glanced around Starbuck's nervously. "And you can have it all, if you want. Especially since I wouldn't know where else to send it. It's certainly not anything her family or her friends would be interested in. But you might find something interesting in there. Something that will help you with—you know, what you're trying to do."

Her offer had sent my heart into overdrive. "That would be great."

"I'll ship the boxes to you as soon as I pack them up," Coo said. "Just give me the address you want me to use. And while you're doing that, I'll give you my cell phone number in case you want to get in touch with me again."

I jotted down my home address, 59 Sugar Maple Way.

Somehow, having the boxes delivered to my house seemed more private than having them show up at Lickety Splits.

Then something else occurred to me. "Do you happen to have Savannah's address?"

"I do," Coo said. "She had a party there a couple of months ago, so I have it in my phone. I'll text it to you . . ."

I lingered at Starbucks for a few minutes after Coo raced off, scraping the last of the foamed milk off the sides of the paper cup with my wooden stirrer. My head was spinning from the opposing stories I'd heard from two women who had known Savannah Crane well.

Amanda had insisted that Savannah and Timothy were the happiest couple on earth. But Coo had said that recently there had been tension in their relationship.

Amanda had claimed that Ragnar Bruin was stalking Savannah and that she was convinced that the director was her friend's killer. Coo, meanwhile, said she had witnessed Savannah texting him and sending him cute little presents.

I had already known that Savannah had had two men in her life, one of whom was married. But Coo's take on the murder victim's complicated relationships had cast them both in an entirely different light.

At this point, I didn't know who—or what—to believe. But that only made me more determined than ever to find out.

Chapter 8

First-class passengers on the *Titanic* were treated
to French ice cream for dessert, according to the
April 14, 1912, menu. Second-class passengers
had to settle for plain, egg-free American
ice cream.

—Everybody Loves Ice Cream: The Whole Scoop on
America's Favorite Treat, *by Shannon Jackson Arnold*

Even though it was close to lunchtime, my visit to Starbucks and my inability to resist scones had left me full. As I walked to the subway, I noticed that the delicatessens and takeout restaurants I passed were already buzzing with the office crowd. I found myself missing being part of the hustle-bustle of city living.

But that feeling only lasted about ten seconds. Instead, I found myself appreciating the freedom of my life in Wolfert's Roost. Nowadays, I could have lunch anytime I felt like it. And I could take as much time as I wanted, as long as Lickety Splits was taken care of.

Thanks to Coo, I had added one more destination to my list. And this one was taking me to Brooklyn. I got on the subway after consulting the New York City Transit app on my phone. Forty minutes later, I climbed up the station's concrete steps and found myself in a different world.

The buildings around me weren't towering high-rises, the way they were in Manhattan. Here, the streets were lined with shops, with just a few floors of apartments above them. You could tell you were in place where each neighborhood had its own personality.

Unfortunately, this particularly neighborhood's personality was that of someone who hadn't quite gotten his act together.

While most of the businesses I walked past were staples of everyday life, like hair dressers and small food markets, there were also several pawn shops and a check-cashing place. There were quite a few empty shops, too, boarded up tight and decorated with aggressive slashes of graffiti.

Savannah Crane lived *here*? I thought, anxiously checking the address Coo had texted me.

But I knew that neighborhoods could change from block to block, so I kept on walking. By the time I got to the address that Coo had given me, the buildings were a bit cleaner, and there were more bakeries and dry cleaners than pawn shops. But the area still wasn't what I'd expected.

I stopped when I spotted the number on the address on my phone screen: 304. It was stenciled on the glass door of a shop that sold ninety-nine-cent items, the kind of place I love to browse in. Next to it was a second door with the same number. To the right there were a dozen buzzers, along with handwritten or typed names next to them.

The buzzer for Apartment 5A had a strip of bright-green duct tape next to it. The name CRANE was handwritten on it in black.

I peered through the glass window set into the door. It would have benefited greatly from a good scrubbing. Inside, I could see a small foyer that was a far cry from elegant.

A woman came up behind me. She carried two plastic tote bags filled with groceries in one hand and a leash in the other.

At the end was a small, fluffy black dog that immediately began barking at me with the ferocity of a pit bull.

"Going inside?" the woman asked cheerfully.

"Uh, no," I said. "I was just . . . I'm on the way out."

She nodded. And then, gesturing at the bags she was carrying, she commented, "Boy, at times like this I really wish I lived in an elevator building. Anyway, have a good day!"

"You, too," I replied.

So this building didn't even have an elevator. Which meant that Savannah Crane had lived in what was commonly called a five-story walk-up.

I was more puzzled than ever. How could Savannah have owned a weekend house in the Hudson Valley, yet lived in a seedy neighborhood like this?

I supposed that Timothy could have helped. But he, too, was an aspiring actor, with even fewer credits than she had. He certainly wasn't enjoying an explosive career. True, it was possible that he had a lucrative day job. Then again, it would be difficult to go to auditions if you were a stockbroker on Wall Street.

I headed back to the subway, anxious to move on to the next place on my list.

Reaching the address I'd found online for Monarch Cinema Props required getting myself from Brooklyn to Queens. While these two boroughs actually border each other, with Queens directly above Brooklyn, traveling from one to the other required a seemingly endlessly long subway ride back through Manhattan.

When I finally emerged from the subway station in Long Island City, I found myself surrounded by large, flat industrial buildings. I walked several blocks, then finally spotted my destination.

I had thought Amanda was exaggerating when she'd said

that Monarch occupied a one-hundred-thousand-square-foot space. But as I stood outside the warehouse-like building, I could see that it sprawled across an entire city block.

As soon as I walked in through the main entrance, I noticed a big sign that listed five floors and what was on each of them. Drapery and linens were on the fourth floor. Pews, confessionals, and religious artifacts were on five, garden ornaments on three. There was also furniture on every one of the floors, arranged by period. Mid-Century modern, sixties, and seventies on the fourth floor; Colonial, Asian, and 19th-century French on the second.

As I peered beyond the sign and into the building, I saw a mind-boggling amount of stuff on display.

Neatly arranged inside the nondescript building were dozens of leather couches and chairs, a dozen statues of frightening Samurai swordsmen, and a cluster of at least thirty coatracks of different styles and sizes. Along the wall to my left were shelves that ran all the way up to the high ceiling. One eight-foot side section was crowded with clusters of artificial flowers. The one next to it held stacks of silver trays. Another was filled with old-fashioned toys, like wooden animals on wheels and metal wind-up toys. Another group of shelves was crammed with hundreds of ceramic figurines, ranging from a few inches high to almost two feet: ladies in long dresses, ballerinas, soldiers on horseback, dogs, lions, even little castles.

And from the long corridors that stretched ahead of me, I could tell that the display area extended far beyond what I could see. Directly in front of me were rows of office chairs. They were neatly lined up on two levels, with one platform right above the other. I spotted at least twenty padded, black office chairs, followed by another twenty white ones, and behind that a row of wooden ones. Carefully arranged in front of them were conference tables: ovals and rectangles, wooden and glass, small and large.

The place reminded me of a giant thrift store, one that was extremely organized and only carried items that were in perfect condition. Once again, I thought about how much Emma would love seeing a place like this. At the very least, I had to tell her all about it.

A receptionist sat behind a counter at the front, just like at Alpha Industries. Only this particular woman had hot-pink, spiky hair and glasses with thick, perfectly round black frames.

"I'm here to see Amanda Huffner," I told her.

"Do you have an appointment?" she asked automatically.

"Just tell her Kate McKay is here," I replied.

She nodded, then picked up the phone. "Amanda? Kate McKay is here to see you."

Less than two minutes later, Amanda emerged from behind the row of Samurai swordsmen. Her wavy, dark brown hair was pulled back into a loose ponytail, and she was wearing denim overalls.

"Kate!" she said, sounding a little out of breath. "This is a surprise! But such a nice one."

She glanced back at the receptionist, then turned back and loudly said, "Let me show you around, Ms. McKay. I'm sure you'll find that Monarch has everything you need."

Once we'd stepped away, she whispered, "Ella is such a busybody. For some reason, she's really weird about having friends come here during the workday."

She hit the elevator button, and we rode up to the fourth floor.

"There's nobody up here right now," she explained as we stepped out. "That'll give us a chance to talk without anyone overhearing."

We had just walked into the 1950s. In front of me were five television sets from that era, big hulking contraptions that were half the size of a refrigerator. Just past them were groupings of furniture arranged to create the feeling of a little room, just like in furniture stores. We sat down on a boxy orange couch, surrounded by two white leather lounge chairs, a blond coffee table, and several white plastic lamps that looked as if they had come from outer space.

"Do you recognize any of this?" Amanda asked, smiling as she gestured at the pretend room we were sitting in.

"I'm afraid not," I admitted.

"These were used in *Tom's Story*," she said. "Remember the scene where Marnie Merrill tells Alan Prescott that he's the father of her teenage son?"

"I do remember that scene," I told her. "But I don't remember the furniture at all."

She laughed. "It's funny; most people never even notice the props in a movie. But it's so important in setting the tone for each scene. Maybe the audience isn't aware of them when they're done correctly, but they sure would be if anybody got it wrong! Like in that scene, what if there had been a flat-screen TV? Can you imagine how strange that would have looked?"

"It makes perfect sense that everything has to belong," I said, nodding. "So I guess a big part of your job is to make sure that everything looks as if it should be there."

Glancing around, I joked, "The next time I want to buy furniture, I think I'll just come here and order up an entire room."

But Amanda was shaking her head. "Actually, Monarch doesn't sell any of its props. It's our policy.

"In fact," she went on, "Ragnar Bruin—" She paused to make a face. "That *monster* Ragnar Bruin wanted to buy one of the chairs that had been used in his movie *Pirates*. Apparently, he and the star, Jimmy Dorp, are great friends, and he wanted to give it to him as a birthday present." She shrugged. "My boss said no, and he refused to budge. Of course, I was secretly pleased, given how I feel about the guy.

"But enough Hollywood gossip," she said. She dropped her hands into her lap and looked at me expectantly. "What can I do for you?"

"It's funny that you brought up Ragnar, since that's why I'm here." I took a deep breath. "I was hoping you'd be able to help me come up with an excuse to meet with him."

A look of horror crossed her face. "No!" she cried. "That's not a good idea, Kate. The man is dangerous! I'm convinced that he's responsible for what happened to Savannah! And if he found out that you knew what was going on between him and her, I don't know what he'd do!"

"But I'd be meeting him at his office," I told her, still hoping I could change her mind. "I don't think he'd make a scene in front of the people who work for him."

Amanda shook her head hard. "Kate, you have no idea. I'm sorry, but I'm definitely against you having anything to do with that man. It's just too risky."

Her insistence that I keep away from him fueled my theory that when it came to the true nature of Savannah's relationship with Ragnar, Amanda was the one who was lying, not Coo. But I had no choice but to play along.

"I suppose you're right," I said. "It was just an idea."

"A *terrible* idea," she agreed. She must have figured that she really had convinced me to see things her way, since she stood up.

"Look, I should get back to work," Amanda said, still agitated. I wondered if being afraid of getting caught goofing off was the real reason. "You need to go."

"Of course," I said, gathering up my things. "Thanks for your time."

"You can let yourself out," she said. "I have a couple of things to do up here. But honestly, Kate? Stay as far away from that creep as you can. I'm serious."

As I rode down in the elevator, I was still mulling over Amanda's strong reaction to the idea of me talking to Ragnar. She was determined to keep me away from him, which made me more curious than ever to meet the man.

And even though she'd been unwilling to help me come up with a way of getting through the door of Ragnar Bruin's office, during our short conversation she'd inadvertently done exactly that.

It was late afternoon by the time I left Monarch and headed back to the subway. After my long day running around the city, I was glad I didn't have to get back on the train to go home. But in addition to being tired, I was also looking forward to seeing my work friend, Becca Collins.

Becca and I had worked at the same public relations firm for two years. While I'd been friendly with most of the people who worked there, she and I had developed a special bond almost from the beginning. She was one of those people who just *got* me.

Even so, I hadn't yet decided whether I'd tell her about what had really brought me to the city. Since Becca had been a work friend, there were some limits to what we told each other.

I figured I'd decide once we were together. I knew that sometimes it was possible to maintain a friendship after two people no longer worked together, and sometimes it wasn't.

At a small corner grocery, I plucked a bouquet from the dozens on display outside, a happy profusion of mixed blossoms in bright shades of yellow and orange. I also picked up a hunk of cheese and two boxes of interesting crackers. The tremendous selection that was available, even in a tiny place like this, gave me a pang of regret over no longer having access to the abundance of choices that city living offered.

But trudging down the street lugging my purse, my tote

bag, the groceries, and the bouquet reminded me that the urban experience had its negatives, too.

Becca's apartment building was a stark contrast to Savannah Crane's. It was a white brick high-rise, at least twenty-five stories tall, with a sleek lobby decorated in black and silver.

The doorman buzzed Becca's apartment, then nodded at me after she gave him the go-ahead. I shared my elevator ride to the fifteenth floor with a jogger and an old man with a slow-moving Westie on a leash. For a moment, I let myself pretend that I lived there and that I was still a city gal.

"Kate!" Becca squealed when she opened the door. She threw her arms around me even though my hands were both full, which made for a pretty one-sided hug. "It's so great to see you!"

Despite the fact that she'd probably gotten home from work only minutes before, she had already changed into stretchy black sweatpants and a faded Nine Inch Nails T-shirt. Her long, dark brown hair had been pulled back into a loose ponytail. I was a little taken aback since I was used to seeing her in business clothes and more eye makeup than I had ever felt comfortable wearing.

I handed her the flowers and the snacks. "I figured we could talk for a while before we went out to eat."

"I've already ordered in," she announced. "I got Thai food from that place you told me about on Second Avenue. They have a new owner, but the food is just as good. And they still have the same red curry dish you put me on to!"

"Sounds great," I said sincerely.

"How about some coffee while we wait?" she offered. "Or tea? Or a glass of wine?"

"Tea sounds great," I said. "Do you have any herbal tea?"

Five minutes later, Becca and I were sitting in her small living room, nursing mugs of tea and admiring the flowers, now standing tall on the coffee table in a cylindrical glass vase. She was settled on the couch with her bare feet tucked under her. I was curled up in a comfy upholstered chair that took up a good twenty-five percent of the compact room. I was surprised by how the rooms in a New York City apartment suddenly struck me as so absurdly small.

"So tell me how you are!" Becca demanded. "I was thinking today that just about everything in your life changed—let's see—not even a year ago! You must be totally overwhelmed! I mean, you moved from the most fabulous city in the world to a teensy little town upstate, you went from living alone in a cute apartment to living with your *grandmother* in a big old house, you gave up your glamorous PR job and opened a *store*, of all things . . ."

"It's true," I agreed. "A lot *has* changed in my life."

I wondered if I was simply being too sensitive or if Becca's pronouncements really did border on criticism. Or at least sounded a lot more judgmental than they needed to be. But I'd certainly reached a decision about whether or not to tell her the truth about what had brought me to the city today. The answer was no.

"My niece Emma has come to stay with Grams and me, too," I added. "She's my older sister Julie's daughter. She's eighteen, and she's taking some time off before going to college. She wants to figure out what direction she wants to go in."

Becca nodded. "That's right," she said. "I remember you emailing me something about that. So even more has changed! Now you're also living with a *teenager*! That must be . . . well, interesting!" She paused to sip her tea. "But I guess what matters is whether you're happy with the changes you've made. Are you?"

I thought for a few seconds. "You know, Becca, I really am."

"But you must miss the city!" she insisted.

I drank some of my tea as I gave her question some thought. "I don't, at least most of the time. I certainly thought I would. I also expected that I'd be coming back every chance I got. But I'm finding that small-town life suits me better than I ever would have expected."

"Tell me more about what it's like," Becca demanded. "I mean, honestly, living in your hometown again? That's something I can't even imagine. Do you feel like you're in high school again? Do you wake up in a sweat in the middle of the night, worried about a math test—or about having to play field hockey again?"

I laughed. "Surprisingly, no. It feels . . . comfortable. Yeah, I guess that's the best way to describe it. When I look back at my years in the city, I realize it was much more work than living where I am now. Standing in the rain waiting for a bus, crowding into the subway every morning, carrying groceries and everything else I needed blocks and blocks every day . . ." I shrugged. "Maybe I'm just getting lazy in my old age."

"I get that," Becca said earnestly. "But really, going back to the same place where you grew up? I bet there are still plenty of people around from your childhood. That must be weird. Old friends, old enemies . . ."

"Sure there are," I replied. "But I'm actually finding that that's one of the nicest things about being back. My best friend from high school, Willow Baines, still lives in town. She runs a yoga studio now, but she works in my shop from time to time. She's helped out at a few catering events, too.

"And I've run into some other people that I grew up with," I continued. "Like Pete Bonano, who used to be our star football player. He's our local friendly police officer now."

I paused to take another sip of tea. Given the way this conversation with Becca was going, I was debating whether to bring up the other old friend who lived in town.

But even before I'd decided, the words popped out of my

mouth. "And then there's Jake. Jake Pratt. You may remember me mentioning him. He and I have actually . . ."

I let my voice trail off, not certain how to finish that sentence. Gotten back in touch? Struck up a friendship? Nervously entertained the idea of picking up again where we left off?

"Wait a minute." Becca banged her mug down on the coffee table and stared at me intensely. "Jake? Jake, the old high school flame? The one you never got over, the one you talked about endlessly—"

"I didn't talk about him endlessly," I said crossly.

"Maybe not *endlessly*," Becca said. "But he definitely came up in the conversation from time to time. Especially when you'd had a cosmopolitan or two."

"Really?" I said, blinking. I wasn't playing dumb. I honestly didn't remember.

Becca rolled her eyes. "I love you dearly, Kate, but sometimes I felt that if I had to listen to you go on and on about how blue his eyes were one more time . . ."

"They're amazingly blue," I commented. "The bluest I've ever seen."

"Or about how the two of you were soul mates," Becca said, grinning. Then she grew serious. "And then there was that awful thing that happened when he stood you up at—what was it, the homecoming dance?"

"The prom," I told her. I swallowed hard. "At the end of our senior year. The very end."

"That's right. Now I remember." Becca's face lit up again. "So you two are back in touch?"

"Yup." I suddenly pretended to find my mug so fascinating that I couldn't take my eyes off it.

Becca sighed impatiently. "Tell me!" she demanded. "What's going on exactly?"

"Nothing," I replied with a shrug.

"Nothing?" Becca repeated, sounding incredulous. "*Nothing?* Here you two were the Romeo and Juliet of Wilbur's Rooster, or whatever that town of yours is called, and you both find yourselves living in the same place fifteen years after you were torn apart like—like, well, like Romeo and Juliet . . . You've got to tell me more about what's going on with that, girlfriend."

I grimaced. "I'm not sure what's going on. I mean, I think he wants to pick up where we left off."

Becca let out a loud groan. I blinked, not sure if she was thrilled or horrified.

"That is so-o-o-o romantic!" she cried.

Okay, so she was thrilled.

"That is like something in a movie," she went on. "Here's this guy who you considered the love of your life, and then you lost him, and now he's in the picture again, so you two can go right back to where you were before—"

"It's not that simple," I interrupted. "At least, not from my perspective."

"Meaning?"

"Meaning I'm not sure how I feel about him," I told her.

Becca cast me a strange look. "You mean you're not sure how you feel about Jake, the person? Or you're not sure how you feel about getting back together with someone who broke your heart once upon a time?"

"Both," I told her. "And there's a third thing, too. I'm not sure I want to be involved with anybody right now."

Becca let out another loud noise, this one more of a moan. And this time, I was pretty sure it was meant to express being horrified, not thrilled.

"Kate McKay, what is *wrong* with you?" she demanded. "Here's this guy, who from the way you've always talked about him is *perfect* for you if not perfect in the absolute sense. He's nice, he's normal, he's stable, he's got those incredible blue eyes . . . and he's crazy about you!"

"But—"

"And you're crazy about him!" Becca went on. "Or at least you were once. And now you get a chance to see if you're still crazy about him, if even after fifteen years you two still feel that you were made for each other, and you're not jumping right in to find out?"

I frowned. "If you put it *that* way—"

"What other way is there to put it?" Becca cried. "Kate, I don't think you have any idea how hard it is to find a nice guy these days. All the guys I meet are boring or nerds or workaholics or chronically unemployed—or else they have something else seriously wrong with them. Have you forgotten how hard it is to find somebody you have real chemistry with?"

I was about to answer, but she kept going. "Do you really not remember all those horrid blind dates you went on? And what about the time you tried that dating service where you have lunch with a bunch of guys, like an assembly line, and all you got out of it was indigestion?"

"True," I told her. "But—"

"You have got to take the word 'but' out of your vocabulary," Becca insisted. "This Jake guy is definitely someone you have to take seriously. How can you just walk away from what could turn out to be the most important opportunity of your life? At least, your personal life. Your 'and they lived happily ever after' life?"

"No one lives happily ever after," I pointed out.

"Of course not," Becca agreed. "But you want to do everything you can to increase the odds of keeping the word 'happy' in the equation."

"Okay, I'll think about what you're saying," I told her.

Ready to change the subject, I glanced around her apartment and said, "Hey, that's a great lamp. I love the turquoise shade. Where did you get it?"

And then we were off on Becca's second favorite topic, after my love life. And that was her favorite web sites for shopping online.

Chapter 9

Rainbow Sherbet was invented by Emanuel
Goren while working at Sealtest Dairies,
Philadelphia, Pennsylvania, during the early
1950s. He is credited by them in conceptualizing
the three-nozzle design to fill the containers
simultaneously with three flavors, thus creating
the 'Rainbow' effect of the confection.

—*https://en.wikipedia.org/wiki/Rainbow_sherbet*

Spending the night on Becca's fold-out couch meant listening to a never-ending lullaby of honking horns, groaning trucks, and the occasional siren. When I woke up in the middle of the night, my head thick with sleep, for a few seconds I thought I was still back in my old apartment, living my old life.

But as I turned over and pulled my pillow over my head, I knew that as much fun as that old life had been, I felt more comfortable than ever in my *new* life.

I stayed at Becca's until mid-morning. I actually experienced a sense of relief when she went off to work and I had the luxury of lingering in her apartment for another couple of hours. As I savored a second cup of coffee, I plotted out my surprise visit to Ragnar Bruin's office.

By late morning, as I trudged up the stairs leading out of

the Midtown subway station that was closest to his office, I was pretty sure that I'd be able to carry off the scheme I'd come up with. Just like the day before, it was going to require a bit of acting. But I was growing increasingly confident about my abilities in the theater arts.

The building that housed the famous director's office was as different from Alpha Industries' building as I could imagine. Just as Coo had said, it was located mere steps away. But while Alpha Industries stood on a busy corner of Sixth Avenue, a major thoroughfare that was lined with towering office buildings, Ragnar Bruin's New York headquarters were located in a quaint, five-story brownstone on a much quieter side street.

In fact, it appeared that his offices occupied the entire building. That was pretty impressive, given the price of New York real estate. Then again, the man had had a ridiculously impressive career. That point was driven home by the giant movie posters covering every inch of wall space. As I walked into the front entryway, I immediately spotted posters for three of the films I knew he'd directed, *Pirates*, *The Hartford Trilogy*, and *Too Much Time*. But there were also posters for half a dozen other films I knew of but hadn't realized were his.

The furnishings were as funky as the building itself. They appeared to be deliberately mismatched: a burgundy-velvet Victorian couch paired with a glass-and-chrome coffee table straight out of the 1980s, a Noguchi-style floor lamp with a crinkled paper shade at the edge of a lush, deep-red Oriental rug that looked like a souvenir that Marco Polo had brought home. Then there were the fun touches: a jukebox, an old-fashioned movie camera that looked like it dated back to the 1920s, and a neon sculpture that spelled out "Go Away."

The receptionist was similarly unique. She was dressed in a salmon-colored suit with a 1940s look, complete with wide shoulders and a peplum waist. Her bright-red lipstick, a startling contrast to her espresso-brown skin, was another 40s touch. But she had several piercings on her face, and her head was shaved. An homage to the punk era, I assumed.

Trying not to stare at the safety pin jutting out of her nose, I took a deep breath and said, "Good morning. My name is Kate McKay, and I'd like to see Mr. Bruin."

"Do you have an appointment?" she asked, barely glancing up from her computer screen.

I'd had a feeling that that would be her first question, and I was ready with an answer. "I won't need one when he hears the reason I'm here."

She looked up, her expression skeptical. "And what exactly is the reason?"

"Just tell him it's about the Jimmy Dorp chair," I replied. "The one at Monarch Cinema Props."

Her face lit up. "The Jimmy Dorp chair?" she repeated excitedly. She was already pressing one of the buttons on her phone. "I'm sure Ragnar will want to talk to you about *that*."

Two minutes later, she was ushering me into the famous director's office. I knew it had to be his because it was huge, with a tremendous window that overlooked the street.

The room was so sparsely furnished that I couldn't tell if the various pieces were intentionally mismatched or not. A clear Lucite table that served as a desk was at one end of the spacious office, and a lime-green couch and two matching chairs were at the other. Hanging on the stark white walls were more framed posters for movies Ragnar had made.

Interestingly, I didn't see a picture of his wife on his desk. In fact, there was nothing on his desk but a small laptop computer.

And sitting at that desk was the man himself. He was tall; that was apparent even though he was seated. His nose was unusually long and crooked, and despite his Scandinavian first name—a name I recognized as a legendary Norse hero from watching the TV series *Vikings*—he had a wild mane of long dark hair and piercing dark eyes.

Partly because of his size and partly because of his status, he had an air of importance about him. Somehow, he managed to exude power.

I breezed into his office, doing my best to present the picture of self-assurance.

"I'm Kate McKay," I said, sitting down even before being invited to, "and I have good news, Mr. Bruin."

"Good news about the Jimmy Dorp chair?" he asked eagerly. "Is that what I heard you two talking about?"

I could already see that my ploy was working.

"As you know, Monarch has a policy of not selling any of its props," I went on, trying to give off the same air of confidence. I took care not to say anything about me actually *working* at Monarch or even about me representing the company. "But Monarch came up with another idea: the craftspeople there can make you a chair that's identical to the one you wanted. Would that work?"

He thought for a few seconds. "It's not quite the same thing, is it? So, of course, I wouldn't be willing to pay as much."

I started to panic. I hadn't anticipated talking about money. But I quickly came up with a good answer: "No one has gotten as far as determining a price," I told him. "At this point, Monarch just wants to find out if you're interested."

"I'm interested," Ragnar said, running his long fingers through his mane of dark hair excitedly.

"Wonderful," I replied. "In that case, the designers will figure out the cost. Someone will get back to you as soon as that's been done."

"Excellent!" he said. "Thank you so much for coming in."

We were done, as far as he was concerned. Which meant I had to do some fast thinking.

"Is the chair going to be a gift for your wife?" I asked.

I was surprised when he laughed, a loud, throaty guffaw that made me jump.

"My wife!" he repeated. "You obviously don't read the tabloids."

In response to my confused look, he added, "My wife left me. It's been two months now. In fact, she's already engaged to a French actor. And she's telling everyone who'll listen that divorcing me is the best thing that ever happened to her."

"I'm so sorry," I said.

So much for my theory about Ragnar's wife being a suspect. If she'd left the man and already moved on to someone else, it was hard to believe she'd be jealous enough to want to do away with his paramour.

But I still wanted to find out more. "I suppose couples simply grow apart some times," I commented.

"Or one of them finds their true soul mate," he said, his voice thickening. "The way I did."

I had a feeling I knew where he was going with this. But I wanted to make sure.

"Aren't you lucky!" I exclaimed. "That's something I'm still working on myself. Is it someone else in the industry?"

His expression darkened. "She *was* in the industry. She passed away recently." He swallowed hard before adding, "Savannah Crane. A terrible thing happened to her. It was in all the papers and all over the Internet."

"I did read about that," I told him. "And I'm so sorry."

I found it interesting that he was being so open about his feelings for Savannah. I would have expected that if he really had been stalking her, the way Amanda had insisted, he wouldn't want everyone to know that he had been, well, stalking someone. Which lent credence to Coo's claim that he hadn't been stalking Savannah at all.

"I'm devastated," he went on, his voice thick with emotion. "I had to take down all the photos of her I had here in the office. They make me too sad. I even had to put this away."

He reached into his desk drawer, pulled out a flat sheet, and handed it to me. I studied what looked like a handmade collage consisting of photographs, construction-paper hearts, and other items that had been artfully arranged on a big piece of cardboard.

"Who made this?" I asked, glancing up at him.

"Savannah made it," he replied, his eyes shiny with tears. "She gave it to me for my birthday, back in April. She was extremely creative."

He was right about that. The person who made this had taken half a dozen photographs of Ragnar and Savannah posing together and scattered them across the page. In one photo, they were sitting on a yacht, wearing bathing suits and sun visors. Their arms were wrapped around each other's waists, and they were both beaming. In another, they were dressed in evening clothes, dancing. Their bodies were pressed together tightly. Savannah's head rested on Ragnar's shoulder, and the expression on her face was one of pure bliss.

Interspersed among the photographs were the cut-out paper hearts. Scrawled across them were sayings like, "Love you forever!" and "So glad you're mine!"

If Savannah had actually made this, there was no way that Ragnar had been stalking her. This struck me as concrete evidence that the two of them had been involved in a genuine love affair.

Which meant one of two things. One was that Amanda had been lying when she'd told me about Ragnar and Savannah. The other possibility was that Savannah had been lying to her best friend.

It wasn't until the train that would take me home was pulling out of Penn Station that I realized how exhausted I was.

Simply being in the city had been tiring, I realized. True, I loved all the stimulation: the people hurrying by, the congested traffic, the honking horns and the screeching buses and the rumble of the subway under my feet. Then there was the visual excitement, things I'd paid special attention to over the past thirty-six hours: buildings with ornamentation I'd never noticed before, cafés with signs advertising foods I wasn't familiar with, enticing displays of shoes and fashionable clothes in the shop windows.

When I'd lived in Manhattan, somehow it had all become background noise. But now that I was a country girl again— or at least a Hudson Valley girl—I was shocked by how demanding I had found the city. I had changed. I wasn't used to walking on crowded sidewalks, having to veer around people who were moving too slowly or else being jostled by someone passing me because this time it was me who wasn't fast enough. I jumped every time a car horn bleated angrily. When a fire truck raced by, the shrieking siren was so loud and so shrill that I covered my ears.

As I settled back in my seat and closed my eyes, I could feel myself relaxing. The city was starting to feel farther and farther away. But the information I'd gathered during my two days there began coming into sharper focus. Thanks to what I'd learned, I was starting to put together a list of suspects in Savannah Crane's murder.

Timothy Scott was at the top. Even though he'd come across as someone who had sincerely cared about Savannah, the simple fact that he was her boyfriend meant that he was someone worth looking at. Crimes against women were too frequently perpetrated by the men in their lives. Then there was Coo's claim that things between Timothy and Savannah had been anything but smooth as of late. Given the fact that she appeared to have been honest about Ragnar and Savannah's relationship, I tended to believe her about Timothy, as well.

As for Ragnar, the director's name was the second one on my list. He, too, had been an important man in Savannah's life. But the question of what was really going on between them remained unanswered in my mind, even after seeing the handmade tribute to their love. For all I knew, she hadn't been the person who made it. It was still possible that Amanda had been right about their relationship. Which would mean he could even have made it himself.

Chelsea Atkins was next on the list. Despite her contention that she barely knew Savannah, she had had the most access to the dish of ice cream that had killed her. And I had found her hair in the cabinet, which raised the question of whether she had been tampering with the dishes minutes before Savannah had eaten the ice cream that had killed her.

At this point, I also had to include Amanda Huffner's name on the list. And that was mainly because it seemed possible that she had lied to me about Savannah's relationships with one or both of the men in her life, Timothy and Ragnar. It was possible that Amanda was trying to protect Timothy, mainly by pointing a finger at Ragnar. While I didn't know her motivation, I did know that it was possible that she hadn't been honest with me.

The last name on my list of suspects was Jennifer Jordan. She was a long shot, I knew. But I trusted Emma's instincts, and her insistence that Savannah's rival was worth looking at was something I couldn't ignore.

As the train chugged along toward the Hudson Valley and home sweet home, I began drifting off. Not into sleep, exactly, but more into a meditative state. Yet as I did, I found it more and more difficult to think about Savannah Crane. Instead, I found myself going back to my conversation with Becca.

The one about Jake.

And how I'd be crazy not to give the relationship another chance.

"Have you forgotten how hard it is to find somebody you have real chemistry with?" Becca had said, clearly exasperated over my inability to see what she found so obvious.

What about Brody? I thought. How does he fit into all this—if he fits in at all?

I hoped that my date with him, or whatever it was, would help me resolve that issue.

I guess I really did fall asleep, because I was suddenly jolted awake by the ringing of my phone. As I pulled it out of my purse, I was so disoriented that it took me a few seconds to comprehend the fact that it was Jake who was calling.

I hesitated for a moment, feeling guilty that not long before I'd been thinking about Brody. When I finally answered, my voice was groggy.

"Hi, Jake," I mumbled.

"You and I have a date tomorrow, Kate," he announced. "Well, not a date, exactly. More like an appointment. Wait, that's too formal. Let's just say there's someplace I'm taking you tomorrow. How does four o'clock sound?"

"Wait," I said, still not completely awake. "Where are we going?"

"It's a secret," he replied, sounding positively impish.

"But what should I wear?" I asked. "Should I bring anything? A bottle of wine, a warm jacket . . . a pint of Dark Chocolate Hazelnut?"

He laughed. "Wear whatever you want. And don't bring anything. Should I pick you up at home or at the shop?"

"At home," I told him. That way, I figured, I'd have a chance to freshen up after a long, grueling day with an ice cream scoop.

"Great," Jake said. "See you tomorrow." Then he hung up.

Another mystery, I thought, as I dropped my phone back into my pocketbook. But somehow, unlike the one surrounding Savannah Crane, this mystery made me feel good.

I don't remember the first time I saw Jake Pratt, or even the first time I spoke to him. Our high school was small enough—and our star baseball player was well-known enough—that I, like everybody else, just sort of knew who he was.

Our first serious interaction, however, was wonderfully dramatic.

At the beginning of my junior year, probably in early October, I was standing by my locker at the end of the day when my longtime nemesis, Ashley Winthrop, wandered by. Two members of her entourage were in tow.

But as Ashley sashayed down the hall with two members of her fan club, she stopped at the water fountain a couple of feet away from my locker and loudly said, "Would you believe that I've got not one, not two, but *three* invitations to the Halloween dance? And sadly, I'm sure that some people don't have any! Isn't that the saddest thing you've ever heard? My heart positively *bleeds* for the unpopular girls!"

I could feel her two sidekicks staring at me as Ashley leaned over to take a long sip of water. I could also feel my blood boiling.

I hate you, Ashley Winthrop, I remember thinking, trying to keep my cheeks from turning bright red as I pretended to reorganize my textbooks. I truly hate you.

As if that wasn't bad enough, Ashley then came right over to me and said in a nauseatingly sweet voice, "Why, hello, Kate. I didn't notice you standing there. Are you going to the Halloween dance?"

Just then, out of nowhere, Jake Pratt appeared. Popular Jake Pratt. Gorgeous Jake Pratt.

Independent Jake Pratt, one of the few hot boys at school who refused to get corralled into Ashley's group of popular kids, the ones who ran the school and tormented everyone who wasn't part of their clique.

"Hey, Kate," he said breezily, stopping right behind me and Ashley. "I was wondering if you'd like to go to the Halloween dance with me."

I was certain that my cheeks were the same shade of crimson as the history book I happened to be holding in my hand. But Ashley's nastiness had little to do with it.

"I'd love to, Jake," I said.

"Wow, that's great!" he exclaimed. "You just made my day! My entire week, in fact!"

And he actually sounded as if he meant it.

I turned to Ashley. "So I guess the answer to your question is yes, I *am* going to the Halloween dance."

She just stared at me, her expression one of total shock. This appeared to be one of the few times in her life when she couldn't think of anything to say.

"See you there, Ashley!" I called after her as she and her two ladies-in-waiting slunk away.

I turned to Jake. But instead of feeling grateful, I was furious.

"You didn't need to do that!" I cried. "You don't have to—to feel *sorry* for me! It's not your job to bale me out just because you think I'm—I'm *desperate* or something!"

He just blinked. "I don't think you're desperate," he replied calmly. "And I certainly don't feel sorry for you. I just want to go to the dance with you."

Now it was my turn to be at a loss for words. "You do? I mean you *really* do? You weren't just trying to make a point?"

He laughed. "I must admit that I did overhear what Ashley said. And the timing of me asking you to the dance had everything in the world to do with that. But I've wanted to ask you for days, and, well, I just haven't had the nerve."

"Really?" I croaked, too astonished to handle this moment any more gracefully. "But I didn't even think you knew who I was!"

"Of course, I know who you are," he said. Now *his* cheeks were turning pink. "I've been trying to get up the courage to ask you out ever since—well, ever since Kathy Norwood and I broke up last month."

With a shrug, he added, "I guess I have Ashley to thank for finally presenting me with just the right moment. My intention wasn't to put her in her place, but doing it sure felt good!"

Jake and I went to the Halloween dance. He dressed as a pirate, complete with a colorful stuffed parrot on one shoulder and a fake black mustache. I was a tiger, wearing a fuzzy orange-and-black one-piece suit that Grams whipped up on her sewing machine. We attached some of the fabric to a black headband for ears, and I carefully painted whiskers on my face. But my long tail was the best part, even though I did end up holding onto it most of the evening to keep it from banging into people.

Ashley came as Cleopatra, wearing a flowing white skirt that revealed her bellybutton. With it, she wore a low-cut, gold-sequined bra that prompted Mr. Ambrosiano, a curmudgeonly math teacher and one of the chaperones for the evening, to insist that she wear a Modderplaatz High School sweatshirt over it for the entire evening.

Yet even having her costume ruined didn't stop her. She made a point of flirting with Jake every chance she got until he finally told her, "Look, Ashley, I'm here with Kate. And Kate's the only person I want to dance with. And talk to. And drink that horrible sweet punch with. So why don't you go spend some time with your own date? I'm actually starting to feel sorry for that jerk Tommy Barrett, something I never thought would happen."

That night, Jake kissed me for the first time. The two of us were standing on the porch at Grams's house, saying good night after an absolutely lovely evening. All around us were the glowing jack-o'-lanterns that Grams and I had carved together. They all seemed to be smiling at us, and it was one of those moments I knew I'd remember for the rest of my life.

Which is exactly what it turned out to be.

Chapter 10

Iced dairy products made from the milk of horse,
buffalo, yak, camel, cow, and goat first appeared
during the T'ang Dynasty in China (618–907 AD).
King T'ang himself relished an iced-milk dish
called kumiss. The frosty concoction included
rice, flour, and 'dragon's eyeball powder,' better
known today as camphor, a chemical taken from
the wood of an evergreen tree.

—We All Scream for Ice Cream!
The Scoop on America's Favorite Dessert, *by Lee Wardlaw*

Wednesday morning, when the alarm clock in my bed-room went off, I had to remind myself that during my stay in the city I'd developed a new appreciation for the life I'd made for myself in Wolfert's Roost. And that included getting up with the sun to make ice cream.

Ice cream can sure be a cruel mistress, I thought grumpily as I dragged myself into the bathroom and turned on the shower.

But within half an hour, the steaming hot water and two cups of strong coffee had turned me into a new person. In fact, I was feeling energized enough to walk to Lickety Splits, rather than driving.

As I stepped outside onto the porch, the early-morning air

was crisp, and the sun was shining brightly. It was hard to believe the weather forecaster's gloomy prediction that rain clouds would be moving in by afternoon.

In honor of the upcoming holiday, I decided to whip up a batch of a new flavor I'd been thinking about. I planned to call it Bag o' Tricks and Treats, inspired by my memories of my own haul every Halloween. I started with a rich chocolate ice cream, mixing in chopped-up pieces of the candies that trick-or-treaters love most: Milky Ways, Snickers, M&Ms, and Reese's Peanut Butter Cups.

I was afraid it might be too much. But as I scooped up a small amount and cautiously tasted it, a wave of pleasure immediately rushed over me. For a while, I was transported back to my childhood. Or at least a *fantasy* from my childhood.

This one is going to be a winner, I thought.

And I was right. Bag o' Tricks and Treats turned out to be a big hit with my customers, too, at least my more adventurous ones. While plenty of people came in to Lickety Splits for the usual chocolate, vanilla, and strawberry experience, there were quite a few who stopped into my shop expressly to try whatever new concoction I'd just dreamed up.

Elton Hayes was one of these people. Elton, who owned and operated Let It Brie, the gourmet cheese shop a block or so away, was passionate about food.

He also happened to be one of my first customers that day.

"It's only eleven-thirty, but I'm already on lunch break," he exclaimed as he bustled into my shop. He was short, with chubby cheeks and a waistline to match. Even though he was only a few years older than I was, probably around forty, he had already lost most of his hair. "And I decided that ice cream was on the menu today."

He leaned over the glass display case and studied the tubs of ice cream lined up inside. Rubbing his pudgy hands together, he cooed, "And I can't wait to hear about the extra-special goodies you have in store for your loyal fans today, you ice cream goddess, you!"

I laughed. "How does Bag o' Tricks and Treats sound? It's chocolate ice cream with four kinds of candy mixed in."

Elton rolled his eyes appreciatively. "It sounds like you've brought the ice cream experience to a ridiculous new level. I need some. *Pronto!*"

"Coming up," I said, still laughing. "Cone or cup?"

"I'm going to have to take that in a waffle cone and eat it on the run," Elton said. "I've got a delivery from the Cow Girl Creamery in California that's due any minute. Getting a package from them always feels like Santa arriving on Christmas morning, so I don't want to miss it!"

Even though he insisted on rushing back to Let It Brie, Elton tasted my new concoction as soon as I handed it to him. His eyes grew big.

"Oh, my, Katy McKay," he said breathlessly. "You truly are a genius. If there's an ice cream hall of fame, you deserve to be in it."

I was still chuckling over Elton's appreciation of my ice cream fantasies and fine food in general when the door opened once again. I glanced up, expecting to see another customer. Instead, I encountered a familiar face.

"George!" I exclaimed. "How nice to see you! What brings you into town today?"

"I was doing some errands, so I thought I'd stop in and say hello," he replied congenially. With a wink, he added, "And possibly avail myself of some of your ice cream. I hear it's amazing."

"You mean you haven't tasted any yet?" I asked, surprised.

"Nope," he said. "But as the old saying goes, there's no time like the present."

"In that case," I told him, "you're welcome to sample as many flavors as you'd like. All of them, in fact. And, of course, it's on the house."

"That's certainly the best offer I've had in a long time," he said. He came over to the display counter and earnestly studied the rainbow of three-gallon tubs neatly lined up under the glass. "Let's see," he mused. "Cherry Cheesecake sounds amazing. So does Kahlua and Chocolate. Bag o' Tricks and Treats? I've never heard of that one, but I have a feeling you've come up with something inspired. I can see that I should take advantage of your offer to try as many of these as I have room for!"

He sampled four different flavors, declaring each one the best thing he'd ever tasted.

Finally, he said, "I'd treat myself to a Hudson's Hottest Hot Fudge Sundae made with Chocolate Almond Fudge and Cappuccino Crunch," he commented, "but I shudder to think of what my doctor would say if he ever got wind of it."

So he settled for a scoop of each of those two flavors. I still couldn't resist pouring on a little hot fudge sauce, to which I'd added a touch of cinnamon. It complements both flavors so well that it just seemed wrong not to.

George was grinning like an eight-year-old boy as I set down the oversized tulip dish on the table he'd chosen.

"If you don't mind, I'll join you," I said after scooping myself a much more modest dish of Peach Basic Bliss sorbet. It's one of my Lickety Light selections, a line of frozen treats I developed for people who wanted a snack that was a little less sinful. I sat down in the chair opposite his. "I've already had a few customers, even though it's still early. But as you can see, we're in a bit of a lull right now."

"I'm glad for the company," he said. "Now that I'm retired, I'm finding life a little—well, I hate to use the word 'dull,' so let's just say it's a lot less exciting than it used to be."

"I'm sure it's a big adjustment," I said, savoring a spoonful of the delectably light fruit sorbet with the surprising touch of basil. "What exactly did you do?"

"I sat in an office and did boring things with numbers," he said. "Which I suppose is a good reminder that maybe I shouldn't miss it so much, after all."

I smiled. "It seems to me that building foam pits and haunted houses is a much more fun way to spend your time." Gesturing toward his dish, I said, "And eating ice cream, too, of course. It's my personal belief that there's no better way for anyone to spend their time."

"I'm with you on that," he agreed, chuckling.

Then he grew serious. "So you've had a tough few days," he said. "Are you doing okay?"

"I think so," I told him. Glancing around, I added, "I sure am glad I was able to open the shop again."

"It must feel strange," he commented, glancing around. "Being back in here, I mean. Now that this . . . *thing* has happened here."

"I'm trying really hard not to let it affect my feelings about Lickety Splits," I told him. "And I'm doing okay with that. I adore this place, and that helps a lot."

His expression grew tense. "It didn't happen at this table, did it?"

"No," I assured him. "Savannah Crane was sitting at the table behind us."

He looked relieved.

"Besides, when the movie people were here, the whole place looked different," I said. I gestured at Emma's fabulous Halloween-themed creations. "They had taken all these decorations down. Those paintings of ice cream that Willow made, too. So it wasn't Lickety Splits as I know it." I shrugged. "That helps, too."

"Good," George said. "You seem to be a pretty strong person, Kate. It looks like you've weathered this whole thing just fine."

"I think so," I agreed. I was more than ready to change the subject. "So how's the ice cream?"

"As good as people say it is," he said. "But I actually came by today for another reason. Aside from finally trying your ice cream, that is. And, of course, having a chance to see you again, too."

"What's that?" I asked.

"I wanted to ask you about your grandmother," he said.

"Okay," I said, not sure where this was going. "What about her?"

His cheeks turned the slightest bit pink. "I was just wondering if she'd said anything. About me, I mean."

"Why, George!" I exclaimed. "I do believe you've got a crush on Grams!"

By now his cheeks were definitely pink. "I'd say that's pretty obvious," he said. "But I wondered if she'd said anything about how she feels about me. Or at least what she *thinks* about me. The kind of person I am, whether I'm, oh, I don't know, fun or boring or—or . . ."

I was finding this conversation absolutely charming. "George, I think it's pretty obvious that Grams likes you, too."

"So she hasn't told you anything specific?" he asked.

"Not in so many words," I said. "But I can tell she likes you. In fact, I can't remember the last time I've seen her so happy."

A look of relief crossed his face. "So she thinks I'm okay," he said.

I laughed. "I'd say she thinks you're *very* okay."

"I was hoping that was why she invited me over for dinner tomorrow night," George said, looking relieved. "I wasn't sure if she was just being nice because of all the time I've been putting in on her Halloween Hollow project."

"I'm sure she's grateful for that, too," I said. "But I do think there's more to it."

George grinned. "I'm glad we had this little talk. And I think I'm going to enjoy this ice cream even more."

With that, he dug his spoon into the scoop of Chocolate Almond Fudge and stuck it in his mouth, looking more like that contented eight-year-old boy than ever.

Late that afternoon, Emma came to Lickety Splits for her usual shift, right after her computer class. The two of us usually work side by side, but given her passion for playing the role of matchmaker, today she was more than happy to take over by herself.

I hurried home and changed into nice pants and a rose-colored sweater that Grams had hand-knit and given to me as a Christmas present. Deciding what to wear was tricky since I still had no idea where Jake was taking me or what we were doing. I hoped the outfit I had finally decided upon would be suitable.

I perched on the living room couch and played with my phone while I waited for Jake. Sure enough, at exactly four o'clock, Digger started barking his furry little head off. A few seconds later, I heard the usual creak made by a footstep on the wooden front porch, followed by a knock.

"You're right on time," I greeted Jake. I was relieved to see that he wasn't particularly dressed up, either. He was wearing jeans and a light jacket over a dark blue knit shirt that made his eyes look even bluer than usual. His light brown hair was neatly combed, as if he'd made a point of getting spiffed up for little old me.

"Are you kidding?" he said. "I've been watching the clock all day, waiting for this."

"Then I guess you don't want to come in first," I said, "either for coffee or my standing offer of ice cream. I tried out something new today, and it seems to be a success. It's my own personal tribute to Halloween, called Bag o' Tricks and Treats. It's made with chocolate ice cream, Snickers bars, Milky Ways, M&Ms . . ."

Jake laughed. "It sounds like heaven on earth, but even that can't tempt me. Not today."

"My goodness," I said. "You really are a man with a mission."

As soon as I walked out the front door and saw the car that was parked in the driveway behind Grams's gray Corolla, I froze.

"What is *that*?" I demanded.

"That," he replied, "is my new toy." He was wearing a grin that would have put the Cheshire cat to shame.

"It *looks* like a toy," I told him.

And it did. The Miata sports car in my driveway, which was the same brilliant shade of red as an M&M and at least as shiny, was about the size of a Hot Wheels number a child would find in a Christmas stocking.

"Is this the surprise?" I asked, still shocked. "What you wanted to show me, I mean."

"Nope," he said. "This is the just the chariot that's transporting you *to* the surprise. And I promise that you're going to love riding in it."

I was skeptical. Tootling around in a vehicle that wasn't much bigger than a three-gallon tub of ice cream had never been a top priority for me.

Yet once we were on our way to wherever we were going and Jake began taking the curves in the road just a tad faster than I would have, I had to admit that driving around in a sports car really *was* fun. Especially with the top down.

It didn't hurt that the weather that afternoon could have been expressly ordered for an exhilarating ride in a sporty convertible. Despite the forecaster's prediction of rain late in the day, the sun was still holding its own, shining its heart out with that slightly golden color it takes on in October. The sky was shadowed with gray but could still rightfully be considered blue. And the air was supercharged with the crisp coolness that makes autumn in the Hudson Valley feel as if something magical is about to happen.

Then there were the leaves. All along the road, the trees were decked out in brilliant shades of orange that reminded me of flames, yellows that bordered on gold, and patches of crimson that looked as if they'd been scribbled by a super-creative child with a red Crayola. The Hudson Valley is beautiful at any time of year, but in the fall, the intensity of the colors at every turn make it look like something Walt Disney created rather than a real place.

All in all, I'd have to classify this as a close-to-perfect autumn day.

"Having fun?" Jake asked, turning to me and wearing that big grin again. Or I should say wearing that grin *still*, since I didn't think he'd stopped smiling since he'd climbed in.

"I am," I told him. "And here I'd always thought one car was as good as the next."

"Ah, but this isn't just a car," he corrected me. "This is a *lifestyle*."

I laughed. "So you're a person who has a gleaming red sports car, and I'm somebody who has a red truck," I said.

"And what do you think that says about each of us?" Jake asked.

"I'm not sure," I said, considering his question seriously. "Maybe that you're better at having fun than I am?"

"Or maybe that you're more practical," he said. "Of course, I have a truck, too. More than one. But that's business. This is pleasure. So maybe it just means that I'm more of a car person than you are."

"I'm definitely not a car person," I assured him. Casting

him a sly smile, I added, "But I can see myself turning into one."

Jake threw back his head and laughed. "In that case, I've
already gotten my money's worth out of this baby!"

And then another aspect of Jake's new "lifestyle" occurred
to me.

"Did you just win the lottery or something?" I asked him.

"I'm not that lucky," he replied, "though business has
been good lately. Really good. And something did happen recently: I picked up a great new account. I'm going to be supplying organic dairy products for several local branches of a
big national supermarket chain."

"Congratulations!" I said sincerely. "That's wonderful,
Jake. So is that what's behind this mystery outing? Are we
going somewhere to celebrate?"

He looked over at me and, with one hand, made that locking-
my-lips-with-a-key motion.

"You are such a man of mystery," I teased. "I feel like I'm
going for an afternoon drive with James Bond."

"I don't think this outing will be quite as thrilling," he
said. "Then again, it's pretty exciting for me."

"*More* mystery," I said, pretending to be exasperated. But
I was secretly enjoying this. The sense of embarking on an
adventure, the pleasurable drive . . . and simply being with
Jake.

As soon as he turned off the road, I understood what this
was about. He had pulled into the driveway of an abandoned
store, a low brick building that looked unloved but which
definitely had good bones. It was a good size and had large
windows. It also had a wide, welcoming front door and
plenty of parking. A big FOR SALE sign was out front, along
with the name of a local realtor. Directly underneath it was a
smaller sign that read IN CONTRACT.

"So this is it," I said, climbing out of the car. "The future home of the Flying Frog Farm Stand."

"I'm still not convinced about the 'Flying Frog' part, but otherwise, you're exactly right," Jake replied.

"This place has incredible potential," he said as we stood in the parking lot, studying the building. Pointing at the boarded-up windows, he said, "I'm going to replace the shutters, of course. And I'm thinking of painting them a bright color, something that'll be hard to miss if you're driving by."

"Emma could help you decide on a color," I commented. "She's great at that kind of thing."

"And at some point—maybe not right away—I'd like to add on a wooden porch," he went on. "That would give it a homier look. Maybe paint that a bright color, too, although I might be better leaving off leaving it natural. I'd run hanging baskets of flowers all along it, except in winter when I'd put up tons of Christmas lights—"

"You could hang wreaths along that front wall," I suggested. "Christmas wreaths in the winter, but the rest of the year, maybe you could find a local craftsperson who makes wreaths out of branches and dried flowers." Thoughtfully, I added, "Grams makes those. I wonder if she'd like to start her own cottage industry."

"That's a great idea," he said. Glancing at me, he continued, "I was counting on you to have plenty of those."

"Can we go inside?" I asked.

He reached into the pocket of his khaki pants and pulled out a key. But before we went in, he grabbed something out of the trunk. It turned out to be a big tote bag. It was zipped up so I couldn't see what was inside it.

When we stepped through the front door, I gasped. Even though the exterior had looked as if needed plenty of TLC, I still wasn't prepared for what was inside. The walls had no sheetrock, only wooden studs. The floor was bare concrete with a few cracks. And strewn around the place were planks of wood, empty cardboard boxes, and enough dust and debris to make me sneeze. Which is exactly what I did.

"Whoa," I said. "This place needs a lot of work."

"Yes, but that's not necessarily a bad thing," Jake said. The expression on his face was one of total excitement. He reminded me of that little kid I'd pictured finding the Hot Wheels Miata in his stocking on Christmas morning. "That way, I can start from scratch, making the space exactly the way I want it."

He proceeded to dash around, gesturing with both arms as he explained his vision. "The first thing I'd like to do is build a really attractive shell. Paint the walls a nice color, redo the floor, of course, probably using wood to give it that old-fashioned feeling I want . . . I thought I'd put the counter over here. The refrigerators and freezers will go along that back wall. And back here, I'll put shelves. That's where I'll keep the local food products, like the jams and jellies. And on tables, over here, I'll display the crafts made by local artisans—"

"Wow, I can see you've already put a lot of thought into this," I commented.

His cheeks turned pink. "I have. I've also had a few conversations with Hayley Nielsen. You remember her from school, don't you? She became an interior designer, of all things. And she had a bunch of amazingly good ideas."

I was surprised that I actually experienced a flash of jealousy over Jake's mention of one of the prettiest, most popular girls from our high school days.

"And I've talked to Johnny O'Hare and Danny Melski," Jake went on. "You probably remember them from school, too, right? They were always getting into trouble. But these days, they have a construction company. They've kept it pretty small, and they mainly do local projects. Jobs this size are exactly the kind of thing they specialize in."

"So you're already pretty far along in this process," I observed.

"Yes and no," Jake said. He suddenly seemed overcome with awkwardness. "That depends on you. And whether you're interested in becoming my business partner.

"But we can talk about that later," he went on before I had a chance to say anything. Picking up the tote bag he'd retrieved from the trunk of his car, he added, "For now, I'd like you to join me in celebrating this new venture."

I looked around at our chaotic surroundings. "There's no place to sit."

He held up one finger, as if to say, "Wait." He unzipped the bag and pulled out a red plaid wool blanket dotted with moth holes. "A picnic blanket for m'lady."

So *that* was what was in the bag. A picnic. I could feel the color rise in my cheeks.

With a flourish, he spread the blanket out on the floor. I lowered myself onto it, sitting cross-legged. Jake sat down opposite me with the big bag between us.

"This floor is kind of hard," he said with a frown, rocking from side to side as if to prove his point.

"It's fine," I assured him. I was so tickled by all the effort he'd gone to that I didn't want to say or do anything to ruin the moment. Peering inside the bag, I said, "So what else have you got in there?"

He grinned at me slyly, then pulled out two champagne flutes.

"I hope there's champagne to go with those glasses," I teased.

"Of course there is," he replied.

"I was joking!" I insisted. "And please tell me that those glasses are plastic."

"Crystal," he said.

"I'm impressed."

"Hey, this is an important celebration!" he insisted. "I'm about to—I believe the expression is 'expand my business vertically.'"

I groaned. "And here I thought I'd left the world of big business behind when I gave up my big-city job in public relations!"

"In this part of the world," Jake replied, pushing the champagne bottle stopper with both thumbs, "'big business' means selling organic half-and-half in quart containers instead of just pints."

Laughing, I said, "I can deal with that."

A loud pop echoed through the room. Jake immediately filled the two glasses.

As he handed me one, I asked, "Should we toast your new venture?"

"Not yet," he insisted. "First I have to set everything up."

"Can I help?" I asked as he began pulling more items out of the tote bag.

"Nope," he said as he took out several slabs of cheese, a baguette and a long knife, and a plastic container of fresh fruit, cut up into bite-size pieces. "Today you are my guest of honor. In fact," he continued, "you're the first person I've brought here."

"Really?" I said. "Then I do feel honored."

Jake pointed to the wall behind him. "See that space over there? That's where I picture the ice cream freezer. Horizontal or vertical—your choice."

"Definitely vertical," I said. "It's much easier for customers to see all the flavors that way. And I've already started thinking about what flavors might make sense."

"I was thinking basics—like chocolate, vanilla, and maybe coffee—that would be available every day," Jake said. "But I hoped you'd be willing to add a few of your more creative flavors, too. Two or three at a time, maybe. That way, people would get to try them, but they'd still have to go to your shop to get refills. To try your other flavors, too."

"That sounds like a good plan," I said. I took a deep breath. "Jake, at some point we really do have to discuss your idea about me becoming your partner." Quickly, I added, "I mean, going into business with you."

"Yes, but right now there's something more important we need to do," he said.

"What's that?"

"Eat some cheese," he said. And he handed me a napkin. A *cloth* napkin, the rich yellowish-white color of organic cream.

"The cheese is from Let It Brie," he said. "Elton picked these out for me himself. He promised me that the 'piquant bleu' would be the perfect complement to the fresh strawberries. And if anyone knows cheese, it's Elton."

Jake reached back into the tote bag again. This time he took out two packages of crackers, one with cracked pepper, the other with rosemary.

"Elton also swore on his life that I simply had to get these to go with the cheeses he selected," Jake said.

"I can just hear him," I said, laughing. "I imagine he threatened not to sell you the cheese unless you took the crackers."

"That sounds about right," Jake said. "But I picked these out myself." He brought out a series of small containers: cashew nuts in one, dried cranberries in another, tiny chunks of dried mango and pineapple in a third.

"This is lovely," I said with a sigh. "I'm so glad I didn't eat lunch today. Or much ice cream. At least by my standards." Holding up my glass of champagne, I asked, "*Now* can we make a toast?"

"That moment has arrived," Jake agreed.

I was about to say something bland like, "To your new business." But Jake beat me to it.

"To new possibilities," he said, raising his glass, "and the wonderful fact that life never stops bringing us exciting surprises and unexpected opportunities. None of us ever really knows what amazing experiences are just around the corner. So let's drink to that."

As we clinked our glasses, Jake locked his eyes on mine. "I can't think of anyone I'd rather be with right now."

I didn't know how to respond, so I pretended to be too busy tasting the champagne to talk. It was delightful—crisp and cold and deliciously dry. I took another sip, then another. I could already feel myself relaxing.

"Did Elton instruct you in which cheese we should eat first?" I teased. "I wouldn't want him to sic the cheese police on us."

"I think we have free rein with that," Jake replied. "Of course, he might have strong feelings about which cheese goes with which type of cracker."

"I'm surprised he didn't include written instructions," I joked. "Explicit ones."

"Hey, remember that math teacher we had who'd give an exam and he'd start by saying, 'Take out your pen. Take off the top. Turn over the page. Now begin!'"

"I *do* remember!" I squealed. "Mr. Miller!"

"That's right, Michael Miller." Jake laughed. "What a character! Like we didn't know we were supposed to take the top off our pens before we started writing!"

"And that's something that's a lot easier than knowing what cheese goes with what cracker," I said. "But Mr. Miller wasn't nearly as quirky as Mr. DeMarco. Do you remember all those long stories he used to tell about his kids? What was his son's name?

"Frank David!" Jake replied. "I remember him going on and on about Frank David setting the trash pail on fire. He acted like it was some amusing prank. I wonder where that kid is now!"

"Probably doing ten to fifteen upstate," I said.

I realized I felt warm inside, as if I was glowing. And I was pretty sure it had nothing to do with the champagne. It felt so good, being with Jake again. Someone with whom I had so much shared history, someone who knew me so well . . .

Someone who *used* to know you well, I corrected myself.

But either the champagne or the blissful feeling that had come over me made my usual arguments feel far, far away.

And then I became aware of the rhythmic tapping of rain against the roof.

"That's one of my favorite sounds," I said, glancing upward, as I took another sip of champagne.

"Rain on the roof?" Jake asked.

I nodded. "It always feels so nice and cozy being inside while it's raining. It makes me feel like I'm holed up in a comfortable cabin somewhere, all safe and secure."

"That's because you don't have cows to worry about," he said, smiling.

"True," I said. "No cows in my life."

"But I have to admit that I like that sound, too," Jake said. "It reminds me of when I was a kid and I'd go camping with my uncle. I really loved those trips. The problem was that for some reason, it seemed to rain every time we went! But I came to associate the sound of rain falling against the tent with that same feeling you're talking about, the feeling of being safe and secure."

He was quiet for a few seconds, then added, "My uncle was like a father to me. My real dad was usually passed out on the couch with an empty bottle in his hand, so it was Uncle Steve who did most of the stuff a regular father would do. I don't know if my mom asked him to do it or he took it upon himself, but we did all kinds of cool stuff together."

"I'm so sorry you lost your uncle," I said quietly. "I remember you talking about him a lot, but I never realized he was like a father to you."

"Did I talk about him?" he asked. "I don't recall doing that. But I'm glad I did. I hope I appreciated him enough while he was still around."

With a meaningful look, he said, "We don't always take time to appreciate the people who matter to us while we still have them in our lives. We don't always tell them how much they mean to us. And we should. We should tell them every day. We shouldn't let time slip away without letting them know that they're the most important thing in our lives."

His eyes were fixed on mine. As intense as the moment was, I couldn't bring myself to look away.

"Hey, Kate?" he said softly.

"Yes?"

"I really like the idea of you and me being partners," he said.

I could hear the sound of my own breathing as he reached across the tattered wool blanket and took my hand.

I didn't pull it away.

I knew what was coming next. And I was ready for it to happen.

My heart was racing as Jake leaned forward and gently pushed a strand of hair away from my face. When his lips touched mine lightly, it was almost as if he was asking a question. And I answered it. I kissed him back.

I thought it would be the same, but somehow all the years apart had erased that feeling of first love, as delicious as it had been. We weren't seventeen anymore. We weren't two kids who were in a constant state of giddiness, unable to believe we'd actually found someone who could elicit such strong feelings.

I understood in that moment that the idea I'd been wrestling with, that I'd be going back into the same relationship I'd had with Jake before, dissipated like a burst of smoke.

This time, it all felt brand-new.

Chapter 11

The top-selling Ben and Jerry's flavor is Half-Baked, chocolate and vanilla ice creams mixed with gobs of chocolate chip cookie dough and fudge brownies. Cherry Garcia is next, followed by Chocolate Chip Cookie Dough.

—*http://www.benjerry.com/whats-new/2016/top-flavors-2016*

The following morning, I woke up with butterflies practicing their gymnastics routines in my stomach. Today I had another challenge to confront: my hike with Brody.

I was nervous about it for two reasons. First of all, the word *hiking* was simply not a part of my working vocabulary. In fact, if there was ever anyone who could best be described as indoors-y, that was me. I'm someone whose idea of an adventurous vacation is staying at a hotel that has a rating of four stars instead of five. Who thinks the only boots worth owning are the ones that are made of Italian suede. Who once stayed inside the house for a full week after spotting a man-eating-size raccoon going through the trash can.

Okay, so maybe that's a bit of exaggeration. But the point is that I'm not exactly a nature lover unless I'm viewing it from the inside of a car. Or, better yet, a movie theater.

Yet here I was, about to go hiking. In the mountains.

Second, there was my lingering ambivalence about doing anything at all, indoors or out, with Brody. Especially after yesterday. That kiss had been pretty special. *Jake* was special. Or he at least had the potential to be special.

I reminded myself that going hiking with Brody wasn't necessarily a date. The man was a positive fanatic about the outdoors, so I still believed it was possible that he was just looking for someone to keep him company. Or even someone to turn on to the wonders of being outside simply because he felt that gaining converts was his mission in life.

And even if it *was* a date, Emma had been right about me owing it to myself to explore—well, whatever it was she had said. It had certainly sounded reasonable at the time.

Which left me with the problem of what to wear. I dragged myself out of bed and stood in front of my closet, wondering if I even owned anything suitable for trekking around in the so-called Great Outdoors.

It took me about two seconds to decide on jeans. If there's anything that cowboys and other people who spend lots of time breathing fresh air like, it's jeans. I'd always assumed the reason they were so popular was because they looked good on pretty much everybody. But now that I was thinking about it, I realized it was probably because they were made of rugged fabric that didn't tear easily, they had a little stretch in them, and they had plenty of pockets.

For the top half of my body, I decided on layers. October was unpredictable in the Hudson Valley. It could be pretty warm during the day, especially in the sun. But once the sun got low, it could be positively chilly. Especially in the woods. Not to mention the mountains.

So I pulled a thermal undershirt out of one drawer, a long-sleeved T-shirt out of another, and a fleece vest out of a third. With my bra, I was wearing more layers than a fancy birthday cake.

The last part was the hardest. And that was footwear.

Of course, I'd heard the term "hiking boots," but I didn't own anything that came even close to what I imagined those to be. In the end, I opted for sneakers with thick socks.

I had just put everything on and was studying my reflection in the mirror when Emma walked by and glanced through my open door.

"This is a new look for you," she observed, sounding surprised. "Modeling for the L.L.Bean catalog?"

"I wish," I replied. "I'm going hiking later."

Her eyebrows shot up to the ceiling. "You? Someone who sprays on bug repellent every time she walks by a newsstand that sells *National Geographic*?

"Ha, ha, very funny," I told her. "It's never too late to explore new horizons."

Emma thought for about two seconds before her face lit up. "Brody!" she cried. "Today's your date with him!"

"Bingo," I told her.

"Whoa," she said, folding her arms across her chest and leaning against the door frame. "If I were you, I'd be ready for some pretty serious trekking."

"I can always insist that we turn back," I told her. "Or pretend that I twisted my ankle."

"Just hope he doesn't decide that you're too heavy to carry and that he has no choice but to leave you behind for the wolves," she teased.

I stuck out my tongue.

Growing serious, I told her, "I'm thinking about canceling."

"Kate," she cried, sounding exasperated, "Brody is probably the nicest, sexiest, handsomest man in town! I thought I'd talked you into give him a chance. Why would you change your mind?"

"Jake," I replied simply. I took a deep breath, then said,

"Yesterday he took me to see this new roadside farm stand he just rented. And, well, we ended up kissing."

I expected sympathy. Instead, she looked impatient.

"For goodness sake, Kate, a kiss isn't exactly an engagement ring. Have some fun! Explore your options!" Her expression became grave. "But I do have one piece of advice."

"What's that?" I asked.

"Don't eat too many protein bars on that hike," she said with mock seriousness. "Those things can wreak havoc on your guts if you're not used to them."

I tossed a balled-up pair of socks at her, and she ran away, laughing and shrieking.

For the next several hours, I was busy enough scooping ice cream that I forgot all about my upcoming adventure. But those annoying, super-athletic butterflies returned a few minutes before Brody was due.

When Emma arrived at Lickety Splits around then, ready to take over at the shop, she was upbeat and encouraging. But I still wished I could spend the rest of the day filling cones, drowning sundaes in hot fudge sauce, and making stomachs happy instead of hanging out with Mother Nature.

Brody arrived right on time. I was relieved to see that, like me, he was wearing jeans and layers. The man was a professional, after all, so he knew all about appropriate attire. But I was unnerved by his boots, which looked a lot more substantial than my wimpy Skechers. In fact, his footwear looked suitable for climbing one of the lesser Himalayas.

"All set?" he asked. He flashed his sparkling smile. That alone was enough to ease my anxiety. Emma had certainly been right about him being nice and sexy and handsome. In fact, his eyes looked particularly green today, and his curly blond hair seemed even thicker than I remembered it.

"I'm ready," I told him. I sounded almost convincing.

"Have fun, you two!" Emma called as we headed out the door, toward his truck. "And don't forget what I told you about those protein bars!"

"Have you done much hiking?" Brody asked as we drove out of town, toward the Great Beyond.

"Only in Manhattan," I told him. "I've been known to walk from Fourteenth Street to Times Square in under a half hour."

He laughed. The man had no idea that I was serious.

We road into the Mashawam Preserve, as I expected. But when we reached the parking lot, instead of pulling into one of the spaces, he continued on toward a dirt road at the very back. One that was marked with a sign that read KEEP OUT!

He completely ignored the sign and just kept going. The ride suddenly got very bumpy. "I don't think we're supposed to go in here," I said nervously.

"You mean because of that sign?" he said. "That's only there to keep amateurs from getting hurt."

But I *am* an amateur! I wanted to cry. And not getting hurt is one of my key goals for today!

But it was too late.

We bumped along for another quarter of a mile before we finally stopped. And once we did, there were no parking lots in sight. No people, either. Or signs. Or any traces of civilization. We were, to use a cliché, in the middle of nowhere.

I guess the look on my face was pretty telling because Brody chuckled. "Don't worry, Kate," he said. "I've been here before. There's a great trail right around that bend." Thoughtfully, he added, "Well, maybe not a *trail*, exactly . . ."

By this point, scenes from a PBS documentary about the Donner Pass I'd recently seen were playing through my head. It's only October, I told myself. The snow won't be coming for months. Or weeks, anyway.

We hopped out of the truck. Actually, Brody hopped. I

kind of dragged myself out, gazing at it longingly and wondering if I'd be seeing it again. Next, he grabbed a heavy-looking backpack and shrugged it on. I hoped there was water in it. Lots of water.

But before I had a chance to ask, he reached into his pockets. His eyes glittered impishly as he said, "I brought snacks! There's no reason why we shouldn't enjoy a little fun food while we're hiking!"

He held out both hands so I could inspect his offerings. In his right hand was a bag of those protein snacks Emma had warned me about. The packaging boasted that these were made with chick peas, quinoa, *and* chia seeds. Just seeing those words in print was enough to make my stomach churn. In his left hand was a bag of kale chips.

This, I thought, for a woman whose idea of "fun food" is something that includes whipped cream, a few dozen carbohydrate grams of sugar, at least as many grams of fat, and chocolate.

Still, if there was anything that I'd learned over the past week, it was that I was a pretty good actress.

"Yum!" I cried. "Can't wait!"

I only hoped I'd find some ancient M&Ms or some dry-roasted peanuts in one of the many pockets in my jeans, just in case I got light-headed from all the physical exertion I knew lay ahead.

"All set?" Brody asked. His cheeks were flushed, and his eyes were practically glowing.

He truly loves this! I realized. Lugging heavy equipment through the woods in order to pretend we're squirrels is his idea of a good time!

"I'm as ready as I'll ever be!" I said. I reminded myself that for a few years, back when I was in elementary school, I had been a Girl Scout Brownie. True, we had mainly sold cookies, sung "Kumbaya," and made Thanksgiving centerpieces out of branches and plastic chrysanthemums. But surely some of that group's spiritedness and can-do attitude had sunk in.

We headed into the woods. I was dismayed to find that the "trail" Brody had mentioned turned out to be nothing more than patches of dirt about six inches wide that were scattered here and there. As we trudged through the dense growth, I was pretty sure I could feel the bears watching us. I could even hear them licking their chops.

And Brody, being very tall, had ridiculously long legs. Keeping up with him was a challenge, especially given all the nasty rocks and malicious roots that kept jumping in front of me.

"I should probably have made this clear earlier," I called to him in a wavering voice, "but I'm not exactly what you'd call an outdoor girl. Not that I don't love adventure, but I'm more into adventure that involves maps and vending machines."

Brody laughed. "You are so funny, Kate. I've never met a woman with such a great sense of humor."

Soon afterward, he stopped, looking around and letting out a deep sigh. I, meanwhile, was happy that I was finally getting a chance to catch my breath.

"Isn't this amazing?" he said, his voice filled with reverence. "I feel like I'm truly alive when I'm in the woods like this."

And I'm hoping to get *out* alive, I thought.

Still, I had to admit that he had a point. It *was* beautiful out here. Peaceful, too. No honking cars, no buzzing cell phones . . . maybe this business of being in the middle of nowhere really did have its good points.

"Listen!" he said, his voice dropping to a whisper. "Did you hear that?"

"No, what?" I cried, glancing around. Terror instantly gripped every cell of my body.

"I think that was a blackpoll warbler," he said. "Yes, I'm pretty sure it was."

At least birds don't maul you to death and eat your vital organs, I thought, relieved. Unless they're the ones that starred in Alfred Hitchcock's movie.

We walked on. I did my best to appreciate my surroundings, but I had to admit that they were starting to look pretty much the same. I mostly saw trees. And, of course, those sadistic rocks and roots. I encountered some spiteful vines, too, but I managed to step around them before they had a chance to lunge at me.

"We're almost at the lake," Brody finally said, glancing at me over his shoulder.

"There's a lake up here?" I asked, surprised.

Sure enough, after only another twenty minutes of plodding through the woods, the trees suddenly cleared, and we stepped out onto the shores of a lake.

"Isn't this the most amazing spot you've ever seen in your life?" Brody half-whispered, sounding awed.

I had to admit that it was indeed gorgeous. The lake's calm blue waters glistened in the low afternoon sun, and surrounding it was a spectacular view of mountains, trees, and the clear blue sky.

I found myself wondering if I could find it in myself to share this man's love of communing with nature, making it a major part of my life. I'd actually enjoyed reading about Thoreau's *Walden* when I was in middle school. I'd even gotten an A on the five-page paper I wrote about it. Maybe I was capable of embracing Thoreau's appreciation of the simple life, even if it involved bugs and ugly footwear.

"The sun is getting low in the sky," Brody said after we'd admired the lake for a few minutes. "We should probably start back. Let's take a different route."

"Whatever you say," I said affably. While I'd ended up enjoying this outing more than I'd expected, I was starting to miss the strangest things about civilization. Not only my bed, my bathroom, my coffeepot, and Trader Joe's. But also things like donuts. And I've never even been that big a fan of donuts.

Still, as we headed back into the woods and continued on our way, I tried to remain in the moment. I breathed in the fresh air, raised my face toward the smudge of yellow that was the late-afternoon sun, and tried to remember the lyrics to "The Happy Wanderer." Aside from the "val-de-ree, val-de-rah" part, most of them seemed to have vanished from my head.

We walked a bit farther and suddenly seemed to be on an actual trail. Not Brody's idea of a trail—the Parks Department's idea of a trail, which was more in line with mine. Beneath our feet was a wide pathway that had been put there deliberately. There were even markers, small wooden arrows indicating which way to go as well as an occasional sign indicating the direction of the parking lot.

"We're almost back to civilization," Brody said, sounding a little sad.

Sure enough, there was the parking lot we'd driven past, a few hundred yards in front of us.

But as we walked past it, something odd caught my eye. One of the main paths leading off the paved parking lot was marked with a big sign reading PINE TREE TRAIL. But a high metal fence had been put up across the entryway, along with another sign that warned DO NOT ENTER. Given our natural surroundings, it looked extremely out of place.

"I wonder why that path is closed," I said, thinking aloud. Glancing around, I added, "Especially since it looks as if all the other paths are open."

Brody shrugged. "There could be lots of reasons," he said. "Maybe a tree fell across the path and they're still in the process of clearing it away. Remember that big rainstorm we had last month?"

"Maybe," I said. And, of course, he was right. There could be a lot of reasons why one of the paths in a preserve would be closed off to the public. After all, we ourselves were guilty of ignoring the park's warning, heading down a dirt road that was officially off-limits.

And then, as sudden as a slap, my ears were assaulted by the loud roar of an engine. It seemed to be coming from somewhere beyond the fence, cutting through the silence of the forest. I was beginning to appreciate the sound of that blackpoll warbler.

"Sounds like I was right," Brody observed. "They're obviously doing some kind of work in there."

Maybe it was just as well that we'd hiked along a quieter route, I thought. Even though it meant breaking a few rules.

As we drove back to Wolfert's Roost, the sun was low in the sky. I was tired, I realized, but in a way that felt good. I had enjoyed the workout. And in the end, I had appreciated being in such a spectacular and peaceful setting.

And what about Brody? I asked myself. Did you enjoy being with him, too?

The man must have been reading my mind, because at that very moment he glanced over at me and, with a big smile, said, "That was great. We'll have to do it again sometime soon."

"Definitely," I agreed.

Deep down, I wasn't so sure. But the reason for my uncertainty had nothing to do with hiking. Or even chia-laden protein bars.

After Brody dropped me at my house and I let myself in, all I could think about was a long, hot bath and a big mug of peppermint tea.

"Is that you, Katydid?" Grams called from the kitchen.

"It's me, all right," I called back. "I've made it back from the wilds of the Hudson Valley."

She came out, wearing an apron and drying her hands on a dish towel. From the tantalizing smells coming out of the kitchen, I could tell she'd been baking something delicious.

"How was your hike?" Grams asked eagerly.

"Not bad," I said, surprising myself. "It was actually kind of—fun."

"I'm so glad," she said. "I want to hear all about it, but my Russian tea cookies will be ready in about two minutes. By the way, UPS dropped off some boxes for you this afternoon. I asked the nice delivery man to put them in the living room."

Sure enough; three big cardboard cartons were stacked up next to the coffee table. As soon as I saw them, my heartbeat speeded up. I didn't even have to look at the labels to know what they were: the boxes of Savannah Crane's possessions from work that Coo had packed up for me.

Chapter 12

Ben and Jerry's employees get to take three pints
of ice cream home with them every day.

—http://www.benjerry.com/whats-new/2017/09/ice-cream-
useless-facts

As I distractedly gave Digger his usual stomach scratch-ing, I knelt down to check the mailing labels. Poor Chloe stood by, looking irritated over being neglected.

As I expected, the return address on the boxes was Alpha Industries. The bath and the tea would have to wait.

"I'm going to take these into my room," I called to Grams.

I carried the three boxes through the hallway one at a time, forgetting all about my aching muscles. Then I folded back the handmade quilt that served as my bedspread and deposited them on my bed.

I opened the first box using the sharp edge of my house key. As I pulled back the flaps, my heart was pounding as hard as if it was Christmas morning and I'd just received a very special gift.

But as soon as I saw the three Beanie Babies on top, I felt deflated. In fact, my eyes filled with tears as I was struck by the fact that I was doing more than trying to solve a mystery. I was delving into someone's personal life—a life that had ended much too soon and much too tragically.

Still, I knew I had to go on. I pulled out the floppy stuffed animals, wondering what they had meant to Savannah. I got a partial answer when I noticed that written on the tag that was attached to the furry orange tiger was, "Love you forever! Timothy."

I took out some more items that were typical of what you'd find in anyone's work space. A mug that said, INSTANT HUMAN! JUST ADD COFFEE! A nail file. Coffee stirrers and packets of artificial sweetener. A folding umbrella. Finally, a framed photograph of Savannah and Timothy standing on a beach with their arms around each other, both of them grinning.

That was all there was in the first box. I went on to the second, wondering if I'd find something more meaningful. I was heartened when I saw that it was stuffed with files, dozens of manila folders filled with papers.

I was hopeful as I pulled out the first few folders. But that feeling dissolved as I looked at one after another. Inside the folders there were just forms, lists of numbers, printouts of emails, and other documents that meant nothing to me.

The third box was more of the same. I scrutinized the labels on these folders, too, but I still didn't see anything useful.

Still, I knew that if I was going to uncover anything from Savannah's job that was related to her murder, chances were good that it would be somewhere in these files. And combing through them, page by page, was going to take some serious time.

I immediately felt overwhelmed by the task ahead of me. Could I really figure out enough about what Savannah's job was all about—and what Alpha Industries was involved in— that I could understand if the goings-on at the company where she worked might have been behind someone's decision to kill her?

That task suddenly struck me as impossible.

*   *   *

Having Grams's gentleman caller over for dinner was a welcome distraction from investigating Savannah Crane's murder. But it suddenly felt as if there was a lot to do.

Instead of a long hot bath, I settled for a shower. Then I gulped down a cup of mint tea as I blow-dried my hair and put on my version of a nice outfit: black slacks instead of jeans and a shirt that wasn't bubble-gum pink and didn't have LICKETY SPLITS ICE CREAM SHOPPE embroidered on it.

Emma seemed as excited as I was. When I went into the kitchen, I found that she was already bustling around, taking masses of fresh vegetables out of the refrigerator. She had put a black-and-white-checked Lickety Splits apron over her jeans and T-shirt, and her cloud of black-and-blue hair was pulled back into a bushy ponytail. Grams stood at the sink, scrubbing potatoes and humming.

"Grams, let me do that," Emma insisted. "Why don't you go lie down for a while before George gets here?"

"I don't need to lie down!" Grams insisted, laughing. "Goodness, Emma, I may not be eighteen anymore, but I'm still capable of washing a few potatoes."

"If you insist," Emma said with an exasperated sigh. "In that case, I'll start chopping these veggies. I'm going to mix them with olive oil and garlic and a few other magic ingredients and roast them. Yum!

"And I'm pretty sure everything else is under control," she added thoughtfully, as if she was checking a mental list. "The roast, the biscuits . . . and, of course, I'm leaving dessert up to Kate, since she's our resident Empress of Ice Cream."

Emma glanced up then, noticing for the first time that I'd come into the room.

"If it isn't the bachelorette herself!" she joked. "I can't wait to hear all about your date with Brody!"

I just sighed.

Emma grimaced. "I think I can guess. The man is simply too outdoorsy for you, right?"

"It's not even that," I said. "It's more like . . . there's no real chemistry between us."

"Maybe you're expecting too much, too soon," she suggested. "These things take time. Don't they?"

"I don't know," I said thoughtfully. "With me, it's always been an instant thing. Like I knew from the beginning."

At least, that was how it had been with Jake. By the time our first date at the Halloween dance had ended and he kissed me good night, I knew. That spark had been there since the very start.

And I kind of felt as if that spark was still firing away.

"If you want my opinion, I think you should give it more time," Grams commented, glancing up from the sink.

"I agree with Grams," Emma said. "If I were you, I'd go out with both Jake *and* Brody. Sooner or later, I'd think it would be pretty clear which one of them makes your heart go pitter-pat."

Once again, my niece sounded so logical. Even so, I wasn't so sure I agreed with her.

But before I had a chance to ponder the issue any longer, Grams said, "Goodness, look at the time! George will be here in half an hour. Kate, would you mind setting the table?"

"Not only will I set it," I replied, "I'm going to make it Martha Stewart–worthy. I'm going to use your 'good' china, along with that gorgeous hot-pink-and-orange jacquard tablecloth you bought in the south of France. I'll get out the matching napkins, too."

"And I insist on exiling Digger to the backyard," Emma added, glancing up from the brussels sprouts she was hacking away at with a sharp knife. "I love that doggie to death, but we don't want to overwhelm poor George, especially since this is the first time he's having dinner here."

"You two!" Grams cried. "You're acting as if royalty was coming over!"

"That's because we see you and George as the new Prince Harry and Princess Meghan," Emma said, grinning.

I've always found that preparing for an event is as much fun as the event itself. And tonight was no exception. Between the teasing, the tasting, and the enjoyment of the three of us simply being together, adding George to the mix was just—well, the cherry on top of the ice cream sundae.

Still, Grams seemed pretty excited when he showed up, snappily dressed in a sports coat, a red-and-blue-striped tie, khaki pants, and black shiny loafers. Especially since he'd brought her another bouquet, this time an explosion of blossoms in every color imaginable. Glancing out the window, I saw that he'd pulled up in a sleek black sports car. With the top down, of course.

I'll have to tell Jake about that, I thought, smiling. Maybe the two of them can race sometime—or at least compare notes on horsepower or spark plugs or whatever else sports car enthusiasts like to brag about.

"Thanks for inviting me, Caroline," George greeted Grams. He handed her the flowers, then leaned over and gave her a quick kiss on the cheek. Grams immediately turned pink.

"We're glad you're here!" she replied. And she leaned forward and gave him a kiss on *his* cheek.

The two of them were pretty darned cute together.

Next George handed me a white bakery box.

"I assume that you're in charge of dessert," he said. "And I'm pretty sure that dessert involves ice cream. So I brought these cookies from a fancy bakery. I hoped they'd be a good accompaniment to whatever's on the menu."

"They're perfect," I assured him. I peeked inside the box and found an assortment of butter cookies that would, indeed, go well with the baked Alaska I planned to serve. In honor of Halloween, underneath the baked meringue crust, I was using the Smashed Pumpkins ice cream Emma and I had dreamed up—luscious, pumpkin-flavored ice cream dotted with pecans and pralines. The ice cream was a beautiful pale orange that I thought would look gorgeous with the white meringue shell.

By the time dinner was ready and the four of us sat down at the dining room table, I felt as if we had all known each other for years. George fit right in, making wry observations about our inside jokes and our comfortable banter. He didn't seem the least bit intimidated by the three of us fluttering around him, treating him like—well, like Prince Harry.

We had just begun eating when Emma's phone buzzed. Naturally, she couldn't resist checking it. Her eyes instantly grew as big and round as two Oreos.

"You won't believe what just happened!" she cried, cutting into our chatter about the various Halloween costumes we'd worn when we were children.

Grams and George looked at her expectantly. I also glanced over at her, although I'm sure that my expression was more along the lines of skeptical.

"It's Jennifer Jordan!" Emma went on excitedly. "She's been spotted in the Hudson Valley!"

That *was* interesting.

"Who's Jennifer Jordan?" George asked, spooning himself a generous portion of roasted vegetables. "And why is it important that she's here?"

"You probably don't know about this," Emma explained, "but Kate has been investigating Savannah Crane's murder."

"She's the actress who was killed in Kate's shop," Grams interjected.

Emma nodded. "And Jennifer Jordan is one of the prime suspects."

George looked surprised. "I didn't know Kate was an amateur sleuth."

Grams and Emma exchanged a meaningful look.

"Kate is too much of a risk-taker," Grams said at the exact same time Emma said, "Kate is so amazing!"

Proudly, Emma added, "Kate has already helped with two other cases."

"You mean this isn't the first time Kate has investigated a murder?" George asked, sounding incredulous.

"Let's just say that I've had reason before to look into some local crimes," I muttered, reaching for a biscuit and wishing we could change the subject. I didn't feel comfortable being the center of attention, at least not when people were talking about my past involvement with something so unsavory.

"Kate also happens to be really, really good at snooping around," Emma said.

"But isn't that dangerous?" George asked, his eyes clouded with concern. "If you ask me, dealing with murderers is something that's better left to the professionals."

"Thank you, George," Grams said meaningfully. Turning to me, she said, "See, Kate? I'm not the only one who's worried about you getting messed up in this case."

"But it affects me directly!" I protested. "The horrible thing occurred in *my* shop! And poor Savannah Crane was eating *my* ice cream!"

"It's not the best thing for Lickety Splits' reputation, either," Emma added. "I'm with you, Kate. The sooner this case is solved, the sooner people will forget all about it and we can focus on more important things—like coming up with more fabulous new flavors."

"So who are the suspects in this case of—what's the actress's name again?" George asked.

"Savannah Crane," Emma and I replied in unison.

"I'm putting together a list," I told him. "It includes her boyfriend, a famous movie director, and a few other people who knew her."

"I still think Jennifer Jordan is behind this," Emma insisted. "She's an actress, too, and she and Savannah have been rivals for years. And according to what I read online, Jennifer really wanted this part."

"It sounds as if you've already put a lot of time into this," George observed. "But I'm afraid I'm with Caroline on this. It sounds as if you're treading into dangerous waters. If I were you, I'd put my efforts into making more of that delicious ice cream of yours."

"Here, here," Grams agreed. "Now who's ready for more potatoes?"

I fell into bed as soon as Emma and I finished cleaning up. George had left early, around ten. But even though it wasn't that late, it had been a long, tiring day.

I was sure I'd drift off to sleep immediately. Instead, I lay with my head propped up on the pillow, staring at the shadowy tower of cartons I'd stacked up in the corner.

Finally, I couldn't stand the suspense any longer. I threw back the covers, turned on a light, and hauled one of the two boxes that was stuffed with files back over to the bed.

Just like before, I pulled a bunch of folders out of the carton. But this time, I forced myself to look through the pages inside them, one by one. It appeared that Savannah had created a file for each property Alpha was developing, with all the forms related to every aspect of it from start to finish: its original architectural drawings, its construction, and its financing. And the projects themselves ranged from strip malls to apartment buildings to office complexes.

It was a miracle that it didn't put me to sleep.

But as tedious as it was, I kept looking through files. When I finished that batch, I moved on to another. And another. I was starting to get a feel for the paperwork that went along with each building Alpha Industries was involved in.

But I still had no idea how any of it could have been related to Savannah being murdered—if there was even any connection in the first place.

It was midnight when I finally glanced at the clock. I could hardly believe that I'd spent so much time going through all these pieces of paper. And I could hardly believe that I had absolutely nothing to show for it.

I was ready to give up. In fact, I was squeezing the last wad of paper back into the box when I noticed one more manila file folder.

Up until that moment, I'd missed it completely. That was probably because it was so skinny. Unlike the other folders, which were all at least a half-inch thick, this one appeared to be empty. And it had slipped down to the bottom of the box so that only the top corner was visible. I pulled it out.

Instead of being labeled in the same manner as the others—with a tab that said something like SYLVAN APARTMENTS or FOUR SQUARE OFFICE PARK—the label on this folder was a hand-drawn emoji.

An emoji of a frowning face.

I opened it and found that inside was nothing but a single sheet of paper. A date was handwritten in the top left-hand corner, August 12 of that year. Written in the right-hand corner were the initials HH.

There were two words scrawled across the top, as well. They were written in a different color ink, as if they'd been added at a later date.

Savannah had written MASHAWAM PRESERVE, then underlined each word twice and added two exclamation points.

I was still puzzling over what that could possibly mean as I zeroed in on what was written below. I let out a gasp, feeling as if I'd just been slapped in the face.

It was a handwritten list of five names: Timothy Scott, Amanda Huffner, Chelsea Atkins, Ragnar Bruin, and Jennifer Jordan.

I blinked hard, trying to comprehend the fact that in my

hand was a list of names that was identical to the list of suspects I'd put together. And according to the date on top, Savannah had made this list a little over two months before she was murdered.

I didn't sleep well that night. Gone was all the fatigue from my demanding day of hiking, then helping prepare dinner and entertaining Grams's new beau. Instead, I lay in bed as rigid as a wooden plank, replaying everything that had happened in the past week over and over again.

Finally, after breakfast and before heading into Lickety Splits, I put in a call to Coo. It had occurred to me at around three AM that she was the one person I'd talked to who was most likely to know what this list referred to.

I was surprised that a real person answered, rather than a machine.

"Alpha Investments," a woman greeted me pleasantly. I recognized her voice. She was the receptionist I'd met on Monday.

It took me a few moments to remember Coo's real name.

"May I please speak to Cornelia Jameson?" I asked politely.

"I'm sorry, Ms. Jameson is out of the office today," the receptionist replied. "Would you like her voice mail?"

Darn, I thought. Here I'd been hoping for immediate results. Instead, I said yes.

"It's Kate McKay," I said after the formal, business-y recording, followed by the usual beep. Trying to be as cryptic as I could, I added, "I came across something I'd like to talk to you about. Call me as soon as you can!"

Next, I tried her cell phone. I wasn't surprised that she didn't answer. But when I tried to leave her a message, a recording informed me that her voice-mail box was full.

For the rest of the day, as I scooped out ice cream and

made small talk with customers, I desperately waited to hear back from Coo. All I could think about was that list of names and what it could possibly mean. I must have checked my phone a hundred times.

No response.

Finally, I couldn't stand the suspense anymore. Waiting for the phone to ring—especially when it refused to do so—was simply too frustrating.

So I texted Emma, who I knew was spending the evening with Ethan. I asked if there was any chance the two of them could fill in for me for the rest of the evening. Twenty minutes later, they burst through the door, ready to take over the shop.

It was time for me to do a little more sleuthing.

Emma and Ethan plied me with questions about what I was doing and where I was going. But I remained secretive, partly because I didn't know if I was embarking on a fool's errand.

And that errand was trying to talk to Timothy again. Over the past week, since I'd gone to his house the day after Savannah's murder, his name had popped up again and again.

Yet there was still so much I didn't know. What had his relationship with Savannah been like? Lovey-dovey, as Amanda had insisted, or turbulent, which was Coo's take on it? Had Timothy known about Ragnar Bruin being in her life—and, if so, did he have any insight into what the true nature of their relationship had been?

Then there was the fact that his name was on the mysterious list I'd come across in Savannah's files. Did he know what that list meant—and why his name was on it?

I was hoping that meeting with him again would help me answer some of those questions.

As I drove up to the house in Cold Spring and parked on

the street in front of it, my anxiety level began to climb. I was starting to wonder if I should have told Emma and Ethan where I was headed tonight. Maybe I was taking more of a risk than I realized by coming to Timothy's house. Especially since I was alone.

It didn't help that it was a strangely dark evening, with no stars in the sky. Even the moon was unusually pale, giving the impression that it simply wasn't trying very hard. It was also pretty late by then, almost ten o'clock. There didn't seem to be anyone else around. In fact, the neighborhood felt positively eerie as I got out of my truck.

As if that didn't do enough to create a creepy mood, a few of the houses around me were decorated for Halloween. Tonight, the smirking jack-o'-lanterns looked strangely spooky, their grins evil rather than whimsical. The next-door neighbors had hung rubber vampire bats along their front porch, and I jumped when out of the corner of my eye I noticed them swinging.

Jack-o'-lanterns and fake bats never hurt anyone, I reminded myself, trying to quiet my pounding heart.

Besides, now that I was here, I still wasn't sure whether or not it would be foolhardy to ring the bell. Turning around and leaving was still an option.

I was still trying to decide as I slowly started up the front walkway toward the house. Someone had pulled down the louvered blinds on the living room's big picture window. Even so, I could see that there were lights on inside.

But as I got closer, I noticed that the garden gnome I had damaged the week before was still perched on the windowsill, right where Timothy had deposited it. Next to it was the chunk of his hat that had broken off. When the blinds had been lowered, the bottom slats had gotten caught on the two ceramic pieces, creating a gap that allowed me to see inside.

I suddenly felt my eyes growing as big and round as those sneering pumpkins.

Through the window, I could see Timothy lying on the couch, his shirt off and his hair tousled. There was someone else there, as well. Someone who had also taken off some of her clothes.

Their bodies were intertwined in a way that immediately told me they weren't just watching a movie together.

Timothy sure didn't waste any time, I thought, suddenly angry. And here I thought he was such a nice guy. I'd believed that, even though he and Savannah may have been arguing, he was still in love with her . . .

And then he stood up, smiling at the woman and gesturing toward the kitchen, as if indicating that that was where he was now headed.

Which allowed me to get a good look at his companion.

I had to clasp my hand over my mouth to keep from crying out. The woman who was lying on the couch with Timothy was Amanda.

Chapter 13

Pecans are the most popular nut chunk in the US, and strawberries are the most popular fruit chunk.

—*http://www.benjerry.com/whats-new/2017/09/ice-cream-useless-facts*

I felt as if someone had punched me in the gut. Timothy and Amanda? I thought, feeling dazed. Savannah's boyfriend and the woman who claimed to be her best friend . . . they've been having an *affair?*

I turned and raced back down the front walkway, taking care not to trip. I was trying not to make any noise, either. I was out of breath by the time I reached my truck, but I was pretty sure that at least I'd managed to sneak off the property without being spotted.

But as I started to drive off, I glanced over my shoulder, for some reason taking one last look at the house. And what I saw made my stomach tighten even further.

The blinds in the living room had been pulled all the way up, exposing the silhouettes of two people standing at the window, watching me drive away.

They *saw* me! I thought, instinctively stepping harder on the gas. They know that *I* saw *them*—and that I now know their secret!

As I careened back to Wolfert's Roost, I struggled to sort through all the noise in my head. I started by replaying every word I could remember Amanda saying about Savannah's relationship with Timothy.

She had insisted that the two of them were madly in love, echoing what Timothy had told me. She had said they had even gotten engaged recently. She had sounded so convincing that it had only been Coo's version of recent events, her claim that the two of them had been fighting constantly, that had made me question what Amanda had said.

Then another thought occurred to me: that Detective Stoltz had said there was a good chance that the murderer would return to the scene of the crime. And Amanda had come to Lickety Splits. In fact, she hadn't even pretended to have any reason for coming besides wanting to see the place where Savannah had died.

Were Amanda and Savannah really friends? I wondered. But even if they had been, or at least appeared to be, what I had just discovered proved that Amanda hadn't been a very good friend to Savannah at all.

Amanda also had a good reason to protect Timothy, I realized. That could certainly have been why she had made up that story about Ragnar Bruin stalking Savannah. She could have been trying to shift suspicion away from the victim's boyfriend—always an obvious focus—to the director.

All this told me that what I had learned tonight had three possible implications. One was that Amanda had killed Savannah. Her intention could well have been to get rid of her rival for Timothy's affections. But it was also possible that she had murdered her for some other reason entirely, a reason I hadn't yet identified.

The second possibility was that Timothy was the murderer. He could have killed Savannah for two reasons: either because he was jealous of her affair with Ragnar or because he wanted her out of the picture so he'd be free to continue his relationship with Amanda.

The third possibility was that Timothy and Amanda had acted together.

But as I drove on, winding along Route 9 and noticing how quiet the usually busy road was this late at night, I pondered another issue that had been bubbling along on the back burner of my mind. And that was the question of how either Amanda or Timothy had managed to get into Lickety Splits to put poison into the dish of ice cream right before Savannah ate out of it.

And then a realization popped into my head like a bolt of lightning.

Amanda worked for a props company. While she'd told me that Monarch hadn't handled the props for *Ten Days*, she could easily have been lying.

Which meant she would have had easy access to the set.

I wanted to check with Chelsea Atkins about whether or not Amanda had been telling the truth about that. I made a mental note to send her a text as soon as I got home, asking her to call me the first chance she got.

But as I drove on, I realized that even if Amanda's company, Monarch, hadn't supplied the props for *Ten Days*, the woman *did* work in the movie industry. Which meant it was quite possible that she knew some of the people at the film shoot simply because that was the world she traveled in. She could easily have stopped in, claiming she was there to see how the filming was going or to say hello to a friend.

And maybe no one on the *Ten Days* set had thought to mention it merely because, in their eyes, Amanda popping in to say hello was a non-event.

The same went for Timothy. Since he was Savannah's boyfriend, he, too, could have stopped into Lickety Splits just to say hello. No one would ever have suspected that the reason he was there was not to wish his girlfriend good luck—but, instead, to make use of the poison he had sneaked in.

I was starting to think that the names of the two people who were closest to Savannah both belonged at the very top of my list.

I was still lying in bed early the next morning, going over the same points I'd been ruminating about as I'd driven home the night before, when my cell phone rang.

My first thought was that it was Chelsea, responding to the text I'd sent her the night before. But when I grabbed my phone off the night table and glanced at the screen, I saw a number I didn't recognize.

Still, the area code was Manhattan's 212. I answered immediately.

"Hey, Kate," Coo greeted me breezily. "Sorry I didn't call back sooner. I was in an all-day training seminar yesterday. In fact, since it ate up the whole day, I actually had to come in this morning, on a Saturday, to finish up a couple of things. So I just got your message. Did the boxes arrive?"

"They did," I told her. "Thank you so much for sending them."

"I figured that was what you were calling about," she said. Lowering her voice, she added, "Which is why I'm calling you from my cell phone, rather than Alpha's landline. In case you came across something interesting." She hesitated, then in the same soft voice said, "And it sounds as if you did."

"I'm not sure if I did or not," I replied. "I'm hoping you can tell me if what I found means anything."

I described the list I'd found in Savannah's files, explaining that it had been written two months earlier yet included the names of all five of the suspects I'd identified.

"I'm afraid I have no idea what that list means," Coo said,

sounding frustrated. "I don't even know who Chelsea Who-ever is."

"She's the assistant director on *Ten Days*," I told her. "She claims she'd only met Savannah a few times before filming began. Yet there she is, on the list."

"Timothy, Amanda, Ragnar . . . They're all people Savannah was close to, of course," Coo said, sounding as if she was thinking out loud. "But aside from that, I don't know what they have in common. As for Jennifer Jordan, I'm pretty sure she knew her, but it's not as if they were close friends."

She paused, then asked, "Was there anyplace else where those five names were listed together? Another file, perhaps?"

"Not that I found," I said. "Are you sure you got every-thing out of Savannah's office?"

"I'm positive," she assured me.

"Is it possible that somebody else went into the office be-fore you did and took something out?" I asked. "Maybe another file that would have shed light on what the list Sa-vannah made was all about?"

Coo was silent for several seconds. And then I heard her gasp. "Timothy!" she cried. "Of course. I don't know why I didn't think of this sooner. He could have taken something out of Savannah's files."

"Timothy?" I repeated, confused. "Isn't it unlikely that he would have been able to get into her office?"

"Why not?" Coo asked. Now *she* sounded confused.

"Because I would think that most companies wouldn't want an outsider coming in and going through their files—" I started to explain.

But she interrupted me.

"An outsider?" she said. "What do you mean, an out-sider?"

This conversation seemed to be getting more and more muddled. "I just mean that having someone like Timothy who's not an employee—"

"But Timothy *is* an employee," Coo declared.

I was still trying to understand. "Timothy works at Alpha, too?"

"Of course," Coo replied. "You didn't know that?"

"No, I didn't," I said. My mind was racing as I tried to wrap my head around this new piece of information. "But I thought he was an actor."

"He *is* an actor," Coo said. "Or at least he's trying to be an actor. Which is why it made sense for him to work at his family's firm. That way, he has all the flexibility he needs. After all, when your father is the CEO of a billion-dollar company, it's no problem if you want to take a day off here and there to memorize a script or go to an audition."

"Timothy's father is the CEO of Alpha Industries?" I was still having trouble piecing all this together.

"That's right," Coo said, still sounding surprised that she had to explain all of this to me. "I'm sorry. I just assumed you knew.

"I guess I also figured you knew that Timothy got Savannah her job at Alpha," she continued. "All he had to do was pick up the phone and ask his father to hire her. Savannah and Timothy met through acting, but like everyone else who's trying to break into the business, they both needed a way to pay the bills. Once they were seeing each other, he was more than happy to help her out with that."

My thoughts were reeling. Timothy not only worked at Alpha Industries; he was the boss's son. My earlier suspicions about Timothy's involvement in Savannah's death were growing stronger every second. But I still didn't have a grasp of what had been going on that might have motivated him to kill Savannah.

"There was something else written on that sheet of paper with the list of names," I told Coo. "The initials HH and the name of a local preserve."

Coo was silent for a few minutes. "The only thing I can

think of is Hudson Hideaways. I suppose that could be what the HH stands for."

My heart suddenly began to pound wildly in my chest. "What's Hudson Hideaways?"

"One of the properties Alpha has been developing," Coo replied.

That made sense. After all, nearly every one of Savannah's files had been dedicated to a different property. And if the Hudson Hideaways file was conspicuously absent, it could have been because Timothy had made a point of grabbing it out of Savannah's office.

And I had a hunch about why.

"Is it near the Mashawam Preserve?" I asked, picturing the underlined name of the preserve scrawled at the top of the list, along with two exclamation points. I was beginning to feel as if the pieces of the puzzle I'd been agonizing over were finally starting to fit together.

"Sorry, but I'm afraid I don't know anything about it," she replied. "But I'll see if I can do a little nosing around. It looks like I'm the only person here in the office this morning. Maybe I can find something that'll be useful to you."

The sick feeling I suddenly had in my stomach told me that while Coo didn't have a sense of what all this pointed to, I did. But there was still a lot more I had to find out.

Despite the sense of urgency that engulfed me, the reality was that I had an ice cream shop to run. And because it was a Saturday, I didn't feel comfortable leaving Emma to run Lickety Splits all by herself. On a crisp, sunny autumn weekend like this one, there were bound to be hordes of leaf peepers who hopefully liked ice cream as much as they liked beautiful scenery. In addition, with Halloween growing close, I figured there would be plenty of customers putting in orders for parties and other holiday-related events.

So I spent the entire day at Lickety Splits. Business was as bustling as I'd anticipated, and Emma and I worked nonstop. Smashed Pumpkins turned out to be as popular as we'd hoped it would be. As for Creepy Crawlers, it turned out that Emma had been right. Plenty of people were eager to eat gummy centipedes, candy spiders, and powdered cocoa that looked like dirt. And it wasn't just ten-year-old boys, either. Even a woman I recognized as the head librarian at the Wolfert's Roost Public Library was eager to try it. In fact, she giggled like a little girl as she pulled one of the wriggly candy centipedes out of her scoop of ice cream and stuck the whole thing in her mouth.

It wasn't until late afternoon that things quieted down and I felt I could leave the shop entirely in Emma's hands. As I drove toward the Mashawam Preserve, I was dismayed to see that the sun was already getting low in the sky. Finding my way around in the woods in the dark wasn't exactly something I was likely to be very good at.

But I didn't want to wait any longer. I was too anxious to find out if my hunch was correct.

The sky was rapidly growing darker as I pulled in to the preserve's parking lot. And from the looks of things, in another few minutes I was going to be the only person there. The park closed at sundown, and the three or four cars that remained had their trunks open, with hikers packing away their gear and getting ready to leave.

I climbed out of my truck, dismayed as I watched the last car drive off. I was suddenly all alone in the parking lot, accompanied only by long, eerie shadows and the occasional cry of a bird. The trees rustled ominously. I reminded myself that there was bound to be a breeze up here. Nothing strange about that.

I didn't waste any time. I walked right up to the chain-link fence I'd spotted two days earlier during my hike with Brody.

And I realized that it was probably just as well that no one else was around. I was about to break the law. Or at least do something I wasn't supposed to do.

I glanced around, but I didn't spot any security cameras. So I took a deep breath and began to climb.

Even though I'm not particularly athletic, I'm pretty strong. Maybe hours of standing behind a counter, scooping out ice cream, has helped build the muscles of my arms and legs. But whether or not I had ice cream to thank, I was surprised at how easy I found it to scale that fence. Grabbing the metal with both hands, sticking my toe in, and hauling myself upward brought back childhood memories of having done this before, even though I couldn't remember the exact circumstances.

I'd just reached the top and was about to sling my right leg over the top when I heard a loud *snap*.

I froze.

A few seconds later, as my heart pounded away wildly, I finally dared to look over my shoulder. I expected to see a uniformed park ranger standing below, scowling.

Nothing.

I must be imagining things, I thought, sharply breathing in some fresh air. Or maybe I'd just heard an animal. Or the wind.

I climbed over the top and made my way down, jumping off the fence and onto the dirt path below. Tall trees surrounded me, casting more of those long, creepy shadows ahead of me.

I really should have researched bears, I told myself as I began to walk. As in whether or not there are likely to be any lurking in the woods around here.

But part of me felt that bears weren't the only thing I had to worry about.

And then I heard another unexpected noise. This one was

different. It was more like a cry. A human cry. As if someone had tripped or encountered something unexpected . . .

No one is following you, I told myself firmly. You're just nervous, being out here in the woods all alone, with the sun going down and you sneaking into an area of the park where no one is supposed to go . . .

I quickened my pace. By now I was nearly jogging along the path. Finishing my mission before it got completely dark was starting to feel more and more urgent.

And then I heard another snap.

I whirled my head around, certain this time that this wasn't merely something I'd imagined. And whatever had made that noise wasn't some innocent woodland creature.

Either my imagination was playing cruel tricks on me or someone was following me.

"Who's there?" I called.

The only response was silence.

You're just imagining things, I scolded myself. And who wouldn't, walking around the woods all alone like this? You really have to cut down on the caffeine, young lady. Perhaps even start eating less Cappuccino Crunch. Or maybe create a decaf version.

I walked on, even though I was beginning to wonder if I'd made a mistake in coming here. The farther I got, without any results, the more this mission of mine was starting to seem like a waste of time.

And then I stopped. My mouth had suddenly become dry, and my heart had begun racing again. And this time, my re-action had nothing to do with imaginary sounds.

Directly in front of me was a sign that said, FUTURE HOME OF HUDSON HIDEAWAYS.

Hudson Hideaways—*here*? I thought. On public land? Land that's supposed to be preserved for, well, for forever?

I walked a little farther and let out a gasp. Just beyond the sign was a construction site.

Not just any construction site, either. This one was on such a tremendous scale that it would have seemed horribly out of place anywhere in the Hudson Valley, much less in the middle of a preserve.

There must have been a hundred condos under construction. Spread out before me were row after row of half-built brick town houses, each one two stories high. There was a driveway in front of each, along with a small yard. Dirt roads connected them, but to judge by the size of the trucks parked nearby, I got the feeling that they'd be paved roads before long.

I felt sick. The fact that the gears were turning in my head, putting together all the pieces of the puzzle, did little to alleviate the fact that what I had found was so ugly that I could barely process it.

Alpha Industries had been involved in an illegal construction project. The company must have paid off local officials or engaged in some other type of corrupt practices, unethically gaining the right to build a housing development smack in the middle of a preserve.

And Savannah Crane had found out about it.

I was about to take my line of reasoning to the next step when I heard another strange noise. This time, it was a rustling, followed by a thump that was definitely a human foot landing hard on the dirt-covered road.

And it sounded as if it was right behind me.

I whirled around, instinctively balling my hands into fists. Then I let out a cry as I found myself face-to-face with a tall lean figure dressed entirely in black, including a ski mask that completely concealed my stalker's face.

Chapter 14

The Klondike bar was created by the Isaly Dairy
Company in Mansfield, Ohio, which was founded
in the early 1900s by William Isaly, the son of
Swiss immigrants. It was made by hand-dipping
square pieces of homemade ice cream into Swiss
milk chocolate. In 1922, the company released
five flavors of the chocolate-covered bars: vanilla,
chocolate, strawberry, maple, and cherry.

—https://www.klondikebar.com/about

"Get away from me!" I yelled, feeling the adrenaline
shooting through my veins like a drug.

Every one of my muscles was tense. I was poised to run.
But the terrifying ninja standing in front of me was blocking
my way.

I was also ready to fight, even though I felt fairly helpless
since I had nothing to use as a weapon. I looked around,
frantically searching for a stick or a rock.

But before I had a chance to either fight or flee, the figure
in front of me whipped off the ski mask.

She was a woman. A tall, thin, beautiful woman who shook
out a thick mane of long, jet-black hair.

"I'm sorry if I scared you," she said, flashing me a brilliant
smile.

As soon as I saw that smile, I knew who she was. In some remote part of my brain, stored away with other useless bits of information like my old gym locker combination and Grams's foolproof recipe for perfect cornbread, was the image of this face and the name that went with it.

"You're Jennifer Jordan, aren't you?" I said, feeling as if I was finally emerging from the state of shock I'd been in.

"That's me," she replied. Grimacing, she said, "Which is why I'm wearing this ridiculous getup. You're not the only person who's likely to recognize me. I was afraid I'd run into a bunch of hikers or a Girl Scout troop who'd start hounding me for pictures or an autograph."

With a sigh, she added, "It's the price of fame. It turns out that being a celebrity isn't all it's cracked up to be."

My momentary sense of relief faded as I remembered that Jennifer Jordan was a suspect in Savannah Crane's murder. She was also someone who had followed me deep into the woods, secretively trailing me as I headed into an isolated place.

Not a good sign.

"I'm not alone," I said, raising my chin defiantly. "I'm here with a group of people. In fact, I'm sure they're looking for me—"

"Of course you're alone," she interrupted. "I've been following you since you got out of your car." With a shrug, she said, "But by now I hope you've realized that I'm not exactly someone you should be afraid of."

I had to admit that she had a point. Even here in the woods, with she and I the only people around for miles, it was hard to believe that this disarming woman was a cold-blooded killer. Then again, I'd misjudged people before.

"I thought you'd gone into hiding," I said boldly. "Everyone is saying you've disappeared."

She raised her eyebrows. "Me—disappeared? What are you talking about?"

"The tabloids are saying that you vanished right after Savannah Crane's murder," I explained.

"I didn't *vanish*," she said, sounding even more exasperated. She thought for a few seconds. "I did make a point of staying out of sight, though. I was afraid that those ridiculous supermarket tabloids would drag out those silly stories about us hating each other."

"Do you mean it's not true that you two were archenemies?" I asked.

"It's true that Savannah and I have known each other since our days together in acting school," Jennifer said, sounding frustrated. "And, of course, she and I ended up auditioning for some of the same roles. But so did a hundred other actresses. Sometimes she got the role, sometimes I got it, and most of the time someone else entirely got it. That doesn't mean we hated each other. No one could survive in show business if people took things like that personally."

"But what about the starring role in *Ten Days*?" I demanded. "I heard that you desperately wanted that part."

"Are you kidding? Savannah was *made* for that role," she insisted. "The willowy blond ingénue? That's her to a T. And not me at all." With a sigh, she added, "She would have been amazing in it. It would have turned her into a megastar, and she totally deserved it."

"So if you're not in hiding because of Savannah Crane's murder," I asked, "what are you doing in the Hudson Valley? And why are you in a preserve, following me?"

"Because I wanted to find out for myself if this horrendous housing development had anything to do with what happened to Savannah," Jennifer replied, her big brown eyes filling with tears.

"So you knew about Hudson Hideaways," I said.

She nodded. "I was one of the earliest investors."

The wheels in my brain immediately started to turn. In my mind, as big as a movie screen, I could see the list I'd found in Savannah Crane's files.

So Coo had been right. HH stood for Hudson Hideaways, this sprawling condo complex that was being built illegally in the middle of a preserve. As for the list of names, since Jennifer Jordan was one of the investors, I suspected that everyone else on that list was an investor, too. And every one of those people was someone Jennifer knew personally.

Wanting to confirm what I'd just concluded, I said, "So you invested in Hudson Hideaways, like Savannah's friend Amanda Huffner and the director Ragnar Bruin . . ."

"That's right," Jennifer agreed. "A bunch of people who knew her invested back when we were still operating under the delusion that this was a legitimate development project."

Thoughtfully, she added, "It wasn't until Savannah got in touch with me a few weeks ago that I found out the ugly truth. Alpha had been working with local politicians to gain access to preserved land, bribing them to get them to quietly change its status. Needless to say, it was all done behind closed doors. I knew what a serious risk Savannah was taking by telling me. The whole idea was that no one would find out until Hudson Hideaways had already been built and it was too late."

She paused, then said, "I guess Savannah felt partly responsible since she worked at Alpha. And because of Timothy, too, of course."

"Timothy?" I asked, my ears pricking up. "What did he have to do with Hudson Hideaways?"

Jennifer looked surprised by my question. "He's the one who pitched it to all of us."

"So Timothy was involved in the corruption behind Hudson Hideaways," I said breathlessly, thinking aloud.

"He was up to his ears in it," she replied angrily. "He'd invested tons of his own money, for one thing. And then he'd apparently asked Savannah for the names of her friends, figuring they'd be more likely to go in on something if it was her boyfriend who was pitching it."

So Timothy had used Savannah to get people to invest in what *he* undoubtedly knew was a shady land-development project.

And then *she* found out.

Savannah had made a point of telling all the investors who were friends of hers. And given my sense of her, I had a feeling she had intended to tell a lot more people as soon as she got a chance. Which was why someone who was deeply involved in the project had felt motivated to keep her from doing exactly that.

And that someone, I fully believed, had been Timothy.

I noticed that Jennifer had gone on a few steps farther and was gazing out at the huge construction site that stretched just beyond the spot where we were standing.

"So this is it," I heard Jennifer say mournfully, breaking me out of my reverie. "This is the crummy housing development that cost Savannah Crane her life."

"We don't know that for sure," I said. "I mean, nothing has been proved yet . . ."

But Jennifer looked over at me, and our eyes met as a moment of understanding passed between us.

We were both silent for a few moments, staring at the ugly construction site in front of us. Dozens of tall, magnificent trees had been chopped down and now stood in haphazard piles next to bright yellow tractors and cranes. There were huge, gaping holes behind the houses that were already half-built, marking the places where more buildings would be put up. The ground looked raw, as if it was wounded.

The image was made even worse by the long shadows draped

everywhere like shrouds. Which jolted me back to the reality that the sun was on the verge of setting.

"We should get back," I said. "It's almost dark, and I don't know my way around this place very well."

"The trail is pretty decent," Jennifer said. "My phone has a great flashlight app. But you're right: we should head out." Sadly, she added, "Besides, we're done here. We both saw what we came to see."

"Would you like to come back to my house?" I offered as we started back along the trail. "You could join my family and me for dinner. We even have a guest room where you're welcome to spend the night. But I'm warning you that my grandmother and my niece will both make a terrible fuss over you. You'll have to pose for photos, give autographs—"

"Thanks, but I'm heading back to the city," she said. "I've got to get home. I'm actually in the middle of negotiations for a new movie. The project is just getting off the ground, so the trade papers haven't even written about it yet."

"That sounds exciting," I commented.

"It truly is," she said. "It's an independent movie that focuses on an issue I care about deeply. I'm pretty sure it's going to make a big difference in the way people see things." Grinning, she added, "It's also a once-in-a-lifetime role. Perhaps even one that's Oscar-worthy."

"So your career is about to get back on track," I observed. And then I realized what I'd just said. "Sorry! It's only that I read something online—"

She laughed. "Believe me, I'm used to not having any privacy. And it's true that my career has been in a slump lately. But I really think this new film is going to turn things around for me."

"I'm glad," I told her. And I meant it.

"But can I ask you for one small thing?" I asked as the parking lot came into view. "Could I please get your autograph for my niece? It would mean so much to her."

"It sounds as if you and I should take a selfie together, too," Jennifer said. "You don't want this niece of yours to stop speaking to you, do you?"

A few minutes later, as I watched Jennifer ride away in the taxi that had brought her to the preserve an hour earlier, I was warmed by what a nice person she had turned out to be.

She had also given me some valuable information.

Information that had fully convinced me that it was Timothy who had killed Savannah.

He certainly had a strong motivation. It was very likely that she was about to ruin him. And the fact that she was on the verge of being catapulted to national and even international fame was part of it. While his corrupt dealings were likely to have caught up with him at some point, perhaps even sending him to prison, Savannah's new celebrity status would have enabled her to blow up the story and smear his name on an even larger scale.

The fact that their personal relationship had deteriorated so badly convinced me of his guilt even further. The man had been having an affair, which meant that there was no reason for him to feel protective toward her any longer. His loyalties had clearly shifted elsewhere.

Only one piece of the story was still missing: how he had managed to do it. And at this point, I was hungrier than ever to figure that out.

Which meant getting in touch with someone who was likely to have that information—whether she realized it or not.

Chelsea Atkins was the one person who I knew had been in Lickety Splits the entire time before Savannah's death, which meant she had to have been there when the murderer put poison in the ice cream dish. It was true that she'd been busy, coordinating all the chaos that went along with turning my shop into a movie set. But she was *there*, and she had therefore seen everyone else who had been there.

If someone who wasn't part of the regular crew had been in Lickety Splits for even a few moments, she would know about it.

I tried texting her as soon as I climbed into my truck. Not surprisingly, my phone informed me that there was no service up here in the mountains.

I made a mental note to get in touch with her as soon as I got to my shop. By the time I drove into Wolfert's Roost, I had decided what the text would say. It would definitely include the word "urgent" and it would contain several exclamation points.

It was completely dark by then, with a handful of stars and only a sliver of a moon. While Hudson Street was lit up by streetlights, the fact that it was a Saturday night meant that most of the shops I drove past were closed. All the lights were out at the cheese shop, Let It Brie. The quilt shop, Stitchin' Time, looked positively spooky. The same went for the florist, Petal Pushers, and the hair salon, Lotsa Locks. At least Brody's shop, right across the street from Lickety Splits, was open. But from the looks of things, not much was going on in there.

Things in town seemed so sleepy tonight that I wondered if Lickety Splits was getting any customers. Saturday night usually brought out quite a few people: teenagers hanging out downtown, couples who had just had dinner at one of the restaurants, dog walkers, even day-trippers in search of one more bit of fun before heading back to wherever they'd come from. But tonight, for some reason, downtown felt strangely still.

There were lots of free parking spots, and I spotted one a few doors down from Lickety Splits. As I headed toward it, I rode past my shop.

As I did, I suddenly let out a sound that was a cross between a gasp and a scream. Abruptly, I slammed on the brakes, then rolled down the window as I tried to get a better look at what I thought I was seeing.

Sure enough; it was exactly what I'd thought it was.

Lying on the sidewalk in front of Lickety Splits was the body of what appeared to be a large man. And protruding from his chest was a dagger.

Chapter 15

August 6 is National Root Beer Float Day, honor-
ing the treat consisting of a scoop of vanilla ice
cream floating in a mug of ice-cold root beer. The
root beer float, also known as a "Black Cow," is
believed to have been invented in a mining camp
by Frank J. Wisner, the owner of the Cripple
Creek Cow Mountain Gold Mining Company.

*—https://nationaldaycalendar/national-root-beer-float-day-
august-6/*

Stay calm, I told myself, aware that my heart was pounding
away at jackhammer speed. *Before you deal with this, you
have to park the truck.*

Doing my best to remain in control of my vehicle—and
not cause any accidents—I pulled into the parking space I'd
been heading for. My hands were shaking as I switched off
the ignition. Part of me thought that the next thing I should
do was call 911. But another part of me wanted to investigate before taking any action at all.

So I climbed out of my truck, my cell phone in hand. As I
walked toward my shop, I switched on its flashlight. But
when I was still a good thirty feet away from Lickety Splits, I
suddenly understood what I was looking at.

The man who was lying on the sidewalk was the Frankenstein monster that Emma had created.

But even though *he* wasn't real, the knife that was sticking out of his papier-mâché chest appeared to be *very* real. I leaned down to get a better look, taking care not to touch it, and saw that it was a kitchen knife. From the clean incision it had made into the dummy's paste-and-newspaper chest, it was a very *sharp* kitchen knife.

If this had been any other Halloween season, I might have found it humorous. Clever, even.

But not this Halloween. Not when the sick feeling in the pit of my stomach bore out the first thought that came to mind: that this was meant to be a warning.

Suddenly, I remembered that Emma was alone inside Lickety Splits. I rushed inside, a wave of panic rushing over me.

But it faded as soon as I spotted her standing behind the counter. She was cheerfully chatting with two women who were about Grams's age, meanwhile scooping up a generous amount of Honey Lavender and pushing it down into a sugar cone.

I resisted the urge to ask her if she was all right—at least, until the two customers left, exclaiming over the deliciousness of the Honey Lavender and Cashew Brittle with Sea Salt cones they were carrying out.

"Emma, are you okay?" I demanded.

She looked surprised. "Why wouldn't I be?"

"Did you hear anything strange going on outside?" I asked. "Did you see anyone who was acting funny? Did any of the customers say anything about Frankenstein—?"

"Frankenstein?" Emma repeated, clearly puzzled by all the bizarre questions that were flowing out of my mouth, one after another. "'Anything strange?' Kate, what are you talking about?"

I took a deep breath. "Someone vandalized your Frankenstein monster."

"Oh, no!" she cried, already dashing toward the door. "Is he okay?"

Something about her question struck me as ridiculously funny. Maybe it was a reaction to all the tension of the day or maybe it was simply because I was so tired, but I burst out into uncontrollable laughter.

"Emma, he's not real!" I cried. "Of course, he's okay! Or at least he will be as soon as you patch him up with a little duct tape!"

The look on my niece's face told me she still didn't understand what was going on. Also, that she thought her aunt had lost her mind.

But she hurried outside. I heard a yelp of dismay, and a few seconds later she was back in the shop.

"What does this mean, Kate?" she cried. "Is someone playing a practical joke?"

"That's probably all it is," I told her, realizing that there was no point in frightening her. Especially since I was feeling much calmer now that I was standing in my brightly lit shop, surrounded by multiple tubs of ice cream and one of my favorite people in the entire universe.

And I told myself that that really could be the case. After all, it *was* possible that someone who had wandered by had simply thought that stabbing Frankenstein with a knife would be a good practical joke, a special touch that would carry the horror-themed decorations of my shop to a new level. After all, the young man who'd come into Lickety Splits right after Savannah Crane's murder had assumed that the crime-scene tape was part of my store's tribute to Halloween.

But would that random person happen to have a kitchen knife with him or her? I immediately wondered, that uneasy feeling coming right back. Not very likely. And it wasn't much more likely that the prankster would have been motivated enough to go home to get one, come all the way back, and then carry out what he or she thought was nothing more than a lighthearted bit of theater.

While I would have liked to believe that an attempt at humor was all that was behind this, deep down I knew that Frankenstein had been used to send me a warning. Someone wanted me to know that it was time to abandon my unofficial investigation of Savannah Crane's murder.

If not, that person was telling me, I might end up in the same sorry state as Frankenstein. The difference, of course, was that *I* wasn't made of paper and paste.

In the end, I decided not to tell Detective Stoltz about this incident. At least not yet.

After all, by this point I was fairly certain that I'd identified Savannah's killer. But before I went to Stoltz with my theory, I wanted to talk to Chelsea Atkins. I needed to find out if she'd spotted Timothy Scott at Lickety Splits in the hours before the murder.

I went ahead and texted her, using the word "urgent" and the three exclamation points I'd already decided to include. Then, all I could do was wait.

Since it was a Saturday night, I knew it was unlikely that I'd hear back from Chelsea right away. But that didn't keep me from checking my cell phone every two minutes as Emma and I dragged poor Frankenstein into the shop.

Watching Emma pull that knife out of him was wrenching. Even though she was chattering away, explaining that all she needed to do to fix him up was glue a few strips of painted newspaper over his chest, I couldn't stop thinking about the fact that whoever had done this had the ability to do the exact same thing to me.

I was actually glad that we didn't have many customers that night. And I let Emma handle most of the ice cream seekers who wandered in. I was so preoccupied that I was afraid someone would order Mint Chocolate Chip and instead I'd give them Pistachio 'n' Almond 'n' Fudge Swirl.

My agitated mood continued for the rest of the night. I barely slept, instead wrestling with my sheets and blanket and even my poor pillow. And the few times I did manage to doze off, Timothy's face loomed large in my nightmares.

I was obsessed with proving that he had come into Lickety Splits before the shoot. And I desperately hoped that Chelsea would be able to verify that he had been there, even if only for a minute or two.

The next morning, instead of feeling groggy, I was pumped up with adrenaline from the moment the sun peeked in my window. I jumped out of bed, threw on some clothes, and made a big pot of coffee. As soon as I fueled up, I went off to Lickety Splits. It was still ridiculously early, and given my agitated state, I didn't think I could be quiet enough to keep from waking Emma or Grams way too early on this Sunday morning.

Once I was in my shop, I didn't feel like whipping up fresh batches of ice cream or doing paperwork. Instead, I sat at one of the tables, just thinking.

And trying to will Chelsea to call me back.

When my cell phone finally did buzz, I grabbed it before the first ring had ended. I assumed it was Chelsea. So I was disappointed when I recognized the number as Coo's cell phone.

"Is it too early to call?" she asked anxiously.

"It's fine," I assured her. "I've been up for ages."

I was about to tell her about what I'd learned from Jennifer Jordan—and that I was now convinced that Timothy had killed Savannah. But before I had a chance, she jumped right in with, "I'm sorry, Kate, but even though I scoured the office yesterday, I couldn't find out a single thing about Hudson Hideaways. I even brought home a bunch of files to look through, which is why it's taken me so long to get back to you. I'm here at the office again this morning, still looking. But I'm coming up empty."

She let out a frustrated sigh. "And it doesn't make any sense at all! I know for a fact that it was a property Alpha was developing. I heard people talking about it all the time. But it's as if every shred of paper mentioning it has suddenly vanished."

"Are you sure you looked everywhere?" I asked.

"Absolutely," she insisted. "I even looked through the big boss's files. Or at least I tried to. His secretary's cubicle is right outside his office, and she's got a couple of big file cabinets where she meticulously files every single paper that crosses her desk. I looked through every drawer, but I couldn't find a thing about Hudson Hideaways. It just doesn't make any sense."

"I suppose he could have kept his files in his own office," I said, thinking aloud.

"Good point," Coo agreed. "But that's one place I couldn't look. I'm afraid that good old G.V. keeps his office locked, at least over the weekends."

"G.V.?" I repeated, even though I pretty much knew she was referring to the head of Alpha.

"That's what we call him around the office," she said lightly. "G.V. for George Vernon."

All the blood in my body had turned to ice. "George Vernon?" I repeated, barely able to get the words out.

"That's right," Coo said. "George Vernon Scott. He's the CEO of Alpha Industries. Of course, he's not in the office much these days, since he's in the process of retiring. Not that he's ever been that involved with the day-to-day workings of the company. He's got his minions to do that. Like me," she added with a chuckle.

But I wasn't laughing. "You're telling me that George Vernon is the name of the CEO of Alpha Industries?" I repeated, saying the words aloud as a way of trying to understand them.

"Yes, that's right," Coo said, sounding puzzled by my question. "George Vernon Scott."

"And the man is Timothy's father," I said, still attempting to digest what I'd just learned.

"Right . . ."

I felt both a rush of understanding and a wave of confusion rushing over me at the same time, something I never would have thought was possible.

Everything about George Vernon had been a lie—starting with his name. He had used only his first and middle names to keep Grams and me and everyone else from knowing his true identity.

Then there was his claim that he was retired. Another lie. While he'd pretended to be playing golf a few days a week, in reality he had been going into the city to run his company, Alpha Industries.

And at Thursday night's dinner, he had acted as if he'd never heard of Savannah Crane. Yet she had been an employee he had hired himself, as well as his son's girlfriend—perhaps even his fiancée.

One more lie. A really *big* lie.

That same evening, he had also learned that I was investigating the crime. Which could have led him to vandalize Frankenstein as a warning to me.

My head was spinning. Was it possible that George Vernon Scott had been involved in Savannah's murder? Here I had been so certain that Timothy was responsible. But George was Timothy's father, which only muddied the waters even further . . .

"Coo, I have to go," I said abruptly.

"Sorry I couldn't be more helpful," she said.

I didn't bother to explain that she had been more helpful than she could imagine.

After I hung up, I put down my phone and buried my face in my hands, struggling to focus on the hurricane of thoughts whirling around in my head. But before I had a chance to calm down enough to even begin to sort through them, the door to my shop opened. And in walked Chelsea Atkins.

Chapter 16

The first cookbook in history devoted entirely to
ice creams and sorbets was M. Emy's *L'art de Bien
Faire les Glaces d'Office* (The Art of Making
Frozen Desserts), published in France in 1768.
The title page from the book illustrates a common
opinion of the day that ice cream was a "food fit
for the gods."

—We All Scream for Ice Cream! The Scoop on America's
Favorite Dessert *by Lee Wardlaw*

"You didn't have to come to the shop," I told her. "A
phone call would have been fine."

Chelsea let out a cold laugh. "As if I have anything else
to do. Until this case is cleared up—or until that creepy Detective Stoltz tells me I can leave—I can't go back home to
California. I'm just twiddling my thumbs up here in the
boondocks." Glancing around my shop, she added, "Coming
here actually gave me something to do this morning."

She plopped down at a table. "So tell me: What's so urgent?"

I decided to jump right in. "Chelsea, are you sure no one
came onto the set who didn't belong there?"

"Positive," she replied without hesitation. "Kate, I've been
over this with you before. The police, too, more times than I
care to think about."

"What about Savannah's boyfriend, Timothy?" I asked. "Maybe he stopped in just for a minute . . . ?"

She shook her head. She was clearly growing exasperated as she said, "I'm telling you, Kate, I didn't see anyone who wasn't part of the crew. And Stoltz has questioned them all and concluded that he doesn't have reason to suspect any of them."

I thought for a few seconds, then asked, "Who handled the props for *The Best Ten Days*?" I held my breath as I waited for her answer. Amanda had claimed her company hadn't been involved with this film. But I now knew that she had a penchant for lying.

But I discovered that this time she had been telling the truth when Chelsea replied, "A company called CineProps. They're based in New Jersey. Why?"

"It's a long story," I told her. "But let me ask you something else: do you know Amanda Huffner?"

Chelsea shrugged. "I've never heard of her. Who is she?"

"She was, or at least she says she was, Savannah Crane's best friend," I said. "She also happens to work at a props house, which is why I wondered if she had an excuse to be involved with this film. I thought she might have come onto the set the night before the shoot or early that morning. But the company she works for is called Monarch."

"I've worked with Monarch plenty of times in the past, but not on this film." Scowling, she added, "Honestly, the only people who were there besides the crew members were the people who work for you. All those cheerful people dressed in those bright-pink polo shirts . . ."

Even though I knew that no one from my 'Cream Team had had anything to do with any of this, I said, "Tell me exactly who you remember being there." I knew the answer to this question was beyond obvious, since I had been myself there with Emma, Ethan, and Willow. But I wanted to be absolutely certain I was covering every possible angle.

Chelsea scrunched up her face thoughtfully. "Okay, let me see if I've got this right. You, of course. Then there was the young woman with the curly black hair and the blue streaks . . ."

"My niece, Emma," I told her.

"Right. Then there was another woman, probably around thirty," Chelsea went on. "She had short hair. Really light blond, like almost white."

"That's Willow," I said.

"Right. Then there were the two men—"

I froze. "Two men?" I repeated.

"Yes," she replied. "The young one and the old one."

My heart had begun pounding, and the room suddenly felt very warm.

"Can you describe them?" I asked, trying to sound matter-of-fact.

"Sure," Chelsea said. "The young one—he was probably eighteen or nineteen—had straight black hair that kept falling in his eyes."

"That's Ethan," I said. "Emma's boyfriend."

"Then there was the older guy," Chelsea went on. "He was only here Wednesday night for the setup, though. He didn't show up again on Thursday morning for the actual filming."

"But *I* was at Lickety Splits Thursday night, too," I reminded her, confused. "Only the four of us were there. Emma, Willow, Ethan, and me."

Chelsea shook her head. "He wasn't here the same time you were. He came in afterward. Right after you left, in fact."

"What did this man look like?" I asked, still struggling to keep my voice even.

"Let's see," Chelsea said thoughtfully. "He was nice-looking. Tall and lean, without that paunch that a lot of old men get.

Gray hair, or more like silver maybe . . . and he had this cute habit. It struck me as kind of old-fashioned, but in a charming way."

"What habit?" I asked. By this point, my heart was threatening to burst out of my chest.

"He winked at me," she replied. "Twice. It wasn't flirtatious or anything. It was his way of punctuating what he was saying. Like we were both in on some inside joke."

By that point I thought I really *was* going to explode.

The man she was describing was George Vernon.

Or, more accurately, George Vernon Scott, the CEO of Alpha Industries. The man Savannah Crane had been on the verge of destroying by going public about the corrupt land-development deal he and his company were involved with.

"So this man with the silver hair and the wink came to the shop after the rest of the Lickety Splits employees were gone?" I asked, trying to reconstruct what had happened.

"That's right," Chelsea said. "A few minutes after you and the other three people you mentioned left, he came into the shop. He was wearing a pink shirt, just like I'd seen you and your employees wearing. He said he had to do something with the ice cream or it would all go bad. I didn't want that to happen, so I let him do whatever he had to do."

"Did you see what he did?" I asked.

"No," she said. "I didn't see any reason to pay any attention to what he was up to. I figured he worked for you and that he was simply taking care of business as usual."

"And you're sure he was wearing a pink shirt?"

"That's right," Chelsea replied. "I'm positive about that, since I was thinking about how unusual it was for a dignified older man like him to wear a shirt that was the color of bubble gum—even if it was part of a uniform." She added, "That's why I figured he really must be a Lickety Splits employee."

I was still puzzling over how George had gotten hold of a Lickety Splits shirt when another thought occurred to me.

"By any chance, do you remember if the shirt he was wearing actually had the Lickety Splits logo on it?" I asked.

Chelsea shrugged. "I have no idea. There was so much going on that there was no way I would have noticed a detail like that."

By now, I was able to picture the entire scenario in my mind. George had staked out Lickety Splits, watching the door of the shop from a distance. Once he saw me leave with Emma, Ethan, and Willow, he had come into the shop, pretending that he worked for me. And in order to carry off that little charade, he had worn a pink shirt that was similar in color to the real Lickety Splits T-shirts.

I found myself replaying the conversation I'd had with Amanda when I'd stopped in to see her at work. After she'd pointed out the importance of the props fitting in with the time and place in which the scene was set, I'd commented, "It makes perfect sense that everything has to belong. Part of your job is to make sure everything looks as if it should be there."

Which is exactly what George had done. He had taken great care to make sure he looked as if he belonged at Lickety Splits.

Once he had access to the shop and everything in it, it would have been easy for him to put poison into the ice cream dish that Savannah Crane was going to eat out of. The dish was already out on the table, so he would have had no trouble identifying it. And everyone around him would have been too involved in what they were doing to pay attention to what George was doing.

He was also someone who had returned to the scene of the crime, which was exactly what Detective Stoltz had told me the killer was likely to do. George had come into Lickety Splits a week after Savannah's murder, pretending to ask me about where I thought his relationship with Grams was going.

Now I knew that wasn't the real reason he had come to my shop.

I had been silent for a long time as my mind clicked away. Chelsea must have been growing concerned because she said, "Kate? Are you okay?"

"I'm fine," I assured her, even though at the moment I was feeling anything but fine.

"Do you know who this man is?" she asked anxiously. "It sounds like maybe he wasn't really someone who worked for you."

"I know exactly who he is," I told her.

"Do you think he had anything to do with—?"

But I didn't answer her. I was too busy calling Detective Stoltz.

Even though the age of technology is supposed to make communicating a breeze, it doesn't always play out that way.

Detective Stoltz didn't answer his phone. Instead, I got an annoying message encouraging me to leave a detailed message. I did.

"Detective Stoltz, this is Kate McKay," I said, doing my best not to speak too quickly. "I just found out something really important about what happened at Lickety Splits the night before Savannah Crane's murder. There's a man in town that I'm sure you haven't even considered a suspect. His name is George Vernon Scott, and he's the CEO of a company called Alpha Industries. Savannah worked at his firm. I learned from another employee that Savannah had found out something terrible concerning George's business dealings and she was going to go public with it.

"In addition to that, I just discovered that George snuck into my shop the night before the murder," I went on, by now unable to resist the impulse to talk faster and faster. "The way he managed that is that he was wearing a pink shirt, which people on the set assumed was the same shirt that Lickety Splits' employees wear. The fact that he was here during the setup for the shoot means he could easily have put poison in the ice cream dish that Savannah was going to be eating out of the following morning, and—"

A shrill beep told me that my time had run out. All I could do was hope that Detective Stoltz called me back right away.

In the meantime, I had another important call to make. One that was related to the new realization that was throbbing in my head like a migraine headache: my grandmother was dating a murderer.

It took four rings before anyone at the house answered.

"Come on, come on . . . ," I whispered, ready to jump out of my skin as I listened to what seemed like endless rings.

It was Emma who finally picked up, greeting me with a cheerful, "Hey, Kate!"

"Put Grams on," I demanded.

"She's not here," she replied, the tone of her voice immediately changing. "Kate, what's wrong?"

"Where is she?" I asked, not wanting to take the time to explain.

"She went to the high school gym," Emma said. "She said she planned to meet George there nice and early this morning because they still had a lot to get done on—"

My sense of urgency had instantly escalated into near-panic mode.

"I'll call her there."

"What's going on?" Emma demanded.

I ended the call without answering her question. Then, with shaking hands, I pressed the keys required to call Grams's cell phone.

It rang and rang, my frustration practically making me

jump up and down. Finally, I heard the beginning of her taped message: "Hi! This is Caroline! I can't answer the phone right now—"

"I have to leave," I told Chelsea. She was still sitting opposite me, her expression a combination of confusion, astonishment, and alarm. "Just pull the door closed after you."

I grabbed my jacket and my purse, fumbling for my keys as I dashed out of my shop.

At this very moment, Grams was alone at the gym with a murderer. Which meant I had to get there fast.

I grabbed my jacket and purse, dashed out of Lickety Splits, jumped into my truck, and careened toward the high school. This was one time that I hoped going over the speed limit would attract the attention of Pete Bonano or some other local cop. I could have used the help.

There were hardly any cars in the section of the school parking lot that was closest to the gym. I wasn't surprised, given that it was still early on a Sunday morning. In fact, the only two cars I saw were Grams's gray Corolla and, three or four spaces away, George's black sports car.

I raced around the school building, trying three different doors before I finally found one that opened. Once inside, I ran through the corridors, glad that I still knew my way around the building.

When I neared the gym's double doors, I slowed down. My heart was pounding, and my mouth was dry. As I grabbed one of the handles, I paused to take a few deep breaths.

Finally, I opened the door cautiously and peered inside. I had expected to find the gym in the same condition as the last time I'd been here: a busy, brightly lit space filled with activity.

Instead, the gym was strangely dark. Glancing up, I saw that the windows high above the bleachers had been covered with black paper.

I blinked hard several times, trying to get my eyes to adjust to my dimly lit surroundings. Gradually, I was able to see that there were spots of light in the cavernous space: candles flickering in the windows of the haunted house, pale lights behind the grotesque grins of the jack-o'-lanterns scattered across the fake lawn, strings of orange, pumpkin-shaped lights draped throughout the room.

I had already decided that my strategy should be to start out acting as if nothing was wrong.

"Grams, are you here?" I called gaily. "It's me, Kate. I thought I'd stop by to see how Halloween Hollow is shaping up!"

"Stop right there!" I heard George's voice reply. "I've got your grandmother. And I've got a gun! Don't come any closer or you'll both be sorry!"

Chapter 17

The Joy Ice Cream Cone Company was founded in 1918 by a Lebanese immigrant named Albert George when he and members of his family bought second-hand cone-baking machines and started the George & Thomas Cone Company. Today it is the world's largest ice cream cone company. It produces over 1.5 billion cones a year.

—*https://www.joycone.com/about-us*

It took me a few seconds to locate him. I could barely make out his silhouette, since he was standing behind one of the gnarled trees at the side of the haunted house, half-hidden by shadows. I could also see part of someone else's head, close to his shoulder as if he was grasping that person with one arm.

Grams.

I felt sick. I knew I had to react, to do something. But I still didn't know enough about what was going on to know what that should be.

"What's going on, George?" I asked, trying to sound as calm as I could. "It seems there's been some kind of misunderstanding—"

"There's no misunderstanding," he interrupted, his voice seething with anger. "I know all about everything you've been up to. I've been tracking every move you've made over the past week, ever since you showed up at Alpha."

I gasped. "How did you know about that?"

His response was a cold laugh. "I know everything that goes on there," he replied. "I had my company's offices out-fitted with the best security system in the world. I watched you show up there myself, in real time. Frankly, I was aston-ished when your face appeared on my computer screen."

The man tracks the comings and goings of everyone who works at his company, I marveled. He even monitors every outsider who comes in—including me.

"I immediately got a bad feeling about what you were up to," he went on. "Why else would you be poking around the place where Savannah Crane worked? And when I came to Caroline's house for dinner, you were totally up front about taking it upon yourself to play the role of amateur sleuth.

"So I started paying even closer attention," he continued, "not only to you, but also to everything else that was going on at Alpha. Which is how I happened to catch Cornelia Jameson sneaking around the offices yesterday, going through files. Even *my* files! As if I'd be foolish enough to leave a paper trail, especially after the way all this has played out! But that woman has crossed a line. I can assure you that she'll be fired first thing tomorrow."

She might not want to work there anymore anyway, I was thinking. That is, if Alpha Industries even *exists* after all this comes out . . .

"And, of course, I heard the phone conversations the two of you had about Hudson Hideaways," George declared.

"You bugged her cell phone?" I asked, aghast.

"I don't need to bug anyone's phones," he jeered. "Not when I can already hear every word that's spoken within the walls of my company."

But before I had a chance to reconstruct our conversations

in my mind, he added, "I also know that you've been stalking my son. He told me you showed up at his place in Cold Spring the day after Savannah Crane died. He said he also caught you sneaking around his property on Friday night. He thought he heard a prowler, and when he looked out the window, he saw you driving away in your truck."

I noticed that George had referred to the Cold Spring house as Timothy's place.

"That house doesn't belong to your son," I insisted. "It's Savannah's."

Another icy laugh. "Who do you think financed their little love nest, back when it looked as if the two of them were going to be together forever?" Speaking more to himself than to me, he added, "As if that little fool could have afforded a house on her own! She never was someone who understood the importance of money."

"But your son did," I said as matter-of-factly as I could. "He was certainly helpful with the Hudson Hideaways development."

"My son had nothing to do with that project!" George insisted, sounding offended. "Aside from getting a few people to invest in it, that is. He even invested in it himself. He had no idea about the, shall we say, *complications* that surrounded it."

So George knew I'd learned about his shady Hudson Hideaways deal. I was wondering whether he also knew that I'd identified him as Savannah's killer when he said, "Since you found out about Hudson Hideaways in such short order, I knew it was only a question of time before you figured out why that vile woman had to die—and whose job it was to make sure that happened. Then I drove by your shop this morning and saw that person from the film crew walking in, the one who seemed to be running things. I knew you were on the verge of figuring out who the extra Lickety Splits employee was. And that you'd be running to the police as fast as you could, determined to be a hero.

"But what happened to Savannah was her own fault," he continued. "She was on the verge of becoming a big movie star, someone the press would have listened to. Someone all her fans would have been willing to support in whatever she did. She knew that as well as I did. If she'd only agreed to keep her mouth shut, all I'd have had to deal with were a few local tree huggers that my lawyers could have taken care of. And she could have gone on to become the big movie star she wanted to be. But she wouldn't listen. She was determined to use her new star status to blow this up into a national story.

"That stupid girl intended to ruin me!" George cried, spitting out his words. "Going public with what she considered the scandal of the century! She was too naïve to understand that what I was doing was merely business as usual. Alpha has done hundreds of development projects, and believe me, this isn't the first time we've cut some corners. That's simply the way things are done in property development. Hardworking, forward-thinking people like me work together with other like-minded people, sometimes behind the scenes, to accomplish things that some folks in the community might not appreciate until they've actually been achieved. And if people like me can make a little money that way, then good for us.

"And that idiotic actress had no idea how many people— *good* people—would have been decimated if she'd opened her big mouth," he continued. "Not only me, either. She probably would have destroyed my son's reputation. Then there are all the local officials who had enough vision to be willing to, shall we say, break a few rules in order to make my beautiful new development become a reality."

"Did you move to the Hudson Valley just to make sure Savannah Crane didn't ruin your development deal—and your reputation?" I asked.

"I've had ties to this area for years," he replied. "When I decided to cut back on hours—go into semi-retirement, in a way—this was the obvious place to settle. Then I met your grandmother and, through her, met you and found out that the movie Savannah was making was being filmed in your shop. The perfect opportunity had just fallen into my lap. How could I *not* take advantage of it?"

With a self-satisfied chuckle, he added, "And I've managed to commit what's commonly known as the perfect crime. No one would have ever suspected me. That is, until you came along."

I swallowed hard. "So what happens now?"

He laughed coldly. "You're about to have an unfortunate accident. One that involves a fatal fall." He paused, then said, "And the fact that I'm holding a gun on your beloved grandmother means you're going to do everything I tell you to do so that can happen."

By that point, I was feeling light-headed. Panic was starting to get the best of me.

Stay calm! I instructed myself, taking deep breaths. You need to think your way out of this. Not only for your own sake, either. He's got Grams!

"And we'll start by you going inside the haunted house," George said.

"Inside?" I repeated, the fear I'd been trying to fight off gripping me more ferociously than ever.

"I want you to walk through it, all the way to the back," he said. "And I'd suggest that you step it up. Your grandmother here is starting to look a little pale."

"Whatever you say," I said.

But I had a sense of what his plan was. And I was already hatching a plan of my own.

Walking through the gym toward the haunted house took

me past a disorganized mishmash of supplies. The haphazard pile included building materials, fabric, paper streamers, and several cardboard cartons. One of those cartons, I knew, contained the ingredients for the ice cream sundae station that I'd dropped off a week earlier.

I spotted the box as I walked by the heap. When I was about a foot away from it, I allowed my purse to slide off my shoulder, pretending it was accidental. Quickly I dipped down to grab it. As I did, I picked up something else as well.

And then I had no choice but to go inside the haunted house.

I shuddered as I passed beneath the skull that was hanging over the front door.

It's fake, I reminded myself, noticing that it was glowing in the dim light. Don't even look at it.

As soon as I opened the door, I saw that it was dark enough inside the house that I was going to have difficulty making out my surroundings. My eyes still hadn't adjusted as I stepped inside.

Immediately something white and ghostlike swooshed in front of me, brushing against my face.

"Agh-h-h-h!" I yelled, feeling my pulse triple.

Also not real, I told myself, taking more of those deep breaths. I vaguely remembered George mentioning that he was trying to figure out how to create an effect like that. He'd clearly figured it out.

I assumed that the place was rigged up to be motion sensitive because as I took a few more steps, a strobe light suddenly came on. The effect of the quickly blinking light was jarring. Especially because the room immediately began filling up with puffs of white fog.

The fog machine, I reminded myself. It's nothing more than a silly effect, one that's right out of a Grade B horror movie.

Somehow, it was very effective.

And then I heard strange sounds, soft at first, but quickly growing louder and louder. Low, eerie moans that sounded as if they were coming from something that wasn't quite human. And then, abruptly, the almost hypnotic sound was interrupted by the clanking of chains. I let out a yelp.

"Keep going!" I heard George yell. "Caroline and I are coming into the house right behind you. I've still got a gun on her!"

I hesitated, wondering if I was making a mistake by walking right into the trap that George had obviously set for me. But I didn't have much choice, since he was holding my grandmother at gunpoint. And I was still hoping that I could outsmart him.

I took a few more steps. And felt something brush against my face once again.

But this time it wasn't silky, like the ghost. This was rubbery and cold and—

Spiders! Dozens of spiders were dangling in front of me, the strobe light making them look as if they were swarming around me like bees.

I let out a shriek.

"You're taking too long!" George called to me, his voice angrier than before.

"I'm doing my best," I called back to him weakly.

I did begin to move more quickly, largely to get away from the chilling cloud of spiders brushing against my face and my neck and shoulders. I passed into a second room.

At least there was no strobe light in this one. The light in here was dim, though, just bright enough for me to make out an elaborate chandelier dripping with cobwebs. One wall was mirrors behind a line of life-size skeletons and ghouls and other creepy beings. They stood in pairs on small, rotating platforms that made it appear that they were dancing in front of it. Their dressy evening clothes were tattered, their hair was wild, and their expressions crazed. Soft music played in the background, just off-key enough to sound unpleasant.

And then I felt someone touch me.

I let out another cry, automatically jumping away. It was only then that I saw it was a dry, shriveled hand that jutted out of the wall and was rigged up to grasp whoever walked by.

By that point, I was more than ready to get out of there.

"Where are you?" I demanded. "And where's Grams?"

"We're right behind you," George replied. "Keep going. You're almost there."

I hurried through the ballroom, taking care not to step on the boney feet of the skeleton that was whirling around in front of me, the shreds of its pink skirt dragging on the floor.

Finally, I spotted a door and rushed toward it. As soon as I stepped through it, I encountered a wooden staircase.

I glanced up and saw that it led to the top of the foam pit.

Just as I'd anticipated, this was where George expected me to have my fatal fall.

"Go up the stairs," George commanded.

I began to climb the stairs, every muscle in my body as tense as a tightrope. My mouth was dry, my stomach knotted, and my heart was pounding with sickening force. As I neared the top, I loosened the top of the small bottle I'd grabbed from my box of ice cream ingredients. I desperately hoped I could manage to pull off what I'd planned. But there was one major problem: I didn't know how I could accomplish it without putting Grams at risk.

When I reached the top of the staircase, I found myself standing on the ledge that surrounded the foam pit, just as I'd expected. The deep wooden bowl was still only partly constructed. It was also in the exact condition I'd been anticipating: completely empty.

The gaping hole below me was only half painted, with the boxes of foam rubber that would eventually fill it still stacked up on the ledge that encircled it. Planks of wood jutted out from the sides treacherously. The people who were building this foam pit clearly had a lot of work to do before it would be safe for anyone to use.

I could hear George coming up the stairs. When he reached the top, I saw that he was alone.

"Where's Grams?" I demanded. "What have you done with her?"

He laughed. "She's not here."

I blinked. "But I saw her—"

"What you saw was one of those ridiculous dummies your niece made," he countered gruffly. "That woman hasn't been here the whole time. She's off in some other part of the building, doing an errand I sent her off on."

So he had lied about Grams being held at gunpoint. I was greatly relieved.

I was also relieved that he didn't appear to have a gun after all.

"Here's the plan," he went on, his mouth twisting into an evil grin. "That unfortunate accident I mentioned? You're going to lose your balance and fall into this pit. It'll be a pretty big fall, and the wooden surface is hard. But it won't be enough to kill you. What's going to accomplish that is you getting hit in the head as you go down by one of those two-by-four pieces of wood jutting out." His grin widened as he added, "At least that's what it will look like. What will really happen is that I'm going to give this process a little help."

And then he lunged toward me. He was still at least ten feet away, which gave me just enough time to screw off the lid of the bottle in my hand and spill out dozens of tiny sugar pearls, each one a perfectly round little ball.

George was either too distracted to notice what I'd done or too confused to figure out what it meant, because he kept coming toward me. In the second or two he was in motion, I noticed that he was wearing the same shiny black loafers I'd seen him wear before.

Loafers that no doubt had a slick leather bottom.

Which turned out to be extremely advantageous, since once he was almost close enough to grab me, he instead began slipping and sliding as those smooth soles encountered what amounted to a sheet of treacherous little BBs.

The way his arms flailed around as he tried to regain his balance was almost comical, making him look like a character in a Looney Tunes cartoon. He was also making a noise that made him sound like one: "Who-o-o-oa!"

And then, just as I'd hoped, he slid off the ledge and down into the pit. His head didn't make contact with the wooden planks, the scenario he'd had in mind for me. But when he finally hit the bottom, his leg was twisted in a grotesque way that told me he had most likely broken it.

"Ow-w-w-w!" he yelled. "Help me! I can't get up! Get me out of here!"

But I was too busy dialing 911.

I'd just been assured that both the police and an ambulance were on their way when I heard Grams's voice call, "Katydid? Are you all right? What on earth is going on?"

I saw her standing in the doorway to the gym, holding an armful of construction paper and glue and other supplies. The expression on her face was one of total confusion.

"Is George still here?" she asked. "And for heaven's sake, what are you doing up there? You should come down immediately before you get hurt!"

I had no problem with doing exactly that.

Fifteen minutes later, Grams and I were standing together with our arms around each other, watching two EMTs transport George Vernon Scott out of the gym on a gurney. Officer Pete Bonano had handcuffed him to the edge even though it didn't look like he was going anywhere, given how twisted his leg was.

"He's going to be fine, once he gets that leg taken care of," Pete Bonano said as he strolled over to us. "He'll certainly be in good enough shape to stand trial."

And then someone else came over to us, someone who had showed up at the gym mere minutes after I'd called 911.

"I'm not sure whether or not to thank you," Detective Stoltz told me begrudgingly. "The good news is that you figured out who poisoned Savannah Crane and then managed to catch the killer. The bad news is that you almost got killed yourself in the process."

"But that didn't happen," I pointed out. Trying to add a little levity to the occasion, I added, "And once again, my passion for ice cream saved the day. Can you imagine that there are some people who don't understand how important the regular consumption of ice cream can be to a person's health and safety?"

Detective Stoltz didn't look the least bit amused. In fact, he just sort of grunted. Then he turned and walked away.

But when he had almost reached the double doors, he stopped and turned back. "Good job, Ms. McKay," he called. And then he left.

Once Grams and I were alone, she seemed to crumple, her shoulders sagging as she covered her face with her hands.

"Oh, Kate, I feel like such a fool!" she wailed. "How could I have ever been silly enough to fall for a man like that?"

"George is someone who's very good at covering up who he really is," I assured her. "He's been deceiving a lot of people for a very long time."

Sadly, I added, "Unfortunately, Savannah Crane was one of the few people who *wasn't* deceived. And in the end, it cost her her life."

We were both silent for a while, still thinking about the

horrific events of the past week and a half. Finally, I took a deep breath and slung my arm around Grams's shoulders.

"Come on, Grams," I said. "Let's go home."

Grams looked astonished. "Go home? When there's still so much to do? I've got my painting crew coming any minute now, and I have to be around to tell them which walls to make black and which ones to make gray. Then there's Arnie, a crackerjack bingo player who happens to be a retired electrician. He's going to help put in more lighting. And Marilou is a top-notch seamstress, and she's going to be making costumes for some of the other volunteers to wear . . ."

I started to protest, then stopped myself. My grandmother, I could see, was as unstoppable as I was.

I held up my hands. "I've got an extra pair of these, in case you need them," I told her.

"I can always use more help," Grams replied, smiling. "Any chance you're as handy with a paintbrush as you are with an ice cream scoop?"

"Maybe I'm good with an ice cream scoop," I told her, "but that's nothing compared to what I can do with a few sprinkles."

Chapter 18

In Ireland and Scotland, ice cream cones are called
pokes. In other parts of Britain, they are called
cornets.

—en.wikipedia.org/wiki/Ice_cream_cone

Halloween had never seemed less scary. Or more fun.
The high school gym was swarming with elementary-
school–age kids, laughing and chattering away so enthusiastically that the noise level was nearly ear-shattering. All of
them were wearing costumes. I spotted clowns, pirates, prin-
cesses, mummies, ghosts, Disney characters, and at least six
different versions of Superman, all with a red cape. Some of
the parents, sitting on the bleachers or standing in clusters,
were also wearing costumes, or at least funny wigs or makeup.

I was pleased to see that there was a big crowd of children
around my do-it-yourself ice cream sundae station. It had
been clear from the moment the doors opened that it was
going to be a huge success. Not surprisingly, the fake eyeballs
and the gummy centipedes were turning out to be even more
popular than the M&Ms and Skittles. As for the volunteers
from the senior center who were helping the kids make the
craziest concoctions imaginable, they appeared to be having
even more fun than the little ones.

And the centerpiece for all the Halloween high jinks was
the glorious haunted house. Grams's brainchild was magnifi-

cent, somehow both cute and eerie at the same time. Every element had come out perfectly, from the glowing jack-o'-lanterns to the fake graveyard with its funny sayings. Even the foam pit behind the house looked enticing, thanks to the strings of pumpkin-shaped lights all around it. It was filled to the top with chunks of cushiony foam, and I could hear the children's laughter as they jumped into it—safely.

The schoolchildren weren't the only ones in disguise today. Emma had made good on her promise to whip up some fabulous costumes. She and I were both dressed as witches, wearing the classic, long black dresses they're known to favor. We also had tall black hats, rustic-looking brooms, and enough green makeup on our faces that the two of us were barely recognizable. I turned out to be excellent at cackling, a natural talent I'd never known I possessed. Emma wasn't bad, either.

As for Willow, she had gone the princess route. She had found, at a local thrift store, a shimmery floor-length blue dress with a full skirt. Emma had made it more princess-worthy by cutting the neckline more deeply, making the sleeves really puffy, and sewing twinkly silver sequins along the neckline and hem. Like us, Willow was barely recognizable, thanks to the long blond wig she wore over her pixie cut. Her silver tiara from a costume shop was the perfect finishing touch.

Grams had made her own costume. After all, the woman was undoubtedly the source of Emma's creativity genes. She had decided to come as Raggedy Ann, complete with a starched white apron, red-and-white-striped stockings, and a wig made of bright red yarn.

"This is so much fun!" Emma exclaimed as we stood by the front door, greeting the children as they came in and handing them each a goodie bag filled with toys and sweet treats. "And the kids really seem to be enjoying themselves!"

"They all look so cute in their costumes, too," Willow added. "Check out that pirate over there. He can't be more than six years old. He doesn't look very scary, does he?"

I looked over at the little boy she was talking about. Not only did he not look the least bit threatening, thanks to his mop of curly, orange-red hair and freckled cheeks; he was clearly miserable over the patch he was wearing on one eye, which kept slipping down. He finally grabbed it, yanked it off, and angrily stuffed it into his goodie bag.

"I guess he's more into the treats than the tricks," I said, laughing.

"I just know he's going to love the gummy centipedes," Willow added.

I turned to Grams. "You've really put together something amazing," I told her. "This was such a great idea. But now you'll have to do it every year!"

"It did come out well, didn't it?" she said.

She immediately grew silent. I had a feeling I knew why.

As much fun as the day was turning out to be, it couldn't help but be overshadowed by the events of the previous weeks. Especially by George Vernon. Or George Vernon Scott, to be more accurate.

Willow must have been reading my mind. "I've been meaning to ask you something," she said, nervously looking from me to Grams and back to me again. "How is that man doing? The one who—you know?"

"He's still in the hospital," I said. "But the doctors say he's going to be fine once his broken leg heals."

"He'll certainly be in good enough shape to go straight to jail as soon as he's on his feet again," Emma added. "He's been charged with the first-degree murder of Savannah Crane, the attempted murder of Kate, bribing public officials, breaking land-use laws, and a whole list of other things. It looks like he's going to be spending the rest of his life in jail.

"And he's not the only one who's in trouble," she added. "So are all the local politicians who were involved in this scam. But the best news is that they've already started taking down that horrible Hudson Hideaways project. The land is going back to being preserved, even though it'll take a long time for it to get back to its original state."

Turning to me, Willow said, "Kate, you deserve an award for solving this mystery. The others you've been involved in investigating on your own, too. They should build a statue of you in the Mashawam Preserve."

"I'm just glad this case is finally closed," I said. "Chelsea Atkins is, too. She flew back home to California as soon as Detective Stoltz told her it was okay to leave."

"What about Savannah's boyfriend?" Emma asked. "Is he going to get in trouble?"

"The authorities are definitely looking into the role he played in the Hudson Hideaways project," I told her. More to myself than to anyone else, I muttered, "I wonder if Amanda will still find Timothy attractive once he's been slammed with a bunch of felony charges."

"It sounds as if every last piece of the puzzle has been put in place, thanks to you," Emma said with a sigh. "Thank goodness that ugliness is behind us. Now we can all breathe freely."

"Here, here," Willow agreed.

Grams still looked troubled, however. I knew she was continuing to wrestle with the fact that she had actually been developing feelings for a man who turned out to be completely different from the person he appeared to be.

Talk about a Halloween disguise.

I had a feeling that it would be some time before Grams allowed herself to take another risk. But I was hoping that I'd be able to help her with that.

After all, I had come up with a decision of my own. One

that was very closely related since it involved the possibility of a broken heart.

At practically the same moment I had that thought, Sir Lancelot came through the door. That is, Sir Lancelot with Jake Pratt's face.

He was wearing a suit of armor, or at least pants and a shirt made out of shimmery silver fabric. He had on a head-piece, too, kind of a skullcap thing with silvery mesh hanging around the sides.

The finishing touch was a shield and a sword. Given their flimsy appearance, neither of them looked as if they'd serve him very well in a serious fight, not to mention a joust. Fortunately, it didn't look as if there were any possible challengers around, aside from a little boy of about seven I spotted who was also dressed as a knight. And he didn't look like he was about to challenge anyone. He was too busy pouring about a pint of caramel sauce over a baseball-size scoop of vanilla ice cream that was studded with eyeballs.

As Jake came over to us, he struck a knight-like pose, holding out his shield and raising his sword into the air.

"A knight?" I said, laughing. "Really?"

"Hey, I'm not just *any* knight," he countered, pretending to be offended. "I'm a knight in shining armor."

"Too bad I'm not in need of a rescuer at the moment," I commented.

"I've said this before, and I'll say it again," Jake replied seriously. "I've never thought of you as someone who needs rescuing, Kate."

He thought for a few seconds, then added, "Although you might do well to accept a little assistance whenever you're confronting a killer. By yourself. In a deserted place."

His voice thickened. "If anything ever happened to you, Kate, I don't know what I would do."

The intense look in his blue eyes made me feel as if he really was a knight in shining armor.

I guess Emma picked up on that vibe, because she abruptly said, "Grams, I think we should go check on the candy corn over at the ice cream table. It looks as if they're about to run out. Willow, could you please help us?"

"Certainly!" Willow quickly agreed, gathering up her voluminous blue skirt and skittering after them.

"That was subtle," Jake said, grinning.

"The members of my family aren't exactly known for their subtlety," I commented. I took a deep breath before adding, "Which is why I'm going to come right out and tell you what I've been thinking."

"Okay," Jake said nervously. I could tell from his expression that he didn't expect this to be good news.

"I think your plan to open the roadside stand is a great idea," I told him. "I have no doubt that it's going to do well. But I've decided that I don't want to be your business partner."

He thought for a few seconds. "I guess I'm not surprised," he finally said. "I was hoping for a different answer, of course, but—"

"There's more," I interrupted. "I haven't told you the reason."

He looked at me expectantly as I paused to take another deep breath. "It's because I want to try being your partner . . . in a *different* way."

The tension in his face immediately dissolved. But I wasn't sure I'd made myself clear.

"What I mean is—"

"I know what you mean," he said softly. "I know *exactly* what you mean."

And right there, in the middle of the high school gym, with

a couple of hundred little kids surrounding us, he took me in his arms and kissed me.

"Eww!" I heard a little girl cry. "That knight is kissing a witch! Those two don't belong together!"

I, however, thought the two of us made a fine pair.

Affogato

Affogato, an Italian word that means "drowned," combines two heavenly ingredients: ice cream and espresso. It sounds simple (and it is), but this basic recipe leaves plenty of room for creativity.

While chocolate, vanilla, and coffee are popular flavors for the ice cream, you can use any flavor that you think pairs well with coffee. You can also add Grand Marnier or Amaretto or another flavored liquor, top it off with berries, nuts, amaretti biscuits, or chocolate shavings, or add whatever else suits your fancy. (Chocolate-covered coffee beans, anyone?) You'll soon find yourself saying *"arrivederci"* to more ordinary desserts!

To make four servings:

1 pint of ice cream or gelato
4 shots (about 8 tablespoons) of hot espresso (regular or
    decaf)
whipping cream
sugar

Beat the whipping cream, adding sugar to taste. Scoop the ice cream into attractive serving dishes, pour the hot espresso over it, top with whipped cream and other add-ons, and serve immediately.

Baked Alaska

Baked Alaska is a fun dessert consisting of cold ice cream encased in a warm crust made of either pastry or, more commonly, meringue. It is also known as an *omelette à la norvégienne* or "Norwegian omelette," because Norway, like

Alaska, is cold in the winter. Other names are omelette surprise and *glace au four*.

There are many stories about how it got its name. A popular one is that Charles Ranhofer, chef at the legendary New York City restaurant Delmonico's, named his version Alaska, Florida in 1894 because of its combination of cold and hot.

While the dessert is wonderfully dramatic, it's also easy to make. The most important thing is to keep the ice cream and the cake as cold as possible. One trick is to make the cake base in advance, wrap it up tightly, and freeze it.

4 egg whites
⅛ teaspoon of cream of tartar
½ cup of sugar
1 quart of hard ice cream (you can use more than one flavor)
8-inch-wide, round layer of pound cake, brownies, or other cake, preferably frozen

Beat the egg whites until they are very stiff, gradually adding the cream of tartar and sugar.

Cover the cake layer with the ice cream, arranging it to get the shape you want. One option is to press the ice cream into a bowl and freeze it, creating a dome-shaped ice cream layer.

Cover the ice cream and the side of the cake with the meringue. Sprinkle the meringue with chopped nuts or coconut, if desired.

Bake at 500 degrees Fahrenheit for 5 to 10 minutes, until the tips of the meringue begin to brown. Be sure to keep an eye on it! Serve immediately.

ALLAH'S BOMB

ALSO BY AL J. VENTER

NONFICTION

The Terror Fighters (1969)

Underwater Africa (1971)

Report on Portugal's War in Guiné-Bissau (1973)

Underwater Seychelles (1973)

Portugal's Guerrilla War (1973)

Under the Indian Ocean (1973)

Africa at War (1974)

The Zambezi Salient (1974)

Coloured: Profile of Two Million South Africans (1974)

Africa Today (1977)

Challenge: South Africa in the African Revolutionary Context (1988)

Underwater Mauritius (1989)

War in Angola (1992)

The Chopper Boys: Helicopter Warfare in Africa (1994)

The Iraqi War Debrief: Why Saddam Hussein Was Toppled (2004)

Iran's Nuclear Option: Tehran's Quest for the Atom Bomb (2005)

War Dog: Fighting Other People's Wars (2006)

Cops: Cheating Death (2007)

Diving with Sharks (2007)

FICTION

Soldier of Fortune (1980)

ALLAH'S BOMB

THE ISLAMIC QUEST FOR NUCLEAR WEAPONS

AL J. VENTER

The Lyons Press

Guilford, CT 06437
An imprint of The Globe Pequot Press

The Lyons Press is an imprint of The Globe Pequot Press.

10 9 8 7 6 5 4 3 2 1

Printed in the United States of America

ISBN 978-1-59921-205-0

Library of Congress Cataloging-in-Publication data is available on file.

FOR MARILYN
This could never have happened without you.

A NOTE:

The use of the Divine in the title of this book, *Allah's Bomb*, is neither irreverent nor is it demeaning. On the contrary, its use indicates great respect for the Will of God. Indeed, the average Muslim in the Near East, Europe, or North America will tell you that Islamic states—like their Western or Asian counterparts—have every right to pursue whatever scientific discipline they choose, nuclear included. "It is Allah's Will," they will proudly say. There are also those among them who might even add a touch of rhetoric by quoting one of the most notable phrases from the Qur'an, that most Holy of Books. *Bismillah al rahman al rahim* is the expression most likely to be used, and it is always uttered piously. In the fundamental Arabic idiom of today, the phrase declares that it is God Who decides everything.

CONTENTS

PROLOGUE

A book covering as vast and complex a Middle East and Islamic panoply like this one deserves a personal note.

Since I've been to war, literally, with both Arab and Jew, I should start with the 1982 invasion of Lebanon by the Israeli Defense Force, or as we all called it, the IDF. That conflict, which resulted in thousands of deaths, followed a botched assassination attempt on the life of Shlomo Argov, Israel's ambassador in London.

The invasion took Israeli troops all the way to Beirut, and me and British cameraman George De'Ath with it. In Lebanon we moved about those parts of the country that had been "occupied" by the IDF very much as the mood took us, traveling in a car rented at Hertz in Tel Aviv, like we hacks used to do in those days. Sometimes, when the going became a little hairy, we'd attach ourselves to one of the convoys moving along the coast. Other times, in the interior where the Israeli military presence was sparse, we didn't bother.

In a sense we were "embedded," though we didn't have the customary IDF minder appointed to journalists who worked with the army. Consequently, we were able to come and go just about as we pleased, usually entering Lebanon at the restricted border post at Rosh HaNiqra.

Getting into an IDF camp inside the embattled state was another matter: though they knew exactly who we were, there were M16s pointed at all our heads until we'd passed the final barrier that led inside. These people took no chances; too many lives had already been lost because of slack security.

Once in Beirut, an IDF headquarters was established at Baabda, a not altogether appropriate choice because Lebanon's presidential palace was only a short distance away. The operation itself was code-named "Peace for the Galilee," which we journalists thought hilarious. In a lighter, beer-infused moment, one of the wags declared that whoever back in Jerusalem had thought that one out deserved an award for idiocy. Peace, he declared over drinks at the bar of West Beirut's Commodore Hotel, was as likely to break out in the Levant just then as the prospect of seeing Yasser Arafat riding stark naked on the back of a white stallion down Beirut's Corniche.

For all that, these were interesting times. I was in and out of Beirut, both with the Israelis and with militia forces on either side of the Green Line. All of us became targets at some time or another, though the Commodore, tucked away behind an array of taller buildings, was spared much of the nightly shelling that we'd listen to from our beds, very much as people in other parts of the globe would hear their dogs bark.

While conflict continued, we'd drive down along the coastal highway—or what was left of it—through Tyre and Sidon, sometimes twice a day. I also spent a week on board an Israeli gunship, patrolling the coast for infiltrators. The crew must have numbered about a dozen, and the oldest on board was its captain who couldn't have been more than twenty-two. That's the way this war was fought.

Lebanon's Chouf Mountains were part of it. There I witnessed an impromptu exchange of the remains of former combatants between an IDF unit and a bunch of Druze combatants who didn't take kindly to my camera. The two sides exchanged clusters of bones, most of them gathered together in numbered plastic packages. It was a poignant experience, Druze families of the long-lost gathered together in a pathetic bunch in a nearby mountainside village.

After George left to go home—he always traveled first-class and would make a ritual of ordering Beluga caviar and a fine champagne after takeoff—subsequent peregrinations took me through to the eastern frontiers of Lebanon with Syria, and onto the snow-covered slopes of Mount Hebron with members of the UN NORBATT (Norwegian Battalion) contingent. Along the way I'd be stopped several times by people who called themselves Pasdaran, the forerunners of today's Hezbollah. Only afterwards was I to discover that Pasdaran is the security wing of Iran's Islamic Revolutionary Guard Corps, or, as it is better known, the IRGC.

After the Israelis pulled back into what they called their "Exclusion Zone" and Hezbollah's insurgency started in earnest, I went back to South Lebanon many times—often enough to get on first-name terms with Timur Goksel, the three-packs-of-Marlboro-a-day Turkish media officer at the UN base at Naqoura along the coast. I came out each time with mixed feelings.

One lasting impression of these adventures has remained fixed in my mind all these years—and that was the implacable hatred that the combatants had for each other. The emotion was so tangible you could almost touch it. I realized only long afterwards that while odium, revulsion even, was as much a part of conflict as the situations that created mindless violence, one also sometimes encounters antipathy. But this war was different. I'd covered others—in the Middle East, in parts of Africa and Central America, and elsewhere—but never had I found the sentiments of those involved so totally debased.

At the various Israeli military bases where I would sometimes spend a night, we'd discuss the goings-on among us: the side bombs, Arafat's Al Fatah, the daily ambushes, sniping, the Christian Phalanghists, as well as the systematic killing of one group by another that we only afterwards came to regard as ethnic cleansing. That side of things seemed to have become a feature of hostilities between ethnic Arabs and Christians in this largely mountainside enclave hedged in by Syria and Israel.

Jewish soldiers, it seems, took things a step further, probably because they were following examples set by their parents only a generation before. There wasn't a man among them who hadn't lost a relative in those earlier battles. Many of these troops were reservists, quite a few into middle age. One and all, they regarded the enemy that opposed their presence as subhuman. *Like animals* was something I was to hear often.

Being a visiting foreign correspondent, I'd also spend time with groups of Arab fighters who made up the hundred-odd factions then battling for control of the embattled Lebanon of the early 1980s. Moving between the two groups of combatants presented problems, if only because Western journalists are invariably suspected by Third Worlders—even today—of being spooks. It was also a time when it had become fashionable to grab them as hostages. So like the rest of the media contingent in Lebanon at the time, I tended to tread warily.

I'd also discuss the war with some of the Arab irregulars I encountered—at least those who could manage passable English. But these exchanges had limitations, because even the mention of the word *Israel* would elicit contempt. To most of these zealots, who later became Jihadists, the only word that would do was *Palestine*. It was made quite clear that it would be in all of our best interests if I never forgot that vital minutiae of protocol.

In a sense, it was a bit like my more recent visit to Syria. With a small group of passengers on a local flight, we'd come into Damascus from Larnaca in Cyprus. The only problem was that some of the luggage had gone missing. After a good deal of obfuscation from the most bureaucratically hidebound regime in the Middle East, we were able to establish—horror of horrors—that the bags had erroneously landed in Israel. And because the word *Israel* simply does not exist in the Syrian lexicon—as in George Orwell's famous *1984*, the Jewish Homeland had become an "uncountry"—it took a while to sort out that mess.

Looking back over the years, I see now that the real tragedy faced by both sides was that neither even began to consider that those who opposed them were people, ordinary people, very much like themselves. They too had families, mothers, grandparents, and others who loved them. Many were married with children. That most fundamental of human traits simply never entered the picture, which in this compassionate day and age is tragic beyond compare.

I heard it on both sides of the front, and the language was identical: *They are all barbarians . . . they must be slaughtered . . . their bones must be left to rot for the dogs . . .*

The same theme was constantly reiterated. Which begs the question: When people have such severe views, how does anybody begin to contemplate a settlement? More to the point, could peace ever become a reality in such an emotionally embroiled environment?

That was the eighties. I've been back to Lebanon many times since. In the same week that Princess Diana died in a Parisian car crash, I was taken by car to a South Beirut Shiite stronghold to meet Ibrahim Moussawi, the spokesman for the Hezbollah guerrilla group. The assignation was certainly not helped by the fact that while in the country, I'd been the guest of General Émile Lahoud, then head of the Lebanese armed forces and soon to become its president.

In Moussawi, I found a charming, quiet-spoken Muslim cleric who knew all that he needed to know about me and probably a good deal more, including the fact that only weeks before I'd spent time in an IDF forward base along the Lebanese frontier near Metullah. Asked about Hezbollah's war against the Jewish State, he was almost dismissive: "Just a question of time," he declared with a smile, "and then there will be no more Israel . . . only Palestine . . ."

Since I was on his turf, I couldn't argue. In any event, my brief was a profile of the guerrilla movement for *Jane's Defense Weekly*, and, as it later turned out, quite a good one. To the chagrin of my Israeli friends, I predicted a withdrawal of the IDF from their exclusion zone a year hence. I was off by about a week.

My single lasting impression of the Moussawi meeting—and others, before and after—was that there can never be peace in the Middle East as long as a Jewish Homeland exists. The fanaticism I encountered—in Lebanese military camps, at Hezbollah strong-points south of Sidon and Tyre and along the hills adjoining the Litani River (where there are enough antipersonnel land mines buried in the shallow soil to start another war)—was almost corporeal. There was no letup to this fanaticism, not for a moment.

Nor are you likely to find many run-of-the-mill Israelis on the streets of Haifa, Tel Aviv, or Beersheva who have a kind word to say about their Arab neighbors. The word *intransigence* was coined for today's Middle East.

None of it was for effect, or to impress this visiting scribe. I found people in Syria, Egypt, the Sudan, and elsewhere in the Islamic world as dedicated to removing the State of Israel off the face of the map as the countermanding will to survive that I encountered among Jerusalem's leaders. But what is of real concern is that this new form of holocaust—for that's what it really is, an extermination program—gets the bulk of its inspiration from Iran. Which, essentially, is what this book is all about.

Iran's Supreme Spiritual Guide, Ayatollah Ali Khamenei, has told his people many times that the first objective of the Iranian nation is to reclaim the holy city of Jerusalem for Islam, which is instructive, because after Mecca and Medina, Jerusalem is the third-holiest city in the Islamic world. That issue is something that Khamenei always likes to stress when addressing the Iranian *Majlis* (or Parliament), usually with his head held high and fists clenched.

It is the same each time: "The country that is called Israel and all the Zionists who live there must be annihilated." To which members of the *Majlis*, almost as one, will rise from their seats, punching the air in front of them. The call that echoes through this great hall is in unison: *"Allah-u aqbar!"*—God is Great! We've seen it often enough on network television. Though much of it is grandstanding, what disturbs a lot of people is that these histrionics are a pretty constant theme in today's Tehran. And while these emotions might be condemned by some, we need only to recall events that took place in Europe a few generations earlier.

There, an obscure World War I corporal—born in Austria, mark you—displayed the same kind of racial prejudice that we now find prevalent in Tehran, Qom, Shiraz, Esfahan, and elsewhere in Iran. In his fervor, this so-called racial purist almost succeeded in ridding much of the continent of the people he hated. While comparisons, as the saying goes, are odious, Hitler's abhorrence of the Jews had the same intensity as that displayed by today's Supreme Spiritual leader of Iran and those who follow him.

Yet, closer to home, another dimension has surfaced in recent years, only this one doesn't have an Israeli appendage. Instead, it has to do with the West and is coupled with values held sacred by so many peoples of the developed world.

One example will do, and it deals with an event that took place in the largest teaching hospital in Riyadh, Saudi Arabia. Early in the new millennium, in one of the operating theaters, a complex procedure was taking place with a handful of Saudi surgeons and other staff gathered around a comatose figure. In an adjacent but distant corner, still in view of the medical team, was a television set tuned in to CNN. Nobody took any notice of the silent screen; the set was there for those taking a break, and the volume was turned down.

Suddenly somebody's attention was drawn to a news flash that was accompanied by images of a tall building in flames. Moments later the screen showed an explosion, followed by an aircraft striking the second tower. By now the broadcast had everybody's attention. Somebody turned up the sound, and it didn't take long for those watching to be made aware that this wasn't a Hollywood movie, nor was it a promo for some forthcoming TV event. What they were looking at was a real-time view of one of the historic events of our age.

While there must have been people in operating theaters, offices, workshops, and other places around the globe who watched the same scenes with great shock, our learned doctors in Riyadh reacted differently. As one of the Western nurses present at the time commented—like many other medical personnel, she was in Saudi Arabia on contract—it was like something out of a Three Stooges film. In a moment, the patient was totally forgotten while his doctors dropped their instruments, whooped, and hugged one another in joy. In unison they offered a great cheer for the Great Allah, after which they danced a jig around the operating table. This charade apparently went on for some minutes. I never did get to hear whether the medical team eventually got their act together enough to finish the procedure.

There were many such celebrations throughout the Saudi Kingdom that warm September night. In fact, there was jubilation throughout the Islamic world. Everywhere the word went out, the public was told that the Great Satan had suffered a terrible defeat. Details were only to emerge gradually, and with each disclosure, there would be more joy, more celebration, and further homage paid to Allah. It happened in Cairo, in Amman, in Damascus, and in dozens of Islamic cities, towns, and byways up and down North Africa, the Middle East, and central Asia.

INTRODUCTION

The *schadenfreude* displayed by a group of Islamic doctors at a Riyadh hospital following al-Qaeda's successful bombing of the Twin Towers might have been expected, if only because of the differences between these groups of people. The American experience in Iraq has suggested that the sooner the average American accepts this difference in cultures, the better it will be for his own country and for the world at large. As I've always told my own children, the world is a very different place out there. For a start, Islamic Jihadists feel a huge antipathy toward the West.

A fundamental issue linked to these diversities—which, after all, is what different nations and peoples are all about—is that Islamic societies generally deeply resent the kind of achievements that the West—and increasingly the East—have, with great labor and effort, worked for and adapted to their own particular social and cultural conditions. And let's not make too fine a point of this, these are things that we have also learned to cherish and, when the mood fits, enjoy.

It is the same with political systems that successive generations of Westerners—with the occasional (and sometimes monumental) glitch—have instituted for their societies and which kind of run their show. There are many factors that have enabled the Western world to gain and retain global dominance. While they battled through a succession of wars between them, their leaders were always wise enough to separate church from state. Also, they tended to keep their armed forces under democratic control. While this might be a small point, the arrangement, while not perfect, seems to have avoided the twin perils of theocracy and military dictatorship. Moreover, in almost all cases, economic progress has been based on the free market, which works best within the Western political, social, and legal framework.

Not so in the Arab world, where, since the eighth century, the common term of reference in any framework is the Qur'an. Also, within these communities, "might is inalienably right," and any opposition to the established authority is dealt with in brutal fashion. As a consequence, Arab societies stay mired in the kind of obsessive theocracies from which Christendom partially emerged after the Inquisition. You see it in the way they run feudal structures, many of which are nepotistic to its roots. You can also observe the way they treat their women, very often as inferior beings, particularly Wahhabist Saudis and fundamentalist sects.

More than half the women in the Arab world cannot read or write, and many are not allowed access to gainful employment. They don't even have the right to drive a car, or travel on public transport without an escort, usually a male relative. It is no better in Persian Iran, where the inappropriately named sex police can stop any female on the street and check to see if there is a single strand of hair protruding from her veil.

The problem linked to this kind of illogicality is that these very same people—the inheritors of a great Islamic culture that gave the world some fine traditions, the ability to navigate, and the same system of counting that we use in our everyday lives—have regressed. When last did you hear of something original that might have had an Islamic tag to it? Have these people invented *anything* in the modern world that has been put to everyday use?

This shortcoming has resulted in a tremendous groundswell of resentment among Islamic people not only against Westerners—the same people who created almost all of the systems they use today, like aircraft, cars, computers, modern medicine, and so on—but more recently, increasingly against the East. Industrially, Japan, South Korea, China, and half a dozen other countries have taken on where the West left off. Again, our Islamic friends have become stragglers. They have their oil, but that, too, obviously with a profit motive, was "put on their plate," compliments of the industrialized West.

Stephen Ulph, my Arabist friend who lectures at West Point and is the founder-editor of *Jane's Islamic Affairs Analyst*, phrased it presciently in one of my earlier books.[1] In an essay titled "Arab Progress in Reverse," Ulph makes a rather succinct point: "[I]n a world region that is described as 'richer than it is developed,' the Arab states are alone in demonstrating not only relative weakness . . . but concrete signs of economic, intellectual and cultural regression." If this trend continues unchallenged, he suggests, "the future of the Arabs is likely to be permanently on hold."

His arguments are measured, and in typical Ulph fashion, spare nobody. He lays a lot of the blame for what is going on in the Middle East today at Israel's door, but the predicament in which our Islamic friends now find themselves is their responsibility alone. Ulph quotes Arab writer Mohammad Reza Shalguni, one of the few Oriental thinkers who has dared to go against the flow in his own country, where dissension in the recent past has often led to the ultimate punishment. Shalguni's perception is that since the middle of the twentieth century, "an increasing number of people in Islamic countries have concluded that the only way to escape the domination of the West is to adopt Western Culture." In some fundamentalist sectors, that might almost be equated with asking your best Jewish friend to eat pork.

Not without a strong element of self-deprecation, Shalguni emphasizes the misconception that underpins a culture based on widespread delusion. He writes that part and parcel of this is the titanic struggle "to defend ourselves against a new imperial constantly reinventing itself," a position, says Ulph, that was lampooned by another Arab writer, Hazem Saghiyeh, who contributes to the Pan-Arab *Al-Hayat*, published in London.

The Arab obsession of being bamboozled by the West is possibly best encapsulated by Saghiyeh's comment: "[W]hoever follows the news coming from Egypt—and the positions of most of Egypt's intellectuals, journalists and politicians—begins to think that the world wakes up every morning, rubs its eyes and exclaims: 'Oh my goodness, it's seven, I'm late, I have to start immediately to conspire against Egypt!'"

And these are the same people who now aspire to build nuclear weapons—the same people who might become the target of an Israeli preemptive nuclear strike. The full implications of such an act are simply too terrible to contemplate, but they are real enough to have found space in several Israeli publications recently.

Gill Hoffman[2] reported along these lines in *The Jerusalem Post*, when Ephraim Sneh, Israel's newly installed deputy minister of defense (and a former brigadier-general in the Israeli Defense Force), was quoted. It was Sneh's view that sanctions against Iran were unlikely to work, so Israel must be prepared to thwart Tehran's drive for a nuclear capability "at all costs." Sneh went on: "I am not advocating an Israeli preemptive military action against Iran, and I am aware of all of its possible repercussions; I consider it a last resort. *But even the last resort is sometimes the only resort.*" (author's italics)

One man who phrased it well was Uri Avnery, former publisher and editor-in-chief of the news magazine *Haolam Hazeh*, and who also served three terms in the Knesset (the Israeli Parliament). In an article titled "Who Is Afraid of the Iranian Bomb?" he encapsulated the sentiment of millions of Israelis when he wrote that "if a small and primitive nuclear weapon of the Hiroshima type falls on the building where I live, a large part of the Israeli population will be annihilated. Two or three such bombs are enough to put an end to Israel (together with the neighboring Palestinian territories)."

Avnery's comments begin to make sense when you recall a "sermon" delivered at Tehran University a few years ago by the former Iranian president, Akbar Hashemi Rafsanjani. His words, quoted elsewhere in this book, were to the effect that "if one day . . . the world of Islam is mutually equipped with the kind of weapons which Israel presently possesses, the world's arrogant [colonialist] strategy will then come to a dead end, because the use of an atomic bomb on Israel won't leave anything; however, in the world of Islam [use of a bomb] will just cause harm, and this scenario is not far-fetched." (This speech can be found on the Web in several alternative translations, as are some of Rafsanjani's other topics of discussion, which are equally extreme.)

That said, one simply has to accept that the implications of an Israeli preemptive strike on Iran's nuclear facilities are almost beyond the comprehension of today's mindset, whether it be in the West or the East. Such an attack would likely involve the entire international community, because in order to survive, Israel would almost certainly not hit only its most immediate target. There is a reasonable possibility that it would use the opportunity to neutralize all of the enemies that have been a consistent and niggling threat to the Jewish Homeland since its inception almost sixty years ago. As many as 200 million people or more could ultimately be affected.

And if that were to take place, Allah forbid, then who is to say that Russia, China, or even the United States would stand by and allow this carnage to happen? For a start, the globe's fuel supplies would be impeded not just for years, but possibly for generations. The situation, at its bottom line, is utterly untenable. Yet, as one of my Canadian friends declared, "It stares us in the face."

Nor has Russia been inactive. Moscow is again courting Islamic leaders, much as it did in the Soviet era when the arms-marketing giant, Rosvooruzheniye (today, Rosoboronexport), produced and exported thousands of combat aircraft, armored vehicles, warships, and nuclear missiles, built each year by a network of more than 1,700 research institutes, design centers, and manufacturing plants. Moscow called this monolith its "defense-industrial complex."

Today, these goings-on also include nuclear issues. While the nuclear reactor nearing completion at Bushehr on the Iranian Gulf coast is strictly civilian, its application—if not strictly monitored by either the Russians or an organization like the International Atomic Energy Agency—could be adapted to one of producing plutonium for atomic bombs. While Tehran vows that this will never happen, that it *could never* happen, memories are short. North Korea made exactly the same pledge in the past. We are all aware of what happened at an obscure mountainside site in the vicinity of Chik-tong, P'unggye-yok, in the north of the country during the fall of 2006. Mao Zedong wasn't the first leader to declare that the paper on which agreements are written can be easily discarded.

With this in mind, Egyptian president Hosni Mubarak visited Moscow in early November of 2006, looking for help to establish a domestic nuclear program. An atom bomb program wasn't part of it, members of his entourage assured the press, and not for the first time. There is much evidence (explored in chapter 16) that shows Cairo is not as lily-white as some would like us to believe. Whatever the truth, Russian Security Council secretary Igor Ivanov confirmed that Russia was indeed interested in any future program that involved building nuclear stations in Egypt.

"I expect that Egypt will announce an international tender and that, in competitive conditions, Russia will be successful," Ivanov declared with the aplomb that reflected a done deal. Meanwhile, Egyptian parties were hosted by Russia's state atomic energy agency, Rosatom. A spokesman for Rosatom said the Egyptian government had asked the Russian agency's export unit, Atomstroiexport, to submit a presentation, similar to ones that resulted in Moscow acquiring contracts to build reactors in China and India, as well as the Bushehr reactor in Iran. More recently, Russia landed a contract to build a new nuclear plant in Bulgaria worth more than $5 billion.

As part of the deal, this former Soviet state would train Egyptians at Russian nuclear establishments, very much as it is doing now with Iran, where there are scores (perhaps hundreds) of Iranians studying nuclear-related subjects at universities throughout the Federation.

Were this a matter that involved only governments, the international community could possibly deal with it. Instead, the issue also involves a potential terrorist element. That much was declared by Dr. Mohamed ElBaradei, head of the United Nations watchdog agency, the IAEA. Speaking in an interview with *Netwerk*, the Dutch television program, in May 2006, Dr. ElBaradei said that the world should be a lot more worried about nuclear weapons falling into the hands of terrorists than about Iran's nuclear program.

Dr. ElBaradei was insistent that there was no military solution to the standoff with Iran over its determination to continue its uranium-enrichment program. But, he added, the risk that terrorists could acquire a nuclear weapon was of even greater concern. "Terrorists are a different thing . . . the fear of [them] acquiring nuclear weapons is much more, in my view . . . than a country acquiring nuclear weapons right now."

Also of concern is an increasing number of incidents that involve internationally linked nuclear smugglers. According to the IAEA, there were fifty-eight such incidents in 2002. By the year 2005, the tally was heading for the two hundred mark. In 2004, it noted, Western security agencies had thwarted sixteen attempts to smuggle uranium or plutonium, which, when you do the sums, indicates a dismal success rate of about one interdiction in ten or twelve. And those are only the ones we know about.

Though I deal with nuclear smuggling and its long-term security implications in chapter 2, it is worth mentioning that IAEA investigators believe that the smugglers (who come mainly from former Eastern bloc countries) are interested only in making a quick buck. An IAEA report reads: "They fear that the criminals may have no qualms about selling to jihadist groups."

Al-Qaeda has also made no secret of its desire to obtain a dirty bomb. Its leader in Iraq, Abu Hamza al-Muhajir, called for scientists to join them and experiment with radioactive devices for use against Coalition troops. And let us not forget that even before the 2001 terror attacks, Osama bin Laden invited two Pakistani atomic scientists to visit a training camp in Afghanistan to discuss how to build a bomb using stolen plutonium (see chapter 1). This makes sense in light of the IAEA's sobering revelation that captured al-Qaeda leaders confessed to the CIA that they had attempted to smuggle a radioactive device into the U.S.

The most disturbing issue here is that there appears to be so much of it about. This writer was approached by two of his trading friends during a visit to Johannesburg in 2000. On offer were "two bricks of enriched uranium" held by a Rwandan businessman from Kigali and already smuggled into South Africa. The final price, they told me, had not yet been determined, but was well into five figures, payment in cash and in the inevitable U.S. dollars.

The consignment had originally come from Burundi, an embattled country with a history of violence, though with exceptionally close ties to the Democratic Republic of the Congo. Kigali has been a conduit for illegal Congolese goods for as long as anybody can remember. Though the offer might have been bogus, it could not simply be ignored, and the way law and order works in South Africa (or does not), the South African police are the last people to whom you should report something like this. There's a more-than-even chance *you'd* be the one that is arrested.

And then we had the dreaded Abdul Qadeer Khan, a brilliant Pakistani European-educated scientist who helped put his country's nuclear weapons program on the map. The trouble with A.Q. Khan was simple: He wasn't satisfied with the acclaim he received for that effort, so he established the largest international nuclear smuggling ring the world has ever seen. Khan's efforts also get a lot of attention within these pages, and though there was some satisfaction in Western intelligence when his operation was closed down, more recent reports show that although A.Q. Khan sits out his days under house arrest near Islamabad, this nefarious business continues under another guise.

Andrew Koch (formerly with Britain's Jane's Information Group) revealed some interesting information in July 2006. His report revealed that German, EU, and American officials were of the opinion that Iran had built an equivalent, if not larger, network than the original nuclear smuggling organization established over decades by Khan, to supply prohibited goods for its nuclear and ballistic missile programs.[3]

Quoting various sources, Koch stated that Tehran had principally been seeking material from European and Russian firms, but had included some of the Khan middlemen in the process. "In doing so," Koch explained, "Iran's new network is exploiting many of the same weaknesses and loopholes of the system that Khan's associates used."

In March 2006, for example, Koch said, "German authorities raided dozens of business locations suspected of being connected with illicit sales of nuclear-related goods to Iran in 2004 and 2005. Overall, German officials believe Iran has used as many as one hundred German front companies to help Tehran buy and illegally export a range of defense goods, from military items to nuclear technology. German authorities are prosecuting these and a number of other cases against those believed to have funneled nuclear goods and ballistic missile technology to Iran, as well as Libya and others."

Always on the button, Andrew Koch also revealed that "some of these other cases are part of Pakistani attempts to rebuild a network for supplying the needs of its own nuclear weapons program, which, for years, has relied on illicitly bought high-technology components. Intelligence officials said that this heightened procurement activity by Pakistani agents has been ongoing since at least 2004. What troubles European investigators, they say, is that they believe Pakistan appears to be buying more nuclear equipment than it needed to keep its own program going. Moreover," Koch noted, "because many of the procurement agents had worked for Khan, there are concerns that the nuclear wares could have ultimately been intended for Khan's foreign clients."

Makes you think, doesn't it?

Possibly the most immediate nuclear threat facing the world today is from a terror group exploding an RDD (radiological bomb) in one of the West's preeminent business centers, like Wall Street or London's banking center. Also referred to as a "dirty bomb," an RDD is designed to spread radioactive material over a large area by combining radioactive material with a conventional explosive. It does not involve a nuclear explosion and would be unlikely to result in many immediate deaths, but it could provoke widespread panic and render buildings in the affected area unusable.

Several of the more prominent authorities that I spoke to in compiling this work agree that this threat is imminent. These include Dr. Nic von Wielligh, who has been associated with the IAEA for decades (and spent two sessions on its board of governors), as well as my old pal, Dr. Mike Foley, a geologist specializing in nuclear-related issues at the Pacific Northwest National Laboratory, which hosted me on one of my many fact-finding missions for *Jane's International Defence Review*.

Though I deal with this subject in some detail in chapter 15, it's worth repeating Mike Foley's warning here: "Weapons-radioactive materials could be used in terror acts as pollutants rather than as fissionables." The reason why this is not being addressed, Foley suggests, is because the immense effort required would be extremely expensive. "It would need to expand coverage to everything, including radon waste storage sites, medical waste and the rest," he declared. Worse, there is an awful lot of radioactive waste about, not all of it safeguarded (and in the former Soviet Union, very badly).

An article in Britain's *New Scientist* spelled out some of the risks in its June 2004 issue, which included an IAEA report. This disclosed that there were more than 10,000 sources designed for radiotherapy, each containing 1,000 pellets of cobalt-60. Each pellet emits 100 gigabecquerels of radioactivity, enough to put somebody over their annual safety limit in two minutes. According to the report, "There are also tens of thousands of large radiation sources used by industry as gauges, sterilizers and metal irradiators." The IAEA also expressed particular concern about the security of hundreds of thermogenerators made in Russia and the U.S., in which the heat produced by radioactive decay drives a generator to provide power in remote areas. Just one of them can contain as much strontium-90 as was released by the notorious Chernobyl accident in 1986.

The IAEA's smuggling figures did not include radiation sources that have simply gone missing. "An average of one a day is reported to the U.S. Nuclear Regulatory Commission as lost, stolen or abandoned," read the report. Also, there were still one thousand radioactive sources unaccounted for in Iraq. Of twenty-five sources stolen from the Krakatau steel company in Indonesia in October 2000, only three have been recovered.

According to the IAEA report, "In Tbilisi, Georgia, a taxi driver, Tedo Makeria, stopped by police in May 2003 was found to be carrying lead-lined boxes containing strontium-90 and caesium-137. And in Belarus customs officials seized twenty-six radioactive cargoes between 1996 and 2003, six of them from Russia."

The good news is that so far, only two known incidents that could be classed as radiological terrorism have occurred in Russia. In 1995 Chechen rebels buried a caesium-137 source in Izmailovsky Park in Moscow. That was followed in 1998 when a container of radioactive materials attached to a mine was found by a railway line near Argun in Chechnya.

Even the most sanguine critic of Moscow's activities in Chechnya concedes today that it won't be very long before President Putin's government is faced with the real thing. That was echoed in 2003 when Eliza Manningham-Buller, director-general of the UK's counterintelligence agency, MI5, said it was "only a matter of time" before a crude attack against a major Western city took place.

It is perhaps appropriate that the last word on this issue should come from the International Atomic Energy Agency, which monitors trafficking and inspects nuclear plants to audit their radioactive materials (discussed in detail in chapter 14). Olli Heinonen, deputy director-general of the IAEA, declared not long ago that a dirty bomb was something that needed to be taken very seriously.

"We need to be prepared for anything, because anything could happen . . . terrorists look for the weakest link."

[1] Al J. Venter, *The Iraqi War Debrief*, Casemate Publishers, Philadelphia, 2004.

[2] Gill Hoffman, *The Jerusalem Post*, November 10, 2006.

[3] Andrew Koch, "Investigators Suspect Nuclear Smuggling Network Is Still Active," *Jane's Intelligence Review*, July 1, 2006.

THE VERY REAL THREAT OF NUCLEAR TERRORISM

Last March, the federal government set up a Web site to make public a vast archive of Iraqi documents captured during the war. The Bush administration did so under pressure from Congressional Republicans who had said they hoped to "leverage the Internet" to find new evidence of the prewar dangers posed by Saddam Hussein. But in recent weeks, the site has posted some documents that weapons experts say are a danger themselves: detailed accounts of Iraq's secret nuclear research before the 1991 Persian Gulf War. The documents, the experts say, constitute a basic guide to building an atom bomb.
—"U.S. Web Archive is Said to Reveal a Nuclear Primer," by William J. Broad, *The New York Times*, November 3, 2006

The documents, said Bill Broad, were roughly a dozen in number. He went on to explain that they contained charts, diagrams, and equations, as well as lengthy narratives about bomb building that nuclear experts say go beyond what is available elsewhere on the Internet and in other public forums. "For instance, the papers give detailed information on how to build nuclear firing circuits and triggering explosives, as well as the radioactive cores of atom bombs," Broad explained.

How they got into the public domain is another matter, and something that must have pleased a lot of people—as well as some countries that have recently shown themselves eager to achieve nuclear parity. And al-Qaeda as well, since Stephen Ulph, the London-based editor of *Jane's Islamic Affairs Analyst* and a lecturer at West Point, has repeatedly warned that there are many nuclear tidbits on this movement's Web site, including the basics of building the bomb.

Among documents posted on the Web (and since removed, following pressure from Europe as well as the International Atomic Energy Agency) was one marked "Draft FFCD Version 3 (20.12.95)." This signifies that it was preparatory for the "Full, Final, and Complete Disclosure" that Iraq made to United Nations inspectors in March 1996.

As Broad puts it, "The document carries three diagrams showing cross sections of bomb cores and their diameters." At one stage the site posted a document headed "Summary of technical achievements of Iraq's former nuclear program." Its pages included a good deal about the physical theory of nuclear weapons construction, as well as stuff on the atomic core and high-explosive experiments.

One senior European diplomat, who spoke to Broad on the condition of anonymity, equated U.S. actions to providing any potential enemy a "cookbook," and went on to say that "if you had this, it would short-circuit a lot of things."

For reference purposes, Stephen Ulph was able to pull some of this stuff from his files and it was remarkably explicit. Each was headed with a full-color promotional page, coupled to the appropriate course number, to which had been added the title: "Nuclear Preparation for Mujahideen: The Jihadi Nuclear Bomb." With diagrams, the course went into some detail about components, such as the role of a beryllium reflector in an atom bomb, a hollow plutonium "spark plug" and much else. Many other issues were dealt with in this 49-page document: there was even a breakdown of the MK.84 low frequency E-bomb together with the "lethal footprint" of such a weapon "in relation to altitude." Surprisingly, delivery profiles for GPS/Inertial guided weapons were also discussed.

Another section dealt with hardening a computer room against electronics attack, including instructions for fitting doors with electromagnetic seals. Attention was also given to the ubiquitous "dirty bomb."

It is on the study of ideological materials on the Internet that Ulph is the most forthright.[1] This is his area of abiding interest and he has made a competent study of it, which could be one of the reasons why he was asked to prepare a White paper on the subject for the United States Senate Select Committee on Intelligence. It could also be why a seven-man 60 Minutes crew beat a path to his London door in December 2006 to get him to explain the threat. His views are disconcerting.

For a start, Ulph feels strongly that the Islamic world is undergoing a massive and unopposed revolution to establish its future mindset and worldview.

Jihadis, he declares, "are blending propaganda and education with very thorough indoctrination procedures to shape this means of indoctrination faster and better than the West is able to oppose it. The Internet is their ideal open access distribution medium." As he says, "they have at least a decade head start on us."

Much of this perception comes from his years of research on what he terms the "Jihadi Curriculum" circulating around the ether on the web, and which is to be brought together in a book scheduled for publication in 2007. "It's nothing less than a comprehensive re-education program of books, treatises, encyclopedias and fatwas, meticulously constructed to undermine, re-orient and radicalize," he says.

It is also why normal young Islamic people in the West are persuaded to give up everything and commit suicide in dreadful acts of terror like London experienced in 2005 in its own version of 9/11. As somebody who knew these bombers said afterwards, "they were ordinary lads from ordinary homes."

"Hundreds of tailored works undermine the non-jihadi Muslim's self-image and confidence by attacking his education and his behaviour and detach him from his environment and associates. Accomplished tomes of history support the millenarian Clash of Civilizations, devalue democracy and pluralism and de-legitimize Muslim regimes, leaders and religious authorities. An avalanche of authoritative volumes push his religion's center of gravity towards militant Jihad, the "Absent Obligation" that overrides all other duties—to friends, to parents, to the rule of any secular law. And to fill the moral void, the reader is comforted with manual after manual of Jihad purporting to arm him with the culture, poetry and ethics of the new 'Mujahid Man.' There is enough of a library online," Ulph concludes, "for the reader never to have to leave the parallel universe the Jihadis are creating for themselves."

Ulph maintains that no one doubts the value of the security response to the Jihad phenomenon. "The issue is whether we start and finish in that arena." Up to now, Ulph explains, counter-terrorism has focused on the high profile pronouncements of Jihadi militants on web forums, while ignoring the over 60 percent of information traffic on the Jihadi websites which appear in their law, ethics, culture sections.

"Yet to pay close attention to these writings is not an obscure academic exercise. They are meticulously composed texts, and they are there for a reason. They have direct strategic and tactical implications."

The mujahideen, says Ulph, are devoting much effort to two things: ideological self-confidence and ideological self-defense against their opponents, because they know that this is the make or break issue for them.

"This is what the massive internet library—expanding by the week—is all about. It is a cultural race for the hearts and minds of all Muslims."

He then poses the same question that he asked the Senate Committee: If the mujahideen are investing in this, why aren't we?

"I think it is no exaggeration to say that this is the long-term battle arena—one which, in its significance and future ramifications, dwarfs the arena of bombs and bullets."

He illustrates the point: "Last autumn [2005] a posting on a Jihadi internet forum had this extraordinary title: 'The al-Qaeda organization is now finished.' But the writer then went on to explain: the Jihad is now entering on a new phase 'which the infidels are unaware of, or do not wish to believe.' It turns out that we infidels 'are still fixated on fighting individuals, oblivious to the fact that they are actually fighting an idea, one that has spread across the globe like fire and which is embraced even by those whose faith is a mustard seed.'"

Stephen Ulph sums it up: "There is indeed a bigger struggle going on, an intellectual civil war which we are being dragged into whether we like it or not. Why aren't we educating ourselves about this?"

Concern about Radiological Dispersal Devices (RDDs) intensified in May and June 2002 following revelations that senior al-Qaeda official Abu Zubaydah told his captors that al-Qaeda was interested in producing an RDD and knew how to do it. Adding to worries was the arrest not long before of the alleged al-Qaeda operative, Jose Padilla, in Chicago in May 2002. He was reportedly on a scouting mission for an al-Qaeda operation to attack the United States with an RDD.

Kevin O'Neill, former deputy director of Institute for Science and International Security (ISIS), had his own take on the possibility of terrorist groups acquiring the wherewithal to develop weapons of mass destruction. "Russia today cannot guarantee that nuclear explosive materials have not found their way to proliferating countries in the Middle East or to terrorists seeking nuclear weapons."

O'Neill went on: "The lack of security and accounting of these materials is one of the most troubling and immediate proliferation threats in the post–Cold War world." He added that the Russian economic free fall that began once the nation split into a dozen or more separate republics had a dramatic impact on Moscow's ability to implement upgrades at its nuclear sites. For example: "American Department of Energy officials relate stories of security guards at nuclear establishments leaving their posts to look for food. Also, there were numerous cases of inadequate clothing and heating units for guards, coupled with unreliable communications, as well as cuts to electricity supplies at the various sites housing nuclear materials," O'Neill said.

When I last spoke to him, it was his opinion that the situation has improved, "but that doesn't alter the fact that there was a time, fairly recently, when security gaps within the Russian establishment were horrific." The Americans had a hand in it by providing emergency rations, portable generators, warm clothes, and other items at sites participating in the upgrade programs.

Although it would be impossible to follow every lead that emerged out of the former Soviet Union, it is generally accepted that a lot of strategic material was either mislaid, misappropriated, or stolen during the changeover period. Moscow is full of stories of gangs operating on behalf of the local *mafiya*: You placed your order for whatever it was that you needed in the morning, and before nightfall you'd be told whether it could be filled or not, and what it would cost.

It hardly stretches credibility to accept that a fair proportion eventually found its way to countries like Syria, North Korea, Pakistan, Iraq (under Saddam Hussein), Libya, and, inevitably, Iran. Going solely by what was discovered in Afghanistan after the Taliban had been toppled, terror organizations like al-Qaeda were as much a part of this scenario as any of them.

The broadcast said that documents found in a Kabul building believed to have been used as a safe house by Osama bin Laden's al-Qaeda network contained details about how to produce nuclear weapons. While then U.S. Homeland Security Director Tom Ridge said the information could have been found on the Internet, and it did not necessarily mean bin Laden was able to build a nuclear device, he did concede that U.S. intelligence agencies were working on the matter. The documents, partly destroyed by fire, were in English, German, Arabic, and Urdu, one of the dialects in everyday use in Pakistan.[2]

We also have evidence that A.Q. Khan visited Afghanistan several times when the Taliban still ruled, though Pakistan remains schtumm about the reasons for his visits. Several sources maintain that he met with bin Laden and his lieutenants.

With regard to the fire-ravaged documents recovered in Kabul afterwards, nuclear experts quoted by *The Times* of London said that designs included in the documents suggested that al-Qaeda might have been working on a fission device, similar to the bomb dropped on Nagasaki in 1945. In the same report, the network noted, two Russian men had been arrested for trying to sell cobalt-60, a radioactive material that can be used to carry out radioactive terrorist attacks. Ivan Safranchuk, director of the Moscow branch office of the Center for Defense Information, told the BBC that this was not the first case of people being arrested for attempting to smuggle or sell radioactive materials. While the stuff could not be used for making a nuclear bomb, said Safranchuk, it could be used on a smaller scale, with conventional weapons that could spread radioactivity.

One of the most significant comments on developments in Afghanistan prior to the overthrow of the Taliban came from ISIS president David Albright. In a talk hosted by the Nautilus Institute in January 2002, and titled "Al-Qaeda's Nuclear Program: Through the Window of Seized Documents," Albright said that al-Qaeda managed to develop only limited technological capabilities to produce WMD while it was in this Central Asian state.

However, he declared, "if al-Qaeda had remained there, it would have likely acquired nuclear weapons eventually," adding that the revolutionary movement viewed the acquisition of WMD as a religious obligation. Albright suggested that:

> It could develop only limited technological capabilities in Afghanistan to produce WMD, and few believe al-Qaeda obtained nuclear weapons while it was entrenched there. On the other hand, al-Qaeda's determination to get nuclear weapons, along with its increased ability to obtain outside technical assistance, led to the conclusion that if al-Qaeda had remained in Afghanistan, it would have eventually acquired nuclear weapons.

He concluded with the comment that although al-Qaeda's WMD efforts were in disarray, it remained determined to get WMD.

Also found in Afghanistan, Albright disclosed, were instruction manuals to train recruits to make and use a wide variety of conventional explosives. There were pictures or schematics of intended targets, including nuclear power plants.

In November 2001, says Albright, CNN found an Arabic document titled "Superbomb" in the home of Abu Khabbab, the code name of a senior al-Qaeda official. This document, which was assessed by Albright in cooperation with CNN, had sections that were relatively sophisticated and others that were remarkably inaccurate or naive. More than twenty-five neatly handwritten pages, its unknown author discusses various types of nuclear weapons, the physics of nuclear explosions, properties of nuclear materials needed to make them, and the effects of nuclear weapons.

"It was not systematic in its coverage and [its] author sometimes covered some subjects in depth and others superficially or incorrectly . . . and many critical steps to make a nuclear weapon were missing from the document.

"[He] advocates the use of laser enrichment, which he claims is 'simple.' In reality, laser enrichment is incredibly complex to master. This indicates that [whoever wrote it] possessed only a rudimentary understanding of the knowledge to enrich uranium, or was trying to convince the reader to pursue this enrichment technology for an unstated reason."

In contrast, says Albright, "sections on plutonium and uranium were relatively detailed. Compared to the sections discussing nuclear weapons, these implied that the author was more comfortable writing about the nuclear fuel cycle than nuclear weapons. . . . These documents showed that al-Qaeda was interested in developing a deeper understanding of nuclear weapons and that some of the information suggested that the author understood shortcuts to making crude nuclear explosives."

Prior to that, CNN's David Ensor reported that according to U.S. officials, one hand-drawn diagram uncovered either in a Taliban or al-Qaeda facility showed a design for a "dirty [radiological] bomb." These findings were echoed by former CIA head George Tenet, who told Congress in January 2002 that the United States had uncovered rudimentary diagrams of nuclear weapons in a suspected al-Qaeda house in Kabul. Albright disclosed that these "diagrams, while crude, described the essential components—uranium and high explosives—common to nuclear weapons."

Another interesting disclosure made by him was that al-Qaeda's nuclear effort benefited from the help of two Pakistani nuclear scientists, Sultan Bashiruddin Mahmood and Chaudiri Abdul Majeed. The two men admitted that they had had long discussions with al-Qaeda officials in August 2001 about nuclear, chemical, and biological weapons.[3] Pakistani intelligence officials told *The Washington Post* that they believe the scientists used a charity they had created as a cover to conduct secret talks with bin Laden.

The scientists actually admitted to meetings with bin Laden, as well as his Egyptian second-in-charge, Ayman al-Zawahiri, together with two other al-Qaeda officials at a compound in Kabul. The scientists described bin Laden as being "intensely interested in nuclear, chemical, and biological weapons."

A BEGINNER'S GUIDE TO THE ATOM BOMB

One urban legend that has done the rounds for years is that any good university with an advanced scientific faculty could, with solid application, build the bomb. This is nonsense. If it was that easy, everybody would be doing it, especially if you can master something as obtuse as spherical geometry, a necessary adjunct to nuclear weaponization.

Also, constructing the bomb requires a very substantial industrial and scientific base, and at the end of it, huge amounts of electricity, if only to power some of the installations like centrifuge cascades . . .

The principle is basic, though getting there proved enough of a bind for the few nations that subsequently abandoned their efforts. Which is why there are only nine countries to have successfully detonated the bomb—ten, if Iran cracks it before this book appears on bookstore shelves.

According to Vienna's International Atomic Energy Agency, there are thirty or more states willing and eager to achieve this kind of nuclear parity.

Fundamentally, an atom bomb is fueled by two materials, either of which will provide the necessary atomic oomph—namely, enriched uranium (^{235}U) and plutonium (^{239}Pu). In order to be able to proceed with such a device, whosoever is responsible would need to have available a certain amount of what is referred to as a "critical mass" in order to initiate and sustain the chain reaction that ultimately results in an atomic explosion.

A critical mass can be significantly reduced by making use of materials which release as well as reflect neutrons, and also "contain" or "tamper" the explosive chain reaction, thereby giving it time to build before it blows the device apart. This explosion is truly devastating. When the first atom bomb was tested at Trinity in the Nevada Desert, some of those present said it was "like watching the sun exploding."

You can initiate and sustain an explosive chain reaction in two ways.

The first is the so-called **gun-type** method. It got its name from the "gun" barrel which it employs. The Soviets used the word "cannon." It is instructive that this method was advocated by physicists from the start of the atomic age. It works like this:

At one end of the barrel there is a subcritical chunk of uranium-235, usually referred to as "the projectile." At the other end (see the accompanying sketch), there is a larger piece of subcritical uranium-235, usually referred to as "the target."

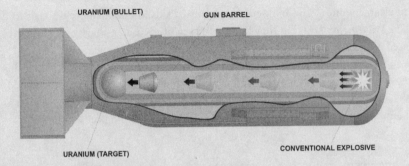

URANIUM (BULLET) GUN BARREL

URANIUM (TARGET) CONVENTIONAL EXPLOSIVE

"Little Boy" (Hiroshima)

To bring together ("assemble") these pieces in order to form a critical mass, a conventional explosive must be used to fire the projectile down the barrel into the target. This has to be achieved at exactly the right speed. Too slow, and the two pieces will prematurely interact before the complete critical mass is fully "assembled," which is what is required to sustain a chain reaction. This can lead to a pre-detonation and result in a less-powerful atomic explosion than planned.

If all goes well, the projectile will strike the target; break the beryllium-polonium neutron source located in a recess in the center of the target; and a flood of neutrons will be released, initiating a chain reaction.

Materials such as boron or tungsten (which surround the target) will reflect escaping neutrons back into the now chain-reacting ^{235}U, in turn, increasing the efficiency of the process and at the same time, containing the explosive energy and giving it time to build. When this energy becomes overwhelming, the device will be blown apart by an explosion—an atomic explosion. Simple, if you know how . . .

A modern gun-design will require roughly 55 pounds of ^{235}U and because the principle underscoring this method is uncomplicated, it can manage without a neutron source (relying on a passing neutron to initiate the chain reaction). For a variety of reasons plutonium is not suited to the gun-type device.

The second method, namely **implosion**, got its name from the way in which it functions: It implodes *into* itself, not outward, as with your usual explosive detonation.

In a sense, an implosion device very much resembles a beach ball, being rounded and about the same size. At its core there rests a gold-plated mass of material (usually plutonium-239, though uranium-235 can also be used). This material may be shaped as either a solid or a hollow sphere, which has at *its* center a beryllium-polonium neutron source.

Around the ^{239}Pu or ^{235}U sphere is a shell which acts as a reflector, as well as a tamper. Around this there is yet another sphere consisting of aluminum-boron. Its purpose is to exercise a squashing (or compressing) inward force. Around this globe are several block-shaped explosive charges and evenly spaced detonators. Because of their three-dimensional shape and purpose—which is the shaping and directing inwards of the shock waves that are created—

these charges are also called "lenses." Finally, a shell of dural or aluminum covers the entire beach-ball form.

When all the explosives are simultaneously detonated, the result is a shock wave that is forced inward and causes the aluminum-boron shell to start compressing (or imploding). When all of these forces reach the core of the device, the neutron source creates huge amounts of neutrons, which start the anticipated chain reaction. The reflector and tamper then function as described above, until the expanding energy can no longer be contained. The bomb is then ripped apart by the huge forces generated by an atomic explosion.

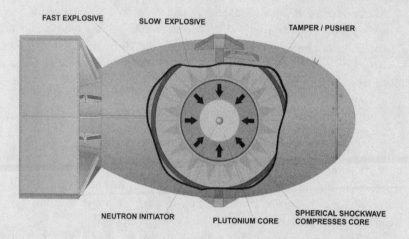

"Fat Man" (Nagasaki)

A modern implosion nuclear device is dictated largely by the measure of scientific expertise employed. Typically, it can incorporate as little as 10 or 20 pounds of plutonium, or a good deal less for a tactical battlefield nuke that might be fired by a conventional 210mm (Israel) or 155mm (U.S. and NATO) artillery shell.

The same principle holds with that modern media favorite, the "suitcase" bomb.

Though bin Laden's people lost their base in Afghanistan and al-Qaeda took a step backwards in trying to acquire nuclear or radiological weapons, the organization remains very much alive. Six years after the overthrow of the Taliban, there have been some subtle—and not so subtle—international changes that might have revived terrorism's nuclear threat.

There are several examples of how this might happen. The first is linked to the discovery of six al-Qaeda training camps in South Africa's KwaZulu-Natal province. Once these had been pinpointed by informers and the issue raised in parliament in Cape Town, they were abandoned. Yet in late 2006, this correspondent was informed that there was at least one al-Qaeda training camp not far from the South African city of Port Elizabeth, which also has a large and active fundamentalist Islamic community.

Not unrelated was a special report produced by CBS's David Martin which identified a second and third tier of al-Qaeda leaders in countries stretching across the globe, South Africa included. In a report in Cape Town's *Sunday Argus* of October 10, 2004, it was disclosed that Martin told a reporter with South Africa's Independent newspaper group that the CIA report apparently included the name and picture of an alleged al-Qaeda leader, said to be based in South Africa.

South Africa's intelligence chief, Ronnie Kasrils—always outspokenly pro-Islam and anti-Israel—cautioned against paranoia. He declined to comment on whether the country's intelligence agencies knew about this, or even whether he had seen the CIA report. Of course he had; it's his job to keep abreast of such developments.

His reaction was along the lines that there were what he termed "elements" or individuals sympathetic or linked to international terrorism in South Africa, but that was also the case in many other countries.

"The minister moved to allay concern in the Muslim community over reports that Muslim schools and theological colleges had been identified as an area for concern, particularly in relation to a large number of students who come from other countries to study here," Martin reported.

The reality, however, is that radical Islam has indeed found uncommonly fertile ground in South Africa. Dating from the apartheid era, Muslim extremists forged links with radical groups in Iran, Syria, Lebanon, Egypt, the Sudan, Algeria, and elsewhere.

Meanwhile, a powerful fundamentalist Islamic movement, calling itself PAGAD—the acronym for People Against Gangsterism and Drugs—took root in South Africa and started a cleansing program of its own. Scores of people regarded as "enemies of society" were killed. PAGAD operatives would often arrive at their homes and shoot them in cold blood, sometimes in the presence of their families. Obviously, quite a few drug dealers and criminals were liquidated, and this pleased some communities where crime was out of hand, though it does indicate something else in a country where the rule of law is supposed to be sacrosanct. Matters weren't helped when the police failed to react in situations where there were sometimes dozens of witnesses. But then, asked another commentator, what else can you expect in a country with almost 20,000 homicides a year?

Emboldened by its actions, PAGAD went a step further and included a political agenda in its brief. Some of its spokesmen started making promises that there would be "an Islamic government in South Africa in the near future." An immediate consequence was a massive mosque-building program in many parts of South Africa, the money coming from Iran.

Shortly afterwards, an even more extreme revolutionary splinter group called Qibla emerged. It was formed in the mid-1990s and maintains strong ties to extremist Middle East Islamic organizations, including al-Qaeda.

The United States views these developments seriously enough to have labeled Qibla a terrorist organization in the State Department's Report on Global Terrorism. It pointed to the powerful anti-Western sentiments espoused by both Qibla and PAGAD. For its part, local police sources have consistently maintained that PAGAD receives a lot of its financial support from Tehran, though that has been downplayed by the government. Recently there has also been a distinct reluctance on the part of the South African police services to provide information about the Islamic group, in part because individual policemen on PAGAD cases have had their homes firebombed and their families threatened.

There is no doubt that both Qibla and PAGAD have a large following among the mainly "colored" masses—meaning people of mixed blood. Part of their attraction, said the *Mail & Guardian* in a linked report, was their basic Islamic militancy, which is not that surprising in a community that boasts five million Muslims. The weekly said that "PAGAD's confrontational conduct and inflammatory rhetoric have attracted publicity, admiration and vilification."

It also pointed out that members of PAGAD's military wing had boasted that some of their members were sent to Iran for military training. More recently, Qibla adherents traveled abroad and joined Hezbollah at the height of the dispute with Israel. Still more have fought for the Khartoum government against southern Nilotic Christians and animists. There is a report of PAGAD having sent some of its cadres to Algeria for training in urban guerrilla warfare. The Sudanese report coincidentally stems from the existence of a PAGAD group in the Eastern Cape named Talaai el Fatah, which is linked to the exiled Egyptian Gama al Islamiya. PAGAD spokespeople routinely deny such reports.

A sociologist at Cape Town University made a study of the PAGAD phenomenon. For his own and his family's safety, he didn't wish to be identified, but he did tell me that one of the reasons why the organization has made such remarkable headway was because South African Muslims are easily influenced by events abroad. "It's all part of the romanticization of the international Islamic struggle," he stated, suggesting that similar sentiments are shared by people of Islamic persuasion in other Third World countries.

"There is also some unease in South Africa at the growth of American cultural and economic dominance. Couple that with admiration for bin Laden,

Libya, and the early theocracy of Iran, together with the formation of militias to fight in places like Chechnya, Iraq, Kashmir, [and] Afghanistan, and you have a potentially explosive mix," he declared.

The formation of an even more extreme group like Qibla, he believed, was symptomatic of the power that PAGAD's leaders now sensed they exercised over the country's Islamic community.

Even more unsettling was the fact that a South African intelligence source disclosed that Libyan leader Muammar Gadhafi had had several meetings with senior PAGAD members in the Zimbabwe capital shortly after the turn of the millennium. On a visit to South and Central Africa, Gadhafi and the usual entourage traveled to the Zimbabwean capital from Lusaka, Zambia, in a motorcade that spanned miles.

It was there that Gadhafi proclaimed on television that "Africa is for the Africans and the whites must all go back to Europe." That was when Gadhafi promised embattled President Mugabe $360 million in oil, and made a $1 million contribution to the funds of his ZANU-PF (Zimbabwe African National Union—Patriotic Front) for the Zimbabwe leader to fight the next election. It was of interest that while in Harare, Gadhafi bought something like twenty homes. London's *Sunday Times* identified one of them as Gracelands, a huge, luxurious complex that belonged to Mugabe's young wife—and this in a country where people are starving.

What is important about all these developments is that Zimbabwe today is a dictatorship like few others. Almost all the white farmers have been driven off their land. Much of the country now lies fallow, and huge stretches have been declared out of bounds to tourists. Nobody dares to question why, except that in Harare today, there are more people of Arabic extraction than there ever were before. Even attempting anything investigative is out; foreign journalists are banned from entering the country without a visa, and very few are being granted.

Moreover, the local media is under siege by government goons. They have a tough-enough job just staying alive without getting involved in something intrusive, and that might embarrass the Harare government. These days, people asking too many questions simply disappear. Which leads to questions that are being asked in London and Washington about some of the goings-on in Zimbabwe's interior. Al-Qaeda enjoys a presence, but nobody is able to question why, or what its extent might be. In other words, bin Laden's cohorts could be up to the same tricks its adherents practiced in Afghanistan, and nobody would be any the wiser.

Getting in and out of the country is a cinch for black people, since its frontiers are porous. But not for non-Africans. As I write, there are refugees from all over Africa heading toward South Africa's "promised land." Also, since Zimbabwe shares borders with five other countries (if you include Namibia's tiny spur in its northwestern corner, where the Zambezi emerges out of Angola), many of them pass unimpeded through "Mugabeland" as they head south. Anybody who pleases could just as easily transit that country again on the way north . . .

Then comes Somalia—isolated, ungovernable, impoverished, and, at a quarter million square miles, about the same size as Afghanistan (and Texas)—possibly next in line to embrace the al-Qaeda mantle as a future headquarters.

Strategically this makes very good sense, especially since there has been a spate of reports of late indicating strong Iranian as well as Hezbollah interest in gaining a foothold in this country, which dominates the approaches to the Suez Canal and the entrance to the Red Sea, as well as the single most important oil route to the West.

One recent report spoke of Iran being one of seven countries to have provided weapons to factions involved in Somalia's ongoing civil war. Others include Libya, Eritrea-Ethiopia, and Syria—an interesting list of conspirators.[4] Reports also talk about arms being exchanged for uranium supplies, though this makes little sense: Somalia has no mines to speak of, and in any event, just about every asset that exists in this embattled state remains under fire, which is why Kofi Annan talks about the country as a "failed state."

Having established that much, there are moves afoot to establish some kind of control over a situation that has teetered on the brink of anarchy for fifteen years. During this time, hundreds of thousands of Somalis have died in the kind of bloody factional chaos that is almost biblical in its ferocity. There seems to be no end in sight. The trouble is that Somalia's former rulers—they called themselves the Union of Islamic Courts (UIC)—who were every bit as radical as the Taliban, were overthrown in late December 2006. But don't write them off yet.

The country was headed by a former Army colonel, Sheikh Hassan Dahir Aweys, who appeared to know what he was doing in trying to stabilize the place. He was in command of a military organization that supplanted the half-dozen Somali warlords who, for more than a decade, divvied up the country and its assets between them, including Mogadishu. He was also instrumental in imposing Islamic *Shari'a* law (which means cutting off the hand of someone caught stealing), and, to his credit, banned qat, that mild amphetamine on which almost the entire Horn of Africa, and parts of the Saudi Peninsula, are hooked.

He brooked no opposition from anybody. When a bunch of Somalis marched into the center of Mogadishu in early November of 2006, protesting the ban, he ordered his troops to open fire, and some were killed: ergo, no more qat, and no more complaints either. Which is how the "New Somalia" is going to work from now on and suggests perhaps a smidgeon of recent historical déjà vu.

For its part, the United States says it will not deal with Aweys because he is on the American list of people "linked to terrorism" since shortly after the 9/11 attacks in 2001. Colonel Aweys was named because he used to head Al-Ittihad al-Islami (AIAI), an Islamist militant group accused of having links to al-Qaeda in the 1990s. It has since emerged that some of those involved in blowing up American embassies in Nairobi and Dar es Salaam in East Africa were linked to these people.

By some accounts, al-Qaeda now has a free hand to accomplish in Somalia what it did in Afghanistan, including possibly toying with weapons of mass destruction. An important difference between the two countries is that Afghanistan was always something of a crossroads in a part of the world where from time immemorial, all roads seemed to converge on Kabul, and that's a tradition that dates back to Alexander the Great.

Not so with Somalia. It was isolated even before the revolutionaries took over, and is a dozen times more so today.

Even foreign aid bodies are affected: most of them have given way before a political program that is calculatedly xenophobic. Consequently, the possibility of setting foot along that stretch of the Indian Ocean coast is almost impossible for anyone who is not an ethnic Somali.

Not unaware of its revolutionary potential, it says a lot that one of the largest United States military counterinsurgency bases in the world is to be found today at Camp Lemonier in Djibouti, the tiny enclave that fringes Somalia's northern frontier. Djibouti is also France's largest foreign military base, host to several thousand French military personnel, including the *13e Démi-Brigade de la Légion Étrangère* (13e DBLE—13th Half-Brigade of the Foreign Legion).

Clearly, something needs to be done. There are reports of U.S. Special Forces having penetrated as far south as Mogadishu in individual raids, but the prospect of gaining a firm foothold remains a distant hope. That could be one of the reasons why Washington has come out in strong support for more Ethiopian military action against the country's uncompromising Islamists.

Obviously, the situation is out of control, not only in Somalia itself, but down the length of East Africa, all the way to Mozambique, where huge swathes of coastline are in the hands of Muslims who make no secret of their admiration for Osama bin Laden. As a diver, I've traveled these byways extensively over many years, and on recent visits, expatriate Somalis were in evidence wherever I went. What were they doing there? Nobody was prepared to say. Preparing for the next attack on one of the American embassies in the region was one wag's reply. Or possibly another go at Israeli commercial interests in Kenya. He was serious.

Remember, it was an al-Qaeda cell, linked to a group of Hezbollah terrorists, that tried to shoot down an Israeli passenger jet about to take off from Mombasa Airport in November 2002. Concurrently, three al-Qaeda-linked terrorists were involved in a suicide car-bombing at the entrance of a local Israeli-owned Mombasa hotel full of tourists: fifteen people died in that onslaught.[5]

Subsequent investigations indicated that the group had ties to Somalia. Indeed, Israeli sources confirmed afterwards that the SAM antiaircraft missiles recovered by Kenya police at Mombassa Airport was found to have come from the same batch as one used in a failed al-Qaeda attack on an American warplane in Saudi Arabia last year. Others had been used in the past by Hezbollah in South Lebanon. The trail followed by these SAMS indicated that they had come into Kenya through Somalia, as had, previously, the explosives used to blow up the two U.S. embassies.

Could the same thing happen again? Western intelligence sources are unanimous that it's only a matter of time. Somalia, they argue, is just across the way, and Nairobi Airport is one of the busiest in Africa. More pertinent—why stop at conventional bombs? East Africa is a flight away from Europe—two, if you're going on to an American destination. And chemical or biological weapons are an easier option when compared to explosives.

Or possibly, in the longer term, something nuclear . . .

Chapter 1 Endnotes:

[1] As one of Europe's leading Arabists, he did a piece for the Jamestown Foundation on the implication of this view. It was titled 'On the Bowing Out of Al-Qaeda' and the web reference can be found at: www.jamestown.org/terrorism/news/article.php?search=1&articleid=2369787.

A brief summary of the range of jihadi works available online can be found in Ulph's article 'A Guide to Jihad on the Web', Jamestown Foundation, at this URL: http://www.jamestown.org/terrorism/news/article.php?articleid=2369531.

[2] Those responsible for uncovering this cache disclosed that details about biological weapons were also found, including formulae for producing the lethal biological poison, ricin. Derived from a toxin protein in castor oil seed, ricin was used to kill Bulgarian dissident Georgi Markov in London in 1978.

[3] Kamran Khan and Molly Moore, "Two Nuclear Experts Briefed Bin Laden, Pakistanis Say," *The Washington Post*, December 12, 2001.

[4] Steven Edwards, "Somalia Risks Becoming Another Iraq, UN Experts Say," *National Post*, Toronto, November 16, 2006.

[5] CDI Terrorism Report: Al Qaeda Attempts to Widen Terror War, Center for Defense Information, Washington, D.C., December 6, 2002.

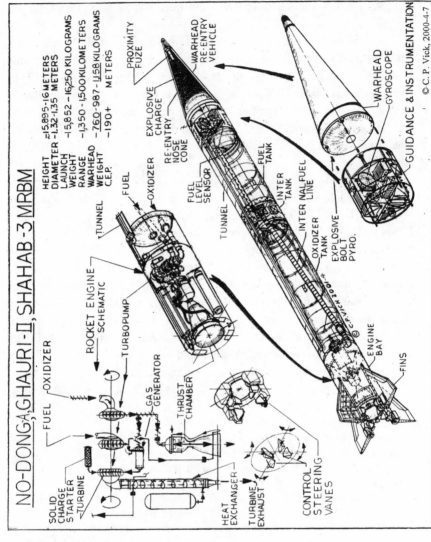

NO-DONG-A, GHAURI-Ⅱ, SHAHAB-3 MRBM

HEIGHT	~15,895-16 METERS
DIAMETER	~1.32-1.35 METERS
LAUNCH WEIGHT	~15,852 - 16,250 KILOGRAMS
RANGE	~1,350 - 1,500 KILOMETERS
WARHEAD WEIGHT	~760-987-1,158 KILOGRAMS
C.E.P.	~190+ METERS

PROXIMITY FUZE

WARHEAD RE-ENTRY VEHICLE

EXPLOSIVE CHARGE

RE-ENTRY NOSE CONE

WARHEAD

GYROSCOPE

GUIDANCE & INSTRUMENTATION

FUEL

OXIDIZER

TUNNEL

FUEL LEVEL SENSOR

INTER TANK

FUEL TANK

INTER NAL FUEL LINE

TUNNEL

OXIDIZER TANK

EXPLOSIVE BOLT PYRO.

ENGINE BAY

FINS

FUEL OXIDIZER

ROCKET ENGINE SCHEMATIC

TURBOPUMP

GAS GENERATOR

THRUST CHAMBER

SOLID CHARGE STARTER TURBINE

HEAT EXCHANGER

TURBINE EXHAUST

CONTROL STEERING VANES

©C.P. Vick, 2000-4-7

© C.P. VICK 2000-4-7

A good deal of international smuggling and intrigue went on over many years to bring this "Troika" medium, range ballistic missile into full production by North Korea (where it is called the No-Dong-A). In Pakistan the same MRBM is called Ghauri and in Iran the Shahab-3. These sketches by Charles Vick of GlobalSecurity.org indicate a fair measure of sophistication. They are indicative of the route being followed by all three countries.

A THRIVING NUCLEAR SMUGGLING INDUSTRY

There are no "legal" rules and regulations in the dense field of intelligence, espionage and collection . . . It seems only logical that the more you know, the safer you are and the greater the chance that you will get things right. That should have been the case with Britain's SIS and Langley but it wasn't . . .

—Ephraim Halevy, head of Israel's Mossad from 1998 to 2002, writing in Britain's *Economist* [1]

Halevy went on to say that it was not by chance that the international statute book had neither chapter nor verse on espionage, "although this has been a vital tool of war from time immemorial.

"We are in the throes of a world war, which is distinct and different from all the wars that the world has hitherto experienced. There are no lines of combat; the enemy is often elusive and escapes identification," Halevy remarked in an Op-Ed that has been culpably underreported.

The thrust of Halevy's argument, which is both disturbing and prescient, is that the world has tended to sit on its hands while a dozen or more nations are gathering many of the materials needed to develop not only nuclear weapons, but chemical and biological WMD as well. Further, they are doing so with the kind of application that is rarely found in Third World countries.

Ephraim Halevy had good reason to make these observations, not least because the media is routinely cluttered with reports of the smuggling of radioactive materials, ranging from nuclear waste that might be used in a radiological (dirty) bomb to sizable quantities of highly enriched uranium (HEU) and plutonium. It has been going on for some time. Vienna's International Atomic Energy Agency (IAEA) issues a report each year, but it is axiomatic that it can only cover those incidents that have made the news. In other words, the perpetrators were arrested while crossing borders or were possibly apprehended at checkpoints along the way to someplace else. Occasionally somebody blows a whistle or the local intelligence community has a field day.

Last year that tally was well into three figures. The problem here is that the list includes only those incidents that we know something about. Which begs the question: How many more nuclear smugglers got away with it? Even worse, this kind of illegal activity has been going on for an awfully long time. It has also taken inordinately long for the developed world to wake up to the reality of the consequences of such actions—the reality that smuggling nuclear constituents could result in a group like al-Qaeda getting their grubby little fingers on it.

Ian Traynor and Ian Cobain of Britain's *Guardian* newspaper[2] said as much in a report in early 2006, which suggested that a large number of European companies—including a handful in the United Kingdom—were the main targets in this kind of illicit trade. Quoting a fifty-five-page confidential report, they declared that the document was "a wake-up call to EU governments, spy agencies and customs officials to keep the ingredients of weapons of mass destruction out of the hands of some of the most unsavory regimes in the Middle East and Far East."

Traynor and Cobain were struck by the sheer mass of detail on the names and locations of suspect players in the global WMD game. "It emphasizes that west European engineering firms, germ laboratories, scientific think-tanks and university campuses are successfully preyed on by multitudes of middlemen, front companies, scholars with hidden agendas and bureaucrats working for the Iranian, Syrian or Pakistani regimes."

Underscoring that report, a court in the town of Alkmaar in the Netherlands convicted Henk Slebos, a sixty-one-year-old Dutch national, of illegally exporting five shipments of dual-use nuclear equipment to Pakistan between 1999 and 2002 for civilian and military purposes. Slebos's company, Slebos Research BV, sold the equipment to the Institute of Industrial Automation in Pakistan, which had links with the research laboratories of the rogue Pakistani scientist, Abdul Qadeer Khan.

Then, on March 28, 2006, German authorities in Potsdam announced that they had uncovered a clandestine network involving at least six German firms that provided equipment to Iran's nuclear program through a Russian front company. The company operated in Berlin in 2003 and 2004, and seven employees, mostly of Russian origin (and whose whereabouts are now unknown), are thought to have organized the network.

Those countries that border Iran have proved to be particularly susceptible to Tehran's attempts at obtaining proscribed materials, and Istanbul has been a constant focus of privateers. The Turkish Customs Directorate disclosed on

May 12, 2006, that an Istanbul trading firm, Step SA, had been serving as the hub of a massive smuggling network that procured internationally controlled dual-use equipment for Iran's nuclear and missile programs. The equipment included huge heat-resistant aluminum containers for nuclear materials and components for missile-guidance systems, much of it manufactured in Western Europe, and in some cases, by subsidiaries of American companies.

The report indicated that Step SA, established and operated by Iranian nationals, had obtained the controlled goods by falsifying export-license end-user certificates to state that the commodities were to be used in Turkey; it then illicitly exported them from Turkey to Iran, again falsifying export-control documents.

According to the July/August 2006 edition of *WMD Insights* (published by the U.S.-based Defense Threat Reduction Agency), what also emerged was that one of the firm's smuggling efforts was the target of a joint operation by the CIA and the Turkish National Intelligence Organization, which seized a shipment headed for Tehran at the Gurbulak border crossing.

The material—almost all of it high-tech—was fabricated by the Italian firm Fond SPA, and left Milan in two trucks. Customs documents stated that the items were destined for Shadi Oil Industries in Iran, believed by Western intelligence to be a front for the Iranian nuclear program. *WMD Insights* reported that the Turkish Atomic Energy Agency subsequently classified the three special-steel containers as dual-use items used in uranium enrichment.

So it goes, with more reports of this kind of illicit activity coming in by the week.

One man who has the full measure of the problem and is prepared to talk about it is Joseph Cirincione, Director for Non-Proliferation at the Carnegie Endowment for International Peace in Washington. He was recently quoted as saying that the authorities were looking for these illegal weapons and transfers in all the wrong places.

According to Cirincione: "North Korea has nuclear weapons. Pakistan has an unstable government, armed fundamentalist Islamic groups and material to build at least 30 nuclear weapons. And nuclear terrorism is as close as Osama bin Laden being able to get his hands on enough of the right materials to build a bomb . . . Those are the more urgent threats," he declared.

More recently, there has even been talk of countries like Egypt and Saudi Arabia developing the bomb. In the Saudi case—with its limited domestic expertise and the country's almost total reliance on a foreign technological labor force—the more likely scenario would be for Riyadh to buy nuclear weapons from a country like Pakistan. In fact, it is the view of John Pike, who leads GlobalSecurity.org, one of the world's leading experts on defense and intelligence, that this has already happened.

There has indeed been a lot going on between Saudi Arabia and Pakistan in recent years. In January 2006, *Cicero*, a German monthly that deals with political affairs, ran a story that alleged Islamabad had been collaborating with Riyadh for several years in what was termed "a secret nuclear program." Three months later *Cicero* came up with more of the same, only this time it was more specific. It quoted Western intelligence sources that claimed Pakistani scientists had been traveling regularly to Saudi Arabia during the past three years. They would disguise themselves as pilgrims attending the Hajj, it said, but once on Arabian Gulf soil, they would simply "disappear" for weeks at a stretch. That time, the magazine averred, was devoted to working on the secret Saudi nuclear project.

Of course the Saudis were furious, but at least they didn't threaten to break off diplomatic relations with Berlin as they had promised to do earlier, when a British newspaper report had displeased the Saudi royal family.

What they couldn't refute was the existence of satellite images of the city of al-Sulayyil, three hundred miles south of Riyadh, which had detected what the magazine called a "secret underground city." It went on to tell readers that al-Sulayyil was home to dozens of missile silos, which allegedly house Pakistani medium-range Ghauri missiles. According to some pundits, these are nuclear-tipped. Previous reports have pinpointed the site as the place where some of the CSS-2 intermediate-range missiles, which Saudi Arabia had purchased from China, had been deployed.

Which raises the question: Why are the Saudis worried about Iran going nuclear? The issue was encapsulated by Kuwaiti journalist Sami Al-Nusf, when he broadcast on the Arab station Al-Rai TV on August 28, 2006.

Sami Al-Nusf: "The Iranian [nuclear] dossier is more dangerous than the Israeli one, and for several reasons. First, the Iranian nuclear reactor is not on the Caspian Sea, but near the Gulf, and six countries use the water of the Gulf for drinking. If the Gulf water is contaminated, six countries will die of thirst. This is not the case with regard to Israel. The same goes for the decision-making. Even though Israel has had nuclear weapons since the 1960s . . . despite the 1973 war and the Arab victory over Israel, it did not even threaten to use these weapons.

"Even during the missile attack on Israel in 1991, it did not threaten to use these weapons. On the other hand, we are familiar with the irrationality of the Iranian approach. This was also the case with Saddam. When he obtained chemical weapons of mass destruction, he immediately used them against the Iranians and the Kurds."

Asian countries also have their problems. India's *Vijay Times* reported[3] that smugglers were sending highly radioactive yellowcake (processed uranium) to Nepal through the clandestine narcotic route via the Jharkhand-Bihar-West Bengal conduit. It was suspected that the destination might be al-Qaeda, said the newspaper. The story went on to allege that yellowcake was so valuable—worth between $600,000 and $900,000 per kilogram—that "smugglers are paid not in currency, but gold," principally by purchasers from the Middle East and Southeast Asia.

However, as the American publication *WMD Insights* pointed out, there were several inaccuracies in the report. First, the world price for yellowcake is roughly $30 per pound, or $66 per kilo, making the black-market price quoted in the article suspect. Second, the product shown in the photo that accompanied the article was a large piece of rock, which might be uranium ore. It was certainly not yellowcake. Also, the link to al-Qaeda was more of an attention-getter and had no real basis in truth, even though this fundamentalist group has been reported as eager to acquire nuclear capability.

URANIUM

The use of uranium dates back to at least AD 79 in its natural oxide form, when it was first used to add color to ceramic glazes, though there are those who say that it had similar uses in earlier civilizations. The German chemist Martin Klaproth discovered uranium in samples of the mineral pitchblende in 1789, though it was first isolated as a metal half a century later by Eugene-Melchior Peligot.

It was only a little more than a century ago that uranium was discovered to be radioactive by French physicist Henri Becquerel. Through his work with uranium metals, he was the first to discover the process of radioactivity.

Some lighting fixtures utilize uranium, as do some photographic chemicals. Phosphate fertilizers often contain high amounts of natural uranium: the mineral material from which they are made is typically high in uranium. Also, people who collect rocks and minerals may have specimens of uranium minerals in their collection, such as pitchblende, uraninite, autunite, uranophane, or coffinite.

When refined, uranium is a silvery white, weakly radioactive metal. Its other significant property is that it is unusually heavy—65 percent more dense than lead.

A naturally occurring element found at low levels in virtually all rock, soil, and water, it can be handled without protection. Significant concentrations of uranium occur in some substances, such as phosphate rock deposits, and minerals such as uraninite in uranium-rich ores. Because uranium has such a long radioactive half-life (almost 500 years for highly enriched ^{238}U), the total amount of it on earth stays almost the same.

When depleted (DU), uranium is used by the military as shielding to protect army tanks, and also in parts of bullets and missiles. The military also uses enriched uranium to power nuclear-propelled U.S. Navy ships and submarines, and in nuclear weapons. DU is also incorporated in helicopter and airplane construction as counterweights on certain wing parts.

Fuel used for naval reactors is typically highly enriched, though the exact values are classified. In nuclear weapons, uranium is also highly enriched, usually to over 90 percent (again, the exact details are classified).

The main use of uranium in the civilian sector is to fuel commercial nuclear power plants, where fuel is typically enriched in uranium-235 to between 2 and 3 percent.

The greatest health risk from large intakes of uranium is toxic damage to the kidneys, because, in addition to being weakly radioactive, uranium is a toxic metal. Uranium exposure also increases your risk of getting cancer due to its radioactivity. Since uranium tends to concentrate in specific locations in the body, risk of cancer is increased to the bone, liver, and blood (leukemia). Inhaled uranium increases the risk of lung cancer.

What does make sense is that reports of uranium-smuggling from India's Jaduguda mine are not new. Thefts from this source were mentioned in Washington reports dated as early as the 1970s. An Office of Technology Assessment Report to Congress dated June 1977, for example, mentioned that a uranium-smuggling operation was uncovered in India in April 1974. From a series of sketchy press accounts at the time, it appears that uranium was being removed from the Jaduguda plant in Bihar and smuggled to Hong Kong through Nepal, where Chinese or Pakistani agents took delivery. Roughly $2.5 million worth of uranium was said to have been involved.

What is also a fact is that yellowcake from Jaduguda remains an essential raw material for both the country's nuclear energy and nuclear weapon programs.

Yellowcake, or uranium concentrate, is a mildly radioactive intermediate material in the nuclear fuel cycle. It is produced at a uranium "mill," usually co-located with a uranium mining operation, which extracts raw uranium from uranium-bearing ore, and then purifies and reconstitutes the uranium product into a solid, powdery form, known as yellowcake (from its yellow color).

Chemically known as U_3O_8, it is sold in multi-ton quantities in international commerce as the raw material for the manufacture of fuel for nuclear power plants. It is also an essential material for the manufacture of nuclear weapons.

Looking at the broader picture with regard to safeguarding (or trying to protect) fissile material, one has to examine some of the machinations in the former Soviet Union (FSU). The scenario is horrendous. To a large degree it helps to explain how North Korea managed to acquire as much fissile material as it did, and how Iran now stands on the brink of testing its own A-bombs.

Following the collapse of the Soviet Union, Washington has not stood idly by—although granted, it took a while to get its act together. In recent years, the so-called Nuclear Material Production, Control and Accounting Program provided more than $150 million for about a hundred projects. What becomes apparent after a bit of research is that some of the money that was designated for "nuclear safety" was never used for the purposes for which it was intended. Rose Gottemoeller, who headed the Department of Energy (DoE) office of nonproliferation before she returned to the private sector, attributed some problems to the "difficulty of opening doors to Russia's weapons-making facilities."

Initially, the interception of a cache of stolen uranium at Batumi, a few miles from the Georgian-Turkish border, prompted a strong reaction from Washington, and was the subject of a report in *The Washington Post*. Washington, the paper suggested, was abuzz following the fury expressed by the U.S. Energy Department at the inability of the Russians to "adequately safeguard nuclear bomb–making materials." The State Department disclosed shortly afterwards that this was the second such incident in two weeks. There have since been many others, and this illegal trend, though slowed, continues today.

According to an American intelligence source, these and many other such events suggested a possible security breakdown either at a former Soviet Union nuclear fuel fabrication factory or at an atomic energy plant; and that this occurred despite Russia and America having signed an agreement on cooperation in the monitoring and safeguarding of nuclear material.

Then followed a Tbilisi report that told of a quantity of uranium pellets found in the possession of Valiko Chkmivadze, a sixty-year-old Georgian with a history of illegally trading in fissile materials. Chkmivadze had previously been arrested by Turkish authorities on suspicion of dealing in smuggled uranium, but was never brought to trial. No one is prepared to say why.

Turkish nationals (with their country bordering on several countries that have sketchy political agendas) seem to have taken the lead in smuggling prohibited material. There are scores of smuggling attempts on record that show Turkey was used as a conduit. In early 2000, for instance, a man was apprehended with a "certificate for the purchase of uranium-235," together with a quantity of uranium in a 5-pound lead container. Its origin was given as Moldova, and the illegal substance was recovered at Dounav Most, on the Bulgarian-Turkish border.

About the same time, roughly 10 pounds of "non-active" solid uranium, together with 13 pounds of "active" plutonium from the "secure" Ulba Metallurgy Plant in Ust-Kamenogorsk, Kazakhstan, was taken from a man arrested in Istanbul. Four Turkish nationals and three Kazakhs were linked to this man later, and one member of the gang was a Kazakh army colonel. This incident was followed by another, when thirteen cylinders of uranium marked UPAT UKA3 M8 and destined for Iran were seized at the town of Van in Turkey. In a separate incident at Bursa, also in the Turkish state, about a quarter-pound of enriched uranium from Azerbaijan was recovered.

Interestingly, there were also two shipments of almost 3 pounds of highly enriched uranium (HEU) recovered out of Georgia. One lot was impounded in Switzerland and the other in Yalova, Turkey. Both were destined for Libya. That was followed by more than 5 pounds of enriched ^{235}U intercepted in Istanbul. Once it was established that it was intended for Iran, several Turkish nationals and suspect Iranian secret service agents were arrested.

Following these disclosures, a State Department official told me that there were other nuclear-related issues that remained unresolved. For instance, U.S. nonproliferation and disarmament experts had difficulty in trying to get the Russians to disclose specific details of their fissile material stocks. These referred mainly to plutonium, though highly enriched uranium was part of it. The imbroglio, he stated, stemmed from the fact that U.S. nuclear facilities, curiously, had the same problem with their own statistics.

"Each time we ask them to give us an *exact* rundown, they counter by asking us whether we can do the same. Of course we cannot, because this is an incredibly complex issue," the specialist disclosed. Speaking on the condition of anonymity, he said that the last time a survey of stocks of U.S. plutonium was done, "there was an uncertainty of about 2.8 metric tons [MT] of plutonium at American nuclear plants. In addition, losses to waste were put at about 3.4 MT."

Part of the reason for this, he explained, was that while the plutonium manufacturing process is very well understood in general, there were some specifics about which the scientists were still a little uncertain. This was more marked in the early days. For instance, numerous computational irregularities at the beginning were really only resolved in the 1970s; these might have included things like how much plutonium a specific reactor might produce, or how long the facility had been operational.

"One needs to keep in mind that apart from some pretty obvious uncertainties, a lot of this stuff is still classified. Restrictions apply as much to Russia as to America," he stated, stressing that the so-called "missing" plutonium at U.S. nuclear establishments hadn't actually been stolen. Instead, there were several other factors involved.

"These range from trying to estimate the amount of plutonium still trapped in transuranic waste [TRU], to possibly something as mundane as inadequately kept books," the specialist said. Since the first plutonium was produced in 1944, the industry had to "feel its way" through a successive series of phases and establish its own parameters.

In order to comprehend how and why fissile or nuclear material goes missing in Russia, one needs to look carefully at how Department of Energy stocks are stored and managed in America. Some striking differences come to light. For example, the DoE disclosed that in the United States before 1978, inventory differences were identified as "materials unaccounted for," or MUF. At various times, MUF included the fractional amounts of nuclear materials lost in regular day-to-day operations. These were listed as normal operating losses. There were also accidental losses, as well as materials possibly removed from a facility for quality control and safeguards analysis.

He also made the point that since it was not prudent to discount the fact that a small inventory difference in U.S. stocks might be due to theft, all losses were invariably investigated, analyzed, and resolved to ascertain whether an actual theft or diversion had taken place. If necessary, a spokesman stated, an entire operation might be shut down until these differences were resolved.

It was his view that matters for the Americans had improved markedly since the seventies. It was worth noting, he added, that almost 70 percent of inventory differences had occurred during a period when the learning curve was being established, largely through a complex process of trial and error.

In answer to a query, the DoE released details relating to American plutonium removals from the period beginning in 1944 through September 1994 (there had been very little change in the previous six or eight years).

Of a total of 111.4 metric tons of plutonium produced or acquired in the half-century (of which 85 percent was weapons-grade), only 12 MT was removed from the DoE/Department of Defense inventory. Of this, 3.4 MT was expended in wartime and nuclear tests; 2.8 MT was due to inventory differences; 3.4 MT was waste (normal operating losses); 1.2 MT was consumed by fission and transmutation, while 0.4 MT was lost to decay and other removals. A total of 0.1 MT was transferred to U.S. civilian industry, and 0.7 MT went to foreign countries, details of which remain secret.

PLUTONIUM

The use of plutonium in an atom bomb (as an alternative to highly enriched uranium) means "cooking" ^{238}U, which involves substantial energy/heat signatures. It was the respected Dr. Siegfried Hecker, director emeritus at Los Alamos National Laboratory, who told my old friend Eric Croddy[1] how "amazingly wacky and difficult are the metallurgical properties of plutonium." Hecker added: "I still don't know how anybody can figure out how to get plutonium into the shape of a ball when you consider that its physical properties tend to change depending on what day of the week it is."

[1] Eric Croddy, *Chemical and Biological Warfare: A Comprehensive Survey for the Concerned Citizen* (with Clarissa Perez-Armendariz and John Hart), Copernicus Books, New York, 2002.

It was also Sig Hecker who declared that plutonium is an element at odds with itself. "With little provocation, it can change its density by as much as 25 percent; it can be as brittle as glass or as malleable as aluminum; it expands when it solidifies, and its freshly machined silvery surface will tarnish in minutes, producing nearly every color in the rainbow."[2]

Hecker went on to say that to make matters even more complex, plutonium ages from the outside in and from the inside out. It reacts vigorously with its environment—particularly with oxygen, hydrogen, and water—ultimately degrading its properties from the surface to the interior. In addition, plutonium's continuous radioactive decay causes self-irradiation damage that can fundamentally change its properties over time. Only physicists would think of using such a material . . .

A radioactive, silvery, metallic chemical element, the most important isotope of plutonium is ^{239}Pu, which is most frequently used in nuclear weapons, such as in the recent North Korean nuclear test.

The isotope ^{240}Pu, in contrast, undergoes spontaneous fission very readily, and is produced when ^{239}Pu is exposed to neutrons. Moreover, the presence of ^{240}Pu in a material limits its nuclear-bomb potential, since it emits neutrons randomly, increasing the difficulty of accurately initiating the **chain reaction** at the desired instant, and thus reducing the bomb's reliability and power.

Hecker goes on to explain that plutonium of an enrichment consistency of more than about 90 percent ^{239}Pu is called weapons-grade plutonium. Plutonium obtained from commercial reactors, in contrast, generally contains at least 20 percent ^{240}Pu, and is called reactor-grade plutonium.

But the stuff can be deadly if not correctly handled or controlled, as we saw on April 26, 1986, with the explosion and fire at the Chernobyl nuclear reactor in the former Soviet Union.

Dr. Nic von Wielligh told me that there were several incidents in the early days. When two naked plutonium hemispheres come together, they tend to cause the now-assembled mass to start chain-reacting, and although this would not necessarily cause a nuclear explosion, lethal radiation is released in the process. There is also a release of the highly dangerous "blue flash," which is symptomatic of neutron radiation.

Otto Frisch—co-author with Rudolf Peierls of the "Frisch-Peierls Memorandum"—conceived of an experiment that illustrated just such an explosive chain reaction late in 1944. Called the "dragon" or "drop" experiment, this entailed dropping a slug of uranium-235 hydride through a space between blocks of uranium hydride. The device used to facilitate this was a 10-foot-high iron frame appropriately called "the guillotine." The experiment was a success, and produced the world's first chain reaction using prompt neutrons. The late, great Richard Feynman likened it to "tickling the dragon's tail." If not performed with care, the consequences can be (and have been) fatal.

One such accident involved Los Alamos scientist Harry K. Daghlian Jr., who suffered fatal radiation poisoning in 1945 after dropping a tungsten carbide brick onto a mass of plutonium. The brick acted as a neutron reflector, bringing the mass to criticality.[3]

---

[2] *Los Alamos Science 26* (2000): pp. 16–23, on 16. Online at www.fas.org/sgp/othergov/doe/lanl/pubs/00818006.pdf.

[3] http://en.wikipedia.org/wiki/Plutonium.

Nine months later, scientist Louis Slotin accidentally irradiated himself during a similar incident, when a critical mass experiment with two half-spheres of plutonium took a wrong turn. Realizing immediately what had happened, he quickly disassembled the device, likely saving the lives of seven fellow scientists nearby. Slotin died of radiation poisoning nine days later.

Prior to his own accident, Daghlian was involved with a series of experiments at the Los Alamos Omega Site concerning the critical masses of a 13-pound sphere of plutonium (^{239}Pu, or, in the argot of the time, "49 metal") in various tungsten carbide (WC) tamper arrangements. After dinner one night, Daghlian attended a scientific lecture which prompted him to think about returning to Omega Site that evening to test another assembly, rather than the following morning as originally planned. This was against safety regulations on two counts: Nobody was supposed to perform a potentially hazardous experiment alone after hours.

Once in the lab, Daghlian set about removing the plutonium metal sphere from the vault and constructing the planned assembly. Using the audible "clicks" of his monitoring instruments as a guide, he quickly completed four layers.

His pace slowed as he started the fifth layer, and he finished half of it. As he attempted to place another brick over the center of the assembly with his left hand, clicks from the radioactive monitor suddenly alerted him to the possibility that it had gone supercritical.

He immediately started withdrawing his left hand when the brick fell from his grasp into the center of the assembly. Reacting instinctively, he pushed the brick from the assembly with his right hand, which developed a tingling sensation as it was enveloped in the characteristic blue glow that surrounded the sphere.

A security guard was seated with his back to the assembly some twelve feet away, but even so, the guard couldn't miss the rapid succession of instrument clicks, or the thud of the falling brick coupled with the distinctive bright blue flash of light. At that moment, Daghlian's large figure was standing limply with his arms suspended at his sides while he attempted to rationally assess the situation. After a few moments, he decided to partially dismantle the assembly to a more stable configuration, which was fortunate, or the radiation could have been worse. By chance, another graduate student had just arrived at Omega, and she drove Daghlian to the hospital at Los Alamos.

A source who was forthcoming when I visited the Hanford nuclear facility in Washington a few years ago disclosed that the core of the problem with shortages lay with the production process. The system had always been fraught with uncertainties, he declared. For instance, nuclear physicists were aware from the start that plutonium was subject to a variety of natural losses.

"Some of it was trapped in process lines and waste streams [and it is still there], some tons of it." There is even more in liquid waste dump grounds. Another 880 pounds decayed.

Until fairly recently it was believed that radioactive waste products that had been left standing for many years (and sometimes for decades) might be close to criticality—which means initiating a chain reaction such as what occurred at Chernobyl. Consequently, for a long time the authorities were simply unwilling to tamper with it. Some was certainly unstable, but at facilities like Hanford, Savannah River, and Los Alamos, cleanup programs resulted in much of it being stabilized and stored in preparation for the move to the Waste Isolation Pilot Plant at Carlsbad, New Mexico. Thus, claimed the man from the State Department, exactly the same situation prevailed for Russian or FSU nuclear processing plants when faced with similar problems.

"The only real difference between the two countries is that while it is all but impossible to get into Hanford or Colorado's Rocky Flats undetected—never mind try to take something out illegally—that has not always been the case in Russia since the collapse of the Soviet Union," he stated.

"Not only were these installations badly guarded until fairly recently, but we have discovered that some of the sophisticated monitoring equipment supplied free by Washington was sometimes not put into service. Or it was declared unworkable, perhaps not properly understood, faulty, or possibly subjected to power cuts." In one or two instances, he confided, the equipment was never even installed.

More important, he said, "Until fairly recently, Russian security personnel were often not paid for months at a stretch," although things have improved a lot. It was so bad, he suggested, that staff sometimes lacked the motivation to do a proper job, especially during the winter months when some of the guards were more interested in keeping themselves warm than watching dials. "You can accept that it is probably a lot worse on an empty stomach."

One consequence of purported Russian nuclear disparities was that such issues were always somewhere near the top of most agendas wherever there was a meeting between Russian and American heads of state. As one official at State phrased it, "Bush and Putin have taken on very much where Clinton and Yeltsin left off."

Early in 2000, for example, Reuters reported that a woman had been arrested in Vladivostok for trying to sell radioactive metal. Although she was employed at a base at Bolshoi Kamen (near the home of the Russian Pacific Fleet), the alloy wasn't from there, stated Grigory Pavlenko, a director of the Zvezda maintenance plant. What he did confirm was the fact that his company serviced nuclear submarines and worked with nuclear fuels.

In a statement, the police in Vladivostok said that their investigation showed that the stolen ^{238}U and other rare metals probably came from one of the many atomic plants in the region. Police and factory investigators checked stocks but could find no missing atomic materials.

The woman was arrested after she tried to sell a 6-pound piece of radioactive metal for $65,000. It had been kept in a local lockup garage near her home, and at the time of the arrest, had been wrapped in newspaper and was being carried about in a shopping bag. What astonished the investigators was that the substance exceeded safe radiation levels by more than two and a half thousand times, a Russian source disclosed.[4]

In another incident, Kyrgyz security service agents arrested an Uzbeki national trying to smuggle 13 pounds of plutonium aboard a flight to the United Arab Emirates. The man said that he had been offered $16,000 to smuggle the shipment out of the country. The plutonium, used in the detonation devices of nuclear bombs, had been carefully packed in a rubber container. Unconfirmed reports indicated that it was intended for Iran. As with the Vladivostok incident, the ITAR-TASS news agency said afterwards that the origins of the radioactive metal could not be established.

Richard Meserve, at the time the chairman of the U.S. National Research Council (part of the U.S. National Academy of Science), issued a statement shortly thereafter.[5] He said that although joint efforts by Russia and America had strengthened security at many sites, "we believe that terrorist groups or rogue nations have more opportunity to gain access to Russian plutonium and highly enriched uranium than we had previously estimated." Moscow spokesman Yuri Bespalko immediately countered this by declaring that "the safety and protection of Russian nuclear materials met and, in some ways, even exceeded international standards."

Shortly afterwards, Bellona, the Norwegian nuclear watchdog organization, reported that the Russian security police had arrested five people in St. Petersburg for trying to sell a radioactive Californium-252 source, as well as 37 pounds of mercury from the nuclear icebreaker base Atomflot, in Murmansk. Police said that the radiation source "could be used for the perfect murder."

Californium-252 is a strong emitter of neutron radiation and is used to start up nuclear reactors. It was customarily stored in containers of about 450 pounds on board the *Imandra*, a Russian fleet supply ship. A single man used a bucket-sized container to transfer the material to an icebreaker. After it had been depleted, the vessel would be transferred to the Atomflot storage facility.

Bellona has made an issue many times over the fact that there are aspects of the case that simply don't make sense. In recent years, it says, the DoE (through a program called Material Protection and Accountability) supplied both the *Imandra* and the Atomflot base with physical protection equipment. Also, radiation detectors had been installed at the entrance to the Arctic base. Because the stolen material emitted radiation 350 times higher than background levels, it should automatically have triggered those electronic alarms that were already in place, courtesy of the Americans. They did concede that the stuff could have been taken through a hole in the fence—or possibly that the equipment wasn't working or the guards might have been bribed to look the other way.

Questions have also been raised about the ease with which the Russian Federal Security Service (FSB) police made the arrests, and whether the operation wasn't a setup to convince Washington that they were doing a good job protecting Russian nuclear assets.[6]

In a related comment, the U.S. Department of Energy's Pacific Northwest National Laboratory (PNNL) in Washington State suggested (during this writer's visit) that what was often overlooked in trying to assess the Russian problem was the "weapons-radioactive materials that could be used in terrorist acts as pollutants rather than as fissionables." It was indicated that part of the reason why this issue was not being confronted was that "it would need to expand coverage to everything including radon waste-storage sites, medical waste and the rest."

It was also the view of PNNL's Dr. Michael Foley that in the long term, radioactive contamination by hostile elements could very well become a serious security threat—a sentiment, incidentally, echoed by other specialists dealing with such issues.[7]

Other incidents involving the illegal movement of radioactive materials or equipment include the following:

- A theft at the Kola nuclear power plant, when thieves removed two items that were part of the automatic radiation monitoring system at the facility's fourth reactor unit. For a full day the plant lost control over radiation levels, but managed to regain it.[8] The thieves were never identified, and there were indications that the goods might have been targeted for outside or foreign interests.

- A short while before, a theft in the Kola plant's turbine machinery led to an automatic shutdown of its No. 1 reactor unit. Kola Nuclear Power Plant operates four VVVR-440 reactors commissioned between 1973 and 1984.

- A conscript on board one of Russia's Northern Fleet nuclear submarines at the Vidyaevo base pillaged more than twenty lengths of palladium-vanadium wire from the reactor room at about the same time. The significance here is that it could have been highly radioactive. The Murmansk newspaper *Polyarnaya Pravda* reported that the wire was used in communications systems of vital control devices on board nuclear submarines. When removed, they prevented the installation from being operated. The next day the sailor sold the wire to a naval petty officer for $45. Vidyaevo is a base for Russian Akula-class submarines, the most advanced attack-class submarines in Moscow's navy. In September 1998, another conscript shot eight of his mates and hijacked an Akula-class submarine at Skalisty on the Kola Peninsula. He was killed by Speznatz troops after a twenty-three-hour standoff.

- Six containers with radioactive cesium-137 were stolen from a refinery in Volvograd in May 1998. Each of the 300-pound containers held a single capsule with about 1 cm^3 cesium-137. If taken out of its container, the capsule could radiate up to 400 roentgens/hour. Volvograd police spokesman Pyotr Lazarev disclosed that the cesium was used in electronic equipment that monitors chemical processes in the oil refinery, and that the thieves would probably try to sell the isotopes abroad. He added that there was a certain demand on the black market for cesium, which could be used by terrorists in "dirty bombs" and other terrorist acts. The Volvograd theft was the second that month: Two containers of cesium were stolen from a cobalt smelter in the southern Siberian republic of Tuva, but later recovered.

- The previous March, a number of radioactive pipes were stolen from the premises of the Chernobyl nuclear power plant. In a theft characterized by Deutsche Presse-Agentur as "not the first of its kind."

- Smugglers attempted to move into Kazakhstan a quantity of weapons-grade ^{235}U that had been stolen in Novosibirsk in March 1997, according to a local paper, *Novaya Sibir*. A year later, the gang was smashed by a police follow-up team shortly before they were due to hand over the uranium pellets. Again, the origins of the uranium were not identified. Questioned about the incident, Vladimir Orlov, director of the Center for Political Studies in Moscow, said that by then, more than twenty criminal cases had been launched in Russia—and all were related to the theft of radioactive materials. In an article in *Nuclear Control*, Bellona quotes Orlov as saying that "the possibilities to smuggle nuclear materials for organized professionals remains quite high."

- Also in 1997, a cache of almost 9 pounds of uranium was seized by police at the home of a man in the north Caucasus town of Ivanov. Police traced its source to the nuclear research center at Sarov (formerly the "closed city" of Arzamas-16), from where it had been stolen three years before. Meanwhile, the report said, it had been kept at the man's home in a metal cylinder inside a lead isolator.[9]

- V. N. Obarevich, head of the Inspectorate for State Oversight of Nuclear Weapons Security, told the Russian Duma (Parliament) in October 1996: "I really cannot imagine how people who work with nuclear weapons are managing to live, especially at the Ministry of Defense. People have no money. They do not have the means to live. A major who is going to be doing technical maintenance on nuclear munitions tomorrow is fainting from hunger today. How can these nuclear weapons be serviced? And these are nuclear weapons that require materials as well. There's no more money with which to buy these materials . . . as I understand it, things are getting worse.[10] At our [nuclear warfare] facilities, 70 percent of the technical security devices have become worn out, and 20 percent have been in operation for two or three service-life periods. While this was going on, attempts were made to repair the facilities, but it took a while. Though things have changed, most control and checkpoints then did not have resources for detecting the unauthorized transport of nuclear materials, metal, or explosives." This was the gist of a statement to the Russian Parliament by Lev Ryabev, deputy minister of the Russian Ministry of Atomic Energy.

- In 1998, a U.S. team visiting the Kurchatov Institute in Moscow was shown a building containing 220 pounds of HEU that was totally unguarded.[11] The Institute apparently could not afford the $200-a-month salary for one guard, never mind the full quota for round-the-clock surveillance that would have been regarded as essential anywhere else.

- A report in *Nuclear Fuel*[12] stated that the 6-pound cache of HEU grabbed in a car in Prague late in 1994 matched the specifics of similar material seized in Germany four months earlier. Following a tip-off, a number of people (including a Russian atomic scientist from the Nuclear Research Center at Rez) were arrested. The report states that the material found in containers identifying them as from the ex-Soviet Black Sea fleet had been stolen from a stockpile at Chelyabinsk-65. A correction later said that all of it had originally come from Mayak, and was only part of what had been seized in Prague and Germany. A year later, 0.4 grams of the same material was being offered as a sample for sale in Prague.

There are more issues in the former Soviet Union that need attention, some of them urgently, if only because they are also nuclear-linked. For instance, nuclear safety in the Russian Arctic, where redundant former USSR strategic missile submarines are being dismantled, is a cause for grave concern, especially in

Western Europe. Conditions there are bad enough to have prompted Nikolay Yegorov, Russia's deputy atomic energy minister, to comment that with nothing being done, "matters worsen every year . . . and could turn into a catastrophe worse than Chernobyl."

Norwegian watchdog organization Bellona (www.bellona.org) specifically targets work (or more appropriately, the lack of it) being done in several "closed cities" in the remote Kola Peninsula. Some nuclear storage sites are only a twenty-minute drive from the Norwegian border. Bellona issued a report[13] which stated that more than 45,000 spent nuclear fuel elements were being stored in the region. That was a while back, and clearly, many of these have been moved, though recent reports suggest that the problem remains critical. Some of these assets were in temporary onshore storage tanks. Others were placed aboard a variety of run-down service vessels. In the old days, excess or spent nuclear fuel elements would have been transported by rail to the Mayak reprocessing plant in Siberia; this still occurs, but it is a slow process. Many elements are stockpiled to await shipment, and unfortunately, there are an awful lot of people who know it.

In some of the Arctic naval ports, says Bellona, many of the discarded reactors of Yankee- and Delta-class dismantled submarines still contain their nuclear fuel elements, and a number have been left unattended for years, often lying where they were abandoned along the shore. More ominous, however, is the fact that the concrete tanks in which the spent nuclear fuel elements were being stored were so run-down, the stability of their radioactive contents was threatened.

The report went on to explain that the distance between each "stored" nuclear element was only about an inch, and that the concrete separating them had developed cracks, some serious, because of extreme temperatures which can sometimes plummet to minus 60 degrees.

"There is consequently a substantial risk for criticality. Because of the sheer volume of nuclear fuels stored, a meltdown in the Russian Arctic would in all likelihood be on a much bigger scale than anything yet experienced this century. It could, conceivably, affect the entire Northern Hemisphere."

Chapter 2 Endnotes:

1 Ephraim Halevy, "By Invitation," *The Economist*, London, July 31, 2004.

2 Ian Traynor and Ian Cobain, *The Guardian*, London, January 8, 2006.

3 "Indian Report: Smugglers Send Processed Uranium to Nepal, Bangladesh," *Vijay Times*, May 3, 2006, OSC document FEA20060503022603.

4 *The Washington Post*, November 6, 1999.

5 Internal State Department memo, dd September 6, 1999.

6 "Bellona: Nuclear Icebreakers Base Robbed," by Igor Kudrik, July 14, 1999.

7 Personal interview, PNNL Hanford, Washington.

8 *Polyarnaya Pravda*, a Murmansk daily, May 28, 1999.

9 Interfax, Moscow.

10 *Yaderny Kontrol Digest #5*: Stenographic Record of the Parliamentary Hearings on Issues Concerning the Security of Hazardous Nuclear Facilities, October 1997.

11 Elisabeth Rindskopf, "Where Nuclear Peril Lies Waiting," *Chicago Tribune*, October 12, 1998.

12 Mark Hibbs, "Smuggled HEU seized in Germany, Prague came from Mayak Stockpile, Police Say," *Nuclear Fuel*, September 21, 1998.

13 "Naval Nuclear Waste Management in Northwest Russia," Bellona, Norway, www.bellona.org.

HOW LIBYA ATTEMPTED TO ACQUIRE NUCLEAR WEAPONS

With nuclear proliferation unchecked, the world stands on the brink of an Armageddon, the likes of which mankind has never experienced before . . .
—Ariel Sharon, former Israeli premier

Were the plot not quite so convoluted, the attempt by Muammar Gadhafi to acquire nuclear weapons for his Socialist People's Libyan Arab Jamahiriya might have made for a pretty good treatment by a Hollywood mogul. Spanning decades, his quest for the atom bomb has all the ingredients of a modern thriller. There's intrigue galore, lots of cadavers, and enough subterfuge to populate half a dozen thrillers by the likes of John le Carré or Frederick Forsyth. By comparison, Ian Fleming might have been a rank amateur.

As much of an arch revolutionary as before, Gadhafi likes to tell people he's reformed. He no longer likes to topple governments, like those of his neighbors, he tells those who inquire about his past. Since achieving power in the 1960s, Colonel Gadhafi has been a very active revolutionary. There have been several attempts to invade his southern neighbor, Chad. Also, he's been stirring the tumultuous Sudanese pot for decades. There also came a time when Gadhafi sent thousands of his troops to bolster the tyrant Idi Amin in faraway Uganda, but then the Tanzanian army invaded and locals turned on these dissolute Arab "invaders" and slaughtered them in batches.

More recently, it has emerged in trials and public hearings in Sierra Leone and Liberia that Libya was behind the machinations of both former president Charles Taylor of Liberia and his protégé, the disgraced Sierra Leone army sergeant Foday Sankoh, who headed Sierra Leone's Revolutionary United Front. Both men had been trained in insurgency in Libya, and almost all the money and materiel used in both wars—and subsequently—arrived by air in West Africa at Gadhafi's behest.

It was the prospect of collaring Sierra Leone's very substantial diamond assets that was at the core of it; and to the Libyan leader, it didn't seem to matter that conservative estimates placed casualties in both conflicts at close to a million souls, the majority of them innocent women and children. These issues are dealt with in *War Dog*, my last book on the subject.[1]

There have been other ignominious adventures, and as happened so often in the past, having been caught short, Gadhafi will proclaim that he is innocent of his crimes on every public platform to which he is allowed access. Memories die hard, however.

Muammar Abu Minuar al-Gadhafi, pundits will remind you, was the brain behind the bombings of two passenger aircraft in the 1980s that left hundreds dead. The first, just before Christmas in 1988, was a Pan Am jet that exploded 30,000 feet in the air above the tiny Scottish hamlet of Lockerbie. The other was the not-so-well-publicized downing of a French plane with almost two hundred people on board that had taken off a short while before from the Central African city of Brazzaville. Again, there was a Libyan-made explosive secreted on board, primed to explode over the Sahara Desert.

The weathered, dissipated face of this picture-book dictator never displays emotion when he discusses any of it. Indeed, Gadhafi continues to plead his innocence, as he always does when the subject is broached by the occasional reporter who visits him in his tent at his desert hideout south of Tripoli. The fact that he paid $2 million in compensation to each of the families of the victims he murdered says a lot. It is commendable that some of the families of the bereaved refused to accept the oligarch's "blood money."

Nor did he stop there. At one stage, Hermann Eilts—the recently deceased former American ambassador to Cairo, and erstwhile advisor to Henry Kissinger—had to dodge a Libyan hit team sent to assassinate him. That came after Gadhafi tried to murder President Reagan. Like so many of his adventures, he routinely denied both attempts. Instead, as was customary after his plots had been exposed and made public, he'd demand that evidence be produced.

Like all scoundrels, this one was finally, if not brought to book, then held to be culpable. Figuratively, of course, because he remains at the head of a nation of almost six million people in a country roughly the size of Alaska, and which includes a hefty chunk of the largest desert on the globe.

Gadhafi made many mistakes in a career that one of his biographers described as "illustrious." But the most damning of all was possibly getting involved with a Pakistani by the name of A.Q. Khan, whose decades-long specialty was smuggling components for nuclear weapons. It was perhaps axiomatic that the Libyan leader would eventually approach Khan, because there would come a time when Gadhafi decided he would like to have a bomb of his own.

Like Gadhafi, A.Q. Khan, a European-educated former metallurgist, walked the remarkably thin line of legality, and he did so with the aplomb of a professional. A passionate nationalist who despised India, the country of his birth, he was singularly motivated during his early years to help Pakistan achieve nuclear parity. Indeed, that objective eventually became a consuming passion for no other reason than the fact that India already had nuclear weapons and had defeated Pakistan several times on the battlefield. India, Khan would tell his friends without any kind of equivocation, was the hated enemy. India must be destroyed, he would say, and though he would sometimes laugh uproariously, A.Q. Khan was dead serious.

Having helped his country get the bomb—and, as a consequence, become an acclaimed national hero—he is regarded as a demigod by millions of his fellow Pakistanis. He used his connections to set his sights on other objectives, which to some seemed a natural progression.

Khan had worked closely for many years with a number of like-minded countries. He'd traded secrets with North Korea (in exchange for guided missile data), obtained atom bomb specifications from China, and at one stage, even dealt with Iraq. Khan had already ingratiated himself with the followers of the late Ayatollah Ruhollah Musavi Khomeini, the much-revered spiritual guide and founder of contemporary Iran. We witness the consequences of this connection in what is happening in Tehran at present.

Not satisfied with sitting back and enjoying fame and glory, it seemed logical that A.Q. Khan should expand his business and make some money in the process. In the end, declares one of his biographers, he made more than a billion dollars, much of it going into Pakistani government coffers. He personally saw to it that he was never was left short; the man acquired properties and businesses with interests both at home and in more than a dozen countries. There were other activities. Portrayed by his hagiographers as "a giving soul," A.Q. Khan became involved in hundreds of charities. He even had his own cricket team, the A.Q. Khan Eleven, which would sometimes play visiting international teams with the proceeds going to this welfare fund or that.

He was busy in other directions as well. Over the years he continued to nurture ties that were regarded by some as "almost intimate" with several of Pakistan's leaders. To them, having saved the country from utter disaster, he was appropriately portrayed as Allah's Gift. Since he could do no wrong, they simply let him get on with whatever he was doing at the time. In the process, it is said, by those who followed his peregrinations (twenty-eight countries at last count), A.Q. Khan established the biggest nuclear smuggling enterprise the international community has ever experienced.

Iran soon became his biggest single cash customer. Having faced disaster on the battlefield in the six-year war with Saddam Hussein's Iraq, Tehran's leaders had already decided that the country would need essential nuclear know-how if it were to build the ultimate deterrent—its own atom bomb. But as we now know, this was something beyond the scope of this country's indigenous scientific community. So the technology had to be bought, and it seems that A.Q. Khan was eager to oblige. Payment was apparently mostly in cash—American dollars—although one source talks of gold bars.

Nobody is certain how much Tehran eventually paid for all of this, except that one of the details that emerged from the subsequent in-house Pakistani government investigation of the Khan operation was that finances were never a problem. Tehran's theocrats had loads of it. Indeed, in a report carried by the prestigious Monterey Institute for International Affairs in February 2004, a former Pakistani official involved in the Tehran deal was told by General Mirza Aslam Beg, then Pakistani army vice chief of staff, that "Iran is prepared to give whatever it takes: $6 billion, $10 billion. We can sell the bomb to [them] at any price . . ."

Such a colorful character is bound to attract interest, and over the years the media has made much of him. Stories about A.Q. Khan are legend—even though he has been shamed and lives under house arrest in Pakistan. While most agree that it was greed that got him in the end, his is both a gripping and fascinating chronicle of drama, subterfuge, and deceit.

Much of this activity is dealt with in the best book I've seen on the subject, by Gordon Corera, a security correspondent for the BBC. The book is titled *Shopping for Bombs: Nuclear Proliferation, Global Insecurity and the Rise and Fall of the A.Q. Khan Network.*[2]

There is no less interest in the United States in this figure, who remains as charismatic today as he was when he still strode tall. William Langewiesche, a national correspondent for *The Atlantic Monthly*, did a two-part series on A.Q. Khan that is a veritable mini-book.[3]

A.Q. Khan's efforts at illegal nuclear proliferation are regarded by pundits who have studied his methods as nothing short of profound, all the more so since he was at it for decades and employed thousands, the majority in his factories back home. In one sense, with his proliferation of weapons of mass destruction, the man turned the global strategic balance on its head. With time, A.Q. Khan, in his high-wire dealings, made contact with many countries that were eager to acquire nuclear know-how. One of them was Libya. So far, nobody has identified the fourth, although both Syria and Saudi Arabia have been mentioned in this context, and according to Corera, the connection was solid enough for money to have exchanged hands. When Khan spoke cash, nobody was under any illusion that he meant anything less than tens of millions of dollars.

That this obscure North African leader aspired to go nuclear surprised a lot of us, even after former Israeli prime minister Ariel Sharon told his Knesset about eighteen months before the story broke that he believed Libya might be the first Arab country to go nuclear. I was doing a series of reports at the time for *Jane's Islamic Affairs Analyst*, and the news sounded like hype. I wasn't the only skeptic. We were all aware that the Israelis have been extraordinarily adept at putting disinformation about, particularly when it involved their Arab enemies, but when the same source repeats something three or four times, you tend to take notice. Looking back, there were some very good reasons for disbelief, especially when you consider that this North African Berber nation is better known for camel herding than for high-tech enterprise. What we were yet to discover was that the Libyan leader had already decided several years before that it might take a nuclear arsenal to make him a leader of consequence.

His nuclear aspirations reportedly first surfaced in 1970, when he approached Beijing. Look at the facts: For years Muammar Gadhafi had been trying to make his mark among the fifty-odd countries that today comprise the African Union, or what was once known as the Addis Ababa–based Organization of African Unity. His attempts at destabilizing his neighbors, as well as several states further afield, had met with little success. Several times he tried to invade Chad, a huge desert state to Libya's immediate south. His forces were always rebuffed, usually with the help of the French. The same held true with the always-volatile Sudan, a constant media presence these days with news about Darfur. At one stage he even had a hand in trying to foment revolution in oil-rich Nigeria, which today supplies North America with about 15 percent of its crude oil.[4]

On Chad, Gadhafi even hired a bunch of American mercenaries to fly an aircraft to the outskirts of Ndjamena, the capital. Dana Drenkowski—a veteran of two hundred combat missions in Vietnam and today a San Francisco lawyer—was hired for the job in the 1970s, for a relatively fat fee of $12,000. What should have been an easy eight weeks of work went sour when some of the tribal leaders involved in the insurrection turned against their leader. Dana and his friends managed to escape, and then, only by a whisker. In fact, they were lucky to get their plane off the ground.

The group managed to fly to Sabha, one of Libya's notorious terrorist training camps in the Sahara, where they shared quarters with revolutionaries from just about everywhere, including cadres from the Japanese Red Army, members of the Baader-Meinhof gang, and a bunch of IRA malcontents. I also detail that remarkable little episode in *War Dog*, where Dana tells all.

Gadhafi, according to some of those who have met him, is both an opportunist and a blusterer. Even the most unsophisticated African leader regards him as, if not a buffoon, then certainly not the brightest boy in his class. Also, his paranoia verges on hysteria. On state visits he will arrive with an entourage of a thousand or more, including squads of security personnel composed mostly of specially chosen women and enough hardware, electronic monitoring equipment, and reinforced limousines to fill half a dozen forty-foot shipping containers.

On a visit to South Africa and Zimbabwe recently, he moved around in a convoy of 150 vehicles, many of them armor-plated. On the road, Gadhafi's heavies insisted that all other traffic be halted. Their leader needed to pass unimpeded, his security would tell their hosts. For the organizers, getting the show moving could be agony, which is one of the reasons why so many African leaders decline offers of a visit by this otherwise esteemed leader. He tried the same trick late in 2006, when he arrived in Nigeria with several planeloads of his goons and an array of weapons that awed his hosts. The Nigerians would have none of it. When Gadhafi said he was going to go home, they said he must do as he saw fit. In the end Gadhafi accepted the same bodyguard as others who arrived for the conference.

Always eager to score points in a bid to uplift his teetering prestige, the Libyan leader sought to acquire weapons of mass destruction for his country very early on in his leadership.[5] Obviously, the Cold War helped. With the United States out of the picture after he'd been branded a rogue by Washington, the Soviets used the opportunity to supplant America's influence in North Africa, not only in the Libyan oil fields, but also in its armed forces. Moscow wasn't shy about providing whatever services were required by this surrogate client state, and none of it came free.

By the early 1980s, Gadhafi had acquired a series of basic nuclear components that included a modest 10-megawatt (MWt) research reactor, which he sited at a nuclear research establishment at Tajura, about ten miles east of Tripoli. This pool-type power unit was fueled with 80 percent highly enriched uranium (HEU), and the facility employed almost a thousand scientists and technicians, mostly foreign nationals or Libyans who had been trained abroad.

Another segment of the deal involved Moscow handing over almost 50 pounds of HEU, which when enriched to weapons-grade is used for arming nuclear weapons. This was instead used to fuel the Tajura reactor. Although Tajura was no great guns as reactors go, its use, said Ali Gashut, director of the center, was focused largely on medical purposes. He wouldn't comment when asked whether the place was used as a training ground for Libya's bomb makers.

In all other respects, the Tajura nuclear facility was perfectly legal, the original transaction to acquire it having taken place under the auspices of what is commonly known as the Nuclear Non-Proliferation Treaty, or NPT. This allows for the international transport of certain "qualified" nuclear assets, or know-how. In certain respects the arrangement is loose enough for even politically "tainted" countries to qualify.

What had not yet emerged, however, was that the Libyan leader had already been involved in one or more secret missions to smuggle yellowcake from Niger, through Libya and on to Pakistan.[6] This is a uranium-oxide concentrate that is used in preparation for uranium enrichment.

At about this time, Libya also broke NPT protocols and exported several more illegal substances (including more yellowcake) to an undisclosed country, in all probability North Korea. Details leaked out along the way, because Moscow eventually backed out of a deal to supply Gadhafi with two larger 440-MWt reactors.

Though the timeline is uncertain, Gadhafi must have made his initial approach to A.Q. Khan, the nuclear arms marketer, in the early 1990s. His representatives had already conducted a series of secret meetings with Khan's agents in Morocco, one of which was attended by Khan himself, with subsequent encounters held in Turkey or in one of the Gulf States.

One of the upshots was that members of the Pakistani's worldwide network shipped a consignment of partly processed uranium directly to Libya aboard a Pakistani plane in 2001. Though this was hardly the start of Gadhafi's secret nuclear program, it did (according to a report released afterwards by Malaysian government sources) provide him with the fuel stock, as well as the designs and equipment to make a nuclear bomb.[7]

It is also worth mentioning that a number of complete centrifuges were flown to Libya from Pakistan, in all probability P-1 models that were based on a design stolen by Khan from the Netherlands in 1975.

The report talks about Project Machine Shop 1001, which was an effort to build a manufacturing plant in Libya capable of making centrifuge components. Also disclosed was the fact that the project was supervised by a British national named Peter Griffin, an engineer who joined the Khan network in the early 1980s. His role was to provide plans for Machine Shop 1001, together with a lathe. Machines for the workshop arrived from companies in Spain and Italy, usually trans-shipped through Dubai. Additionally, Griffin arranged for seven or eight Libyan technicians to spend time in Spain to learn how to operate this equipment.

THE CENTRIFUGE: ON THE ROAD TO MAKING A BOMB

Few people are aware of the circumstances under which the modern-day centrifuge was invented by a Dr. Zippe, a German scientist who was kidnapped by the Soviets shortly after World War II ended. Hustled off behind the Iron Curtain, he was ordered to find an easy way to produce uranium's rare ^{235}U isotope. Having done so, he returned to Germany a free man, only to have the Americans order him to repeat the process.

The underlying principle behind the centrifuge—the same device that Iran is currently using to enrich uranium in its controversial nuclear program—has been around for a very long

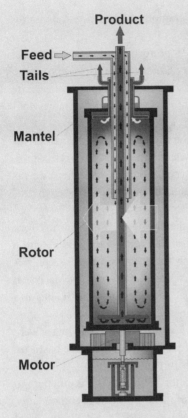

Product

Feed

Tails

Mantel

Rotor

Motor

time. Greatly simplified, think of the humble milk churn that our grandparents used on farms to separate the cream to make butter. The centrifuge does much the same thing, removing the fractionally lighter uranium-235 isotope from the slightly heavier (1.26 percent) uranium-238. Centrifugal force employed in a cylinder (thus, centrifuge) that spins at a rate of anything up to 90,000 revolutions per minute achieves this objective.

Clearly, this is a hugely complex operation which needs a massive electrical and industrial input. It is also why the technical nitty-gritty associated with centrifuge production has remained a closely guarded secret for two generations—at least until the devious A.Q. Khan arrived in the Netherlands. He started poking around and making notes at a top-secret European uranium installation (Urenco) about a quarter-century ago. Designs, specifications, and blueprints that he stole and smuggled back to Pakistan (with a lot of help from the Pakistani embassy in The Hague, it can now be revealed) ultimately laid the foundations for that country's atom bomb project.

Khan also passed on the secrets of the Zippe-type centrifuge to North Korea, while another German scientist sold the plans to Saddam Hussein, who used them to develop his own bomb (see chapter 6).

What it comes down to essentially is that natural uranium consists of two isotopes, of which—in the jargon preferred by our scientist friends—the greater part is ^{238}U (99.3 percent), with a tiny percentage (about 0.7 percent) being ^{235}U.

If natural uranium is "enriched" (or purified) to a level of about 5 percent of uranium-235, it can then be used as fuel for light-water nuclear reactors. However, the enriched version that has 90 percent or more of ^{235}U is what proliferators are looking at as fuel for nuclear weapons.

Because the enrichment process involves such tiny percentages, producing enough weapons-grade uranium can only be achieved by connecting together large numbers of centrifuges in what is known in the trade as a "cascade." These involve hundreds, thousands—indeed, sometimes tens of thousands—of centrifuges. The uranium-235 collected "cascades" toward a collecting point.

Obviously, there is much more to the operation than this simplistic explanation allows. Basically, the energy that it takes to separate ^{238}U and ^{235}U isotopes is expressed as "separative work units," or SWUs. The percentage of ^{235}U ultimately left in the depleted uranium-238 "tail" is referred to as a percentage "tails assay." For instance, if the U-235 left in a tail amounts to about 0.3 percent, then it would be accepted by those involved in the process that the enrichment plant producing this material is operating with a "tails assay" of 0.3 percent. In more practical terms, with a tail of 0.3 percent, it would take about 3,000 SWUs to produce about 32 pounds of weapons-grade uranium, enriched to 90 percent. That would come from less than 4 tons of uranium "feed."

Considering the extreme stresses under which centrifuges operate, careful attention has to be paid to the construction of these devices; again, no easy task. We know now that it took Pakistani scientists—in conjunction with a slew of foreigners—several years to iron out their own centrifuge glitches, details of which have since been passed on to Iran.

Centrifuge construction demands only the strongest and purest metals, the most prominent of which is referred to as "maraging steel," though earlier versions of centrifuges incorporated aluminum. Great care must also be taken to ensure that the devices are sensitively balanced. A centrifuge which fails, commented one source, can be likened to an exploding bomb.

It was an innocuously named 6,404-ton tramp steamer, the *BBC China*, which ultimately became the key to unraveling this extremely complex nuclear conundrum. Built in 2000 and originally named *Beluga Superstition*, the ship was owned by Bremen-headquartered Beluga Superstition Shipping Ltd., part of Beluga Shipping GmbH in Bremen. In the meantime, it had been chartered to a neighboring Bremen company called BBC Chartering & Logistic.

Something about the itinerary or movements of the *BBC China* must have alerted Western intelligence agencies, because the ship was being tracked even before it got to Dubai to pick up what is called in the trade a "mixed cargo." According to Sven Anderson of BBC Chartering & Logistic, there was nothing suspicious in the cargo manifest, but the people involved "clearly knew what they were looking for."

What emerged afterwards was that the *BBC China* was followed from the Persian Gulf all the way through the Red Sea and its Suez transition into the Mediterranean. There, shortly afterwards, a NATO-led naval task force took charge. Following a message from his German bosses, the master allowed them to escort his ship into the southern Italian port of Taranto.

"That was the first time that either the owner or the firm that chartered the ship realized that the *BBC China* was being tracked," Anderson told Janet Porter of the London shipping paper, *Lloyd's List*.

In Taranto, without fuss or bother, it took intelligence agents just two hours to identify and discreetly unload five large containers. The ship was then allowed

BUILDING "GOD'S BOMB" WITH A LITTLE HELP FROM OUTSIDE: CONCERNS WHICH ALLEGEDLY SUPPLIED—OR WOULD HAVE SUPPLIED—COMPONENTS TO LIBYA'S GAS CENTRIFUGE PROGRAM

RING MAGNETS

KRL - Pakistan

POWER SUPPLY

EKA - Turkey

ETI Elektroteknik - Turkey

KRL - Pakistan

SMB Computers - Dubai

FLOW-FORMING OR BALANCING EQUIPMENT

Hanbando Balance Inc - South Korea

KRL - Pakistan

Traco - Switzerland

Tradefin Eng - South Africa

VACUUM PUMPS

Krisch Eng - South Africa

KRL - Pakistan

Tradefin Eng - South Africa

NON-CORROSIVE PIPES AND VALVES

CETEC - Switzerland

SMB Computers - Dubai

Tradefin Eng - South Africa

KRL - Pakistan

ALUMINUM OR MARAGING STEEL

Bikar Mettale Asia - Singapore

ETI Elektroteknik - Turkey

KRL - Pakistan

SCOPE - Malaysia

END-CAP AND BAFFLES

KRL - Pakistan

SCOPE - Malaysia

SMB Computers - Dubai

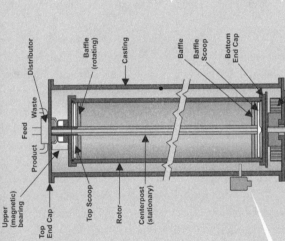

Labels on diagram: Upper (magnetic) bearing, Distributor, Feed, Waste, Product, Top End Cap, Top Scoop, Baffle (rotating), Casting, Rotor, Centerpost (stationary), Baffle, Baffle, Scoop, Bottom End Cap, Electromagnetic Motor, Oil, Lower Bearing

to proceed to Libya and other North African destinations. Commented one of the ship's owners, "It was all very orderly and civilized, and apparently done well away from public gaze . . ."

What wasn't mentioned until five months later was that the containers were marked USED MACHINE PARTS. When subsequently opened by American and British intelligence agents, in conjunction with International Atomic Energy Agency officials, they discovered thousands of centrifuge parts which could be used to enrich uranium—all manufactured in Malaysia by the A.Q. Khan network. The *BBC China* had on board a veritable trove of equipment which could ultimately be used for making an atom bomb.

Shortly afterwards, accosted about the cargo, Libyan officials, at Gadhafi's behest, admitted that they had been dabbling in nuclear research, but that was only after this recalcitrant Libyan leader had been warned that if he did not "come clean" on the issue, he and his nation would have to accept the consequences. In the interim an IAEA official was handed a stack of documents in the very same way they had received them—stuffed into two shopping bags from "Good Look" tailors in Islamabad. With that, all Libya's facilities were thrown open for inspection.

The head of the IAEA, the Egyptian-born Dr. Mohamed ElBaradei, took a while to go public on what was discovered at Libya's nuclear sites. Under some Western pressure he was obliged to concede that there were "surprises" in store for his team.

"It was an eye-opener to see how much material was being shifted from one country to the other," he said after inspecting several facilities. He admitted to being surprised by the extent of the black-market network.

What emerged, he explained, "was the existence of a shadowy network of middlemen involved in nuclear-related matters who tended to circumvent national export controls. These measures were supposed to control the movement of weapons of mass destruction. What I encountered in Libya proved that these controls are simply not working."

According to Judith Miller of *The New York Times*, who scoured these reports, "the UN inspectors were flabbergasted. The designs were for a bomb that could, if 'properly' unleashed, devastate a city. The plans had apparently arrived in Libya more than two years before through a nuclear proliferation racket that spanned at least nine countries on three continents."[8]

Chapter 3 Endnotes:

1 Al J. Venter, *War Dog: Fighting Other People's Wars*, Casemate Publishers, Philadelphia, 2006.

2 Oxford University Press, 2006.

3 William Langewiesche, "The Wrath of Khan: How A.Q. Khan Made Pakistan a Nuclear Power," *The Atlantic Monthly*, November 2005.

4 Nigeria has also recently emerged in the sights of al-Qaeda. A document issued by the movement in 2005 stresses the vulnerability of this West African country and the economic harm that might result should it be destabilized and its huge oil industry disrupted. One report mentions a jump of $100 per barrel in the oil price should that be allowed to happen.

5 Bruno Tertrais, senior research fellow, Fondation pour la Recherche Strategique, "Pakistan's Nuclear Exports: Was There a State Strategy?" Final Draft, August 12, 2006, paper prepared for the Non-Proliferation Education Centre; fn 43 pp. 6–7.

6 Yellowcake, in preparation for uranium enrichment, is converted to uranium hexafluoride gas (or UF_6), and is the basis for acquiring weapons-grade uranium.

7 Report released by the inspector general of police, "In Relation to the Investigation on the Alleged Production of Components for Libya's Uranium Enrichment Program," Royal Malaysia Police Office, Kuala Lumpur, February 20, 2004.

8 Judith Miller, "How Gadhafi Lost His Groove," *The New York Times*, May 16, 2006.

CHAPTER 4

THE LEGACY OF A.Q. KHAN

To understand A.Q. Khan, you have to understand ego, greed, nationalism and Islamic identity.
—David E. Sanger, *The New York Times*

Number 109 Ocean View Drive in Cape Town's Sea Point suburb is a choice address in South Africa. Stand on one of several balconies on this garden-laced three-level mansion, and on a good day you can easily scan thirty miles out to sea. It's not for nothing that this tree-lined enclave on the road between Green Point and Camps Bay is referred to by some as "Millionaires Row."

When the weather's right, the vista from these lower slopes of Cape Town's famous Signal Hill allows a gull's-eye view of Robben Island. Those who have followed recent history will recall that this was where former president Nelson Mandela was held in close custody for many years by the old apartheid regime.

Until recently, this Ocean View address was also the home and offices of Top-Cape Technologies (Pty) Ltd., owned by fifty-one-year-old Hungarian-born Israeli citizen Asher Karni. An enterprising fellow, he made major in the Israeli Defense Force before immigrating to the shores of the South Atlantic. Asher Karni was a model citizen. Moreover, he was thoroughly at home in one of the largest Jewish communities in the Southern Hemisphere. He and his wife were respected members of Sea Point's Beit Midrash congregation, where he taught the Torah. Occasionally he would stand in for rabbi Jonathan Altman when there was a need.

In an article published after his arrest in the United States, the Israeli newspaper *Haaretz* said that Karni spent his first few years in South Africa with Bnei Akiva, where he acted as a mentor to Jewish youth. In fact, the report read, he encouraged many of them to do their *aliya* in the Promised Land. Almost everyone who came into contact with Asher Karni felt he was one upstanding *mensch*. Finally, he resigned his religious obligations and joined a local electrical company, Eagle Technology, owned and run by a prominent couple, Alan and Diana Bearman, together with their son Nathan.

On the face of it, the firm's Greenmarket Square outlet—while competing with a huge Afrocentric open-air market on the cobblestones outside—sold everyday items like electrical appliances, coffee machines, and the like. But its real interests lay in sophisticated security-linked electronic items. In fact, Eagle Technology had made good money during the apartheid years by importing sensitive high-tech equipment which found a ready application within the country's security establishment. Frankly, with a black government in power and many of the country's ills being blamed on racism, this is not something you talk about in South Africa today.

Being ex-military, Asher Karni was almost made for the job. He understood what was required of him and this he did well; both he and the company prospered. While he remained with Eagle Technology, he brought in business from all over the world. At his peak he was easily earning $10,000 a month; going by South African standards, where even earning $1,000 a month is good money, he was bringing in a fortune.

So it comes as a bit of a surprise to learn that for all his newfound wealth and good intentions, Asher Karni began doing some additional business on the side as a smuggler. Again, he took the obvious route and concentrated solely on high-tech goods—only these were nuclear-related, and intended for Pakistan's atom bomb program.

Among items Karni secretly dealt with were triggered spark-gaps, esoteric technological instruments that have a variety of functions and which can be used in nuclear weapons, specifically to set them off. He ordered 66 from an American firm—part of a larger consignment of 200—and took delivery in Cape Town. The triggers were then forwarded to a Pakistani businessman, Humayun Khan, who, as an intermediary, used a Dubai address. (Humayun Khan, although not related to A.Q. Khan—the name is as common in Pakistan as Smith might be in London—was one of a host of shadowy figures working out of Pakistan in illegal nuclear-proliferation enterprises.)

One needs to explain that triggered spark-gaps are a very unusual item for anybody to acquire. They are rated—apart from actual uranium and other radioactive material—among the most tightly restricted items in the world, listed as number 2,641 on the control list. In fact, the Bureau of Industry and Security of the U.S. Department of Commerce categorized them as what is known in the trade as "dual-use" items; these might have either a civilian or a military application. Because of civilian needs—they are used in machines for pulverizing kidney stones—it is quite legal to sell them to South Africa, but certainly not to Pakistan, North Korea, or Iran, all countries suspected of using them in their nuclear weapons programs. If they want them—even one—a shipper must request an export license.

In the 1990s, when the Iraqi Health Ministry asked for small numbers of the devices for several of their hospitals, Vienna's International Atomic Energy Agency (IAEA) confirmed the proper use of each of them.

"The only way for the Iraqis to get a new trigger," said Mark Gwozdecky, an IAEA spokesman, "was to send back the one they used." The surveillance system worked, he said, and the agency was confident that none were diverted to nonmedical purposes.

Although Humayun Khan will deny that he had anything to do with his namesake, others involved with Abdul Qadeer Khan, who have since agreed to talk, said there were scores of such people involved in the illicit trade. One British operative told Gordon Corera that some were even competing against each other: They would bid for the same contracts, deal with the same clients, and often manipulate prices to the advantage of one or the other.

The fact that Humayun Khan was into the same business points pretty conclusively to his ties to the illegal network. He was described by one source as an Islamabad businessman with exceptionally close links to Pakistan's military. American government officials suggest ties to militant Islamic groups, some of which are suspected to be arming fighters in the Kashmiri conflict.

Also, the triggers weren't a one-off job; Karni worked for his Pakistani bosses for a very long time, and though the Americans admit to nothing, this was one job among many. Once he'd been nabbed, it took the authorities months to go through all his documents, which included information housed on several computer hard drives. It later emerged that Karni was a key element in this game—a small cog in a big wheel, perhaps, but a vital ingredient nonetheless—which could be why, in his customs declaration to his American counterpart, he declared that the triggers were to be used in equipment installed in Johannesburg's Chris Hani Baragwanath Hospital.

In subsequent investigations, the doctor responsible for dealing with such matters admitted that he might use a couple of the devices each year. He suggested that it would take a lifetime to use up all sixty-six that Karni had ordered.

The gravity of Asher Karni's actions were underscored by a more recent visit to South Africa by retired major-general M. K. Paul, controller of the National Institute for Advanced Studies in Bangalore, India. General Paul told those present at the South African Institute of International Affairs at Witwatersrand University (now the University of Johannesburg) that Karni's actions had "upset the delicate nuclear balance in south Asia between India and Pakistan."

While only some of what took place between Karni and his Pakistani handlers emerged at the time of his sentencing—as was revealed by U.S. attorney

Kenneth L. Wainstein, in the American capital on August 5, 2005—it was also no secret that much of what Karni disclosed during lengthy debriefing sessions (behind closed doors and arranged by the FBI) remains sealed.

Corey Hinderstein, formerly at the Institute for Science and International Security (ISIS), told me when we last met at her Washington office that she had seen the file. She confirmed that only essentials were made public. In fact, without being specific, she disclosed that there was much more, and—possibly true to form, for this was no hero—Karni revealed all, which was why he got only thirty months in jail.

The background to all this makes for an epic tale. U.S. attorney Wainstein told the presiding judge in Washington, D.C., that in August 2002, Pakistani businessman Humayun Khan approached Karni and asked him to help acquire certain models of oscilloscopes manufactured by an Oregon company, Tektronix, Inc. What Khan did not disclose then was that those models could be used for testing in the development of nuclear weapons and missile-delivery systems. For that reason, said Wainstein, the U.S. Department of Commerce required licenses for their export to certain countries, Pakistan included.

Khan did ease the passage of events a little by telling Karni that he was an authorized distributor for Tektronix in Pakistan, which he was, it has since been revealed.

At that stage Karni had already set up Top-Cape Technologies at his Ocean View address, through which he came to channel all his business. On the trigger request, he told Khan, he'd help, even though the Pakistani warned him that they were subject to American export controls. Notably, Karni was cautioned not to disclose the ultimate destination of the goods—not to a single soul.

After several false leads, Karni eventually got hold of one of the Tektronix-controlled oscilloscopes in March 2003 from a firm in Plainview, New York. The firm was directed to send it to Cape Town. Karni re-exported it to Khan in Pakistan, the deal taking place without the requisite licenses. Two additional oscilloscopes were bought five months later, and again illegally diverted to Khan. For much of the rest of the year, the two men worked to fill a $1.3 million order for the triggered spark-gaps that eventually resulted in Karni's arrest. Avoiding specifics, Khan told him that they were for a third party in Pakistan.

The spark-gaps that Khan sought were manufactured by PerkinElmer Optoelectronics of Salem, Massachusetts. Because of the sensitive nature of the deal, Karni first made inquiries of PerkinElmer's French sales representative. It took a little while, but eventually Karni was quoted a price. At the same time, he was told that he would need to certify that the product would remain in South Africa, and, more salient, that it would not be used for nuclear purposes. Karni forwarded this information to Khan, and because of the sensitivity of the deal, he initially declined to pursue the order. But Khan was assertive and the Pakistani prevailed. The money was remarkable, even by Karni's standards: This one job would have earned him millions.

Court documents from Washington detail the rest of the story:

"In July 2003, an anonymous source [in Cape Town] informed agents of the Office of Export Enforcement of the Department of Commerce and Immigration and Customs Enforcement of the Department of Homeland Security that Karni was in the process of using a broker in Secaucus, New Jersey, to obtain 200 PerkinElmer triggered spark gaps for ultimate shipment to Pakistan through South Africa. The agents approached PerkinElmer, which agreed to cooperate in the investigation but to render [them] inoperable."

Three months later, U.S. agents were able to track the first installment of sixty-six triggered spark-gaps to Top-Cape in South Africa, and then on to Pakistan through the United Arab Emirates.

One of the people who helped get Asher Karni arrested was Cape Town attorney Michael Bagraim, a fellow Jew. More important, by the time this rumpus had started, Bagraim was chairperson of the South African Jewish Board of Deputies, a powerful position in a country with such a large Jewish population, and its chief spokesman for anything affecting the community, Parliament included. Following Karni's arrest and sentencing in the United States, Bagraim told a Cape Town newspaper that he believed it was possible Karni did not understand the enormity of what he was doing.

"But then again, being Jewish possibly made it worse . . . if he really sold nuclear material as he is accused of doing, then he deserved what he got," Bagraim said. "He might have been unwitting, but even so, it is a hard lesson to others not to deal in weapons of mass destruction. If this conviction stops someone like that, then I applaud it."

Getting involved with Pakistani nuclear middlemen was probably the worst mistake of Asher Karni's life. It wasn't his last. Despite earlier visits to his premises in Cape Town by investigators, he blundered badly when he flew to the U.S. on a skiing holiday with his wife and daughters. The authorities grabbed him when he stepped off the plane at Denver International Airport.

Britain's Jane's Information Group has given a good deal of coverage to the Pakistani weapons of mass destruction imbroglio in recent years, particularly since that country's forces remain active in a number of military theaters in the Middle East and further afield.

One of its flagship publications, *Jane's Intelligence Review* (for which this author wrote for some years), went further.[1] Andrew Koch, *JIR*'s former Washington-based correspondent, published a report on events relating to the

A.Q. Khan network on July 1, 2006, which included the fact that the hugely publicized smuggling operation, though declared moribund by Islamabad, just isn't so. And this in spite of the fact that three years before, the world was told by President George W. Bush that the Khan network had been neutralized.

Koch makes some prescient observations, including the reality that the Khan network and its middlemen successfully used "the conveniences of the time." This involved "front companies in pliant jurisdictions, flexible communications and travel, swiftness and anonymity of international finance. Most of the participants—particularly in Europe and South Africa—were market-savvy rather than geopolitically inspired . . . the culprits used loopholes in the new global marketplace to sidestep international restrictions that were often too cumbersome or unwieldy to keep up with changing tactics," declared Koch.

Although the arrests of A.Q. Khan; his deputy, a Sri Lankan named Buhary Seyed Abu Tahir; and several other senior members of their network eliminated a major source of nuclear weapons–related goods for would-be proliferators, it did not end the trade in nuclear wares. In fact, says Koch, recent evidence suggested that part of the Khan network continues to flourish today.

One senior international investigator told Jane's: "There is no reason to believe this is the whole story"—a comment which Koch says sums up a widely held view regarding known information on the enterprise to date. He also made the point that parts of the organization are yet to be uncovered. Moreover, Koch tells us, this includes individuals who are more senior in Khan's illegal establishment than first thought.

Koch goes on: "Recent clues that have been uncovered by law-enforcement officials, international nuclear inspectors, and intelligence operatives, support this contention. One major piece of evidence was that Iranian agents and to a lesser degree, Pakistani ones have attempted numerous illicit nuclear-related purchases since 2003. That suggests that such a reconfiguration of suppliers is occurring and that atomic goods continue to be available for those with the means and desire to buy them. While these new suppliers cannot provide the one-stop shopping that Khan offered, and are insufficient by themselves for moving a nuclear weapons program very far forward, they point to the likelihood that some tentacles of the network have yet to be discovered."

Key points mentioned by Koch include:

- Iranian and, to a lesser degree, Pakistani agents have attempted numerous illicit nuclear-related purchases since 2003.

- Tehran has been seeking material from European and Russian firms and has included some of the Khan middlemen in the process.

- Heightened procurement activity by Pakistani agents has occurred since at least 2004.

What is interesting about Khan's network is that he didn't keep it "home-grown." He ran the full international gamut in recruiting people who might be useful. Some were exceptionally well placed to fulfill their role, for which each one of them was handsomely paid. They recruited anybody who might be useful, including, as we have seen, a former major in the Israeli Defense Force.

Among others were a handful of British, Malaysians, Swiss, Indians, South Africans, and Sri Lankans, together with the inevitable bunch of Germans. Which makes one wonder why so many of these otherwise respectable North Europeans so often get themselves involved in illegal nuclear smuggling operations. A bunch of them were arrested after Saddam Hussein's nuclear operations were destroyed following Gulf War 1. Still more have been named in recent reports, which detail South African and Brazilian quests for the bomb.

Of the more prominent Germans in the operation, Gotthard Lerch has been described as the "main contractor" for Khan's deputy and principal operating officer, Buhary Seyed Abu Tahir. Lerch has since been brought to trial in Germany, charged with illegally helping to build a uranium-enrichment plant in South Africa that was ultimately destined for Libya. But more of that later.

There was also Heinz Mebus, who managed to ingratiate himself with Khan at an early age when they were classmates. Mebus was to become an important link in filling Tehran's "want lists," and was actually involved in the first centrifuge transfers to Iran in the 1980s. Another German was the technician Gerhard Wisser, who owned Krisch Engineering at Vanderbijlpark near Johannesburg, the same firm hired by Khan to build the illegal Libyan uranium plant. Otto Heilingbrunner was yet another German, and one of Lerch's associates.

Among other Europeans linked to Khan was his longtime associate, Swiss national Urs Tinner, fingered as the man who, until 2003, was responsible for the production of centrifuge parts in Malaysia. Bold to a fault—stupid, say some—Urs Tinner also recruited his father, Frederick, together with brother Marco, into this nefarious network. Over lengthy periods, all three men were associated with illegal nuclear operations in Libya and Iran.

Frederick Tinner's specialty, as president of the Swiss firm CETEC, was to act as a procuring agent for many of the European components needed by Khan. It was an ideal setup, since most people believe the Swiss are squeaky-clean when it comes to moral issues.

Then came a British father-and-son combination in Peter and Paul Griffin. Peter Griffin actually designed Gadhafi's "Project Machine Shop 1001," which involved acquiring high-tech equipment from several European countries. Much of this stuff was trans-shipped to Libya through Dubai, where Griffin Junior ran Gulf Technical Industries, a convenient arrangement since Khan himself spent a lot of time in the Gulf state.

At the top of Khan's external network was the Indian-born Mohamed Farook (also spelled "Farouq"), who had the ultimate say in most things in which the group was involved. Like his nephew Tahir, he too was based in Dubai, where both men were linked to a company called SMB Computers. That company, together with several others linked to A.Q. Khan, seemed to vaporize immediately when the Libyan link to Khan had been pinpointed.

That came shortly after the German ship *BBC China* was seized by a NATO-led naval task force after it had entered the Mediterranean (see chapter 3).

At first glance, it seems just a little absurd that a single individual—a disgraced Pakistani metallurgist who ran the world's most successful nuclear smuggling operation—might have strategically turned the world on its head. Granted, A.Q. Khan didn't work alone. There is little doubt that his government was very much in on the act; how else to explain their accomplishments, knowing that they were dealing with huge transfers of money that would have been channeled through the country's national banking system, and which were bound to attract attention. What later emerged was that a "billion dollars or more" was involved over the thirty-year period. The cold truth is that one of the consequences of A.Q. Khan's actions was the fact that North Korea became the ninth country to detonate a nuclear weapon. And by all accounts, Iran is almost there as well. That, in turn, has triggered a nuclear race in the Middle East.

In late October 2006, Dr. Mohamed ElBaradei, head of the United Nations–sponsored International Atomic Energy Agency, disclosed that apart from thirty-something other countries interested in acquiring nuclear parity, the half-dozen Arab states in the hunt included Egypt, Saudi Arabia, Syria, and Algeria. It is worth a mention that all four countries at one time or another had surreptitiously dabbled in things nuclear, though none would admit as much today. They are also of one voice that their intentions are peaceful, which says little when you recall that Pakistan and North Korea were of a similar mind before they tested their bombs.

If nothing else, Abdul Qadeer Khan has led a charmed life. Though in disgrace and said to be ailing, he enjoys the status of a nationally acclaimed hero in Pakistan, even if he wasn't born there. His parents, originally from Bophal, had slipped across the border from India after the subdivision of the subcontinent, which was both bloody and traumatic. In fact, it affected young Khan so much that for the rest of his life, he could never utter the words "Hindu" or "Hindi" without embellishing them with a curse. As one of his biographers pointed out, a good deal of what Khan did in making Pakistan proficient in the nuclear domain was achieved with one eye on similar events across the border to his immediate east.

The Khan family suffered their fair share of travails, although they quickly managed to pick up the pieces in their new environment. Khan's father became the headmaster of a local school, and the illustrious Abdul Qadeer, having been sent abroad to study in 1972, earned a doctorate in metallurgical engineering from the Catholic University of Leuven in Belgium. Within months, A.Q. Khan had started work at a research laboratory, which was linked to Ultra-Centrifuge Nederland (UCN). Some of that work involved classified research into the Urenco uranium-enriching project. It wasn't long before Khan was allowed access to Urenco's advanced UCN enrichment facility in Holland, in order to familiarize himself with centrifuge operations.

As a metallurgist, it was to be expected that he would be involved in this phase of production: special steels was his professional forté, especially where they were linked to strengthening metal centrifuge components. While Khan was not officially cleared to visit the facility, it emerged after he had left the country that he had done so many times—with or without the consent of his employers.

In the meantime, he met and married Hendrina, a South African–born Dutch girl, and they set about raising a family.

The date May 18, 1974, changed everything for the still-youthful Pakistani, when India conducted its first nuclear test. A press release issued by the New Delhi government referred to it as "a peaceful nuclear explosion." It is not all that surprising, therefore, that four months later, Khan wrote a personal note to Pakistan's prime minister, Zulfikar Ali Bhutto, delivered to the office of the president by a personal friend. The thrust of the message: He had unusual scientific services and expertise to offer his country.

Alarmed at India's nuclear progress—and having been involved in several wars with their more preponderant neighbor—Pakistan had meanwhile initiated a nuclear program of its own. By mid-1975, Islamabad acquired the basics for an enrichment program from European agents. It was all legitimate.

A.Q. Khan's timely letter to his prime minister had obviously had the required effect, and to the consternation of his Dutch bosses, Khan started taking an inordinate amount of interest in nuclear-related projects that were not part of his domain. That was in 1975, only a few years after he graduated; this fresh-faced scientist was already making waves. The matter was compounded by the detailed questions he liked to ask, many of them dealing with issues that were regarded by European governments as top-secret. By now the Dutch were alarmed, and there was pressure put on Khan's bosses to move him to less-sensitive projects.

Khan must have been aware that he was being watched, which could be why he suddenly left Holland in December 1975. In the family baggage was a batch of classified Urenco blueprints, together with lists of European suppliers, many of whom he would be contacting in the years ahead. A lot more such information had already been passed on to Pakistani intelligence agents operating out of their embassy in The Hague. There is no doubt—A.Q. Khan was sharp.

Back home, his former bosses discovered shortly afterwards, the still-youthful Khan was to begin immediate work on a project, where he would focus exclusively on developing an indigenous uranium-enrichment capability. This would be Pakistan's first, and in Khan's view, a possible long-term counter to India's military dominance. By now others had discovered his duplicity, and not long afterwards, the Netherlands government took its first steps to indict Abdul Qadeer Khan for criminal espionage. The only problem was, the bird had flown.

After he'd left Holland, Khan formally told his company that he had problems at home and had decided to stay in Pakistan. It is interesting to note that although Khan visited Europe often in later years, and there were outstanding warrants for his arrest, it was Langley that prevented its European counterparts from arresting him. The CIA maintained that they wanted to keep track of Khan's movements.

Initially, on his return home, A.Q. Khan worked in centrifuge-related projects within the confines of the Pakistan Atomic Energy Commission (PAEC), headed by a namesake, Munir Ahmad Khan. From the start, the two men were suspicious of each other, which led to dissention and a series of confrontations that soon became public.

In a bid to stabilize a situation that was to have an impact on Pakistan's nuclear weapons program, which was both strategic and critical, the upshot came when Khan was given autonomy and control over Pakistani uranium-enrichment programs from July 1976 onwards. That was when he founded his own company, Engineering Research Laboratory (ERL), at Kahuta, about an hour's drive out of the capital. Meanwhile, the rival PAEC went ahead with programs of its own, related to both nuclear power and nuclear weapons.

Khan's uranium-enrichment program was based largely upon developing an indigenous gas-centrifuge system, which he dubbed Pak-1. In fact, there was nothing new about it; it was little more than a modification of Urenco's first-generation design. Nor was it something that came easily. He had difficulty in the early days producing aluminum rotors that would pass a rigorous "spin" test, to which all centrifuges are subjected, to ascertain whether they are able to maintain the extreme speeds needed to "spin off" uranium-235.

It was only in the 1990s that Khan was able to develop his more advanced Pak-2, a modification of Urenco's second-generation design, which had steel rotors.

Khan continued with research that would later contribute toward Pakistan's first generation of nuclear weapons. But this labor—and that of others involved in similar projects—had already attracted attention from the West. In 1979 Islamabad was cut off from all U.S. financial and military support. This impasse was short-lived, however, thanks to the Soviet Union. Following Moscow's invasion of Afghanistan, Washington had no option but to reestablish friendly ties with the embattled country's nearest neighbor. In fact, for the duration of the Afghan War, it was Pakistan that played a seminal role in channeling aid and equipment to a variety of mujahedeen factions fighting in the mountainous north. The situation was consolidated after Ronald Reagan was elected in 1980.

There was more progress on the domestic front in the early 1980s. A.Q. Khan—having initiated strong contacts through his government with a variety of countries, China included—managed to acquire the plans for Beijing's first atom bomb, which was tested fifteen years before at Lop Nor. The event made the man, and Khan was showered with plaudits. From then on, there would be no looking back.

Nobody is certain exactly when Khan and his entourage decided to make money on the side by selling some of the nuclear secrets he'd stolen, or subsequently had had a hand in developing. Word has it that about the time the Soviets were driven out of Afghanistan, Khan was quietly approached by an Arab state, purportedly Saudi Arabia—perhaps even Syria—with a request for nuclear assistance.

By then, we are told by Michael Laufer (who compiled an A.Q. Khan Nuclear Chronology[2]), Khan's early successes with the Pakistani uranium-enrichment program were "followed by the more advanced design and technologies of the P-2 centrifuge, an adapted version of the German G-2 that can spin twice as fast as the previous P-1 design."

According to Laufer, Khan was left with an excess inventory of P-1 components, and he began to purchase additional P-2 components that he would ultimately export through many of the same channels he had used to import centrifuge components. Notably, he adds, "Khan makes nuclear sales in this period to Iran and offers technologies to Iraq and possibly others." That was followed by a secret nuclear deal signed by Pakistan and Iran, and the provision for groups of Iranians to study nuclear-related sciences at Pakistani institutions, something that didn't please Washington and led to a good deal of friction. Relations between the two Islamic states were good enough for Khan to visit the Iranian nuclear facility at Bushehr on the Gulf several times.

In 1987, Laufer reckons, Khan is believed to have made a centrifuge deal with Iran to help build a cascade of 50,000 P-1 centrifuges. He adds that Tehran may also have received centrifuge drawings through the offices of an unknown foreign intermediary around this time.

Khan's firm—by this time, renamed the Khan Research Laboratories (KRL)—"begins to publish publicly available technical papers that outline some of the more advanced design features Khan has developed. The papers include information that would normally be classified [in the West] and show that KRL is competent in many aspects of centrifuge design and operation. The papers also include specifications for centrifuges with maraging steel that can spin faster than earlier aluminum designs.

"Later, in 1991, KRL publishes details on how to etch grooves around the bottom bearing to incorporate lubricants. These technical developments are important for Khan's P-2 centrifuges."

Almost exactly a decade later, on May 11, 1998, India detonated five devices in nuclear tests that included at least one thermonuclear—or hydrogen—bomb. Pakistan responded less than three weeks afterwards with its own first six tests, and became the eighth country in the world to possess nuclear weapons. Since that day, Abdul Qadeer Khan has been hailed by one and all in Pakistan as a national hero. This is the man, some of his countrymen maintain—taking a distinctly unsubtle swipe at what is regarded by many of his fellow countrymen as unwarranted Western opprobrium—that can do no wrong.

In an interview with Elizabeth Dougherty, *The Atlantic*'s William Langewiesche sheds some light on how this all came about. His comments are interesting because he met many of the players involved, and also went to Pakistan to do some extremely thorough field research. Langewiesche's view is that Khan succeeded (where others didn't) because he was so very aggressive: "He was very effective. He was a great organizer and manager. People say he's a great scientist and a brilliant scientist. But it wasn't science that mattered, it was management. He was highly energetic and had an unlimited budget. That helped, but had it not been for him, it would have been someone else."

As he explains, there were many different reasons for Khan's success. The Pakistani military—which runs the Pakistani army and Musharraf, says Langewiesche—"does not want the real story to come out because it will definitely implicate them. There's just no question about that. They don't want Khan's export activity to be explored fully out of political self-preservation."

Langewiesche goes on: "It's important to realize that the United States, unlike Pakistan, is a very large and complex country politically. Pakistan has a lot of people, but it's actually a very small country because the great majority of people are extremely poor and basically don't count politically. Pakistan is a dictatorship with very small elite running it as if it's a small country. . ."

David Albright and Corey Hinderstein studied A.Q. Khan's activities for *The Washington Quarterly*.[3] They make the point that his setup was first and foremost, "an elaborate and highly successful illicit procurement network that Khan created in the 1970s to supply Pakistan's gas-centrifuge program, which has been used to produce weapons-grade uranium for Pakistan's nuclear weapons program.

"Khan and his associates slowly expanded their import operation, however, into a transnational illegal network that also exported gas centrifuges and production capabilities, as well as designs for nuclear weapons, to other mostly Muslim countries to turn a profit and provide additional business for their international collaborators. In addition to money, Khan was also motivated by pan-Islamism and hostility to Western controls on nuclear technology."

Most significant, they say, is the fact that it caused enormous damage to efforts aimed at stopping the spread of nuclear weapons, to U.S. national security, and to international peace and stability.

"Without assistance from the network, it is unlikely that Iran would have been able to develop the ability to enrich uranium using gas centrifuges—now that country's most advanced and threatening nuclear program."

This leads to one of Khan's many tentacles, which by this point stretched all the way across the Indian Ocean, again to South Africa. South African national Johan Meyer, owner of Tradefin—a local company with links to a clique of German nuclear proliferators—was arrested on suspicion of manufacturing centrifuge parts and equipment for the original Libyan nuclear weapons program. This was no simple matter; it spanned years, cost millions, and subsequent investigations have indicated that there were people involved who knew first, that the project was nuclear-related, and more important, that it was intended for Libya, one of the arch revolutionary states of the modern period. Moreover, Meyer had been involved in South Africa's nuclear program, so he knew the score. It is perhaps no accident that Gadhafi and *both* South African presidents in the post-apartheid period have regularly visited each other.

With so much that is unsavory taking place in that country since Nelson Mandela's African National Congress took over the government—and the fact that the ANC, for generations, was staunchly communist (its national trade-union structure remains so) as well as being outspokenly anti-American—one can only speculate as to why this has been allowed to happen. Many of these shenanigans are detailed in chapters 11 and 12.[4]

Government ignorance is no excuse. Too many people in South Africa—a state with one of the most intrusive intelligence organizations on the continent—

were in the know. Also, huge amounts of money arrived directly from Libya, peculiar in an age with so many significant money-laundering stopgaps. In addition, the Krisch project wasn't the only one built; others had preceded it, and had been ferreted out of the country to Pakistan. Unusual, say some observers, never mind the fact that people talk. And Pretoria knew nothing about it . . .

Then, when American authorities asked the South Africans, as a matter of great urgency, to look into what was going on at Krisch Engineering in December 2003, it took until September 2004—nine months—for them to do so. That, in itself, says a lot. When they eventually did act, eleven shipping containers, fully loaded and ready to go, were seized, which was when British, American, and IAEA officials descended on the scene to have a look for themselves. Dr. Nic von Wielligh was brought in to monitor South African government interests.

What has subsequently been pieced together is that apart from Meyer, two foreign nationals with permanent South African residency status were, as the court records show, "implicated in the manufacture of products meant to enrich uranium—and facilitate its supply to Libya." These were Daniel Geiges, a Swiss citizen and a director of Krisch Engineering, and Gerhard Wisser, also German and the firm's managing director. Wisser also arranged for two Libyans to come to South Africa and inspect the completed project.

Brought to court the first time, the State showed that some of these individuals were linked to South Africa's Nuclear Energy Corporation of SA (NECSA), a government body, as well as to the Abdul Qadeer Khan network.

Wisser, it has since transpired, had a long history of involvement with Khan. Shortly thereafter, the Swiss national Urs Tinner was nabbed in Germany for complicity. That was followed by the arrest of another German, regarded as pivotal to the operation, and this is where things start to get interesting. In the 1970s and early 1980s, according to Albright and Hinderstein, Lerch was employed by Leybold Heraeus, a German company that developed and produced vacuum products and technology. Before undergoing significant internal reform in the early 1990s, Leybold Heraeus and its sister companies had been major suppliers to many secret nuclear weapons programs, including those in Iraq, Iran, South Africa, and Pakistan. In this instance, Leybold Heraeus—where Lerch worked—supplied a prototype valve which was "clandestinely exported" to South Africa. When asked about it, a spokesperson for Leybold refused to comment, saying that the company was cooperating with "relevant institutions."

A South African weekly paper, the *Mail & Guardian*, laid it on the line in a brilliant exposé on the subterfuge. It showed that Meyer had turned State witness early on and blown the whistle on his pals. It also emerged that Krisch Engineering—and specifically Wisser and Geiges—had worked on the apartheid nuclear weapons program. It also disclosed that Geiges had approached Meyer "in the late 1980s" to manufacture part of a nuclear-enrichment plant, ordered by "a client" of Krisch Engineering. It was built at his South African factory and exported. Meyer, said the *Mail & Guardian*, had subsequently established that the client was Pakistan.

There were other deals, some of them involving Pakistan's archenemy, India. The charge sheet claims: "In the late 1980s and early 1990s, [Wisser] commissioned one of his employees to produce flow meter units which were specifically designed for a UF_6 [the processed uranium ready for enrichment] application. They were delivered to India."

The most ambitious project was yet to come, one that implicated all the major players. In July 1999, says the charge sheet, Wisser traveled to Dubai for technical discussions with Lerch and others. Later that year, Geiges, drawn into the project by Wisser, approached Meyer to help. Most of the manufacturing was to be done at Meyer's Tradefin.

In the Gulf, they had met the A.Q. Khan network's chief money man, Buhary Seyed Abu Tahir, who was subsequently arrested in Malaysia, where he had arranged for the materiel found on the *BBC China* to be engineered by a company co-owned by the Malaysian prime minister's son.

Meanwhile, Meyer opened a Swiss account. When asked about it, Wisser claimed that Meyer received $6 million for what he maintained was only a water purification plant. Personally, he admitted to receiving a commission of about a million U.S. dollars, although the German magazine *Der Spiegel* reports that German investigators believe he received up to ten times as much.

Also spelled out were details of what had been manufactured. This included all the equipment to service a cascade of 5,832 centrifuges, the machines central to nuclear enrichment. There were also units made to feed uranium hexafluoride gas (UF_6) into the centrifuges and extract the enriched product and waste, as well as the piping systems to connect the centrifuges and control, regulate, and monitor the systems.

The specialized centrifuge cylinders would also have been manufactured at Tradefin. Controlled manufacturing machinery was illicitly shipped to South Africa for this, but was shipped back to Dubai after that part of the project was abandoned. Wisser allegedly arranged for Tahir to be informed that the machine was on its way back with the following words: "The gift has been dispatched with DHL." The machine was eventually recovered in Libya by U.S. investigators.

Plans were made to export the plant via Mozambique. A fake contract for "high purification water treatment plants," supposedly destined for Jordan, was drawn up, signed by "Professor Tahir." But then the *BBC China* was stopped in Italy, and the Libyan nuclear program abandoned.

Wisser destroyed evidence at Krisch Engineering and traveled to Dubai for further instructions. From there, he sent a frantic text message to Meyer: "The bird must be destroyed, feathers and all . . . They have fed us to the dogs."

Meyer didn't comply. The "bird"—the better part of a nuclear-enrichment plant ordered by Libya, we now know—survived.

Chapter 4 Endnotes:

1   Andrew Koch, "Investigators Suspect Nuclear Smuggling Network is Still Active," *Jane's Intelligence Review*, London, July 1, 2006.

2   A.Q. Khan Nuclear Chronology, by Michael Laufer, Proliferation Brief, vol. 8, no 8, Carnegie Endowment for International Peace, Washington, D.C.

3   *The Washington Quarterly* 28.2 (2005), pp. 111–28 (The Center for Strategic and International Studies and the Massachusetts Institute of Technology).

4   *Iran's Nuclear Option—Tehran's Quest for the Atom Bomb*, Casemate Publishers, Philadelphia, 2005, pp. 353–55.

5   He eventually went public with it, adequately illustrated at Pakistan's first international arms bazaar in 2000. At the booth of the Khan Research Laboratories (KRL), available for all was a Pak-2 brochure together with a ten-page catalog of specialty items like high-voltage switches, vacuum pumps, gauges, and power supplies. It was all for sale, KRL representatives told anybody who inquired about availability.

6   Stefaans Brummer, "SA's Nuclear Bazaar," *Mail & Guardian*, Johannesburg, March 24, 2006.

CHAPTER 5

A NUCLEAR IRAN

> If one day . . . the world of Islam is mutually equipped with the kind of weapons which Israel presently possesses, the world's arrogant [colonialist] strategy will then come to a dead end, because the use of an atomic bomb on Israel won't leave anything behind . . ."
> —Former Iranian president Akbar Hashemi-Rafsanjani, speaking to graduates at Tehran University

Somebody said something on one of the network news reports not long ago to this effect: The first time anybody will know whether Iran has the bomb or not is when they use it. It's a simplistic deduction, but as we heard from Uri Avnery in the introduction to this book, the sentiment causes an awful lot of sleepless nights in the Jewish Homeland.

What we do know is that it was Pakistan's A.Q. Khan who supplied Libya with enough hardware to build the bomb. Had Gadhafi not been checked, he'd probably also have it by now. The North Koreans were also at the receiving end of Khan's benevolence, as a host of intelligence agencies on both sides of the Atlantic have been able to discover. So too were Tehran's mullahs.

What is understood in the broadest terms is that the trail that led from Pakistan to Libya included a similar road that led to Iran. The Libyan connection was more sophisticated. It was left to Dr. Mohamed ElBaradei, head of Vienna's International Atomic Energy Agency, to fill in some of the gaps after he'd cleared house in Tripoli and Gadhafi's illegal acquisitions had been shipped off to the States.

Hardly effusive in dealing with the media—in fact, interviewing him is like pulling teeth—he was surprisingly forthcoming. He admitted to being astonished at what he discovered in North Africa, and talked about "the existence of a shadowy network of middlemen involved in nuclear-related matters who tended to circumvent national export controls. These measures were supposed to control the movement of weapons of mass destruction. What I encountered in Libya proved that these controls are simply not working."

Though he is invariably loath to admit IAEA shortcomings, because that is supposed to be America's game—Washington is suspicious of just about everything that the UN body does—he did concede that the agency had been taken by surprise. By inference, he suggested, so had the entire Western intelligence community.

As another commentator explained, the smuggling network was, and still is, global. It stretches from Germany to Dubai, from Malaysia to South Africa, and from China to south Asia. It involves middlemen and suppliers, significant numbers of both. What is striking about a string of recent disclosures, experts say, is how many roads appear to lead back to the Khan Research Laboratories in Kahuta, where Pakistan's own bomb was developed.

Earlier, in an interview with the French newspaper *Le Monde*, the IAEA's Dr. ElBaradei suggested that there were dozens of countries that would be capable in the long term of manufacturing nuclear weapons. He underscored an urgent need to reinforce and update the Nuclear Non-Proliferation Treaty (NPT).[1]

The treaty, he said, came into force in 1970 and had been overtaken by a world "in which developing nuclear arms has become attractive not only to many countries, but also to terrorist groups." Under current international law, he added, there was nothing illicit in a non-nuclear state conducting uranium-enriching activities, or even in possessing military-grade nuclear material. Should any country decide to break its commitment to the NPT, experts believe that it "could produce a weapon in a comparatively short time. We are on the verge of just such a catastrophe with North Korea."

Since then, North Korea has done what it said it would do. And the perception in Washington, London, Cairo, Moscow, and Beijing is that exactly the same holds true for Iran.

Fortunately, not everybody associated with the IAEA is as reticent as Dr. El-Baradei. Following the old South African apartheid regime handing over power to Nelson Mandela, this former racist state was once again voted onto the board of governors in Vienna. The move made sense. During the volatile apartheid era—which included a spate of wars along the largely hostile frontiers with Black Africa—South Africa had built itself six atom bombs.

The man appointed to oversee South Africa's interests in Vienna was Dr. Nic von Wielligh, a physicist who had served his country's Atomic Energy Corporation (now South African Nuclear Energy Corporation—NECSA) for twenty-four years. With a very good understanding of that period, he was appointed to the position by the venerable Madiba himself.

Having spent years dealing with Tehran's representatives while associated with the IAEA—intermittently from 1985 onwards to his retirement in 2002—Dr. von Wielligh had some interesting things to say when I met him at his home outside Pretoria. What emerged from this impromptu discussion was the fact that the good doctor had many opportunities to observe Iran at work at the IAEA, most times at close quarters. He talks candidly about the 1995 and 2000 Nuclear Non-Proliferation Treaty (NPT) Revue Conferences, or, in the lingo, Revcons, which he attended.

"I must confess that I was struck by [the] very sharp and formidable [Iranian] negotiating skills. Especially in 2000, they got in the end [wording in the text of the Final Document] what they'd set out to obtain all along," he declared.

As a team, the South African physicist found the Iranians both relentless and focused, "and by this I do not necessarily mean in any kind of negative sense. What I want to emphasize is that the Iranian way of doing things is the age-old Middle-East way of bargaining. Their recent stop-and-go tactics with the IAEA are typical of this.

"I don't think that we, accustomed to the more clinical Western approach, always appreciate this way of doing things—especially the U.S., to which other cultures don't exist. Obviously Iran has much to hide, but this is compounded by their traditional way of doing things."

Some of the observations that Dr. von Wielligh was able to make at the IAEA are instructive. They point to a pattern for the future which most Western governments find unsettling. He was also able to listen to Iranian complaints that they sometimes felt themselves excluded by the Arab-speaking countries. "And that, in spite of their common religion, of course compounded by the variants thereof," he added.

His association with the Iranian contingent at the agency wasn't all business. While these Middle Eastern envoys liked to keep to themselves and invariably stuck together, even when out on the town, there was the occasional informal session, he told me. "I found them if not actually genial, then polite and well-mannered. They'd enjoy a little small talk, though clearly, anything to do with politics back home wasn't on the agenda. Once that was over, it was back to the negotiating table."

Dr. von Wielligh explained how Iran concluded a comprehensive Safeguards Agreement with the IAEA as far back as December 1974, after being one of the first countries to sign the NPT (while still ruled by the Shah). "The recent discoveries in Iran are clearly a violation of the requirements of that Safeguards Agreement."

As he suggests, the IAEA is often taken to task because they have not discovered undeclared activities. Not always rightly so, he elaborated, making the point that a Comprehensive Safeguards Agreement has some important limitations built into it, due to the way in which it was negotiated decades ago (not by the IAEA, but by its Member States).

Dr. von Wielligh continues:

Inspectors cannot just roam about in a host country and inspect what they wish. There are strict limitations to access and information. Furthermore, it was only the other day that new methods—for example, so-called environmental analysis—have become available through which the analysis of swipe samples can yield important information on undeclared activities based on very small samples.

Due to these limitations Saddam [and Iran] could run undeclared and un-detected activities next to plants that were being inspected by the IAEA for many years. But it was precisely through environmental sampling that undeclared ac-tivities were uncovered in Iran.

More salient, Dr. von Wielligh stressed, was the fact that in terms of Com-prehensive Safeguards, there is simply no obligation for any country to report uranium mining operations.

In fact, uranium comes under safeguards only when it has reached a certain pu-rity as UF_6, or has been processed into a pure-enough form as an oxide for use as fuel in heavy water reactors.

In all fairness then, it must be clear why Hans Blix [and others] visited Iran many times in the past without detecting any undeclared activities. They had no right to inspect or visit facilities *not declared* to them, due solely to the way the Agreement was structured by the Member States, including the USA.

Due to these limitations, and after the discoveries in Iraq, the Additional Protocol was negotiated. This now gives the IAEA access to substantially more information and places to inspect, the latter at very short notice under certain circumstances. Information on mining, the production of ore concentrates, fuel cycle–related research and development (R&D) activities—even when no nu-clear material is present—and the manufacture of nuclear-related equipment, together with the import/export of Trigger List items and the rest must now be submitted.

Thus, with a comprehensive and focused analysis of all the information at its disposal (including satellite photos, information submitted by intelligence agencies, and open source literature), the IAEA is now in a much better position to detect undeclared material and activities.

This former South African diplomat at the IAEA then added his own two bits' worth about terrorists acquiring nuclear weapons.

It's my view that in spite of the general nature of bomb design being known [with actual blueprints having been available in Libya], the problem has always been the availability of the nuclear material for the bomb core.

This is still the main obstacle and requires a huge amount of financial and technological resources to overcome. It is my belief, therefore, that groups or states inclined toward fostering terror will rather settle for a so-called "dirty bomb" or a Radiological Dispersal Device. [As explained by the Web site of the U.S. Nuclear Regulatory Commission, this type of bomb—also called an RDD—"combines a conventional explosive, such as dynamite, with radioactive material."]

It is simple to construct using conventional explosives available to them, mixed with radioactive nuclear waste or other commercially available radioisotopes which are not by far as well guarded as HEU or Plutonium.

In Western terms, the handling of radioactively hot material without the necessary sophisticated technical means would be a problem from a safety point of view—though not for terrorists willing to give up their lives. The radioactive contamination spread by such a bomb, while not necessarily deadly, will create great and lasting panic among the public who is so afraid of radioactivity.

This, unfortunately, is exactly what terrorists want, he declared.

In a rare interview given to an American network in May 1995, former Iranian president Rafsanjani told the ABC television network that his country neither had nuclear weapons nor was it seeking to acquire or to develop them. "If [Washington] can prove a single case, then we will accept all other allegations," he declared on camera.[2]

Even now, more than a decade later, Rafsanjani's statement remains significant for several reasons, the first being that he was not telling the truth. In fact, he, like the rest his theocratic friends, have been lying fluently from Day One.

By the time he issued this challenge, as the Iranians themselves have since told us—and as they disclosed to the IAEA after the second invasion of Iraq by the American-led Coalition Forces—the Iranian nuclear program was already eight years old. More salient, it was one of those rare occasions that anyone in Iran (least of all the head of state) had allowed himself to be drawn out on the subject.

In one of his comments on this issue, former secretary of state Warren Christopher went on record as saying: "[B]ased on a wide variety of data, we know that since the mid-1980s, Iran has had an organized structure dedicated to acquiring and developing nuclear weapons.

"In organization, programs, procurement, and covert activities," he declared, "Iran is pursuing the classic route to nuclear weapons which has been followed by almost all states that have recently sought a nuclear capability." He referred specifically to Iraq, where, because of a weak industrial infrastructure that could not support the demands of a nuclear effort, it needed to seek expertise from abroad—very much as Iran is doing today—in terms of personnel, technology, equipment, and materials for building weapons of mass destruction.

While Tehran denies that it is building an atomic bomb, the West has assembled a very substantial body of evidence suggesting the contrary.

Though Iran originally signed the Nuclear Non-Proliferation Treaty (NPT)—as, coincidentally, had Iraq—it was secretly pursuing a broad, organized effort to develop nuclear weapons. According to the Chicago-based *Bulletin of the Atomic Scientists*, there are those who implicate the (Iranian) defense ministry in illegal foreign procurement activities and possible nuclear weapons work.[3] The Pakistani connection, as some call it, is also involved, to the point where *The Washington Post* recalled that Clinton told Yeltsin at one of their first summits that America had evidence Iran was pursuing a nuclear weapons acquisition blueprint. It had been drawn up at least four years earlier with the aid of Pakistani officials, Clinton disclosed.[4]

Already in 1995, *The New York Times* mentioned that senior American and Israeli officials had revealed that "Iran might be able to build a bomb in five years." The consensus in Washington a decade later is that this Shiite nation is further ahead "in the race towards nuclear parity than Iraq was when the UN Special Commission for Iraq (UNSCOM) halted Saddam's nuclear program."

Pakistan's involvement with Iran is linked to more substantive issues, particularly with regard to some of the acknowledged alliances in the region. India's border dispute with China has clearly resulted in closer Pakistani-Chinese ties, and, by inference, a deepening friendship between China and Iran.

Since the mid-1980s, China has been another of Iran's suppliers of nuclear-related technologies. Beijing supplied three sub-critical and zero-power reactors, as well as an electromagnetic isotope separation (EMIS) machine for enriching uranium, which features in several programs for producing nuclear weapons, South Africa's too, during the formative years of its program.

A small, 80 kW thermal research reactor followed. Washington acknowledges that while none of this hardware is capable of producing more than small quantities of nuclear weapons' material, EMIS machines can be reverse-engineered.

Significantly, reckons David Albright, China also helped Iran create nuclear fuel facilities for uranium mining, fuel fabrication, uranium purification, and zirconium tube production (see *Jane's Pointer*, February 1998). Already in the pipeline (despite strong American protests) were facilities to produce uranium metal and uranium hexafluoride (UF_6).

It's worth mentioning that in his day, Saddam Hussein also received some Indian aid in developing weapons, which seriously displeased the Tehran regime. But that was before the first Gulf War, and for some time, there had been speculation in intelligence circles about a "rogue alliance between Iraq and Iran." Alliance or not, it's worth recalling that the two countries remained deeply suspicious of each other until the end. Reasons stemmed as much from Saddam's persecution of his own Shiite majority as from the terrible damage and loss of life (a million-plus) caused by the horrific eight-year war between the two nations.

Looking back, it would seem that India's involvement with Iraq, while low-key, could have been one of the reasons why Saddam very publicly supported India's nuclear tests. At about that time the Sunday edition of a Baghdad weekly owned by one of the dictator's sons announced that India had agreed to enroll several groups of Iraqi engineers "in advanced technological courses." The training was unspecified, but America was concerned at the time that Iraq might acquire illicit assistance in the nuclear or ballistic missile areas.[5]

A lot of what has been going on in Iran until recently—the country hosted scores of visits by IAEA inspectors before they were expelled—took place in yesterday's Iraq.

Like Iran's relationship with Saddam Hussein's Iraq, Iran's association with the International Atomic Energy Agency has always been precarious. It was punctuated by periods of cooperation and apparent goodwill one moment, followed by uncompromising and intransigent stonewalling the next. This much is clearly reflected in the IAEA "restricted distribution" Board of Governors report, titled Implementation of the NPT Agreement in the Islamic Republic of Iran, dated 27 February 2006 (GOV/2006/15). It reads, in part:

As noted in the Director General's report . . . the Agency has repeatedly requested Iran to provide additional information on certain issues related to its enrichment program. Iran declined to discuss these matters at the 12–14 February 2006 meeting in Tehran . . . The Agency reiterated that it was essential to resolve these questions so that the Agency can verify the correctness and completeness of Iran's declarations, particularly in light of the two decades of concealed activities . . .*(continues on page 72)*

ENRICHING URANIUM

Despite the hullabaloo about Third World states breaking accords to achieve a nuclear option, it's a pretty fundamental reality that nuclear power—in all its forms—is here to stay. There are almost 500 nuclear power reactors in the world, either operating or in the process of construction. In a few years, we could have double that number. Every one of them requires "uranium enriched in the uranium-235 isotope" (or ^{235}U, in scientific language) for their fuel. Several processes are employed, but we'll stick with the two that are most commonly used.

First the basics:[1] Uranium is found in nature, and consists largely of two isotopes, uranium-235 and uranium-238. The production of energy in nuclear reactors is from the "fissioning" or splitting of the ^{235}U atoms, a process which releases energy in the form of heat. Uranium-235 is the main fissionable isotope of uranium.

Natural uranium contains 0.7 percent of the ^{235}U isotope. The remaining 99.3 percent is mostly the uranium-238 isotope, which does not contribute directly to the fission process (though it does so indirectly by the formation of fissile isotopes of plutonium).

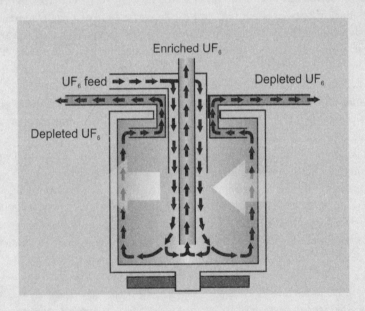

Some reactors—for example, the Canadian-designed CANDU and the British Magnox reactors—use natural uranium as their fuel. Most present-day reactors (light water reactors, or LWRs) use enriched uranium, where the proportion of the ^{235}U isotope has been increased from 0.7 percent to about 3, or up to 5 percent. (For comparison, uranium used for nuclear weapons would have to be enriched in plants specially designed to achieve at least 90 percent ^{235}U in content.)

There is also the Pebble Bed Modular Reactor (PBMR), a new type of high-temperature helium gas–cooled nuclear reactor, which builds and advances on worldwide nuclear operators' experience of older reactor designs. Reckoned by its designers to be a practical and cost-effective solution to most of the logistics of generating electricity, the system has particular reference to South Africa today. Regarded as low-cost, relatively simple in design, and cheaper than conventional nuclear reactors, ten PBMR reactors produce 1,100 MWe (enough for more than 300,000 homes), and would occupy an area of no more than three football fields.

Conversion

Uranium generally exits the mining process as the concentrate of a stable oxide known as U_3O_8, [or as a peroxide]. It still contains some impurities, and prior to enrichment has to be further refined before being converted to uranium hexafluoride (UF_6), commonly referred to as "hex" (see below). Conversion plants are operating commercially in the USA, Canada, France, the UK, and Russia.

After initial refining, which may involve the production of uranyl nitrate, uranium trioxide is reduced in a kiln by hydrogen to uranium dioxide (UO_2). This is then reacted in another kiln with hydrogen fluoride (HF) to form uranium tetrafluoride (UF_4). The tetrafluoride is then fed into a fluidized bed reactor with gaseous fluorine to produce UF_6. Removal of impurities takes place at each step. When suitably refined, it is ready to be introduced into the enrichment process proper.

The UF_6, particularly if moist, is highly corrosive. When warm it is a gas, suitable for use in the enrichment process. At lower temperature and under moderate pressure, the UF_6 can be liquefied. The liquid is run into specially designed steel shipping cylinders which are thick-walled and weigh over 15 tons when full. As it cools, the liquid UF_6 within the cylinder becomes a white crystalline solid and is shipped in this form.

The siting, environmental, and security management of a conversion plant is subject to the regulations that are in effect for any chemical processing plant involving fluorine-based chemicals.

Enrichment

A number of enrichment processes have been demonstrated in the laboratory, but only two—the gaseous diffusion process and the centrifuge process—are operating on a commercial scale. In both of these, UF_6 gas is used as the feed material. Molecules of UF_6 with U-235 atoms are about 1 percent lighter than the rest, and this difference in mass is the basis of both processes.

Large commercial enrichment plants are in operation in France, Germany, the Netherlands, the UK, the USA, and Russia, with smaller plants dotted elsewhere around the globe. New centrifuge plants are being built in France and the USA.

---

[1] Uranium Enrichment: Nuclear Issues Briefing Paper 33, November 2006, Uranium Information Center, Melbourne, Australia: http://www.uic.com.au/nip33.htm. Also Heriot, I. D. (1988), Uranium Enrichment by Centrifuge, Report EUR 11486, Commission of the European Communities, Brussels; Kehoe, R. B. (2002), The Enriching Troika: A History of Urenco to the Year 2000, Urenco, Marlow, UK; Wilson, P. D., ed. (1996), The Nuclear Fuel Cycle: From Ore to Wastes, Oxford University Press, Oxford, UK.

Since it will be difficult to establish a definitive conclusion with respect to the origin of all of the contamination, it is essential for the Agency to make progress in ascertaining the scope and chronology of Iran's centrifuge enrichment program. The implementation of the Additional Protocol and Iran's full cooperation in this regard are essential for the Agency to be able to provide the required assurance concerning the absence of undeclared nuclear material and activities in Iran.

While a similar IAEA resolution two years previously "welcomed Iran's offer of active cooperation and openness and its positive response to the demands of the Board in the resolution adopted," the one that followed "strongly deplored Iran's past failures and breaches of its obligations to comply with the provisions of the Safeguards Agreement as reported by the Director General." It went on to urge Tehran to adhere strictly to its obligations in both "letter and spirit."

Part of this problem stems from what, in nuclear inspection parlance, is meant by "correct, complete and final pictures" of Iran's past and present nuclear programs.

There was a time when Tehran decided to come clean on its nuclear programs in 2003 (after Gulf War 2, which caused a nervous flutter not only in Libya, but also in Iran). By all accounts it seemed that things would proceed accordingly. Tehran assured the agency that weapons inspectors would be invited to Iran to see the various sites, make observations, install monitors, and so on. Shortly afterwards, the theocrats would backtrack and demand that all such activity stop.

It hasn't been lost on any of these people that ongoing Iranian problems are exactly the same as those experienced in Iraq under Saddam Hussein. Like Iraq in the past, Tehran would offer "full and final" reports. Then, once the inspectors had detected anomalies or nondisclosures, a debate would follow. This could become quite furious in private, but occasionally public sentiments were voiced. Press reports would follow in the government-controlled media that tended to inculcate bad feelings all round.

Then, almost on schedule, another "full and final" report would appear and the cycle of duplicity would be repeated. Most times, the Atomic Energy Organization of Iran (AEOI) would provide just enough information and background to keep the inspectors at bay, and, as Dr. von Wielligh observed, history has a way of repeating itself. The Iranians were doing exactly as the Iraqis had done: They were buying time. It was an endless, inconclusive business, he added, in one sense, a bit like the game of catch-me-if-you-can, with rather more serious consequences for the international community if, in the end, not everything was brought to light. North Korea's actions certainly validated that one.

Matters can be further compounded by language and innuendo, the sort that tends to emerge from exchanges between Tehran and the West. Take one example:

Following the adoption by the UN nuclear organization of a "compromise" solution to an Iranian nuclear dossier in November 2003, Tehran promptly hailed the deal as a "victory for Iran and an obvious failure for America and Israel," even though the Jewish State had absolutely nothing to do with it. Which raises another question: What exactly do we know about things nuclear in Iran? The international community has batches of satellite images of the goings-on at Natanz and Arak, two nondescript towns a few hours south of Tehran. These show a heavy-water plant similar to the nuclear-related heavy-water facilities used in Pakistan's atom bomb program at Arak.

Photos taken of the Natanz facility show something akin to a uranium-enrichment plant coupled to a centrifuge facility, which the Iranians say is really only surface workings. The rest, a recent report out of Tehran disclosed, was secreted far below ground and out of reach of just about everything short of a thermonuclear—meaning hydrogen bomb—preemptive strike.

David Albright confirmed that work conducted in both centers might be related to the production of highly enriched uranium and heavy water, which, he explained, could be used for the production of nuclear weapons. Interestingly, the disclosures come in the wake of strong denials by Mohammed Javad Zarif, Iran's ambassador to the United Nations, that his country is building atom bombs. *The New York Times* had already upped the ante on March 11, 2004, when Craig S. Smith declared that the alarm had been raised over the quality of uranium found in Iran.[6]

Smith reported that United Nations nuclear inspectors had discovered traces of extremely highly enriched uranium in Iran of a purity for use in a nuclear bomb. Some of this stuff had been enriched to 90 percent of the rare 235 isotope. He also made the point that while the IAEA had previously admitted to finding "weapons-grade" traces in a preliminary search in 2003, it had not revealed that some of it had reached such a high degree of enrichment. So far, nobody had had the temerity to ask, why not?

What was also disconcerting was that Iran's defense minister, Ali Shamkhani, disclosed for the first time on March 10, 2004, that the Iranian military had produced centrifuges to enrich uranium. He added the rider that these were strictly for civilian use, according to an Associated Press report from Tehran. A senior American official quoted afterwards by Smith had his own view of the subject: "It's rather strange, don't you think, that the military gets involved in the electric power–generating business, or that they forgot to mention this before when they were 'fully disclosing' all details of their program?"

What *is* clear is that there are peculiar goings-on in Iran at present, all the more so once Tehran blocked further nuclear-related inspections.

Issues were further compounded when Iran disclosed that it had conducted a successful test of its much-vaunted Shahab-3 missile in October 2006, which, some Americans sources maintain, can carry a one-ton payload as far as 1,300 miles, or well beyond Israeli territory. The timing of Iran's announcement about the Shahab-3 and the size of its payload suggested that the missile could very well be intended to carry a nuclear warhead.

Remember—the Shahab medium-range ballistic missile and all its variants underscores Iran's close links with the other members of this infamous troika. In Pakistan the same MRBM is called the Ghauri, and in North Korea, No-Dong.

Looking back, there is simply no question that Saddam Hussein's confrontational and often unpredictable actions played a significant role in causing Tehran to look at the nuclear option as an alternative to conventional styles of warfare.

The two countries fought a fierce eight-year war which, while it lasted, was utterly unrelenting. At the end of it, more than a million Iranian casualties were left on the battlefield. Though official tallies are vague, the number of Iranian troops KIA is something along the order of 300,000. Thus, it came as no surprise when America's Central Intelligence Agency told Congress in the mid-1980s that there was every indication that Iran was driven to build nuclear weapons because it feared that its bellicose neighbor Iraq might be doing the same.

That need became especially urgent, a well-placed intelligence source in the American capital told Jane's, after the original UN monitoring body, the UN Special Commission (UNSCOM), was forced out of Iraq in 1997. It didn't help that there were endless debates in the UN Security Council about how its successor might be reconstituted.

It was David Albright's view at the time that the Iranians were being driven to produce the weapon for no better reason than to prevent being annihilated as a nation. "Tehran was alarmed at what they knew [was] taking place just across the border. They didn't want to be caught short a second time," he reckoned.

There are a variety of indications that a lot more might be happening in Iran at the present time than most Western observers would like to believe. For instance, Iranian attempts to buy highly enriched uranium (HEU) and plutonium on the East European black market are well sourced. A number of incidents are documented. Also, Tehran has been shopping for nuclear technical know-how. Moreover, the authorities are aware that the Iranians recruited foreign specialists for its WMD research and development programs, including a number of South African scientists who were formerly involved in their own country's now-defunct missile programs. Other reports mention Russians and Pakistanis.[7]

Since then, the going rate for someone with the required skills in that country has increased to well beyond $10,000 a month. Since rocket scientists from Pretoria's program have been helping Iran hone these skills for quite a few years, it would seem a natural progression to employ those with other advanced scientific skills, especially if they are unable to earn a living in their own country.[8]

On the nuclear side, research has been taking place at various locations. The IAEA knows of many of them, including the Tehran Nuclear Research Center (TNRC), which includes hot cells located in the Jabr Ibn Hayan Laboratories, the Natanz site, Karaj, the well-publicized heavy-water facility at Arak, and the Esfahan Nuclear Technology Center (ENTC), along with a host of others. Until its nuclear assets were dismantled and moved, there was also the innocuously named Kalaye Electric Company, though that is hardly the end of the story. There are many more nuclear assets that remain hidden, and in a country as xenophobic as Iran, they are extremely difficult to trace.

Noteworthy is Tehran's October 21, 2003, letter to the IAEA, acknowledging that it had conducted laboratory and bench-scale conversion experiments in the Uranium Conversion Laboratory (UCL) at the former Radiochemical Laboratories located at the TNRC, and at the Jabr Ibn Hayan Laboratories. For these purposes, scientists used nuclear fuel that had been imported in 1977, 1982, and 1991.[9] It also admitted to having transferred "relevant dismantled equipment used in these processes at the TNRC" to the Radioactive Waste Storage Facility at Karaj.

In a country bigger and, in places, as remote as the Yukon, it is impossible to keep track of all developments. Some details are known. According to Iranian expatriate sources (including those with the dissident insurgent group, *Mujahedin-e-Khalq*), there is a cadre of between three and four thousand personnel at work at various nuclear-related sites in Isfahan, south of the capital. Work at Isfahan, where, it is said (but not confirmed) that many nuclear-related facilities are located half a mile underground. A second, secret weapons design center is located at Moallam Kelaieh near the Caspian Sea.

Two more nuclear research sites are at the nuclear power plant at Bushehr on the Gulf, where Russian crews are building Iran's only nuclear power station (partially destroyed during the war with Iraq). Still more is going on at Tehran's Sharif University, long suspected to be the cradle of Iran's nuclear program.

An Israeli diplomatic source in Washington told this writer that because so much attention was given to this institution in the past, it was to be expected that the Iranians would fragment their nuclear activities. "They would do what you expect them to do and spread them about the country," he declared, adding that following the Israeli Air Force attack on Iraq's 40-MWt materials test reactor, Tammuz-1, at Osiraq in June 1981, Tehran was taking no chances.

From a country that at first allowed religious principles to dictate an aversion to nuclear weapons, and then, halfway through the war with Iraq, to do an abrupt about-face, it is interesting that so much was achieved in such a short time.

Already in 1989, Rafsanjani had observed that Iran simply could not ignore the nuclear reality in the modern world. Nor was the possibility of Iran exploring chemical and biological warfare ruled out. At a speech to military officers, he stated, "Chemical and biological weapons are the poor man's atomic bombs and can easily be produced. We should at least consider them for our defense." He went on: "Although the use of such weapons is inhuman, the [Iran-Iraq] war taught us that international laws are only scraps of paper."

Since then, it has been all systems go at trying to acquire foreign WMD expertise and technology in all three basic nuclear, biological, and chemical (NBC) disciplines. Pakistan, for instance, was asked for uranium gas centrifuge technology and agreed to train Iranian nuclear scientists at its Institute for Nuclear Science and Technology near Islamabad. We are now aware that this association was far more extensive than anybody thought possible.

Islamabad's role, it is now revealed, was decisive in Iran acquiring the level of advanced nuclear technology necessary to make bombs. This emerged when A.Q. Khan confessed in a twelve-page document presented to his president, Pervez Musharraf, to sharing his country's nuclear technology with Iran, Libya, and North Korea.

In turn, the IAEA was given a list of at least five scientists and officials associated with Khan's brainchild, the Kahuta Research Laboratories (KRL), since renamed Khan's Research Laboratories, a uranium-enrichment plant located just outside the capital city of Islamabad. Moreover, none of it was for free; the money involved resulted in tens of millions of dollars transferred into Pakistani bank accounts, prompting just about everybody who has taken an intrusive look into the scandal to suggest that it was simply impossible for the government *not* to be aware of what was going on.[10]

In retrospect, this caused severe damage. Said Michael Krepon, former director of the Henry L. Stimson Center, "If only half of this is true, it suggests a huge breakdown in [proliferation] oversight that must be repaired."[11]

Argentina was also approached in the early days about acquiring nuclear expertise and equipment and, until U.S. pressure was brought to bear, responded favorably. So, too, was Cuba. Similarly, reactors were sought from China, Russia, and India. Others contacted include Poland, Czechoslovakia, and Italy. The results, as far as can be reckoned, have been mixed, since Washington managed to block only some of these efforts.

Meanwhile, Beijing entered the picture. U.S. officials believe that China constructed a uranium hexafluoride (UF_6) plant under a secret nuclear cooperation agreement signed in 1991.[12] This allows yellowcake to be transformed into 93 percent pure HEU using gas ultracentrifuges. This intelligence was coupled with reports circulating in the Russian media of a shipment of uranium hexafluoride gas going directly from China to Iran in late 1994. Of note, too, were March 1995 reports[13] that "Iran is now capable of producing UF_6 gas in research installations run by the AEOI."

This was followed by a report in the American publication *Nuclear Fuel* that it had uncovered a joint U.S.-German sting operation in which former Soviet nuclear warheads were offered to the Islamic Republic of Iran for $3 million apiece.[14]

A Hanover (Germany) businessman, who suggested the deal to an Iranian procurement officer in 1993, testified to German prosecutors shortly afterwards. Specifics remain classified, but what is clear is that attempts to buy nuclear warheads—as well as a variety of other military items—appear to fall within the jurisdiction of Iran's Defense Industries Organization (DIO), which, claims German Intelligence, is a clandestine nuclear and military procurement agency.

The list was originally brought to the attention of Bonn's Ministry of Defense by an Iranian, who had shown a German a letter of introduction from the Atomic Energy Organization of Iran (AEOI). The witness said that terms of sale were discussed after the prospective Iranian buyer had cleared the matter with the Ministry of Defense in Tehran.

There was also the visit to South Africa shortly afterwards by Reza Amrollahi, head of AEOI, and at that stage, deputy president for Iran's atomic affairs. This event remains controversial. What we know is that Minister Amrollahi approached Dr. Waldo Stumpf, chief executive of the South African Atomic Energy Corporation (AEC), with a "shopping list" of items required for the manufacture of atomic bombs. The details are in *Iran's Nuclear Option* (Chapter 7, pages 156–64), having first been published in London by Jane's *International Defense Review* in the December 1997 issue.

Less than a decade before, South Africa, under the auspices of Pretoria's apartheid regime, had built six A-bombs with yields ranging from more than 4 KT to about 20 KT. The Boers obviously had the know-how. South Africa's nuclear arsenal was subsequently dismantled under the auspices of the IAEA and several Western monitoring agencies, including the Americans. But even that didn't prevent Tehran from making contact with some of the hard-line Muslims that emerged in President Mandela's cabinet after President de Klerk formally handed over power.

AEC's chief executive, Waldo Stumpf, issued lengthy disclaimers afterwards (including one before South Africa's Parliament in Cape Town). He denied that he had any knowledge of a meeting with Amrollahi, even though he told this writer that it had happened at his Pelindaba office in 1997. Also, his immediate boss at the time, former minister Pik Botha, confirmed to Mungo Soggot of the Johannesburg *Mail & Guardian* that the event had, in fact, taken place. Moreover, said Botha, when contacted by Soggot, "not only did it happen, but I was there." As the then minister for mineral and energy affairs, the South African AEC and its boss, Stumpf, was part of Minister Botha's responsibility.

It is also instructive that some of the critics of this report have never bothered to check sources. They're all there, from Pik Botha, a former cabinet minister in Mandela's cabinet, to one of South Africa's leading investigative journalists, who was then working for a paper linked to London's *Guardian*.

There is also Clifford Beal, former American-born editor of Jane's *International Defense Review*, to whom I first confided the report.

Chapter 5 Endnotes:

1 Al J. Venter, "An 'irregular' nuclear proliferation," *Jane's Terrorism and Security Monitor*, February 1, 2004.

2 Al J. Venter, *Iran's Nuclear Option: Tehran's Quest for the Atom Bomb*, Casemate Publishers, Philadelphia, and Greenhill Books, London, 2005.

3 David Albright, *Bulletin of the Atomic Scientists*, Chicago, July/August 1995.

4 Jim Hoagland, *The Washington Post*, May 17, 1995.

5 ISIS Issue Brief, "India's Nuclear Tests: Will They Open New Possibilities for Iraq to Exploit?" Washington, D.C., May 28, 1998.

6 Craig S. Smith, "Alarm Raised Over Quality of Uranium Found in Iran," *The New York Times*, March 11, 2004.

7 *Jane's International Defense Review*, London, September 1997.

8 Venter, *Iran's Nuclear Option*.

9 See IAEA GOV/2003/75, paras. 20–24.

10 Among those taken into custody were three scientists: former director general of the KRL, Mohamed Farook, and two other close aides of Khan. Others were administrators and security personnel of the KRL, including two former military brigadiers and Khan's personal staff officer.

11 Worse, Khan has been characterized as a "hard-core nationalist and a very ambitious person," by A. H. Nayyar, a physicist at Quaid-e-Azam University in Islamabad. "He's in for fame and money."

12 A volatile compound of uranium and fluorine, UF_6 is a solid at atmospheric pressure and room temperature, but can be transformed into a gas by heating.

13 Iranfax quoting government sources.

14 *Nuclear Fuel*, August 27, 1997.

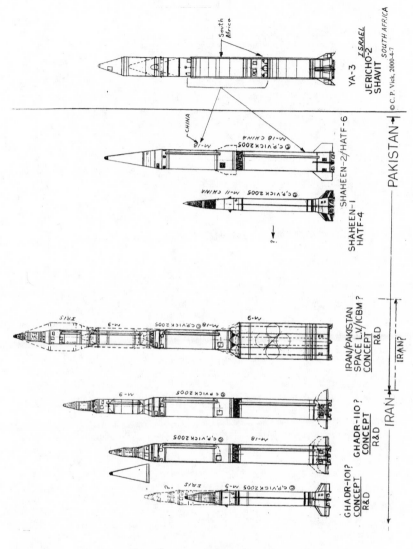

Charles Vick of GlobalSecurity.org compares some of the missiles either developed or still being worked on by both Iran and Pakistan where there is every indication of a substantial interchange of information, facilities, intelligence and ideas. It is a supreme irony that one of Islamabad's principal allies is Iran, America's most vituperative foe.

For comparison Vick also includes views of Israel's Jericho-2/Shavit where he also matches South Africa's YA-3's [RSA-3] second stage to that of Pakistan's Shaheen-2's first and second stages.

Note too, the sophistication of Iran's three-stage Ghadr-110 ICBM (intercontinental ballistic missile) which, when in production, will put the U.S. East Coast well within range.

HOW SADDAM HUSSEIN ALMOST BUILT HIS BOMB

After President Saddam Hussein stopped a United Nations strip-search of his country for real or imagined stocks of weapons of mass destruction in the late 1990s, nobody really knew what he had been doing in the interim. For its part, Tehran was alarmed at the lack of any kind of monitoring process in place. The story behind Baghdad's bid to build a nuclear weapon makes it a remarkable mix of deception, intrigue, and political power play, as well as downright greed on the part of some of those in both the East and the West who lent a hand. This was to have been the first *Arab* bomb: Iraq's atom bomb.

What the aftermath of Operation Desert Storm did for those involved in the Middle East was to stir the recurrent nightmare of a major Israeli-Arab conflict involving nuclear weapons. This dreadful scenario continues to haunt strategists on both sides of the Atlantic. Looking back, there are quite a few arms specialists who concede that the prospect of Saddam getting a bomb of his own was a close-run thing.

The scientific boffins reckon that while Iraq had serious problems with some of the more arcane disciplines associated with building a nuclear weapon, Baghdad, using indigenous facilities, might have been as little as two or three years from producing the first Arab atom bomb. Others talk about six or eight months. And while it was Pakistan that built the first *Islamic* bomb, there was a brief window when Islamabad began to share some of its secrets associated with weapons of mass destruction with Baghdad.

Some specialists also maintain that had he taken the shortcut (which is what his Iranian neighbors are suspected of doing right now, with plutonium and weapons-grade uranium bought on the former Soviet Union [FSU] black market), that objective might have been achieved even sooner.

It is worth noting that it was Saddam Hussein's original intention, once it became clear that the invasion of Kuwait would be fiercely opposed, to use his safeguarded highly enriched uranium (HEU)—covered by the Nuclear Non-Proliferation Treaty (NPT)—for the construction of a single nuclear device. Had he succeeded, he might well have had his bomb within a year. And while he would still have lacked the means to deliver it to target, he was spending a lot of money and effort working on that aspect as well.

United States National Intelligence estimates said at the time: "Iraq [with a supply of HEU] could build such a device in six months to a year." At the same time, it concluded that the final product was fraught, and, in any event, it would have been "too big to deliver by missile."

Vienna's International Atomic Energy Agency (IAEA), and by inference, the major powers, were very much aware that when the Coalition forces launched Desert Storm, Iraq had in stock a total of more than 30 pounds of fresh Russian-supplied, 80 percent enriched uranium, as well as 26 pounds of lightly irradiated, 93 percent uranium, together with about a pound of 93 percent HEU, the last two items bought from France.

All had been subject to IAEA scrutiny, which, according to Dr. David Kay (chief inspector of the three early UN nuclear weapons inspection programs in post–Gulf War Iraq), had been cleverly manipulated by Baghdad. The point made here by several observers is the fact that Saddam was in possession of HEU, and like it or not, that gave him leverage.

During the course of subsequent weapons searches, the Iraqis were obliged to admit to UN inspectors that after the IAEA made their routine inspection of this material in November 1990 (following the invasion of Kuwait, but before the Allies started bombing), they intended to divert all their HEU and further enrich a portion of it.[1] Indeed, they were planning to convert it to metal "buttons" for the final weaponization process, which should have taken place by April 1991. The intention was to present the world with a fait accompli: that Iraq had its bomb.

Israeli sources in Washington have suggested to this author that in order to do this, Saddam Hussein might have exercised one of two options:

- He could have test-fired his first atom bomb in the desert at a site to be built near the Saudi Arabian border. This would have demonstrated to the world that Iraq had nuclear capability (and thus, possibly, bring about a stalemate in the Kuwaiti issue with his forces still ensconced at the head of the Gulf). As it was, he was preempted by the invasion.

- Alternatively, there is a school of thought that believed he might have considered trying to transport such a bomb to Israel, possibly by boat, for detonation in the roadstead to Haifa harbor. This is a premise that did the rounds in Beirut during the mid-1990s and thought to have originally been mooted by Iran's Pasdaran, or Revolutionary Guards (author's visit to Lebanon, August 1997).

Significantly, people involved in such things have maintained all along that it is not necessary to *physically* land a nuclear weapon on American soil in order to cause destruction. Such a device could be detonated while still on board a ship in New York (or any other) harbor.

It is clear that the biggest shock of postwar IAEA inspections was the discovery that Iraq had a very substantial electromagnetic isotope separation (EMIS) program for the envisaged production of an A-bomb. It was vast. Numerous buildings were constructed at Al-Tuwaitha, about twenty miles south of Baghdad. These housed the research and development phases of both the EMIS and gaseous diffusion enrichment programs.

The diffusion program (which lasted from 1982 until mid-1987) occupied three large buildings. Interestingly, the EMIS project was located in other structures at Al-Tuwaitha, which disconcerted a lot of the staff working there. They were only too aware of what had happened at Osiraq in June 1981, when the Israelis bombed that reactor. They knew, too, that Israel had already complained about the huge conglomeration of buildings at the complex. When Saddam added still more structures, it did little for morale.

In the meantime, though, his EMIS program had a home. EMIS is such a large and energy-intensive technology that intelligence agencies have always assumed that with modern electronic and satellite-surveillance techniques, they would easily be able to detect such a development, even in its infancy.

More significant, neither Russia nor America believed that any nation would pursue "obsolete" calutron technology in a bomb program. It was outdated, World War II stuff, the experts argued. In any event, the U.S. abandoned that route soon after Japan capitulated. Yet the detail is there, in print, among documentation that was declassified years ago. For decades it has been available for public inspection by anybody who knows where to look.

After Iraq lost the war and the first of the international inspectors arrived, they uncovered what was termed at the time "a remarkable clandestine nuclear materials production and weapons design program of unexpected size and sophistication."[2] The total value of the program was initially estimated at about $5 billion. Later estimates put it at double that figure. Dr. David Kay, in his testimony before the U.S. Senate Foreign Relations Committee in October 1991, reckoned that there were about 7,000 scientists and 20,000 workers involved on the nuclear side alone, never mind all those still working on chemical and biological programs, as well as missile-delivery systems.

One of the most comprehensive accounts of how the Iraqis managed to befuddle the West is contained in a report that Kay wrote for the Center for Strategic and International Studies at the Massachusetts Institute of Technology. Another was authored by Dr. Khidir Hamza, at the time the most senior Iraqi nuclear physicist to defect to the West. He detailed the extent of his (and others') work in a report published in the *Bulletin of the Atomic Scientists*[3] and, subsequently, in his book, *Saddam's Bomb Maker*. Dr. Hamza now lives in the U.S. with his family, all of whom the CIA successfully smuggled out of Iraq.

Kay pointed out that in terms of Security Council Resolution 687, Iraq was required to give the UN precise details of the quantities and locations of all its nuclear, chemical, biological, and ballistic missile stockpiles. These listings were designed to provide a touchstone for subsequent inspection activities, and were to lead to the eventual dismantling of Iraq's WMD.

"What really happened was that just about every detail that emanated from Baghdad thereafter was misleading," Dr. Kay subsequently stated. "On the nuclear front, the scale of deception was even greater," declared Kay. "Iraq's initial declaration on April 19, 1991, was that it had no proscribed nuclear materials. This was amended eight days later to acknowledge that it had only what was reported to the IAEA before the war, as well as a peaceful research program centered on the Al-Tuwaitha Nuclear Research Center."

Subsequent inspections found something altogether different. It soon became clear that Iraq had been involved in a massive nuclear weapons program (certainly the largest in any Third World country outside India and Pakistan) for some years. Kay writes: "At the time of the invasion of Kuwait, [Iraq] had begun the start-up for industrial-scale enrichment using calutrons, and had acquired the material, designs, and much of the equipment for perhaps 20,000 modern centrifuges. Design, component testing, and construction of manufacturing facilities for actual bomb production were well advanced."

UN inspectors determined at about this time that the electromagnetic isotope separation program had put Iraq just eighteen to thirty months from having enough material for between one and three atom bombs. (It is worth noting that prior to going pro-Iraq in the early years of this millennium, former UNSCOM inspector Scott Ritter confirmed to this writer that there were possibly three or four such bombs. Indeed, he was about to uncover them in September 1998, when the State Department halted his vigorous inspection program.)

The UN Action Team also found a great deal of sophisticated European centrifuge technology. This seemed to indicate a leak of substantial—and as yet, unspecified—proportions from the triple-nation (Germany, the Netherlands, and Britain) Uranium Enrichment Company, better known as Urenco, possibly through Pakistan's A.Q. Khan network.

What quickly became apparent was that there were detailed plans for building an "implosion" nuclear device which can use either HEU or plutonium. This type of weapon contains a mass of nuclear material—in this case, HEU—at its core. Iraqi scientists envisioned building an implosion device with conventional explosives around the central mass detonating simultaneously; this has the effect of compressing fissile material into a supercritical mass. At that instant, neutrons are injected into the material to initiate a chain reaction and explosion. (China uses something similar in their warheads with HEU.)

The appropriately named "Fat Man," an American atom bomb dropped on the city of Nagasaki that caused about 60,000 immediate deaths (and another 70,000 from radiation sickness in the years that followed), was such a weapon. It had a yield of less than 20 KT. Achieving this much was no easy task. Vienna's IAEA discovered early on that the Iraqis appeared to be just starting to comprehend the extremely complex principles associated with spherical geography linked to this kind of weapons research.

Another IAEA inspector told this writer that Iraqi scientists were planning a device with a solid core of about 40 pounds of weapons-grade uranium. It would have included a reflector of natural uranium metal about an inch thick, and a tamper of hardened iron. An atom bomb of this type would weigh about a ton, with an outer diameter of about 36 inches (just less than a meter), making it significantly smaller and lighter than the devices developed by Robert Oppenheimer and his Los Alamos club in the mid-1940s.

The circumference would still have precluded it from being fitted to Scuds, the only missile available to Baghdad.

Astonishment has always been expressed at the "true breadth of Saddam's nuclear weapons enterprise," as well as the amount of maneuvering—both adroit and malfeasant—that was needed to keep it hidden from prying eyes, both on the ground and above it, says David Albright. He spent time with the IAEA Action Team in Iraq and is president of Washington's Institute for Science and International Security (ISIS). These discoveries shook the international nonproliferation regime, and the tremors persist today, since there are now other nations getting into the act, North Korea and Iran included.

What was revealed early on in Iraq was a succession of critical weaknesses in inspection routines, export controls, and in intelligence gathering. There was also a huge gap with many of the agencies involved in the sharing of these assets. Albright reckons that the reality of those first disclosures, and the well-founded suspicion that more lay ahead, led to the initial assumption that Saddam was "on the brink" of putting his own atomic weapon on the international table.

Yet while the Iraqi nuclear program involved tens of thousands of people, no one in the West was even vaguely aware until long afterwards of the numbers of Iraqi students that had been sent abroad to acquire the necessary expertise. These youngsters—and some not-so-young academics—were rarely sent either to the same universities or countries, which made it difficult for any single authority to appreciate the breadth of technical skills being acquired by Baghdad. It also presented problems for the world community in terms of keeping track of individual Iraqi scientists. The two exceptions, peculiarly, were France and Italy, who together hosted about four hundred Iraqis; yet none were officially approached about the subjects or courses that they were actually following. Dr. Hamza told me that nearly all the current leaders of the program were drawn from those batches of trainees.

Dr. Kay highlighted this development with a disturbing observation. While in Iraq, he said, he dealt for months with a senior Iraqi scientist whose entire university training—from undergraduate level, all the way through to his doctorate—had been in the United States. His first real job was at an American nuclear power plant. Yet, declared Kay, all basic data on or pictures of this key individual could not be found at any of the academic institutions where he was purported to have spent time. In retrospect, the issue has something of a *Dr. Strangelove* resonance about it.

It is interesting that the Iraqi experience (together with developments that followed September 11) has since led to a significant tightening up of IAEA inspection procedures. Essentially, this was designed to prevent such things from happening again. You only need to look at developments in Iran right now to show that history appears to be repeating itself there.[4]

There have been other anomalies. It is no longer a secret that prior to Desert Storm, the Iraqis received generous amounts of tactical aid from what later became their chief antagonists, the Americans. During the Iran-Iraq War, while Washington was providing arms to Iran in the hope of getting their hostages in Lebanon freed, it was also rushing classified satellite intelligence to Baghdad almost as soon as it came in. This gave Baghdad a good idea of what the Americans were able to see, what they could detect from looking at such images, and, by inference, how they could be fooled. With time, they would use this knowledge to good advantage.[5]

Before that, Baghdad managed to gain IAEA acceptance by placing Abdul-Wahid Al-Saji, a mild-mannered Iraqi physicist, in a position to serve his country as a bona fide inspector. Gradually, the Iraqis came to understand the agency's machinations, and this knowledge ultimately proved useful to Baghdad's weapons program in obtaining nuclear technology.

According to Dr. Hamza, the agency accepted Iraq's importation of HEU for its research reactor without ever evaluating the possibility that it might be diverted for military use. Most important, Iraqis were able to gain a complete understanding of IAEA inspection procedures and processes. Iraqi officials were also alerted to the success of satellite remote sensing in uncovering clandestine and, especially, underground activities. For this reason, with few exceptions, Saddam built almost no underground facilities.

Kay makes instructive comments about the way the Iraqis demonstrated their ability to understand the limitations of U.S. technical collection systems, and of how data gathered by such systems were interpreted by the experts.

The catalogue is long. It includes the erection of buildings within buildings [Tuwaitha]; deliberately constructing structures designed to the same plans and for the same purposes to look different [Ash Sharqat and Tarmiya]; hiding power and water feeds to mislead as to facility use [Tarmiya]; disguising operational state [Al Atheer]; diminishing the value of a facility by apparent low security and lack of defenses [Tarmiya]; severely reducing off-site emissions [Tuwaitha and Tarmiya]; moving critical pieces of equipment as well as dispersing and placing some facilities below ground level.

For his part, Hamza points out that even though Al-Tuwaitha had 100-foot-high berms (which should have attracted suspicion that the plant was being used for other purposes), good effort went into carefully escorting IAEA inspectors each time they arrived. Customarily they were shunted along predesignated paths that exposed no buildings where secret research was being conducted. Also, answers to possibly difficult questions would be endlessly rehearsed, sometimes for days beforehand.

It was only after Desert Storm, when Vienna received aerial photos of the site, that the IAEA learned about many other buildings that they had never been allowed to get near.

When the bombings were done, the Pentagon had to concede that while Iraq had suffered through the most sophisticated aerial bombardment in history, the country had emerged, in the words of former U.S. Air Force chief of staff, Merrill A. McPeak, with enough nascent nuclear capability to produce weapons early in the new millennium.

Now that there have been two invasions of Iraq, there is a sentiment among some of the experts at UN headquarters in New York that Iraq might have gone nuclear if UN sanctions had been prematurely lifted.

Saddam was always eager to make use of his assets in what he termed "the interests of Islamic hegemony," especially if the ultimate target was to have been the Jewish Homeland. We know too that after the first Gulf War, he managed to get some of his WMD assets to Libya. These were then forwarded overland to the Sudan.[6]

Meanwhile, in the decade that followed Operation Desert Storm, Syria continued to demonstrate an interest in acquiring WMD of its own. By early 1997, Israeli reports said that Damascus had tipped some of its Scud-C missiles deployed along the southern (Israeli) front with Sarin and the even more deadly VX nerve gas. This prompted an Israeli Defense Force (IDF) spokesman to declare that if such weapons were used against the Israeli state, it would automatically be followed by nuclear retaliation—harsh words in an already-tough environment.

According to Paul Stokes, a former UNSCOM Action Team deputy leader, frequent inspections prevented Iraq from conducting nuclear weapons development work at declared sites after the end of the war. There was evidence—including a good deal from defectors who had come across to the West—that this did not prevent Saddam's people from going ahead elsewhere, in clear violation of a variety of Security Council resolutions. Dr. Kay provided explicit evidence of such deceptions in his MIT report; it was often a nightmare of duplicity, he said.

He told this correspondent that, among those who had originally worked with the UN in the region (before they were expelled), it was common knowledge that the Iraqis had stalled, obfuscated, or confused wherever and whomever they could. They did what they had to do in order to hide what had been going on.

For instance, declared Dr. Kay, one of the conclusions reached in 1997 was that while the Iraqis claimed to have had little success with the centrifuge enrichment program, there was a mismatch between the sophistication of the materials that they admitted to having imported and those that were actually turned over to UN inspection.[7] This gap raised real concerns that a hidden centrifuge facility still remained to be found. There are other examples.

It took the defection of Saddam's son-in-law, General Hussein Kamel, former head of the Ministry of Industry and Military Industrialization (MIMI), to expose the full extent of what Iraq had achieved after Desert Storm. Once he was safely ensconced in Jordan, Iraq had no option but to hand over to the IAEA half a million pages of secreted documents (from the "chicken farm"), as well as almost 20 tons of high-strength maraging steel and stocks of carbon fiber for more than 1,000 gas centrifuges, all of which (and much more) Kamel had detailed in his debrief. Some of these items, according to Scott Ritter on his return to the U.S., were linked to material believed to be still hidden.

There was good reason for this supposition. Iraq is known to have subsequently tried to acquire hydrofluoric acid—a chemical used in the production of uranium hexafluoride feedstock. Scientists use it in gas centrifuge and other enrichment processes, and as a purging agent to remove industrial residues from centrifuges and calutron parts. According to Michael Eisenstadt, a military affairs fellow at the Washington Institute for Near East Policy, it raised questions—notwithstanding the IAEA monitoring process—about the status of the Iraqi nuclear program.[8]

In the simplest terms, the Iraqi nuclear program covered a period from 1976 (when construction on the French-supplied Tammuz 1RR/PPR reactor began) to mid-1991, when all major nuclear work was halted by the Gulf War. In between, the most significant highlights included the following:

1981: Destruction of the nearly completed Tammuz reactor at Osiraq by Israeli warplanes

1982: Research concerning various gas-enrichment methods gets into full swing

1987: Lab-scale quantities of Low-Enriched Uranium (LEU) produced by calutrons, now referred to as "Baghdadtrons" (LEU contains more than 0.71 and less than 20 percent ^{235}U)

1987–88: Construction of the Ash Sharqat calutron enrichment plant begins

1989: Construction begins at the Al Furat centrifuge production facility

1990: Initiation of crash program using diverted reactor fuel

1991: Work halted by war as the IAEA and UNSCOM weapons strip-search began

1999: Abrupt ending of both UNSCOM and IAEA monitoring of Iraq's weapons and nuclear programs

The Israeli Air Force bombing of the Osiraq reactor (and subsequent developments) highlighted at a very early stage the fact that Iraq was fostering a nuclear weapons interest.

Saddam Hussein had bought two nuclear reactors from France—a 40-megawatt thermal research reactor, which was destroyed, and the 800-kilowatt thermal "Isis"—as well as a fuel manufacturing plant together with nuclear fuel-reprocessing facilities, all under the cover of acquiring the expertise needed to eventually build and operate nuclear power plants and recycle nuclear fuel.

What is remarkable is that nobody in the West ever seriously questioned the logic of these programs, coming, as they were, from Iraq, the country with the second-largest oil reserves in the world (as is the case with Iran today, with equally formidable resources). It is lost on almost nobody that both countries are the last nations on earth that need to generate electricity by building nuclear assets.

These deals were followed by further purchases, this time from Italy. It included a radiochemistry laboratory in 1978, which included three "hot cells" used for the reprocessing of plutonium. Until destroyed in the Gulf War, they were operating at Al-Tuwaitha. Meanwhile, Iraq became a signatory to the Nuclear Non-Proliferation Treaty. Iran also subsequently signed.

Dr. Jafar Dhia Jafar, leader of Iraq's nuclear-weapons effort (even though his curriculum vitae includes the notation that he was jailed for twenty months by Saddam for "political crimes"), claims it was the Israeli bombing of Osiraq that originally prompted his government to proceed with a secret uranium-enrichment program. Educated at the University of Manchester and Imperial College, London, he spent four years thereafter working at CERN, the European accelerator center in Switzerland. Of particular note here is the fact that this man was among the first of Saddam's "most wanted," who cut a deal with the Americans to come in from the cold after Baghdad fell in April 2003. He is currently living in Paris.

It was Jafar's view that the Israeli bombing of the Osiraq nuclear facility cost his country almost a billion dollars. Yet, he says, the world community neither punished nor seriously admonished the Jewish State for what was clearly an act of war. This was one of the factors, he believes, that caused Iraq to resort to subterfuge. As he described it during the inspection phase to UN inspectors: "Let the Israelis believe they destroyed our nuclear capacity. Accept the sympathy offered for this aggression and then proceed in secret with an atom bomb program—which is what we did."

Already in 1982, the Iraqis had begun to explore electromagnetic isotope separation at Al-Tuwaitha, which eventually became the principal focus of nuclear research in the country. Baghdad was confident that its scientific establishment had the necessary skills and technology to master this extremely difficult process. They also reached out in other directions: gas centrifuge, gaseous diffusion, chemical enrichment, and laser isotope separation.

To begin with, time, together with good money and effort, went into gaseous diffusion. This route was abandoned when some technical problems proved insurmountable. Also, Saddam's agents were having trouble getting their hands on essential equipment on the open market, much of which had been embargoed by the West. Looking at the lists of material seized after Desert Storm, they appear to have been remarkably successful.

Starting in the late 1980s, Iraqi scientists began working on centrifuge enrichment as a possible alternative, or as a source of LEU for EMIS. They had hoped to achieve a production output of about 30 pounds of 93 percent weapons-grade uranium a year at each of the EMIS production units that they intended to build.

"Originally, the gaseous diffusion elements would have provided low-enriched uranium as a feedstock for the EMIS plants, dramatically increasing HEU production," Jafar explained during an interview.

The Tarmiya complex on the Tigris River (built by a Yugoslavian firm, Federal Directorate of Supply and Procurement) and its "twin" at Ash Sharqat (a few hundred miles to the north of Baghdad) were designated to support industrial-scale EMIS production. While there were numerous problems of a technical nature, the two plants, jointly, could have ultimately produced between 60 and 200 pounds of weapons-grade HEU a year, giving Iraq the capacity to build up to four atomic bombs a year. But for that, they would have had to operate successfully.

A small plutonium separation program was started in the mid-1970s. Following contact with SNIA-Techint of Italy, a facility was established in Baghdad for research on fuel processing under IAEA safeguards. This laboratory was eventually able to separate small quantities of plutonium—again, contrary to NPT safeguards agreements.

Kay's observations about some of the deception techniques employed by Baghdad are interesting. Iraq, he maintains, was able to use the strong desire of Western providers of technology to make sales in order to effectively conceal the true purposes of its efforts. Thus, they were able to extract a considerable amount of proprietary information from these firms without compensation. He gives the classic example that lay at the heart of Iraq's efforts to obtain technology for the chemical enrichment (Chemex) of uranium:

At the time there were two suppliers in the world of chemical-enrichment technology—one Japanese, the other French. In the mid-1980s, Iraq initiated preliminary discussions with both, indicating a desire to acquire this capability. In the end, they concentrated solely on France. Iraq engaged the French company in lengthy negotiations, which would soon assume a familiar pattern. Each time Iraq would say that it needed "only a little more data" to make a decision.

The French would reveal more. The cycle would begin again later, and this went on for several years. Finally, after the suppliers had disclosed just about all the technology involved, Baghdad announced that it was too expensive and was abandoning all interest in going ahead. Iraqi scientists were then able to begin the clandestine development of Chemex on their own.

Shortly thereafter, Washington's ISIS chief, David Albright, stressed that in the evaluation of enrichment technologies, the Iraqis saw many advantages in EMIS technology, the first being that the procedure involves large and static pieces of equipment.[9]

Baghdad regarded this as preferable to gas centrifuge programs, which required advanced engineering technology and was perhaps ill-suited to a developing country with a limited industrial base, he told me. For example, the rotors on gas centrifuges move at seven or eight times the speed of sound, and the slightest instability can, in an instant, cause bearings to fail and rotors to crash. It is common knowledge that Pakistan battled with this technique for years; an intelligence source has indicated to this writer that for all their success in exploding a bomb, it took years for them to master it.

The advantages of following the antiquated EMIS route are important, especially since they might well apply to other developing countries intent on something similar. These include:

(a) EMIS is well documented in the open literature;

(b) the basic scientific and technical problems associated with the operation of EMIS separators are relatively straightforward to master;

(c) the computational software and main equipment are often not on international export-control lists, making procurement easy;

(d) the design and manufacture of the main equipment for prototypes can be accomplished indigenously;

(e) the feed material is relatively easy to produce and handle;

(f) final enrichment can be handled in two stages in machines that act independently of each other (one or more separator failures do not affect the operation of other separators); and

(g) LEU feed can be used for a substantial increase in productivity.

Recent disclosures have indicated that as we go to press, Iran appears to be involved in a similar process. Like Iraq, Tehran is happy to keep its options open with regard to gas centrifuge technology, and laser as well as chemical separation. This is not unusual. Both IAEA and British Intelligence sources inform us that there are at least three dozen countries—all of them Third World—intent on acquiring this kind of expertise.[10]

In pre-invasion Iraq, meanwhile, atom bomb design (weaponization) was the responsibility of scientists and technicians at Al Atheer, which—when he opened the plant about thirty miles south of the capital—the Iraqi minister responsible said was to be "like Los Alamos."

By the time David Kay and his IAEA Action Team associates visited the site, which was bombed by the Allies during the first Gulf War, the Iraqis had managed to acquire a variety of advanced equipment, much of it on Western export-control (and thus embargoed) lists. Included were such items as high-speed streak cameras (from Hamamatsu Photonics of Japan) and maraging steel (which was found elsewhere in Iraq) from European suppliers.

Al Atheer was also linked to sophisticated work in metallurgy, chemistry, and detonation engineering. Here, the Swiss company Asea Brown Boveri provided a state-of-the-art cold isostatic press, which could be used to shape explosive charges. More Swiss firms that supplied equipment to Iraq included Acomel SA of Neuchâtel (five high-frequency inverters suitable for centrifuge cascades), and, among other shipments, 700 uranium hexafluoride–resistant bellows-valves from Balzer AG and VAT AG (together with the American company, Nupro).

There is no doubt that in pursuing his objective to acquire a bomb, Saddam relied heavily on foreign technical resources for much of it. The bulk, curiously, came not from his old allies, the Soviets (or their cohorts), but from free Europe. David Albright and Mark Hibbs stated in their reports that Iraq's "Petrochemical Project Three"—a code name for the secret program (conducted under the auspices of MIMI)—received massive infusions of money and resources. Like America's redundant Manhattan Project, Iraq sought a number of different technical avenues to the bomb.[11]

The Iraqi leader sent out a minor army of secret agents to establish an elaborate procurement network that had operatives throughout the developed world. Even Africa was covered, since South Africa (through Armscor) had much potential. By then the apartheid regime had supplied Iraq with the vaunted G5 howitzer, a 155mm artillery piece which, until silenced in the first Gulf War, was used to good effect against Coalition Forces in Desert Storm. The entire program was subject to the most stringent secrecy. There wasn't an Iraqi legation abroad that was not involved. Curiously, Gerald Bull (the Canadian maverick arms developer who was involved in Saddam's "Super Gun" when Israel's Mossad killed him in Belgium) also had a hand in developing the G5. He was assassinated outside his Belgium apartment, in itself a remarkable story of intrigue and betrayal.

Ostensibly, everything that was acquired for Saddam's nuclear program was intended for what his agents liked to term "civil and peaceful use." Purchases were hidden behind such innocuous pursuits as dairy production, car and truck manufacture, as well as oil refining. But it did not take the West very long to click: Iraq was covering up its real activities and, more disconcerting, it was happening at a breathtaking scale and pace.

Many of the bulky calutron pole magnets used to enrich uranium were produced in Austria by a state-owned firm that shipped the finished products to Iraq—half by truck through Turkey and the rest shipped through Hamburg. The Austrians never asked about the purpose of this equipment, and the Iraqis volunteered nothing. Much the same story applied to high-quality copper that was used to wrap these magnets. It was produced in Finland to Iraqi specifications.[12]

Hundreds of tons of HMX, or High Melting Explosives—regarded by specialist demolition experts as the "big brother" of the better-known RDX (some of which would be used in the A-bomb program)—was imported from Carlos Cardoen of Chile, a man very well known to Pretoria. This man eventually built a plant in Iraq to manufacture cluster bombs. Cardoen came under investigation by the U.S. Justice Department immediately afterwards.

Germany (both pre- and post-unification) featured prominently in almost every phase of the Iraqi nuclear program, so much so that it is impossible that Bonn could *not* have been aware of the extent of it. German companies included international conglomerates like Siemens AG (a workshop for "tube processing"); H&H Metalform (flow-forming machines to make steel maraging rotor tubes for centrifuges); Neue Magdeburger Werkzeugmaschinen GmbH (aluminum forgings and a CNC machine to machine casings); Rhein-Bayern Fahrzeugbau GmbH (almost a quarter-million magnetizable ferrite spacers for centrifuges); oxidation furnaces from Degussa AG and Leybold Heraeus (electron beam welder); centrifuge balancing machines from Reutlinger und Sohne KG; Arthur Pfeiffer Vakuumtechnik GmbH (vacuum induction furnace); and a host of other companies and products. It has been suggested by Western intelligence agencies that some companies doing work of a similar nature might now have shifted their focus toward Iran.

H&H was contracted by Baghdad for centrifuge assistance and served, while doing so, as a conduit for advanced technical expertise, material, and equipment for the Iraqi nuclear effort. Much of the financing for the project was handled by the scandal-ridden Bank of Credit and Commerce International (BCCI) before it folded. Subsequently, the Atlanta-based branch of an Italian bank, Banco Nationale da Lavore (BNL), was placed under investigation in the U.S.

British companies were involved too, and some remained under a cloud of suspicion for years afterwards. These included Endshire Export Marketing, a company that met an order for ring magnets which had come from Inwako GmbH, a firm directed by the German arms dealer Simon Heiner. Britain's Special Intelligence Service (SIS), aware by now that the magnets were intended for a nuclear program, let the shipment proceed in order to try to establish what technical route the Iraqis were taking. London tends to work closely with Langley on such matters.

It also transpired that the Technology Development Group, a company co-directed by an Iraqi intelligence agent, Safa Al-Haboudi, was an associate of some of the German firms involved. Al-Haboudi eventually implicated the British firm Matrix Churchill, as he was a member of that company's senior management, as well. Matrix Churchill offered a lucrative, long-term contract for a tool shop (ostensibly for automobile parts manufacturing) to the Swiss metal-working combine, Schmiedemeccanica SA.

The records show that some of these exports never got through. Once alerted, the West came down hard. Swiss and German customs officials halted a shipment of special computer numerically controlled (CNC) machines for making the endcaps and baffles of centrifuges. Earlier, Iraqi operators were caught trying to smuggle detonation capacitors from CSI Technologies of California. This material would have been incorporated into an implosion-type bomb.

For all the help that Baghdad received from abroad, there were some serious technological gaps. Iraqi electronics expertise, for instance, did not warrant close scrutiny. Baghdad, it was discovered later, was having difficulty developing adequate capacitors and bridge-wire detonators. Rolf Ekeus, the former head of UNSCOM, said that while Iraq had blueprints and considerable knowledge, it tended to lag a bit with the engineering aspects. Also, Baghdad had been noticeably slowed by its inability to obtain what it needed from overseas as Western government controls began to stymie deliveries.[13]

It is important to observe that during its subterfuge stage, Iraq was not alone in this sort of skullduggery. The newsletter *Nuclear Fuel* reported on June 20, 1994, that several shipments of pre-formed tubes for scoops in gas centrifuges from the German metalworking firm Team GmbH were shipped to Pakistan after being declared in customs documents as "bodies for ballpoint pens." There are other examples, including several still under wraps.

Looking at the bigger picture, it is clear that this targeted Arab nation was able to demonstrate an astonishing level of enterprise by getting as far as it did. It is of concern that more countries wish to emulate it.

Basic items—factories, electrical supply, power equipment—were easy to buy. But, as Albright explained, "the more specific the equipment Iraq sought, the more export controls began to bite. Crucial transfers of components were thus effectively blocked."

Orders were subdivided into subcomponents that, on paper, looked innocuous. Or machines were bought to manufacture something back home. Middlemen and unethical companies in the hundreds were bribed to disguise final destinations or to falsify end-user certificates in much the same way as South Africa (under UN sanctions) stocked its arsenal with embargoed items of choice.

German technicians were secretly hired to work on the Arab enrichment project. Once the IAEA went to work and uncovered names, some of these people were charged with treason as, ultimately, will South African scientists who have been helping Tehran build WMD.

In Iraq's case, several were jailed. Among these individuals were Bruno Stemmler, Walter Busse, and Karl-Heinz Schaab. It was Schaab and Stemmler who provided Saddam with classified centrifuge blueprints. The three men had worked on the centrifuge program at MAN Technologie AG of Munich, and had come to Iraq under the sponsorship of the German company H&H Metalform. Together, they operated efficiently as a team and met many of Iraq's technical requirements. They also assisted in locating international suppliers. Some were companies with whom they had previously been associated.

In the end, says Albright, their assistance greatly accelerated Iraq's gas centrifuge design process, noting: "It sped the acquisition of necessary materials, know-how and equipment for manufacture." During an earlier period, some Iraqis had already spent time in Urenco training programs in order to familiarize themselves with complex centrifuge-related procedures.

What does all of this tell us? While the Iraqi nuclear program was effectively halted in the end, Iran, according to some sources, might right now be further ahead than was Saddam by the time UNSCOM had begun its search.

Worse, should Tehran have managed to acquire a supply of weapons-grade uranium on the Russian or Ukrainian black markets—and there is a lot of conjecture right now that the mullahs might have done exactly that—it is not impossible that they are on the brink of their own atomic revolution. The implications are chilling.

As Dr. David Kay observed, "[T]he failed efforts of both IAEA safeguards inspectors and national intelligence authorities to detect—prior to the Gulf War—a nuclear weapons program of the magnitude and advanced character of Iraq's, should stand as a monument to the fallibility of on-site inspection and national intelligence when faced by a determined opponent."[14]

He maintained that those words should be cast in concrete and embedded into the floor of Washington's Capitol.

Kay: "The Iraqi military buildup, as well as multiple failures of its timely detection, is an experience rich in lessons. Correctly understood, it may help the West detect other covert weapons programs and, equally important, U.S. understanding of the limits of its ability to guarantee timely detection."[15]

Chapter 6 Endnotes:

[1] David Albright and Robert Kelley, "Has Iraq Come Clean at Last?" *Bulletin of the Atomic Scientists*, November/December 1995.

[2] Jay C. Davis and David A. Kay, "Iraq's Secret Nuclear Weapons Program," *Physics Today*, July 1992.

[3] Khidir Hamza, *Bulletin of the Atomic Scientists*, September/October 1998.

[4] Until Iranian opposition groups pinpointed several sites—among them, the one at Natanz, where they claimed Tehran was involved with nuclear work (small centrifuges were found for enriching uranium)—the Iranians prevented IAEA staff from setting up environmental monitoring units in some areas where the Atomic Energy Organization of Iran was active. They were particularly restrictive at some newly established uranium processing plants. See "Inspectors in Iran Examine Machines to Enrich Uranium," *The New York Times*, February 23, 2003.

[5] William Burrows and Robert Windrem, *Critical Mass*, Simon & Schuster, New York, 1994; Davis and Kay, "Iraq's Secret Nuclear Weapons Program."

[6] Davis and Kay, "Iraq's Secret Nuclear Weapons Program."

[7] *Pointer*, supplement to *Jane's Intelligence Review*, London, March 1998.

[8] Michael Eisenstadt, *Like a Phoenix from the Ashes? The Future of Iraqi Military Power*, The Washington Institute of Near East Policy, 1993.

[9] David Albright, Frans Berkhout, and William Walker, *Plutonium and Highly Enriched Uranium 1996*, OUP, 1997.

[10] Statements by the head of the International Atomic Energy Agency in October/November 2006 about unusual nuclear proliferation among Third World states; in particular, six Arab countries who gave notice early November 2006 about going nuclear. Check the IAEA Web site for details (www.iaea.org).

[11] David Albright and Mark Hibbs, "Iraq's Shop-Till-You-Drop Nuclear Program," *Bulletin of the Atomic Scientists*, April 1992.

[12] Dr. David Kay, "Denial and Deception Practices of WMD Proliferators: Iraq and Beyond," The Center for Strategic and International Studies and Massachusetts Institute of Technology, *The Washington Quarterly*, Winter 1995.

[13] Albright and Hibbs, "Iraq's Shop-Till-You-Drop."

[14] Kay, "Denial and Deception Practices of WMD Proliferators."

[15] Note also Iraqi attempts to acquire krytons: In March 1991, Iraq attempted to illegally import krytons from CIS Technologies Inc. of the U.S. Several years earlier, Iraq had imported weapons-quality capacitors from other American concerns. IAEA investigators have also found about 230 metric tons of high-energy explosive HMX in Iraq that may have been purchased from Czechoslovakia (Monterey Institute, CNS, Iraqi Nuclear Abstracts: 1992, http://cns.miis.edu/research/iraq/iraqnu92.htm).

CHAPTER 7

THE MAJOR NUCLEAR PLAYERS

> I have sworn upon the altar of God eternal hostility against
> every form of tyranny over the minds of men.
> —Thomas Jefferson (1800)

The development of nuclear weapons over more than sixty years is well documented. One of the most interesting publications on the subject remains Richard Rhodes's Pulitzer Prize–winning *The Making of the Atomic Bomb* (Simon & Schuster, New York, 1986). Reprinted innumerable times, it has become something of an iconic source on the subject, not least to this writer. In fact, as Dr. Jonathan Tucker of the Monterey Institute of International Studies commented when we discussed this work, "It is such an incredibly complex story, yet it has been handled almost like an adventure story . . . lots of drama . . . keeps you on the edge, which is unusual for a scientific work."

Adventure it certainly is, because Richard Rhodes manages to encapsulate many of the more important elements of developing the bomb. He breathes a gusty life into the major players in a way that I doubt has been done before with such an esoteric subject.

Here is an overview of today's major players:

The United States of America
What we do know about America's role is that the expatriate Hungarian scientist, Leo Szilard, fearing that Nazi Germany might become the first country to actually construct such an explosive device, tried very early on to warn the Americans. But he was frustrated by his failure to interest either the American army or navy in his line of thought, which, by implication, included the possibilities and dangers residing in nuclear fission. Aided by fellow expatriate Hungarians Eugene Wigner and Edward Teller, Szilard expressed his concerns in a

letter to FDR. The letter, dated August 2, 1939, was drafted by Leo Szilard and signed by Albert Einstein, the great man himself.

Industrialist Alexander Sachs, a newly acquired friend who had access to President Roosevelt, delivered the letter (together with a memorandum from Szilard) on October 11, 1939. During a second meeting with Sachs early the next day, the president told his secretary, General Edwin M. ("Pa") Watson, that "this requires action."

How to actually achieve a nuclear explosion would be postulated by a young Berkeley physicist, J. Robert Oppenheimer, in a National Academy of Sciences (NAS) report. According to Oppenheimer, the way to create such an explosion was by "bringing quickly together a sufficient mass of element 235-Uranium."

A team of chemists at Berkeley subsequently headed up by Glenn T. Seaborg early in 1941 identified another fissile material called element 94. A year later, it would be renamed "plutonium" by Seaborg. All this, and much besides, is recorded by Rhodes in his book, and taken together, it makes for some of his most compelling chapters.

In June 1942, FDR ordered an all-out effort to build the bomb. He placed the huge construction projects under the authority of the U.S. Army Corps of Engineers. An associate body was established, with its headquarters in the borough of Manhattan, New York City, which was why the project assumed the name "Manhattan Project." U.S. Army colonel Leslie R. Groves was chosen to follow up Colonel James C. Marshall as commander.

In a separate research project in Chicago, it took six more months for Italian national Enrico Fermi—one of the great minds of the last century—to achieve the world's first self-sustaining chain reaction. The way was now finally clear for a large-scale effort to produce plutonium (^{239}Pu).

Dr. Robert Oppenheimer, who had been involved with nuclear fission since 1939, and who had proved himself the natural leader of this dynamic task force, had by then already been asked by Groves to head up a still-to-be established laboratory. In order to preserve secrecy, it was decided that the focus of this one establishment (which would eventually employ thousands) would be on weapons physics research and design. Oppenheimer suggested to Groves that a suitable site (aptly code-named Site Y) might be found in New Mexico, where the Los Alamos Ranch School was situated.

Work was started in April 1943 on the application of both uranium-235 and plutonium-239. The method was dubbed "gun" devices, or weapons. In contrast, a plutonium gun weapon called "Thin Man" was shelved when it was found in 1944 that high neutron emissions could possibly cause the weapon to predetonate. Work continued on "Little Boy," a smaller uranium gun-type weapon.

While success with the latter appeared to be ensured, the efficacy of the implosion device remained uncertain. The scientists decided that it should be tested before being operationally deployed. A site in the Jornada del Muerto region of the Alamogordo Bombing Range in New Mexico was selected. That test will forever be known as Trinity, and the world's first atom bomb as "the Gadget."

Thus, on the morning of July 16, 1945, the world entered a new and uncertain age when the tower-mounted bomb was detonated. Its 13.4 pounds of ^{239}Pu yielded an explosion equivalent to about 21,000 tons of TNT, although others have used the figure of 15,000 pounds. Either way, that was one mighty bang, and its two successors killed an awful lot of people.

"Little Boy" (or Unit L11) was deployed operationally on August 6, 1945. Its 140 pounds of high-enriched ^{235}U (80 to 85 percent) obliterated large parts of the city of Hiroshima, with an explosion in the magnitude of roughly 15 kilotons (KT). It was the first time that nuclear weapons had been used against fellow members of the human race. It was also not the last, and going by what is taking place east of Suez today, that won't be the end of it . . .

NUCLEAR FISSION

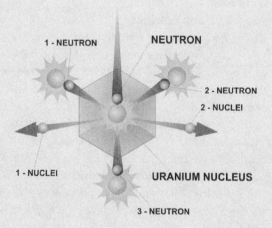

One scientist, when asked to explain nuclear fission, declared that the principle behind it was easy enough to understand but extremely difficult to apply.

Essentially, the nucleus of a uranium atom contains protons, which are positively charged particles, and neutrons (as the name implies, with no charge), all powerfully bonded. When a neutron from outside collides, it becomes unstable. If this atom is uranium-235 (^{235}U), the added neutron increases the molecular mass of the nucleus with resultant instability.

What takes place then is that the uranium atom splits into two separate atoms (thus, splitting the atom), and several neutrons are forced out at great speed along with a small amount of energy. The process continues countless times over, neutrons colliding with uranium atoms that, in turn, lead to the creation of self-sustaining chain reactions. All of this occurs within a time span of millionths of a second. If there is enough uranium present, those same tiny amounts of energy mount up to create an enormous explosion, together with widespread radiation—which can be just as deadly as an explosion, although death will not be instantaneous.

This then is the fission bomb, otherwise known as an atomic or atom bomb. It has been explained by one source as a fission reactor designed to liberate as much energy as rapidly as possible before the released energy causes the reactor to explode (and the chain reaction to stop). Worthy of note here is that it was the great Dr. Enrico Fermi who, in Rome in 1934, stumbled upon the momentous discovery that the shooting of neutrons at uranium resulted in the splitting of the uranium atom, or uranium fission.

Development of nuclear weapons was the prime motivation behind early research into nuclear fission, and resulted in the U.S. Army's Los Alamos–based Manhattan Project of World War II. Two of the first three bombs produced there were dropped on Japan, which ended the war in the Pacific.

The Union of Soviet Socialist Republics

The Soviet Union, having emerged from the most destructive war in its lengthy history with Nazi Germany, had a good idea of what had been taking place at Los Alamos over the previous two years, but what Moscow lacked were specifics.

When the news of nuclear fission first reached the Soviet Union (whether through a letter from Frédéric Joliot-Curie to Abram Fedorovich Ioffe, or by the arrival of scientific journals from the West), it was to cause a good deal of speculation among Soviet physicists. Certainly they knew *what* it was. In the summer of 1939, during a seminar held at the Leningrad Physico-Technical Institute, Yuli B. Khariton and Yakov B. Zeldovich emphasized the importance of fission by stating that a single atomic bomb would be able to destroy Moscow.

While the Soviets were made aware through a multiple succession of spy networks of British and American efforts to build the bomb, serious work on a "Motherland Weapon" only started after World War II had ended. Intelligence that came from both UK- and U.S.-based sources saved the Soviets at least two years of research and development.

During this period, crucial information on the implosion device would arrive from the American-based Klaus Fuchs and David Greenglass. It supplemented work already done, with the first trace quantities of plutonium having been chemically separated at Igor Kurchatov's Laboratory 2 in Moscow in October of 1944.

Meanwhile, Stalin directed his gulag-master and intelligence chief, Lavrenti P. Beria, to oversee the Soviet bomb effort. In a meeting that took place in mid-August of 1945, with Boris L. Vannikov (People's Commissar of Munitions) and leading physicist Igor Kurchatov, Stalin laid squarely on the table what has since become known as his momentous "single demand": "Provide us with a nuclear weapon in the shortest possible time!"

The State Defense Committee set up shortly afterwards was named the "Special Committee on the Atomic Bomb," and was chaired by Beria. The Soviet bomb program was given the code name "Operation Borodino," and Kurchatov was named scientific director.

A production reactor, the F-1 (Physics 1), was built in 1946 on the grounds of Laboratory 2, and went critical on Christmas Day of that year, with Kurchatov at the controls. It was a carbon copy of the U.S. Hanford 305 reactor.

The test site for detonating the first Soviet nuclear weapon had already been selected in 1947 in Kazakhstan, almost 100 miles northwest of the city of Semipalatinsk. The area was subsequently code-named Semipalatinsk-21 (also called the Polygon), and the device was dubbed Josef-1 (or Joe-1), after you-know-who. Having been secured to the top of a tower, it was finally tested on August 29, 1949. The blast, code-named *Pervaya Molniya* (First Lightning), had a yield of ~20 KT.

The designation chosen for the Soviet "Fat Man"—an almost exact copy of its U.S. namesake—was RDS-1.

Great Britain

Quietly and without fuss, Britain was also forging ahead with its own nuclear weapons program.

Originally, George Thomson, a professor of physics at the Imperial College, London, had already in 1939 sought to focus British attention on the inherent military potential of the bomb. Thomson was alerted to this danger when he saw a letter by Frédéric Joliot-Curie, Hans von Halban, and Lew Kowarski, which had been published in the April 22, 1939, issue of *Nature*, revealing that 3.5 secondary neutrons were released per fission.

He consequently contacted General Ismay, secretary of the Committee of Imperial Defense, who in turn involved Sir Henry Tizard, chairman of the Committee on the Scientific Survey of Air Defense (better known as the Tizard Committee). Tizard was not convinced, and little came of Thomson's initiative.

By the early 1940s a British nuclear weapons program wasn't even under consideration. This was abruptly changed by two German refugee scientists at the University of Birmingham: Otto Frisch and Rudolf Peierls. They wrote a three-page technical memorandum titled "On the Construction of a 'Super-bomb'; based on a Nuclear Chain Reaction in Uranium." The outcome, as well as a general report written by them, would forever change the face of warfare. The memo only reached Tizard in March, through the good offices of the New Zealand physicist, Mark Oliphant.

The Frisch-Peierls Memorandum, as it came to be known (see Appendix A), immediately raised interest at the government level. It not only explained theoretically how to build a nuclear bomb, but also dealt fairly accurately with its potential devastating use. Frisch and Peierls estimated that a fast fission explosion could be achieved with as little as a couple of pounds of pure uranium-235. That was followed by the establishment of the "Maud Committee," which decided that a bomb could be made from as little as 22 pounds of ^{235}U.

Then the unexpected happened. After approving two reports in July 1941, the "Maud Committee" was disbanded, possibly for financial reasons—Britain was struggling with the war. Those involved were aghast; they felt this matter was too serious to be ignored, which was probably why its details reached prime minister Winston Churchill that August. Following the advice of Lord Cherwell, his influential personal scientific advisor, Churchill wrote to his chiefs of staff, telling them that he was very much in favor of such work being carried forward—and so it was. The records show that the work "was pursued at all speed." Responding to one of his critics, Churchill wrote that not to have done so, in the face of a possible Nazi bomb, would have been foolish.

Expecting at least some help from their American cousins, the British were disappointed that nothing was forthcoming. For its part, Washington remained tight-lipped about its own nuclear program, and the prospect of a direct appeal by Churchill to Roosevelt was considered. The situation needed to be redressed.

On May 25, 1943, during a visit to the White House, Churchill elicited a promise from Roosevelt for a sweeping exchange of information. Roosevelt's instruction in this regard was telegraphed to Vannevar Bush in London two months later (after a suitable period of repentance and subsequent procrastination), directing him to "renew" the complete exchange of information with London.

Plans for building Britain's own atom bomb were laid even as war raged. The decision-making process started in Washington in May 1944, and recommended a postwar program that would enable the country to produce a militarily significant number of bombs (the figure ten was mooted). The gist of the discussion: It was to be done within the shortest possible time.

But the war was to end and a new government elected in Britain before anything tangible resulted. It was only on January 8, 1947, that a committee of six members of the government (known as Gen 163) met at 10 Downing Street and decided that Britain should have the bomb. This decision was influenced by two considerations. First, to have the capability to independently deter the Soviet Union should Moscow develop the bomb; and second, for the influence and prestige that seemed to accrue with the possession of nuclear weapons. Thus, an Atomic Energy Committee was established in February 1947.

Britain's bomb-building project was obliquely referred to as "High Explosives Research" (HER), and the first official indication of such a program emerged in May 1948, when minister of defense A. V. Alexander indicated as much in the House of Commons in reply to a question.

Responsible for designing Britain's first atom bomb was scientist William Penny, who initially worked out of the Armament Research Establishment, Kent. More such work took place at Woolwich Arsenal, a military firing range at Shoeburyness, and at Foulness Island, where warhead explosive assemblies were later tested.

Weapons electronics production work was established at Woolwich Common, while environmental testing of the explosive assemblies was carried out at Oxfordness in Suffolk. Security and cooperation considerations eventually convinced the British to concentrate work at a single locale, much as the Americans did at Los Alamos. The consequence of that decision was that the Atomic Weapons Research Establishment (AWRE) ultimately found a home at Aldermaston in Berkshire, in April 1950.

Development of Britain's Mk1 fission bomb proceeded with close cooperation between the scientists and the Royal Air Force (RAF). In the end, an August 1952 deadline was set for completion of the core, and only met with the help of some Canadian plutonium. That first device contained about 15 pounds of ^{239}Pu and incorporated a polonium (and presumably beryllium) initiator with a uranium tamper.

The British closely followed the design of the original "Fat Man," although their device would sport a more sophisticated core. Since a nuclear device could not be tested on the British mainland itself, prime minister Clement Attlee opened secret negotiations with Australian premier Robert Menzies late in 1950 to use as a testing base the Monte Bello Islands, an archipelago off the northwest coast of Australia. Formal sanction was granted by Canberra the following year.

The non-nuclear assembly of the first British device was dispatched to Monte Bello via Simonstown and the Cape of Good Hope aboard the frigate HMS *Plym* in June 1952. Its plutonium core arrived three months later aboard a Sunderland flying boat, after a three-day flight. Encased in a watertight caisson beneath the *Plym*, then anchored off Trimouille Island, Monte Bello, Operation Hurricane took place at midnight on October 3, 1952.

The yield of this first British atom bomb was a respectable 25 KT.

France

Like Britain, France took longer to launch its nuclear weapons program. The event, known as Gerboise Bleue, detonated on top of a tower at the Reggane Proving Grounds in the Tanezrouft Desert, French Algeria, with a yield in the order of 60 to 79 KT. The bomb was a plutonium-fueled, implosion-assembly nuclear device, and was referred to in Paris as Type A. This was also the first "indigenous" bomb to be exploded by a country joining this exclusive club, which was not a carbon (or near) copy of the U.S. "Fat Man" (as was the Soviet RDS-1 and Britain's Hurricane).

It took a while to get there, however, and the original April 1939 letter by Joliot-Curie, von Halban, and Kowarski played a significant role. That document concluded that it was uranium's rare ^{235}U isotope which fissioned and made a chain reaction possible—even in natural uranium. The importance of this observation may be deduced from three secret patents which Joliot-Curie registered a month later—two concerning the production of energy, and the third dealing with explosives. Already in 1935, Joliot-Curie had recognized the possibility of achieving an "explosive nuclear chain reaction."

For their part, von Halban and Kowarski eventually ended up in Canada as part of the British contribution to the U.S. Manhattan Project, as would three Frenchmen: Pierre Auger, Jules Guéron, and Bertrand Goldschmidt.

These five scientists were leading physicists in pre-Vichy France. When General Charles de Gaulle, leader of the Free French, visited Ottawa in July 1944, Guéron went on to inform him about the atom bomb and its potential impact on international politics. It was actually the first such communication to reach a Frenchman of significant political stature.

Sadly, the presence of French scientists in the Manhattan Project also contributed toward the sometimes-strained relations between Britain and America in this sphere of activity. Washington was concerned that secret information would be passed back to Paris. Indeed, the last thing that the U.S. wanted was another nuclear partner. It was felt at the time that additional influences might usurp America's perceived leadership role in what was then still very much of a nuclear monopoly.

The French believed otherwise. After the war, Paris set about the task of building a nuclear infrastructure of its own. The first step in this momentous chapter was a decree in October 1945 by General Charles de Gaulle that established a French nuclear energy agency. Called the Commissariat à l'Énergie Atomique (CEA), Raoul Dautry was appointed its administrator-general, with Joliot-Curie named as its high commissioner.

With the exception of von Halban, all the leading French physicists who had been involved with the Manhattan Project returned to France within a year.

Although none were formally released from their wartime pledges of secrecy, it would be simplistic to accept that they would withhold details of such important research once on home ground again.

While the Saclay Nuclear Research Centre near Versailles was being established, the CEA took over an old fortress on the outskirts of Paris—the Fort de Châtillon—where France's first nuclear reactor was erected.

The year 1948 was a milestone for French nuclear aspirations. Uranium was discovered near Limoges, while the first French reactor, called EL-1, or ZOE (Zero power, uranium oxide fuel, and *eau lourde*—heavy water—moderated), was built under the direction of Lew Kowarski. The reactor went critical in December.

The first milligram-quantity of French plutonium was extracted in November 1949 at a lab-scale facility at Le Bouchet, using a technique developed by Bertrand Goldschmidt. The next year, an event of even greater significance occurred during a meeting held at the Saclay, when Goldschmidt successfully argued in favor of a program of plutonium-producing power-reactors as opposed to research-reactors. A French bomb at that stage was not even a matter for discussion.

It was only in 1952 that the French military started taking an active interest in nuclear weapons. That came when a small group of army officers under the direction of Colonel Charles Ailleret, of the Commandement des armes spéciales, began preliminary studies on the requirements for a nuclear weapon detonation.

Like many other historical reversals, it took the war in French Indochina to create an awareness of the potential of nuclear weapons. That sentiment surfaced in parliamentary and military circles after the disastrous French defeat at Dien Bien Phu, Indochina, in May 1954. Another factor had been the failure of French premier Pierre Mendès-France to interest the United States and the Soviet Union in a policy of nuclear disarmament. Meanwhile, as in the Middle East today, there were Frenchmen not yet aware of the difference in status between the nuclear "haves" and "have-nots."

It was Mendès-France who called a cabinet-level interministerial meeting to discuss the issue shortly afterwards, which was when he asked about the time frame. He demanded answers to two specific questions: how long it would take to develop a home-built atom bomb; and second, the feasibility of France constructing its own nuclear-powered submarine (an SSN). Two days later, General Albert Buchalet agreed to head up a secret nuclear weapons unit within the CEA. It was named the Bureau d'Études Générales (BEG).

By now, May 1956, BEG had expanded sufficiently for it to be transformed into a department—the Département des techniques nouvelles (DTN). The issue was not yet a fait accompli, as there were still powerful political elements in the country's government—many of them communist—that were opposed to France going nuclear. But that, too, was short-lived, because the Suez Canal crisis (referred to as the Suez Fiasco by the media) emerged shortly afterwards.

On July 26, 1956, Egyptian president Nasser did the unthinkable and nationalized the Suez Canal. It was Egypt's waterway, he declared to his nation in a radio broadcast, adding forcefully that the time had come to reassert Egyptian sovereignty. In other words, foreign ownership of a major Egyptian strategic asset was not acceptable.

To redress the situation, Israel, Britain, and France decided that the only solution to an Arab leader grabbing a significant European asset—and a hugely strategic one at that—would have to involve the military. A Franco-British landing took place on November 5 at Port Said, preceded by an Israeli land assault six days before. British and French forces were ostensibly there to pacify the situation, but in reality, it was nothing of the sort: Paris and London wanted their canal back.

Issues were compounded when Soviet premier Nikolai Bulganin condemned these actions with a "barely veiled . . . threat to use nuclear missiles to end the fight . . ." And that, essentially, was the end of it. The war in Egypt ended as suddenly as it had begun, with both countries in disgrace.

At that stage, to the chagrin of the French leadership, a decision still had to be made at the government level regarding whether or not to acquire nuclear weapons. Abandoned by its friends and allies, the humiliation faced by Paris (and London) was as visible as its hugely embarrassing impotence. An immediate consequence was a new protocol signed weeks later between the CEA and the French Armed Forces. It covered research on all aspects of a nuclear explosive device, as well as the acquisition of plutonium for this purpose.

Further, the French military was charged with working on the preparations for testing an atom bomb.

The People's Republic of China

The Chinese Communist Party was presumably aware of the American Manhattan Project from its inception in 1942, thanks in part to members and sympathizers within the Soviet intelligence-gathering apparatus in the West (such as "Sonia"—Ursula Hamburger).

It certainly knew that the U.S. project was on track by 1944. Ironically, while Mao Zedong was initially dismissive of the atom bomb (he described it as a "paper tiger" during an interview in 1946), Kang Sheng, his spymaster, was at the same time running a campaign to lure home expatriate Chinese scientists who had received training in Western technology. Some of these specialists might have been involved in nuclear weapons and other sensitive projects that included missile development.

While the Sino-Soviet Treaty of Friendship, Alliance and Mutual Assistance of 1950 served to provide the People's Republic of China (PRC) with an implied nuclear umbrella, this did not prevent U.S. threats to use the bomb during the Korean War (1950–53) and, thereafter, during the critical 1954–1955 Taiwan Strait Crisis.

An early result of these developments took place in early 1955 during an enlarged meeting of revolutionary China's Central Secretariat. Presided over by Mao and held in Zhongnanhai, the political and state center in the Forbidden City, it was resolved that the People's Republic would have its own "Manhattan Project." It was dubbed Project 02.

Because of the perceived urgency, the group also decided to enlist Soviet help. Between January 1955 and September 1958, six accords were signed by the two countries, the most important pertaining to the delivery of a prototype Soviet atom bomb. There were also agreements for the provision of a nuclear reactor and a cyclotron, as well as a joint survey for uranium in the PRC.

Prudent, as always, Mao didn't put all his trust in Moscow. China went ahead and followed a second, indigenous route to the bomb. Besides the Soviets, unofficial help allegedly also came by way of the Joliot-Curies in late 1949, when Frédéric and Irène assisted Qian Sanqiang, one of their former students, in purchasing the PRC's first nuclear instruments in Europe. That was followed by Irène Joliot-Curie giving Yang Chengzong 10 grams of radium salt in October 1951.

More assistance might have come from Dr. Bruno Pontecorvo, who had worked in Canada for the Anglo-Canadian team that contributed toward the Manhattan Project from 1943 onwards. He followed that with a stint in the UK at the Harwell nuclear research center. Then, to the surprise of many of his colleagues, he defected to the Soviet Union with his family in October 1950.

With the benefit of hindsight, America's initial reticence to get more parties involved in its earlier phases of nuclear research seems to have been well founded. Soviet advisors, equipment, and data started to arrive in China in 1958. Unfortunately so too did Mao's catastrophic Great Leap Forward, which resulted in social, political, commercial, and industrial havoc throughout the country. It had a direct bearing on slowing China's nuclear aspirations.

In a bid to stop the rot and possibly reverse this trend with regard to the country's defenses, the PRC's all-powerful Central Committee approved several ad hoc commissions to allow nuclear-related work to continue without interruption. Their nuclear path was further spelled out by the Central Military Commission during a conference held in 1958, and chaired by the Great Leader himself. This event produced what was termed "The Guidelines for Developing Nuclear Weapons," the most revealing being the development of both fissile and thermonuclear warheads, as well as a clutch of long-range delivery missiles. It was stressed that these programs would enjoy precedence over the country's reconstruction. That June—the month during which the country's Soviet-supplied reactor and cyclotron started operating—Mao said that China would acquire nuclear weapons within a decade. He was proved right.

Things were not going so well on the international front, however. China's newfound intimacy with the Soviets would not see out the decade. Differences were not merely ideological. It soon emerged that Khrushchev and Mao had very different perceptions about the consequences of a nuclear war. Beijing, studiously diplomatic in its dealings with Moscow, was already aware that the Soviet Union had secretly decided to renege on its undertaking to supply a prototype bomb. A Soviet letter dated June 20, 1959, formally notified the People's Republic of China of this decision.

Undeterred, work on the Chinese bomb went ahead. They were not only fast-tracking the highly enriched uranium route to the bomb, but also working on a plutonium core. In 1958 the Chinese laid plans for their first plutonium-producing reactor. This was situated in Jiuquan Prefecture, Gansu Province. A Soviet-designed, graphite-moderated, natural-uranium light-water reactor (LWR) was adapted for this purpose, and on-site work initiated in February 1960.

The "Three Hard Years" of 1960–62 followed, coupled with social unrest and food shortages. It was to be expected that the nuclear program would be slowed as a consequence. Although plant construction and equipment installation at the uranium-enrichment site was about complete by the end of 1961, it was nowhere near operational. The Lanzhou Gaseous Diffusion Plant was now labeled a "national crusade."

Late in 1962, Mao's Second Ministry directed that ^{235}U production be brought forward to the beginning of 1964, which was when a youthful Lanzhou scientist, Wang Chengxiao, proposed a revised production plan that would enable the original schedule to be constrained by six months. Thus, in January 1964, the first highly enriched uranium was produced. As was noted afterwards in some of Mao's papers, the national crusade had paid off.

It was only discovered years later that Beijing—like Pakistan, Iraq, Iran, and North Korea afterwards—benefited immensely from details gleaned from open publications in the West. Source material which had been unclassified (prematurely, as we now accept), such as the so-called Smyth Report, *Effects of Nuclear Weapons* by Gladstone and Dolan, Jungk's *Brighter than a Thousand Suns,* and Groves's *Now It Can Be Told: The Story of the Manhattan Project* all played revealing roles.

Not only was the implosion technique detailed in these reports and publications, but also the manner in which it could be achieved, vis-à-vis the use of spherically arranged high-explosive "lenses." This information had its place in enabling the Chinese to work out their own theoretical designs. Soviet advisors also unwittingly contributed to the Chinese program when they left behind important scraps of paper. Among other technical information, these provided their former protégés with vital design details for implosion "lenses" ultimately used in the bomb. More aid came from clues garnered from Soviet and U.S. test sites. The Chinese collected debris from the periphery and carefully examined them for clues.

Nuclear weapons design in China, meanwhile, was being handled under the auspices of the Ninth Bureau, which had been initiated at the transitional Beijing Nuclear Weapons Research Institute in the late 1950s. Bureau head Li Jue was fortunate in having the services of three senior nuclear scientists—Wang Ganchang, Peng Huanwu, and Guo Yonghuai—who had been assigned to the Northwest Nuclear Weapons Research and Design Academy (Ninth Academy), then still quartered at the Beijing Institute.

While most of the credit for designing the country's first bomb went to these three scientists, the "father" of the Chinese bomb was to be Deng Jiaxian, who after years of study in the U.S. was accorded a PhD by an American university. He went on to make very substantial contributions to the bomb's theoretical design.

China's first nuclear explosive device was named "596," a not-so-subtle reminder of Khrushchev's June 1959 action when he reneged on the delivery of a prototype bomb to the PRC.

Early in 1961 China had to make a final decision about what type of nuclear device it would produce, with quantity being the prime objective. First came the A-1, an implosion device. In contrast, the A-2 was gun-type. Although the A-1 became first choice, it is interesting that work on the A-2 was never abandoned—obviously as a backup should A-1 fail.

After approximately thirty months of work, and some 1,000 test shots, the design was perfected by September 1962. In September of the following year, Deng and three groups of theorists under his leadership completed the draft design of the device at the Beijing Institute. In November 1963, another important milestone was reached when a hydrodynamic test was carried out using a half-size model of the explosive package.

The Nuclear Component Manufacturing Plant, also at Jiuquan, began machining the first HEU "ball" into a bomb core at the end of April 1964. Appropriate to this communist state, it completed the task on May Day 1964. Final assembly of 596—which weighed in at 3,400 pounds, including a ton of high explosives and more than 24 detonators—took only 72 hours.

The first atom bomb was completed three months later, and finally detonated at the Lop Nor (Lop Nur) Nuclear Weapons Test Base in China's far western Gobi

Desert, on the morning of October 16, 1964. The People's Republic of China formally became the world's fifth official nuclear power.

Israel already had the bomb (see chapter 9)—unofficially, of course—and India followed soon afterwards. Then came South Africa. But Pretoria eschewed a nuclear option shortly before the white-led apartheid regime handed over power to president Nelson Mandela, so far the only country in the world to have done so.

Then came Pakistan. And now we have North Korea. London bookmakers are hedging their bets that of the thirty other countries that Dr. Mohamed El-Baradei (head of Vienna's International Atomic Energy Agency) says are honing their skills to develop some kind of nuclear capability, Iran will be next.

LISE MEITNER: MOTHER OF NUCLEAR FISSION

Marcia Bartusiak did a wonderful piece in *The Washington Post* some years ago titled "The Woman Behind the Bomb." It dealt with Austrian Lise Meitner, who was one of the best experimentalists in nuclear fission in an age when hardly anybody was aware that such a concept even existed.[1]

In the world of nuclear physics, it seems men have always predominated. Yet the youthful Lise Meitner—she was also Otto Frisch's aunt and inspiration—was prodigious enough in her output to be given her own physics section in the prestigious Kaiser Wilhelm Institute for Chemistry when still in her early thirties. On top of which, she was a Jew, which was something unheard of until then.

Indeed, Albert Einstein was so impressed with her work that he referred to her affectionately as "our Marie Curie." It is significant that in his book on the subject, *The Making of the Atomic Bomb*, author Richard Rhodes devoted a sizable chunk to Meitner's work on nuclear fission. With all that, as Bartusiak observes, it is peculiar that today, this great lady's name "has diminished to a footnote."

Lise Meitner quickly made her mark with her perceptive realization that the atomic nucleus could be split in two, which, as Marcia Bartusiak points out, "was the first step in a cascading step of discoveries that would relentlessly lead to the atomic bomb." In the midst of these revelations, Lise Meitner had to flee from Nazi Germany, which effectively cut her off from her laboratory and her colleagues. While exile saved her life, it undoubtedly cost her a Nobel Prize nomination and a prominent niche in some annals of physics.

More recently Ruth Lewin Sime, a chemist at Sacramento City College, wrote the definitive scientific biography of Meitner, titled *Lise Meitner: A Life in Physics*.[2] It is an insightful work about a woman's devotion to science. Also, it reads easily, and among a host of other informa-

---

[1] *The Washington Post*, March 17, 1996.

[2] Ruth Lewin Sime, *Lise Meitner: A Life In Physics*, University of California Press.

tion, lays bare some of the scientific claptrap that emerged in Germany as Adolf Hitler moved to a pivotal position of power that ultimately led to disaster.

Lisa Meitner was born in Vienna in 1878. As Marcia Bartusiak tells us, she was one of eight children, and her father, Phillip Meitner, was among the first group of Jewish men to practice law in Austria. Bartusiak writes:

> As with Curie [but rare for a woman at the turn of the century], the intellectual atmosphere that surrounded Meitner as a child nurtured her scientific proclivity. Only the second woman to obtain a doctoral degree in physics at the University of Vienna, she was soon drawn into the novel study of radioactivity.
>
> In 1907 she moved to Berlin, the mecca of theoretical physics, where she was introduced to Einstein and Max Planck, father of the quantum theory. More important, she met Otto Hahn, who became her closest collaborator and a valued friend. They were an interdisciplinary yin and yang: Hahn, the chemist, Meitner, the physicist. While he was methodical, she was bold.
>
> Together, in 1917, they discovered a new element, protactinium.
>
> Despite the terrible gender discriminations of the time (especially in Germany), Meitner's deft abilities could not be ignored.

Sadly, history has not been very kind to her.

North Korean & Iranian Missiles

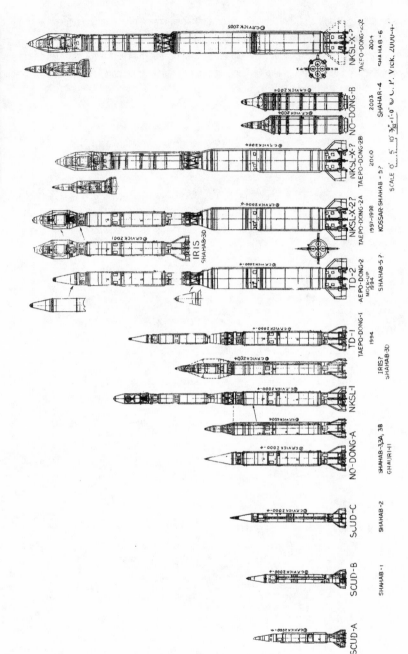

AN UNCHECKED NUCLEAR IRAN

> If Iran develops a military nuclear project—against whom will it direct it? According to the Iranian president's statement, it is not directed against Israel, but is for peaceful purposes, for energy. Iran has oil and gas reserves that will last it for dozens, if not hundreds, of years. I don't think it's true that this project is for energy purposes. If only this nuclear project were directed against Israel, but it isn't. We have experience with this kind of regime—whether the former Iraqi regime, or the totalitarian regimes in Iran and elsewhere. They want to intimidate their neighbors.
>
> —Interview with Kuwaiti MP, Dr. Walid Al-Tabtabai (Al Jazeera Television, August 30, 2006)

A dilemma that faces the West is its consistently failed attempts to penetrate Iran's security mantle, including the machinations of that country's secretive Pasdaran or IRGC (the Islamic Revolutionary Guard Corps, Tehran's most secret security body), to whom the nation is subject.

There have been efforts made to "get inside," obviously—many of them—not only within the Tehran political and military establishment, but also, as the Israelis would like, into the labyrinth of its principal expatriate surrogate, Hezbollah, but very few have been successful.

Indeed, in the shadowy world of spooks and subterfuge, this kind of thing goes on all the time. What we've been able to gather from those in the know is that Iran's is an inordinately difficult carapace to pierce. Like the tortoise, the country's public face tends to disappear behind an immutable array of screens, mostly impenetrable. Then, when things subside, its functionaries emerge once more.

Paula A. DeSutter, today assistant secretary for verification and compliance in the Bush administration, said it best when she remarked: "The Iranian government is not easy to understand. There is a gap between its rhetoric and its actions; between its sense of grievance and its inflammatory behavior, and between its ideological and national interests. Nor are its actions consistent."

The reality is that to make headway in Iran, almost any kind of breakthrough would have to start and end with a single premise: If you are not Iranian and, specifically, Shiite, you are excluded from just about everything in this theocracy that, fundamentalist Saudi Wahhabism apart, is unique in the world of Islam.

Obviously, religion, race, and ethnicity, as well as political orientation, have their place, but the people who make it work are almost exclusively the descendants of The Twelvers, the twelfth Imam "who has never died" and is the focus of Iran's doctrine of *velayat-e faqih*. Essentially, this implies political guardianship of the country and its people "by scholars trained in religious law." Western media often refer to this section of the community as mullahs, which is disparaging. It is also unkind, since the average Iranian mullah is at the bottom of the heap of a huge body of educated clergy, some of whom are as likely to throw Socrates or Plato's *Republic* at you as a discourse on Pythagoras's views on the life of man.

Nor are you allowed to forget that Iran—that Great Persian Empire of yesteryear—stems from some pretty awesome historical traditions. Its early leaders embraced swathes of empire that at one stage stretched from the Mediterranean to the Indian subcontinent, each one of them acquired by conquest. This includes almost all of the present-day Middle East, which is one of the reasons why the average Iranian looks down his nose at his Arab neighbors.

Not referring to Iranians as Arabs is the very first lesson that prospective Western diplomats destined for a Tehran posting are taught. The fact is, in order to make any kind of headway in contemporary Iran, you need to speak Farsi. Arabic—in any of its multifarious dialects—simply won't do.

There is also an almost inbred, millennia-old paranoia that the visitor is likely to encounter the moment he steps off the curb. Some call it the Esfahan Syndrome, named after that fine central Iranian city south of the Caspian that seems always to have produced good carpets. Today Esfahan plays hosts to one of the country's biggest underground nuclear establishments, said by some to be secreted half a mile down and, as a consequence, impervious to anything short of a ground or subterranean burst, high-order thermonuclear strike.

Though things have eased fractionally in recent years, Westerners are only grudgingly welcome in the country. Visa applications can take a month to process, though anybody from a country enjoying favored-nation status, like South Africa, can get one in a week. An office attached to the Pasdaran vets all prospective applications.

The movement of non-residents in the country, including diplomats, is closely monitored. While staying at any hotel, either in the capital or in the interior, chances are that your baggage is more than likely to be searched. To question something as sensitive as the country's nuclear weapons program would invite a lot of attention.

There have been a few breaks. Iranian opposition groups tend to keep close tabs on developments and appear to be well funded by Langley.

Then, occasionally, the Iranians slip up, like they did in late 2006 when certain nuclear materials were discovered in a waste facility which the International Atomic Energy Agency had been examining. George Jahn of the Associated Press reported on November 14 that IAEA inspectors found the "unexplained plutonium and highly enriched uranium traces" and asked Tehran to explain. Some answers were provided but none was satisfactory.

The Iran of today is different if you scratch under the surface a little. You have the Iranian population-at-large—especially the younger set—who are not nearly as anti-Western or anti-American as their parents might have been. Beyond the everyday image that most of us nurture of contemporary Iran today, linked as it is to a harsh system of political and religious control, Americans are a lot more popular than most foreigners are likely to expect. It also helps that there is a huge expatriate community of Iranians—some put the figure in excess of a million—and through the interchange of ideas (combined with the Internet), this helps to foster inquiry and often enough, dissention. It also encourages interest in just about everything non-Iranian, including the West's preoccupation with Iran's putative weapons of mass destruction.

There are also Iran's expatriate politicians, quite a bunch of them who have dissociated themselves from the old leadership, including some notable individuals such as former Iranian president Abol Hassan Bani Sadr, who lives in exile in Paris and still gives interviews. Sadr and quite a few others have created their own underground contacts, some of them within the government itself. These are the people who, with time, have been sapped of their original enthusiasm for the Great Revolution. Others are simply disillusioned with the country's politics, overwhelmed by the kind of restrictive religiosity that prevents women from displaying a single strand of hair or open flesh, be it on their arms or necks. Still more of them see a Tehran establishment succumbing to those most elemental blunders of all totalitarian regimes—greed, corruption, and nepotism. Most of these people tend to abominate Tehran's ruling elite, and one effect over the years has been more defections to the West than anybody would like to admit.

Given the swirling brew of sentiment in Iran today, details occasionally emerge more by design than by accident. Much valuable data on the country's nuclear program was provided by Iranian general Sardar Shafagh, formerly a member of the Islamic Revolutionary Guard Corps (IRGC), and, in his day, a key player in the country's uranium-enrichment program. He disappeared in Moscow in mid-1995 while negotiating contracts with the Russian organization Minatom. According to Bani Sadr, he had with him a batch of important documents. As he will ask, invariably with a smile, who knows where these are now?

On a practical level, Iranian's WMD program falls squarely within the ambit and control of the IRGC, better known in Iranian circles as the Pasdaran. Created in the early days of the revolution, the Pasdaran takes the lead in the production and employment of nuclear, chemical, and biological weapons, and as all Western intelligence agencies are aware, its activities are shuttered behind a formidable veil of secrecy.

Only the trusted few are allowed into its inner sanctum with clearances dominated by the country's powerful religious interests and, in particular, by Iran's Supreme Spiritual Leader. As someone said, paraphrasing a verse out of that other Great Book, it would be easier for a camel to get through the eye of a needle than for a non-Shiite to be accepted within the ranks of the Pasdaran.

Paula A. DeSutter wrote an insightful thesis on the Iranian IRGC and its role in the country's nuclear establishment for the Center for Counterproliferation Research at Washington's National Defense University.[1] She tells us that the role of the Pasdaran extends far beyond the country's frontiers. It is the inspiration and main source of succor behind the anti-Israel Hezbollah movement in southern Lebanon. More recently, Pasdaran has been said to have links with al-Qaeda.

For some years the Pasdaran was involved in a comprehensive training program involving Sudan's security personnel. The Pasdaran negotiated the lease to the Sudan's two main Red Sea ports, Suakin and Port Sudan. Again, one might ask for what purpose, since Iran is hardly a regional power in the Indian Ocean. But as some of us have observed, having acquired submarines and maritime cruise missiles that might soon be tipped with who-knows-what, Tehran is slowly getting there.

Ms. DeSutter's assessment is comprehensive. She describes the IRGC as an effective post-revolutionary unit that "has not only survived, but thrived . . . with a structure reminiscent of the old Bolshevik Red Army." As she observes, the IRGC would be the "focal point for Iranian efforts to 'export the revolution.'" It says a lot that by the end of the Iran-Iraq war, the IRGC was directing thirty-seven secret weapons-development projects and working closely with another revolutionary entity that acted as its "Corps of Engineers," the "Construction Jihad," or "Crusade for Reconstruction."

More bizarre is the fact that the IRGC is answerable to no one but the man who inherited the title "Supreme Spiritual Guide" from the late Ayatollah

Khomeini. The role of Iran's present-day Supremo, Sayyid Ali Hoseini-Khamenei, within government, supersedes even that of the country's titular head of state, the controversial, outspoken—and some would say, fiery—President Mahmoud Ahmadinejad.

This man likes to make statements that his colleagues sometimes regard as tongue-in-cheek outrageous. Like the one the Associated Press reported on October 23, 2006, when he told a gathering on Tehran's outskirts that "Iran's nuclear capability has increased tenfold despite Western pressure to roll back its atomic program."

While there have been some differences of opinion regarding the nuclear road that Tehran has chosen to develop its nuclear weapons programs, all indications remain that the focus of that country's nuclear interests in the new millennium is centered on a trilogy of systems comprising uranium enrichment (gas centrifuge); a laser isotope system that is somewhere between AVLIS (atomic vapor laser isotope separation) and MLIS (molecular laser); as well as a weapons-oriented means of delivery that is largely of North Korean extraction (the No-Dong family of missiles, re-branded "Shahab" in Iran).

This hasn't been easy. As Saddam Hussein quickly discovered when he was still at the helm, the three systems are fraught with the most complex disciplines. Certainly, none are suited to the infrastructure, human resources, or doctrines of developing or Third World countries. Furthermore, they are formidable drains on the economy, though with 7 percent of the world's oil resources, that is of little or no consequence to Tehran's leaders. However, as Iraq was to discover once it had moved into the second stage of this kind of weapons development prior to Gulf War 1, there are some things that money simply can't buy.

What is different from nuclear programs followed by other rogue nuclear states—South Africa included—is that with Iran, there is also a plutonium component to its program, which means that it might additionally be fixed on an implosion device (such as the one used at Nagasaki), as opposed to the simpler "gun-type" of atom bomb (Hiroshima).

Additionally, the Iranians are stuck with the reality that their country is hardly first-tier industrially orientated. Nor is it technologically advanced, in the South Korean or Japanese sense, and certainly not scientifically adept enough to go it alone. Though there are many expatriate Iranians perfectly at home in advanced Western research establishments, coupled with thousands more in the upper echelons of industry, finance, academia, and the rest, in just about every country on earth, they—like so many Jews in Hitler's Germany—took the gap while they still could, the majority heading for the United States and Canada.

Some of what we know was made public in the U.S. Congressional Research Service Report for Congress by Sharon Squassoni, specialist in national defense, foreign affairs, defense, and trade division. In a submission titled "Iran's Nuclear Program: Recent Developments," dated September 6, 2006, American lawmakers were told that Iran's current plans were to construct seven nuclear power plants (1000 MW each) by 2025. This was extremely ambitious, particularly for a state with such vast fuel reserves, members were told.

Squassoni submitted that it was Iran's argument—as it had been in the 1970s—"that nuclear power is necessary for rising domestic energy consumption, while oil and gas are needed to generate foreign currency. Few observers believe that such an ambitious program is necessary or economic for Iran." Iran also repeatedly asserted that its nuclear program was strictly peaceful, stating in May 2003 that "we consider the acquiring, development, and use of nuclear weapons inhuman, immoral, illegal, and against our basic principles. They have no place in Iran's defense doctrine."

However, the CRS report went on, "two decades of clandestine activities have raised questions about Iran's intentions, and Iran's use of centrifuge enrichment technology makes detection of clandestine enrichment very difficult. In fact, the preferred approach to rebuilding world confidence in Iran since 2003 has been to persuade Iran to suspend enrichment and reprocessing, perhaps indefinitely."

A subsection of the CRS report, headed WHAT INSPECTIONS REVEALED, covers the 2002 disclosures by the National Council of Resistance of Iran (NCR) which gave information about nuclear sites at Natanz (uranium enrichment) and Arak (heavy-water production):

> Three years of intensive inspections by the IAEA revealed significant undeclared Iranian efforts in uranium enrichment [including centrifuge, atomic vapor laser and molecular laser isotope separation techniques] and separation of plutonium, as well as undeclared imported material. Iranian officials have delayed inspections, changed explanations for discrepancies, cleaned up facilities, and in one case, Lavizan-Shian, razed a site.
>
> According to IAEA director general Mohamed ElBaradei, "Iran tried to cover up many of their activities, and they learned the hard way."

Among other activities, Congress was informed, was that Iran admitted in 2003 that it conducted "bench scale" uranium conversion experiments in the 1990s (required to be reported to the IAEA), and later, conceded that it had used for those experiments some safeguarded material that had been declared lost in other processes (a safeguards violation). This came from Iranian officials only after A.Q. Khan's *mea culpa* broadcast to the Pakistani nation that he had supplied several countries with equipment to make atom bombs.

Clearly, Iran has come a long way in the twenty years that it admits to having clandestinely dabbled in the nuclear domain. For much of the time, it received succor from the north, first from the former Soviet Union (FSU), and more recently, from the same sources in modern-day Russia. Looking at the broader scenario, the idea of Moscow's leaders providing Tehran with the wherewithal to create an independent nuclear establishment—with or without Nuclear Non-Proliferation Treaty (NPT) safeguards, primitive or otherwise—makes about as much sense as it would for the Americans to equip Cuba with ICBMs.

There are several reasons. The first is that Iran borders several FSU states, just about all of them with powerful Islamic traditions that go back almost forever. Thirty minutes spent looking at news reports out of the region reveals that Moscow is today viewed with great suspicion, and indeed, deep-rooted odium by almost all the countries that have embraced the Islamic faith. This is a consequence of what has been going on in the tiny southern enclave of Chechnya, which is largely Islamic.

The truth is, the Kremlin's leaders, one and all, have been mindlessly brutal in their handling of any kind of Chechnik opposition in a conflict that has left several hundred thousand people dead, wounded, or dispossessed. This crisis—another bitter rivalry between Islam and forces that oppose the tenets of the Qur'an—is decades old. No wonder, then, that Chechnya has become a most prolific al-Qaeda recruiting ground for fighters willing to lay down their lives for the cause.

Sentiments expressed on Islamic Web sites are explicit about the issue. Routinely they display examples of Muslims being targeted in Chechnya, and that it is Russian troops doing the killing. Some are filled with horrifying images of human-rights transgressions. An impression that lingers is one of intransigence and culpability on the part of the Kremlin that is unforgiving. As far as any Muslim is concerned—devout or otherwise—this war has become personal. In the eyes of Allah, many feel that what has taken place is unconscionable. In a word, Chechnya might even be regarded as Russia's intifada.

An interesting sidelight is the public reaction of some Islamic countries. Pakistan's *Jamaat-e-Islami*, in a recent publication titled "Memorandum on the Situation in Chechnya," declared that the Russians were using chemical weapons against the civilian population.[2] It made a rather ominous correlation: what the one party can do, so might the other.

Some Western observers have noted that it would be a rather supreme irony if one of the states which in the past has received help from Moscow in developing weapons of mass destruction—we know about Iraq, Syria, Pakistan,

Libya, and others—was now to supply somewhat similar assets to a group of anti-Moscow rebels in Chechnya. Nor has it been lost on the Kremlin that should relations between Moscow and Tehran go sour, Iran might eventually be at the forefront of mullah ire.

It doesn't take a scientist to appreciate Moscow's dilemma. Almost all the southern states of the FSU, and now, part of the Commonwealth of Independent States (CRS), have preponderant Islamic populations. There is not a Muslim leader among them that has not been critical of how the Chechnyans and their culture have been abused. For their part, most of those who regard Grozny as pivotal are Muslim. As fighters they have proved formidable. Events in Iraq, Afghanistan, Kosovo, and elsewhere have hosted cadres from the tiny enclave while aiding their Muslim comrades-in-arms. That situation—and the subsequent murder of hundreds of innocents, schoolchildren included, in Moscow, Dagestan, and elsewhere—has placed Chechnyan insurgents at the forefront of international terrorism.

We also have a fairly recent example of Chechnyan separatists taking a radiological bomb (an RDD device) and placing it in one of the Moscow suburbs. They tipped off the media before it was detonated, largely as a warning to show what they really could do if they set their minds to it.

There are senior Russian leaders who believe that a real threat exists from rogue or rebel elements. In late 2006 Russia's air force commander Vladimir Mikhailov declared that it was increasingly probable that terrorists could launch a nuclear strike against Russia or Western countries sometime in the future.

"Terrorist organizations and the countries harboring them would not be deterred by a retaliatory strike," he said. He added that the long-term implications were chilling for all."

There have been other revelations, including those made by Dr. Fred Wehling, a senior research associate at the Center for Nonproliferation Studies, Monterey Institute of International Studies. He told this writer that while Russian missile exports to Syria had become an issue, it should not detract from what was going on with nuclear and ballistic missiles between Moscow and Tehran.

The author of *Irresolute Princes: Kremlin Decision Making in Middle East Crises, 1967–1973* (St. Martin's Press, 1997), Dr. Wehling published his findings in the Winter 1999 edition of *The Nonproliferation Review*.[3] He stated that the Russian government's apparent support for—or its inability to prevent transfers to Iran of—technology related to nuclear weapons and ballistics missiles, had raised serious concerns in the U.S., Israel, and other countries.

Both Washington and Jerusalem protested vigorously at the diplomatic level once this involvement became known. The U.S., he said, had applied economic sanctions on Russian firms and research institutes suspected of transferring sensitive technology to Tehran. Wehling cites the July 28, 1998, "Statement by the President Expanding the President's Executive Order on Weapons of Mass Destruction."

Yet, he says, "Russia's Ministry of Atomic Energy [Minatom] for some time afterwards continued aggressively to promote exports of nuclear technology and materials to Iran." Likewise, Russian missile firms and research institutes, strapped for cash and short of orders while the country remains mired in an economic crisis, looked to Tehran and other countries of proliferation concern for markets for their products and technology.

Russian environmentalist Aleksey Yablokov supported this view. He went on record as saying that the U.S. might very well have legitimate reasons to suspect Russian institutes of cooperating with Iran in "strategic areas," adding that initial Minatom plans for cooperation with Iran included a military component. It was notable that this was all going on in spite of former president Yeltsin's assurance in 1994 that this military component in all exports to Iran would be removed. By the time it had been halted—and under President Putin, there is no interchange of these technologies that the West is aware of—it was too late.

It was Yablokov's view that individual Russian defense organizations had become involved in supplying sensitive nuclear technology to Iran. He referred to the fact that an Iranian spy was arrested in Moscow at about that time for obtaining technical information on missiles, and that one of the sanctioned facilities was known to be developing a chemical component of missile fuel for Tehran interests.

Apart from the billion-dollar VVER-1000 light-water power reactor deal at Bushehr, the construction of several more nuclear reactors are mooted. These include three additional power reactors of unspecified size, one 30–50 MWt research reactor, and a 40 MWt heavy-water research reactor. There are also ongoing discussions regarding a nuclear APWS-40 desalinization plant. If signed, these contracts will ultimately be worth $2 to $3 billion.

News of the 40 MWt heavy-water reactor first appeared when U.S. intelligence sources reported that Russia's Scientific Research and Design Institute of Power Technology (NIKIET) and another nuclear research institute (probably the Mendeleev University of Chemical Technology) were in the process of negotiating a nuclear reactor sale to Iran.

Months later, Washington announced that it had imposed sanctions on both bodies, as well as against the Moscow Aviation Institute (MAI). What later emerged was that there was only one specialist from MAI involved with Iran, and once this emerged, he was pushed out. According to initial reports, though, negotiations over the sale had been ongoing for more than six months. While no equipment was ever shipped, personnel and blueprints were exchanged—the bottom line being that the more Iran gets involved in nuclear disciplines, the sooner it will be able to go it alone without any kind of foreign oversight. And that also means ultimately developing the full range of nuclear weapons, including the hydrogen bomb.

The reports raised concerns about the personal involvement of several former Russian ministers of atomic energy, including professor Eugene O. Adamov, the same man who, until his appointment as Russia's nuke chief in 1998, had served as a director of NIKIET. His has been something of a devious career. Apart from his links with Tehran, he was picked up in Switzerland on a U.S. warrant for, among other things, allegedly laundering $9 million in funding from the U.S. Department of Energy, money intended for safeguarding Russia's misplaced or badly guarded nuclear assets, an issue dealt with in some detail in chapter 2.

Dr. Fred Wehling quotes U.S. nonproliferation expert Gary Milhollin on the 40 MWt reactor as saying: "If Iran succeeds in importing a research reactor like this, it will open the way to making a bomb."

Also highlighted in the report in the category of enrichment, mining, and milling is a uranium conversion facility. There had been nuclear materials transfers planned for LEU fuel rods for the VVER-1000 reactor, including 2,000 tons of natural uranium, as well as training for Iranian physicists and technicians at the Kurchatov Institute and the Novovoronezh Nuclear Power Plant.

It is interesting that Viktor Mikhailov, former first deputy minister of atomic energy, was quoted on a Kremlin International News Broadcast, saying that Russia had helped Iran design a uranium mine. Work had already started in 1992, with preliminary studies for a facility that would have an annual output of between 100 and 200 MT. Mikhailov added that even then, Iran was seeking Russian assistance in uranium and isotope enrichment.

There were also issues related to missile proliferation. Articles in the Western press reported that Trud (located in Samara) and Energomash (Moscow region) transferred technology related to the FSU RD-214 and RD-216 rocket engine (which was being incorporated into Tehran's SS-4 medium-range rocket). It follows that this development would ultimately allow the engines to be made compatible to Tehran's Shahab-5 and Shahab-6 ICBM/satellite launchers.

Intelligence sources maintain that the news was the result of a well-placed Israeli "leak," followed by quick denials by both the Russian president and his prime minister, and carried by ITAR-TASS and *Voprosy besopasnosti*. According to GlobalSecurity.org's Charles P. Vick, who interfaced with several reliable U.S. sources, the real story was based on an official letter from Trud's N. D. Kuznetsov

Research and Engineering Complex. Apparently the issue had originally been discussed with Tehran way back in 1994. Trud maintains today that it was uninterested in the project, which hardly makes sense in an economy desperately short of funds following the breakup of the FSU.

One of the significant developments linked to this news was the testimony before Congress by former CIA director George Tenet. Though relations between Russia and America had improved markedly, he averred that there were some notable gaps. Despite sanctions, Russia was "backsliding" on its commitments to restrict the transfer of missile technology to Iran. While he accepted that there were positive signs in Moscow's performance on this issue at the time, there was no sustained improvement. In the previous six months, he disclosed that expertise and materials from Russia had assisted Iranian missile programs in training and testing, among other areas.

That followed a statement by the then first deputy prime minister, Yuriy Maslyukov. He declared that Russia was willing to tighten controls on exports of missile technology to Iran *if the U.S. could offer proof of illicit transfers.* He added cryptically that the onus lay with Washington, an old Soviet ploy that seems to have increasingly resurfaced as more disclosures about illicit Moscow links surface.

Shortly afterwards, his colleague, the then Russian minister of defense, Igor Sergeyev, stated that control over nonproliferation of nuclear missile technologies did exist in Russia. Referring to the U.S. imposing sanctions on various Russian bodies, Sergeyev maintained that those institutes could not in any event "supply Iran with missile technologies they did not possess." He suggested that the sanctions issue was being used as a pretext for something that was not yet clear. "While every country has the right to apply sanctions, what America has done is unethical," Sergeyev is quoted as saying in *V.Rossii yest kontrol za neraprostraneniyem raketno-yadernykh tekhnologii-Minoborony.*

It is of interest that these and other issues were again discussed in meetings between former vice president Gore and the then Russian prime minister, Yevgeniy Primakov, while attending the World Economic Forum in Davos, Switzerland. That was shortly before the Russian security service (FSB) issued a statement that U.S. sanctions may well have resulted from misunderstandings or incomplete work by American intelligence agencies. According to the statement, "The decision to impose sanctions indicates a U.S. bias against Russian agencies that cooperate with Iran and other foreign countries."

Though much of this is history, it leads to some interesting speculation when one sees exactly what Iran has been searching for in its quest for more sophisticated weapons of mass destruction. The issue points toward specific objectives, some regarded by military specialists as offensive. Among other Russian missile exports to Iran in that period were the following:

- 21 tons of maraging steel of unknown manufacture (but possibly Inor Production Association and exported by MOSO and Yevropalas 2000)

- Composite material used for ballistic warheads, manufactured by NII Grafit

- Unspecified missile guidance components from the Polyrus Scientific Research Institute and 620 kilograms of special alloys and foils from Inor Production Association and exported by Moscow's arms marketing organization, Rosvooruzheniye

- The alleged exportation of wind tunnel and related facilities from the Russian Central Aerohydrodynamic Institute (TsAGI) and exported by Rosvooruzheniye

Instructive in this regard are comments made in closed session by former Israeli Mossad head Ephraim Halevy to a closed session of the NATO Council in Brussels on June 26, 2002. The ambassadors of all nineteen NATO countries took part in the meeting, and Halevy had the following to say about Tehran's missile program.

In recent years, Iran has invested gigantic sums in the development of launch systems, mainly surface-to-surface missiles originally based on North Korean expertise. The Shahab-3, with a range of 800 miles, has been tested successfully. Iranian Defense Minister Shamkhani publicly stated that Iran is trying to increase its range, carrying capability, and "destructive capability." Iran is also involved in the research and development of even longer-range missiles, which can reach Europe and in the distant future, even the United States. The Iranian defense minister denied this in public, but our view is different. This effort is being conducted under the cover of launching civilian satellites. I have to tell you that I see no reason for this entry into developing such long-range missiles. Who and what are the potential targets of these systems? I do not know.

Since then, the Iranian military tested their latest version of the Shahab-3A, or "Shooting Star." It has continued to do so ever since, with a huge display of missiles in the "Great Prophet-II" military exercises, held toward the end of 2006. Early reports indicate a weapon with multiple warheads that include softball-sized bomblets. Whether these are conventional or otherwise is unknown.

The single Shahab-3A launched during the exercise is capable of a touchdown range of almost 1,000 miles, which brings all of Israel within striking distance. Mirim/No-Dong-B/Shahab-4 has been flight-demonstrated to 1,860 miles, but was apparently capable of almost 2,500 miles, which would encompass a big slice of Europe. The Shahab-3B, in contrast, managed only about half that distance. Meanwhile, it would appear that the Shahab-3B tankage was lengthened and the engine uprated with a Block-II warhead mass reduction.

There are two potential nuclear warheads: Block-I is 2,550 pounds implosion type for Shahab-3 and 3A; and the Block-II, gun-type, which is capable of lifting 1,430 pounds for Shahab-3B, according to Charles Vick. The fact that Iran did not launch either the Shahab-3B or Shahab-4 during these exercises is significant; they could be nuclear-related, a reality not lost on the West.

Also significant are the comments made by the Federation of American Scientists on its Web site (www.fas.org). In referring to the Iranian missile program, the FAS made the interesting point that "for many years, there has been a lack of understanding of the origination of Iran's strategic ballistic missile program. Equally absent from the public discussion about the Missile Technology Control Regime (MTRC) is the exchange of information between North Korean and Iranian launch vehicle strategic ballistic missile programs and the Chinese support of both."

The issues, raised by Walid Al-Tabtabai and former Mossad boss Ephraim Halevy, need to be addressed in more detail in order to understand Iran's intentions. These conclusions are based on comments made during a series of personal communications between this author and Charles Vick of GlobalSecurity.org.

Essentially, in order to guarantee the survivability of their revolution—and indeed, to export it successfully beyond their borders—the Iranian leaders not only had to acquire the full range of weapons of mass destruction, inclusive of nuclear, but also they had to be able to deliver these "onto the heads of our enemies," to paraphrase an aside made by the country's Supreme Spiritual Guide.

With huge North Korean aid, combined with solid South African scientific input,[4] Tehran has developed and fielded its Shahab missile. To do this, it had to import a number of No-Dong-B projectiles (called Shahab-4 locally). The country is also working on a vehicle conceptualized as the multistage Ghadr-110, "the lance aimed at the heart of Satan, whose great cities dot the New World."

The first of these, and especially the Shahab-3B, have been tested and are regarded by Western experts as "mature and operational." The earlier version, the No-Dong-A, was also developed with varying degrees of participation by North Korea and Pakistan (where it is called the Ghauri-II). It bears a striking design resemblance to early Soviet SS-N-4/R-13 and SS-N-5/R-21 SLBM designs. To this end, all three countries must have had substantial Russian aid, official or otherwise. Also, the missile's Scud ancestry speaks for itself. This single-stage liquid-propelled Shahab-3, 3A, and the uprated Shahab-3B can deliver a payload of about 1,430 pounds over a distance of roughly 1,250 miles.

The latest mark to come out of Iran is the Shahab-4, or, as it is known in North Korea, the No-Dong-B/Mirim. Apparently tested for the first time in Iran on January 17, 2006—probably in a bid to avoid the kind of political backlash such a test would bring if carried out from North Korea itself—the missile can traverse some 1,800 miles, while a modified version can manage an additional 600 miles. This single-stage liquid-propelled vehicle is said to be able to deliver the same-sized warhead more than double the distance of the earlier variant. According to Vick, the only known FSU platform that would correspond to these performance figures would have been an uprated FSU SS-N-6/SS-NX-13 design.

Since the Soviet Union had widely deployed the SS-N-6 SLBM on board its SSBN submarines, its protégé has been quickly pressed into service among those rogue states who have it, and, according to Vick, Russian specialists were almost certainly involved. Of the initial order of eighteen missiles, Iran received its first batch from North Korea in December of 2005.

There are also solid propulsion missiles involved. One of these, conceptualized by Vick as the multistage Ghadr-110, appears to be similar to the solid-propelled Pakistani Shaheen-2 (Hatf-6). The two-stage Shaheen-2 has widely been reported as being based on the People's Republic of China's M-18 missile (of similar propulsion and configuration). According to information supplied at a display of Shaheen-2 (on its TEL), its length is 54 feet, with a diameter of just under 4 feet 6 inches, and a weight of 50,000+ pounds. Range is a more modest 1,250 miles. Vick reckons that the reentry vehicle (RV) mass appears to be somewhere around a ton.

Vick illustrates two Ghadr-110 concepts, the first of which is similar to the Shaheen-2, besides its "baby bottle-necked" RV such as a gun-type nuclear device would require. This RV has also been spotted on Iran's Shahab-3B.

Vick's other missile illustration is of interest. It shows a three-stage vehicle, with the first and (shortened) second stage plainly coming from the M-18, topped off with a third (also shortened) M-9 propulsion stage. At the sharp end resides a gun-type RV. This conceptual illustration is of a vehicle about 67 feet long. Assuming a base diameter of 4 feet 6 inches, then its launch weight should be in the region of roughly 30 tons. One needs to compare this missile with the U.S. LGM-30F Minuteman-II ICBM in order to establish a realistic size parameter. The Minuteman-II had a length of 54.99 feet, a base diameter of 6.17 feet, and a weight of roughly 72,765 pounds. It could hurl its single 1,500-pound warhead almost 5,779 miles.

Apart from alleged Chinese M-18/M-9 or JL-1 contributions to the Iranian Ghadr-110, this missile could just as easily have had an even shadier forerunner. The Israeli–South African family of Jericho-2/Shavit/RSA-3 missiles/launchers encapsulated main (and second) propulsion stage with a diameter of 4.3 feet. If so, asks Vick, could this perhaps form the basis of the Ghadr-110? China might have acquired the technical specifications from Pretoria in a missile deal it allegedly had with the apartheid government in the late 1980s. It could just as easily have passed these specs on to Pakistan, where they would have gone from there directly to Iran.

As we are already aware, Iran had already benefited by employing South African missile engineers who found themselves unemployed when the apartheid government folded in 1994. And that certainly would never have happened without joint government collusion at the highest levels. More sobering still is the reality that the new missiles put the entire Eastern American seaboard in range of such a vehicle, with its 1,430-pound payload.

Compounding factors with regard to U.S. ABM-defenses against such an attack would be "stealth," "multiple," or even "maneuvering" warheads.

ROCKET ENGINE SCHEMATIC
NO-DONG-A, GHAURI-II, SHAHAB-3 MRBM

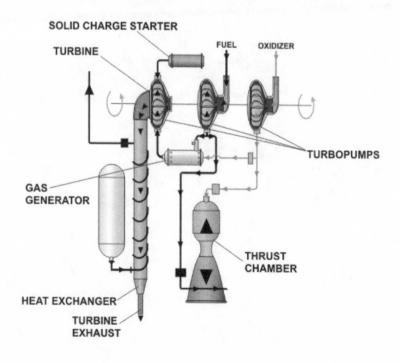

Chapter 8 Endnotes:

1 Paula DeSutter, "Denial and Jeopardy: Deterring Iranian Use of NBC Weapons," National Defense University Center for Counterproliferation Research, Washington, D.C., 1997.

2 Central Information Department, *Jamaat-e-Islami*, Lahore, Pakistan (www.jamaat.org).

3 Fred Wehling, "Russian Nuclear and Missile Exports to Iran," *The Nonproliferation Review*, Monterey Institute of International Studies, Winter 1999, vol. 6, no. 2, pp. 134–43.

4 Al J. Venter, *Iran's Nuclear Option: Tehran's Quest for the Atom Bomb*, Casemate Publishers, Philadelphia, 2005, chapt. 9, pp. 195–212.

ISRAEL'S NUCLEAR CAPABILITY: AN ASSESSMENT

> As the eponymous character in *Dr. Strangelove* observes,
> "Isn't the whole point of a Doomsday Machine . . . lost if
> you keep it a secret?"
> —"Israel's Nukes," *The Economist*, April 24, 2004

Though hardly a major power, Israel has been the dominant force in the Middle East for decades. Strategically, it warrants a lot of attention—which is why it is appropriate that the Federation of American Scientists was able to comment recently that "based on the plausible upper and lower bounds of operating practices at the Dimona Reactor, Israel could have produced enough plutonium for at least 100 nuclear weapons, but probably not significantly more than 200 weapons."

What is also true is that after maintaining a transparent charade for decades, the Jewish State no longer denies that it has a formidable nuclear capability, nor that it would use these weapons if the nation were threatened with annihilation. That warning was leveled at Syria by the Israeli government not long after Damascus deployed Scud missiles tipped with Sarin and VX nerve gases along its southern frontier in the late 1990s. In this regard, the Lebanese Hezbollah insurgent movement should probably also take note.

More recently, the head of the country's National Security Council, Ephraim Halevy (having just stepped down as chief of the Mossad), declared that any kind of "mega-terror attack" on his people would open options for retaliation that hitherto were "unacceptable to public opinion." Speaking in the aftermath of twin terror attacks in Mombassa, Kenya, on an Israeli-owned hotel and a Tel Aviv–registered Boeing 757-400 with 272 passengers and crew on board, Mr. Halevy said that Jerusalem needed to examine the new reality created by the country's enemies. Israel's neighbors perfectly understand the implications of what has been termed by some as Israel's capacity for "ultimate retaliation."

Already in June 1996, *Al-Quds Al-Arabi* was quoted as saying that Israeli commanders "have their fingers on the triggers of 300 nuclear warheads, modern factories for the manufacture of missiles and satellites." While its editors weren't specific as to how these numbers had been computed, that figure has been repeated numerous times in just about every publication in the Arab world. Several authoritative sources have been more specific. In 1976, *Time* magazine quoted reliable Israeli and American sources and disclosed that Israel had thirteen nuclear bombs.[1]

Ten years later, the jailed Israeli nuclear dissident Mordechai Vanunu revealed that the real figure was somewhere between 100 and 200 fission bombs, and that the tally included a number of fusion weapons. By February 1997, according to a report in *Jane's Intelligence Review*, the stockpile had been upped to "400 deliverable thermonuclear and nuclear weapons."

What is clear from numerous sources—several of them intentionally leaked by the Israeli government to create a "fear factor" among its Arab adversaries—is that nuclear ambiguity fostered by the Tel Aviv government for decades appears to have served its purpose; well enough, at the very least, to have prevented another war. In the words of Nicholas Valry, who published "Israel's Silent Gamble with the Bomb" in *New Scientist* on December 12, 1974, "Israel [has] used their existence to guarantee a continuing supply of American conventional weapons, a policy likely to continue."

In the subsequent period, the Jewish Homeland has moved from producing basic fission weapons to fielding American 175mm and 203mm self-propelled artillery pieces capable of firing nuclear shells and manufacturing low-yield neutron bombs. Some evidence has been published in the West that it has "micronukes" as well as "tinynukes," both of which would be useful for attacking point targets and other tactical or barrier (mining) uses.[2]

Notably, the word in Jerusalem is that tinynukes are said to be deployed on the Golan to prevent attack by the Syrians, as happened in 1973. However, a repetition of this is unlikely due to Israel's state-of-the-art electronic and optical surveillance systems, including satellites.

It is perhaps ironic that the Germans, of all nations, have given Israel its most powerful potential striking power by providing three Dolphin-class Type 800 submarines, built by Emden's Thyssen Nordseewerke and Howaldtswerke-Deutsche Werft in Kiel. The security blanket drawn over these craft has been almost impossible to penetrate. What is known is that Jerusalem has embarked on a program of creating an additional strike capability with nuclear cruise missiles. This gives Israel a kind of capacity that could well change the arms race in the Middle East, especially if it could operate within Iranian territorial waters in the Gulf.[3]

A senior Israeli defense official confirmed to the U.S. Natural Resources Defense Council in Washington, D.C., that the Dolphins (which cost $300 million each) would carry modified U.S. Harpoon anti-ship missiles. He conceded that making them "nuclear capable" would require an Israeli-developed warhead and guidance kit for land-attack targets, both of which the country is known to have been working on for some years. A test of a cruise missile from one of these Dolphin boats was held in May 2000 off Sri Lanka, and may suggest a long-range air-breathing derivative of either of the indigenously developed Gabriel or Popeye family of missiles.

It is instructive, too, that Washington rejected Jerusalem's request for a dozen long-range BGM-109 Tomahawk cruise missiles, the same weapon which exists in a nuclear-tipped version for delivery by America's attack undersea craft, though that ban might since have been lifted. Whatever the case, Israel is forging ahead and has ordered two more Dolphins from Germany.

Throughout its comparatively short history, Israel has vigorously pursued a nuclear objective. The idea of acquiring fission weapons first took hold after many talented Jewish scientists immigrated to Palestine after World War II. Once the program was on track, it reportedly even conducted underground nuclear tests on domestic soil.

The West German army magazine *Wehrtechnik* claimed in its June 1976 issue that the first such underground tests in the Negev took place in 1963. Other reports mention a nuclear test at Al-Naqab, also in the Negev, on November 2, 1966.[4] The government was accused of performing another nuclear test near Eilat on May 28, 1998, by a member of its own Knesset [Parliament]. Egyptian scientists made similar charges immediately afterwards, both of which were denied by the Israeli deputy defense minister.

That Israel tested nuclear weapons in the south Indian Ocean on September 22, 1979, at a time when Israel was still cozy with South Africa's apartheid government, has again come to the fore of late. South Africa's deputy foreign minister, Aziz Pahad, was quoted in the Israeli daily *Ha'aretz* as saying that there "was definitely a nuclear test." He also confirmed that the bomb was South African.

An Israeli reporter added that "this was the first time an official spokesman of the South African Government had actually admitted that the flash was the result of a nuclear test. The statement contradicts declarations by his predecessors that South Africa never ever conducted such tests."

Then, to obfuscate matters, Pahad backtracked, claiming afterwards that he had never made the statement attributed to him. His press secretary told the *Albuquerque Journal* (July 11, 1997) that the deputy minister "did not admit" that a nuclear test took place. Instead, she insisted that he had been quoted out of context. More significant is the fact that three nuclear blasts were specifically mentioned, and the circumstances confirmed by the U.S. Embassy in Pretoria.

American writer Seymour Hersh was even more forthright in his analysis of the issue.[5] Referring to a brilliant "nuclear explosion–type" flash picked up by the U.S. Vela satellite, he explained that the blast was the third test of a neutron bomb. "The first two were hidden in clouds to fool the satellite, and the third was an accident; the weather cleared."

There have been at least four occasions since 1967 that crises in the Middle East have brought the Israeli nation to nuclear alert.

In his book, *The Sword and the Olive*, Israeli commentator Martin van Creveld recalls that prior to the 1967 war, Israel—with substantial help from the French—worked furiously to develop at least one atom bomb before the outbreak of hostilities. The fact that war was imminent was obvious to everybody. Nasser was of the opinion that it would take the Israelis another year to achieve their nuclear objective.

In fact, by the time Cairo sent in its troops to blockade the Straits of Tiran, the strategic gateway to Israel's southern port of Eilat—this was the final act that precipitated the Six-Day War—Israel had managed to construct two gun-type bombs, each with a yield of between 17 and 20 kilotons.

While some purists differ with this assertion, at least one other knowledgeable U.S. observer, Harold Hough, seems to concur by noting that the first atom bombs in the Israeli arsenal were indeed gun-assembly devices. They used HEU covertly acquired in the U.S. from the now-defunct Nuclear Materials and Equipment Corporation (NUMEC).

Before and following its disbandment, NUMEC was enmeshed in controversy, with some investigators claiming that Israel obtained its first batches of highly enriched uranium from this Pennsylvanian facility. The *Pittsburgh Tribune-Review* did a fascinating three-part series on the subject; titled "Government Agencies Investigate Missing Uranium, NUMEC," the series started on August 25, 2002, and provides a host of controversial insights.

Interestingly, the Egyptians were very much aware of what was going on in the Negev at Dimona, where the French, a decade before, had started building the secret EL-102 underground nuclear reactor that was to process plutonium to provide fissile material for Israel's nuclear weapons program. There were even Arab plans to bomb the facility, but these were later quashed by Nasser for fear of infuriating the Americans, and possibly involving U.S. forces in what was regarded as a strictly regional conflict. Indeed, Israel considered Egyptian Air Force overflights of Dimona on May 16, 1967, directly linked to a pre-strike reconnaissance.

The second Israeli nuclear alert came on October 6, 1973, when Egypt and Syria launched a surprise attack that was later termed the Yom Kippur War. A third took place soon afterwards. Moscow, in a bid to limit a major military disaster after one of Egypt's armies had been isolated by the Israeli Defense Force (IDF) east of the Suez, consigned a batch of nuclear weapons to Cairo in an attempt to boost flagging morale.

The American *Aviation and Flight Magazine* claimed that the two Soviet Scud brigades deployed in Egypt in late October 1973 were equipped with nuclear warheads. Another report speaks of Washington having detected nuclear trace emissions from a ship that the U.S. shadowed after it had left the Dardanelles, though neither of these reports is backed by hard evidence. To be fair, Langley rarely issues statements about its operations.

Israel did go on full nuclear alert once more after seven Scud missiles were fired at Tel Aviv and Haifa by Iraq on January 18, 1991. This time, according to Colonel Warner D. "Rocky" Farr (author of a comprehensive paper titled *The Third Temple's Holy of Holies: Israel's Nuclear Weapons*[6] published by the USAF Counterproliferation Center), the alert lasted the duration of the war, a total of forty-three days. It was then that the Shamir government warned that if the Iraqis were to use chemical warheads, Israel would retaliate with nuclear weapons.

Perhaps the closest that Israel has come to using nuclear weapons was after Egypt and Syria jointly launched the Yom Kippur War in October of 1973. It was a two-pronged invasion from the north and south that was not only brilliantly timed but masterfully executed. The Arab armies of both countries pushed onto Israel soil, the Egyptians having to ford the Suez Canal in a manner not envisaged before and involving the use of high-power water jets to wash away Israeli sand defenses around her strong points. Additional armored elements from Iraq, with limited help from Jordan, gave support along Syrian lines in the Golan.

Caught short, the IDF was not prepared for a war. Despite well-timed warnings of an invasion, hubris from past military victories came into play, resulting in only a small number of regular forces and ill-equipped reservists being on duty at the time. Israel's defense lines crumbled. Within days alarming reports of stockpile depletions filtered through to the defense ministry. Issues were exacerbated by Russia's support for the enemy; Egyptian and Syrian air and ground losses were made up almost immediately on orders from Moscow. Colonel Farr encapsulates that critical week in his paper:

Defense Minister Moshe Dayan, obviously not at his best at a press briefing, was, according to *Time* magazine, rattled enough to later tell the prime minister that "this is the end of the third temple," referring to an impending collapse of the State of Israel. "Temple" was also code for nuclear weapons.

Prime Minister Golda Meier and her "kitchen cabinet" made the decision on the night of October 8, and the Israelis assembled more than a dozen 20-kiloton atomic bombs. [The number and, in fact, the entire story, says Farr, was later leaked by the Israelis.]

Although most probably plutonium devices, one source reports that all were enriched uranium bombs. The Jericho missiles at Hirbat Zachariah and the nuclear strike F-4s at Tel Nof were armed and prepared for action against Syrian and Egyptian targets. Also targeted was Damascus, with nuclear-capable long-range artillery, although it is not certain that the IDF by then had developed a nuclear artillery shell capability. U.S. Secretary of State Henry Kissinger was notified of the alert several hours later.

With that news, President Ford allowed an aerial resupply pipeline to the Holy Land to be started, and Israeli aircraft began picking up supplies later the same day. The first U.S. flights touched down on October 14.

The rest is history, except that it is not generally acknowledged that the munitions air bridge over the Atlantic became the biggest supply operation to take place since the end of World War II. It was matched in intensity by a similar aerial pipeline between the USSR and Arab capitals involved in the invasion.

Though Dimona is no longer the only nuclear facility in Israel (and if one is to judge by the number of compensation claims in Israeli courts, it is now badly dated), the nuclear facility has played a remarkable role in the country's bid to achieve nuclear parity. In the 1960s it already had a plutonium/tritium production reactor and an underground chemical separation plant, as well as nuclear component fabrication facilities.

The United States first became aware of Dimona's existence after U-2 flights in 1958 captured the facility's construction, but it was not identified as a nuclear site until two years later.[7]

Although France initially helped in developing the Israeli nuclear program, President de Gaulle eventually stopped this association, largely because of pressure from Washington and the fact that the link was alienating many of France's former colonies, several of whom had large Muslim communities. By then Israel had what it needed to go it alone, except that it had to turn to South Africa and Argentina for the uranium which had previously come from Niger, Gabon, and the Central African Republic.

Initially, the Franco-Israeli connection prospered on the basis of solid mutual interests. When the United States embargoed certain nuclear-enabling computer technology from France, Israel breached the gap, got what was needed, and passed it on to Paris. For a while there were Israeli scientists directly involved in the French nuclear program. In return for this technical know-how, the French shipped back to Israel reprocessed plutonium. They also gave the Jewish State several ingredients for nuclear weapons construction; apart from the reactor, there was also a factory for plutonium extraction from spent fuel and, most important, initial design specifications.

Similarly, when France conducted its first nuclear tests in the Pacific, the Israelis were allowed "unrestricted" access. (This is according to Avner Cohen, who wrote *Israel's Nuclear History*).[8] Such was the depth of association that one expert postulated the French nuclear tests in 1960 made two nuclear powers, not one. What comes across forcibly is that the level of subterfuge employed by Israel to achieve its nuclear goal makes Saddam Hussein look like a rank amateur in deceiving the IAEA. Obfuscating weapons inspectors about the true purpose of Dimona warrants a comprehensive study of its own.

Colonel Farr cites various sources that indicate the lengths to which Israel went to conceal what was going on at Dimona. Initially, it called the place a manganese plant. As U.S.-Israeli relations soured (because Jerusalem ignored the American call for transparency), an agreement was reached in 1962 to allow inspectors on-site. But this also became a farce. According to Farr:

Inspectors saw only the above-ground part of the buildings, not the many levels underground, and the visit frequency was never more than once a year [twice a year had originally been agreed upon]. The above-ground areas had simulated control rooms, while access to all underground areas was kept hidden while inspectors were present. Elevators leading to the secret underground plutonium reprocessing plant were actually bricked over.

Then, in a complicated undercover operation, 200 tons of uranium oxide (yellowcake) was bought from a West German front company and transferred from one ship to another on the high seas.[9]

For several years, Israel had to rely solely on the F-4Es that it had acquired from the United States should it need to use its nuclear arsenal. Leonard Spector, the deputy director of the Center for Nonproliferation Studies, Monterey Institute of International Studies, disclosed in 1986—at a time when Israel was producing between three and five bombs a year—that these were delivered with their nuclear capable hardware intact.[10]

Since then, the F-16 has become the backbone of the Israeli Air Force (IAF), and the long-range Boeing F-16I *Sufa* (Storm) version—which can hit at targets almost 3,000 miles away with a 36.7-ton takeoff weight—is today the aircraft of choice for any kind of envisaged nuclear strike. Such an operation would obviously involve aerial refueling.

In 1999, the IAF bought fifty F-16Is (with a maximum speed at altitude in the region of Mach 2) at a cost of $2.5 billion, and the first started arriving in early 2003. The contract gave Jerusalem an option for sixty more, with delivery through 2008. Some of its F-15I *Ra'am* (Thunder) combat aircraft may be similarly tasked.

Nobody that doesn't need to know is certain where the bulk of these aircraft are based, or whether they're spread about the country (and the Israelis aren't saying). Apart from Tel Nof, other bases mentioned in this regard are Nevatim (southeast of Beersheba), Ramon (in the Negev), and Ramat-David (in the north of the country).[11]

Jerusalem's quest for a missile capability began at roughly the same time it began work on an indigenous atom bomb. In the early 1960s the Jewish State signed an agreement with the French company Dassault to produce a surface-to-surface ballistic missile with a range of about 200 miles, and the ability to carry a 1,600-pound payload. Specifications included a circular error probable (CEP) of a thousand meters. The first thirty missiles were delivered three years later.

A year later, following the Six-Day War, Paris embargoed any new equipment transfers, and once more, Israel was forced to go it alone.

First off the Israeli production line was the ubiquitous "Jericho" missile (a Western designation), which the CIA cited in 1974 as evidence that Israel had nuclear weapons. Langley declared at the time that such a missile made little sense as a conventional weapon, and in any event was "designed to accommodate nuclear warheads."

The Jericho II (with some striking similarities to the U.S. Pershing II) followed, with its first test in May 1974. It reached its objective of 500 miles. A year later, according to the U.S. Arms Control and Disarmament Agency, its range was almost doubled. Since then, there is evidence that the range of the Jericho II has been increased to about 1,000 miles, which brings most of the major Islamic players within range.

The *Bulletin of the Atomic Scientists* disclosed in late 2002 that after Israel launched several Ofek satellites into orbit atop *Shavit* (Comet) three-stage rockets in 1988, this missile might be converted into a long-range ballistic missile with a potential range of up to 4,000 miles. Significantly, with the loss of its missile test beds along the South African Cape coast, Israeli rocket launches now take place from the Palmikhim air base north of Tel Aviv, and unusually, are fired westwards across the Mediterranean and against the earth's rotation. This adjustment requires even more thrust, and test results achieved with the Jericho II to date could probably be increased.

That said, weapons such as the Jericho ballistic missile system take decades to develop. Its foundations were laid in 1974 by the Israel–South Africa (ISSA) Agreement, which made provision for the development of such a vehicle under the code name "Burglar."

By 1977 the missile was under development. Ironically, Iran—then still under the Shah—also participated for a short while, until he was ousted by a resurgent theocratic revolt. The original partners continued, and the first Jericho 11 (or YA-3 in Israeli parlance) was fired in 1986.

Its large, solid-propelled motors had reportedly benefited from technology acquired from within France and/or the U.S. In fact, components from America proved especially valuable as far as its Inertial Navigation System was concerned. By adding a third stage to Jericho 11, the Israelis turned this missile into the Shavit satellite launcher, which they used to orbit their first satellite, Ofeq 1, on September 19, 1988.

The South African equivalent of the Shavit, called RSA 3, died when apartheid ended.

It's worth mentioning that in its two-stage Jericho II guise, the weapon was deployed between the late 1980s and early 1990, and can be launched from mobile launchers, flatbed railcars, or under-earth silos. Although specifics are lacking, about sixty of these nuclear-tipped missiles are reportedly stationed at Hirbat Zachariah. Its conservative payload/range estimate is in the region of 3,000 pounds, which can be hurled something like 1,250 miles.

Entering service in mid-2005, however, was the three-stage Jericho III (YA-4), which has a payload/range curve of about 650 pounds/3,750 miles. Some pundits claim that these missiles may each be armed with two or three low-yield warheads equipped with MIRVs (Multiple Independently Targeted Reentry Vehicles).

There have been a few hiccups along the way. In April 2000, Israel test-launched a Jericho missile into the Mediterranean without informing the U.S. in advance. It impacted close to an American warship that reportedly thought it was under attack.

Martin van Creveld has also speculated—which he rarely does without good reason—that Jerusalem is currently pursuing an R&D program to provide MIRVs on their missiles.

Chapter 9 Endnotes:

1 *Time*, April 12, 1976.

2 Thomas W. Dowler and Joseph H. Howard II, "Countering the Threat of the Well-Armed Tyrant: A Modest Proposal for Small Nuclear Weapons," *Strategic Review* 19, no. 4 (Fall 1999).

3 "Israel Begins Test of Nuclear Missile Submarines," *Irish Times*, July 2, 1998.

4 Taysir N. Nashif, *Nuclear Weapons in the Middle East: Dimensions and Responsibilities*, Kingston Press, Princeton, NJ, 1984.

5 Seymour M. Hersh, *The Samson Option: Israel's Nuclear Arsenal and American Foreign Policy*, Random House, New York, 1991.

6   "Future War Series No. 2," published by the Air War College, Air University, Maxwell Air Force Base, Alabama, in September 1999. For a long time, this was regarded by many authorities as one of the most complete assessments of Israeli nuclear capability to appear in print.

7   Federation of American Scientists: "Nuclear Weapons," www.fas.org/nuke/guide/israel/nuke.

8   *Journal of Israeli History* 16, no. 2 (1995), pp. 159–94; see http://www.seas.gwu.edu/nsarchive/israel, where much of it is posted.

9   Quoted in Steve Weissman and Herbert Krosney, *The Islamic Bomb: The Nuclear Threat to Israel and the Middle East*, Times Books, New York, 1981.

10 *Journal of International Affairs* 40, no. 1 (1986).

11 "Israeli Nuclear Forces, 2002," *Bulletin of the Atomic Scientists*, September/October 2002.

ISLAMIC NUCLEAR HOPEFULS

India and Pakistan, by some estimates, were the forerunners of a new kind of nuclear power, ahead of the field but hardly alone. Iraq may be solved . . . but Iran is believed to be moving rapidly toward acquiring nukes . . . Syria [is] watched with suspicion. Experts talk speculatively of the ripple effects—of a nuclear Iran inspiring nuclear lust in Egypt, Turkey, even Saudi Arabia, of a nuclear North Korea prompting a breakout in Japan, South Korea, even Taiwan.
—Bill Keller, *The New York Times*, May 4, 2003

On November 4, 2006, the International Atomic Energy Agency (IAEA) released a report that was astonishingly low-key. The headline in the London *Times* that day read SIX ARAB STATES JOIN RUSH TO GO NUCLEAR. They were named as Algeria, Egypt, Morocco, and Saudi Arabia, with Tunisia and the United Arab Emirates also showing an interest, the British newspaper disclosed.

Several commentators were quoted about the development and were almost unanimous in the view that Iran's race to acquire nuclear weapons was the fulcrum. *The Times* suggested that "the sudden rush to nuclear power had raised suspicions that the real intention of the countries fingered was to acquire nuclear technology which could be used for the first Arab atomic bomb."

While Iran looms large as the potential frontrunner among countries next to detonate a nuclear test device, that is only part of the story. Three of the six countries mentioned were previously linked to real or imagined nuclear weapons programs. Saudi Arabia is thought by some intelligence operatives to already have the bomb, bought at a hefty price from Pakistan and tipped atop either Pakistani Ghauri-IIs or North Korean No-Dong missiles (which, with Iranian Shahab-3s, come essentially from the same stable).

Both Egypt and Algeria had nuclear programs in the past. Both continue to claim that they were intended solely for peaceful purposes, even though great secrecy surrounded both. North Korea said much the same until it tested its first bomb in late 2006. So does Tehran. Of course, they're all lying, and for very good reasons. Their common objective was possibly encapsulated by Mark Fitzpatrick, an expert on nuclear proliferation at the IAEA, when he declared that the sudden drive for nuclear expertise by these Islamic countries was to provide the Arabs with what he termed a "security hedge."

"If Iran was not on the path to a nuclear weapons capability, you would probably not see this sudden rush," Fitzpatrick said.

Dr. Mohamed ElBaradei, head of the IAEA, made much the same noises at the United Nations a few months before. He reckoned that by developing technology at the core of peaceful nuclear energy programs, these could quickly be switched to making weapons. He called the errant countries "virtual new weapons states."

UN officials have since mentioned a host of states currently heading along the nuclear path and that could feasibly go on to build the bomb. The tally includes Indonesia, which, with a population of 200 million, is the globe's fourth most populous country. More significant, about 90 percent of its people are Muslim, and we've already seen the havoc that some of its fundamentalist malcontents have visited on Western tourist resorts like Bali.

Apart from Indonesia and the six states already mentioned, UN officials told reporters that countries considering developing nuclear programs in the future include Bangladesh, Ghana, Jordan, Namibia, Moldova, Nigeria, Poland, Thailand, Turkey, Vietnam, and Yemen. That doesn't include some that take a more than casual interest, like Brazil, Taiwan, South Korea, and Syria. There are several others on the periphery, including Japan and Kazakhstan.

South Africa went a step further. Ronnie Kasrils, the South African intelligence minister—and a card-carrying, outspokenly anti-Israel Jewish member of the S.A. Communist Party—arranged a closed meeting for his intelligence staff in Pretoria recently, having invited a prominent local professor to address the group. The thrust of his presentation was that South Africa should once again build nuclear weapons. This action would not only return South Africa to the forefront of African politics, but in an unstable world, the country would also be able to look after itself in the event of serious trouble. No question that South Africa has done it before; and it could build the bomb again. The old apartheid regime, remember, built six atom bombs, which were later dismantled under British, American, and IAEA auspices. This issue and its implications for Africa are dealt with in more detail in the next chapter.

While unraveling the complex and extremely widespread two-decade-long smuggling career of the disgraced Pakistani metallurgist Dr. A.Q. Khan, what has emerged from his clandestine "proliferation period" was the reality that he visited quite a few Muslim states; in fact, he went to almost thirty countries. These included Iran (many times), Egypt (numerous visits), Syria (at least three times, officially), Morocco, Saudi Arabia (several visits), Kazakhstan, Tunisia, Turkey (many visits because of the monitoring role played by his agents there), the Sudan, Malaysia (constantly), Indonesia, Algeria, and Kuwait, as well as Dubai and Abu Dhabi. He even had a holiday home in the United Arab Emirates, which was convenient because it was easy-come-and-go from there to Iran.

We've already seen the extent of these activities, but there is more, a good deal of it detailed in what is likely to be the first in a plethora of A.Q. Khan titles. The latest and far and away the best was written by Gordon Corera, a security correspondent for the BBC. Well placed to handle his Oxford University Press brief, Corera's book is titled *Shopping for Bombs: Nuclear Proliferation, Global Insecurity, and the Rise and Fall of the A.Q. Khan Network*. It should be required reading for everyone who is concerned about the fate of our next generation.

Corera carefully tracks the rise and fall of Khan, as well as his role in the devastating spread of nuclear weapons technology over the past thirty years. He paints a scenario that is both vivid and disturbing. Employing clever detective work and connections in the right places, Corera includes the role of several intelligence agencies, including Britain's SIS.

Although the list of some of the states below is partial, it is nonetheless sobering. More worrying is the fact that they're at it again. Egypt, most prominent among the Arabs, is dealt with in detail in chapter 16.

Algeria

America is again concerned with what is happening along the southwestern shores of the Mediterranean. When I discussed the issue with David Albright (president of Washington's Institute for Science and International Security—ISIS) a while back, he expressed disquiet at the fact that in the foreseeable future, Algeria might have the capacity to produce nuclear weapons–usable plutonium.

Albright told me that recent disclosures have indicated China has been the principal supplier of nuclear technology to Algiers since the two countries signed a secret accord in 1983. This involved the construction of the nuclear complex near Birine. It also included the Es Salam reactor, a hot cell laboratory, and other facilities for the production of radioisotopes.

Of significance is the fact that Es Salam is a heavy-water reactor with 15 MWt capability. Such a plant, Albright maintains, is able to produce military-grade plutonium that might be used in the construction of a nuclear bomb. The facility was opened in 1993, and an American intelligence source told him that the Algerian atomic program, as a consequence, exceeds its civil need. The Algerians also received Argentinean assistance at some stage, but this was stopped after Washington issued a spate of demarches.

A Spanish intelligence report quoted by Madrid's *El País* on August 23, 1998, disclosed that Algeria had concluded the second phase of its nuclear program.[1] This was the construction of the hot cell laboratory, where this country's scientists would be able to dismantle nuclear fuel produced from its reactor, a single before plutonium is obtained. The third and final phase would consist of the construction of a radioisotope production laboratory with the capability to extract plutonium from the nuclear fuel first irradiated in the reactor and then dismantled in the hot cells, the two Spanish reporters wrote.

Argentina's role was that it originally sold Algeria the 1MWt Nur research reactor in 1989. Though militarily irrelevant, the step did commit Buenos Aires to a significant level of nuclear cooperation with the Arabs. There was a link to Es Salam, and the West found this disquieting.

What worried the Americans at the time (and the Spanish, in particular, because the Iberian Peninsula is separated from North Africa only by a narrowing Mediterranean) was that while Algeria renounced nuclear weapons, and had signed the same Nuclear Non-Proliferation Treaty (NPT) that most other countries had signed, there was evidence that nuclear work was moving forward.

ISIS maintains that this information was the basis of a report produced by the Spanish secret service (*Centro Superior de Información de la Defensa*, or CESID) and presented to the Madrid government. CESID, he disclosed, was unequivocal about the development. It described the clandestine program as threatening, and highlighted the implications of tolerating a calculated Algerian deception regarding military objectives.

Meanwhile, in a confidential Washington, D.C., intelligence briefing afterwards, it was noted that the Algerian armed forces were in possession of a variety of delivery vehicles including bombers, missile launchers, and Soviet-made rockets, all theoretically capable of carrying nuclear weapons. Algeria also has access to underground sites where, before independence, France carried out its own tests with nuclear weapons.

There are several other Islamic states that might have an interest in what is happening in Algeria today. The original French nuclear testing sites in the Sahara, it is argued by pundits, might be ideal for testing an Iranian-built atom bomb. The fact that Algerian ties with Tehran are excellent hasn't been lost on some Western observers. More recently, there were problems when the IAEA discovered that about six pounds of enriched uranium and some heavy water and various pieces of natural uranium supplied by China had not been declared.

What is notable here is that the Es Salam reactor has the theoretical capacity to produce about seven pounds of plutonium annually. Without strict monitoring, it wouldn't be difficult for small quantities to be diverted for military purposes. Further, Algeria depends on outside suppliers of nuclear fuel. The

IAEA had also confirmed the purchase of 150 tons of uranium concentrate from Nigeria in 1984. Its main limitation now, the Spanish document stated, was technical: Algeria's inability to undertake a military nuclear program on its own. However, the discovery of uranium in the southern Hoggar mountain region puts the country in a special category within the context of the Islamic quest for nuclear parity.

It is interesting that all documentation related to the project has been classified as secret by the Algerian authorities, which, says the Spanish report, "is surprising because everything about its nuclear efforts are supposed to be peaceful."

Second, with Algeria's abundant energy resources, especially natural gas (the country is a major international supplier), the Spanish intelligence agency says that Algeria simply has no need to take the nuclear route. Like Iran, it has enough power resources for a dozen generations. The only conclusion reached by CESID, and contained in its confidential report, was that the goings-on at Es Salam had military objectives. It is significant that Washington concurs.

The most recent development came during May of 2006, when an eleven-member Algerian delegation visited South Korea to discuss bilateral nuclear cooperation. News reports stated that the Algerian delegation was led by Mohamed Derdour, commissioner of the National Commission on Atomic Energy. This was preceded by President Roh Moo-hyun's visit to Algiers in March 2006. Since then, news reports have stated, the two countries have become fast friends.

Syria

Of all the countries in the Near East known to possess weapons of mass destruction (WMD), the one that has consistently remained below the radar is Syria, Israel's nearest hostile neighbor.

Animosities go deep, to the extent that there have been reports for years that Damascus has tipped "several hundred" of its limited-range Scud missiles with either Sarin or VX nerve gas, and has warned that if the Jewish State invades, these weapons will be unleashed against Israel's northern cities. At this moment, Israeli intelligence maintains, there are between 200 and 400 of these missiles pointed south. Also, the threat is sufficient for Jerusalem to have prevented the Israeli Defense Force from launching a preemptive attack on Syria during the anti-Hezbollah invasion of South Lebanon in the summer of 2006.

Whatever it is that the Syrians have in their unconventional arsenal, it has Israel worried. While the country has invested a fortune in what is termed "an effective missile shield," nobody believes that should Syria simultaneously launch 50, 100, or 200 missiles into Israeli territory, that every one of them would be intercepted or brought down short. "Short" could also mean dropping a VX-tipped Scud intended for Haifa onto one of the settlements around Tiberius.

Nor is anybody forgetting the controversial events that surrounded Russian lieutenant general Anatoly Kuntsevich, a 1958 graduate of the (Soviet) Military Academy of Chemical Defense, and an author of over two hundred works on weapons of mass destruction. Kuntsevich's claim to notoriety is that he was suddenly and inexplicably dismissed from his post as head of the Center of Eco-toximetry at the Academy of Sciences Institute of Chemical Physics. This happened after a furious exchange with his fellow generals when he was charged with helping smuggle a quantity of chemical warfare (CW) nerve agent precursors to Damascus.

Unlike most of his colleagues (many of whom made no secret of the fact that they despised Arabs), Kuntsevich—always regarded as a maverick among his peers and very outspoken—had apparently continued to maintain close ties with the Syrian president and his military advisors.

Kuntsevich's political sentiments can perhaps be gauged from the fact that while this drama was unraveling, he tried to win a parliamentary seat in the Russian Duma with the late Zhirinovsky's reactionary party, which was characterized by numerous anti-Semitic utterances while the election process went on. It is also noteworthy that Kuntsevich (who shared the Lenin Prize for his work in binary chemical weapons with three other former Soviet scientists[2]) never actually denied his actions. He simply justified his contacts with Syria on the basis that it was part of a deal that had been authorized under a "long-standing contract obligation" with the Assad regime.

The debate about Syria's WMD goes on. The Israeli newspaper *Yedi'ot Aharanot*, quoting Harold Hough, an independent U.S. analyst, reached the following conclusions after studying satellite imagery of suspected Syrian missile deployment sites. The Scud-C missile has an estimated circular error probable (CEP) of about a mile. That made it improbable that it could hit specific military targets. More likely, said Hough, the Scud-C would deliver a chemical warhead to create mass casualties and havoc.

While most systems behind contemporary Scud missiles of the kind deployed in the Middle East date from World War II, it remains a reasonably potent close-range weapon, especially if tipped with a chemical weapon. Advances made by both Iran (with South African rocket scientists' help), as well as North Korea, have added markedly to this clumsy weapon's efficacy.

There must also be a reason why Syrian Scud-C deployments include a relatively high ratio of launchers to missiles. This enables the youthful President Bashar el-Assad to launch most of his ballistic missiles in a limited number of salvos; in other words, he can get a lot of them away before the Israelis are able to retaliate. Most Scuds, worldwide, are matched to about one launcher for every ten missiles. In contrast, Hough stated, Syria appears to have one launcher for every two of its missiles. East Germany in its heyday, he reckons, had a 1:5 ratio for its nuclear and chemically armed Scuds, though the Soviets retained strict control over East Germany's nuclear capability throughout the Cold War period.

It is clear that Jerusalem is aware of the potential Arab missile threat— acutely so. Damascus, they say, has the largest and most advanced chemical weapon (CW) capability in the Arab world. Only Egypt and Iran are anywhere close as contenders. Moreover, apart from Scuds, the Syrians have developed chemical gravity bombs for delivery by aircraft.

Historically, Syrian CW development was spurred by a succession of disastrous military defeats at the hands of Israel in 1967, 1973, and again in 1982, when it lost a huge proportion of its air force in a two-day aerial confrontation, without a single Israeli fighter having been brought down. There were almost one hundred Syrian Air Force jets destroyed in combat.

There are indications that as early as 1972, Syrian CW scientists began serious work on their WMD programs as a possible counter to overwhelming Israeli military supremacy. By 1986, the current President Assad's father possessed an arsenal of both blister and nerve agents. There is evidence— including testimony from Russian specialists now living in the United States— that he got help from the Soviets. Trouble is, while there was still some Russian involvement in these departments until recently, this has been a difficult issue to pin down. At present just about everybody in the FSU is in denial. The situation, said one Moscow-based British journalist, is almost a bit like Germany after it capitulated in 1945: you had to go far to find anybody who admitted to having saluted Hitler.

Very recently it was estimated that Syrian stockpiles of nerve gas and other CW agents could be measured in terms of "hundreds of tons." Agents include Sarin, VX, and mustard gas. Less than a single drop of VX on a man's skin will kill him, Eric Croddy explains in his most recent book, *Chemical and Biological Warfare: A Comprehensive Survey for the Concerned Citizen* (a must if you're concerned about the possibility of the West's unseen enemies using these weapons against America's civilian population).[3]

While Assad's CW program remains dependent on foreign chemicals and equipment, much of the work is now being conducted at a facility north of Damascus known as CERS (*Centre d'Études et de Recherche Scientifique*). Other production facilities for WMD are near Damascus, Aleppo, and Homs.[4]

One *Jane's* source maintains that hundreds of tons of nerve agents are being produced in Syria annually. Damascus denies it, even though satellite photos of all of Syria's WMD are available on the Web.

In an exchange of correspondence with this writer, Brigadier-General (Res.) Aryeh Shalev of Tel Aviv's Jaffee Center for Strategic Studies said that in the long term, it was not impossible that Syria could go to war in a bid to recapture the Golan Heights, even though the statement was made prior to Operation Iraqi Freedom. There were a number of imponderables to such a scenario, he warned. "If the young Assad decides to take that course, then he will start as his father Hafez did in 1973, with a surprise attack. He is likely to take advantage of the positive ratio, for Syria, of the numbers of active armed forces (compared to Israel)." General Shalev explained that this was because Syria's armed forces "are always on an active footing, whereas Israel needs at least forty-eight hours for mobilization and deployment." Under special circumstances, he added, Assad might just be tempted to capitalize on this advantage. Like his departed father, the Syrian president would like to see his flag over the Heights.[5]

The main hurdle then, as now, has been the IDF's determination—for clearly delineated strategic reasons—to hold on to its three early-warning electronic outposts. There is one on Mount Hermon, and others have been built on the eastern crest of the Heights, including Lucifer, the most extensive of them all.

I was able to view these sites at fairly close range from the UN Area of Separation, about an hour's drive south of Damascus. All three installations, with their powerful arrays of aerials, radar masts, and defenses, might easily have been mistaken for a *Star Wars* film set. Though I visited the place under the auspices of the UN mission in Damascus while on a visit to Syria a few years ago, I was warned not to be seen there with a camera.

The Israeli government has always maintained that the status of the Golan facilities was not negotiable, even though that of Jewish settlers on the heights, as with their counterparts in the Sinai a generation ago, might ultimately be.

There is some concern, too, in the way that Syria, in spite of its impoverished economy, has been beefing up its armed forces. The latest development in this regard is that President Assad, with Saudi and some Iranian financial help, launched an ambitious program to strengthen his armored corps and acquire a more modern and effective missile arsenal in the new millennium. Almost all the hardware ordered, as had been the tradition for decades, came from Russia. As I was to see during my own visit, Moscow continues to maintain a large cadre of military advisors and technicians (said to be about a thousand) in Syria.

According to Shalev, one of that country's objectives for embarking on such a program would be to bolster the country's weakened image in the Arab world. Now, with Saddam gone, the issue might not warrant the same priority.[6]

On the nuclear front, there is much conjecture that Syria might be the fourth country helped by the disgraced Pakistani scientist, A.Q. Khan, to embark on a nuclear weapons program. Nothing has come to light in this regard except that there is much talk in Islamabad about that mysterious "fourth country." Others maintain that it might be either Saudi Arabia or Egypt, both of whom are known to have attempted to resuscitate nascent nuclear weapons programs. Either way, a lot of money had already changed hands between Khan and the phantom state before Pakistani nuclear weapons proliferators were disgraced.

There is a reason for all this. Allegations that Syria desires nuclear weapons capability is old news. However, such suspicions are not corroborated by any examination of open sources, and are even contradicted by some national intelligence services. Instead, the contemporary perception surrounding Syria's nuclear intentions are due to other policies it pursues, such as its chemical weapons program and its unsettling role in Lebanese politics, together with Damascus's sponsorship of terrorism, which remains unbridled. It was Syrian secret agents that assassinated Lebanese prime minister Rafiq Hariri in 2005. Also, U.S. officials have issued warnings about a putative Syrian nuclear weapons program.

Going back a while, former U.S. senator Jesse Helms reported before a Senate committee in the early 1990s that there were "credible reports" that "China is engaged in furthering the nuclear weapons ambitions of Syria and Iran." Helms provided no evidence to back his statement, except that he was shy to exploit confidential CIA sources.

The Stockholm International Peace Research Institute (SIPRI) did report that Argentina concluded negotiations with Syria for the sale of a $100 million 10MWt isotope production reactor (research reactor) in 1990, but that was shelved under pressure from Washington.

SIPRI: "Under the deal Argentina's state-controlled company INVAP would supply the reactor and the *Comisión Nacional de Energía Atómica* (CNEA) would supply Syria with uranium hexafluoride enriched to a maximum of 20 percent as reactor fuel. The 'nuclear centre' was to include a radiological protection centre and a hot cell for producing radioisotopes. However, the Argentine government blocked the sale."

According to some accounts, this was an effort by Argentina to be seen as a responsible player in the nuclear domain in a bid to join the nuclear suppliers group (NSG).

Other reports alleged that Argentina assured Israeli government sources that the deal would not be completed until Syria signed a peace agreement with Israel. Lending credence to information of Israeli pressure was a *Jerusalem Post* article which reported that then Argentine foreign minister Guido Di Tella said that his country was mindful of objections by any party who deemed a sale of nuclear technology as a potential security threat: "Not only [do] we have to judge that it is not interfering with the process or with security, but both Israel and Syria [must] believe the same."

Of significance here is a 2003 version of the CIA's "Unclassified Report to Congress on the Acquisition of Technology Relating to Weapons of Mass Destruction and Advanced Conventional Munitions." It contained only a single paragraph related to Syria's nuclear program, noting that: "Syria—an NPT signatory with full-scope IAEA safeguards—has a nuclear research center at Dayr Al Hajar. Russia and Syria have continued their long-standing agreements on cooperation regarding nuclear energy, although specific assistance has not yet materialized. Broader access to foreign expertise provides opportunities to expand its indigenous capabilities and we are looking at Syrian nuclear intentions with growing concern."

Saudi Arabia

For some years there have been reports that the Saudis might have acquired nuclear weapons, in all likelihood bought from Pakistan for the kind of money only a major oil-producing country could afford. In terms of numbers, billions of dollars have been mentioned, although much of that is speculation.

There are some specifics, however. Ariel Levite, principal deputy director-general for policy at the Israel Atomic Energy Commission, told Britain's *Jane's Intelligence Review* (July 1, 2006 issue) that a likely scenario with regard to the Saudis getting the bomb is an arrangement with Pakistan, whereby Riyadh is afforded some sort of nuclear umbrella in the event that Iran develops a nuclear bomb.

John Pike, of GlobalSecurity.org, was even more forthright. He also cited the Iranian bogey, but his view was that this desert kingdom might have gone nuclear for several reasons. Once Tehran acquires the bomb, he added, echoing many voices in the Middle East, there will be no stopping Shiite regional dominance. Pike, Levite, and others also point to Tehran's undermining role in an embattled Iraq, together with some of the actions of Hezbollah, Iran's revolutionary protégé in Lebanon.

More salient, Shiites make up about 10 percent of the Islamic world, most of the rest being Sunni, with a tiny proportion of Sufis. Saudi Arabia, consequently, is preponderantly Sunni, and over the years Riyadh has discriminated—often ruthlessly—against its minority Shiite population.

Former Kuwaiti minister Dr. Ahmad Al-Rubei covered some of the bases during an interview that aired on Al-Rai TV on March 6, 2006. "What we are facing is madness. I call this madness. The Iranian nuclear activities must cease," declared Dr. Al-Rubei. "We must stop saying that since Israel has a nuclear bomb, we must also have a nuclear bomb. This logic is wrong."

His logic was conclusive: "Let's assume you have a nuclear weapon. You can either use it or not. If you don't use it—what is it for? If you do use it—who's your enemy? Let's assume it is Israel. Go and drop it on Israel. Would you say to it: 'Oh my Islamic nuclear bomb, if you don't mind, strike the Jews and spare the non-Jews.' There are a million Palestinians in Israel. Or maybe you plan to kill them along with [the Jews]?

"Let's assume you kill them and call it a sacrifice for the Arab and Islamic nation; what about the neighbors in the region, the people of the West Bank and Gaza, Amman, and Damascus?"

Dr. Al-Rubei's reasoning is that possession of nuclear weapons is not to be taken lightly. It is not a weapon that one drops on ten people in order to kill them, he suggests. Rather, "It is mass killing of human beings, and so, what's going on is madness."

There have been numerous reports of Saudis buying nuclear weapons, including one by Arnaud de Borchgrave of *The Washington Times*—a man with more intelligence contacts than just about any other journalist in Washington. He reported on October 22, 2003, that Saudi Arabia may have concluded a secret agreement on "nuclear cooperation" that will provide the Saudis with nuclear-weapons technology in exchange for cheap oil. That bit came from what he termed "a ranking Pakistani insider."

The disclosure came at the end of a twenty-six-hour state visit to Islamabad by crown prince Abdullah bin Abdulaziz—at the time, Saudi Arabia's de facto ruler. He arrived in Pakistan with an entourage of two hundred, including his foreign minister, Prince Saud Al Faisal, together with several ranking cabinet ministers. De Borchgrave also disclosed that Prince Sultan bin Abdul Aziz Al Saud, the pro-American defense minister (and at the time, next in line to the throne after the crown prince), was not part of the group.

Quoting a Pakistani source, who de Borchgrave maintained had proved reliable for many years, the visit "will be vehemently denied by both countries, but future events will confirm that Pakistan has agreed to provide [Saudi Arabia] with the wherewithal for a nuclear deterrent."

As predicted, Saudi Arabia—which has faced strong international suspicion for years that it was seeking a nuclear capability through Pakistan—denied the claim.

Another tidbit shared by de Borchgrave was that the CIA believed Pakistan had already passed on the requisite nuclear know-how. It had worked with North Korea in exchange for missile technology. According to a Pakistani source, reports de Borchgrave, "A Pakistani C-130 was spotted by satellite loading North Korean missiles at Pyongyang airport last year [one of many such flights in recent years]. Pakistan, which is estimated to have between 35 and 60 nuclear weapons, said this was a straight purchase for cash and strongly denied a nuclear quid pro quo.

"Both Pakistan and Saudi Arabia," the Pakistani source reckoned, tended to "see a world that is moving from nonproliferation to proliferation of nuclear weapons."

Other points raised by this Washington editor-at-large that pointed to Saudi-Pakistani defense and nuclear links included:

- A new policy paper by Simon Henderson, an analyst with the Washington Institute for Near East Policy, noted that Prince Sultan visited Pakistan's highly restricted Kahuta uranium-enrichment and missile-assembly factory in 1999, an event that prompted a formal diplomatic complaint from Washington.

- A son of Prince Abdullah attended Pakistan's test-firing (in 2002) of its Ghauri-class missile, which has a range of 950 miles and could be used to deliver a nuclear payload.

- President George W. Bush was reported to have confronted Pakistan's president Pervez Musharraf over the Saudi nuclear issue during his visit to Camp David in 2003. The then deputy secretary of state, Richard Armitage, also raised the matter during a trip to Islamabad afterwards, according to Mr. Henderson's paper. According to Henderson, "Apart from proliferation concerns, Washington likely harbors more general fears about what would happen if either of the regimes in Riyadh or Islamabad became radically Islamic."

- GlobalSecurity.org, a well-connected Internet defense site, found in a recent survey that Saudi Arabia has the infrastructure to exploit such nuclear exports very quickly. "While there is no direct evidence that Saudi Arabia has chosen a nuclear option, the Saudis have in place a foundation for building a nuclear deterrent," John Pike stated.

A March 2004 paper by Akaki Dvali, a graduate research assistant at the Center for Nonproliferation Studies (CNS), Monterey Institute of International Studies, asked the question: Will Saudi Arabia acquire nuclear weapons?

Dvali quoted a September 2003 article in London's *Guardian* that alleged the Saudis were putting serious effort toward acquiring nuclear weapons. The paper referred to a strategy paper, supposedly considered at the highest levels in Riyadh, which laid out three options for maintaining national security:

1. Acquiring a nuclear capability as a deterrent;

2. Maintaining or entering into an alliance with an existing nuclear power that would offer protection; and

3. Trying to reach a regional agreement for a nuclear-free Middle East.

Dvali writes: "According to the *Guardian* article, the discussion of the strategy paper was triggered by the current instability in the Middle East, Riyadh's estrangement from Washington, and the subsequent weakening of its reliance on the U.S. nuclear umbrella. However, the day after [it appeared], the Saudi government forcefully denied all allegations put forward by the newspaper. The Saudi Embassy in Washington reacted to the reports, and called them 'baseless and totally false.'"

He went on: "Saudi Deputy Foreign Minister Prince Turki Bin-Muhammad also dismissed the allegations and noted that the Kingdom has always been known for its position in support of making the Middle East region free of weapons of mass destruction."

Corroborating what both de Borchgrave and Dvali said was a report on September 21, 2003, by Ian Mather, *The Scotsman*'s diplomatic correspondent. Mather noted that "the prospect of Saudi Arabia building a nuclear arsenal raises a nightmare scenario in the Middle East." Mather added that the Saudi government was considering alternative options, one of which is to acquire a nuclear deterrent. "The other choices are to maintain or enter into an alliance with an existing nuclear power that would offer protection, or to try to reach a regional agreement on a nuclear-free Middle East," according to a leaked Saudi government strategy document.

Daniel Neep, head of the Middle East and North Africa Programme at the Royal United Services Institute in London, added his circumspect input by noting that "the Saudis would have to be very thick-skinned not to realize that there are problems with the Saudi-U.S. relationship." Neep added that it would not be unusual for Saudi Arabia to look at the nuclear option "without it necessarily meaning that there was any firm desire on the part of Saudi Arabia to develop nuclear weapons."

Neep rounded off this scenario by noting that "the possibility that a country for whom money would be no object is even discussing internally the idea of having its own nuclear deterrent, adds a dangerous new dimension in a region already torn apart by the chaos in Iraq and the collapse of the Middle East road map."

A salient and related issue not raised in any of these reports is the fact that China has already approached the Saudis with offers to sell them modern missile systems. While it did get long-range CSS-2 ballistic missiles from Beijing in 1988, and still more recently, Saudi officials discussed buying new Pakistani intermediate-range missiles capable of carrying nuclear warheads.

Indonesia
Indonesia's 200-something million people (compared to Pakistan's 160 million) makes it the world's fourth most populous nation. The fact that nine-tenths of the people there are Islamic tends to focus attention. There have been several anti-Western terror attacks by Indonesian Muslim radicals, and the consensus is that there will be more.

This island state is also one of the countries which the IAEA believes might be interested in acquiring the bomb. It won't be for the first time, either. Robert M. Cornejo gives us some details of that episode in his report "When Sukarno Sought the Bomb: Indonesian Nuclear Aspirations in the Mid-1960s," published in the summer 2000 edition of *The Nonproliferation Review*.[7]

What has become clear in recent years is that Indonesia has proved to be a fertile spawning ground of a variety of terrorist groups, al-Qaeda included. The revolutionary ethos is fueled by a combination of religious intransigence, poverty, and Wahhabist financial contributions from countries in the Gulf, Saudi Arabia, and the West (see chapter 17).

One of many quandaries facing the authorities of this multi-island state is the hugely intimidating mass of numbers. The island of Java, for instance, is one of the most densely populated areas in the world, with more than 100 million people living in an area the size of New York State. Nor is the situation ameliorated by age differences, as more than half the population is twenty years old or younger.

While a few gaps and questions remain, it appears that Indonesia has largely succeeded in developing an indigenous nuclear fuel cycle, according to the Stockholm International Peace Research Institute. The Swedish watchdog organization reports:

Unfortunately, it is difficult to ascertain via open sources how viable the cycle is without international assistance. Evidence indicates that Indonesia's work in the fields of uranium milling, processing, and conversion has [thus far] only been conducted on a laboratory scale. However, several notable nuclear facilities have been established. Three research reactors are currently in operation, and a fourth is planned. Indonesia has announced ambitious plans to construct multiple nuclear power reactors [with international assistance] in the future.

SIPRI goes on to warn that while Indonesia operates under IAEA safeguards, and (since 1966) has pursued only peaceful applications for its nuclear technology, it is conceivable that, should it adopt a radical shift in its nuclear policy (Islamic-linked pressure, possibly), Indonesia could pursue uranium-enrichment and weaponization programs.

Additionally, SIPRI declares, "The perceived threat posed by the questionable security of Indonesia's radioactive waste-management facilities has engendered much scrutiny from international observers. While there is little open-source evidence to suggest that Indonesia would actively proliferate technology to non-nuclear nations, it is conceivable that terrorist organizations could utilize its spent waste in a radiological device [or 'dirty bomb']."

Kazakhstan

At independence in 1991, Kazakhstan was among the four states of the former Soviet Union to inherit nuclear weapons, acquiring with it the status of the fourth-largest nuclear power in the world. FirstWatch International, another august body closely monitoring nuclear developments worldwide, reckons that the new acquisitions included thousands of nuclear warheads, intercontinental ballistic missiles (ICBMs), cruise missiles, and the world's largest testing facility (where 456 nuclear tests took place over a fifty-year period).

United Nations officials maintain, however, that this has not prevented further development of Kazakhstan's nuclear fuel cycle resources, which include extensive uranium mining zones and fuel processing and fabrication technologies. Kazakhstan, UN officials say, aims to become the world's largest producer and exporter of uranium in the next five years.

The country is taking advantage of its position to offer those services for export. While its overall intent appears peaceful, Kazakhstan has made known its desire to operate all steps of the nuclear fuel cycle. If Kazakhstan decides to undertake enrichment or reprocessing capabilities, that will certainly be of concern to the international community—especially Moscow—as a potential source of weapon material.

At present, Kazakhstan's nuclear strategic significance lies not in its capabilities (which are polished by decades of being part of one of the world's two nuclear superpowers), nor in its intent, which appears to be anti-proliferation. Instead, it lies in the risk of nuclear security and proliferation by virtue of its location and circumstances. Kazakhstan's geographic position makes it strategically important to current international nonproliferation efforts. It is the only Central Asian country sharing borders with both Russia and China, and with states of nuclear-transit significance, such as Uzbekistan, Turkmenistan, and Kyrgyzstan. Iran, too, is just across the way.

At the core of this activity, says SIPRI, is the Ulba Metallurgical Plant (UMP), the world's largest fuel-fabrication facility. This is the same strategic installation that became a focus of attention of Iranian secret agents during the breakup of the Soviet Union. The giant Ulba nuclear plant was where Iranians were active in trying to acquire HEU, and this activity was only halted by removing stocks of this strategic material to the U.S. for safekeeping.

In its more than half a century of existence, Ulba produced low-enriched uranium fuel pellets used in half of the reactors of Soviet design. During the Soviet era, UMP also produced HEU fuel for military purposes (the secret Alfa submarine project, nuclear-powered satellites, et al.).

Fortunately for the West, the plant appeared to have halted HEU-related activities in the 1980s.

Chapter 10 Endnotes:

1 CESID warns that Algeria can have the capacity to produce military plutonium in two years. The Algerian atomic program exceeds its civil need, according to a confidential report. M. Gonzáles and J. M. Larraya, *El País*, Madrid, August 23, 1998.

2 A. Gayev, A. Kisletsov, and V. Petrunin.

3 Eric Croddy, with Clarissa Perez-Armendariz and John Hart, *Chemical and Biological Warfare: A Comprehensive Survey for the Concerned Citizen*, Copernicus Books, New York, 2002.

4 See also J. Michael Waller, "The Chemical Weapons Cover-up," *The Wall Street Journal*, February 13, 1997, p. 18.

5 Personal interview.

6 See also Matthew Moore, "Jakarta's Nuclear Dream," *The Age Online*, August 22, 2003.

7 Personal interview with the author.

HALF A DOZEN ATOM BOMBS FOR A ROGUE STATE

> The South African nuclear program was an extreme re-
> sponse to its own "identity crisis." Nuclear weapons became
> a means to achieving a long-term end of a closer affiliation
> with the West. A South Africa yearning to be identified as a
> Western nation—and receive guarantees of its security—
> rationalized the need for a nuclear deterrent.
>
> —USAF Lieutenant Colonel Roy E. Horton III, "Out of (South) Africa: Pretoria's
> Nuclear Weapons Experience," USAF Institute for National Security Studies,
> August 1999

If any of today's Islamic nuclear hopefuls are going to build the bomb, they will have to look at the first of the "rogue" states to have done so.

South Africa went nuclear before Pakistan and North Korea. With a strong Israeli component, it also developed a variety of missile-delivery systems, several of which were successfully tested before Washington threatened economic sanctions if the entire program wasn't immediately abandoned. It was, within six weeks—but more of that later.

During the apartheid era, a relatively small group of South African scientists and weapons technicians built six atom bombs. It is notable that they did so in about seven years, and in total secrecy, a scenario that might appeal to some prospective nuclear hopefuls.

Since then, under a new government, this heavily industrialized country at the southern tip of the African continent has remained a player—most times, as the following chapter will show, clandestinely. It has also, to the consternation of its former Western partners, developed powerful ties with countries routinely shunned by Europe and America, including Iran, Syria, North Korea, Cuba, the Sudan, and Zimbabwe, together with a few others that remain marginal.

But first, we need to know how South Africa cracked the nuclear code that resulted in its constructing six nuclear devices with yields of up to 24 KT. What is significant is that in developing its nuclear weapons program, South Africa worked entirely on its own. It built large facilities that allowed it to enrich uranium, and handled the weaponization of all six bombs in specially created "factories" near the capital. Only South Africans who were actually born in the country were allowed into the program; even dual passport holders, no matter how distinguished their scientific abilities, were excluded.

Yet, when that country's white leaders decided that after two decades of largely black-white conflict along its northern borders that they'd had enough and that the time had perhaps come for a majority government, Pretoria altogether abandoned the project. It notified both Washington and London that it was doing so. Both countries, again in secrecy, together with the International Atomic Energy Agency (IAEA), set about dismantling the program and turning the bombs into scrap. All weapons-grade uranium produced over the years was checked, verified, and tabulated; once removed from the warheads, it was placed in safe custody.

Thus, it was all the more surprising when Intelligence Chief Ronnie Kasrils, one of President Thabo Mbeki's top ministers, got together a number of his intelligence operatives, who were addressed by Professor Renfrew Christie, dean of research at the University of the Western Cape. And South Africa being what it is—almost a one-party state—Kasrils would almost certainly have had to get the nod from his boss to have done that.

It came as no surprise that Christie warned of possible future wars in Africa. But it astonished everybody when he suggested that South Africa should again look to building the bomb. It needed to "quickly be able to revert to a nuclear weapons state if it became vital to the country's interests," was the thrust of his argument. The professor noted that South Africa still retained a stockpile of weapons-grade highly enriched uranium derived from the country's former nuclear weapons program, and reminded everyone that technical knowledge of South Africa's former atomic bombs was contained on CDs held by the current government.

"The presentation was greeted with loud applause from the intelligence community," reported Cape Town's *Weekend Argus*.

Is it not ironic, therefore, that the presentation came as South Africa's special representative on disarmament, Abdul Minty, chaired the fiftieth session of the International Atomic Energy Agency (IAEA) in Vienna. That was followed by the South African minister of minerals and energy declaring that South Africa strongly supported the Convention on Nuclear Safety. She called on nuclear-weapon states to reaffirm their commitments and undertakings to systematically and progressively eliminate their nuclear-weapon arsenals.

As somebody else commented, perhaps a little blithely, *C'est l'Afrique . . .*

The fact is that if South Africa set the scene for anybody else considering building an atom bomb—and that tally might very well include the terrorist organization al-Qaeda—it would probably take the same road as South Africa did in the 1970s and 1980s. Pretoria chose to build "gun-type" bombs instead of implosion devices for a variety of reasons, not least being the fact that uranium is readily available as a secondary product from the country's huge gold-mining industry. Also, gun types do not need testing—in theory, at least.[1]

"Little Boy," the American gun-type device developed at the Los Alamos nuclear facility during World War II, and dropped over Hiroshima, was such a weapon. It was never tested, as were subsequently built implosion bombs in Nevada. Dr. Robert Oppenheimer's scientists were confident enough that the systems employed in their research and the subsequent manufacture of the bomb were foolproof, which was why they were able to go ahead and deploy the weapon without a test-base verification.

Other countries that dabbled in gun-type weapons, which use highly enriched uranium (HEU—also referred to as weapons-grade uranium), included Switzerland. Zurich started with plutonium and then moved on to HEU, before it abandoned explosive nuclear research altogether. It would be reasonable to assume that the Swiss could sequentially have considered building implosion *as well as* gun devices. Activities in the 1977–1988 time frame included evaluating the possibility of a lash-up or makeshift nuclear bomb, as well as issues related to the triggering mechanism—although there is nothing specific on which type of assembly they actually had in mind.

Israel built a few HEU devices and then moved on to plutonium implosion bombs, before tackling awesome thermonuclear complexities. That the Jewish State has the hydrogen bomb—lots of them—is no longer in doubt. Numbers are of necessity vague, but one American source suggested a total nuclear stockpile somewhere in the vicinity of two hundred. Again, this might be pure speculation.

Then we have Libya, which was well on its way toward producing the bomb before Western pressure (and threats) halted those efforts. What is known is that Gadhafi had an initial preference for gun devices, not only because these are relatively uncomplicated to build, but more important, because he would not have to test them—an event that would almost certainly have brought with it even more UN sanctions. The possibility of more American air strikes might have been part of the equation that caused him to come clean.

That Libya had an interest in implosion devices as well was witnessed by data on the so-called A.Q. Khan device, which the country had in its possession and handed over to Western inspectors when it decided to tell all.

Saddam Hussein's first atom bomb would have been an HEU-fueled implosion device called "The Mechanism." Evidence uncovered by UN inspectors attached to UNSCOM found that the Iraqis also intended to produce tungsten-carbide, a good gun-type reflector/tamper material. The neutron initiator designs uncovered, say the experts, are better suited to a gun-type than an implosion bomb (see chapter 6).

The first atom bombs produced by Pakistan (dealt with more comprehensively in chapter 13) were based on a proven People's Republic of China missile-warhead design that it received in 1983. This made use of HEU and includes an implosion-assembly process. However, more recent technical drawings out of Islamabad suggest work on a gun-type device (possibly in conjunction with North Korea and Iran).

Brazil, as far as the Americans have been able to establish (and also dealt with in some detail in chapter 13), may have taken both roads in their Solimões Project. Like their Pretoria counterparts, Brazil initiated its nuclear program with HEU, and was therefore spoiled for choice in being able to choose either a gun or an implosion design. While news did emerge in 1986 of a test site at a military reservation in Cachimbo, southern Pará State, and of shafts about a yard in diameter (and about 1,000 feet deep), this does imply the implosion option, though it doesn't rule out gun-type either.

For its part, South Africa produced its first deployable atom bomb less than a decade after it started nuclear weapons research. Five more were to follow.

One of the first questions asked by the ANC after taking power was why the West insisted on South Africa's nuclear weapons program being neutralized prior to the takeover. Didn't they trust us? was a question asked by one of Mandela's functionaries. Subsequent events at the southern tip of the African continent suggest that the decision was not only wise, it was also sensible in the light of the new South Africa's unbridled anti-West political approach.

The path toward nuclear parity taken by South Africa in the last quarter of the twentieth century is interesting. In a presentation given in Castiglioncello, Italy, in 1995, at the conference "Fifty Years After Hiroshima," Dr. Waldo Stumpf, former head of the Atomic Energy Corporation of South Africa, presented a paper titled "South Africa's Nuclear Deterrent Strategy." While never personally involved with nuclear weapons work, his comments are incisive. They provide the kind of overview which, until then, had been lacking.

Dr. Stumpf told his fellow delegates:

> Though the Atomic Energy Board was established in 1948 by Act of Parliament and assumed general nuclear research and development activities at its Pelindaba site near Pretoria in 1961, all activities in the early years were based on the

peaceful uses of nuclear technology, especially since South Africa was [and still is] a prominent producer of uranium. It was to be accepted that attention was given to uranium enrichment technology as a means to mineral beneficiation.

Other sources suggest that research into the military implications of a nuclear capability reportedly was already undertaken by South Africa in the 1950s. Yet another report, based on an interview with the South African Soviet spy Dieter Gerhardt, suggests that the country began to develop an independent nuclear option in 1964. Interestingly, Dr. Ampie Roux, who helped initiate South Africa's nuclear weapons program, declared in 1960 that South Africa was "capable of producing a nuclear weapon if it was prepared to isolate the best brains in the country, and give them all the funds they needed."

In his Italian presentation, Dr. Stumpf makes the point that none of it was easy. Some of the technical problems linked to nuclear weapon design, he admitted, can be awesome.

After encouraging laboratory results were achieved in 1969 with an indigenous uranium-enrichment process based on a stationary wall vortex tube, approval was given for the further development of the process on an industrial scale. At the same time the construction of a pilot plant to prove the process was begun.

This work was undertaken within the newly created [1970] Uranium Enrichment Corporation on the Valindaba site which lies immediately adjacent to Pelindaba. Construction of a Pilot Enrichment Plant, which the South Africans called the Y Plant, went ahead in 1971 and the first stages at the lower end of the cascade commissioned by the end of 1974.

Full cascade operation was initiated in March 1977, Dr. Stumpf recalled, which was about half the time it took Pakistan to achieve the same results. "Due to the long equilibrium time of the plant [the time necessary to establish the full enrichment gradient], the first and relatively small quantity of high enriched uranium hexafluoride (UF_6) was withdrawn from the plant only in January 1978." Significant here is the fact that this substance—a volatile compound of uranium and fluoride—is the feedstock in the uranium-enrichment process, which ultimately becomes the core of the bomb.

During all of 1978 and most of 1979, more uranium hexafluoride was withdrawn from the plant and converted to HEU in its metal form. This material was still of relatively low enrichment (about 80 percent ^{235}U).

Then came disaster. At one stage, Dr. Stumpf explained, the plant had what was termed a "massive catalytic in-process gas reaction between the feedstock and the carrier gas, hydrogen." Work at the facility was halted for almost a year.

However, there are those who maintain today that the flow of HEU was never actually interrupted and that the nine months' supply was used to fuel one or more atom bombs, which were tested in conjunction with the Israelis in extreme southern latitudes. It was kept well out of the public eye, one source told me.

It will be recalled that shortly after, in September 1979, there was a huge international rumpus over distinct "double flashes" detected by a U.S. Vela satellite more than a thousand miles south of Cape Town. This data offered strong evidence that the flash had been caused by a low-yield nuclear explosion.

In June 1980, the CIA reported to the U.S. National Security Council that the two- to three-kiloton nuclear test had probably involved Israel and South Africa. Meanwhile, U.S. intelligence confirmed that it had tracked frequent visits to South Africa by Israeli nuclear scientists, technicians, and defense officials in the years preceding the incident, and concluded that "clandestine arrangements between South Africa and Israel for joint nuclear testing operations might have been negotiable."

Because of its potentially adverse political impact, Washington had to strive to find a way to avoid calling this event "an Israeli–South African test." The publication *The Message* was more conclusive when it noted that: "An affirmative report might have affected the ongoing negotiations over the creation of Zimbabwe [then Rhodesia] in which South African cooperation was needed and [possibly] upset the recently negotiated Camp David accords between Israel and Egypt."[2]

Such speculation was fueled in 1986 when Israeli nuclear technician Mordechai Vanunu was interviewed by the London *Sunday Times*. Vanunu said it was common knowledge at Dimona that South African metallurgists, technicians, and scientists were there on joint technical exchange programs.

The Vela satellite issue remains contentious. Both Israel and South Africa continue to deny that nuclear weapons were tested, even though a member of Nelson Mandela's cabinet told a newspaper shortly after the ANC had taken over that the flashes had indeed been nuclear. It's worth mentioning that he retracted his statement soon afterwards.

Whatever the truth, it remains Stumpf's view that valuable lessons were learned from South Africa's brief but productive nuclear experience. What he told the delegates at Castiglioncello says much, not only in respect to the South African nuclear weapons program, but also about similar programs to follow, including those in North Korea, Iran, and elsewhere:

- Although the technology of uranium enrichment and unsophisticated nuclear weapons is of a very high level, it is still within the bounds of a reasonably advanced industrialized country, and therefore, is not in itself an insurmountable barrier. This is particularly so where the technical goals are relatively modest, as with South Africa's gun-type devices without neutron initiators.

- Although the vast Iraqi nuclear weapons program and the huge financial and human resources it required may leave the impression of a self-limiting constraint, the South African experience proved otherwise.

- Although international political isolation may be an instrument to contain individual cases of nuclear proliferation, a point in such an isolation campaign may be reached where it actually becomes counterproductive and really pushes the would-be proliferator toward full proliferation. In the case of South Africa, this point was probably reached when the U.S. cut off contractual supplies of fuel to both its Safari and Koeberg [commercial] reactors, together with punitive financial measures applied by the American administration at the time. What little leverage the U.S. had over the South African nuclear program was consequently lost.

- Where proliferation occurred due to a real or perceived political threat, a reversal toward de-proliferation may occur upon removal or neutralization of the threat, whether real or perceived. This means that international pressure by a superpower from outside the region on a would-be proliferator can be helpful, but only up to a point. In the final instance, regional tensions must be resolved before the cause of nonproliferation can be fully realized. This was the case with South Africa, and is probably so in the Middle East, South Asia, and the Korean peninsula.

- The reversal from a position of nuclear proliferation to a truly and permanent status of nonproliferation within the Nuclear Non-Proliferation Treaty (NPT) will probably not be achieved by technical or military/strategic decisions, but rather, requires a fundamental political decision by the leader(s) of the country. The "rollback" option for a so-called threshold non-nuclear weapon state is not an easy path to follow, as the NPT and its instruments were not designed to deal with such an eventuality. The international community should therefore take care in its application of pressure on the process of normalization where a threshold state already has taken the fundamental decision to embark on this road. South Africa experienced a lot of unnecessary international pressure during the "completeness investigation" by the IAEA, which, under different circumstances, could have even derailed the process.

- For a "threshold state" that has taken the political decision to "roll back" and then to achieve international credibility and acceptance within the NPT is [difficult]. It can be eased considerably, however, by a sustained policy of full openness and transparency with the IAEA. Once more, this is a political decision.

United States Air Force veteran and intelligence specialist Lieutenant Colonel Roy E. Horton III added the results of his own study of the South African nuclear saga in Occasional Paper #27, completed for the USAF Institute for National Security Studies in August 1999.

Horton felt it was possible that South Africa leapfrogged the testing phases and concentrated on the weaponization and delivery of its nuclear explosive device. As he declared in his thesis, "Afrikaners are [by their nature] a contingency-minded people and, as such, probably would prefer to have a deliverable nuclear weapon rather than be forced to develop one hastily in the face of a worsening security situation."

Thus, he maintained, the ebb and flow of the South African nuclear deterrent effort was all the more remarkable given the small number of personnel involved (1,000 in total and no more than 300 at any one period). Those actually responsible for key programmatic decisions reportedly never numbered more than between 6 and 12 individuals. In fact, South Africa's nuclear weapons program was minuscule compared to that of other states; for example, there were about 25,000 people working on the Iraqi bomb prior to the first Gulf War.

On March 26, 1993, the London *Sunday Times* published an interview with a former South African nuclear scientist who was involved in the weapons program until the mid-1970s. He said that while he was at Pelindaba, there were about thirty scientists working on the bomb project.

According to Horton:

Decisions emerged from the synthesis of four basic groups—the scientists, politicians, the military, and technocrats—who shaped the focus and direction of the program. The scientific zeal and drive of the Atomic Energy Board's Ampie Roux and Wally Grant, who headed UCOR [the uranium enrichment plant] . . . to demonstrate that South Africa could make a nuclear device established the technical foundation for the program.

Yet, as this officer observes, their work was not done in isolation from the political leadership, the support of the military on military-to-military cooperation matters, and the technocrats responsible for actual weapons production.

Horton continues:

> The strong leadership of [South Africa's] ruling National Party supported [nuclear] research during the 1950s and 1960s, before molding it into a key element of national strategy in the 1970s. Prime Minister B. J. Vorster presided over the decision to pursue "peaceful nuclear explosives" and the aborted Kalahari nuclear test.

The military exerted strong influence within the State Security Council (SSC), but their role focused primarily on domestic security and conventional military operations. Two defense ministers oversaw the nuclear program: P. W. Botha and his handpicked successor, General Magnus Malan. Under Botha, the defense minister's power was merged with that of the prime minister's in supporting the nuclear deterrent program. With Malan, it would appear that the military's direct influence over the course of the nuclear deterrent program was more limited, although they remained engaged at some level as the ultimate customer for nuclear weapons.

Finally, explains the colonel, there were the technocrats—the engineers at Armscor (the South African Armaments Corporation).

This group exerted heavy influence over the nuclear program, he reckons, particularly during its critical middle stage. Armscor managing director Tielman de Waal headed a corporation that not only produced nuclear weapons, but also established the capability to mate them with ballistic missiles.

Horton notes: "There are also indications that Armscor was involved in more than just producing munitions—it also worked in developing the nuclear strategy itself. Together, these four groups formed a partnership that conceived, produced, and then discarded South Africa's nuclear deterrent." Yet, in the end, he maintains, the political leadership exerted the pivotal influence over the program's progress.

South Africa eventually possessed six devices in its nuclear arsenal, each containing about 120 pounds of highly enriched uranium (HEU), together with enough HEU for a seventh device. The devices were stored unassembled, with their front and rear portions kept in separate vaults. In order to prevent premature detonation, they were designed to arm only when a certain altitude was reached, whether this was achieved on locally produced MRBMs (such as the RSA-3) or SAAF jets.

According to Dr. von Wielligh, who spent several years with the IAEA in Vienna, the figures mentioned by Horton are strictly guesswork, since the quantities used are proliferation-sensitive and were therefore never published.

At the same time, suggests Signe Landgren, a researcher at SIPRI, the Stockholm International Peace Research Institute, South Africa was developing "long-range missiles capable of carrying nuclear warheads." His study stated that in November 1989, the CIA confirmed that a joint South African–Israeli test of the "Arniston" missile, which could carry a nuclear warhead over 1,200 miles, had taken place.

The name "Arniston," coincidentally, was given to the South African RSA-3 medium-range ballistic missile by the CIA because that Cape fishing village was the closest to the test-firing range. Its official name is Waenhuiskrans.

By the late 1980s, says Horton, South Africa was in the process of preparing to upgrade its seven gun-type weapons. Quoting David Albright, Horton noted that Armscor had plans to "replace the seven cannon-type devices with seven upgraded devices, when they reach the end of their estimated life by the year 2000."[3]

He also mentioned a report carried in the January 12, 1989, issue of *Nucleonics Week*, which cited nuclear collaboration between Argentina's Comisión Nacional de Energia Atómica (CNEA) and South Africa. This, he states, mentions the sharing of design information on nuclear fuel cycle technology with South Africa. Von Wielligh counters this by stating that nuclear fuel cycle technology is a very broad term, which could include completely harmless, peaceful topics such as mining, conversion, enrichment, and fuel fabrication, as well as waste handling and disposal.

"I am not aware of this specific example of cooperation with Argentina, and it definitely had nothing to do with the weapons program," this former IAEA board member told me when I visited his Pretoria home.

One of the questions most often asked about South Africa's nuclear weapons program is why these people should have thought it necessary to build such a weapon in the first place. The immediate answer, as with Israel today, could probably be encapsulated in a single word—survival. By the time de Klerk and his National Party cabinet made the decision to call a halt to racial discrimination, the nation had become distinctly war weary. Twenty years of conflict, said one parliamentarian at the time, is enough.

Pretoria's most determined adversary was Angola. Its seasoned and well-blooded army, FAPLA (*Forças Armadas Populares de Libertação de Angola*), was not only equipped and trained by the Soviet Bloc, but also bolstered by Soviet, North Korean, and Yugoslav advisors and technicians, as well as by 50,000 Cuban troops.

Because of South Africa's apartheid laws, the issue was further exacerbated by a UN-imposed arms embargo. Pretoria was prevented from acquiring most kinds of advanced foreign military hardware it needed to contain the threat from the north. That included military aircraft.

While a lot of weapons that emerged from South African factories were well designed, tested, and battle-honed, the outlay dug great holes into the country's budget. The range of goods coming out of hundreds of arms factories included the full panoply of infantry squad weapons and infantry fighting vehicles. These included the Ratel and Rooikat, as well as the Buffel (buffalo) troop carrier, together with a range of mine-protected vehicles. Some of these were indispensable in the conflict then being waged by the "white south" against Moscow's surrogates in Angola, and several variants have since seen good service with the UN and other bodies in places as diverse as Kosovo, South Lebanon, and Rwanda.

Also built locally were some outstanding artillery pieces. The 155mm G5 howitzer remains a fine weapon and is good enough to have been exported to many countries in the Near East, including Iraq when that country was at war with Iran. Add to this tally a complement of mortar and rocket systems, mines, claymores, and the rest, and the South African Defence Force (SADF) was more than adequately equipped to deal with just about all the vagaries encountered in its ground war.

In addition, the country produced enough third-generation communications equipment coupled with an outstanding level of medical backup for South Africa to make for a formidable adversary, even by today's standards. Not bad for a Third Worlder.

What Pretoria didn't have an answer for was air power. Unable to build its own fighters and support aircraft, the South African Air Force could not counter the squadrons of MiG-23s and Sukhoi strike aircraft, as well as Mi-24 helicopter gunships, with which the Angolan Air Force had been equipped. These machines were flown by Cuban, East German, and Soviet pilots, and, it is said, by some Vietnamese veterans of their own conflict with the Americans.

Obviously, South Africa's apartheid leaders had to look for another remedy if they were going to prevent its troops from being overwhelmed, and it was for this reason that the bomb was first considered. Domestic needs also pointed South Africa in the direction of a nuclear option. As Dr. Waldo Stumpf declared, South Africa's political isolation was coupled with a growing nuclear isolation. "During the seventies, some of the nuclear weapon states and in particular the U.S. increasingly started to apply unilateral restrictions on nuclear trade or exchange of information and technology with South Africa," he wrote.

Stumpf goes on:

In 1976, the U.S. government unilaterally refused further exports under a long-standing contract between America and Pretoria of fuel elements for the Safari research reactor, which had been under IAEA safeguards since its commissioning in 1965. South Africa's prepaid payment for the canceled consignment was also retained by the Carter Administration: its return was approved only after Reagan had taken office in 1981.

In 1978 the United States Congress enacted the Nuclear Non-Proliferation Act (NNPA), which precluded the transfer of any kind of nuclear technology to countries not party to the NPT. This act was applied retroactively on all previous agreements and contracts and directly led to the refusal of export permits to South Africa for the shipment to France of its own uranium, already enriched by the U.S. Department of Energy for the Koeberg Nuclear Power station.

Though the bombs produced by Pretoria might have been regarded as an unwieldy effort to join the world's ultra-exclusive Nuclear Club—they were clumsy, overly bulky, and of a World War II vintage—the South Africans in the end achieved their initial objective in constructing six of them. It was only a question of time before Armscor scientists would be able to limit their size and weight, which would have allowed them to be deployed in the country's burgeoning guided missile program.

The first bomb built at the Circle (where weaponization took place) and which was compatible with standard aircraft-borne delivery systems was in December 1982. However, the long gestation period between the completion of this one and the first "qualified and inventory-certified device" (August 1987) is extraordinary. One opinion voiced is that Armscor had to engineer, qualify, and certify its devices for delivery both by guided glide-bombs as well as ballistic missiles.

It is interesting to note that a collaborative effort had already been initiated with Israel on missile development. The Jewish State had fielded its first ballistic missile, the Jericho-1, and was in the process of working on the longer-range Jericho-2 (which could carry a one-ton payload about 1,000 miles). Some of the testing for these weapons took place at the Overberg Test Range, in part because Israel has no eastward-facing test range of its own.

Its scientists, meanwhile, were involved in trying to perfect the bomb so that it could be delivered by one of four missile projects on which the country was focused. At that stage, Pretoria's first fissile devices were so bulky that, should they have had to be used, the only aircraft available for the task would have been obsolete British-built Buccaneer strike aircraft.

It is significant that South Africa, like Israel, never boasted about its nuclear capability. In part, this was due to a policy termed "deliberate uncertainty," which, in some political quarters, is sometimes more effective in achieving results than revealing all. At the same time, both Washington and London were aware that Pretoria was fast approaching the point where it would have had the clout to militarily reshape things in its corner of the globe.

Though hardly a match for any of the major powers, it wasn't lost on strategists abroad that atom bombs dropped onto the heads of the inhabitants of several African capitals had implications that could affect events far beyond Africa. This was before Mandela's release and the Cold War was still real. One authority disclosed to this writer that any form of chemical or biological weapons intended for use against South African forces (or within South Africa itself) would have tipped the balance, very much as Israel has warned Syria that it would retaliate "to maximum effect" were Damascus to launch any of its nerve gas–tipped Scuds against the Jewish Homeland.

Essentially, though, Pretoria would have followed the logic which Washington employed in 1945 to bomb Hiroshima and Nagasaki, viz., to strike at "war plants surrounded by workers' homes." It's about then that the West got serious about bringing Southern Africa's brush-fire wars to a close.

By the late 1980s Chester Crocker, U.S. undersecretary of state for Africa, began a series of negotiations that involved South Africa, Angola, Portugal, Cuba, and the United States, as well as the Soviet Union. The fact that Pretoria had the bomb and wasn't boasting about it was probably the single most powerful motive for peace in the region.

It is notable that South Africa had a "deterrent strategy" in place when all this was happening, described when President de Klerk made his first disclosures about South Africa having the bomb. It was based on three phases:

- **Phase one:** The first was the "strategic uncertainty" issue during which its nuclear capability would be neither acknowledged nor denied. (As Dr. von Wielligh points out, no real offensive tactical application of nuclear weapons was then foreseen—as was later the case—which was why there was no deliberate effort initially to construct a smaller, lighter weapon.)

- **Phase two:** Should its territory be threatened militarily, then the government would covertly acknowledge the existence of its nuclear weapons to leading Western governments, particularly the United States.

- **Phase three:** If this partial disclosure failed to lead to the required assistance in defusing the situation, the government would publicly acknowledge its capability or demonstrate its potency with an underground test.

The South Africans employed a specific strategy, calculated to bring Western governments to South Africa's aid in the event of an overwhelming attack by Soviet-supported military forces in southern Africa. However, it was the view of some Africa watchers at the time that the prime objective in developing its limited nuclear capability was to force the West, particularly the United States, to provide a guarantee of sorts to offset the Soviet Union's capacity for what was termed "nuclear escalation dominance."

This might very well have happened had the country actually been invaded from the north by a Soviet-led Angolan expeditionary force: with air dominance, they certainly had the ability. In retrospect, this was a scenario that was not impossible if the Namibian war was expanded (with Soviet support) to include a second front in Caprivi. It could be argued that the nuclear card was merely a political bluff intended to blackmail the United States (and other Western powers) into coming to Pretoria's assistance should the country be on the verge of being overrun. Nevertheless, in the end, it worked.[4]

Another reason for espousing such a doctrine was the desire for Pretoria to increase Western concerns about South Africa's nuclear intentions, which led to the establishment by 1977 of Vastrap, a potential nuclear testing site in the remotest corner of the Kalahari Desert where Pretoria had hoped to conduct an underground nuclear test.

Preparations were being made at the time for a dummy run (an "instrumented" test without an actual nuclear core). We now know that preparations for this event were detected by Soviet satellite surveillance and subsequently abandoned, after, it has been suggested, Washington threatened to prohibit sales of commercial aircraft and parts, which would effectively have grounded South African Airways' mainly Boeing fleet.

Common sense dictates that such a threat is unlikely to have been made by the U.S. in the case of a mere "instrumented" or "cold" test. First, because it could have taken place in complete secrecy in one of the country's worked-out and deep (miles!) mineshafts on the then Witwatersrand. Second, because the argument that the depleted uranium core would have caused radioactivity is not valid. It would have been a formality to have sealed off entire sections of the mine to prevent leakage, and the superpowers would have been none the wiser. The attempted use, in this instance, of a purpose-built test site, in plain view of those who were able to detect and identify such a site (by satellite), suggests that something more substantial than a mere instrumented test might have taken place had it happened.

Though the country never intentionally moved beyond phase one, this exercise did result in convincing both Moscow and Washington that the Boers were deadly serious about their nuclear capability. In turn, it resulted in the West putting pressure on the Soviet Union and Cuba to withdraw from Angola. Whether the weapons and the strategy ever served this purpose has never been proved, and is consequently impossible to determine.

An article carried by *The Risk Report*[5] and titled "South Africa's Nuclear Autopsy" disclosed that South African scientists—like their North Korean and Iranian counterparts—routinely culled open-source literature, including U.S. Navy manuals on nuclear weapon systems, safety, and design. And, according to Dr. Stumpf, the man who inherited South Africa's nuclear establishment, "Less than five or ten people had an oversight of the entire program."

In short, though, a handful of bombs were produced. This was always a remarkably modern nuclear weapons program. For some tasks, says one report, more sophisticated equipment was needed, so Pretoria resorted to a massive clandestine program that included subterfuge and smuggling.

"I am not at liberty to divulge anything that we import . . . we do not identify our suppliers." This was all that Dr. Stumpf, CEO of South Africa's Atomic Energy Corporation, would say when he fielded related questions during a 1993 meeting at the South African embassy in Washington. He added that South Africa "had no help from anybody on nuclear weapons technology. . . . We gave no help to anybody and we received no help. On other things, yes . . . [but] not on enrichment technology, not on nuclear weapons technology."

Stumpf admitted that South Africa imported nuclear materials over the years, including low-enriched uranium, but he would not say from where. As Dr. von Wielligh reminds us, the imported LEU was never part of the nuclear weapons program, but intended solely for use in reactors.

Not so with South Africa's guided missile program. According to *The Risk Report*, Israel was South Africa's most important missile supplier, hands down. Pretoria got most of what it needed from Tel Aviv, and for much of it, the course was very much a two-way highway. Exchanges included the transfer of approximately 50 tons of South African yellowcake, in exchange for 30 grams of tritium, the heaviest hydrogen isotope customarily used to boost the explosive power of atom bombs. In the end, Israel would receive 600 tons of yellowcake.

Incorporated into the core of the bomb, a tritium plug can quite substantially raise the yield of, for instance, a 20 KT bomb. Pakistan claims to have thermonuclear capability, but in the view of American nuclear physicist Dr. Bogdan Maglich (at one stage one of the departmental heads of CERN, the European Organization for Nuclear Research in Geneva), "That's a clever bit of disinformation in a bid to counter New Delhi's advances in this field."

The tritium received from Israel never found a home in the South African nuclear weapons program. Instead, with a half-life of just over twelve years, most had deteriorated by the time a halt was called to weapons production. At one stage, after the country had abandoned its nuclear weapons program, some tritium was commercially used to illuminate advertising billboards, but nobody can tell whether it was successful or not.

TRITIUM

The first time I met David Albright, we sat in a small restaurant not far from his house in Georgetown and discussed tritium—the heaviest hydrogen isotope customarily used to boost the explosive power of atom bombs.

Though I forget his exact words, he described its unstable properties thus: "Controlling tritium is like turning a glass of water upside down and trying to prevent the spill." He added that while the analogy might be a bit wide of the mark, it gave an idea of what was involved. Point taken . . .

The fact is that tritium has several important uses, the most significant as a component in the triggering mechanism in thermonuclear (fusion) weapons. Also, because it has a half-life of a bit more than twelve years, very large quantities of tritium are required for the maintenance of the nation's nuclear weapons capabilities.

It is also used as a booster for atomic bombs. While Pakistan claims to have thermonuclear capability, the consensus is that it has only fission (or atom) bombs, which its scientists boost to allow for higher explosive yields; of course, this could change. Typically, this is done by injecting a small amount of tritium gas (as little as 2 or 3 grams, or a fraction of an ounce) into the weapon's fission core before initiation. While such devices are usually referred to as "boosted" weapons, they are more properly called "fusion-boosted fission weapons."

What happens during the course of a blast involving tritium is a high release of neutrons as the tritium fuses together. This is due to extremely high temperatures caused by the building atomic explosion—which, in turn, increases the efficiency of the chain reaction, and consequently produces a much larger yield.

The first such boosted bomb was tested by the United States on May 24, 1951, using a core of HEU. It delivered an explosion of 45 kilotons (roughly 45,000 tons of high explosives), or about twice the yield had this isotope not been inserted.

A valuable, toxic, and radioactive substance, South Africa is believed to have traded a large consignment of yellowcake with Israel for about an ounce (30 grams) of tritium. It's worth mentioning that tritium is also produced commercially in reactors. It finds use in various self-luminescent devices, such as exit signs in buildings, aircraft dials, gauges, luminous paints, and wristwatches. Tritium is also used in life science research, and in studies investigating the metabolism of potential new drugs.

It was first discovered at Cambridge's Cavendish Laboratory in 1934 by Ernest Rutherford, one of the most famous physicists of all time, who was born in New Zealand; Australian Mark Oliphant; and German national Paul Harteck, who returned to his homeland before the start of World War II.

The secrecy that surrounded its A-bomb efforts often forced Pretoria to make do with low-tech equipment. "These guys were immensely proud of what they achieved under sanctions," said a U.S. State Department official once Pretoria had opened its doors to IAEA and American inspection. "They came up with their own homespun technology," he added.

From the late 1970s through early 1990, South Africa produced HEU at its pilot-scale enrichment plant at Pelindaba. The key technology, claimed an American-based report, was called "split-nozzle gaseous diffusion," which was rumored to have been supplied by West Germany in the early 1970s. But this is wrong.

Dr. von Wielligh uses this opportunity to remind us that there is no enrichment process with that name. Rather, the different types of enrichment processes are:

- Gas centrifuge (the most common method today)

- Gaseous diffusion (originally used in the U.S. for the Manhattan Project)

- Thermal diffusion (also used for the Manhattan Project)

- Aerodynamic methods (separation nozzles or vortex tubes)

- Chemical or ion exchange (not really used in practice)

- Laser-based enrichment (AVLIS, MLIS, etc.)

- Electromagnetic processes (EMIS, etc.)

He also mentions a German company, STEAG, that became involved in an economic study of the vortex, or the UCOR vortex tube, method of uranium enrichment. This gave rise to the misconception that South Africa obtained its isotope separation technology from Germany, i.e., the so-called "Becker process," an aerodynamic method of making use of separation nozzles.

Dr. von Wielligh stresses that this is not the same as the South African process, though both methods are based on aerodynamic phenomena. That's where any similarity ends, he told me.

Backing this development, Dr. Ampie Roux, president of the South African Atomic Energy Board, maintained at the time that 90 percent of the plant was manufactured in South Africa. The foreign content was purchased "through normal channels and was in no way crucial for the completion of the project," he declared.

Obviously, the need for total secrecy made this kind of shopping difficult. According to the industry newsletter, *NuclearFuel*, South Africa needed tungsten, which is useful for making neutron reflectors for bomb packages. As von Wielligh tells us, tungsten serves to reflect escaping neutrons back into the core of the bomb, thereby reducing the quantity of nuclear material needed for criticality. But since the Nuclear Suppliers Group (NSG) has controlled almost all tungsten for export since the late 1970s, Pretoria had to find secret sources in the then Rhodesia (Zimbabwe), Zambia, and Zaire (the Democratic Republic of the Congo), according to one U.S. analyst. At the same time, no one is willing to say exactly who sold what to whom.

Something that surprised IAEA inspectors (who visited South African nuclear plants once the country had decided to tell all) was that much of the equipment was low-tech.

"They were very creative," a U.S. participant commented. He reported that South African scientists regularly adapted lower-tech equipment to complex tasks. For example, two-axis machine tools normally used for simple manufacturing were reportedly adapted to create complex three-dimensional shapes for South Africa's gun-type nuclear bomb.

The issue of South Africa's nuclear weapons—and indeed, the full spectrum of its weapons of mass destruction—is the subject of a forthcoming book by Nicholas Paul Badenhorst and Pierre Victor.

Chapter 11 Endnotes:

1 See Stephen Laufer and Arthur Gavshon, "The real reasons for SA's nukes," *The Weekly Mail*, March 26 to April 1, 1993, p. 3.

2 *The Message*, The Jewish-Broederbond Syndicate, Chapter 3, Arms Industry. When accessed on April 22, 2005, http://www.islam.co.za/themessage/thesis/thesis_5/toc.htm.

3 David Albright, "South Africa's Secret Nuclear Weapons," ISIS Report, Washington, D.C., May 1994, p. 14.

4 A concept not as far-fetched as it sounds, since it was part of the Kremlin's strategic battle plan to eventually control all of southern Africa and its minerals, just as it wanted to dominate the Middle East with its oil. With Soviet, Cuban, North Korean, and other help, the military objective in Angola was to subjugate Unita forces in Eastern Angola and force South Africa to fight a "second war" in Caprivi (the first was already ongoing in Ovamboland). Pretoria did not have the additional manpower and would have had to pull its forces back to the Orange River. Together with a popular uprising in South Africa's townships—which took place anyway—a Russian-backed invasion force could then have moved on to South African soil.

5 *The Risk Report* 2, no. 1 (January/February 1996), pp. 4–5, 10.

CHAPTER 12

THE KARACHI CONNECTION

One of the observations made by some of those who flew around the globe with newly ensconced President Nelson Mandela was the number of Asians in his entourage. This led to the phrase "the Karachi Connection." It stuck—as it did with the man who filled his shoes when the much-revered Madiba retired.

After South Africa's old apartheid regime neutralized its atom bomb program—then still very much under wraps in the subcontinent, even though the rest of the world by now was aware of these things—the recently elected black government in South Africa looked comfortable with its acquired status of "being totally non-aligned either to one power block or the other." At least that was the way it was phrased by Mandela at an international function.

There was a lot else going on under the covers in the new "Rainbow South Africa." Some of it, including an al-Qaeda presence that was unmasked after a tip-off and exposed in the South African Parliament, was of concern to the West. But since South Africa was the biggest economic power in Africa and one of the few that boasted a viable democracy, nobody was eager to rock this boat. In any event, attention was focused elsewhere, since the Middle East was going off the tracks.

That did not prevent South Africa from becoming a favorite destination among nations or countries that Washington had labeled "rogue." They arrived in droves: Syrians, Libyans, Cubans, and an astonishing number of Iranians. There were even North Koreans who, once there, were allowed to travel about without their government "minders."

Iran's representatives had been coming in considerable numbers even before the transition to majority rule had taken place. Almost overnight their maddrassas sprang up wherever there were enough receptive Muslims to provide a congregation. The upshot of that period resulted in South Africa playing host to one of the largest Islamic fundamentalist groups outside the Middle East, which is how it stands at present. It also recently caused the Malaysian government to ask questions about why so many of its citizens were heading to South Africa for their education.

Meanwhile, things weren't helped by a succession of earlier visits by President Mandela to Libya, then already fostering insurrection into Sierra Leone from Liberia.

A new cartel of South African cabinet ministers was commuting between Pretoria and Tripoli, quite a few of them sidetracking to Damascus and Tehran as well. There was so much truck with the mullahs that Washington at one stage raised objections: There were those in the U.S. State Department who believed that the South Africans might be too inexperienced or naive to appreciate the pitfalls of such associations.

But the West was duped. The wily South Africans, with years in exile, were as accomplished in foreign affairs as their counterparts in Europe and America. In fact, they knew exactly what they were doing. A meeting between Mandela and the then Iranian president, Ali Akbar Rafsanjani, raised enough eyebrows for a furious Rafsanjani to declare that "Iran and South Africa will not allow the United States to determine our fate and our destiny."

There were also indications that Iran was recruiting South African nuclear scientists to work in its own nascent atomic energy program. Whatever the truth, Rafsanjani's remarks did not rest comfortably in the West.

President Clinton's well-publicized tour of Africa followed, during which he made an issue of South Africa's close relationship with Libya. The White House also made known that it was less than pleased with Mandela's resistance to U.S. sanctions against both Iraq and Cuba. One or two foreign policy analysts speculated at the time that, caught as it was between the aspirations of a previously deprived population and a stringent recession, South Africa could opt to sell nuclear or other technology as it pleased.

That possibility may well have spurred Clinton's vehement opposition to the $2 billion deal made by South Africa to supply Syria with updated tank-cannon stabilizing equipment, the first of several such deals which culminated in South African night-vision goggles having been found among Hezbollah combatants in South Lebanon during the 2006 Israeli invasion.

Indeed, it went further. Within a year of President Mandela taking over the government, South Africa began to take a strongly pro-Palestinian approach in anything to do with Israel. That was followed by a display of some pretty outspoken sentiments that were critical of America's role in the Middle East. Indeed, even in retirement today, Mandela rarely has a good word to say about Washington, and it is also worth noting that he has been consistently vocal about the "innocence" of Saddam Hussein.

It follows, then, that there are few non-Islamic countries quite as vituperative about the U.S. presence in Baghdad and Operation Iraqi Freedom as the current leaders of the "new" South Africa. The country's media also followed this trend.

Clearly, under the new black African order, there was much in modern-day South Africa to interest the Iranians. The country has sprawling, ultramodern cities with resplendent residential suburbs that occasionally eclipse what places like Sydney, Long Island, Geneva, and Los Angeles have to offer—though to be fair, with the exodus of so many educated whites, things have become a little tarnished. Johannesburg, Durban, and Cape Town boast some of the biggest shopping malls in the world, offset by sprawling, suppurating slums which have become synonymous with Africa in the twenty-first century.

Anomalies apart, South Africa remains home to the biggest industrial infrastructure on the continent of Africa, a legacy of the former racist regime. It is also blessed with the most sophisticated road, rail, and telecommunications grids on the continent of Africa. In fact, there are more miles of rail tracks laid within its borders than in the rest of the continent put together. Most important to anybody from the Middle East, South Africa, until recently, was the tenth-largest exporter in the world of weapons.

Having just emerged from a two-decade war in Angola and Namibia, the array of sophisticated military hardware produced was impressive. Indeed, it still is. Much is of a kind and quality that those Islamic countries out of favor with the West had, until then, only been able to view from a distance. Moreover, a lot of it was advanced. The laser tank sights that Syria wanted are produced by Eloptro, a subsidiary of the one-time giant arms manufacturer Armscor. There is a 155mm self-propelled artillery system capable of lobbing base-bleed projectiles almost thirty miles, which is farther than any comparable American artillery piece (and includes the G6, a self-propelled version of the same weapon).

There is also an in-flight refueling system, a stand-off guided bomb, an air-to-air missile family, a new-era torpedo, a fresh generation of tactical "frequency-hopping" radios, as well as unmanned aerial vehicles which could easily be mistaken for clones of similar craft manufactured in Israel.

There is also a huge range of munitions, some of which is now being sold in Europe (and were recently bought by the U.S. Army to supplement its stocks), and some limited-range guided missiles from Kentron. Some of this stuff, it might be recalled, was designed and built in conjunction with Israeli engineers working alongside their South African counterparts in South African arms factories.

Even the British army had a stake. In January 2003 the minister of defense in London placed a $10 million order with Denel for a hundred LH 40C hand-held laser rangefinders. This was hardly the kind of thing you were likely to encounter in any downtown Karachi or Cairo industrial estate.

Other exchanges of military technology in joint ventures reportedly included technical knowledge acquired from the canceled Israeli "Lavi" fighter program, some of which was applied to the South African Air Force Cheetah fighter (which is basically an upgraded French Mirage). For the Iranians, the original joint Israeli–South African space program was a bonus.

Very little changed when President Thabo Mbeki took over as head of state, especially since the new incumbent tended to surround himself with people like Dr. Essop Pahad, who was appointed a cabinet minister after the 2004 general elections. Pahad, like his brother Aziz (a deputy minister of foreign affairs), is regarded as a powerful proponent of stronger South African ties with the Islamic world, and is said by those who know him to have fostered Iranian, Iraqi (under Saddam), and Libyan associations for almost as long as he has been politically active. Judging by recent public pronouncements, Pahad is no friend of Washington.

For Tehran, these developments were a bonus. Overnight, with President de Klerk sent into the political wilderness (although he was still to pick up a Nobel Peace Prize with Mandela), the single biggest draw card must have been Pretoria's history of building atom bombs. Even more appealing to the maladroit theocratic mindset was the fact that the bomb had been built in Pretoria in the relatively short space of seven years.

What also emerged was that in the apartheid era, South Africa had been involved in the largest ballistic missile project in Africa. A good deal of the research and development (as well as production) had been handled, again in record time, in conjunction with Israeli rocket scientists. Unlike the bomb program, work on missile projects was still ongoing in the early 1990s. But with de Klerk about to vacate the presidency, strong pressure from Washington resulted in those projects being shelved. It all happened astonishingly quickly, with the result that just about everybody linked to the country's rocket programs were out of work in the relatively short time of about six weeks.

This move resulted in a good bit of acrimony, the Americans being perceived as having interfered in what many regarded as a perfectly legitimate scientific and commercial pursuit. There had even been talk at one stage of developing—again, with Israeli help—a South African satellite. An immediate consequence was still more unemployment, this time among a rather select scientific group.

South Africa had been working on the RSA-2 missile at the time, what had been dubbed by the CIA as the "Arniston." A variation of the Israelis' Jericho II, there were several launches in the direction of Marion Island in the south Indian Ocean, more than a thousand miles distant.

Iranian visitors to South Africa asked permission to examine these achievements and, where still possible, they were given it. Relations between Pretoria and Tehran soon progressed to a reciprocal most-favored-nation status. Consequently, while groups of Iranians set up businesses in all of the country's commercial centers, there were strings of their countrymen touring South African weapons factories, combined with a lot of meetings behind closed doors.

South African–Israeli relations were meanwhile put on hold. In fact, it got so bad that security at Jerusalem's legation in Pretoria was upgraded to the highest level. Even trying to park a car in the street outside (as I did several times prior to going to the Middle East) drew an immediate response from the embassy's security guards.

Things came to a head in May 2004 when there was talk in Pretoria of actually severing relations with Jerusalem.

There is no question that Tehran was intrigued by South Africa's nuclear capability. By its own admission to the IAEA in late 2003, Iran had already been many years into a fairly sophisticated nuclear program and, by some accounts, was having a hard time of it. Nobody is sure—or rather, nobody in South Africa is prepared to say—at what stage Tehran finally decided to grasp the nuclear nettle and put forward a case for some kind of cooperation. Nor would it have been made in public.

In attempting to build the bomb, Iran's nuclear physicists, as with the Iraqis before them, had been flummoxed by some of the hugely complex disciplines involved. But Iran is a rich country, with enough royalties from oil to finance a dozen WMD programs, especially on something that is regarded by Tehran's ruling clique as of national importance. The problem here is that money simply can't buy everything. Also, issues would have been compounded had Iran needed to start its nuclear program from scratch, as they were probably obliged to do.

Like their South African counterparts, they too would have had to get past some of the complex principles related to issues like nuclear physics, uranium enrichment, stabilizing the HEU core in a gun-type atom bomb, and so on. There would have been hiccups in designing and building molds for an implosion device had they decided to walk that road, never mind having to grapple with things as arcane as spherical geography, all of which would be associated with this kind of device.

South Africa, Iran knew very well, had already been there. When you speak to a South African nuclear scientist today—somebody who was involved in the original project—likely as not he will admit to having been perplexed by some of the skills the team needed to inculcate. But not for long, because South Africans are an enterprising and innovative people.

In spite of setbacks—and there were many—Pretoria eventually mastered the complex technology of nuclear weapon construction, be it only enough to produce six bombs, and the Iranians wanted a share of it.

It was perhaps to be expected that with a new government in place—coupled to a still-radical political party that remains demonstrably anti-Washington—that some of the nuclear know-how garnered by South Africa's nuclear physicists would eventually reach Tehran, if not by coercion, then "for services rendered," possibly as a trade-off for oil.

How some of it happened came to me by chance in late May 1997. At very short notice I'd asked for and was given an opportunity to meet the man who was then in charge of that country's nuclear program, Dr. Waldo Stumpf. From Johannesburg, while on a visit to South Africa from the United States, I called his office for an appointment, telling his secretary that I needed advice for an article that I was doing for Britain's Jane's Information Group. It was nuclear-related, I explained, something about Iraq.

The half-dozen South African atom bombs that had been built in the 1970s and 1980s were history, but I was aware that Dr. Stumpf, a quiet-spoken, round-faced scientist, had been around in the industry for many years, and if anybody could help, it would be him.

I'd taken him by surprise, he admitted. He was leaving the next day for Syria. "But come along anyway and let's see what we can do." The drive to Pelindaba, on the outskirts of Pretoria, should normally have taken me fifty minutes; I got there in less than thirty. After some fairly stringent security checks at the gate, I was ushered into the office of the man who was the chief executive officer of Necsa, the Nuclear Energy Corporation of South Africa, a position that Dr. Stumpf held for eleven years, from 1990 to 2001. In the earlier period it was still called the Atomic Energy Corporation.

Because of time constraints, I'd expected the meeting to last perhaps ten minutes. Instead, it was more than an hour before I left Pelindaba.

Dr. Waldo Stumpf, a Fellow of the South African Academy of Engineering, has an impressive array of academic credentials. He holds a BSc Eng (Metallurgy) from the University of Pretoria and a PhD from Sheffield in the UK, apart from a string of other qualifications, most of them engineering. After completing his studies in Britain in 1968 on microstructural aspects of ferritic chromium steels during hot working, he taught a postgraduate course on phase transformations in solids within the department.

Professionally, his particular area of interest lies in the optimization of physical properties of metals and alloys through microstructural optimization by the design of heat treatment or hot working processes, or by alloy design. It's quite a mouthful, but underscores his background. Also, it's not all that different from the studies in Europe of Dr. A.Q. Khan.

Having finished our business, Dr. Stumpf questioned me about my own activities as a correspondent. I'd already published twenty books, and though most were esoteric and nonfiction, he was familiar with my work and my television documentaries. Had he not been, I probably wouldn't have gotten through the door, as this was a very busy man. He also asked a few questions about forays into some of the Arab countries. I had only recently returned from Damascus.

It was then that the tone of our discussion turned conspiratorial. Almost offhandedly, he admitted that a few months before, he'd played host at his Pelindaba nuclear establishment to a group of Iranians. Among them, he confided, was Iran's deputy minister of atomic affairs, Reza Amrollahi.

"I got a call from the president's office in Cape Town soon after getting into the office that morning—not President Mandela himself, but one of his aides. I was told that a high-level party from Tehran, including Minister Amrollahi—who I already knew from international meetings that we'd both attended—was on its way to Pretoria. There were no ifs or buts: the group would arrive by noon," Dr. Stumpf said.

What was immediately troubling, Stumpf confided, was the haste in which the visit had been arranged. Nothing was according to form. If there had been time, he would have liked to have had one of the international observers present, someone from the IAEA. In any event, the IAEA has a monitoring role in South Africa, and the agency doesn't have personnel permanently stationed there.

"But I knew that there was no question that I had to have somebody else in the office while discussions took place. These were sensitive issues. It wouldn't be in either my or Pelindaba's interest to meet alone with an Iranian deputy minister, especially someone involved with nuclear issues. So I called Pik Botha," said Dr. Stumpf.

Botha, a veteran South African politician last seen holding a post in the cabinet of his erstwhile ANC "enemy," had been South Africa's minister of mineral and energy affairs until the post was taken over by Penuell Maduna. Fortunately, he was in Pretoria that day. As Stumpf explained, Pelindaba fell within Botha's bailiwick. "I phoned the minister, told him what was happening, and asked him to come over. He'd arrive within the hour, he replied."

The Iranian party got to Pelindaba in good time, just as Cape Town had said they would. According to Stumpf, the encounter was formal but friendly. For a short while they talked about Minister Amrollahi's visit to South Africa, what he had seen, and what was still planned on his itinerary. "Then the man handed me a file, and I knew exactly what it was," said Dr. Stumpf. "Not a big pile of papers; just a few lists."

The documents, Stumpf explained, contained a comprehensive catalog of items needed to make the bomb. There were some advanced things asked for, like blueprints; industrial, chemical, and laboratory equipment; and other essentials required for this kind of weapon production.

"Obviously we were stunned," Stumpf confided, saying that the request was rejected, politely, but very much out of hand.

Stumpf told the Iranian minister that the provisions of the Nuclear Non-Proliferation Treaty didn't allow either himself or any member of his staff to comply with such demands. He pointed out that not only had South Africa recently signed the NPT, but as everybody present was aware, South Africa had destroyed its entire nuclear weapons arsenal. Additionally, every document relating to the manufacture of atom bombs had been shredded in the presence of IAEA and American and British officials. He also said that since Iran was an NPT signatory, the visit, if anything, was compromising. "We South Africans were being asked to break international law."

Stumpf admitted to having been floored initially by the Iranian's effrontery. More to the point, he told me, he was actually embarrassed. What surprised him the most was that it was almost as if the man had been primed to expect him to comply. It was a bad call, he reckoned.

Stumpf took the opportunity to also remind me of what had happened not very long before in Iraq, following Operation Desert Storm. Once the names of European scientists recruited by Saddam Hussein to work in his nuclear weapons program had been circulated in the weapons strip-search by the IAEA Action Team and UNSCOM, warrants of arrest went out through Interpol. Two of those involved in the Iraqi effort—both Germans—had been charged with treason. At that stage, one was still in jail, Stumpf added.

Aware that he might have exceeded his brief in telling me all this, Waldo Stumpf insisted that everything about the incident remain off the record. For a month or two afterward, it stayed that way. At the same time, I was troubled, especially because of the long-term international security implications of what had taken place, and to which I was now a party. I felt that it might be too potent an issue to put to rest.

Back in London afterward, I mentioned my meeting with Dr. Stumpf to Clifford Beal, the American-born editor of *Jane's International Defence Review* (IDR). I was worried by what I'd been told, I said. I suggested that if it were true that Iran *was* seriously interested in building the bomb, then the ramifications might be incalculable. The lives of untold numbers of people could be affected if things ever got to the fruition stage. Not only that, but the new South African government would have been complicit in helping an aberrant Islamic state—a patently anti-Western one at that—develop a device that might tip the balance of power in a region half the size of Europe.

I felt that the international community had a right to know, was basically what I told Clifford Beal, and he agreed. On the last point, Beal's view at the time was that I should follow the dictates of my conscience. He knew my style and was familiar with the way I worked. By then I'd been contributing to IDR—first in Geneva, and afterwards in Coulsdon, Sussex—for a quarter century. The article was finally published in the September 1997 issue of Jane's *International Defence Review*, which appeared late August. Days later it was picked up by London's *Times* under the headline IRAN SOUGHT PRETORIA NUCLEAR DEAL.

For the record—and because I was aware that I'd betrayed a trust—I'd gone one step further. Just before IDR went to press, I contacted Phillip van Niekerk, an old friend from Sierra Leone's mercenary days, where we'd covered the activities of Executive Outcomes while working in West Africa. At that stage Phillip ran South Africa's most politically outspoken weekly, *The Mail & Guardian*, then still partly owned by Britain's *Guardian* newspaper. His job as editor gradually allowed him to assume the role of an aggressive watchdog in covering polemical government activities, of which there were already quite a lot.

I was in a quandary about the matter and said as much. So I laid out the basics, which up to that point of my interview with Stumpf were based solely on the basis of "I said–he said." What I needed, I suggested, was some help to back up my report. Phillip agreed to look into the matter. If it passed muster, he said, he'd run the story a week after it appeared in London. In retrospect, it was good that he did. *The Mail & Guardian* editor tasked Mungo Soggot, a senior investigative journalist on the paper, to look into it, which he did.

Consequently, when former cabinet minister Pik Botha was asked by Soggot in a phone call to his home in Pretoria a day or two later whether Amrollahi's visit had in fact taken place, and whether the learned Dr. Stumpf had been presented with a nuclear "shopping list," Mr. Botha replied very emphatically that not only was he aware of the event, but, he said, "I was there when it happened."

Once the articles appeared, the South African government reacted with vigor. Within days the issue was raised in Parliament in Cape Town, and I was branded a liar. In answer to a parliamentary question, Stumpf declared: "The entire story is fiction . . . Venter made it all up." The only time he had ever met with any Iranian official, he admitted, was at a dinner in the presence of a large number of people. Dr. Stumpf also denied that deputy minister Reza Amrollahi had ever visited South Africa.

What quickly became clear was that the learned doctor had been well primed, or as one of his colleagues tartly commented, "It was either that or his pension went out the window . . ."

With that, Pretoria went into overdrive. The South African government issued a statement on September 11, 1997, with Penuell Maduna, mineral and energy affairs minister, declaring: "The country's Atomic Energy Corporation

[AEC] had never been involved in business transactions with Iran. Nor were any being considered at present."

In a written reply to National Party member Johan Marais, when the issue was tabled in Parliament, came the announcement that the Atomic Energy Corporation CEO, Dr. Waldo Stumpf, "had never held a meeting with Iran's deputy minister of atomic affairs, Reza Amrollahi, as claimed by local and foreign news media."

There is no disputing that Reza Amrollahi had been in the country at the time in question and that the meeting took place, if only because the circumstances were verified—first by Stumpf himself (to me personally), and afterward by Pik Botha to Mungo Soggot, who, though a colleague, is somebody that I've never met. Curiously, that was followed by an admission in 2003, when Tehran told the IAEA that it had been trying to build an atom bomb for almost two decades. That alone should have vindicated the argument.

Unquestionably, both Botha and Stumpf must have been put under severe pressure by the South African authorities to recant. Why else would they have reacted the way they did?

It is worth noting that though this writer was vilified in Parliament, the issue was then allowed to rest. Not a word more was said about the matter. I've even been back to South Africa several times since, and though the authorities were aware of my presence, there was no reaction from the government during these subsequent visits.

For his part, Dr. Waldo Stumpf, highly regarded by his peers, had every opportunity to test my claims in court. He could have leveled defamation charges. He might have even sued Jane's Information Group in Britain for libel, and for good measure, *The Mail & Guardian*. Nor has he reacted to my most recent book on the Iranian nuclear program, *Iran's Nuclear Option* (published in the United States in 2005), where I repeated my account of those events. I certainly would have done something had I believed that my professional honor was at stake. Instead, nothing has been done, which is a pity because it would have given us all an opportunity to test the truth in the public eye.

There were several other nuclear-related matters that occurred at about the same time, which makes WMD-related issues in South Africa even more intriguing. Some involved Iran, and should have alerted Washington that there were devious things happening. Among others, these included:

- An attempt to export a zirconium tube factory from a South African Atomic Energy Corporation (AEC) establishment to China, with the possibility of it being redirected to Iran (*Jane's Pointer*, February 1, 1998).

Zirconium cladding is used for nuclear elements, and would be needed for Iran's nuclear effort at the Bushehr (or other, planned) reactors. The plant was prepared for dispatch from Pelindaba without necessary end-user certificates and other clarifications having been completed by the South African government. Western intelligence sources were aware at the time that China had been contracted to build such a factory for the Tehran government, and fears were expressed in Washington that the South African shipment might ultimately be diverted to the Near East (*NuclearFuel*, December 29, 1997).

- The disappearance of drums of fissile waste material from Pelindaba, which, despite a winding down of the country's nuclear weapons program, was still one of the most closely guarded establishments in Africa. Such things are serious, according to Dr. Ben Sanders of the Program for Promoting Nuclear Nonproliferation. He was aware of waste from discarded medical radiation sources stolen from a facility in Brazil in the early nineties. It was eventually found, dumped next to a slum, and some children playing there were contaminated.

- There have also been questions asked as to exactly how much weapons-grade uranium South Africa produced while the Pretoria regime was engaged in its atom bomb project. At issue is not so much whether the figures for the amount of highly enriched uranium provided by South Africa's Atomic Energy Corporation were accurate (all were subjected to lengthy audits by Vienna's IAEA), but rather, why Pretoria never allowed unrestricted access to official records for analysis.

Bearing in mind that during the 1970s and 1980s, South Africa was involved in producing six fission bombs in the 20 kiloton (KT) range, there have been other disturbing developments in post-apartheid South Africa.

One of these is the fact that Nelson Mandela's cabinet contained an inordinate number of Asians, almost all of them of Islamic orientation. This was strange, considering that the country's Asian population makes up perhaps 5 percent of the whole. By mid-1997, these included Dullah Omar (Justice and Intelligence Services), M. V. Moosa (Constitutional Development), Kadar Asmal (Water Affairs), and Aziz Pahad (deputy minister of Foreign Affairs), as well as his brother, Essop Pahad (who was deputy minister in the office of the president).

All these notables, closely bonded over years in opposing apartheid—either in jail or in exile—advocated strong ties with their friends in the Islamic world, Iran included. Most were (and still are, as we're constantly being reminded) demonstrably hostile toward the United States, Britain, and other Western interests. Not for nothing was the term "South Africa's Karachi Connection" coined, though arguably their links might have been stronger with Tripoli and Tehran (and, of course Havana,) than Islamabad.

The same holds with Mandela's successor, President Mbeki. Some of his closest advisors (not necessarily in the cabinet) are Islamic, and have included quite a few of the same people that served under Madiba: Dullah Omar, Aziz Pahad, and Kadar Asmal (who by now has gone on to become chairman of the National Conventional Arms Control Committee), as well as Abdul Minty, whose brief included responsibility for Pelindaba and other nuclear assets. With time, this clique moved on to positions that demonstrated powerful clout.

According to Washington sources, some of these people, as is their right, traveled extensively, as does Mbeki today. (His critics jibe that he spends more time abroad than at home.) Countries often visited by some of his ministers include Iran, the Sudan, Syria, Cuba, Libya, and, when Saddam Hussein was still around, Iraq. Minty is known to have kept ties to Iran's spiritual leader, Ali Khamenei, another reason why so many followers of this theocracy have been able to move into South Africa with such ease.

It says something that the sale of sensitive nuclear material intended for Tehran, using China as an intermediary (without first having followed the standard procedures prescribed by the Nuclear Suppliers Group), took place on Minty's watch, who, interestingly enough, has moved on to oversee South Africa's interests at the IAEA.

The shipment of a zirconium tube factory to China sometime during 1997 is a classic case study in an attempt at unconventional proliferation.

Zirconium is a grayish-white lustrous metal commonly used in an alloy form (i.e., zircalloy) to encase fuel rods in nuclear reactors, and here too there is a Tehran connection. With Iran striving for self-sufficiency in all aspects of its domestic nuclear program, it would ultimately be in need of zirconium tubes, great numbers of them. However, under restrictions imposed by the international NSG, Tehran is forbidden to acquire them from any supplier in the West.

There is an easy way to overcome this imbroglio. Tehran might have taken advantage of its close ties to Moscow and possibly bought such a plant from them. After all, the Russians have supplied most of Iran's nuclear needs and, indeed, with the Bushehr reactor, continue to do so. Instead, what emerged in 1997, the same year that Dr. Waldo Stumpf recanted on his original story, was strong evidence that the Iranian government—in complicity with Beijing—tried to secure a surplus zirconium tube factory in South Africa.

What we do know is that the packing up and dispatch of a disused zirconium plant at Pelindaba had progressed to the point where it was about to be shipped out of the country without mandatory end-user certificates when somebody blew the whistle. The publication *NuclearFuel* stated in its December 19, 1997, issue that Washington feared the plant might end up in Iran, since China had contracted with Tehran to build a zirconium plant at one of its nuclear facilities a short while before. The South African plant would have been an ideal stopgap.

The story emerged after a group of about forty Chinese technicians entered South Africa on "business" visas in August 1997. They spent months at Pelindaba getting the plant ready for shipment. It was already packed into reinforced cases when the tip came, though nobody is prepared to say on whose authority this was done. Only after details surfaced in a South African newspaper file did the police raid the place. They promptly arrested all these foreigners for what was termed on the charge sheets as "illegally working in the country." Business visas, the police said, did not permit aliens to work in South Africa, and certainly not a large number of mainland Chinese.

Then followed the first surprise: On ministerial authority, the Chinese contingent was released from custody, even though the Ministry of Home Affairs was explicit that the activity of the group had violated the terms of their stay. An observation made by a Western diplomat was that the Chinese had gained regular and routine access to an extremely high-security nuclear establishment. And though this went on for months, nobody questioned their presence. Another source claimed that the group put in ten- and twelve-hour shifts, six days a week. Somebody was in a hurry.

What also concerned those familiar with what was going on was that while the original contract for the sale was concluded between South Africa and China in the summer of 1997, almost nothing was made public about the deal. It hadn't even gone through Parliament, which is a prerequisite for state-owned enterprises. In fact, it only became newsworthy when the so-called "illegals" were arrested.

Had this event not caught the eye of an alert journalist, somebody in government told me, there might have been nothing to prevent the entire plant from leaving the country. And that would have taken place even though South Africa is a signatory to the Nuclear Suppliers Group. According to David Albright, the NSG provides clear dual-use guidelines for the export of such equipment.

"It would appear that these were not observed," Albright stated. This is pertinent because under South African government regulations, the Council for Nonproliferation of Weapons of Mass Destruction of the Department of Trade and Industry—an interdepartmental export-control body headed by the same Mr. Abdul Minty who now sits on the IAEA board of governors in Vienna—should have known what was going on. Pelindaba being a high-security government installation, of course they knew. Only nothing was said, and one must ask why this was allowed to happen, and on whose authority.

Also, such shipments require end-user certificates, classifying them as dual-use or nuclear-related equipment. The South African government has always been aware that such transfers cannot take place without official sanction.

At issue here, said *NuclearFuel*, was a plant that had been used until 1993 to make zirconium tubing for fuel loaded at the two Koeberg nuclear reactors just north of Cape Town. The sequence of events went something like this:

In early 1997, South Africa's Atomic Energy Commission requested tenders for the sale of the zirconium facility. Brokered in the Channel Islands by a firm calling itself Pacific Development Services, a deal was concluded with the China National Nonferrous Industry Corporation at Shaanzi in north-central China. The price, quoted by Dr. Stumpf, was $4.6 million.

Still more peculiar was that subsequent attempts by the media to make contact either with the broker or his company failed. This raises another matter: If the deal between the governments of China and South Africa was legitimate, why would anyone have involved an obscure middleman who is not only untraceable, but has yet to come forward to clarify some of the more sensitive issues? Clearly, something stinks.

Dr. Stumpf had said in a public statement afterwards, "We will get an end-user statement from China before the plant leaves South Africa."

The background to the zirconium plant is interesting. Originally it had been part of a nuclear fuel production complex for the Cape Town nuclear power plant at Koeberg and cost $42 million to build. Since final qualification of the plant for nuclear-grade zirconium alloy cladding was achieved in 1988, it had produced 75,000 tubes for the Cape's reactors. The plant was shut down in 1993 after international sanctions against South Africa were lifted and cheaper tubes became available from France.

The AEC has since stated that it had tried to convert the zirconium factory to non-nuclear use, but failed because of "the very specialized nature of the installation."

According to a statement issued at the time by the South African Ministry of Foreign Affairs, "There are three pieces of equipment in the zirconium plant which require official authorization under the Nuclear Suppliers Group dual-use guidelines." Stumpf described these as CNC machine tools used to make complex molds.

Washington's comments on the subject included a statement that, independent of a pledge provided by China to cease nuclear trade with Iran (in exchange for nonproliferation certification by the Americans), it was not impossible that Beijing could still go through with the export to Tehran.

Questioned about the Iranian link, Stumpf said that the sale to China was limited only to equipment in the plant. "China won't get any transfer of technology," he added.

The Iranian connection with South Africa did not end there. Following the appearance of an article about the sale of the tube factory in *Pointer*, another Jane's publication ("Is Iran in RSA-China Zirconium Deal?"), Mr. Abdul Minty wrote a letter of protest to the Jane's Information Group in Britain. Dated March 9, 1998, the letter states: ". . . the article is filled with half truths and innuendo and the author's 'investigation' uses as a basis another inaccurate report appearing in *NuclearFuel*" (published in Washington, D.C., January 12, 1998). Minty also says that South African relations with the United States in regard to nuclear matters are exemplary.

The thrust of the article is inaccurate, he goes on. "It indicates, incorrectly, that the whole contract was done under cover of darkness and even with the hope that the zirconium tube plant could leave [the country] without anyone knowing that South Africa had not complied with all the requirements of the Nuclear Suppliers Group [NSG]."

That is "clearly not part of this government's policy nor style," Abdul Minty declared.

So what are the facts?

- Details of the contract came to light after police, acting on a tip-off, raided Pelindaba because the Chinese group involved had originally entered South Africa on business visas. On prima facie evidence, they had no right to be in the country for any other purpose, never mind have access to and work in a nuclear-sensitive installation.

- As a result of that action, a journalist with the *Independent* newspaper group broke the story.

- The application to export the equipment on the Nuclear Suppliers Group dual-use equipment list was made five days *after* the paper first reported the account of the planned sale to China. This was confirmed in a letter from Stumpf, to the editor of *NuclearFuel*, dated January 13, 1998.

- According to a subsequent report in *NuclearFuel* (March 9, 1998), only after the story appeared in the press was it disclosed that the Chinese had been working at Pelindaba. This, too, was in Stumpf's letter.

- Following these developments, according to *NuclearFuel*, "Western officials and experts raised concern that South Africa's export control regime was not functioning smoothly."

There were more conflicting exchanges, this time among South African officials involved in the fracas. Reliable sources in Washington indicate that there may have been serious differences between Stumpf and Minty, but not enough to have had Stumpf removed from office (though he has subsequently been replaced).

On March 4, 1998, Minty challenged Stumpf's account. He explained to Mark Hibbs, author of the original article in *NuclearFuel*, that following press reports, he had personally investigated the matter, and "determined that the AEC application had not been submitted to the Secretariat of the export control revue body last December" (as Stumpf said it had). Instead, said Minty, "it was delivered by hand courier on January 5 of this year."

Minty also confirmed that visas issued to the Chinese were perfectly in order. "They had been processed by the Department of Home Affairs and were valid." In his letter to *Jane's Intelligence Review*, Minty rejected the concept that there had been some unease in Washington about what was going on at Pelindaba.

Commenting, *NuclearFuel* stated in a report (March 9, 1998) that "when press reports of a planned export to China were aired, officials at the Department of State said that America would raise the issue with South Africa, in part, because China [in an apparently separate transaction] had agreed to export a zirconium tube plant to Iran, a country that Washington believes aims to develop a nuclear weapons capability."

The publication also stated that two U.S. nonproliferation officials had observed that, in their view, the record of the export-permitting process in South Africa indicated that procedural mistakes had likely been made.

Another issue involving Armscor was highlighted by *NuclearFuel* at about the same time. The magazine observed that Armscor, the organization that had previously been responsible for South Africa's clandestine nuclear weapons program, appears to be involved in an ongoing political battle with South Africa's black leadership. *NuclearFuel* stated that "the firm's role in nuclear arms control matters has been blunted." For his part, Minty denied all of it: "It is simply not true that there is any friction with Armscor," he commented.

But Minty's following statement (according to Mark Hibbs, author of the original article) spelled out a more damning scenario. He stated very clearly that Armscor played almost no role in the nuclear export control process, even though Armscor personnel (of all people in a country where such expertise is limited) would under normal circumstances have been the best equipped to do so. After all, it was they who originally built South Africa's arsenal of atom bombs, Hibbs suggested.

In addition, with regard to the exclusion of Armscor from NPC's subordinate Control Committee, the document declared: "Armscor has no direct role whatever in matters related to nuclear issues other than its collective role as a member of the NPC, where its primary task is to provide an input in dual-use technologies and equipment which form part of conventional weapons systems."

Not for nothing did some South African press reports question the possibility of the existence of what was termed "a hidden agenda."

CHAPTER 13

NORTH KOREA, PAKISTAN, AND THE REST

> Neither Stalin nor Mao Tse-tung nor Adolf Hitler came
> close to George Orwell's blueprint for a hierarchical world
> tyranny. The gold medalist in Orwell's *1984* Hades-on-
> Earth sweepstakes, beyond Stalin's wildest excesses, is
> diminutive Kim Jong-il, whose Mao suits, elevator shoes,
> and Elvis-style bouffant hair only enhance his wicked
> gnome-like figure.
> —"Korea's Dr. Strangelove," Arnaud de Borchgrave, *The Washington Times*,
> October 20, 2006

Though some of the smaller countries that make up the nine-member "nuclear weapons club" are not Islamic, it is instructive to see how they went about acquiring the bomb. Apart from China, North Korea is the only other Asian state in this exclusive little community with nuclear weapons capability.

North Korea

Arnaud de Borchgrave goes on to tell us that back in 1983, Kim Il-sung—a man picked personally by Stalin after World War II to rule the new Soviet puppet state, the Democratic People's Republic of Korea—assigned his son, Kim Jong-il, to organize the liquidation of the South Korean government. As we have seen, that was a disaster. South Korea has prospered like few other countries, even in the West.

All the while, the dictatorial father-and-son team dabbled in weapons of mass destruction. Nuclear weapons apart, North Korea is believed to have substantial chemical and biological weapons research facilities, and herein lies an interesting little vignette.

Dr. Margaret Isaacson, an international authority and advisor to the World Health Organization on tropical medicines, and also a good family friend with whom my wife and I traveled occasionally before she passed on, gave us a bit of news of her own following her return to South Africa from the Congo in the late 1990s.

North of Kamina, toward the Congo's southwestern border with Angola, there had been an outbreak of Ebola, or what the medical world calls "Ebola hemorrhagic fever," one of the most virulent viral diseases known to humankind. Ebola can cause death in 90 percent of those it infects. Like Marburg hemorrhagic fever, there's an international red alert when there is Ebola about, and the World Health Organization goes into overdrive.

What was unusual about this outbreak, she told us—Margaret was charged with bringing back to Johannesburg some of the blood samples for further research—was that she encountered a two-man North Korean medical team at one of the infected villages. They had arrived in the country a few days before and, her Congolese escort told her, had made a beeline for the area where they too were taking samples. When she questioned one of the North Koreans about the purpose of his visit, after she'd heard him talking to somebody else in fluent English, he backed off, claiming that he spoke only Korean.

Interesting, said Dr. Isaacson, who'd spent enough years in Israeli medical establishments to understand the significance of the North Korean scouting trip. As she tartly commented, "They certainly weren't there on a vacation." According to Dr. Isaacson, it wasn't impossible that the North Koreans were taking samples of Ebola for use as a weapon later.

There are many people who are interested in what is going on north of Korea's 38th parallel. Among them is Arnaud de Borchgrave, one of the best informed observers of the international scene. His reporting is accentuated by the kind of incisive, cynical outlook that tends to cut to the chase if he suspects duplicity. Pyongyang has been a favorite for a very long time. As he says, for the four years between 1994 and 1998, between two and three million North Koreans died of starvation and hunger-related illnesses.

"Those caught attempting to escape across the Yalu River into China were executed at first and later confined to a Korean gulag for reeducation," said de Borchgrave. He added that South Korea's "sunshine policy" of aid and limited investment clearly failed to prevent or, for that matter, even slow, Pyongyang's nuclear weapons and missile delivery effort. Now this has culminated in a nuclear test, and in a country that can neither support nor feed its citizens.

There has been a good deal of controversy as to why North Korea has taken the nuclear road it did. Grandstanding was obviously a part of it. So was being totally overshadowed economically by its southern namesake neighbor.

One source maintains that a successful American program of nuclear psychological warfare against the Democratic People's Republic of Korea (DPRK) during the Korean War years (1950–1953) probably kindled its interest in the first place. Regardless, in 1964 North Korea established the Yongbyon Nuclear Research Center, some sixty miles north of Pyongyang. It would become the cradle of its nuclear activities, "peaceful" as well as otherwise.

The next step was procuring a small (800kW-4MWt) HEU-fueled IRT-2M research reactor, as well as a 0.1MWt critical assembly, from the Soviet Union the following year. The ITR reactor went critical in 1967. Its weapons intentions, probably never in doubt, came with an unconfirmed report that suggested DPRK nuclear scientists had been present at China's first nuclear test in October 1964. Eleven years later North Korea was separating small quantities of plutonium from Soviet-supplied irradiated fuel. They used "hot cells" at a radiochemical laboratory built at Pyongyang with Soviet assistance.

Its next—and most notable—weapons pointer occurred in 1980 when Pyongyang started construction on a 5MW MAGNOX experimental power reactor at Yongbyon, this time without foreign assistance (though Charles Vick, a senior fellow at GlobalSecurity.org suggests that the reactor might be termed 5MWt [thermal] instead of 5MWe [electrical], conceding too that one can probably argue both ways).

The uranium and graphite required for this endeavor was mined and purified indigenously. Though locally built, it was certainly based on foreign designs, such as the British Calder Hall MAGNOX reactor, a Canadian heavy-water research reactor, as well as the French G1 power/plutonium production reactor. The facility went online in January 1986, and started operating at full power in October 1987. It is capable of producing approximately 15 pounds of weapons-grade plutonium a year.

Meanwhile, despite huge internal problems that included failed harvests and starvation on an almost biblical scale, the DPRK continued to cooperate with other like-minded countries, such as Romania and East Germany (before unification), as well as Czechoslovakia and Cuba. Technology, expertise, equipment, material, and training from advanced countries, such as the then Federal Republic of Germany, Japan, France, the then Soviet Union, and the People's Republic of China, were readily accepted, and it is interesting that the country did not discriminate between potential nuclear beneficiaries, whether they were ideologically friendly or hostile. Through it all, though, two countries stand out above all others in the rush to acquire a nuclear capability: Pakistan and Iran.

Pakistan reportedly forged nuclear (and missile) contacts with North Korea between 1985 and 1988. An agreement that was said to have been signed in January 1989 with Tehran may have covered nuclear development as well as the development of nuclear warheads for missiles. One particular area of activity pertaining to this agreement appears to have been the development of plutonium-fueled warheads, using clandestinely acquired Chinese technology and subsystems.

In 1989, the 5MW reactor was shut down for several months, followed by "low power runs" in 1990 and 1991. It is not impossible that the North Koreans might have used the breaks to unload fuel, allowing Pyongyang to amass between 15 and 30 pounds of plutonium. That was followed by the completion, in 1992, of North Korea's first, rudimentary, implosion device. When the reactor was shut down for refueling in April 1994, it was estimated that the 8,000 spent fuel rods might have contained as much as 70 pounds of weapons-grade ^{239}Pu.

Analysis of DPRK-separated plutonium by the IAEA in 1992 indicated that indeed, reprocessing had taken place four times during the preceding three years, and as was expected, the revelation caused a furor. North Korea threatened to withdraw from the NPT, not that it made much difference whether it was a member or not anyway.

Washington "saved" the day with the so-called "Agreed Framework," signed on October 12, 1994. The DPRK undertook to freeze its plutonium production program and to eventually dismantle its existing nuclear facilities, in exchange for fuel oil, economic cooperation, and the construction of two modern light-water nuclear power plants. The West was certainly taken for a ride on that one, because it had little effect on North Korea's ultimate goal.

Enter Pakistan—or more accurately, the nuclear proliferator A.Q. Khan. Pakistan's lack of funds—coupled with a desire for missile technology that fringed on desperation in the face of what was regarded as an aggressive India—was the motive.

From 1994 onwards, North Korea received large numbers of P-1 and P-2 centrifuges. Also passed on were drawings, sketches, technical data, and even depleted uranium hexafluoride gas, courtesy of the A.Q. Khan "network." In turn Pakistan got the No-Dong-A missiles it sought, and thus was born the Ghauri-II missile, as it was rebranded.

Although Khan later publicly "confessed" his nuclear transgressions (once again providing no details)—for which he was pardoned by President Musharraf—it is almost impossible that such transfers could have taken place without the knowledge of the Pakistani government. Flights between Islamabad and Pyongyang were taking place at almost weekly intervals, many of them involving Pakistani Air Force C-130s, with huge amounts of stuff moving in both directions. This begs the question: Did China know of these transfers, through its airspace and all? If so, this would clearly imply a degree of complicity on its part.

The scale of North Korea's uranium-enrichment program is not generally appreciated. Washington has identified at least three sites where suspected enrichment tests were conducted. These are the Academy of Sciences near Pyongyang, together with sites in the Hagap region and Yehong-dong.

In November 2002 North Korea restarted its 5MW reactor and resumed reprocessing plutonium, for what were termed "peaceful nuclear activities."

During a visit of an American delegation to the DPRK in January 2004, a government spokesman told the group that all 8,000 spent fuel rods in the Radiochemical Laboratory at the facility at Yongbyon had been reprocessed. Also disclosed was the fact that it had been achieved in a single continuous process: it was begun mid-January 2003 and completed five months later, no small achievement.

North Korea finally carried out its first nuclear test on October 9, 2006, in the general vicinity of the Chik-tong, P'unggye-yok, site in the north of the country. The core of the bomb was plutonium, and the yield somewhere around 550 tons of TNT. This is in contrast to the 4 KT–range test yield it reportedly informed the PRC about just before the event.

Initially, the low yield led to speculation that the test was a fizzle, or, alternatively, a fission primary for a thermonuclear device—something in which Pakistan would certainly be interested. Again, Charles Vick of GlobalSecurity.org comes to the rescue, estimating that between 12 and 13 pounds of plutonium would be required by the North Koreans per nuclear device, and that half a kiloton to a 4 KT yield might have been achieved with as little as between 5 and 7 pounds. Makes good sense . . .

Pakistan

It was a succession of wars with India—four in all, so far—that caused Pakistan to go nuclear.

Of them all, the most serious was the conflict in December 1971, when New Delhi's forces intervened in what was then known as East Pakistan, today an independent Bangladesh. After a defeat that was described as "crushing" by the media, Pakistan's military leadership retreated from the political battlefield and civilian rule was reestablished. The new leader, and president, was Zulfikar Ali Bhutto, the acknowledged father of Pakistan's atom bomb.

The formal decision to proceed with its construction was taken in January 1972 during a meeting called by Bhutto and held in Multan, in the Punjab. It was a historic event, with some of the scientists invited traveling from Europe and America to attend. From it would emerge two of the three men who would play a crucial role in the country's nuclear weapons project: Munir Ahmad Khan, the recently appointed chairman of the Pakistan Atomic Energy Commission (PAEC)—and no relative of Abdul Qadeer—and S. A. Butt, the man who would head up Pakistan's worldwide purchasing network, much of it covert. For funds, Saudi Arabia and Libya stepped up to the plate.

Pakistan's first attempts were to follow the plutonium route. It contracted a French firm in 1974 to design and act as the principal engineering contractor for the construction of a reprocessing plant at Chasma. Named the Kundian Nuclear Complex (KNC-2), the facility became of interest to Washington, who pressured France to abandon the contract. As with most lucrative export orders, the Elysée Palace responded warily, and it took the French three years to halt supplies of components. More pressure followed, and the French terminated the project the following year.

China came to Pakistan's rescue, in part because of close ties that had meanwhile been fostered between Moscow and New Delhi.

Since the relatively easy route to the bomb had been denied Pakistan, the alternative that remained was uranium isotope separation—which was where Dr. Abdul Qadeer Khan emerged. An expatriate Pakistani and a European-trained metallurgist, Khan had been working for the Physical Dynamics Research Laboratory (FDO) in Amsterdam since 1972. He'd managed to gain access to highly classified ultracentrifuge uranium-enrichment technology pertaining to the URENCO enrichment plant at Almelo, Holland, and told his government so.

By late 1975, Dr. Khan apparently had all that he required to duplicate the technology he'd been accessing, and returned home in December. Commented one contemporary historian: If Zulfikar Ali Bhutto was the father of the Pakistani A-bomb, then A.Q. Khan was its midwife.

A crash program to construct an enrichment plant followed, at a location that would become synonymous with Pakistan's nuclear weapon efforts, namely Kahuta, a tiny village near Islamabad. This is where Khan established his Engineering Research Laboratory—to be renamed the A.Q. Khan Research Laboratories (or KRL) in 1981. In the meantime, Butt's purchasing organization was at work getting many of the components for the undertaking. Pakistan's uranium-enrichment initiative entered the record books as Project 706 and was made autonomous from the Pakistan Atomic Energy Commission in 1976.

A crucial stage of the project was passed in June 1978, when the principle was successfully tested for the first time. An entire plant for converting uranium into uranium hexafluoride feedstock for Kahuta had been smuggled into Pakistan from China between the years 1977 and 1980, where it was assembled and put into operation at Dera Ghazi Khan. Matters were eased by the fact that the country mines its own uranium, at Baghalchar (Dera Ghazi Khan), and afterwards at Qabul Khel, which together produce more than enough ore to supply all of Kahuta's needs.

The plant entered its full-functioning phase in the early 1980s, with China reportedly supplying expertise and also hexafluoride feedstock. In February 1984, A.Q. Khan stated that Kahuta had produced its first enriched uranium.

Reports of a second enrichment facility emerged in Washington. This was finally pinpointed in the mid-1990s, first at Golra Sharif, and later at Wah (at the so-called Gadwal facilities). Actual confirmation remained elusive.

Besides uranium enrichment, Pakistan never abandoned its plutonium efforts. Consequently, it wasn't surprising that work began in the mid-1980s on a 40–70MWt unsafeguarded research reactor, once more with Chinese help. This reactor was completed at Khushab, and its two principal stages commissioned in March 1996 and April 1998. Khushab is apparently able to generate sufficient fissile material for a couple of bombs a year. Notably, the "New Labs" reprocessing facility at the Pakistan Institute of Nuclear Science and Technology (PINSTECH) had already been "hot-tested" in the late 1980s. Unsafeguarded heavy-water production falls under Multan, Karachi, and to a lesser extent, Khushab.

A tritium purification and storage plant, which was first test-operated in 1987, is located at a heavily guarded paramilitary site about 100 miles south of Rawalpindi.

Work on developing the Pakistani nuclear arsenal started shortly after the Indian nuclear test of 1974.

A team headed up by Hafeez Qureshi of PINSTECH and Dr. Zaman Sheikh of the Defense Science & Technology Organization (DESTO) was charged with the work at Wah, where a secondary enrichment plant is reportedly sited. The team subsequently became known as "The Wah Group," with work imaginatively code-named "Research."

An important juncture in Pakistan's quest toward the bomb was reached on March 11, 1983, when the first cold test of a nuclear device was conducted in the Kirana Hills near Sargodha. Khan Research Laboratories (KRL) would independently cold-test a nuclear device near Kahuta a year later, incorporating a design that appears to have been of KRL's own making.

The year 1983 proved momentous in other directions. Pakistan was at the receiving end of a proven warhead design from Beijing, from which, ultimately, its own design(s) would emerge. Originally tested in the People's Republic of China in October 1966 (its fourth nuclear detonation), with an almost 3,000-pound warhead containing an HEU implosion-assembly core, the bomb yielded an explosion in the order of 12+ KT. Its upper yield is believed to be 25 KT.

Perhaps more salient, China that year also supplied Pakistan with enriched uranium sufficient to construct two bombs.

After a successful hydrodynamic test in mid-1985, it was logical that weaponization would follow. Fabrication and testing of key non-nuclear weapons components—and reportedly also weapons assembly—was assigned to the Pakistani Ordnance Factories at Wah. Fabrication of enriched-uranium hemispheres went to the KRL/Kahuta enrichment plant, though there are some who believe this would also have been accomplished at PINSTECH.

The first Pakistani (and probably also Indian) nuclear alert and near-arming was arguably caused by Operation Brass Tacks, a series of large-scale Indian military exercises which took place near the border with Pakistan beginning in late 1986. Pakistan had cold-tested a nuclear device in Chagai (in Baluchistan province) a month or two before, and had reportedly produced sufficient enriched uranium to build at least one device, which is probably something that New Delhi got wind of.

The Indians had little to fear. At that stage, anything produced by Pakistan had still not been missile-configured. In fact, for some years the accepted wisdom was that if it came to actual war, the "devices" would have to be delivered to target by Pakistani Air Force Hercules C-130s and pushed out the back. It would be dropped by parachute to give the plane time to put distance between itself and the anticipated blast. Only one Pakistani C-130 had supposedly been configured for this purpose.

Due to ongoing tension between Pakistan and India, 1987 was also the year that Pakistan reportedly switched from R&D to bomb production, at the very least, of the non-nuclear components. Reports reached Washington not long afterwards that the Pakistani atom bomb weighed a mere 400 pounds, which was a considerable achievement for a country with little previous nuclear experience. The push for perfection went on.

When violence again flared in Kashmir, in late 1989, there was some concern in Europe and America that clashes could result in a nuclear conflict between Pakistan and India.

In two months, starting in May 1990, Pakistan finally "crossed the line" by machining cores for seven 20KT bombs. Regardless of their weapons' reported Chinese ancestry, it was Pakistani scientists, working largely by themselves, that by mid-1996 had achieved results with a new series of boosted weapons. A missile warhead followed in short order.

Although it is now common knowledge that Pakistan responded to India's nuclear tests with six of its own—starting on May 28, 1988 at Ras Koh Hills in Chagai—it has never been able to counter India's thermonuclear challenge, though there are those who say that Islamabad might be on the brink of getting there.

Considering that Saudi Arabia had offered Pakistan $800 million for assistance to produce a thermonuclear bomb in 1988, and given Pakistan's nuclear and missile interaction with North Korea (ties forged between 1985 and 1988)—as well as the joint nuclear-weapons development agreement it had brokered with Iran in 1991—there is some evidence that far from being the "fizzle" that some observers claimed the North Korean 2006 nuclear test was, it could just as feasibly have been a test of a fission-primary for a thermonuclear weapon. This might have been carried out by the Democratic People's Republic of Korea (DPRK) on its own behalf, as well as in the interests of Pakistan and Iran.

It gets worse. John Pike of GlobalSecurity.org is of the opinion that the last Pakistani nuclear test in May 1998, which was held in great secrecy at Kharan, might have been that of a North Korean plutonium-fueled device. His argument runs along the lines that the Pakistani nuclear tests at Chagai took place to the acclaim of a large number of people. Pike contends that the blanket ban at Kharan was necessary because it was a North Korean bomb.

Pike's associate, Charles Vick, notes that information supplied by North Korean defectors confirmed that one or more nuclear plutonium fuel transfers took place from their peninsula to Pakistan. Whether it was intended for use as a weapons fuel contribution or as a weapon remains uncertain. He remains tantalizing when he notes that a test by Pakistan of a North Korean nuclear weapon seems plausible based on fuel evidence acquired by American Air Force Technical Applications Center air-sample analysis.

The supposition makes sense: Why so much publicity with one test and a total blackout on the other?

Brazil

By some accounts, Brazil today might arguably be just as focused as Iran in developing an advanced and sophisticated nuclear program. While there is no evidence that the largest of the South American countries might be trying to build the bomb, there are some who maintain that this is exactly what is taking place. As someone else was heard to comment, the only reason why nobody is getting into a tizz about Brazil's nuclear intentions is because its leaders don't wish to remove the State of Israel off the face of the map. The same argument applies to Japan.

The Federation of American Scientists (FAS) has its own views on the issue. Brazil, it says, began decades ago to pursue a covert nuclear weapons program in response to something similar taking place in Argentina, since discontinued. It might be recalled that Argentina in those days was ruled by a brutal military junta.

For its part, Brazil initially developed a relatively modest nuclear power program together with enrichment facilities (including a large ultracentrifuge enrichment plant and several laboratory-scale facilities). There was also a limited reprocessing capability, a guided missile program, and a uranium mining and processing industry, as well as fuel fabrication facilities. This was done principally to counter nuclear advances in Argentina: the two states were at loggerheads for more than a century and have only recently patched up their differences.

For its much-discussed nuclear weapons program, says the FAS on its Web site (www.fas.org): "Brazil was supplied with nuclear materials and equipment by West Germany [which offered reactors, enrichment, and reprocessing facilities], France, and the U.S." Its strength, adds the Federation, is that Brazil has a dependable raw material base for developing atomic power engineering. It also boasts a highly skilled scientific community, with "cadres who have been trained, as well as relative technologies for enriching uranium." Most important, there are several nuclear research centers.

The crux is that Brazil's nuclear capabilities are now the most advanced in South and Central America.

West Germany's involvement in the Brazilian nuclear project is interesting, if only because Bonn did not require IAEA safeguards.

John Pike of GlobalSecurity.org tells us that following a 1975 agreement, Brazil transferred technology from its power plant projects to a secret program to develop an atom bomb. Code-named Solimões, after a river in the Amazon, this clandestine project was started in 1975 and eventually came to be known publicly as the Parallel Program.

A decade later, President José Sarney announced that his country had enriched uranium successfully on a laboratory scale up to 20 percent. Already at that stage, says Pike, some observers predicted that Brazil would have nuclear-weapons capability by the turn of the century. Officially, the entire program was abandoned a few years later with his successor, President Collor de Mello, symbolically closing a nuclear test site at Cachimbo, in Pará State. That October, de Mello formally exposed the military's secret plan to develop an atom bomb.

Subsequent disclosures showed that the IAEv had designed two atomic devices, one with a yield of 20 to 30 kilotons, and a second with a yield of about 12 kilotons. It was also revealed that Brazil's military regime secretly exported eight tons of uranium to Iraq in 1981.

Brazil first successfully enriched uranium in late 1986, which led to the construction of a pilot-scale gas centrifuge facility at the Aramar Research Center, in Ipero, near Sao Paulo. In this regard, many observers still believe that the Aramar centrifuges were initially based on a Urenco design, which Brazil is alleged to have obtained clandestinely with the help of several German scientists, including Bruno Stemmler and Karl-Heinz Schaab. Both men were later fingered as having assisted Saddam Hussein with his uranium-enrichment centrifuge program.

Schaab worked for many years as a specialist at MAN New Technology in Munich, a major contract company that developed components for the gas-ultracentrifuge. The same separation technology can be applied to the enrichment of weapons-grade uranium, which was why European governments had so strictly categorized it. Schaab's aptitude, as it appeared in court documents, was ultra-specific, "focused on the core of the centrifuge, the so-called rotor."

This man seemed to have little compunction in handing over years of complex and secret European research to his newfound friends abroad. Up to that point, he had already cost the Munich company millions of dollars. At his trial, after returning voluntarily to Germany from Brazil, where he had fled, Schaab admitted that he sold classified MAN blueprints of a subcritical centrifuge to the Iraqis for $40,000. Thirty-six carbon fiber rotors, equipment, and technical assistance for about a million dollars followed soon afterwards.

Brazil is believed to have improved the centrifuge design passed on by Schaab, substituting stronger carbon fiber for special maraging steel to manufacture the units' high-speed rotors and developing a unique, electromagnetic bottom bearing.

Noteworthy is Alfred Hempel, another German who was involved in clandestine nuclear activities at about the same time. Hempel supplied nuclear items to many countries, including Pakistan, India, and South Africa, before he died in 1989. He was instrumental in selling hundreds of tons of heavy water, an item used in natural uranium-driven reactors as a moderator for regulating neutron-flow, thus gaining plutonium directly from the natural uranium without the difficult process of enrichment. Correspondence found in subsequent investigations revealed that Hempel declared his heavy-water shipments as "Coca Cola."

Hempel's ties to Brazil have a significant link to one of the cogs of the A.Q. Khan nuclear smuggling empire. Following a session of intrusive sleuthing, a London *Times* correspondent uncovered the German's links to Pakistan's Pakland Corporation, a family import-export business owned by the Humayun Khan family (who was subsequently linked to the Israeli traitor Asher Karni in Cape Town).

In fact, Hempel had been a purchasing agent for them as far back as 1975. At the time, Pakland was negotiating at least one deal for suspected nuclear weapons material with Hempel. The consensus in Washington and London today is that this former Nazi and central figure in the then already-burgeoning global nuclear bazaar did as much to spread nuclear weapons in his day as did Abdul Qadeer Khan.

And perhaps a good deal more, said Gary Milhollin, founder of the Washington-based Wisconsin Project on Nuclear Arms Control. During the 1970s and '80s, Hempel used cargo planes, bribes, and a secret network of operatives to supply countries in South Asia, Africa (including South Africa's apartheid regime), South America, and the Middle East with nuclear weapons materials. Like A.Q. Khan, Hempel made millions. Despite years of scrutiny by nuclear proliferation watchdogs, he escaped detection and died in his own bed.

The gas centrifuges operating at Resende are believed to be based upon the improved Aramar designs. However, Brazil has refused to allow outsiders to see the units. The argument proferred is that they are based on proprietary technology, including the new electromagnetic bearing. In particular, Brazil insisted that the centrifuges be shrouded when the IAEA inspects the Resende facility; the UN agency acquiesced in this restriction after determining that it can adequately monitor the installation by tracking flows in and out of the centrifuges, without observing the units directly. Some analysts believe that the true reason behind Brazil's refusal to show the centrifuges is that this would reveal them to be based on the improperly obtained German design.

Another similarity between the Brazilian and Iranian nuclear programs has been that both countries have refused to ratify an amendment to their respective inspection agreements with the agency, known as the "Additional Protocol," which would grant the IAEA expanded inspection rights. Although Brazil, these days, is not suspected of harboring nuclear weapon ambitions, it, too, has refused to accept an Additional Protocol amendment to its inspection agreement with the IAEA. The reasons for Brazil's reluctance are not clear.

In 2004, Brazilian officials were reported to have complained that the inspection arrangements under the Additional Protocol were "too rigid," that they unnecessarily applied to research institutes and universities, and that they might facilitate "technological piracy."

In September 2005, the head of the Brazilian National Nuclear Energy Commission, Odair Gonçalves, stated, without explanation, that Brazil had delayed its decision and was studying the matter. He rejected the suggestion that Brazil feared having to disclose details about its nuclear history prior to joining the NPT in 1994.

Taiwan

The East Asian country of Taiwan that was founded as an offshoot of mainland China by the legendary Chiang Kai-shek, following the rise to power of Mao Zedong, began its nuclear weapons program after the 1964 Chinese nuclear test.

Yana Feldman and Jack Boureston of FirstWatch International (FWI) inform us that Taiwan's Defense Ministry proposed what became known as the "Hsin Chu Program," a $140 million project drafted by the military's Chungshan Institute of Science and Technology, and aimed at developing nuclear weapons.

The Hsin Chu Program, they explained, would consist of a heavy-water reactor, a heavy-water production plant, a reprocessing research laboratory, and a future plutonium separation plant, all to be supplied by what was then still a West German firm, Siemens.

Boureston and Feldman have issued the following comments, recorded by SIPRI, the Stockholm International Peace Research Institute:

Ta-You Wu, President Chiang Kai-shek's science adviser, was asked by the President to review the proposal. According to his report, which was made public in 1988, Wu argued vigorously against the development of nuclear weapons, charging that they would run "counter to Taiwan's national security interests." Wu made several recommendations to the President that were adopted, including the establishment of a civilian nuclear energy committee to oversee the development of the nuclear program [Taiwan's Atomic Energy Council]. This significantly narrowed the influence of the military. Wu also advocated a more open and realistic approach to nuclear development, such as the acquisition of a safeguarded nuclear reactor and importation of heavy water legally.

Although Chiang Kai-shek in principle supported Wu's arguments against pursuing a nuclear weapons option, internal debate ensued over whether to proceed with buying a heavy-water reactor [that could facilitate development of a weapon] or to pursue a more open nuclear program and buy a light-water reactor [more proliferation-resistant].

The debate continued until 1969 when, in a compromise, Taiwan's Power Company bought light-water reactors and the newly created Institute for Nuclear Energy Research purchased a 40MW thermal, natural-uranium, heavy-water research reactor from Canada (TRR), the same model supplied to India, which it used to produce plutonium for its first nuclear explosion in 1974.

Through the early and mid-1970s, Taiwan proceeded to build or purchase a fuel production plant, two reprocessing facilities, and a plutonium chemistry laboratory, raising concerns about and contributing to ambiguity surrounding its reprocessing capability that still persist today.

QUESTIONING THE ROLE OF THE INTERNATIONAL ATOMIC ENERGY AGENCY

Proliferation Security Initiative makes intelligence actionable.

—John Negroponte, director of National Intelligence

The incident barely made news, except that it had far-reaching consequences for the international community.

On December 10, 2002, acting on a tip from an American intelligence source, a Spanish warship on patrol in the Indian Ocean as part of the U.S.-led war in Afghanistan, stopped the *So San*, a North Korean cargo ship en route to Yemen. In the ship's hold, carefully secreted amid 40,000 bags of cement, inspectors found fifteen Scud missiles armed with conventional warheads. Though dangerous, the cargo was not illegal, and Spain lacked the legal authority to seize the weapons. The following day the Spanish allowed the ship to continue its voyage.

What also emerged a little later was that the Spanish navy barely had the authority to stop the ship in the first place: Under international maritime law, a ship on the high seas may only be searched if it is without nationality, or if it is stopped by the nation with which it is registered. Spanish officials were only able to board the *So San* because the vessel had numerous problems with its registration and other paperwork.

This incident is among several others which highlight an international security situation that should be under control, but isn't. It was also among several factors that prompted a frustrated Bush administration to launch the Proliferation Security Initiative (PSI) the following year. Essentially, PSI is an effort aimed at attempting to stop the spread of weapons of mass destruction (WMD) and related materials. By some accounts, and in spite of a lot of criticism, it is arguably the best of several systems that have been considered, especially since the PSI has been likened by some countries to an invasion of privacy.

What is interesting here is that the countries that have been the most vocal about its implementation are those with the most to lose from the PSI's sometimes spontaneous and often unheralded searches. The majority, almost to a nation, are Third World, and among them, curiously, is China.

The system has had some success. Though most of its activities are restricted, its officers have admitted (off the record, naturally) that there have been "more than twenty" such interdictions, the most noteworthy being the seizure of the German tramp steamer *BBC China* on its way to Libya. That incident, which laid bare Gadhafi's clandestine efforts to acquire an atom bomb, is discussed in chapter 3.

There were originally ten mostly Western states that joined the United States in creating PSI in 2003. The concept, its founders said, was to shape and promote the initiative. They were Australia, France, Germany, Italy, Japan, the Netherlands, Poland, Portugal, Spain, and the United Kingdom. Since then, the tally has doubled and now includes, among others, Turkey, Canada, Norway, Russia, and Singapore, together with sixty more that have voiced support. What is notable is that PSI participants have tended to downplay the concept of membership, explaining in a press statement that PSI is "an activity, not an organization."

Nor are these restricted to water. Should intelligence arrive about the movement of a shipment of an illegal nuclear substance across borders, PSI-participating states would do something about it—and therein lies the rub. The International Atomic Energy Agency (IAEA) maintains that nuclear matters fall within its domain and nobody else's. America and its friends argue otherwise, for no better reason than the IAEA has lost the trust of the majority of the countries that matter. Years of procrastination, prevarication, hand-wringing, and sometimes infuriating inactivity in the face of what can best be described as the kind of blatant in-your-face proliferation that has hallmarked Iran's nuclear program is only half the story. The other is the inability of the United Nations to vote on issues of critical international interest.

When last was there a unanimous and unambiguous censure of Iran's nuclear program? More to the point, the action taken against North Korea is regarded in most informed circles as little more than a wrist slap. Make no mistake; there are countries with similar agendas that are watching. Quite a few—including Iran, Syria, Saudi Arabia, Brazil, Taiwan, and Japan—have noted the inability of the world body to take determined action against real or potential nuclear proliferators. The matter is further compounded by the fact that the IAEA is a prominent and well-established United Nations body. The lead against transgressors should come from Vienna. But it does not. The suggested course of action is invariably something about getting around the table again and talking some more. And some more . . .

The few times that the UN has censured a country, as it did with Iraq under Saddam Hussein (with the formation of UNSCOM, the United Nations Special Commission [in Iraq]), things have moved ahead. But then again, only in fits and starts. More significant, the IAEA's role in Iran has been what some British commentators have called "an unmitigated disaster." And when resolutions are passed by the UN Security Council, they are simply disregarded by the transgressors.

Again, Iran and North Korea come to mind, as does Saddam Hussein's Iraq prior to two invasions. But there is more.

One Washington official to whom I spoke raised another nagging issue. He was candid about what he termed a "disappointing lack of security" within the IAEA.

"The place leaks like the proverbial sieve," he suggested. "Intelligence that arrives in Vienna in the morning is sometimes on the desks of interested parties in Tehran, Damascus, and, as we've discovered, even Pyongyang, often on the same day."

We have the example of *BBC China*: Following the seizure of the German ship en route from the Persian Gulf to Libya, items intended for a clandestine atom bomb program were discovered on board. Once it was all over, an IAEA spokesperson declared that Libya was years away from producing a nuclear weapon.

In sharp contrast, British and American officials who had been making secret visits to Libya's weapons laboratories countered that statement with one of their own. They released a report that claimed Libya's Colonel Gadhafi was "well on his way" to making a nuclear bomb. If they were right, said *The New York Times* at the time, then Libya posed a far more serious threat than that detected by UN inspection teams.

"We saw uranium enrichment going ahead," said one senior diplomat with knowledge of the British-U.S. inspections. "We were satisfied that they were in the process of developing a weapon." The official added: "Libya was third on our list of concern after North Korea and Iran."

When such anomalies happen and the issue is of significant international importance, who does one believe? More pertinent, how does one establish veracity with a UN organization that is notoriously uncommunicative?

I had a taste of that medicine for myself while working on *Iran's Nuclear Option: Tehran's Quest for the Atomic Bomb*. While I had good contacts through the offices of Ewen Buchanan, who manned the old Iraqi UNSCOM office at UN headquarters in New York, I couldn't get past first base. I was stonewalled whenever I would contact the offices of the IAEA. And this was the public face of that organization.

Dr. Nic von Wielligh, who worked for many years with the IAEA's board of governors, has his own views on the PSI, and they are not flattering. In a personal note to this writer, he suggested that the new body had usurped the role of the IAEA[1]. According to von Wielligh:

> The meeting between ElBaradei and Bush in March 2004 [a year after the PSI came into being] had more to it than just Iran. In an address to the National Defense University a month before, Bush proposed seven measures to counter proliferation, some of which greatly alarmed people at the IAEA.
>
> The first was the Proliferation Security Initiative (PSI), a combined military/intelligence effort to take direct action against proliferators, thereby bypassing the IAEA and making it look ineffective because it does not have the same powers to seize material, freeze assets and prosecute.
>
> [Bush] further suggested a special committee ("governments in good standing with the IAEA") within the Board of the IAEA, something unheard of and probably consisting of countries that joined the PSI. This would create an "inner cabinet" that would effectively run the IAEA's business and create a lot of conflict within the organization's membership.
>
> Bush also suggested that "proliferators" should not serve on the Board. It would be impossible to agree on who is a "proliferator" [and who is not] within the IAEA, given the strong influence of the Group of 77 + China. These are mostly developing countries, many of which are Arab-speaking and who resent the overriding influence of the USA and its allies in the IAEA.

Dr. von Wielligh clearly has a case. But his sentiments do not detract from the fact that since its inception, the PSI has been involved in more than twenty operations, details of which remain classified, largely to protect sources and national interests.[2]

There has been serious criticism leveled at the way the IAEA handled their investigations in Iraq. In an interview with the author, the president of America's Nuclear Control Institute, Paul Leventhal, maintained that the history of IAEA inspections in Iraq was flawed from the start. "In 1990, immediately after Iraq invaded Kuwait, the IAEA safeguards chief, Mr. Jon Jennekins, declared Iraq to be a 'solid citizen' under the NPT. Its cooperation in nuclear matters, Jennekins declared to the delight of the Iraqis, had been 'exemplary.'"

Then, following a report on IAEA activities by Jonathan Broder in *The New York Times*, the IAEA refused to comment.[3] "[The IAEA] denies that its inspectors were soft on Iraq before the war, saying that under the Nuclear Non-Proliferation Treaty they were allowed to inspect only those installations that Iraq had declared," Broder reported.

David Albright, president of the Institute for Science and International Security (ISIS), a Washington arms-control organization, echoed this view when he told me that the IAEA system was never geared to detect nuclear weaponization. He is correct; it never was, and Dr. von Wielligh puts the issue firmly in perspective. Indirectly both men underscore one of the reasons why the PSI exists today.

"In terms of safeguards obligations, there is *nothing* that prevents a country from building and running conversion, enrichment, fuel fabrication, and even reprocessing plants," maintains von Wielligh. "The IAEA is often taken to task because they have not discovered the undeclared activities and not always rightly so. A Comprehensive Safeguards Agreement has some important limitations built into it, due to the way in which it was negotiated decades ago [not by the IAEA but by its member states]," he declares.

Dr. von Wielligh continues:

Inspectors cannot roam about and inspect what they wish. There are strict limitations to access and information. Furthermore, it was only recently that new methods—for example, the so-called environmental analysis—have become available through which the analysis of swipe samples can yield important information on undeclared activities based on very small samples. Due to these limitations Saddam [and Iran] could run undeclared and undetected activities next to plants which we at the IAEA were inspecting for many years, but it was precisely through environmental sampling that undeclared activities were recently discovered in Iran.

Due to these limitations, and after the discoveries in Iraq, the *Additional Protocol* was negotiated which now gives the IAEA access to substantially more information and places to inspect, the latter at very short notice under certain circumstances. Information on mining, the production of ore concentrates, fuel cycle–related R&D activities [even when no nuclear material is present], the manufacture of nuclear-related equipment, and the import/export of Trigger List items must now be submitted. Together with a comprehensive and focused analysis of all the information at its disposal (including satellite photos, information submitted by intelligence agencies, and open-source literature), the IAEA is now in a much better position to detect undeclared material and activities.

There is little doubt that prior to Gulf War 1—and here we are talking about the 1980s and the early 1990s—Saddam Hussein led the world on a merry dance with regard to his weapons of mass destruction. And as UN-backed weapons inspectors were to discover, there were many.

The Iraqi leader instituted a most elaborate program of obfuscation to prevent the IAEA from uncovering what he possessed, and what he might at that stage have been working on. One Iraqi physicist who defected to the West explained that "we understood what the [IAEA] inspector's limits were. This individual wasn't allowed to ask any questions of Iraqi personnel at these installations, outside of these limits. So once [the IAEA inspector] arrived at a nuclear plant, he would be taken along a set path and answered only within the scope of what he was permitted to inquire about. Then he would leave.

"All the while, right next door, we would be working on whatever we were doing at the time to enrich uranium or design an atom bomb," said the physicist. And make no mistake—Iraq almost had the bomb. Saddam Hussein was stopped by Colin Powell's first invasion, under the mantle of Operation Desert Storm (discussed in some detail in chapter 6).

It was notable, said this former Iraqi physicist, that when news first emerged that Iraq was working on fissile material, "we were terrified that we would receive questions from the inspectors. But even that didn't happen when international news reports claimed that we were doing something illegal. They didn't ask us any questions. They simply gave us the benefit of the doubt and never even asked us what we were doing or why we were doing it. The IAEA unreservedly, during years of ongoing inspections, accepted Iraq's story about its nuclear program being nothing more than a small research lab," he added.

And that's the way it stayed until the 1995 defection of General Kamel, Saddam's son-in-law, who disclosed the whereabouts of hundreds of thousands of pages of documents on one of his farms, all of which were subsequently turned over.

In a book on the history of the IAEA, David Fischer declared in mitigation that "any other arms control or disarmament treaty, for instance the Chemical Weapons Convention or Biological Weapons Convention, could run into similar problems." The Iraqi case, Fischer said, showed that a determined and authoritarian state with very large financial resources and a skilled and dedicated nuclear establishment could defy its obligations under the NPT and evade detection "for many years."

Indeed, Iran's leaders have followed suit, having learned some good lessons from how Iraq did it. This evasion, suggested Fischer, "may have been helped by the fact that during the Iran-Iraq War, Western governments tended to tilt toward Iraq, which, as all are aware, also received help from the Soviet Union."

Fischer goes on: "Whether the clandestine [nuclear] program would have remained undetected once the large electromagnetic isotope separation (EMIS) plants went into full production is still an open question." So, too, was the uniqueness of Iraq's circumstances: its internal political structure and its technical and financial resources, as well as its regional and international political environment.

And let us not forget the level of fear instilled into the masses by Saddam's security goons.

One need carefully examine the official function of IAEA to understand what went wrong in Iraq, and, more pertinently, what is going askew in Iran and North Korea today. More important, the international community has a right to know.

The IAEA was originally established as an autonomous organization under the United Nations Charter in 1957. It offers a broad range of services and programs based on the needs of its 130 member states (which includes Israel).

The first function of the IAEA Safeguards Division is essentially to ensure that inventories of known fissile materials such as HEU or plutonium are accounted for within annual error margins (about 17.5 pounds of ^{239}Pu and 55 pounds of HEU). Broadly speaking, the purpose of the monitoring process is to detect possible diversions of what may be very small quantities of material from civil to military use. Stocks are usually monitored on a biannual basis.

In Iraq, the duties of the IAEA and UNSCOM were strictly delineated, the latter being thoroughly intrusive—a vigorous international police action, if you like—in trying to uncover Saddam's weapons of mass destruction. For his part, Saddam did everything he could to hinder the search. Curiously (with subtle support from the French, Beijing, and Moscow), Baghdad was astonishingly successful in this kind of obscurantism, and again, we're talking about the period between Gulf Wars 1 and 2 and not the present catastrophe.

One also needs to bear in mind that Iraq still had the fuel it intended to use in the original partly completed Osiraq nuclear reactor, which was destroyed in an Israeli air strike in the 1970s and which the IAEA inspected regularly. It is (or was) roughly 90 pounds of HEU, with an average enrichment of 84 percent, and contained in 175 fuel elements.

By the time it was all removed, Iraq's processing line to make weapons-grade HEU was all but "ready to go, and it would have taken Saddam only months to complete the task," the Iraqi defector told the Americans. But that's a story in itself. When the HEU was eventually shipped out of the country after Coalition forces had taken over, the IAEA had a difficult job in finding a country to accept it for safekeeping, because some of it had already been irradiated.

And now Iran . . .

Iran's relationship with the International Atomic Energy Agency has always been precarious, punctuated by periods of cooperation and apparent goodwill one moment and intransigent stonewalling the next. That much is clearly reflected in the IAEA "restricted distribution" Board of Governors report, titled "Implementation of the NPT Agreement in the Islamic Republic of Iran, dated February 24, 2004."

While the first resolution the previous September "welcomed Iran's offer of active cooperation and openness and its positive response to the demands of the Board in the resolution adopted," the second "strongly deplored Iran's past failures and breaches of its obligations to comply with the provisions of the Safeguards Agreement as reported by the Director General." It went on to urge Tehran to adhere strictly to its obligations in both "letter and spirit."

Part of the problem stemmed from what, in nuclear-inspection parlance, is meant by "correct, complete, and final pictures" of Iran's past and present nuclear programs—and let's face it: Tehran has played that card with the flourish of a professional.

There have been times when the Iranians decided to come clean, as they did in 2003, and things would proceed accordingly. Weapons inspectors would be invited to Iran to see various nuclear sites, make observations, install monitors, and so on. That would be followed by a demand that all such activity stop.

It hasn't been lost on any of those involved that problems encountered by the IAEA in Iran in 2004 and afterward were little more than the Saddam Hussein routine all over again. Like Iraq in the past, the Iranians would offer "full and final" reports. Then, once the inspectors detected anomalies or nondisclosures, a furious debate would follow, sometimes in private but more often in public. Next would come the requisite press reports, which invariably inculcated bad feeling all around. Then there would be another "full and final" report, and the cycle would be repeated.

Matters are sometimes compounded by language and innuendo, the sort that has emerged from exchanges between Tehran and the West. Take one example:

Following the adoption by the UN nuclear organization of a "compromise" solution to Iran's nuclear dossier in November 2003, Tehran promptly hailed the deal as a "victory for Iran and an obvious failure for America and Israel," even though the Jewish State had nothing to do with negotiations. While the deal "strongly deplored" Iran's eighteen-year covert nuclear activities, the IAEA—having previously gone through the wringer when faced with similar problems in Iraq—refused to refer Tehran's deceptions to the UN Security Council for possible sanctions.

Inspections went well for several months. Then Tehran suddenly called off a nuclear inspection mission scheduled for the weeks ahead. Questioned about reasons why, the Iranian representative at the IAEA, Pirooz Hosseini, was quoted as saying something about the gesture not being politically motivated, but rather that it was due to "the approaching of the Iranian New Year." This delay—critical and timely for the mullahs—came as non-aligned and Western diplomats were struggling to break a deadlock at the IAEA over a U.S. resolution which would condemn Tehran's leaders for hiding parts of its nuclear program. This was followed with a statement by the Iranian foreign minister, Kamal Kharrazi, "that it is our perfectly legitimate right to enrich uranium."

As one American official in Vienna noted, Why else would Iran be enriching uranium to weapons-grade if it did not intend to build the bomb? Mohamed ElBaradei's top-level talks with President Bush in Washington followed soon afterwards in March 2004. Thereafter ElBaradei briefed a U.S. congressional committee about what his organization had uncovered in Iran. Though there was no comment on the issue, there is little doubt that recent disclosures in Pakistan about A.Q. Khan and his associates providing rogue states (Iran included) with nuclear expertise featured prominently in these talks.

According to *The Wall Street Journal*, the Bush and ElBaradei meeting covered a wide range of topics, including IAEA verification of Iran's nuclear efforts, as well as ideas on how to control what appeared to be burgeoning nuclear proliferation in the international community. They dealt with the urgent need to restrict the number of countries that can enrich uranium and reprocess plutonium for use in nuclear fuel or bombs.

On Tehran, the IAEA chief couldn't have been more explicit. While acknowledging that Iran had provided help, it was obvious that all was not well with the inspection program when he declared that "my answer is that the jury is still out."

Clearly, there are things going on in Iran that worry ElBaradei. One of his statements read: "We would like to continue to work hard on inspecting Iran before we come to a conclusion. We expect full cooperation, full transparency, if Iran wants to prove that its program is for peaceful purposes."

Which begs the question: On what aspect of the Iranian nuclear program does the IAEA think Tehran is holding out? Is it unthinkable that Iran might have completed construction of its first atom bomb and is now preparing for a test? Certainly, that would allow a measure of transparency, with the argument in Tehran running along the lines of showing the West what it wants to see, and letting us get on with real issues.

For ElBaradei to have been as forthright as he was after meeting the American president indicates that there must be something substantial in the Iranian nuclear domain that he believes has not yet been disclosed. For what other reason would he have said what he did? Neither ElBaradei nor Washington are telling. Yet, if you'd gone on to read details of the Washington meeting in Tehran's English press, things couldn't have been rosier. Iran had complied with all the IAEA's demands and everybody was happy, was the thrust of one of the reports in *Iran News*.

Things changed rapidly after Mohamed ElBaradei's Washington visit. A day later, a report in *IranMania News* accused the IAEA chief of "playing the role of mediator between Tehran and arch-foe Washington" during his U.S. visit.[4]

"The Islamic Republic has not tasked Dr. ElBaradei with any message for the American leadership," said foreign ministry spokesman Hamid Reza Asefi, quoted by the Iranian Students News Agency (ISNA). Washington's reply was forthright, coming from State Department spokesman Adam Ereli: "The fact is that Iran knows what those issues of concern are [terrorism, nuclear program, support for terrorist groups]. We haven't seen movement on any of those things," he declared.

That was followed by an impassioned outburst from Hassan Rowhani, the official in charge of Iran's nuclear program, when he criticized Britain, France, and Germany for not defending Tehran's views at recent talks on international inspections. The previous week, the IAEA, for once, had adopted a tough resolution that raised questions over Iran's failure to declare its possession of certain equipment and materials which could be used to make nuclear weapons.

"The IAEA resolution was not drafted in a fair way," said Rowhani, head of his country's Supreme National Security Council.

What then do we know about things nuclear in Iran? The international community does have batches of satellite images of the goings-on at Natanz and Arak, two nondescript towns a hundred or so miles south of Tehran. These show a heavy-water plant at Arak, similar to the nuclear-related heavy-water facilities used in Pakistan's atom bomb program. Photos taken of the Natanz facility show something akin to a uranium-enrichment plant coupled with a centrifuge facility.

It is not that the Americans—or, for that matter, Whitehall—don't know about such things. Earlier, John Bolton, former undersecretary of state for Arms Control and International Security and more recently at the United Nations from where he has also departed, testified before a congressional committee that the U.S. has seen indications for some time that Iran was developing a clandestine nuclear weapons program.

He revealed in a closed session that Iran was developing "a uranium mine, a uranium conversion facility, a large uranium-enrichment facility designed to house tens of thousands of centrifuges, together with a heavy-water production plant," adding that such a facility would support the production of highly enriched uranium and plutonium for nuclear weapons.

"While Iran claims that its nuclear program is peaceful and transparent, we are convinced it is otherwise," Bolton declared. "One unmistakable indicator of military intent is the secrecy and lack of transparency surrounding Iran's nuclear activities," he suggested.

While Bolton is long gone from arms control, the dual United Nations Security Council and IAEA problem regarding nations that illegally proliferate nuclear weapons persists. Take a news report filed by Steve Gutterman and Edith M. Lederer of the Associated Press from Moscow, which appeared in early November 2006. It read:[5]

> Russian and China indicated that they will not support a draft UN resolution imposing tough sanctions on Iran for its refusal to halt its nuclear enrichment program.
>
> The comments by Russia's foreign minister and China's UN ambassador were the strongest reactions yet to the draft by the two key UN Security Council members, and signaled difficult negotiations ahead on the resolution drawn up by Britain, France, and Germany.
>
> "We cannot support measures that in essence are aimed at isolating Iran from the outside world, including isolating people who are called upon to conduct negotiations on the nuclear program," the Interfax news agency quoted Russian foreign minister Sergey Lavrov as saying . . .
>
> China's UN Ambassador Wang Guangya declared that there were still different views on what kind of actions the council needs to do under the current circumstances. Wang admitted that the major concern was that "some members want tough sanctions like those in the resolution that the council approved on October 14 to punish North Korea for conducting a nuclear test."

Nobody is certain how long it will take China to publicly accept the gravity of this matter. The Kremlin will probably emerge from its nuclear hiatus when the first radiological bomb is detonated in Moscow by Chechnyan terrorists.

Or it might even be a crude atom bomb, possibly supplied by al-Qaeda . . .

Chapter 14 Endnotes:

1 Dr. von Wielligh did concede that Iran concluded a comprehensive Safeguards Agreement with the IAEA as far back as December 1974, after being one of the first countries to sign the NPT. "The recent discoveries in Iran are clearly a violation of the requirements of their Safeguards Agreement," he told me.

2 South Africa acquired some strange bedfellows following the accession to power of President Nelson Mandela. He had not been in office long before the head of Tehran's Atomic Energy Organization of Iran and deputy president for Iran's Atomic Affairs, Reza Amrollahi, arrived at the Pelindaba offices of Dr. Waldo Stumpf, chief executive of the South African Atomic Energy Corporation (AEC). Amrollahi told Stumpf that he had a "shopping list" of items required for the manufacture of atomic bombs. Despite vocal South African and Iranian protestations to the contrary (the issue was even raised in Parliament in Cape Town), Pik Botha, then a minister in the new black government, subsequently confirmed the incident. He told Mungo Soggot, a senior writer on Johannesburg's *Mail & Guardian*, that this was not only what happened, but that he

was there, *and at Stumpf's insistence.* For a more complete report on that event, see *Jane's International Defence Review*, September 1997.

3 Jonathan Broder, "Saddam's Bomb," *The New York Times*, October 1, 2000; "Arms Control and Verification—Safeguards in a Changing World," International Atomic Energy Agency, Vienna, 1997.

4 *IranMania* News, Tehran, March 18, 2004.

5 "Russia, China, Won't Back Iran Sanctions," Steve Gutterman and Edith M. Lederer, The Associated Press, Moscow, November 2, 2006. Associated Press writer Vladimir Isachenkov contributed to this report. Edith M. Lederer reported from the United Nations.

CHAPTER 15

THE OTHER SIDE OF THE COIN: NUCLEAR SCAMS

> Smuggling throughout the whole of Central and Eastern Europe has been on the upswing since the breakup of the former Soviet Union. Economic conditions are prompting smugglers to transport items ranging from blue jeans to nuclear reactor components. Because border crossings lack funds, adequately trained personnel, and technology, the smuggled goods have a better chance of making it through.
> —Dr. William Cliff, program manager for international border security in Pacific Northwest's National Security Division

One of the problems facing the international community in attempting to regulate nuclear proliferation is that the trade has attracted its own brand of counterfeiter and, as might be expected, organized crime. The stakes are high, quite often reaching into the millions, and those duped include bin Laden's al-Qaeda. In the early days, he was offered a canister of fake highly enriched uranium which, his agents were told, if spread about "would poison your enemies with radioactivity."

Nuclear scams have been big business for some time. Most transactions involving radioactive material have been between former Soviet Union (FSU) countries and the three or four more prominent pariah states in the Middle East. American sources maintain that they are aware of several transactions where both Iranian and Iraqi agents have been hoodwinked, and that millions of dollars were involved in deals that had gone sour.

"The trouble is," warned a spokesman for America's Pacific Northwest National Laboratory (PNNL), which lies adjacent to Washington State's huge Hanford nuclear complex, "what the seller or smuggler actually offloads, may well be dangerously radioactive." The authorities are aware that deaths have resulted from individuals unknowingly handling radioactive materials.

Until recently, few outsiders were aware that a multimillion-dollar industry involving some of the best swindlers in the game existed. Many of those who are doing the "trading" are either Russian or Ukrainian, though at one time or another, nationals from just about every country that once made up the FSU have been implicated. Also, the work can be dangerous. The number of people murdered because they were involved in so-called "red mercury" scams in South Africa over two decades has almost reached the double figure, which, for a scam, is preposterous. (Though specifics are sparse, red mercury traffickers in Europe and the Middle East have not been inactive.)

The reason for doing so is basic. Red mercury is an extremely sophisticated technological fraud that over the past ten or twelve years has generated a lot of cash. Though purported to be a "substitute radioactive component" in nuclear-weapons development (and compared by some crafty operators to the heaviest hydrogen isotope, tritium), that's all nonsense.

Such is the extent of trade in this substance that several books have appeared on the subject. One of them, *The Mini-Nuke Conspiracy: How Mandela Inherited a Nuclear Nightmare*, by Peter Hounam and Steve McQuillan (Faber & Faber, London, 1995), even showed exploded drawings of red-mercury nuclear devices (page 292) as published in an article by nuclear analyst Dr. Frank Barnaby in *Jane's International Defence Review* in 1994.

Other nuclear shams involve osmium-187, Philippine "uranium," Southeast Asian "uranium," as well as radiation gauges. The Americans state that osmium only recently emerged as a common nuclear trafficking scam in the FSU. Hanford officials reckon it has no known weapons application, nor is it radioactive.

One of the tasks being taught by American specialists at Richland in Washington State is the ability of customs or border guards to recognize this danger and blow the whistle, "not only for their own protection but for others as well," said an instructor.

What is true is that there is a variety of osmium isotopes found in abundance in nature. Osmium-186, for example, while produced only in milligrams in the U.S. (and in kilogram quantities in Russia), is a naturally occurring, radioactive alpha emitter. Non-nuclear uses include it as an alloy agent and, in the past, in the production of phonographs and ballpoint pens. Also, PNNL scientists point out, there are no international laws against the sale or transfer of osmium. Also, there is no need to separate the isotopes of osmium for commercial purposes.

Scam prices can sometimes turn heads. "Candium" (another fake Russian radioactive substance) sells upwards of $25,000/pound. One hustler tried to off-load a kilo of osmium-187 to an Iranian agent for $70 million. "Obviously if there weren't takers, the market wouldn't exist," the specialist declared. He added that there were a lot of what he termed "basket cases" out there "and some of them have really big bucks." Nuclear physicists at Richland stress that in the wrong hands, some radioactive materials or sources might be used for terror or extortion.

The facility's 6-inch-thick, 600-page handbook—which is given to every student on arrival at the facility and in his own language (including Cyrillic script for Russian speakers)—cites the case of a group of Chechen separatists who, in 1995, threatened to use radioactive dispersal devices in Russia. They even staged a media event to prove that they actually possessed a radioactive substance.

One of the scientists involved with training (who asked not to be identified, since he travels frequently throughout Eastern Europe) said that while there were any number of dirty tricks, there are also legal radioactive isotopes in abundance, the majority serving a good purpose. Technetium-99, for instance, is used for brain, thyroid, and lung images; chromium-51 is involved in red blood cell tests; cobalt-60 is used for external-beam radiotherapy; and ytterbium-169 in spinal fluid studies. Likewise, iridium-132 is used as an internal radiotherapy source, and the two xenon isotopes, xenon-133 and xenon-127, feature in lung-ventilation function tests.

At the same time, there are numerous legal applications of radiation sources. These include examining welds in the steel industry, well logging medical research and moisture sensing. Other applications that might emit radiation include smoke detectors, airport runway lights, lighthouses in Russia, the Russian space program (for power on spacecraft), and the dismantling of old reactors.

In the shadowy world of nonproliferation of weapons of mass destruction (WMD), say the Americans, times are bad—which is why there are Russians, Slovenians, Georgians, and Azerbaijanis, as well as border-enforcement personnel from a host of other Central and East European countries, manning posts in the sand and sagebrush around the American government nuclear facility near the banks of the Columbia River in Eastern Washington.

Eastern European groups—as well as parties from Asia and the Middle East—are a constant feature of the place. A batch of twenty-four Russians—many of them paramilitary customs officers and headed by a major general—arrived at PNNL's hazard training facility for a two-week course just before I got there. They represented 50,000 customs officers in the Russian Federation, complementing more than 250,000 border guards. The hazard program was developed under the sponsorship of the Pentagon's counterproliferation program, with technical direction by the U.S. Customs Service.

The job can be difficult. PNNL specialists warned that with the global miniaturization of WMD, the most basic "gun-type" atom bomb might have a diameter of only 6 inches and could weigh 50 pounds. This would obviously be representative of a lash-up, minimum-frills device.

Similarly, something thermonuclear might be just 8 inches across and tip the scales at less than 150 pounds. Part of the course is devoted to demonstrating that chemical or biological weapons could arrive in a variety of containers. These include grenades, mines, artillery shells, aerial bombs, spray or storage tanks, or, possibly, a missile warhead. PNNL science and engineering associate Ann Jarrell warned that a pathogen could be smuggled into a country in something as basic as powdered eggs.

Elaborate procedures on the best ways of preventing weapons smuggling are being held several times a year on a rotational basis at the $30 million facility. Training sessions are code-named Interdict/RADACAD (interdiction of materials associated with mass destruction weapons, and RADACAD for Radiation Academy), and they last for two weeks. Courses are held with a range of props that you are likely to find at any East or Central European border post, harbor, railway station, or airport.

Trucks, railway cars (both passenger and freight oil tankers), and more are being scrutinized for nuclear, chemical, biological, and missile components and technology. U.S. Customs—in conjunction with the departments of defense, energy, and state—have not only been lifting the veil on procedures in many of these countries abroad (which only a short time ago were secret), but also the U.S. taxpayer is picking up the tab.

Subjects handled at Interdict/RADACAD are diverse. They include arcane issues such as the threat assessment of WMD, nuclear concepts, advanced detection techniques, nuclear technology identification (both trigger list and dual-use list), as well as missile technology, which includes on-site examination of the innards of a Scud missile and its components.

Russia's Scud missile—and updated versions that flowed from the original design—gets a lot of attention at PNNL's Hammer site, which is to be expected, since many countries have the missile, including North Korea and several Islamic states like Iraq, Iran, and Syria.

The smuggling of Scud components has been a problem for years. This was underscored prior to the second invasion of Iraq by the UN Special Commission (on Iraq), investigating that country's illegal acquisition of dozens of rocket gyros. Originally retrieved from redundant Russian submarine-launched ballistic missiles (SLBMs), boxes of the stuff were smuggled to Baghdad. One of the conclusions subsequently reached was that it would have been impossible to remove such sophisticated devices from the original missiles without the authorities being aware of it. It would have been equally difficult to take them out of the country if there had not been some sort of collusion from on high. Moscow has never adequately explained how large numbers of such sensitive devices were clandestinely shipped abroad.

While some of the gyros that reached Baghdad were later dumped into the Euphrates after UNSCOM got word of them, more were seized at Amman Airport when American agents, acting in concert with the Jordanians, acted on a tip-off. And although some of those involved were arrested, the bigger fish were never identified.

Because outdated Russian missiles are notoriously inaccurate, the gyros were apparently to have been used in Iraqi Scuds. Specialists accept that late-generation ICBM gyros would markedly increase their reliability.

Among Scud components that participants are instructed to look for are several instrument-section components (range accelerometers, horizon gyros, vertical gyros/lateral accelerometers, flight computers, and gyro mounting boards). Engine components include regulator and stabilizer valves (as well as balance diaphragms), turbo pumps (both turbine wheels and inducer impellers), fuel and oxidizer injectors, as well as thrust vector control sets and jet vanes. The latter are made of high-grade steels to counter excessive temperatures generated by rocket engines.

Other WMD component parts listed as having been smuggled abroad include chemical weapon spray parts (actuators, swaybraces, dissemination nozzles, outlet cutters, and more). Similarly, instructors accentuate the illegal transportation of the 152mm chemical tube artillery shell, of which the students are given a cutaway diagram. They are also provided with nuclear weapons schematics and a cutaway of a chemical or biological cluster bomb.

Subjects for study are diverse, and include radiation protection, as well as elements of biological warfare. Time is spent viewing the operations and use of sensitive equipment at a fully functional international border crossing—in this case, at Blaine, on the Washington–British Columbian border.

The two-week training session covers a lot of ground. Usually numbering a couple of dozen participants from two *compatible* East European countries (representatives of Chechnya and Russia, for instance, in the same course might lead to problems), classes are in English with simultaneous translation into home tongues.

The PNNL laboratory—with a staff of about 3,500 when I got there coupled to an annual budget in excess of $500 million—is one of nine national multi-program laboratories in the U.S. It was created in 1965 when the government's research laboratory at the Department of Energy's site at Hanford, along the upper Columbia River, was separated from Hanford's existing nuclear operations.

Because of Project Amber (a classroom program initiated in 1994), the Interdict/RADACAD program has resulted in perhaps a thousand or more foreign officers from dozens of countries having been trained in a variety of anti-WMD detection disciplines over the years. More were put through their paces in similar disciplines on-site in Poland, Estonia, and Uzbekistan, as well as a number of other Central and East European states. Ultimately, extensions of Project Amber will include Cyprus, Turkey, Malta, and elsewhere—if this hasn't already happened—underscoring their strategic potential in the Mediterranean, especially since some of these countries are eager to become members of the European Union.

There have been some notable interdictions over the past three years, some involving past students:

- 22 tons of radioactive contaminated concentrate detained near Krasnoyarsk. The stuff appears to have been sent to Russia to be dumped.

- An American company in 1996 shipped 78 tons of radioactive scrap steel from Houston to China.

- Radioactive sources sent scrap metal from the Czech Republic to Italy. Many people near the path of the train were given medical exams.

- Contaminated scrap copper from Poland got turned back at the German border. It eventually found its way to Slovakia, where it was processed and went out as product.

- Two tons of radioactive tungsten was found entering Lithuania from Belarus. The driver transporting the load was seriously radiated.

- Mexican cables contaminated with radioactive metal were sent to the U.S.

- A large consignment of uranium-235 was interdicted in Bulgaria, apparently en route to the Middle East.

Items offered to participants include a couple of state-of-the-art portable detection devices: a Material Identification System (MIS), and an Ultrasonic Pulse Echo (ultrasound) instrument. An unspecified number have already been sent to other Central and East European (as well as FSU) governments.

The first device discriminates between a variety of strategic metals, some of them used in WMD. Composed of a laptop computer with a plug-in instrument card that fits in a CD/floppy disk port, it operates with a handheld probe.

Among the problems encountered by border guards is the fact that most metals (including those used for strategic purposes) are rather similar in appearance. It is difficult, if not impossible, for a border inspector to visually determine whether a particular metal is what it's purported to be. And since advanced weapons programs require advanced types of steel, MIS—based on non-contact electrical conductivity—can tell whether a batch of metals in a cargo is pressure-vessel steel or cold-rolled; similarly with graphite, which might be used for nuclear-reactor development. Participants are warned to regard any batches of sharp-edged carbon with great suspicion, since its only possible use is nuclear-related.

The Ultrasonic Pulse Echo, in contrast, is based on advanced ultrasound technology, and was developed by UN officials after the Gulf War specifically to inspect chemical weapons stockpiles and discarded munitions. This instrument can also discover, virtually in real time, hidden packages or cavities in a container that might hold drugs or other prohibited material. U.S. government agencies have ordered dozens more for use at East European border crossings.

Other advanced equipment used in the training include:

- a *gamma and neutron spectrometer*, to identify radioactive isotopes such as nuclear weapons material (^{239}Pu, ^{235}U, and ^{233}U), as well as commercial and medical isotopes;

- a *radiation pager*, which alerts border guards that there might be a radioactive substance present;

- a *gamma densitometer*, which is used to locate items hidden behind walls and in tires or other cavities in shipping containers or liquid tanks;

- a *fiber-optic scope*, for viewing inside dashboards, fuel tanks, and so forth; and

- an *electronic measuring tape*, for exposing hidden compartments and false walls.

It is interesting that the U.S. government is also providing almost every Central and East European customs service with numbers of X-ray detection vehicles. Costing about $300,000 each, a classified number have gone to Russia, with more to follow. For their size, the vehicles are well equipped. While 10,000 ordinary packages might be scanned without prompting a reaction, anything radioactive will immediately trigger an alarm, which also makes it an ideal tool for post offices and baggage handling areas at airports. For this purpose, each vehicle is fitted with a forward scanner and backscatter X-ray, which, together with a variety of other systems, are able to detect the full spectrum of nuclear-related materials. These include plutonium, uranium, carbons, lithium, beryllium, and zirconium, together with all substances covered by the Nuclear Suppliers Group.

There are several programmed moves afoot to stop the trafficking of nuclear materials, almost all initiated at American behest.

One of these involves intrusive new advances in the United States that allows fiber-optic technology to be embedded in roads of several East European and East Asian nations. These are being laid specifically to detect smuggled nuclear weapons. A research program launched at PNNL has developed what the laboratory calls "a one-of-a-kind scintillating optical fiber for sensing both neutrons and gamma rays."

Named PUMA—for Plutonium Measurement and Analysis—the sensor is designed to be embedded in a variety of materials, or literally, "wrapped like fingers around objects of different sizes for content analyses." Also, it is adaptable to a wide range of applications, including environmental restoration, cancer treatment, and the nonproliferation of WMD.

Most important, it can be embedded into asphalt roads to detect the transportation of unauthorized or diverted nuclear weapons material. Alternatively, it can be wrapped around drums and other containers to inventory contents. Last heard, Nuesafe LLC was licensed to commercially manufacture the technology under the PUMA name in the U.S.

When I visited Hanford, the head of program research was Dr. Mary Bliss. She advised that developments at the laboratory were quite revolutionary, and that the sensors could be used for body-worn detectors for nuclear materials, as well as airborne weapons detection. Portable monitors, she reckoned, were the single biggest commercial application.

Unlike the gas tube, she explained, "PNNL sensors are less sensitive to vibration. They are also rugged and flexible and versatile in both length and numbers, ranging from about a quarter-inch to two yards long, and may consist of a single fiber or clusters of tens of thousands of fibers." There was an important advantage: High-speed electronics could be utilized to give detectors "an improved, dynamic range, which is simply not feasible with gas tubes," Dr. Bliss said.

PUMA is based on the rationale that ionizing radiation interacts with the scintillating fibers and produces light. It works like this: Light is trapped within the fiber and goes to its end, where conversion to an electrical signal takes place. This can be interpreted as either a neutron or a gamma-ray interaction, depending on size.

A spokesperson for PNNL stated that teams of materials, nuclear, optical, and electrical scientists began testing applications of fiber-optic radiation sensors at the lab about twenty years ago, and this testing has been going on ever since.

Until now, the single biggest problem facing the West has been detecting secret nuclear blasts. There is real fear in Washington, London, and elsewhere that more countries might follow India and Pakistan in testing nuclear weapons, and

North Korea immediately springs to mind. So, too, with Iran, if one is to judge from the enormous amount of illegal fissile material that appears to have been headed there. Tehran, we're all aware, is eager to join the "Nuclear Club."

The refusal of the U.S. Senate to ratify the Comprehensive Test Ban Treaty (CTBT) complicates matters still further.

Several new monitoring developments are already impacting the industry. Indeed, a succession of revolutionary U.S. monitoring procedures is likely, if not to permanently eliminate secret nuclear tests, then at least be able to detect them, which they did following North Korea's first underground nuclear tests in October 2006.

Systems developed involve technology one hundred times more sensitive than the best previously available for detecting nuclear blasts. Monitoring stations on all five continents will cover applicable seismic, hydro-acoustic, infrasound, and radionuclide data.

Just about everybody that I spoke to on this subject agreed that with the CTBT stymied, new monitoring systems are urgently needed to provide for total global verification. The monitoring of nuclear testing will be more intensive than ever before, and, as we go to press, several new systems are being put in place. These include a network of more than 300 stations worldwide incorporating new instruments such as those developed by PNNL and operated for the DoE.

During treaty negotiations, the U.S. Department of Defense was tasked to spearhead an international effort to develop a prototype international data center (IDC) at the Center for Monitoring Research in Arlington, Virginia. There are several reasons. The first is to support future test ban treaty negotiations. Another is to test new concepts necessary for effective global monitoring. Yet another is to establish an infrastructure for cooperative, international verification. Finally, the objective is to provide the foundation for a future international test ban data center to be located in Vienna, Austria. Such a center is envisaged to include a communications system, the prototype IDC, as well as an international on-site inspection component to monitor compliance.

PNNL has produced several systems to monitor nuclear debris: a Radionuclide Aerosol Sampler/Analyzer (RASA) that measures radioactive debris from aboveground nuclear weapons testing (regardless of where or when the bombs were detonated); and ARSA, an Automated Radioxenon Sampler/Analyzer. This device fills the CTBT requirement for near-real-time, ultra-sensitive field measurement of short-lived noble gases. Like its counterpart RASA, ARSA operates automatically.

All programs are remotely programmable, and both projects are funded by the DoE's Office of Nonproliferation and Security, again from Washington.

Dr. Harry Miley of PNNL was responsible for the development of RASA (in conjunction with researchers at DME Corporation, Orlando, Florida), which was given The Most Outstanding Technology Development with Commercial Potential Award by *R&D Magazine.*

Essentially, Miley explained, the analyzer passes air through a large-area, low-pressure drop filter at a high rate of flow for selectable time periods. This action captures verifiable airborne trace particles on six strips of filter paper that are packaged in a single bundle to be analyzed by a gamma-ray detector. In so doing, he detailed, the system actually captures a part of the nuclear weapon: "Minute, yes, but still a verifiable part," he explained.

The resultant spectra are then transmitted to central data locations thousands of miles away. It simultaneously achieves a very high sensitivity coupled with a low-power/small footprint.

He went on to say that since short-lived fission products have no natural background, weapon blasts could also be easily discriminated from reactor accidents. Thus, he said, a simple one-kiloton atmospheric blast will be detected by multiple isotopes at multiple stations.

Special features within the system archived each sample, said Miley. They then identified them with their own unique bar codes. Containing a 90 percent relative-efficiency germanium detector, he reckoned that the new technology— which identifies debris in an environment of ubiquitous radon background— was one hundred times more sensitive than its nearest commercial rival.

The U.S. Air Force and the DoE have authorized DME Corporation to sell RASA units to all potential CTBT participants and other interested parties.

The philosophy behind detecting xenon in the ARSA process, in contrast, stems from the fact that it homes in on all the byproducts of a nuclear blast. Radioxenon is a particularly useful signature of an underground nuclear explosion, for no other reason than it is the most likely radioactive debris to escape. In layman's terms, explained Miley, we actually end up with a physical piece of that explosion—microscopic, but something tangible nonetheless.

What happens is that the high-volume analyzer passes filtered air through an aluminum oxide bed for the removal of moisture and carbon dioxide, then through a charcoal sorption-held-bed near 100° C for xenon collection. The gas is then thermally desorbed, purified, and measured by beta-coincidence X-/gamma-ray spectrometry. That done, gamma-ray spectra are automatically transmitted to appropriate organizations. The gas samples, meanwhile, are tagged and retained for a later central laboratory confirmatory process.

Notable is the fact that ARSA continuously separates xenon from the atmosphere at a flow rate of $48m^3$ per eight-hour collection period. The system has a sensitivity of about 0.1mBq per cubic meter of air in the subsequent twenty-four-hour period, during which four of the samples can be measured simultaneously.

ARSA was field-tested in April 1997 in New York City. The first units were delivered to the USAF not long afterwards, and work progressed on commercial units.

Yet, as we have recently seen, none of these systems is perfect. Many of us have followed the agonizing death in a British hospital of Alexander "Sasha" Litvinenko, former Russian security services spy and outspoken critic of Russian President Vladimir Putin, after he had been mysteriously contaminated with polonium-210. This is a dangerously toxic and radioactive alpha-emitting isotope.

That incident was followed by government disclosures that several British Airways passenger jets on the Moscow run had been contaminated by something radioactive.

While Putin screams innocence, this reprehensible event took place on his watch. As the Russian Supremo—and a former KGB operative himself—he should be able to keep his security goons in tow. This president has clearly not been able to do so and as a consequence, he has disgraced both himself and the Russian people. But then again, this is about the fourth poisoning that we know about in the Former Soviet Union in recent years.

There are other, disturbing implications. Since it is nuclear related, Russian polonium could only have come from a state or parastatal institution, even though it is readily available in the West: Polonium-210 can show up in everything from atom bombs to paint or even cigarette smoke. Iran made relatively large amounts in secret efforts to develop nuclear arms while North Korea probably used it to trigger its recent nuclear blast.

The inference here is that if persons or groups unknown can get hold of polonium-210, what else can they lay their hands on? More to the point, where would they stop should there be a foreign party with an unlimited budget willing to foot the bill?

How did it get on aircraft? Nobody in Moscow is prepared to say, which is unusual since there is an array of sensors in place at all Russian international airports to prevent just such an event from taking place. Consequently, it is of concern to intelligence agencies just about everywhere that someone was still able to smuggle so highly a radioactive substance on board. The stuff shouldn't have got past the first monitor.

At the time of going to press there were half a dozen more people believed to have been contaminated by polonium-210, though none as severely affected as Litvinenko.

CHAPTER 16

ISRAEL AND AN ADVERSARIAL EGYPT: RECIPE FOR CONFLICT

Once the Saudis are in the hunt [for nuclear weapons], Egypt will need nuclear weapons to keep it from becoming irrelevant to the regional power balance—and sure enough, last month Gamal Mubarak, President Mubarak's son and Egypt's heir apparent, very publicly announced that Egypt should pursue a nuclear program.

—"Islam, Terror and the Second Nuclear Age" by Noah Feldman, adjunct senior fellow at the Council on Foreign Relations, *The New York Times*, October 29, 2006

Britain's *Jane's Islamic Affairs Analyst* published an article early 2005 about Egypt going nuclear.[1] That vignette resulted in some humorous banter among several of my Arab friends. There was also incredulity. It just couldn't happen, I was assured. The trouble with that argument is that we're in an age when things tend to change by the day, or as someone commented, sometimes by the hour.

Take the statement delivered by Gamal Mubarak, deputy secretary-general of Egypt's National Democratic Party, and aired on Al-Mihwar TV on September 20, 2006. He very clearly indicated his country's interest in acquiring a nuclear capability. This did not presuppose interest in trying to develop the bomb, he stressed. "We are talking about using nuclear energy for peaceful purposes." Mubarak suggested that Egypt was not the only country eager to acquire a nuclear foothold. "Many developing countries have preceded us in this regard, and the world cooperated with them and helped them, so they could use nuclear energy as alternative energy in the future," said the deputy secretary-general.

What is clear to any Middle East watcher in these interesting times is that Cairo—following North Korea having detonated its first test bomb—has entered a new and rejuvenated phase on nuclear issues. In late November of 2006, with President Hosni Mubarak on the verge of a visit to Moscow, an Egyptian press report stated that the nation would turn to Russia and Cairo for help "in relaunching Egypt's nuclear program." There was the usual abundance of "peaceful" good intentions, which wears thin when one is that focused on an issue that has distinct military connotations.

What was also notable about the press release was the statement that all this was being done "following a twenty-year freeze in the country's nuclear program," when there is good evidence that this is just not so. The fact is, for a while there has been an argument doing the rounds that Egypt could "go nuclear" if it wished. Indeed, questioned on the issue recently, several Egyptian nuclear scientists contended that their country had both the expertise and the raw materials to enrich ^{235}U or produce plutonium. They were quite blunt about it.

A glance at Egypt's "nuclear map" tells you why. There is a solid depth of uranium resources throughout the country, coupled with an industrial base that is not dissimilar to that of Pakistan. If Cairo were to do it illegally, there are a host of countries with nuclear physicists, some of them out of work. Among them are Russians, Iraqis, Brazilians, and the inevitable South Africans, who, we are now aware, have not been altogether inactive in Iran.

Nor has Egypt emerged from the issue crisply lily-white. According to "evidence," said to have been uncovered in early 2004 by American and British inspectors attached to the International Atomic Energy Agency (IAEA), Libya and Egypt were actually involved in some kind of nuclear technical cooperation until late 2003.

The matter was compounded when the French newspaper *Liberation* disclosed in late 2004 that before Libya was forced to abandon its nuclear weapons program, it had "worked . . . secretly for the Egyptians." Significant, too, is that President Gadhafi's uranium-enrichment program on the outskirts of Tripoli was more advanced than first conceded.

The French paper also raised the point that IAEA director Dr. Mohamed ElBaradei is himself an Egyptian, and without presenting any kind of evidence, it declared that he was suspected of preventing his staff from—as the French paper put it—"truly plunging into this dossier." It didn't help that some Americans agree, irrespective of the fact that ElBaradei is a lawyer by profession and has no real technical knowledge of any of the disciplines involved.

It comes as no surprise, therefore, that as a consequence, some pretty tough words are being traded at the UN, in the Middle East, and among members of the IAEA, and some are focused on whether Egypt has or has not made illegal nuclear material.

Quoting diplomats at the UN atomic watchdog agency, George Jahn of the Associated Press said the IAEA had found evidence of secret nuclear experiments in Egypt that could be used in a weapons program. The material was taken to Europe for analysis and evaluation.

EGYPT'S NUCLEAR CAPABILITIES

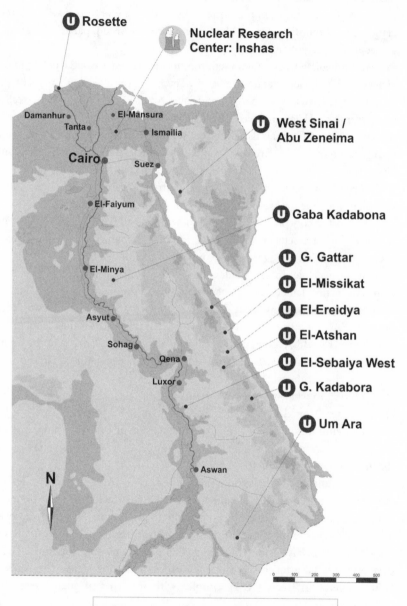

U Rosette

Nuclear Research Center: Inshas

Damanhur
Tanta
El-Mansura
Ismailia

U West Sinai / Abu Zeneima

Cairo
Suez

El-Faiyum

U Gaba Kadabona

El-Minya

U G. Gattar

U El-Missikat

Asyut

U El-Ereidya

Sohag

U El-Atshan

Qena

U El-Sebaiya West

Luxor

U G. Kadabora

U Um Ara

N

Aswan

0   100   200   300   400   500

 NUCLEAR RESEARCH CENTER

 URANIUM DEPOSITS

While most of this work was carried out in the 1970s and 1980s, an IAEA source has since admitted that the agency was looking at some of these experiments possibly having been performed as recently as a year or two ago. This revelation comes months after the IAEA discovered plutonium particles in an area adjacent to an Egyptian nuclear facility.

An immediate reaction followed from former Israeli Mossad chief, Ephraim Halevy. It was his view that it was not only Egypt that was linked to reports of illegal nuclear activity, but so was Syria and Saudi Arabia. Referring to what he called a "nuclear leap," Halevy revealed that the Pakistani nuclear scientist A.Q. Khan—the same man who ran an illegal nuclear supply network under the noses of his own government, which stretched from Libya at one extreme to South Africa and North Korea on the other—had visited the Egyptian capital during this critical period. He had done so several times. Neither Cairo nor Islamabad have been willing to explain what the irrepressible Khan might have been doing there.

Within the context of illegal nuclear weapons activity, *The Jerusalem Post* followed with a disclosure of its own. Quoting unnamed Israeli intelligence sources, it said that one of the three Arab states mentioned by Halevy had made what it termed "significant strides towards becoming a nuclear power." The country was not named, though personally, my money is on Saudi Arabia.

For its part, Washington said that it supported a "thorough investigation" by the IAEA. Not lost on any of those involved in this fracas is the reality of the U.S. taxpayer having paid Egypt $2 billion a year since the signing of the Camp David accords with Israel, largely in a bid to maintain the status quo in the most volatile region of the world.

Reacting to what has been construed in Cairo as a challenge, Egypt's foreign minister, Ahmad Abu al-Ghait, was adamant that his country was not involved in running secret nuclear experiments. Egypt's nuclear program was strictly for peaceful purposes, he stressed—as does every other Egyptian in authority that you get to talk to.

What Minister al-Ghait could not refute was an IAEA source who leaked the news that the controversial haul mentioned earlier included "some pounds" of uranium metal which could be processed into plutonium. Also recovered was an undisclosed amount of uranium tetrafluoride, a precursor to uranium hexafluoride gas, which is customarily enriched into weapons-grade uranium. These developments have taken place in spite of Egypt having signed the Nuclear Non-Proliferation Treaty (NPT), coupled with an active safeguard agreement with Vienna.

Egypt might have good reason to desire nuclear parity. For decades, it scrupulously maintained a delicate balance by championing nuclear nonproliferation in the Middle East to address its economic and industrial needs, and, at the same time, seeking a guarantee of security against the Israeli nuclear threat. Matters have since been compounded by a distinctly more militant approach by some senior Egyptian military officers, government officials, and scholars, all of whom are seeking to develop what the Egyptian weekly *Al-Ahram* has consistently called "the Arab deterrent."

Israeli professor Gerald Steinberg, an expert on nuclear proliferation at Bar-Ilan University's BESA Center for Strategic Studies, observed that these sentiments took off radically after 1998, in the wake of nuclear tests conducted by India and Pakistan. He is of the opinion that "it is possible that the combination [of those tests] and Iraqi-Iranian nuclear developments triggered an Egyptian decision to resume research on developing nuclear weapons."

Professor Steinberg gives good reason for Cairo moving in this direction. He says: "Egypt sees itself as a leading power in the Arab world. It would feel at a loss if other Arab countries had nuclear weapons and were more advanced technologically as a consequence."

Critics of this moral dichotomy point to Israel's consistent refusal to ratify the nonproliferation treaty. Another issue is the perceived double standard in relation to the development of nuclear weapons by the Jewish State, something accepted by the U.S., yet when an Islamic country wants to do the same, the Americans become apoplexic. As one of my Arab colleagues said, Israel has yet to account for its own nuclear weapons program, which is vast.

A problem that confronts most Westerners who visit Egypt these days is that they tend to paint images of the country with the broadest of brushes. Invariably, perspective is superseded by events, and the reason is simple: Egypt has more faces than its forty-six historical dynasties, though its pride is often greater than its accomplishments.

The asphyxiating, polluted, and overpopulated gloss of *Umm al-dunya* ("Mother of the World")—as Cairo is still lovingly referred to by some—is juxtaposed a thousand times over by the appalling squalor of tiny hamlets, villages, and towns up and down the length of the Nile. To some, it's a life of abysmal, dehumanizing misery. Observe that this is not Cairo or Alexandria, but rather, the real fabric of Egyptian society, one that comprises about two-thirds of a nation where the population hovers somewhere around 70 million.

Also, it is impossible to understand modern Egypt without knowing something about what goes on outside the big cities. Very few people, including some who are considered authorities on the Middle East, ever see that side of things in a country where it is not always easy to get off the beaten tourist track. I did it when I made half a dozen television documentaries along the length of the Nile in the 1980s.

At the same time, Cairo has a good deal going for it, even though many expatriates living there might disagree, sometimes vigorously.

Al-Qahira ("The Victorious"), as one writer commented, seduces some and revolts others. In its own lethargic way, this city of six-laned highways and ten bridges works. Its recently inaugurated underground rail-grid and a steady loosening of economic ties to the state, coupled with a host of new, private, and independent associations and institutions, seem to have turned things around. With 12 or 14 million people (who really knows?), the UN says Cairo is the most densely populated large urban area anywhere—the greatest metropolis in its quadrant on earth.

It's also a city that can stifle. The people there are often morbidly suspicious of anything not ethnic. To many, foreigners are, a priori, infidels, and routinely, Israelis are relegated to a category that is sometimes deemed subhuman. Very few non-Arab observers have discerned this nation's interior cast of mind, and frankly, it shows. While Americans are tolerated by the majority of people living there, President Bush and his entire cabinet are considered Zionist surrogates.

It goes further. There is a curious free-floating hostility toward anything American, and, according to one Arab authority,[2] a conviction "that the U.S. is somehow engaged with Israel in an attempt to diminish and hem in Egypt's power and influence." This condition is constantly being articulated, both in the media and in private, in spite of Washington having granted Egypt "most-favored nation" status and passing on all that aid—free, gratis, and for nothing.

Moreover, it has been doing so since 1978. Work it out for yourself: roughly $2 billion a year for almost thirty years.

To hard-line Arabists, it is of little concern that Egypt simply wouldn't survive without it. Rather, it's more a question of principle, loosely based on the precept that you are either for their ideals and culture or, so many of them conclude, you must be against it. Mostly it's a black-and-white issue, and sadly, there are pathetically few grays in this cloistered Muslim world where, among women, the use of the *hijab* (Islamic dress) has tripled in the past ten years.

Egypt's nuclear history has a direct bearing on current developments in the Middle East. The country's indigenous nuclear weapons program—called Operation Cleopatra, and aimed at producing nuclear warheads with which to arm its missiles—had been moribund since the Six-Day War of 1967. It was terminated by incoming President Sadat who, for years, had downplayed the Israeli nuclear threat. It was again raised by President Mubarak after he took power, though clandestine nuclear activity or not, he has always made a very public issue of acceding to the tenets of the Nuclear Non-Proliferation Treaty.

Cairo first threatened to start work on developing the atom bomb when concerns over Israel's activities at Dimona grew in the early 1960s. It initially approached the Soviet Union and China with requests for the bomb, but was rebuffed by both. It was only after it was bowled over in the June 1967 war that Egypt signed the nonproliferation treaty.

Earlier, in 1956, Egypt's nuclear program began with the installation of a U.S. radioisotope at the Egyptian National Research Center. According to the Monterey Institute of International Studies, this was followed by the installation of a Soviet-built Van der Graaf–type 2MWt reactor at Inshas by Moscow. Although this device continues to manufacture radioisotopes for scientific and industrial research projects, it has no known plutonium production capability. Energy shortages and reports of an Israeli nuclear program in the 1960s, and intelligence that Israel had built two nuclear weapons, prompted a push for nuclear development and bids from the U.S. and West Germany for a 150 MWt plant, ostensibly to desalinate seawater at Borg El Arab. The program was abandoned as Cairo's relationship with the West deteriorated.

In 1975, Egypt said it would sign an agreement with the Soviets for a 460MWe reactor, leading to the possibility that the U.S. would supply what was needed. But this was also abandoned when Washington's inspection measures proved too intrusive. In the early 1980s, Egypt had hoped to ink a deal to buy two nuclear reactors, which would have included fuel supplies and technical expertise, but the agreement collapsed due to lack of funding from the U.S. Export/Import Bank and fears of dependence on the West.

The Stockholm International Peace Research Institute (SIPRI) maintains that through its relationship with the IAEA, Egypt has received a good deal of technical assistance in uranium exploration and analysis, milling techniques, and nuclear safety. Egypt's Atomic Energy Authority (AEA) has also participated in bilateral and multilateral programs to facilitate information and expert exchanges, training, technology transfers, and receiving technical equipment.

At the same time, there are various components missing in the country's nuclear infrastructure. The AEA has yet to establish facilities in the fields of uranium mining, milling, conversion, enrichment, or reprocessing, although experimentation has probably occurred in all but enrichment processes. Indeed, some analysts have characterized Egypt's nuclear fuel cycle as being one of a "dual-use" nature.

For instance, in 1996, the authors of *The Risk Report* claimed, "Argentina is building a nuclear reactor in Egypt that will give Cairo its first access to bomb quantities of fissile material, with possibly enough plutonium to make one nuclear weapon per year."

Argentina's 22MWt pool-type light-water reactor does burn enriched uranium and produce plutonium. However, in 1997, when the Argentinean ETTR-2 reactor was built and went on stream, it was subjected to full IAEA safeguards, which made diversion of its spent fuel improbable. This does not preclude possible irradiation of uranium targets which may go undetected. Also, Egypt has a hot-cell laboratory, which may be used to reprocess irradiated targets or provide minuscule amounts of fuel on a laboratory scale. Some Israelis reckon that Cairo has other facilities to develop nuclear weapons.

Last, Egypt may once again be seeking new technologies from Russia and China. Recently, the press reported that both countries offered to sell Egypt a nuclear power reactor, and right now China may be discussing the possibility of constructing a uranium-enrichment plant in Egypt. That said, there is no way anybody can ignore the fact that Egypt's relations with its northeastern neighbor are sorrowful.

Take a few recent examples: Ben Lynfield wrote in *The Jerusalem Post*[3] not long ago that so many years "after the signing of the peace treaty, Egypt and Israel find themselves not so much in a cold peace, but, according to some, in a cold war ..." That might have been in reaction to what Mohammad al-Takhlawi penned some months before in the Egyptian magazine *October*, though in typical Israeli fashion, it is doubtful that Lynfield would have waited six months to reply. The Egyptian said: "The Torah makes clear that quarreling and strife are among the foundations of the 'Israeli personality' ... [that the Jew] is a man of conflict who sows enmity with his hidden fingers throughout the world."[4]

Another commentator, Mustafa Mahmoud, declared at about the same time that "Satan worship is part of Judaism."[5] Some of this rhetoric is hyperbole, while much of it, sadly, is not.

Anybody not familiar with the nuances of Middle East realpolitik might regard any of these shots as little short of war talk, though other recent Egyptian media portrayals equating Israeli leaders as Nazis and terrorists did go way over the edge. Nor is it as bad as calling Jews "descendants of the apes," as was done at a May 1998 U.S. rally sponsored by the Washington-based Council on American-Islamic Relations, a radical organization that seems to be doing its best to give Muslims a bad name.

Comments like those in the Cairo press are commonplace. Some take an even stronger anti-Semitic line. Quite a few talk of Jewish manipulation of conflicts to achieve what are termed "distinctly Israeli objectives." Wahya Abu Thawkra wrote in *Al-Akhbar* that the Holocaust was an Israeli myth invented to "blackmail the world into supporting Zionism."

Notable, too, was that in that run-up to the twentieth anniversary of the Israeli-Egyptian peace accord, the only Egyptians that paid any real attention to that historic milestone were several members of the Egyptian parliament. They launched a vigorous effort to annul it. Because their protests never really gathered momentum, the gesture failed to elicit support. In any event, if it looked like it was going anywhere, President Mubarak's people would almost certainly have squashed it.

Under normal circumstances, such utterances shouldn't raise hackles. We all know that Arab journalists, like their Western counterparts, rarely pull punches. In fact, when the mood takes them, they can be as opprobrious as hell. Further, nobody wants another war. The difference this time around is that relations between the two countries are about as strained as they've been since the accord was signed.

Egyptian analysts not only see little basis for a closer relationship or cooperation between Israel and Egypt, but also the prevalent view in Cairo is that both are now rivals for regional primacy. They view the cloistered coziness between Israel and Turkey as a very distinct threat, and hail Israel's perceived defeat by a raggedy bunch of Hezbollah guerrillas—who took on all that the Israeli Army, backed by overwhelming air power, could throw at them and promptly hurled it back.

No doubt, relations between the two states have taken a knock. Of the twenty-two fields of cooperation envisaged in the peace treaty that originally brought them together, only agriculture has grown. Cairo even shuns cooperation on tourism, though it wasn't too long ago that the place swarmed with Jewish visitors, not always on their best behavior. With disruption back home getting worse, Israelis have become distinctly wary of visiting their biggest neighbor.

A while back, another dimension crept into the dichotomy. In Israel it was underscored in *The Jerusalem Post* under the headline EGYPT THE NEW ENEMY?

Arieh O'Sullivan offered a challenge in a page-one lead: "The army doesn't want to say it out loud, but behind closed doors the IDF [Israeli Defense Force] is changing its attitude about Egypt." At the time, O'Sullivan disclosed that Egyptian armed forces made a deal to buy 10,800 rounds of 120mm smoothbore KEW-A1 ammunition for its M1A1 battle tanks. This was no ordinary purchase, he wrote, noting, "It is the 'silver bullet' of armor-piercing artillery, made of depleted uranium [DU], and is said to be able to defeat any armor system on earth."

Then he added something that chilled sentiments in both countries. Decades of "cold peace" have never eliminated the deep-rooted insecurities and mutual distrust between the IDF and the Egyptian armed forces, he declared. O'Sullivan went on to say: "While the peace treaty has given Israel's military leaders some breathing space in its planning, the command structure has never taken its eyes off our southern neighbor and war plans still call for a hefty reserve force to be set aside for dealing with Egypt, no matter where confrontation breaks out."

Were these comments merely the speculative ramblings of another Israeli hack, they might have been ignored. They were not.

O'Sullivan—like al-Takhlawi and Mahmoud—networks very competently within his own community. Also, many years of peace and growth aside, Jerusalem really is concerned about its long-term relations with its Arab neighbors; so much so that several Israeli think tanks recently offered prognostications about the possibility of a future war in the region. While nobody wants conflict, only a fool would ignore the portents, if not from across the border then from an extremely hostile and totally disaffected Palestinian minority in its own backyard.

When asked how he saw future Egyptian-Israeli relations, Daniel Pipes was pessimistic. He told me he has good reason to be, since he lived in Cairo for several years, speaks Arabic, and is closely associated with the Middle East Forum in the United States, as well as being an author of three books on Islam.

"The problem is simple," Pipes reckoned. "Arabs in general, Egyptians in particular, have not had the requisite change of heart toward Israel. Yes, their governments sign treaties with Israel, but no, the populations still are not reconciled to the permanent existence of a sovereign Jewish state in the Middle East. Until that happens, the Arab-Israeli conflict will go on," Pipes declared. At the same time, he said, Egypt wasn't (as some observers have suggested) about to succumb to Islamic fundamentalism.

It is of some consequence that the tank-round deal came after the U.S. administration agreed to sell Egypt a $3 billion arms package that included twenty-four advanced F-16D fighter jets, 200 more M1 Abrams tanks (assembled in Egypt), and a PAC-3 Patriot air-defense missile system. Like the present Israeli prime minister, Mubarak will use his annual U.S. aid package to pay for this hardware.

Accept the basics, the most zealous adherents aver, and in his wisdom Allah—glorified and exalted is He—will provide.

The slogan of both the Muslim Brotherhood in Egypt and the Islamic Jihad across the border in the so-called Occupied Territories says it all: "Islam is the Answer." Many of these people are increasingly questioning Western values. Others have asked why they should not be allowed to try "something of our own."

That "something," as Geraldine Brooks has stated in her writings, can take many forms. Formerly with the Cairo bureau of *The Wall Street Journal*, Brooks believes it can include extremists rampaging down the Pyramids Road, torching tourist clubs that serve alcohol, or, in rural Egypt, a sheikh urging the ban on the sale of zucchini and eggplants because stuffing the long, fleshy vegetables might give women lewd thoughts.

In Cairo, says Brooks, a writer mocking that pronouncement was gunned down and killed outside his office.[6] Like their counterparts across the Suez, this kind of logic is reinforced by history, much of it recent.

It's the same in Luxor and Aswan in Upper Egypt, and in the country's second city on the Mediterranean. While there are many modern buildings going up in Alexandria, you only need to move on a few hundred meters from the coast-hugging Corniche to sense that Durrell's *Justine* might be a present-day apparition. There is change, yes, but many crippling mores remain rooted. For instance, according to Amnesty International's Human Rights Information Pack, it was estimated that more than 90 percent of Egyptian women had undergone some form of female genital mutilation[7] (though I personally believe that this statistic, like so many of Amnesty International's not-always-even-handed pronouncements, to be inflated). At the same time, even a single little girl having her clitoris removed with a razor is one too many.

In the end, however, it's the heat and the endless throng of humanity that stultifies. Walk through the back streets of Egypt's two largest conurbations—it is actually reasonably safe for most Westerners to do so—and you can sometimes detect an overwhelming sense of hopelessness. It envelops much of Egypt's richly textured society, where contrasts are often so stark and unpleasant that they startle; the hopeless crush of traffic bedlam and unending crowds depress just about everybody.

Max Rodenbeck, a correspondent for Britain's *Economist* who has lived much of his life in Cairo, published an excellent book about the place not long ago. It is titled *Cairo—The City Victorious*.[8] For him, Cairo "fits as snugly as an old shoe," and, as he observes, ". . . not one generation in Cairo's five millennia of incarnations has failed to whine about decline, and still the city has endured."

It's the same beyond urban limits. While filming in the Delta a few years ago, we visited a small settlement in the back of beyond, northeast of Cairo and not far from a provincial capital, Damietta. There, tiny piles of amphora stacked near the road caught our eye. It was all handmade, and we wanted to view it from up close. In the end, despite the protestations of our government-appointed minders, we spent a day filming the lives of the two men responsible for this remarkable output.

Most confining were the terrible conditions under which they worked. Their equipment and the dingy, damp "workshop" predated Christendom. The only recognizable contemporary touch was a bare electric bulb in the middle of a mud-walled shack. Bare backs were arched over the huge stone wheels, on which the vessels were shaped and which they powered with their feet, creating a scene that was very much as it has always been.

Both men started their day at dawn. They kept at it, shaping mud into bulbous, watertight containers, sometimes for twelve hours at a stretch. Their idea of a rest was a smoke break. Their women brought them lunch, which they ate in the workplace because it was too hot to go outside. It was a life numbed by drudgery. Each family, we were told, had seven or eight children, though one of them had recently died of waterborne infections. It might have been bilharzia, endemic in the Nile since time began.

Yes, they could read, they told our driver, who interpreted, "but only the Koran." Yes, they were comfortable: "Nobody goes hungry and we have television," or as the interlocutor tried to explain, "they actually know no better." For them, it was a question of the eternal cycle of putting bread on the table. Most evenings were spent at coffeehouses, where they would gather to chat, smoke their hookahs, and perhaps watch football.

Only one thing was ever allowed to interrupt the evening's proceedings, and that was the TV news. When it came to recent events—perhaps among the Kurds, or a Muslim-backed revolt somewhere east of the Urals, and more recently, Iraq and Afghanistan—we quickly learned that the average Egyptian peasant is probably better informed about events beyond their own frontiers than most Texans. Therein lies another imbroglio: While not everybody votes, or is even aware of Mubarak's prowess as a leader or his long-term goals, Egypt is an astonishingly politicized society. Ultimately, that could be its undoing.

The calculus of Egypt's survival in the twenty-first century rests solely on its ability to survive intact as a nation. In trying to maintain this ideal, it faces the same formidable obstacles that confront so many other developing world entities, Islamic ones especially. These include religious fundamentalism, poverty, widespread unemployment, and an economic base that needs to grow a lot faster than it is doing in the face of an expanding population that could touch 100 million in the next generation. In short, Cairo's leaders face a conundrum: Those with the least might, ultimately, seek support from those who offer the most, even if it is in the life beyond. We've seen such influences at work in Iran and among suicide bombers in Iraq and Israel. Until very recently, the same phenomena could be observed, among others, in Yemen, Afghanistan, Algeria, and the Sudan.

Fouad Ajami, Arab author and academic, wrote that Egypt is both the Arab world's most accomplished state and one of its poorest.[9] It's a tough combination, and is difficult on Egypt's pride and on those states in the Arab world that have to deal with it, he said. "Egypt makes a fascinating study of the role of perceptions in politics as the world changes and power and wealth slip away to others. The memories of centrality and preeminence remain," he declared.

Ajami also reckoned that Egypt was where Arab history came into focus. It did so with Nasser and his brand of revolution. It continues to do so today. It is a nation of strong, freethinking post-Imperial leaders—Nasser, Sadat, and Mubarak—all of whom have left their mark, not only among their own people but also on the Islamic world of the new millennium.

But the rumblings in Egypt's corridors of power foreshadow problems of a far more serious nature than anything that we have observed since the end of Hitler's War, and fundamentalism is only one of them. Another is a peace process that has atrophied. Both are serious developments, because the Egyptian role epitomizes both the possibilities as well as the limitations of Arab history.

Egypt's performance has been referred to by some observers as a desperate trapeze act. As Ajami said, the Arabs are always fixated, often applauding, and, at other times, full of derision. If a concept is not fulfilled in Cairo, it has little chance elsewhere in the Arab world, and this is not helped by Egypt losing its race with modernity, he suggests. As one critic put it to me years ago, "If Egypt farts, the smell permeates the entire Arab world . . ."

A fascinating insight into how Egyptians think politically was recently provided by a poll conducted throughout the country. Almost 1,400 Egyptians were asked for their candid opinion about their country, their government, their intercommunal relationships, and, not least, their aspirations. Three-quarters funded by the Ford Foundation, there were some strategic overtones. The results found that 68.7 percent of those asked preferred to be ruled by a democracy. Only 18 percent opted for what was termed "a just dictatorship." At the same time, barely a tenth were actual members of political parties.

Roughly 41 percent of those Muslims asked said they voted in the last elections, compared to 38.5 percent of Christians who did. Interestingly, almost four-fifths of those polled believed that there was equality between Muslims and Copts, which some apologists say trashes the perception of strife between the two major religions in this Arab country. Press freedom was scrutinized. About 56 percent believed that it was "extensive," which is illuminating, since it's no secret that most editors follow the party line. Either that, or they'd be without a job.

Overall, the poll suggested more than a modicum of optimism for the future. Only a small proportion felt that the country would not be able to deal with a serious foreign military or economic threat exemplified by a possible suspension of U.S. largesse. More pertinent, when asked about the nation's ability to confront an Israeli military onslaught, the message that emerged was clear: 86.5 percent thought that Egypt was "very capable" of doing so.

For their part, the Israelis have also assessed something of an Arab-related doomsday scenario, encapsulated in a book published by the Washington Institute.[10] Its appendix lists "Five Scenarios for War" between Israel and its neighbors, "each of which," say the authors, "illustrates the variety of demands on the Israeli military." The five scenarios are:

1. An *Insurrection in Palestine* by a spontaneous popular uprising, sustained guerrilla warfare sponsored by the PA [Palestinian Authority] . . . independent terrorist action . . . or a combination of all three.

2. *Israeli Intervention in Jordan*, particularly "in the event of a move to bring Palestinians into the West Bank and Gaza under unified Palestinian rule."

3. *Violation or Abrogation of the Peace Treaty with Egypt.*

4. *War with Syria*, which might result either from a preplanned Syrian attack on the Golan or from a deteriorating situation in South Lebanon, where Iranian-supported Hezbollah guerrillas have inflicted casualties on Israel. [This assessment was made prior to the 2006 Israeli invasion of South Lebanon, and things might be perceived very differently today.]

5. *Weapons of Mass Destruction from the Outer Ring*—from states such as Iraq or Iran [or others that might be acquiring WMD], as well as the means of delivering them. The authors suggest that a nonconventional attack would most probably occur against a backdrop of a protracted and bloody guerrilla war with the Palestinians in the West Bank and Gaza, or a regional conflict in which Israel is targeted to deter U.S. intervention.

In short, as Eliot Cohen (professor of strategic studies at Johns Hopkins), Michael Eisenstadt (senior fellow at the Washington Institute for Near East Studies), and Andrew Bacevich (executive director of the Johns Hopkins Foreign Policy Institute) observed, the Jewish State is facing more military threats than ever before. "And they are having to cope with all these threats simultaneously."[11]

The authors suggest that it is not particularly difficult to construct a "super-scenario" that would join at least four of the above scripts together simultaneously, though an invasion of Jordan, considering recent developments, is far-fetched as things stand at present. Let's not forget, however, that Jordan has a history of its leaders being assassinated by political malcontents.

Martin van Creveld, a military historian at the Hebrew University who, over the years, has acquired a reputation as a rather brilliant alarmist (and who has been proved right more often than some of his critics are prepared to admit), made another assessment at about the same time. In his own book, he argued that the IDF today is heavily bureaucratized, no longer aggressive or imaginative, and is overreliant on technology.[12] Though things have improved markedly with the two intifadas, he wrote that "it bears little resemblance to the superb fighting machine that it once was."

Van Creveld went on: The IDF's conscripts are "scandalously underpaid," and its officer corps pampered and spoiled; the army has become "soft, bloated, strife-ridden, responsibility-shy and dishonest."

Though this was penned before the "War with Hezbollah," as some call it, van Creveld reckoned that both the quantity and quality of training had dropped. Morale had declined and there is "hardly an officer left who has commanded so much as a brigade in a *real* war . . . and one shudders to think what IDF commanders and troops would do under full-scale attack" by real-life soldiers armed not with rocks and knives (like the Palestinians) but with missiles, cannons, and tanks (like the Egyptians).

How sad that Israel's 2006 invasion of Lebanon validated all these sentiments and, one needs to ask, at what cost in lives lost?

Cohen, Eisenstadt, and Bacevich maintain that militarily, the Middle East is "undergoing profound changes." Their observations include the assessment that Israel's famed "militia model" of well-trained reservists has become obsolete, and that there has been a drop in what they termed "soldier motivation." As a result, they suggest, the IDF is being forced to become "small, elite, and professional," a process that will convert it to an "Americanized officer corps," and lead to the partial abandonment of universal subscription.

Of course, much of this has been said before. Prior to the 1956 Sinai Campaign, premier David Ben-Gurion expressed concern that a new "espresso generation" would not fight as well as its predecessors did in the War of Independence of 1948. With that in mind, there are specialists in Egypt who accumulate and analyze such data and, no doubt, they have already passed it on where it can do the most good. Indubitably, Cairo's media got some of it. At the end of the day, Egypt rigorously observes the Machiavellian dictum that to maintain peace, you need to prepare for war.

Its armed forces have almost completed a ten-year modernization plan, and about half of its tanks are Western, says *Jane's World Armies*. This includes 555 American M1s. Similarly, eleven of its twelve divisions are now fully mechanized or armored, and its claims that it has cut its army strength from 600,000 to about half that in the past twenty years appears to have been realized. All this has been achieved in a bid to establish a more mobile and efficient force.

The most striking gains have been made with its air force, which *Middle East Military Balance* has described as undergoing "the most far-reaching transformation of any air force in the Middle East." It adds that "Egyptian aircraft are equipped with such interception-enhancement precision-guided munitions systems as infrared and advanced electromagnetic missiles which, until recently, even the Israelis did not have." It labeled the Egyptian Air Force (EAF) "a potent deterrence," and that Jerusalem would have to take Egypt into consideration, even if it were not directly involved in hostilities on another front.

More prescient, it reckoned that the EAF had the ability to block Red Sea or Mediterranean sea lanes, the thesis being that this was "a factor which cannot be lost on historians who know what took place in 1956 and 1967. Both those wars were started because of an Egyptian sea blockade on the Jewish state." (See *Middle East Policy*, June 1998, "The Oldest Threat: Water in the Middle East."[13])

After the Gulf War, no country outside Iraq is more aware of the danger faced by any society of the indiscriminate use of missiles than Egypt. It has some; it's just that Israel has more.

The word out of Jerusalem is that Cairo (with North Korean help) now has North Korean No-Dong medium-range ballistic missiles, which not only puts any location in Israel within its range, but a good deal more besides. Most worrisome is the fact that the Egyptians appear eager to go that extra mile and acquire more sophisticated projectiles, a sentiment dictated largely by the perception (quoted in *Al-Quds Al-Arabi* on June 27, 1996) that Israeli military commanders "had their fingers on the triggers of 300 nuclear warheads, modern factories for the manufacture of missiles and satellites . . ."

According to the Intelligence Resource Program of the Federation of American Scientists, Egypt's missile production capacity is second only to Israel in the region. Project 333 (or *Thalathat*) was initiated during the early 1960s, with the 1,000-mile-range al Ra'id Medium-Range Ballistic Missile (MRBM) on the drawing board. It was planned to carry a 1,200-pound warhead. There is no record that either the al Ra'id or any other missiles being worked on at the time ever entered service.

There have been other developments, including indigenous production of Scuds with North Korean help. An enhanced Scud-C (called Protect-T), with a range/payload of 280 miles/1 ton, was developed, followed (with assistance from the French combine SNPE) by the Sakr-80 as a replacement for the aging Frog.

Since then, protocols were signed between Egypt and Argentina (on the Badr-2000, which parallels the Condor II) to produce newer versions of Soviet antiaircraft missiles. While the Argentinean connection was subsequently scuttled following U.S. pressure, Cairo is still not a member of the Missile Technology Control Regime (MTCR), an informal association of countries that share the goal of nonproliferation.

Similarly, the Egyptian navy is now considered the largest and most powerful in the Eastern Mediterranean, and has vessels big enough to transport large numbers of troops over fairly long distances. *The Military Balance* also stated that unlike Saudi Arabia or Indonesia, both of which acquired sophisticated equipment only to see it all rust because they didn't have properly trained personnel to operate it, Egypt does not have that problem. Cairo looks after what it has with the kind of application not often seen in the Arab world.

Meanwhile, it is Arieh O'Sullivan's opinion that while IDF commanders are reluctant to speak publicly on the Egyptian arms buildup (since the two countries are formally at peace), some of them have privately expressed concern over its aggressive character. A few have described these improvements as "amazing" and "scary."

Whereas Egypt has been a marginal actor in the IDF threat assessment, this is no longer the case, O'Sullivan stated.[14] In short, the IDF is caught in a double bind. It sees the Egyptian army preparing to fight, yet it hesitates to call Egypt an enemy out of fear of turning it into one. At the same time, he quotes senior IDF sources as saying that the probability of Israel going to war with Egypt is close to zero, partially because of Cairo's strong strategic relationship with the U.S., which seems to have created a sense of dependence among Egyptian leaders, "and injects conservatism" into the picture.

However, all that could change if any of one of three events took place. O'Sullivan listed them as follows:

1. Israel goes to war with Syria, and as a consequence, Egypt sees this as Israeli aggression (it could then join in an Arab coalition);

2. There could be a full-scale conflict between Jews and Palestinians;

3. Or, realistically, a fundamentalist coup in Egypt, which the IDF (in its quaint phraseology) terms "an uncontrollable event."

O'Sullivan went on to say that while Egypt is more secular than other Muslim-dominated countries, the clash between Islamic fundamentalism and more moderate influences in the country does pose a serious long-term threat to the nation's internal stability.

There are other imponderables, and one of these involves WMD. According to Western intelligence sources, there are at least a dozen countries that are looking for chemical or biological solutions to their problems, among them Syria, Libya, Iran, North Korea, and Iraq. Egypt is also part of the equation. Quoting Agence France Presse,[15] the Arabic-language, London-based *Al-Hayat* last April published a report datelined Cairo, by John Hart. It was headed JIHAD OBTAINED BIOCHEMICAL WEAPONS FROM EX-SOVIET BLOC. A similar story appeared in Cairo in *Al-Sharq Al-Awsat*, monitored by Washington's Foreign Broadcast Information Service (FBIS).

Both reports maintained that cadres loyal to Osama bin Laden in Egypt might have acquired a quantity of biological weapons through the mail. The *Al-Sharq* report stated that factories in former Warsaw Pact countries and some "Eastern" states were supplying deadly diseases such as Ebola, anthrax, and salmonella to whoever wanted them without verifying the identity of the importer. Thus, it said, an organization with close ties to the bin Laden terror group active in Egypt was able to acquire anthrax from a source in an East Asian country for the equivalent of $3,695 plus freight. A Czech laboratory agreed to supply what appeared to be botulinum toxin for $7,500 per sample.

Egyptian security agencies that conducted an investigation into the case of the "returned Albanian Arabs" over a four-month period, compiled a 20,000-word dossier, part of which was examined by a journalist from *Al-Sharq Al-Awsat*. The "first defendant," Ahmad Ibrahim al-Najar, revealed details of the transactions in a 143-page confession. The case was referred to Egypt's "military justice." Al-Najar told prosecutors that the head of his group was none other than Ayman al-Zawahiri, Osama bin Laden's elusive deputy, who had a $25 million bounty on his head when we went to press. That man has been active for a long time, it seems.

Meanwhile, Cairo has a WMD program or two of its own. In a comprehensive report[16] on the arms race in the Middle East, America's *Bulletin of the Atomic Scientists* stated that a Special National Intelligence Estimate (which represents the combined wisdom of the CIA, Defense Intelligence Agency [DIA], and the National Security Agency) reported that the first country to obtain chemical weapons training, indoctrination, and material in the Middle East was Egypt. It concluded that it might have been motivated by Israel's construction of the Dimona nuclear reactor in 1958.

Egypt was also the first country in the region to use chemical weapons. It employed phosgene and mustard agents against Yemeni Royalist forces in the mid-sixties, confirmed personally by former SAS colonel Jim Johnson, who commanded the clandestine British strike force that seriously damaged the Egyptian war effort in the south of the Arabian Peninsula. His photos of this operation are remarkable, almost all never published.[17]

Some reports believe that Cairo used an organophosphate nerve agent. Moreover, a 1990 DIA study, titled "Offensive Chemical Warfare Programs in the Middle East," concluded that Egypt was continuing to conduct research related to chemical agents. (It identified a production facility, but details were scrubbed in a pre-release security vetting.)

A 1996 United States Arms Control and Disarmament Agency report stated that ". . . Egypt developed biological warfare agents by 1972 . . . and there is no evidence to indicate that it had eliminated this capability and it remains likely that the Egyptian capability to conduct biological warfare continues to exist . . ."

Asked about Egyptian chem/bio programs, John Pike, head of the Federation of American Scientists, told me that his organization had some leads on facility locations, but that he was not prepared to go into detail until satellite imagery had been completed.[18]

In his latest book, titled *Chemical and Biological Warfare: A Comprehensive Survey for the Concerned Citizen*, Eric Croddy, formerly a senior research associate at the Monterey Institute of International Studies, and now an intelligence analyst at Pacific Command in Hawaii, lists thirteen biological warfare agents on which Egypt is suspected to have been working. These include anthrax, botulinum, plague, cholera, tularemia, glanders, smallpox, and others. Croddy states that already in the early 1970s, President Anwar Sadat hinted that an Egyptian biological weapons (BW) stockpile existed.[19]

Croddy points to cooperation between Egyptian and Iraqi CBW experts in the late 1980s and early 1990s, and it warrants attention that President Mubarak has refused to ratify the international Biological and Toxic Weapons Conference (BTWC) Treaty, ostensibly because Israel, too, is culpable.

On chemical weapon production, Croddy quotes 1992 reports that Egypt had procured some 340 tons of chemical weapon precursors from India and Hungary to manufacture nerve agents. He also records that Cairo had been working with Russian and North Korean engineers to design improved ballistic missiles that could deliver these weapons. "Additional evidence suggests that from raw materials and intermediaries [such as phosphorus pentasulphide, a VX precursor] to the finished product, Egypt almost has a complete indigenous capacity to produce chemical weapons," Croddy declared.[20]

At the end of it, we must never forget the comments of Rebecca Stevens and Amin Tarzi, of the Center for Nonproliferation Studies (CNS). These two specialists stated at the Sixth Review Conference of the Parties to the Treaty on the Non-Proliferation of Nuclear Weapons that "in all four of the Arab-Israeli wars, the Egyptians led the Arab side both in the military-political field and in the intangible emotional impetus."

Chapter 16 Endnotes:

1 *Jane's Islamic Affairs Analyst*, London, February 1, 2005.

2 Quoted by Martin Kramer, citing Ajami in "Rude Awakening," *The National Interest*, Washington, D.C., pp. 93–96.

3 Ben Lynfield, *The Jerusalem Post*, March 31, 1999.

4 *October*, Cairo, October 11, 1998.

5 *October*, Cairo, October 4, 1998.

6 Geraldine Brooks, *Nine Parts of Desire: The Hidden World of Islamic Women*, Penguin, London, 1996.

7 In Egypt, clitoridectomy, excision, and infibulation are widely practiced in spite of having been banned by presidential decree in 1958 (overturned in June 1997 by an Egyptian court, even though the Sheikh of al-Azhar, the highest religious authority in the country,

declared his support for the ban). The dispute—which sometimes has the intensity of the U.S. pro/anti-abortion debate—continues.

8 Max Rodenbeck, *Cairo—The City Victorious*, Alfred A. Knopf, New York, 1998.

9 Fouad Ajami, *The Arab Predicament*, Cambridge University Press, 1992.

10 Eliot A. Cohen, Michael J. Eisenstadt, and Andrew J. Bacevich, *Knives, Tanks and Missiles: Israel's Security Revolution*, Washington Institute of Near East Studies, Washington, D.C., 1997.

11 *Commentary*, New York, October 1998, pp. 58–60.

12 Martin van Creveld, *The Sword and the Olive: A Critical History of the Israeli Defense Force*, Public Affairs, 1998.

13 Al J. Venter, *Jane's Intelligence Review*, "The Oldest Threat in the Middle East," January 1998.

14 Arieh O'Sullivan, "Egypt the New Enemy?" *The Jerusalem Post*.

15 Agence France Presse, Subject lexis nexis, April 20, 1999: Author John Hart.

16 E. J. Hogendoorn, "Chemical Weapons Atlas," *Bulletin of the Atomic Scientists*, Chicago, September/October 1997.

17 Personal interview at the home of Colonel Jim Johnson, Marlborough, UK, 2006. Britain and France, in the early 1960s, began a large, long-term covert mercenary operation in Yemen led by Colonel James "Jim" Johnson, formerly commander of 21 SAS. It was a "joint" venture, with Israel providing airdrops and Saudi Arabia's defense minister, Prince Sultan, responsible for finances. One of the young British SAS officers involved was Captain Peter de la Billiere, who was to return to the Arabian peninsula thirty years later as commander of British forces in Operation Desert Storm.

18 Author's communication with John Pike.

19 Eric Croddy, with Clarissa Perez-Armendariz and John Hart. *Chemical and Biological Warfare: A Comprehensive Survey for the Concerned Citizen*, Copernicus Books, New York, 2002.

20 Personal interview.

FOLLOWING TERROR'S MONEY TRAIL

Financing and fund-raising are difficult topics for research when dealing with organizations in general, to say nothing of clandestine ones . . .
—*Targeting Terrorist Financing in the Middle East*: Reuven Paz, erstwhile academic director of the International Policy Institute for Counter-Terrorism (ICT), Herzliya, Israel

Countering international terrorism has a specific link to tracing the money that funds it. Without one, the other cannot operate effectively, since terrorism is only as effective as the money that funds it. That includes nuclear terror, which, by its very nature, is expensive. A solid nuclear weapons program can drain a country of funds.

Though Hezbollah has yet to look to the bomb as a way of gaining a Middle East platform—and, as a consequence, more of an international image—that prospect has been mooted often enough. The Iranian connection could ultimately be useful, especially since many of its followers—like its leader Sayyed Hassan Nasrallah, originally from East Beirut's Bourji Hammoud neighborhood—have spent years at Iranian maddrassas, universities, and insurgent training camps. Many of the movement's cadres, though born in Lebanon, are regarded by their contemporaries as more Iranian in their thoughts, actions, and loyalties than some Iranians who haven't been put through the mill.

That might be expected because Hezbollah, as I demonstrated in my *Iran's Nuclear Option*, remains an active Iranian surrogate organization. It has both political as well as guerrilla components in its makeup, its leaders having extended activities well beyond Lebanon's borders. One example: Hezbollah has recently been linked to several overseas bombings and murders. In October 2006, Argentine prosecutors accused Hezbollah of masterminding the 1994 bombing of a Jewish community center in Argentina, which left 85 people dead and 300 injured.

While most of Hezbollah's financial needs are matched by Iran—an estimated $100/$200 million a year, with a similar amount coming from local and subscription sources within the Levant—the demands made on the organization are enormous. This makes it essential for The Party of God to be able to move cash around without impediment.

With September 11 behind us, that is no longer possible. Hundreds of millions in terrorist assets have been blocked in the U.S. since the attacks on the Twin Towers and the Pentagon, a significant increase over the $200 million-odd that was seized by the end of 2002. Britain took a similar approach. UK chancellor Gordon Brown ordered his banks to freeze the assets of Hamas's new leaders early in the new millennium, including those of the late Abdel Aziz al-Rantissi. By March 2005, the BBC noted, more than $150 million in terrorist assets had been frozen in that country, while almost $7 million had been approved for counterterrorist training abroad.

In a related development, a U.S. General Accounting Office (GAO) report found that terrorist organizations, Hezbollah included, continue to earn and transfer funds variously, including crimes involving precious stones and metals, drugs, and counterfeit goods.[1]

An independent American report at about the same time centered on the matter of countering the funding of international terrorism. Washington's Council on Foreign Relations released a study of the complex methodology of terrorist financing.

Titled "Terrorist Financing," it details the nature and extent of a vast secret underground movement of currencies. It underscored the fact that some terrorist organizations such as al-Qaeda are wealthy enough to provide dysfunctional host governments (like the Sudan, Somalia, and Afghanistan) with financial succor, and not the other way around.

Authors of the report stated that according to several published accounts, al-Qaeda sometimes employed illicit air logistics networks previously used by the Taliban and various African insurgency movements to transport gold and other assets. In this, bin Laden's lieutenants have been remarkably adept, especially "since he built al-Qaeda's financial network from the foundation of a system originally designed to channel resources to the mujahedeen fighting the Soviets."

Almost without exclusion, Islamic terrorist groups make use of the ancient *hawala* or *hundi* underground banking system. This allows the transfer of cash without the actual physical movement of money. It is a cash business "that leaves behind few, if any written or electronic records . . . it operates out of nondescript storefronts and countless bazaars and souks such as you find anywhere in the Islamic world, from Casablanca to Cairo and beyond," maintains a U.S. Independent Task Force inquiry.

It reaches both small villages throughout many regions and large cities around the world. Moreover, it is quick, efficient, reliable, and inexpensive, and draws from a long tradition of providing anonymous services. Most salient, "members of families who have been in the business for generations primarily staff the system." It is almost entirely unregulated around the world, including in the United States and Canada. Significantly, says the report, "the *hawala* system often interacts with similar alternative banking systems operating in other parts of the globe, such as *fei ch'ien, phoc kuan, hui k'uan, ch'iao hui*, and *nging sing kek*." All the *hawala* system needs to operate is a network of *hawaladars* (operators), a good level of trust, and open phone lines. According to the U.S. Independent Task Force report, it works like this:

Customers in one city hand their local *hawaladar* some money. He then contacts his counterpart across the world, who would distribute money out of his own resources to the intended recipient. The volume of transactions flowing through the system in both directions is such that two *hawaladars* rarely have concerns about settlement.

The trust between and among *hawaladars*—who are in many cases related through familial, clan, or ethnic associations—allows them to carry each other's debts for long periods before finding ways to clear them. What is clear is that the entire system, says the report, "appears to be almost custom-made for a terror organization like al-Qaeda." Hezbollah and Hamas would also slot into this category. Some of the money used to fund the London transport bombings in the summer of 2005 was transmitted in this manner.

The report goes on to say that whenever these methods are unavailable, bin Laden and his associates rely on the alternative and oldest method of moving cash; that is, by physically shifting it from one place to another. "Cash smuggling is rampant throughout the Middle East . . . it is abetted by weak border controls and a cash-based culture very much *unlike* Western credit- and electronic-based economies."

The Iranians, Hamas, Hezbollah, al-Qaeda, and the rest also move assets in the form of precious metals and gemstones, "which can be easily and anonymously transferred to cash in any number of souks across the region. The gold trade and the *hawala* system are especially symbiotic, flourishing in the same locales and offering complementary services to those who are looking to move assets across borders," the report states, adding that bin Laden's cadres often rely on "traditional smuggling routes and methods used by drug traffickers, arms smugglers, and other organized criminal groups."

There are a number of intractable problems facing the West in a bid to motivate the tracking of illegal cash flows between terrorist movements, and one of the most important is manpower. While the U.S. Treasury's Office of Foreign

Asset Controls (OFAC) has more than a hundred staff members working full-time on the implementation of financial sanctions (and is still understaffed), the Bank of England, until recently, had only seven. The French Ministry of Finance had two people working part-time, and the German Bundesbank, just one. Similarly, the European Commission in Brussels had only a single individual with a part-time assistant for this extensive work, though that has since been improved by the addition of a few more.

Also, while blocking the flow of money to terrorists may be one of the best ways to stop terror altogether, Treasury department officials have many times stated that this is an extremely difficult task without international cooperation. There are those who regard it as impossible. The overwhelming bulk of terrorist assets reside and flow beyond U.S. borders, David Aufhauser, the department's general counsel, told a House of Representatives Financial Services subcommittee.

Aufhauser cited the distinction made by some countries—including European and Persian Gulf nations—between the political/social and military wings of Hamas as a major obstacle in financial actions against the organization. It was his view that it was impossible to separate the two: give to the political wing of any Arab grouping and there will be some—and often substantial—trickle down to its military affiliates.[2] This, Aufhauser declared, is what is taking place both with Hamas and Hezbollah.

The Independent Task Force inquiry that provided the *hawala* details—for a time under the chairmanship of Maurice R. Greenberg—also disclosed that while financial networks like that established by Osama bin Laden had been disrupted in the wake of 9/11, they had certainly not been destroyed. A conclusion reached was that the most important source of financing for Muslim terrorist groups was not only the continuous fund-raising efforts centered on Islamic organizations, but the fact that they span the globe. Right now, a lot of effort is going into refocusing terrorist financial support efforts in Asia, the task force report declared recently.

Islamic financial institutions that have helped terrorist groups like al-Qaeda in the past (there are many that continue to do so) "are built upon a foundation of charities, nongovernmental organizations, mosques, Web sites, intermediaries, facilitators, banks, and other financial institutions." It also notes that while some donors were aware that their cash was used for illicit purposes, many believed that they were helping to fund legitimate humanitarian efforts.

Al-Qaeda, the report suggests, moved its funds both through the global financial system as well as the quagmire of Islamic banking. At the same time there was a lot more of it transferred through the underground *hawala* system and other domestic or "family" money-transfer mechanisms. These involve a worldwide network of businesses and charities. Some—including those in Iran—are used as a cover for transferring large sums of money.

It also employs such time-honored methods as bulk cash smuggling and the global trade in gold to move and store value. Nor is al-Qaeda alone in using these means: For decades the IRA hustled charities in such cities as Boston and New York to raise funds. They, too, needed to get that cash "back home" undetected, and they were remarkably successful—again, with a modicum of sympathetic political help.

Among welfare organizations that have been publicly identified by the U.S. government as supplying funds to terrorists are the Afghanistan-based Afghan Support Committee, the Al Rashid Trust and Wafa Humanitarian Organization (Pakistan), the Revival of Islamic Heritage Society (Kuwait), and the Saudi-based Al-Haramain organization, as well as the Holy Land Foundation for Relief and Development, which is also to be found in the United States.

These charities and their affiliates—along with others like them that have not yet been publicly designated by the authorities, or even uncovered by intelligence agencies—"have operated internationally, raising, moving, and simultaneously holding their money in a variety countries." The report makes the point that the amounts run into many millions of dollars, and in al-Qaeda's case, hundreds of millions.

An interesting paper published in Israel before September 11 by Reuven Paz, ICT Academic Director, was titled "Targeting Terrorist Financing in the Middle East." Presented at the International Conference on Countering Terrorism through Enhanced International Cooperation, its theme provides those interested with a cogent insight into the subject.[3]

While the paper doesn't deal specifically with Islam or Islamic groups, or with the notion of confrontation between Islam and the West, it does examine the views and perceptions of Islamist terrorist groups toward Western culture. It also touches on the way in which these groups present this confrontation as a *clash of civilizations* (in the tradition of Samuel P. Huntington),[4] or more appropriately, Islam versus the West.

For this reason, Reuven Paz uses the term "Islamists" (or "Islamist terrorist groups"), which applies to those Islamic groups that use the radical and militant interpretation of Islam in order to portray the religious duty of *Jihad* as meaning the use of violence and indiscriminate terrorism.

Paz backs the notion that these same groups often misinterpret Orthodox Islam, and many of their perceptions are in dispute in the Arab and Muslim world. Yet, they influence many believers in the Muslim world as well as Muslim communities in the West. As he says, this influence is the consequence of a combination of political, social, economic, and cultural confrontations "under the guise of religious expressions."

Paz acknowledges that financing and fund-raising are difficult topics for research when dealing with organizations in general, to say nothing of clandestine ones. The tendency of both the individual and community is to keep this issue private, far from public eyes. Dealing with secretive groups, consequently, is much more difficult, and in the case of Islamist terrorist groups, perhaps the most difficult of all.[5]

These groups, he suggests, are in many cases unique, compared, for instance, to other kinds of known terrorist groups, such as nationalists, Marxists, or Anarchists (like Baader-Meinhof in Germany or Italy's Red Army factions).

This uniqueness is the consequence of two main factors: One is the Islamic religious element, in which charity is one of the most important duties and is used as the primary means to disguise financial activity. The other is the relatively widespread support given to the Islamic movements and organizations for political, social, or cultural reasons. Above all, there is the reality that these are religious groups, or at least they like to pass themselves off as such. This is of overwhelming benefit in societies in which Islam is deeply rooted and highly respected among the vast majority of the Arab and Muslim world.

This religious element is most important when financing terrorist groups. In recent years there has been a decline in the sponsoring of terrorism by states, as pointed out in the 1999 report "Patterns of Global Terrorism," published annually by the U.S. State Department.

What this means is that *public support* for terrorist groups has become the most essential element in fund-raising, and the main source of finances. Indeed, contrary to what many believe, public fund-raising from individuals is the most important element in the finances of many institutes, associations, and public organizations. Researches and surveys in the U.S. have indicated this. We should therefore focus on this point with regard to the financing of terrorist groups in the Middle East.

Public support for such Islamist terrorist groups, vital to their success and financial prospects, is the consequence of two social and psychological factors underlying the Islamic social-political renaissance:

- Islamic and Islamist movements and groups have succeeded in the past three decades in fostering in Arab and Muslim societies the notion of a kind of global cultural war, in which they confront a global conspiracy against Islam as a religion, culture, and way of life. Thus, concepts synonymous in the Western political culture with terrorism and political violence are now viewed by many in the Islamic world to be Islamic religious duties. Such concepts include *Jihad* (holy war), *Takfir* (refutation), *Istishhad* (martyrdom, including by suicide), and *Shahid* (martyr).

The central notion, common to most of the Islamic movements and groups—those that carry out terrorism and political violence, and those that justify it and feed the atmosphere that promotes such activity—is that of being in a state of siege, which calls for self-defense. To the believers in this concept, the confrontation justifies the use of all means—particularly when these means are given religious legitimacy.

- Many of the Islamist and Islamic movements and groups have succeeded in convincing many in the Muslim world that they represent the true contemporary interpretation of Islam. Moreover, most of these groups developed out of the perceived need to return to the fundamental sources of Islam. Thus, they based their views on Islamic scholars like Ibn Hanbal (seventh century), Ibn Taymiyyah (fourteenth century), and Ibn 'Abd al-Wahhab (eighteenth century), all of whom were leading fundamentalist religious scholars as well as the most unyielding in doctrine.

It is consequent, maintained Reuven, that the success of the Islamist movements lies in the elemental diversity of Islam. However, in one respect, it also owes much to the lack of a single Islamic center that enjoys the confidence of the vast majority of the Muslim world, and the control of the modern secular regimes in the Muslim world over the religious establishments, on the other.

Those establishments are viewed by large parts of the public as civil servants of the secular state, whose interpretations and rulings conform to the interests of the state. Thus, Islamic and Islamist groups and individuals have become the spiritual guides of quite a large population, and maintain a great deal of power and influence.

Most of the Islamic movements and groups, primarily those that emerged during and after the 1960s, present the Arab and Muslim regimes—in some cases, rightfully—as symbols of arbitrary oppression and the distortion of the social justice rooted in Islam. Thus they encourage their followers to sympathize with and support those who present themselves as the protectors of the weaker elements of society. In many cases they manage to recruit to their side elements of social, political, and cultural protest against Arab and Muslim regimes.

These elements also see themselves as standing against the alleged global conspirators: the United States, Israel, and the Jews. In essence, it is literally everybody of Islamic faith against the Western "Crusader" heretic culture, and just about all else in the West.

The majority of authorities dealing with the subject tend to underscore the difficulties they face in coming to grips with the machinations of financial terror.

In its report, America's General Accounting Office (GAO) said that the full extent of terrorists' use of alternative-financing mechanisms is unknown, due in part to the lack of data collection and analysis by the federal government. Its report also noted that the U.S. departments of the Treasury and of Justice have not yet produced a report, required under the United States' National Money Laundering Strategy, on illegal money transfers via trade in precious stones and commodities.

Outlining the challenges facing law enforcement, the GAO said that U.S. federal agencies have found it extraordinarily difficult to infiltrate terrorist and criminal networks, and that such networks are extremely adept at switching from one method of financing to another. In line with these developments, the U.S. Department of the Treasury has created a new unit that will set strategy and policy for combating terrorist financing. Treasury disclosed that the new Executive Office for Terrorist Financing and Financial Crimes would work with the financial services industry to locate terror-related accounts and groups.

The unit now oversees Treasury's Financial Crimes Enforcement Network (FinCEN), an investigative and information-gathering bureau, and the Office of Foreign Asset Controls (OFAC), which carries out U.S. orders blocking bank accounts and freezing assets of suspected terrorist groups and their supporters.

Several countries followed the American example of monitoring the international—and often illicit—flow of cash, and among the first was Canada. Only weeks after September 11, former ministers Paul Martin (Finance) and John Manley (Foreign Affairs) announced the implementation of a series of tough new regulations aimed at suppressing the financing of terrorism and at freezing the assets of listed persons in Canada.

The regulations implemented a key measure in United Nations Resolution 1373, which was unanimously adopted by the UN Security Council on September 28, 2001. Since Canada's implementation of the system, it has been regarded by many nations as a benchmark to follow. It is worth taking a closer look at its provisions:

A New Listing Provision: The regulation established a list of any persons and organizations that have committed, attempted to commit, or participated in a terrorist act or facilitated the commission of a terrorist act.

Freezing of Assets: No person in Canada or Canadian outside Canada is permitted to knowingly deal directly or indirectly with any asset owned or controlled by a listed person.

Prohibition of Terrorist Fund-Raising: The regulation prohibits the provision and collection of funds to listed persons.

A New Reporting Requirement: Any person who deals in assets they believe are owned or controlled by a listed person must report this information to the Royal Canadian Mounted Police and Canadian Security Intelligence Service.

A New Compliance Regime for Financial Institutions: These institutions must determine if they have any assets that belong to a listed person. Federally regulated financial institutions must confirm their compliance with this requirement and disclose the results to the Office of the Superintendent of Financial Institutions.

While not watertight, Canada, working in conjunction with the U.S. authorities, has had considerable success in interdicting the movement of illegal money from (or to) its large domestic Islamic community. According to Canadian Minister Martin, "the ability to freeze assets is a powerful tool in combating terrorist financing," and, as a consequence, cutting off their access to funding, the activities of these groups are impaired, he added.

Meanwhile, a Canadian finance house has also published a short note on the most common money-laundering methods in operation in many Western states. These are worth noting, and include:

Nominees: This is one of the most common methods of laundering and hiding assets. A launderer uses family members, friends, or associates who are trusted within the community, and who will not attract attention, to conduct transactions on their behalf. The use of nominees facilitates the concealment of the source and ownership of the funds involved. CAs may be used as nominees.

Structuring or "Smurfing": Many inconspicuous individuals deposit cash or buy bank drafts at various institutions, or one individual carries out transactions for amounts less than the amount that must be reported to the government, and the cash is subsequently transferred to a central account. These individuals, commonly referred to as "smurfs," normally do not attract attention, as they deal in funds that are below reporting thresholds and they might appear to be conducting ordinary transactions.

Asset Purchases with Bulk Cash: Individuals purchase big-ticket items such as cars, boats, and real estate. In many cases, launderers use the assets but distance themselves by having the assets registered in the name of a friend or relative. The assets may also be resold to further launder the proceeds.

Exchange Transactions: Individuals often use the proceeds of crime to buy foreign currency that can then be transferred to offshore bank accounts anywhere in the world.

Currency Smuggling: Funds are moved across borders to disguise their source and ownership, and to avoid being exposed to the law and systems that record money entering into the financial system. Funds are smuggled in various ways (by mail, courier, and body-packing), often to countries with strict bank secrecy laws.

Gambling in Casinos: Individuals bring cash to a casino and buy gambling chips. After gaming and placing just a few bets, the gambler redeems the remainder of the chips and requests a casino check.

Black-Market Peso Exchange: An underground network of currency brokers with offices in North America, the Caribbean, and South America allows drug traffickers to exchange pesos for U.S. dollars. The dollars stay in the United States and are bought by South American (mainly Colombian) companies, which use them to buy American goods for sale back home.

In some ways, the United States is severely disadvantaged by the fact that most illegal money transfers take place not on American soil but abroad.

Getting cash into America by means other than bank transfers is easy: clandestine "tourists" can bring in huge amounts of cash in their baggage without declaring the fact that they have more than $10,000 in cash with them. The problem is dispensing it without drawing attention. Banks in the U.S. are required by law to report any suspicious domestic transactions; the same holds true with the movement of any amount in excess of $10,000.

What emerged was that terrorists like to employ a variety of alternative-financing mechanisms to earn, move, and store their assets based on common factors that make these mechanisms attractive to terrorist and criminal groups alike. For all three purposes—earning, moving, and storing—terrorists aim to operate in relative obscurity, using mechanisms involving close-knit networks and industries lacking transparency.

More specifically, terrorists first earn funds through highly profitable crimes involving commodities such as contraband cigarettes, counterfeit goods, and illicit drugs. For example, according to U.S. law enforcement officials, Hezbollah earned an estimated profit of $1.5 million on United States soil between 1996 and 2000 by purchasing cigarettes in a low-tax state for a lower price and selling them in a high-tax state at a higher price. As we have seen, charitable organizations are also a lucrative conduit.

Second, to move assets, terrorists seek out mechanisms that enable them to conceal or launder their assets through nontransparent trade or financial transactions, such as the use of charities, informal banking systems, bulk cash, and commodities that may serve as forms of currency, such as precious stones and metals.

Third, to store assets, they may use similar commodities, because they are likely to maintain value over a longer period of time and are easy to buy and sell outside the formal banking system.

Owing to the criminal nature of their use of alternative-financing mechanisms and the lack of systematic data collection and analysis, the extent of terrorists' use of alternative-financing mechanisms is not known. U.S. law enforcement agencies—and specifically the FBI, which leads terrorist financing investigations—do not systematically collect and analyze data on these mechanisms, though obviously, there is a lot in the pipeline.

In monitoring terrorists' use of alternative-financing mechanisms, the U.S. government faces a number of significant challenges, a few of which include accessibility, adaptability of terrorists, and competing priorities.

First, according to law enforcement agencies and researchers, it is difficult to access or infiltrate ethnically or criminally based networks that operate in a nontransparent manner, such as informal banking systems or the precious stones and other commodities industries.

Second, the ability of terrorists to adapt their methods hinders efforts to target high-risk industries and implement effective mechanisms for monitoring high-risk industry trade and financial flows. According to the FBI, once terrorists know that an industry they use to earn or move assets is being watched, they may switch to an alternative commodity or industry.

Finally, competing priorities create challenges to federal and state officials' efforts to use and enforce applicable U.S. laws and regulations in monitoring terrorists' use of alternative-financing mechanisms.

For example, although the Internal Revenue Service agreed in 2002 to begin developing a system as allowed by law to share with states data that would improve oversight and could be used to deter terrorist financing in charities, it had not made this initiative a priority due to competing priorities.

In this report, it was recommended that the director of the FBI, in consultation with relevant U.S. government agencies, systematically collected and analyzed information involving terrorists' use of alternative-financing mechanisms.

Chapter 17 Endnotes:

[1] A copy of the report can be found on the GAO Web site, http://www.gao.gov/new.items/d04142.pdf.

2   In two cases, in 1990 and 1992, a "special courier" arrived at Israel's Ben Gurion Airport with suitcases crammed with $100,000 each. The money was for Hamas activists, he told the Israelis. In his interrogation and trial, he confessed that the cash was aimed at the reorganization of the terrorist activity of the movement. It was also conceded that had it been legitimately sent to someone with Hamas connections on the pretext of it being used for welfare purposes, there would have been no means of checking that that was the case.

3   http://www.ict.org.il/articles/articledet.cfm?articleid=137.

4   Samuel P. Huntington, *The Clash of Civilizations and the Remaking of World Order*, Simon & Schuster, New York, 1998.

5   When Reuven Paz's paper appeared in October 2000, he observed that even in such reports as the State Department's annual "Patterns of Global Terrorism," there was no serious analysis of the issue of financing terrorism. He went on: "The issue is also not dealt with in the Arab media in the Middle East, though there was an outstanding example of openness in the Arab press in an article of "Abd al-Rahman al-Rashid, *Arab News* (Saudi Arabia), October 11, 1998." Clearly, all that changed after September 11.

EPILOGUE:

AN OMINOUS LAST WORD

Israel will not be the first country in the region to use nuclear weapons. Nor will it be the second.
—Attributed to the late Israeli prime minister, Yitzhak Rabin, during a Washington meeting

Late in 2005, British author Frederick Forsyth was preparing to write his latest novel, *The Afghan*, which covers a remarkable amount of material on Islamic fundamentalist groups—al-Qaeda included. I had my customary lunch with this old friend from our "Biafra Days" at his favorite London hotel, and among those invited were Stephen Ulph and Rupert Pengelley, colleagues from Jane's who specialize (respectively) in Islamic affairs and contemporary weapons systems. Both men had something of interest for Freddie.

One of the more telling asides that emerged at our table was the way the Moroccan government had been countering Jihadist terror groups, a bunch of whom had killed almost two hundred people in a series of extremely well-coordinated bomb attacks on the Madrid transport system in March 2004. Members of those cells, many of whom have since been either arrested or killed, were closely linked to al-Qaeda, their leader apparently having been in contact with Osama bin Laden. Freddie mentioned that he'd spoken to the head of Moroccan security in Rabat, who said: "When these people shave off their beards and don Western clothes, then I start to worry . . . I know that another attack is waiting to happen."

Not every insurgency specialist is aware of this technique, which was also used by Mohamed Atta prior to 9/11. When he got his fateful call, Atta was as hirsute as they come, several months' growth of beard covering his face. Like the Madrid bombers, he adopted Western attire, which immediately made him indistinguishable from those he mixed with on his forays in and out of the United States. Some of the radicals involved in the London bombings were similarly nondescript, as they were described by friends and neighbors. There was a beard here and there, but overall, these were "quite ordinary lads."

The Madrid bombers went a step further, however. In accordance with instructions received from their handlers, they were allowed to blend freely with non-Muslims, and not vicariously either; several of them spent time with European girls, even drinking liquor. The idea, as it was explained by Ulph, was essentially to "become as one with the masses," which is not all that far removed from Mao's dictum of "swimming with the fishes."

Indeed, the *Takfiri* ("excommunicationist") ideology that almost overwhelmed Algeria from the early nineties onward, which I detail in the following pages, actually allows for this kind of assimilation within society as part of its war strategy. This is exactly the same tactic now being employed under a variety of guises against the West.

Brian Robinson has his own take on what is happening in parts of the Islamic world. A former commander of the Rhodesian Special Air Services, he was briefly seconded to 22 SAS in Hereford in the United Kingdom, prior to Ian Smith's unilateral declaration of independence. Colonel Robinson went through that entire African war, coordinating a host of counterinsurgency cross-border raids into Mozambique and Zambia. He put his feet up in Durban after the war ended, but not for long. Robinson was offered, and accepted, the job of military advisor to the chief of staff of the United Arab Emirates Armed Forces in Abu Dhabi. His immediate boss was H. H. Sheikh Mohammed bin Zayed Al Nahyan, who, when the president died, went on to become the UAE crown prince.

Tasked with looking into the security of the UAE, which included border movement and control, it took Robinson about a month to tell the government that there was no border-control plan in place in the UAE. Though he was only to discover this afterwards, the UAE powers-that-be did not take too kindly to such an observation—especially when it was delivered by someone who was neither an Arab nor a UAE national.

Colonel Robinson's conclusions are disturbing, because much of what he found was related to the potential movement of terrorists. As he says, without good communications—which includes easy border access with countries of choice—organizations like al-Qaeda simply cannot function. The research that displeased his superiors disclosed several factors that pointed to some kind of unsubtle collaboration between the UAE and al-Qaeda leaders; essentially, payoffs to avoid cities like Dubai, Abu Dhabi, and Al Fujayrah becoming targets.

This is nothing new in the Gulf. Western intelligence agencies have long been aware that the nearby enclave of Qatar—which also hosts the controversial and sometimes disruptive Al Jazeera television network—long ago reached an accord with bin Laden's people. This is one of the reasons why of all the television networks in the world, and particularly those catering to Islamic audiences, Al Jazeera is invariably the first to provide the latest on Osama.

It was no different in Abu Dhabi, Robinson maintains. He suggests that critics of these views should look at the facts: According to Robinson, all five of the Emirates are especially vulnerable to attack by any kind of dedicated adversary. Yet, as Western-oriented as they are, the first real onslaught still has to happen. And when it does, he warns, the implications of such attacks could seriously destabilize the region.

"Attacks against the UAE economy—namely its oil installations from either the land or the sea against key points such as the Al Taweelah site—would be a formality for a well-trained Islamic special forces unit such as those operating today in Iraq or Afghanistan," says Robinson. "It would almost certainly be concurrent with terrorism in Saudi Arabia." The objective, he suggests, is to destabilize the Saudi economy and create insurrection against the House of Saud. At the same time, hits would take place against anything in the region that might be related to the United States. Robinson continues: "Such actions could include assassinations of high-profile UAE leaders and military or police headquarters, which, at best, are lightly guarded. There might be high-impact acts of terrorism against the civilian population that could cause multiple casualties—or even the detonation of a floating improvised explosives device [IED] in one of the local harbors, which could cause total port dislocation."

Another scenario mooted while he served as military advisor in Abu Dhabi included the possibility of a terrorist group crashing an airliner into a major oil field. This could result in hydrogen sulfide chemical fallout, leading to destruction on a vast scale. More likely would be terrorist group incursions involving the use of heavy vehicle movement through international borders, where only random searches take place. Robinson feels the same thing could happen with any one of the hundreds of Arab dhows and commercial vessels that use UAE ports each week, since they are rarely subjected to stringent searches. It is also no secret, he discloses, that UAE container terminals are notorious for providing opportunities for the introduction of contraband traffic.

"Then you also have the problem of illegal immigrants entering by foot via the Oman, using the broken terrain of the Jebel," says Robinson. Adding that there are times—many of them—when there might be perhaps as little as two dozen border guards on duty at any one time for land, sea and air approaches through the entire country

How did the UAE leadership react to Colonel Robinson's assessment? He was ignored, and his contract was not renewed, even though he pointed out that when you have a situation where there were sometimes only a couple of dozen security officers on duty at any one time, these things are likely to happen. This underscores Robinson's thesis that "in putting forward proposals for tighter security controls in the Emirates, I seemed to have countered a host of under-the-counter arrangements and payoffs already in place that [are keeping] al-Qaeda at bay."

Robinson believes that these unofficial arrangements in the UAE provide al-Qaeda and other Islamic terrorist organizations with the kind of easily accessible comfort zones that they can find nowhere else on earth. As he points out, the Emirates were used as transit and meeting points for some of the terrorists involved in both 9/11 and the 2005 bomb attacks in London. While Robinson has nothing tangible to prove this contention, when you look at the facts, things start to fall into place.

It could be a lot worse, of course. We only have to look at the way recent history unfolded to underscore some of the horrific excesses that fundamentalist Islamic groups are capable of when they set their minds to it. Algeria is one example. Things got so bad in this North African Arab state that even bin Laden eventually dissociated himself, and al-Qaeda, from the kind of mindless brutalities that were taking place there.

Events in Algeria are worth a quick look, if only because Egypt's President Mubarak constantly reminds his followers that if precautions are not taken and strict rule of law followed, exactly the same situation could develop along the Nile.

As with Egypt, Algeria entered a phase of holding national elections, which, though blatantly one-sided, still allowed the populace a voice. The only difference was that the results of the Algerian elections of 1991 were canceled by the military, and this gesture resulted in monumental social strife. It also gave rise to a variety of militant Islamist organizations, including the Groupes Islamiques Armés (Armed Muslim Groups), a loose cell-type structure under regional chiefs or emirs that waged war against the Algerian state.

One of the more powerful of these tribal leaders was Antar Zouabri, who issued his famous sixty-page fatwa in 1997, decreeing that all Algerian people were infidels and therefore legitimate targets. He even ordered Islamist fighters who did not recognize him as their leader to be killed. As part of this Takfiri doctrine, Zouabri issued a *diktat* that nocturnal "raids" were to be mounted against villages and remote communities, and that women and girls could be raped as part of the spoils of war. It was this record of violence that caused al-Qaeda to distance itself from Zouabri's activities, which was when another emir, Hassan Hattab, was encouraged to defect to form the rival Groupe Salafiste pour la Prédication et le Combat (Salafist Group for Call and Combat—GSPC). Civil war raged, leading to horrendous casualty figures. Several independent sources have put the death toll at over 150,000 people.

There is not a single Islamic leader who hasn't closely monitored these developments over the years, only too aware that should things become untenable at home, there will always be a bunch of radical Jihadists—exactly as happened in Algeria—waiting in the wings to create an Islamic revolution of their own. It happened in Afghanistan, and as I write this, it is waiting to happen in Iraq.

Even radical Syria has its own homegrown Takfiri entities. A steady stream of reports emerging from Damascus declare that Syrian security forces have been battling a Takfiri group that calls itself Tanzim Jund al-Sham lil-Jihad wal-Tawhid (Organization of the Army of [Greater Syria] for Jihad and Monotheism). Extremely well organized, this group set to work some years ago, anathematizing not only the Syrian state and its institutions, "but also the sheiks of mosques and the institution of the Friday prayer." It has its own command structure, printing presses, and even sends its recruits abroad for training, some to Pakistan's "lawless" northern frontier areas.

It is interesting to see how an organization like this gets to work. The Saudi newspaper *Al Watan* said the "Tanzim Group" had divided Syria up into five zones, each constituting an "Islamic emirate" with its own emir and organizational structure. The newspaper noted that the scope of these revolutionaries extends well beyond Syria's borders and includes not only Palestine, Lebanon, and Jordan, but also Egypt and Iraq.

Al Watan explained that the division of Syria into operational zones suggested an Algerian model, since that country had been similarly divvied up by the mujahedeen. It also disclosed that close connections between members of Jihadist groups in both countries was illustrated recently by the capture at Damascus of Sakir Adil, the Algerian webmaster of the GSPC Web site, www.jihadalgeria.com.

Morocco has taken particular note of all these developments. Always a moderate, reasonable, and pro-Western country, the Rabat government has consistently been targeted, both by ultra-extreme Jihadists as well as by al-Qaeda. When you discuss these matters with Moroccan security personnel, you will hear that the "Takfiri Syndrome" (as it is called) is constantly out there somewhere.

It is interesting to note that exactly the same situation holds true for Tunisia, another moderate North African Arab country. It is also applicable to the United Arab Emirates, which, as Brian Robinson declares, though under the protection of the West, could easily become unhinged should security falter.

To get something of a handle on international terrorism, one needs to carefully examine some of the publications that routinely appear in Washington. Of significance were the declassified key judgments of the National Intelligence Estimate, titled "Trends in Global Terrorism: Implications for the United States," dated April 2006. This document disclosed that new Jihadist networks and cells—all with powerful anti-American agendas—were increasingly likely to emerge in the future, adding that "the confluence of shared purpose and dispersed actors will make it harder to find and undermine Jihadist groups."

The report continues:

> We assess that the operational threat from self-radicalized cells will grow in importance to U.S. counterterrorism efforts, particularly abroad, but also in the Homeland. . . . The Jihadists regard Europe as an important venue for attacking Western interests. Extremist networks inside the extensive Muslim diasporas in Europe facilitate recruitment and staging for urban attacks, as illustrated by the 2004 Madrid and 2005 London bombings.
>
> We assess that the Iraq Jihad is shaping a new generation of terrorist leaders and operatives; perceived Jihadist success there would inspire more fighters to continue the struggle elsewhere.

Indeed, the report states that the Iraq conflict has become something of a *cause célèbre* for Jihadists, since it breeds a deep resentment of U.S. involvement in the Muslim world. It also cultivates supporters for a global Jihadist movement, very much like the one envisaged by the Syrian Muslim underground movement.

According to the report,

> Should Jihadists leaving Iraq perceive themselves, and be perceived, to have failed, we judge fewer fighters will be inspired to carry on the fight.
>
> We [consequently] assess that the underlying factors fueling the spread of the movement outweigh its vulnerabilities and are likely to do so for the duration of the timeframe of this Estimate.

The report lists four basic underlying factors that fuel the spread of the Jihadist movement. The first of these is termed "Entrenched grievances," such as corruption, injustice, and the dominant fear of Western influences. In turn, this leads to "anger, humiliation, and a sense of powerlessness."

Second comes the Iraqi Jihad, and third, the slow pace of real and sustained economic, social, and political reforms in many Muslim-majority nations. Last is possibly the most important factor of all: a pervasive anti-American sentiment among most Muslims. Jihadists exploit all of these issues.

This concurs with Brian Robinson's prognostications following his experiences on the ground in the United Arab Emirates: Other affiliated extremist organizations, principally Sunni-oriented (such as Jemaah Islamiya, Ansar al-Sunnah, and several North African groups), unless countered, are likely to expand their reach and become more capable of multiple and/or mass-casualty attacks outside their traditional areas of operation.

Israel, like it or not, remains a dominant factor within the Middle East equation. It can neither be wished away, nor are its multifarious enemies likely to vaporize—in the figurative sense—anytime soon, even though that analogy does have significance. And let's face it: There are those who would like exactly that to happen. Iranian president Mahmoud Ahmadinejad is one of the strongest proponents of a Doomsday scenario that forebodes terrible carnage.

Should Iran, or one of its surrogates, like Hezbollah (or even al-Qaeda) achieve the ultimate objective and detonate one or more atom bombs on Israeli soil, the measure of Jewish retaliation would be on a scale that is utterly incomprehensible. It is almost as if Armageddon and its dreadful implications were intended to presage just such a horror. The number of deaths that would result is likely to be in the tens of millions, and, in all probability, several major Islamic capital cities would be eradicated, which powerfully suggests that such threats should not be taken lightly.

This is not just idle chatter. Proponents of a nuclear holocaust have some powerful Israeli voices too. Though not directly advocating their use, Israeli prime minister Ehud Olmert obliterated forty years of deliberate ambiguity in the second week of December 2006 when he admitted in an interview with Germany's SAT 1 television that Israel possessed nuclear weapons. During the interview, a clearly agitated Olmert declared, "Israel is a democracy and does not threaten anyone . . . Iran explicitly, openly, and publicly threatens to wipe Israel off the map."

What does worry Middle East watchers is that Israel has never signed the Nuclear Non-Proliferation Treaty (NPT), which is designed to prevent the global spread of nuclear arms. As a result, it is not subject to inspections or the threat of sanctions by the United Nations nuclear watchdog, the IAEA, something that Islamic states—and Iran in particular—make a lot of noise about, maintaining that the time has come to level the playing fields.

While all this was going on, Iranian president Mahmoud Ahmadinejad spoke in his typical controversial style at a conference in Tehran in December 2006, stating that Israel's days are numbered. "Just as the USSR disappeared, soon the Zionist regime will disappear," he declared to the applause of participants who were taking part in a two-day forum that attempted to debunk claims that six million Jews died at the hands of Nazi Germany during World War II. The sad truth is that if some of these issues weren't quite so serious, this pantomime, under less austere circumstances, might have evolved into quite an entertaining farce.

Glenn Beck attempted to explain the origins of anti-West sentiments recently on his CNN program, *The Extremist Agenda*, which showed the extent of brainwashing propaganda that Muslim children are exposed to, often starting as early as age three. One of these segments explained how "Sabbath breakers and polytheists, Jews and Christians had been punished by Allah by turning them into apes and pigs." There were also cartoons that depicted the glory of blowing oneself up for Allah. Quoting Walid Shoebat, a former Islamic terrorist turned author who produced the report "Why I left Jihad," Beck mentions songs that Arab children are taught from day one in school, with lyrics like "Allah loves the Arabs, but has turned the Jews into apes and pigs."

Also brought out were anti-Jewish films, one of which showed Jews cutting the eyes out of a little Arab girl, while another portrayed Jews killing a Christian child to get their blood to make matzo for Passover. As Glenn Beck commented, Hitler would certainly have been proud.

When communities, societies, and sometimes entire countries resort to this kind of drivel, it is almost always inevitable that the monster eventually ends up devouring itself. History is replete with examples of similar events; Nazi Germany and the blood-lusting Pol Pot regime were only two of them.

Stalin was no less efficient in depleting Soviet society of millions of innocents. Here I found Simon Sebag Montefiore's *Stalin: The Court of the Red Tsar* instructive. I regard this book as one of the most explicit exposés of the decade, and historically, it has some bearing on contemporary issues, especially when you look at what takes place when otherwise perfectly well-organized societies go berserk.

The bottom line in the Israeli-Islamic imbroglio is that there is still more violence in the offing. Israel has fought four major wars for its continued existence. It has yet to face the biggest one of all, for its very survival as a nation, and I fear it won't be long in coming. Whether the Jewish State has the ability to overcome the odds stacked against it (which become more preponderant each year) is another matter.

The adversary is not nearly as disorganized as they might have been a generation ago. I spent time in combat in Sierra Leone with a Shiite side-gunner onboard our Mi-24 helicopter gunship, and he was one of the toughest, most competent combatants that I've ever met. He was also outspokenly pro-Hezbollah, an Islamic group, he told me, that would ultimately "save the world."

I detail much of this in my last book, *War Dog*, commenting on the resourcefulness of this man and other Shiites I was to meet during many visits to Lebanon during the past several years. This is the new face of Islam, and one that the Jewish State is obliged to counter if it is to endure.

A few months before this book went to press, the Israeli nation was stunned to learn that some of its military communications infrastructure had reportedly been compromised by Hezbollah electronics specialists during the 2006 invasion of South Lebanon. How they managed to accomplish this, nobody knows, as military communications these days make use of encryption as well as "frequency hopping." What is also true is that frequency hopping does not in itself guarantee security. Although such radios jump across dozens of different channels per second (from a few dozen hops per second for slow hoppers, to thousands for fast hoppers), this does not render them immune to interception, unless the traffic is also protected with at least 128-bit encryption.

The technology behind frequency hopping itself is nothing new, but it is still sophisticated enough to be restricted to relatively few electronics manufacturers worldwide. Initially, three companies were doing it: ITT Cincinnati in the United States, and Britain's RACAL and Grinaker (today part of the Denel Group in South Africa). All three developed VHF combat net radios that incorporated the frequency-hopping equipment.

The RACAL and Grinaker hoppers appeared on the market first, largely as a consequence of private funding. The U.S. model lagged behind, given that it was hamstrung by a painfully slow military procurement process. They ultimately got over that, and today, U.S. sets are considered the best in the world.

So, how would Hezbollah have gotten into the act—monitoring radio communications that frequency-hop several hundred/thousand times a second (even if only for limited periods)? Nobody knows for certain, but since this revolutionary movement has been found to have acquired other equipment from South Africa, it doesn't overly stretch the imagination to figure it out.

Assuming that the Israelis use a communication system such as the U.S. SINCGARS (Single Channel Ground to Air Radio System) or the equivalent, then it is highly unlikely that Hezbollah would indeed have "broken" into their comms system. While a captured radio could have yielded some intelligence for a while, Hezbollah presumably gained information more readily by analyzing IDF signals and unauthorized civilian cell-phone conversations from the front (the encryption of which *can* be cracked), to build up a composite tactical picture of Israeli deployment.

Frequency hoppers apart, some of the most serious security breaches during the 2006 Israeli invasion resulted from IDF troops calling their family members or girlfriends back home on their cell phones, something that they had been explicitly prohibited from doing. These actions would almost certainly have placed entire units in jeopardy. Indeed, there might have even been casualties as a consequence of such mindlessness, especially since sophisticated direction-finding equipment allows an operator to pinpoint the position of anyone using such a phone.

But then that, too, is symptomatic of the new generation of IDF soldiers, something about which Israeli commentator Martin van Creveld, the most prominent military historian at the Hebrew University" has been outspoken for a while now. Van Creveld is not the only one who is concerned about Israel's military machine (something I discuss in some detail in chapter 15).

A military report released in early December 2006 by Michael Lindenstrauss, the Israeli comptroller who is responsible to the Knesset, was scathing about what it termed "the breakdown of standards at top echelons in the IDF." The gist of Lindenstrauss's report was that the military top brass had been operating without adequate training, clear communications, or ethics. "There is a lack of clear language embedded in the IDF that appears in both emergencies as well as regular times . . . This is very dangerous," said Lindenstrauss, who was characterized by Middle East Newsline as one of the severest critics of Israel's military and government. It was also his view that dishonesty among senior commanders had become rampant. He reported investigations of senior officers who had lied about their whereabouts and finances, portraying an Israeli military that had abandoned basic principles and doctrine. Lindenstrauss noted that 82 percent of generals, 68 percent of brigadier generals, and 76 percent of colonels had not graduated from military college.

In an interview with Israel Army Radio, leading Israeli military analyst Ron Ben-Yishai revealed that ground-force units sent to fight Hezbollah lacked basic equipment. According to Ben-Yishai, combat units did not have enough M16s and night-vision systems. There were also questions raised about inadequate supplies of bunker-busting munitions.

Others critical of the disastrous thirty-four-day conflict included retired major general Eliezer Yaari, a former military comptroller. He believes Lindenstrauss's report highlights problems that have long plagued the Israel Defense Forces, and that deficiencies in the army would take years to correct. "If the war [against Syria and Hezbollah] takes place in another year, the IDF will not be ready," Yaari declared.

Reservist brigadier general Nehemia Dagan, a senior air force officer who served as chief education officer, agrees, saying the military has become politicized over the last twenty years. According to Dagan, at least two recent chiefs of staff—Ehud Barak and Shaul Mofaz—used their positions as a springboard for a career in politics. "The army has become politicized," said Dagan. "It must be severed from politics. We are heading down the road to catastrophe."

The immediate impression from these observations—when combined with how Israel fared on the Lebanese battlefield, and the unusually high number of casualties the IDF suffered—is that the Jewish State's current military establishment compares poorly with earlier generations of the Israeli fighting machine. A specialist on the subject at Jane's told this author that what makes matters worse is countries like Egypt, Iran, and Syria seem to take their defense more seriously than their Jewish counterparts. If he is right, then that bodes ill for the future, because at least two of these states are girding for the kind of confrontation that might finally put an end to what some of them refer to as "the myth of Israeli military invincibility."

Certainly, said my friend, the Israeli air force is as invincible as it has ever been. With recent reverses on the ground, it will make it its business to become even more so. What is being ignored, however, is the reality that wars are fought by men on the ground. In the history of warfare, he reminds us, only one modern conflict was won solely by air power—and that was in the old Yugoslavia.

If these were the only problems on the international security spectrum, then perhaps we could deal with them. But they are not.

Dame Eliza Manningham-Buller, head of MI5 (Britain's domestic security body, roughly the equivalent of the U.S. FBI), recently issued a warning: There are at least thirty terror plots that threaten Britain at the present time. She also revealed that her people are keeping something like 1,600 individuals under surveillance. Some of these plots are serious, she declared. "Tomorrow's threat may—I suggest *will*—include the use of chemicals, bacteriological agents, radioactive materials, and even nuclear technology." It is also her view that current-day terror threats in the West will last at least another generation, and that many are linked to al-Qaeda.

Manningham-Buller's warnings came just days after a Londoner, Dhiren Barot, thirty-four, was sentenced to at least forty years in jail for planning a series of attacks which included using a so-called "dirty bomb" (or RDD—a Radiological Dispersal Device).

Only months before, Russia's minister of the interior confirmed that international terrorists were planning attacks to "seize nuclear materials and use them to build weapons of mass destruction," and that in April 2006, a group of conspirators were arrested with 22 kilograms of low-enriched uranium stolen from Elektrostal—a plant that also processes tons of weapons-usable highly enriched uranium (HEU), where multiple thefts have occurred before.

This report was carried by the Nuclear Research Institute, and emphasized that wide gaps still remain when it comes to securing nuclear stockpiles in the rest of the world. It also warned that, even in Russia, there are still major questions about whether the security measures being put in place are sufficient to meet the threat, and whether they will be sustained after American assistance is phased out. According to the report, a recent U.S. Department of Energy study concluded that "there were 128 nuclear research reactors or associated facilities around the world with enough highly enriched uranium to potentially make a bomb—a larger number of facilities than had been previously publicly recognized." It went on: "Unsecured nuclear material doesn't have to be stamped 'Made in Russia' to be used in a terrorist nuclear attack."

Small wonder, then, that an al-Qaeda Web site which contained detailed instructions in Arabic on the construction of atom bombs had almost 60,000 hits in the weeks before it was removed. The manual was posted on a forum titled *Al-Firdaws* ("Paradise"), and contained eighty pages of instructions and pictures of kitchen bomb-making techniques. It was divided into nine lessons under the overall heading "The Nuclear Bomb of Jihad and the Way to Enrich Uranium." It was dedicated as a "gift to the commander of the Jihad fighters, Sheikh Osama bin Laden, for the purpose of Jihad for the sake of Allah."

HOW IT ALL STARTED: THE HISTORIC FRISCH-PEIERLS MEMORANDUM

Anybody who understands a little science and reads the historic Frisch-Peierls Memorandum, penned by these two scientists in 1940—a couple of years before real work started on developing the atom bomb—must accept this document as a remarkable piece of history. Both men were European, and had they pushed alternative buttons, Hitler might have had the bomb before the Allies—which would mean that we'd probably all be speaking German today . . .

Dr. Nic von Wielligh (who served two terms with the IAEA in Vienna) told me that the Frisch-Peierls Memorandum provides astounding insight into the possibility of building a nuclear bomb at a very early stage, when there were still some very big gaps in understanding the problem. "In 1940, the basic scientific or experimental work to establish many of the necessary physical parameters simply had not yet been done," von Wielligh declared.

Much of the drama that lay behind early British research is revealed in a brilliant book titled *Fly in the Cathedral* by former Reuters correspondent, Brian Cathcart. Recently published by Farrar, Straus and Giroux, it is an entertaining account of what went on in the early 1930s at the Cavendish Laboratory in Cambridge, where, in 1932, scientists "brought forth the birth of nuclear physics." It also deals with the commanding presence of one of the finest scientific brains of that era, the New Zealand–born Sir Ernest Rutherford. As he is described: "a barreling, thundering, penetrating presence in the world of physics, a great rowdy boy full of ideas and energy."

Remember, too, that experiments by Rutherford in 1911 had already indicated that the vast majority of an atom's mass was contained in a very small nucleus at its core, made up of protons, surrounded by a web of whirring electrons. In 1932, another famous British physicist, James Chadwick, discovered that the nucleus contained an additional fundamental particle, the neutron, and in the same year, John Cockcroft and Ernest Walton "split the atom" for the first time. This was the first time an atomic nucleus of one element had been successfully changed to a different nucleus by artificial means.

As refugees from across the channel, Frisch and Peierls weren't part of Rutherford's "kindergarten," but like other eminent European scientists—Enrico Fermi, Leo Szilard, Edward Teller, and others—they'd done their homework. All were to make notable discoveries in their respective scientific disciplines.

Dr. Nic von Wielligh commented as follows:

> The pioneering work of Chadwick and Cockcroft/Walton (British) is well known.
>
> However, Frisch and Peierls (both originally of German origin), at the stage that they drew up the famous Memorandum, were anything but. In fact, when Frisch reached England from Denmark where he had been working with Bohr (Danish), the father of the "liquid drop model of the nucleus," he was barred as an "enemy alien" from working on the classified development of radar.
>
> Frisch and Peierls worked in Birmingham under the Australian scientist, Mark Oliphant, who approved and supported the Memorandum.
>
> The insight that Frisch had in the "fissioning" of the uranium nucleus was due to an interpretation by his aunt, Lise Meitner (Austrian), of the work by Otto Hahn (German) who was a chemist and could not interpret the strange results he obtained when bombarding uranium with neutrons.
>
> Lise Meitner could explain the results using Einstein's (originally Swiss) famous formula linking mass and energy.

Dr. von Wielligh goes on to explain that "the eventual development of the bomb, though seen and propagated as an American achievement, would not have been possible without the contributions of Swiss, New Zealand, Australian, British, German, Austrian, Hungarian, Italian, French, Polish, and American scientists—among others.

In short, as one American scientist commented not long ago, "these two guys really knew their stuff, and that was almost seventy years ago . . . It was a huge amount of theoretical stuff for that time."

Judge for yourself:

Frisch-Peierls Memorandum of March 1940

The document opens with the following paragraph:

> Strictly Confidential Memorandum on the properties of a radioactive "super-bomb." The attached detailed report concerns the possibility of constructing a

"super-bomb" which utilizes the energy stored in atomic nuclei as a source of energy. The energy liberated in the explosion of such a super-bomb is about the same as that produced by the explosion of 1,000 tons of dynamite. This energy is liberated in a small volume, in which it will, for an instant, produce a temperature comparable to that in the interior of the sun. The blast from such an explosion would destroy life in a wide area. The size of this area is difficult to estimate, but it will probably cover the centre of a big city. In addition, some part of the energy set free by the bomb goes to produce radioactive substances, and these will emit very powerful and dangerous radiations. The effect of these radiations is greatest immediately after the explosion, but it decays only gradually, and even for days after the explosion, any person entering the affected area will be killed. Some of this radioactivity will be carried along with the wind and will spread the contamination; several miles downwind, this may kill people.

On the construction of a "super-bomb" based on a nuclear chain reaction in uranium:

The possible construction of "super-bombs" based on a nuclear chain reaction in uranium has been discussed a great deal and arguments have been brought forward which seemed to exclude this possibility. We wish here to point out and discuss a possibility which seems to have been overlooked in these earlier discussions.

Uranium consists essentially of two isotopes, 238U (99.3%) and 235U (0.7%). If a uranium nucleus is hit by a neutron, three processes are possible: (1) scattering, whereby the neutron changes directions, and if its energy is above 0.1 MeV, loses energy; (2) capture, when the neutron is taken up by the nucleus; and (3) fission, i.e., the nucleus breaks up into two nuclei of comparable size, with the liberation of an energy of about 200 MeV.

The possibility of chain reaction is given by the fact that neutrons are emitted in the fission and that the number of these neutrons per fission is greater than 1. The most probable value for this figure seems to be 2.3, from two independent determinations.

However, it has been shown that even in a large block of ordinary uranium, no chain reaction would take place, since too many neutrons would be slowed down by inelastic scattering into the energy region where they are strongly absorbed by 238U.

Several people have tried to make chain reactions possible by mixing the uranium with water, which reduces the energy of the neutrons still further and thereby increases their efficiency again. It seems fairly certain, however, that even then it is impossible to sustain a chain reaction.

In any case, no arrangement containing hydrogen and based on the action of slow neutrons could act as an effective super-bomb, because the reaction would be too slow. The time required to slow down a neutron is about 10^{-5} sec, and the average time loss before a neutron hits a uranium nucleus is even 10^{-4}. In the reaction, the number of neutrons would increase exponentially, like where would be at least 10^{-4} sec. When the temperature reaches several thousand degrees, the container of the bomb will break and within 10^{-4} sec the uranium would have expanded sufficiently to let the neutrons escape and so to stop the reaction.

The energy liberated would, therefore, be only a few times the energy required to break the container, i.e., of the same order of magnitude as with ordinary high explosives.

[Niels] Bohr has put forward strong arguments for the suggestion that the fission observed with slow neutrons is to be ascribed to the rare isotope 235U, and that this isotope has, on the whole, a much greater fission probability than the common isotope 238U. Effective methods for the separation of isotopes have been developed recently, of which the method of thermal diffusion is simple enough to permit separation on a fairly large scale.

This permits, in principle, the use of nearly pure 235U in such a bomb, a possibility which apparently has not so far been seriously considered. We have discussed this possibility and come to the conclusion that a moderate amount of 235U would indeed constitute an extremely efficient explosive.

The behavior of 235U under bombardment with fast neutrons is not experimentally, but from rather simple theoretical arguments it can be concluded that almost every collision produces fission and that neutrons of any energy are effective. Therefore, it is not necessary to add hydrogen, and the reaction, depending on the action of fast neutrons, develops with very great rapidity so that a considerable part of the total energy is liberated before the reaction gets stopped on account of the expansion of the material.

The critical radius—i.e., the radius of sphere in which the surplus of neutrons created by the fission is just equal to the loss of neutrons by escape through the surface—is, for a material with a given composition, in a fixed ratio to the mean free path of neutrons, and this in turn is inversely proportional to the density. It therefore pays to bring the material into the densest possible form, i.e., the metallic state, probably sintered or hammered. If we assume for 235, no appreciable scattering, and 2.3 neutrons emitted per fission, then the critical radius is found to be 0.8 times the mean free path. In the metallic state (density 15), and assuming a fission cross section of 10^{-23} cm^2, the mean free path would be 2.6 cm and would be 2.1 cm, corresponding to a mass of 600 grams. A sphere of metallic 235U of a radius greater than would be explosive, and one might think of about 1 kg as suitable size for a bomb.

The speed of the reaction is easy to estimate. The neutrons emitted in the fission have velocities of about 10^{-9} cm/sec, and they have to travel 2.6 cm before hitting a uranium nucleus. For a sphere well above the critical size, the loss through neutron escape would be small, so we may assume that each neutron after a life of 2.6×10^{-9} sec, produces fission, giving birth to two neutrons. In the expression for the increase of neutron density with time, it would be about 4×10^{-9} sec, very much shorter than in the case of a chain reaction depending on slow neutrons.

If the reaction proceeds until most of the uranium is used up, temperatures of the order of 10^{10} degrees and pressure of about 10^{13} atmospheres are produced. It is difficult to predict accurately the behavior of matter under these extreme conditions, and the mathematical difficulties of the problem are considerable. By a rough calculation we get the following expression for the energy liberated before the mass expands so much that the reaction is interrupted:

(M, total mass of uranium; , radius of sphere; , critical radius; , time required for neutron density to multiply by a factor e). For a sphere of radius 4.2 cm (= 2.1 cm), M = 4700 grams, = 4×10^{-9} sec, we find E = 4×10^{20} ergs, which is about one-tenth of the total fission energy. For a radius of about 8 cm (m = 32 kg) the whole fission energy is liberated, according to the formula (1). For small radii the efficiency falls off even faster than indicated by formula (1) because goes up as approaches . The energy liberated by a 5 kg bomb would be equivalent to that of several thousand tons of dynamite, while that of a 1 kg bomb, though about 500 times less, would still be formidable.

It is necessary that such a sphere should be made in two (or more) parts which are brought together first when the explosion is wanted. Once assembled, the bomb would explode within a second or less, since one neutron is sufficient to start the reaction and there are several neutrons passing through the bomb every second, from the cosmic radiation. (Neutrons originating from the action of uranium alpha rays on light-element impurities would be negligible, provided the uranium is reasonably pure.) A sphere with a radius of less than about 3 cm could be made up in two hemispheres, which are pulled together by springs and kept separated by a suitable structure which is removed at the desired moment. A larger sphere would have to be composed of more than two parts, if the parts, taken separately, are to be stable.

It is important that the assembling of the parts should be done as rapidly as possible, in order to minimize the chance of a reaction getting started at a moment when the critical conditions have only just been reached. If this happened, the reaction rate would be much slower and the energy liberation would be considerably reduced; it would, however, always be sufficient to destroy the bomb.

For the separation of the 235U, the method of thermal diffusion, developed by Clusius and others, seems to be the only one which can cope with the large amounts required. A gaseous uranium compound—for example, uranium hexa-fluoride—is placed between two vertical surfaces which are kept at a different temperature. The light isotope tends to get more concentrated near the hot surface, where it is carried upwards by the convection current. Exchange with the current moving downwards along the cold surface produces a fractionating effect, and after some time a state of equilibrium is reached when the gas near the upper end contains markedly more of the light isotope than near the lower end.

For example, a system of two concentric tubes, of 2 mm separation and 3 cm diameter, 150 cm long, would produce a difference of about 40% in the concentration of the rare isotope between its ends without unduly upsetting the equilibrium.

In order to produce large amounts of highly concentrated 235U, a great number of these separating units will have to be used, being arranged in parallel as well as in series. For a daily production of 100 grams of 235U of 90% purity, we estimate that about 100,000 of these tubes would be required. This seems a large number, but it would undoubtedly be possible to design some kind of a system which would have the same effective area in a more compact and less expensive form.

In addition to the destructive effect of the explosion itself, the whole material of the bomb would be transformed into a highly radioactive stage. The energy radiated by these active substances will amount to about 20% of the energy liberated in the explosion, and the radiations would be fatal to living beings even a long time after the explosion.

The fission of uranium results in the formation of a great number of active bodies with periods between, roughly speaking, a second and a year. The resulting radiation is found to decay in such a way that the intensity is about inversely proportional to the time. Even one day after the explosion the radiation will correspond to a power expenditure of the order 1,000 kW, or to the radiation of a hundred tons of radium.

Any estimates of the effects of this radiation on human beings must be rather uncertain because it is difficult to tell what will happen to the radioactive material after the explosion. Most of it will probably be blown into the air and carried away by the wind. This cloud of radioactive material will kill everybody within a strip estimated to be several miles long. If it rained the danger would be even worse because the active material would be carried down to the ground and stick to it, and persons entering the contaminated area would be subjected to dangerous radiations even after days.

If 1% of the active material sticks to the debris in the vicinity of the explosion and if the debris is spread over an area of, say, a square mile, any person entering this area would be in serious danger, even several days after the explosion.

In estimates, the lethal dose penetrating radiation was assumed to be 1,000 roentgens; consultation of a medical specialist on X-ray treatment and perhaps further biological research may enable one to fix the danger limit more accurately.

The main source of uncertainty is our lack of knowledge as to the behavior of materials in such a super-explosion; an expert on high explosives may be able to clarify some of these problems.

Effective protection is hardly possible. Houses would offer protection only at the margins of the danger zone. Deep cellars or tunnels may be comparatively safe from the effects of radiation, provided air can be supplied from an uncontaminated area. (Some of the active substance would be noble gases, which are not stopped by ordinary filters). The irradiation is not felt until hours later, when it may become too late. Therefore, it would be very important to have an organization which determines the exact extent of the danger area, by means of ionization measurements, so that people can be warned from entering it.

What the Frisch-Peierls Memorandum of March 1940 did was to open a new and unusual scientific era. It presented this community with a host of information, some of which had been tabulated before, but not quite as comprehensively. For instance:

- They were aware that it was the U-235 isotope of uranium which was fissionable.

- They knew that when uranium was "split" by a neutron, it released energy and additional neutrons as well. (Their figure of 2.3 is reasonable for the time. What should also be kept in mind here is that the Manhattan Project was still two years away. This was still the dark ages as far as super-bombs were concerned.)

- They knew that it would be "fast" neutrons that would be required to trigger such a bomb, and not "slow" neutrons.

- They postulated using "nearly pure 235U" in such a bomb. (Today, we call it "highly enriched" ^{235}U.)

- They had a sense of how to "separate out" (and thereby enrich) the ^{235}U isotope, and to this end, proposed an existing process called "thermal diffusion."

- Their critical mass examples ranged from 32, to 5, to 1 kilogram for a bomb. Their assertion that a 10-pound bomb would be equivalent to several thousand tons of dynamite is about right.

- They suggested the same method of starting the explosive chain-reaction—by a stray or prompt neutron—just as the South African nuclear devices would have been initiated had these ever been used.

- They had a tentative idea of an assembly method that would eventually emerge as a gun-type device, and also had a clear understanding of the danger of spontaneous fission, and, subsequently, a pre-detonation.

- They understood that large quantities of U-235 could only be produced by a large-scale effort. (Think how big enrichment plants were—and still are!)

- They had a clear idea of radioactive fallout and the dangers that it would pose for a population exposed to the same.

APPENDIX B:

GLOSSARY OF TERMS

AEA—Egypt's Atomic Energy Authority

AEC—Atomic Energy Corporation (South Africa), successor to the Atomic Energy Board (AEB)

AEOI—Atomic Energy Organization of Iran

AFMLS—The (U.S.) Criminal Division's Asset Forfeiture and Money Laundering Section

AI—Amnesty International

Atomic bomb—Nuclear device whose energy comes from the fission of uranium or plutonium

AVLIS—Atomic Vapor Laser Isotope Separation

Ayatollah—Literally, a reflection of Allah. In Iranian Shiite religious circles, it signifies the most learned of teachers; there are an estimated five thousand ayatollahs in Iran alone. Thus, Ayatollah Ozama literally means "most exalted sign of God."

Barrels per day—Production of crude oil or petroleum products is frequently measured in barrels per day, often abbreviated bpd or bd. A barrel is a volume measure of forty-two United States gallons.

Beryllium—A toxic metal possessing a low neutron-absorption cross section and a high melting point, which can be used in nuclear reactors as a moderator or reflector.

BW—Biological Weapons

BWC—Biological Weapons Convention

CANDU—(Canadian deuterium-uranium reactor); the most widely used type of heavy water power reactor. The CANDU reactor employs natural uranium as a fuel and heavy water as a coolant.

Cascade—A connected series of enrichment machines, materials from one being passed to another for further enrichment.

Centrifuge—Used in a uranium-enrichment process that separates gaseous isotopes by rotating them rapidly in a spinning tube, thereby subjecting them to centrifugal force.

CEP—Circular Error Probable (in relation to missile strike accuracy)

Chembio technology—chemical and biological warfare technology

Chemical enrichment—This method of uranium enrichment depends on a slight tendency of uranium-235 (^{235}U) and uranium-238 (^{238}U) to concentrate in different molecules when uranium compounds are continuously brought into contact.

CIA—Central Intelligence Agency

Core—Central portion of a nuclear reactor containing the fuel elements and usually the moderator

Covert Nuclear Trade Analysis Unit—An IAEA security body that has about a half-dozen specialists looking for evidence of deals by the A.Q. Khan network or its imitators.

Critical mass—Minimum mass required to sustain a chain reaction

CTBT—Comprehensive Nuclear Test Ban Treaty

Curie—A measure of radioactivity based on the observed decay rate of approximately 1 gram of radium. The Curie was named in honor of Pierre and Marie Curie, pioneers in the study of radiation. One curie of radioactive material will have 37 billion atomic transformations (disintegrations) in one second.

CW—Chemical Weapons

Depleted uranium—Uranium with a smaller percentage of uranium-235 than the 0.7 percent found in natural uranium

DIA—Defense Intelligence Agency

DoE—Department of Energy (United States), formerly Atomic Energy Commission

Elint—Electronic Intelligence (See **Humint**)

ENTC—Esfahan Nuclear Technology Center

Euratom—European Atomic Energy Commission

EW—Electronic Warfare

Farsi—Official language of Persian Iran

"Fat Man"—Atomic, implosion-type, fission bomb used by the Americans at Nagasaki on August 9, 1945. This is one of the nuclear concepts being assessed but not yet worked on by the Iranians. (See also **"Little Boy"**)

Fatwa—A formal legal opinion by a religious leader or *mojtahed* on a matter of legal law (as in the decree against the life of Salman Rushdie)

FBIS—Foreign Broadcast Information Service

FBR—Fast Breeder Reactor

Fertile material—Material composed of atoms, which readily absorb neutrons to produce fissionable materials. One such element is uranium-238, which becomes plutonium-239 (^{239}Pu) after it absorbs a neutron.

FinCEN—U.S. Treasury's Financial Crimes Enforcement Network, an investigative and information-gathering bureau

Fissile material—Weapons-usable material composed of atoms which fission when irradiated by slow or "thermal" neutrons. The most common examples of fissile materials are uranium-235 (^{235}U) and plutonium-239 (^{239}Pu).

Fission—Fission weapons get their destructive power from the fission (splitting) of atomic nuclei.

FMC—Fuel Manufacturing Plant (intended for construction at Esfahan)

FSU—Former Soviet Union

FTO—Foreign Terrorist Organization

Fusion—Different type of nuclear reaction from the fission process. Involves the fusion together of the nuclei of isotopes of light atoms such as hydrogen (thus, hydrogen bombs). Development of the H-bomb was impossible before the perfection of A-bombs, as this is the trigger of any thermonuclear device.

Gas-centrifuge process—See **Centrifuge**

Gaseous diffusion—A method of isotope separation based on the fact that gas atoms or molecules with different masses will diffuse through a porous barrier (or membrane) at different rates. This method is used to separate uranium-235 from uranium-238.

GW—Gigawatts

HANE—High-altitude nuclear explosion

Heavy water—Water that contains significantly more than the natural proportion (1 in 6,500) of heavy hydrogen (deuterium) atoms to ordinary hydrogen atoms

Heavy-Water Reactor—A reactor that uses heavy water as its moderator and natural uranium as fuel. See **CANDU**

HEU—Highly enriched uranium, or weapons-grade material in which the percentage of uranium-235 nuclei has been increased from the natural level of 0.7 percent to some level greater than 20 percent (usually around 90 percent).

Hezbollah—Lebanese "Party of God" that was founded in 1982 as a terror group. Originally responsible for bombing a U.S. Marine base and two embassies in Beirut. Before becoming a legitimate political party, evolved into a highly motivated guerrilla force that eventually forced the IDF out of Lebanon.

Hezbollahi—Literally, a follower of the Iranian Party of God, transliterated from *Hizballah* (Arabic). Hezbollahis were originally followers of a particular religious figure who eventually came to constitute an unofficial political party.

Humint—Human intelligence gathered by field operatives or agents, as opposed to **sigint** (signal intelligence) or **elint** (electronic intelligence)

IAEA—International Atomic Energy Agency, a United Nations organization with over 170 signatories, based in Vienna, Austria

IAF—Israeli Air Force

IDF—Israeli Defense Force (usually applied to army units)

Iran Nuclear Research Reactor—A heavy-water reactor planned for the Iranian nuclear facility at Arak

IRGC—Islamic Revolutionary Guard Corps; see **Pasdaran**

ISIS—Institute for Science and International Security (Washington)

ISTC—International Science and Technology Center; a Russian body that caters to FSU scientists who were involved in WMD pursuits, helping them find other avenues of employment.

JDW—*Jane's Defense Weekly*

JHL—Jabr Ibn Hayan Laboratories (an Iranian nuclear research center)

JIDR—*Jane's International Defense Review*

JIR—*Jane's Intelligence Review*

Kiloton (KT)—Energy of a nuclear explosion that is equivalent to an explosion of 1,000 tons of TNT

Laser enrichment—An experimental process of uranium enrichment in which lasers are used to separate uranium isotopes

LEO—Low earth orbit (of satellites)

LEU—Low enriched uranium in which the percentage of uranium-235 nuclei has been enriched from the natural level of 0.7 percent to up to 20 percent

"Little Boy"—Gun-type, fission bomb dropped over Hiroshima by the Americans on August 6, 1945. All six South African atom bombs were gun-type. Iran is following this path, among others. See also **"Fat Man"**

LNG—Liquefied natural gas

LPG—Liquefied (liquid) petroleum gas

LRBM—Long-Range Ballistic Missile

MEIB—Middle East Intelligence Bulletin

MLIS—Molecular Laser Isotope Separation

Moderator—A component (usually water, heavy water, or graphite) of some nuclear reactor types that slows neutrons, thereby increasing their chances of fissioning fertile material

MRBM—Medium-Range Ballistic Missile

MTCR—Missile Technology Control Regime

Mullah—Generic term for a member of the Islamic clergy; usually refers to a preacher or other low-ranking cleric who has not earned the right to interpret religious laws

MW—Megawatt

MWth—Megawatt-thermal (usually reactor)

NCRI—National Council of Resistance of Iran (anti-Tehran insurgency group)

NGL—Natural gas liquids

NGO—Nongovernmental Organization

NPT—Nuclear Non-Proliferation Treaty (Treaty on the Non-Proliferation of Nuclear Weapons)

NSG—Nuclear Suppliers Group

NUMEC—Nuclear Materials and Equipment Corporation

OFAC—U.S. Office of Foreign Asset Controls

OPEC—Organization of Petroleum Exporting Countries responsible for coordinating oil policies of major oil-producing countries.

Osiraq—French-built 40MWth nuclear materials test reactor destroyed in air strike by the Israeli Air Force in June 1981

P-1—An earlier, less-advanced centrifuge design of European origin

P-2—A more-advanced centrifuge design now being used in the Pakistani nuclear program, examples of which have been found, without good reason, at Iranian nuclear establishments

Pars Trash—Where centrifuge equipment from the Kalaye Electric Company was stored and concealed from IAEA inspectors until October 2003, when it was presented for inspection to the agency at Natanz

Pasdaran—*Pasdaran-e Enghelab-e Islami*, or Islamic Revolutionary Guard Corps (IRGC), an organization charged with safeguarding the Iranian revolution. This group of ultrasecret activists is responsible solely to Iran's Supreme Spiritual Leader, Sayyid Ali Hoseini-Khamenei

People's Libyan Arab Jamahiriya—Libya

PFEP—Pilot Fuel Enrichment Plant

Po-210 (Polonium-210)—An intensely radioactive alpha-emitting radioisotope that can be used not only for certain civilian applications (such as RTGs—in effect, nuclear batteries), but also, in conjunction with beryllium, for military purposes (specifically as a neutron initiator in some designs of nuclear weapons).

Proliferation Security Initiative—A Washington-inspired security measure that seeks to intercept illicit nuclear trade at sea or in the air.

^{239}Pu—Plutonium: A fissile isotope generated artificially when uranium-238, through irradiation (as in a reactor) captures an extra neutron. It is one of the two fissile materials that have been almost extensively used for the core of nuclear weapons, the other being ^{235}U. (A small amount of nuclear explosives have been made with uranium-233.)

Radioactivity—The spontaneous disintegration of an unstable atomic nucleus resulting in the emission of subatomic particles.

RDD—Radiological Dispersal Device (radiological bomb involving radioactive matter; otherwise known as a dirty bomb)

RepU—Reprocessed uranium

Revcons—NPT Revue Conference (at IAEA)

RME—Reasonably Maximally Exposed

RMEI—Reasonably Maximally Exposed Individual

RTG—Radioisotope thermoelectric generator

RWSF—Radioactive Waste Storage Facility

SAM—Surface-to-air missile

Shiite or **Shi'a**—A member of the smaller of the two great divisions of Islam, representing between 10 and 15 percent of Muslims worldwide (the majority are Sunni). All Shiites support the claims of Ali and his line to presumptive right to the caliphate and leadership of the world Muslim community, and on this issue, more than a millennium ago, they hived off from the Sunnis in the first great schism of Islam. Later schisms have produced further divisions among these people.

Sigint—Signal intelligence (See entry for **humint**)

SRBM—Short-Range Ballistic Missile

SST—State-Sponsored Terrorism

Sunni—A member of the larger of the two great divisions of Islam. The Sunnis, who rejected the claim of Ali's line, believe that they are the true followers of the *sunna*, the guide to proper behavior composed of the Qur'an and the hadith.

SWU—Separative work unit, a measure of the effort required in an enrichment facility to separate uranium of a given uranium-235 content into two fractions, one with a higher percentage and one with a lower percentage.

Tails—Sometimes called tailings; the waste stream of an enrichment facility that contains depleted uranium

tcf—Trillion cubic feet

Thermonuclear bomb—Hydrogen bomb

TNRC—Tehran Nuclear Research Center

Tritium—The heaviest hydrogen isotope customarily used to boost the explosive power of atom bombs. While Pakistan claims to have thermonuclear capability, the consensus is that it has only fission or atom bombs, which its scientists boost with tritium to allow for higher explosive yields.

TRR—Tehran Research Reactor

U—The scientific symbol for uranium: the radioactive element with 92 as its atomic number

UCF—Uranium Conversion Facility (in Iran at Karaj)

UF_6—Uranium hexafluoride: A volatile compound of uranium and fluorine, which, while solid at atmospheric pressure and room temperature, can be transformed into a gas by heating. It is the feedstock in the uranium enrichment process.

Umma—The worldwide community of Islam

UNSCOM—United Nations Special Commission (on Iraq)

UO_2—Uranium dioxide (purified uranium: the form of natural uranium used in heavy-water reactors)

Urenco centrifuges—Urenco is a commercial consortium involving Britain, Germany, and the Netherlands that has developed the gas centrifuge to make LEU for nuclear power reactors.

^{233}U—A fissile isotope bred in fertile thorium-232

^{235}U—Also U-235: the only naturally occurring fissile isotope

^{238}U—Also U-238: Natural uranium is comprised of about 99.3 percent of this substance

U3O8—Uranium oxide: the most common oxide of uranium found in typical ores

Weapons-grade material—Nuclear material of the type most suitable for nuclear weapons

Yellowcake—A concentrate produced during the milling process that contains about 80 percent uranium oxide (U3O8). In preparation for uranium enrichment, the yellowcake is converted to uranium hexafluoride gas (UF_6).

Zirconium—A grayish-white lustrous material which is commonly used in an alloy (zircalloy) to encase fuel rods in nuclear reactors.

With grateful thanks to various International Atomic Energy Agency publications, as well as excerpts from the glossary of *Plutonium and Highly Enriched Uranium* by David Albright, Frans Berkhout, and William Walker, Stockholm International Peace Research Institute (SIPRI) and Oxford University Press, 1997.

ACKNOWLEDGMENTS

Both Iran and North Korea can be thanked for the timely appearance of this book. While I've been covering Tehran's nuclear machinations for many years, principally for a slew of Jane's publications, it was Pyongyang's detonation of its first nuclear device in late October 2006 that set in motion the need for a comprehensive review of Third World nuclear activities and, in particular, those of several Islamic countries. These include Iran, Libya (thankfully since abandoned), Egypt, Algeria, Syria, and the rest.

Nor should we forget that al-Qaeda is still very much in the race. Though it has a way to go, some of the illustrations in this book make clear that Osama bin Laden and his cohorts remain obsessed with weapons of mass destruction. Their Web sites are full of it: nuclear fission, fusion, the pros and cons of implosion as opposed to "gun-type" atom bombs, centrifuges, the role of these intricate devices in enriching uranium, and so on.

Among those of my colleagues who have been invaluable in getting the job done, I must single out my old friend, Stephen Ulph, longtime editor of *Jane's Islamic Affairs Analyst*. We worked together to put that publication on the map less than a decade ago, and by all accounts, it has built up a pretty solid circulation that even includes the likes of Hezbollah and Palestine's Hamas. I'm told that several Iranian embassies subscribe to it.

This book would never have happened without polymath Ulph's application. He has a handle on about a dozen languages—including that of Egypt's Copts. Stephen reads, writes, and speaks Arabic, if not like a native, then well enough to get along in any Islamic city. There are stories of British embassy staff encountering him on a Cairo street surrounded by a large and sometimes animated mob while they listen, perplexed, as this *farangi* debates the latest shenanigans of the West, or what is taking place in the world of Islam at the moment.

Meticulously objective, Stephen is as outspoken about Israel's excesses in the occupied areas as he can be about some of al-Qaeda's less savory exploits. Small wonder that this Fellow of the Jamestown Foundation was recently appointed as a visiting lecturer on Middle East issues at West Point.

This was the same academic, journalist and author who, when I asked for examples of al-Qaeda's cyber programs on weapons of mass destruction, promptly came up with more than two hundred pages of stuff that he'd pulled off the Web. Quite a bit of it was nuclear-related, including the first photo of a suitcase nuke that I'd been able to view from up close. It is not by chance then that Stephen Ulph's next book (to be published in 2007 in the United States and Britain) will deal with the role of terrorist activity in cyberspace, and how that potentially affects millions who follow the precepts of the Qur'an and have access to the Internet.

That development resulted from a talk Stephen gave in Washington in the fall of 2006. After that, his phone didn't stop ringing for months.

Among other colleagues with whom I've worked at Jane's on these and related matters over the years have been Peter Felstead, currently editor of *Jane's Defense Weekly*. There is also Mark Daly, the long-standing editor of *Jane's International Defense Review*, for which I'm pleased to serve as correspondent for Africa and the Middle East.

David Albright of Washington's Institute for Science and International Security (ISIS) was first among the American specialists to lend a hand. He was joined by his former deputy, Corey Hinderstein, who has since moved on to become a director at Washington's prestigious Nuclear Threat Initiative. Paul Brannan, a research analyst at ISIS, was brilliantly forthcoming in the short time that I had to complete this work.

Over several years, I have been helped by many people, quite a few of them involved in my last book, *Iran's Nuclear Option: Tehran's Quest for the Atom Bomb*. Prior to moving to Pacific Command (PACCOM in Hawaii), my old buddy Eric Croddy (then at the Center for Nonproliferation Studies at the Monterey Institute of International Affairs) would occasionally give my lucubrations the once-over before I shipped them off to Coulsdon.

So too with Dr. Terry Wilson, another compadre who, before he retired from the germ warfare facility at the U.S. Army Medical Research Institute of Infectious Diseases (USAMRIID) at Fort Detrick in Maryland, came up with some remarkable revelations on biological warfare. And when I needed photos with which to illustrate some of my offerings to Jane's, Fort Detrick's delightful Stacy Vanderlinde complied when she was able to do so. I've still got some of her photos of anthrax and Ebola viruses on file.

At the Pacific Northwest National Laboratory in Washington State, several individuals stand out, among them Mike Foley; his colleague, author Don Bradley; as well as the irrepressible Bill Cliff, who provided some revelatory material for the chapter on nuclear scams. All three specialists deal with the proliferation of illegal substances that have emerged in Eastern Europe and beyond since the breakup of the former Soviet Union.

Nor should I forget David and Sue Farnsworth of Casemate Publishers, who were kind enough to let me use some of the more salient excerpts that remain relevant in these difficult times. Had Casemate not published my Iranian nuclear book, as well as *The Iraqi War Debrief* (which preceded it), *Allah's Bomb* would probably never have happened.

Another old friend who made a timely contribution to this little volume is somebody from one of yesterday's wars, former Special Air Service colonel Brian Robinson. Brian was the penultimate commander of Rhodesia's SAS regiment, and when that conflict was brought to a close, he moved on to other things. For a while, based in Abu Dhabi and on the cusp of many of the problems facing the Middle East, Brian was military advisor to Sheikh Mohammed bin Zayed Al Nahyan who became the crown prince of the United Arab Emirates (UAE) after President Sheikh Zayed died.

Having read Frederick Forsyth's latest book, *The Afghan*, Brian told me that he was fascinated by Freddie's grasp of al-Qaeda activities in the Gulf, and how bin Laden's "sleepers" would conduct their operations right under the noses of the UAE security establishment. As Brian says, Forsyth clearly had some damn good information, and much of what he wrote was right on the button.

Many other individuals were involved and, in retrospect, I couldn't have finished without the help of missile specialist Charles Vick, who his friends like to call Pat. John Pike, Pat's immediate boss at GlobalSecurity.org, was equally forthcoming, always at the forefront when it concerned the new and the unconventional. A frontrunner while with the Federation of American Scientists and, as we have so often seen on CNN, the BBC and other networks, his prognostications have been a valuable adjunct to many contemporary strategic developments, in particular those taking place right now east of Suez. It was Pat Vick that came up with the goods when I asked him for a series of fresh images of Iran's real or putative missile program.

Of all these individuals, the two people who did the most to guide me through a brief but extremely pressing period are Nick Badenhorst and his coauthor, Pierre Victor; their forthcoming book on the South African atom bomb program will be published in 2007. Though neither an academic nor a physicist, Nick has spent half his life studying trends in contemporary warfare, and from what I was able to observe, he has an eclectic and far-reaching understanding of the topic. He has tended to focus on both nuclear weapons and their delivery systems, paying particular attention to most of the Islamic states that are featured within these pages.

Pierre Victor, coauthor of their upcoming volume on South Africa's atom bomb program, is an artist of note. Apart from Pat Vick's two sketches, the rest of the drawings and maps are his. The fact that Pierre is also the editor of *Veg*, a monthly publication that specializes in strategic issues, obviously adds to his expertise.

Closer to home, I have my editor Tom McCarthy to thank for this book appearing as soon as it did. A day after North Korea's first atom bomb blast, we spoke about possibly putting something out, which might have been expected since I've been writing on related issues for almost as long as I've been receiving checks from Jane's. With the prescience of a professional that was both consummate and dedicated, Tom went right at it with his board, and days later we had the approval to go ahead. There was one proviso, however: I had just thirty days in which to complete the book.

Tom and I were in daily contact throughout, which included weekends. I ended up at one stage questioning him about whether he ever took any time off. His riposte was to ask the same of me.

I have to offer generous salutations to the lady who knocked the book into shape in the few weeks that she had for this august purpose. It couldn't have been a labor of love for Melissa Hayes, but she did sterling work against an impossible deadline. My grateful thanks to you Melissa and here's to the next book.

My old friend Dr Nic von Weilligh requires a nod as well. Having spent a quarter century involved in nuclear work, this remarkable scientist knows his stuff. He has been invaluable with a few of the little asides that I've included here. Thank you Nic and get better soon.

The Stockholm International Peace Research Institute (SIPRI) produces a formidably body of work each year that in its scope and breadth, must have played a significant role in limited any number of threats on the international front. SIPRI was good enough to give me permission to use some of their material for my earlier book on Middle East nuclear issues *Iran's Nuclear Option* and some of it has again been helpful.

For the record, I should mention that it was SIPRI that originally published (in conjunction with Oxford University Press) a book that could only have been an inspiration to researchers like myself. Written by David Albright, Frans Berkhout and William Walker, it is titled *Plutonium and Highly Enriched Uranium 1996: World Inventories, Capabilities and Policies*, SIPRI, Stockholm, 1997.

The good offices of Armor Express in Central Lake, Michigan played an invaluable if inadvertent role in helping me finish this book. Richard, Matt, Pat, Diane, Andy and the rest of the gang all lent a hand when needed, in particular in getting material from one quarter of the globe to the other.

The last person who gets my heartfelt appreciation is Susan Sizemore, a dear and delightful friend and confidante. Though stuck away in Seaside, Oregon, Suzie has been more of an inspiration in my writing than anybody else that I know. Being the web wizard that she is, Suzie has consistently come up with bagsful of surprises as this work progressed. Thank you my dear one.

Al J. Venter
Sault Sainte Marie, Ontario
January 2007

INDEX

Bespalko, Yuri, 29
Bhutto, Zulfikar Ali, 55, 197
bin Abdulaziz, Abdullah, 151
bin Laden, Osama. *See also* al-Qaeda,
    xx, 7, 219
    and Madrid bombings, 263
Bin-Muhammad, Turki, 153
Bliss, Mary, 226
Blix, Hans, 66
Bohr, Niels, 278
Bolton, John, 216
Botha, P. W., 165
Botha, Pik, 78, 181, 183, 184, 217n2
Boureston, Jack, 204–5
Brazil, 142
    nuclear weapons program, 160,
    201–4
Brighter than a Thousand Suns
    (Jungk), 110
Britain. *See* Great Britain
Broad, William J., 1, 2
Broder, Jonathan, 210
Brooks, Geraldine, 240
Brown, Gordon, 252
Buchalet, Albert, 107
Buchanan, Ewen, 209
Bulganin, Nikolai, 108
Bull, Gerald, 93–94
Bulletin of the Atomic Scientists, 68,
    84, 138
Burundi, xx
Bush, George W., 52, 152, 210, 215
Bush, Vannevar, 104
Busse, Walter, 96
Butt, S. A., 197, 198

C
Cairo—The City Victorious
    (Rodenbeck), 241
Californium-252, 29
Canada, 208
    CANDU reactor, 70, 283
    and terrorist funding, 258–60

Carbons, 225
Cardoen, Carlos, 94
Cathcart, Brian, 275
Centrifuges. *See also* Atomic bomb;
    Nuclear weapons, 41–43, 284
    and Brazil's program, 202–3, 204
    enrichment technology and Iran,
    119, 120
    Khan's program, 57–58
    Libya's program, 44, 45
    manufacture of in So. Africa, 61
Chad, 39
Chadwick, James, 275
Chechnya, xxii–xxiii, 121–22
*Chemical and Biological Warfare: A
    Comprehensive Survey for the
    Concerned Citizen* (Croddy),
    147, 249
Chiang Kai-shek, 204, 205
China, 76
    and Egypt's nuclear program, 238
    and Iran's nuclear program, 68–69,
    76–77, 217
    and Khan, 37
    missile programs, 127, 128, 129
    missiles for Saudi Arabia, 153
    and No. Korea's nuclear program, 195
    nuclear aid to Algeria, 143
    nuclear weapons program of,
    108–12
    and Pakistan's nuclear program, 68,
    198, 199
    and Proliferation Security Initiative
    (PSI), 208
    and South African zirconium plant,
    185, 186–90
Chkmivadze, Valiko, 23
Christie, Renfrew, 158
Christopher, Warren, 67–68
Chromium-51, 221
Churchill, Winston, 104
Cirincione, Joseph, 19
Cliff, William, 219

Eritrea-Ethiopia, 13
Esfahan Nuclear Technology Center
(ENTC). *See also* Iran, 75
Estonia, 224

F
Farook, Mohamed, 54
Farr, Warner D., 135–36, 137
Farsi, 116
"Fat Man." *See also* Atomic bomb, 8,
85, 103, 105, 284
Federation of American Scientists
(FAS), 127, 131, 201, 246, 248
Feldman, Noah, 231
Feldman, Yana, 204–5
Fermi, Enrico, 100, 102, 276
Feynman, Richard, 26
Fiber-optic technology, 225, 226
Finland, 94
Fischer, David, 212
Fission. *See also* Atomic bomb;
Nuclear weapons, 101–2,
277, 285
Fitzpatrick, Mark, 142
Fly in the Cathedral (Cathcart), 275
Foley, Bill, 2
Foley, Michael, xxii, 30
Ford, Gerald, 136
Forsyth, Frederick, 263
France
and Iraq's nuclear weapons
program, 90, 91–92
and Israel's nuclear program &
missiles, 134, 136–37, 139
nuclear weapons program of,
106–8, 136
and Pakistan's nuclear program, 198
and PSI, 208
Frequency-hopping, 271
Frisch, Otto. *See also* Frisch-Peierls
Memorandum, 26, 104, 112
Frisch-Peierls Memorandum, 275–82
Fuchs, Klaus, 102

Fusion. *See also* Atomic bomb;
Nuclear weapons, 285

G
Gadhafi, Muammar. *See also* Libya, 12,
35–36, 39–40
nuclear weapons program, 36,
38–39, 40–41, 43–45, 63
Gamma and neutron spectrometer, 225
Gamma densitometer, 225
Gashut, Ali, 40
Geiges, Daniel, 60, 61
Gerhardt, Dieter, 161
Germany
and Iran's nuclear program, 18
and Iraq's nuclear program,
94–95, 96
and PSI, 208
submarines for Israel, 132–33
Ghana, 142
Glasstone, Samuel, 110
Glossary, 283–89
Goksel, Timur, x
Goldschmidt, Bertrand, 106, 107
Gonçalves, Odair, 204
Gore, Al, 125
Gottemoeller, Rose, 23
Great Britain
and Iraqi nuclear program, 95
London bombings, 263
nuclear weapons program of,
103–5
and PSI, 208
and South African weapons, 177
and terrorists' assets, 252
terror plots threatening, 273
Greenberg, Maurice R., 254
Greenglass, David, 102
Griffin, Paul, 53–54
Griffin, Peter, 41, 53–54
Groupes Islamiques Armés (Armed
Muslim Groups), 266
Groves, Leslie R., 100, 110